D0619868

A Scarpetta Omnibus

Volume 2

CRUEL AND UNUSUAL
THE BODY FARM
FROM POTTER'S FIELD

Also by Patricia Cornwell

THE DR KAY SCARPETTA NOVELS

POSTMORTEM (1990)
BODY OF EVIDENCE (1991)
ALL THAT REMAINS (1992)
CAUSE OF DEATH (1996)
UNNATURAL EXPOSURE (1997)
POINT OF ORIGIN (1998)
BLACK NOTICE (1999)
THE LAST PRECINCT (2000)

OTHER FICTION

HORNET'S NEST
SOUTHERN CROSS

SHORT FICTION

SCARPETTA'S WINTER TABLE

NON-FICTION

RUTH, A PORTRAIT: The Story of Ruth Bell Graham

PATRICIA CORNWELL

A SCARPETTA OMNIBUS

Volume 2

CRUEL AND UNUSUAL
THE BODY FARM
FROM POTTER'S FIELD

Three Novels in One Volume

LITTLE, BROWN AND COMPANY

A *Little, Brown* Book

First published in this omnibus edition in 2000
by Little, Brown and Company
Reprinted 2001

A Scarpetta Omnibus Volume 2 © Cornwell Enterprises, Inc. 2000
Cruel and Unusual copyright © Patricia D. Cornwell 1993
The Body Farm copyright © Patricia D. Cornwell 1994
From Potter's Field copyright © Patricia D. Cornwell 1995

The moral right of the author has been asserted.

All rights reserved.
No part of this publication may be reproduced, stored in a retrieval system, or transmitted, in any form or by any means, without the prior permission in writing of the publisher, nor be otherwise circulated in any form of binding or cover other than that in which it is published and without a similar condition including this condition being imposed on the subequent purchaser.

All characters in this publication are fictitious and any resemblance to real persons, living or dead, is purely coincidental.

A CIP catalogue record for this book
is available from the British Library.

ISBN 0 316 85707 6

Printed and bound in Great Britain by
Clays Ltd, St Ives plc

Little, Brown and Company (UK)
Brettenham House
Lancaster Place
London WC2E 7EN

www.littlebrown.co.uk

This book is for
the inimitable Dr. Marcella Fierro.
(You taught Scarpetta well.)

CRUEL AND UNUSUAL

PROLOGUE

(A MEDITATION AT SPRING STREET BY THE DAMNED)

It is two weeks before Christmas. Four days before nothing at all. I lie on my iron bed staring at my dirty bare feet and the white toilet missing its seat, and when cockroaches crawl across the floor I don't jump anymore. I watch them the same way they watch me.

I close my eyes and breathe slow.

I remember raking hay in the heat of day and getting no pay compared to the way white folk live. I dream of roasting peanuts in a tin and when the tomatoes are in eating them like apples. I imagine driving the pickup truck, sweat shining on my face in that no-future place I swore I'd leave.

I can't use the john, blow my nose, or smoke without guards taking notes. There's no clock. I never know the weather. I open my eyes and see a blank wall going on forever. What's a man supposed to feel when he's about to be gone?

Like a sad, sad song. I don't know the words. I can't remember. They say it happened in September when the sky was like a robin's egg and leaves were on fire and falling to the ground. They say a beast got loose in the city. Now there's one less sound.

Killing me won't kill the beast. The dark is his friend, flesh and blood his feast. When you think it's safe to stop looking that's when you'd better start looking, brother.

One sin leads to another.

Ronnie Joe Waddell

1

The Monday I carried Ronnie Joe Waddell's meditation in my pocketbook, I never saw the sun. It was dark out when I drove to work that morning. It was dark again when I drove home. Small raindrops spun in my headlights, the night gloomy with fog and bitterly cold.

I built a fire in my living room and envisioned Virginia farmland and tomatoes ripening in the sun. I imagined a young black man in the hot cab of a pickup truck and wondered if his head had been full of murder back then. Waddell's meditation had been published in the *Richmond Times-Dispatch* and I had taken the clipping to work to add to his growing file. But the business of the day distracted me and his meditation had remained in my pocketbook. I had read it several times. I supposed it would always intrigue me that poetry and cruelty could reside in the same heart.

For the next few hours I paid bills and wrote Christmas cards while the television played mutely. Like the rest of Virginia's citizens, whenever an execution was scheduled I found out from the media whether all appeals had been exhausted or the governor had granted clemency. The news determined whether I went on to bed or drove downtown to the morgue.

At almost ten P.M. my telephone rang. I answered it expecting my deputy chief or some other member of my staff whose evening, like mine, was on hold.

"Hello?" asked a male voice I did not recognize. "I'm trying to reach Kay Scarpetta? Uh, the chief medical examiner, Dr. Scarpetta?"

"Speaking," I said.

"Oh, good. Detective Joe Trent with Henrico County. Found your number in the book. Sorry to bother you at home." He sounded keyed up. "But we've got a situation we really need your help with."

"What's the problem?" I asked, staring tensely at the TV. A commercial was playing. I hoped I wasn't needed at a scene.

"Earlier this evening, a thirteen-year-old white male was abducted after leaving a convenience store on Northside. He was shot in the head and there may be some sexual components involved."

My heart sank as I reached for paper and pen. "Where is the body?" I asked.

"He was found behind a grocery store on Patterson Avenue in the county. I mean, he's not dead. He hasn't regained consciousness but no one's saying right now whether he'll make it. I realize it's not your case since he's not dead. But he's got some injuries that are real odd. They're not like anything I've ever come across. I know you see a lot of different types of injuries. I'm hoping you might have some idea how these were inflicted and why."

"Describe them for me," I said.

"We're talking about two areas. One on his inner right thigh, you know, up high near the groin. The other's in the area of his right shoulder. Chunks of flesh are missing—cut out. And there's weird cuts and scratches around the edges of the wounds. He's at Henrico Doctor's."

"Did you find the excised tissue?" My mind was racing through other cases, looking for something similar.

"Not so far. We've got men out there still searching. But it's possible the assault occurred inside a car."

"Whose car?"

"The assailant's. The grocery store parking lot where the kid was found is a good three or four miles from the convenience store where he was last seen. I'm thinking he got into somebody's car, maybe was forced to."

"You got photographs of the injuries before the doctors started working on him?"

"Yes. But they haven't done much. Because of the amount of skin missing, they'll have to do skin grafts—*full* grafts, is what they said, if that tells you anything."

It told me they had debrided the wounds, had him on intravenous antibiotics, and were waiting to do a gluteal graft. If, however, that was not the case and they had undermined the tissue around the injuries and sutured them, then there wasn't going to be much left for me to see.

"They haven't sutured his wounds," I said.

"That's what I've been told."

"Do you want me to take a look?"

"That would be really great," he said, relieved. "You should be able to see the wounds real well."

"When would you like me to do this?"

"Tomorrow would work."

"All right. What time? The earlier the better."

"Eight hundred hours? I'll meet you in front of the ER."

"I'll be there," I said as the anchorman stared grimly at me. Hanging up, I reached for the remote control and turned up the sound.

". . . Eugenia? Can you tell us if there's been any word from the governor?"

The camera shifted to the Virginia State Penitentiary, where for two hundred years the Commonwealth's worst criminals had been warehoused along a rocky stretch of the James River at the edge of downtown. Sign-carrying protesters and capital punishment enthusiasts gathered in the dark, their faces harsh in the glare of television lights. It chilled my soul that some people were laughing. A pretty, young correspondent in a red coat filled the screen.

"As you know, Bill," she said, "yesterday a telephone line was set up between Governor Norring's office and the penitentiary. Still no word, and that speaks volumes. Historically, when the governor doesn't intend to intervene, he remains silent."

"How are things there? Is it relatively peaceful so far?"

"So far, yes, Bill. I'd say several hundred people are standing vigil out here. And of course, the penitentiary itself is almost empty. All but several dozen of the inmates have already been transported to the new correctional facility in Greensville."

I turned off the TV and moments later was driving east with my doors locked and the radio on. Fatigue seeped through me like anesthesia. I felt dreary and numb. I dreaded executions. I dreaded waiting for someone to die, then running my scalpel through flesh as warm as mine. I was a physician with a law degree. I had been trained to know what gave life and what took it, what was right and what was wrong. Then experience had become my mentor, wiping its feet on that pristine part of myself that was idealistic and analytical. It is disheartening when a thinking person is forced to admit that many clichés are true. There is no justice on this earth. Nothing would ever undo what Ronnie Joe Waddell had done.

He had been on death row nine years. His victim had not been my case because she had been murdered before I had been appointed chief medical examiner of Virginia and had moved to Richmond. But I had reviewed her records. I was well aware of every savage detail. On the morning of September fourth, ten years before, Robyn Naismith called in sick at Channel 8, where she was an anchorwoman. She went out to buy cold remedies and returned home. The next day, her nude, battered body was found in her living room, propped against the TV. A bloody thumbprint recovered from the medicine cabinet was later identified as Ronnie Joe Waddell's.

There were a number of cars parked behind the morgue when I pulled in. My deputy chief, Fielding, was already there. So was my administrator, Ben Stevens, and morgue supervisor, Susan Story. The bay door was open, lights inside dimly illuminating the tarmac beyond, and a capitol police officer was sitting in his marked car smoking. He got out as I parked.

"Safe to keep the bay door open?" I asked. He was a tall, gaunt man with thick white hair. Though I had talked to him many times in the past, I couldn't remember his name.

"Appears okay at the moment, Dr. Scarpetta," he said, zipping up his heavy nylon jacket. "I haven't seen any troublemakers around. But as soon as Corrections gets here I'll close it and make sure it stays closed."

"Fine. As long as you'll be right here in the meantime."

"Yes, ma'am. You can count on that. And we'll have a couple more uniform men back here in case there's a problem. Apparently there's a lot of protesters. I guess you read in the paper about that petition all those people signed and took to the governor. And I heard earlier today some bleeding hearts as far away as California are on a hunger strike."

I glanced around the empty parking lot and across Main Street. A car rushed past, tires swishing over wet pavement. Streetlights were smudges in the fog.

"Hell, not me. I wouldn't even miss a coffee break for Waddell." The officer cupped his hand around his lighter and began puffing on a cigarette. "After what he done to that Naismith girl. You know, I remember watching her on TV. Now, I like my women the same way I like my coffee—sweet and white. But I have to admit, she was the prettiest black girl I ever seen."

I had quit smoking barely two months ago, and it still made me crazy to watch someone else doing it.

"Lord, that must've been close to ten years ago," he went on. "I'll never forget the uproar, though. One of the worst cases we've ever had around here. You'd've thought a grizzly bear got hold of—"

I interrupted him. "You'll let us know what's going on?"

"Yes, ma'am. They'll radio me and I'll give you the word." He headed back to the shelter of his car.

Inside the morgue, fluorescent light bleached the corridor of color, the smell of deodorizer cloying. I passed the small office where funeral homes signed in bodies, then the X-ray room, and the refrigerator, which was really a large refrigerated room with double-decker gurneys and two massive steel doors. The autopsy suite was lit up, stainless steel tables polished bright. Susan was sharpening a long knife and Fielding was labeling blood tubes. Both of them looked as tired and unenthusiastic as I felt.

"Ben's upstairs in the library watching TV," Fielding said to me. "He'll let us know if there are any new developments."

"What's the chance this guy had AIDS?" Susan referred to Waddell as if he already were dead.

"I don't know," I said. "We'll double-glove, take the usual precautions."

"I hope they'll say something if he had it," she persisted. "You know, I don't trust it when they send these prisoners in. I don't think they care if they're HIV positive because it's not their problem. They're not the ones doing the posts and worrying about needle sticks."

Susan had become increasingly paranoid about such occupational hazards as exposure to radiation, chemicals, and diseases. I could not blame her. She was several months pregnant, though it barely showed.

Slipping on a plastic apron, I went back into the locker room and put on greens, covered my shoes with booties, and got two packets of gloves. I inspected the surgical cart parked beside table three. Everything was labeled with Waddell's name, the date, and an autopsy number. The labeled tubes and cartons would go in the trash if Governor Norring interceded at the last minute. Ronnie Waddell would be deleted from the morgue log, his autopsy number assigned to whoever came in next.

At eleven P.M. Ben Stevens came downstairs and shook his head. All of us looked up at the clock. No one spoke. Minutes ticked by.

The capitol police officer walked in, portable radio in hand. I finally remembered his name was Rankin.

"He was pronounced at eleven-oh-five," he said. "Will be here in about fifteen minutes."

The ambulance beeped a warning as it backed into the bay, and when its rear doors swung open, enough Department of Corrections guards hopped out to control a small prison riot. Four of them slid out the stretcher bearing Ronnie Waddell's body. They carried it up the ramp and inside the morgue, metal clacking, feet scuffing, all of us getting out of the way. Lowering the stretcher to the tile floor without bothering to unfold the legs, they propelled it along like a sled on wheels, its passenger strapped in and covered with a bloodstained sheet.

"A nosebleed," one of the guards offered before I could ask the question.

"Who had a nosebleed?" I inquired, noting that the guard's gloved hands were bloody.

"Mr. Waddell did."

"In the ambulance?" I puzzled, for Waddell should not have had a blood pressure by the time he was loaded inside the ambulance.

But the guard was preoccupied with other matters and I did not get an answer. It would have to wait.

We transferred the body to the gurney positioned on top of the floor scale. Busy hands fumbled with unfastening straps and opening the sheet. The door to the autopsy suite quietly shut as the Department of Corrections guards left just as abruptly as they had appeared.

Waddell had been dead exactly twenty-two minutes. I could smell his sweat, his dirty bare feet, and the faint odor of singed flesh. His right pant leg was pushed up above his knee, his calf dressed in fresh gauze applied postmortem to his burns. He was a big, powerful man. The newspapers had called him the *gentle giant*, poetic Ronnie with soulful eyes. Yet there had been a time when he had used the large hands, the massive shoulders and arms before me to rip the life from another human being.

I pulled apart the Velcro fasteners of his light blue denim shirt, checking pockets as I undressed him. Searching for personal effects is pro forma and usually fruitless. Inmates are not supposed to carry anything with them to the electric chair, and I was very surprised when I discovered what appeared to be a letter in the back pocket of his jeans. The envelope had not been opened. Written in bold block letters across the front of it was

EXTREMELY CONFIDENTIAL. PLEASE BURY WITH ME!!

"Make a copy of the envelope and whatever's inside and submit the originals with his personal effects," I said, handing the envelope to Fielding.

He tucked it under the autopsy protocol on a clipboard, mumbling, "Jesus. He's bigger than I am."

"Amazing that anyone could be bigger than you are," Susan said to my bodybuilder deputy chief.

"Good thing he's not been dead long," he added. "Otherwise we'd need the Jaws of Life."

When musclebound people have been dead for hours, they are as uncooperative as marble statues. Rigor had not begun to set in. Waddell was limber as in life. He could have been asleep.

It required all of us to transfer him, facedown, to the autopsy table. He weighed two hundred and fifty-nine pounds. His feet protruded over the table's edge. I was measuring the burns to his leg when the buzzer sounded from the bay. Susan went to see who it was, and shortly Lieutenant Pete Marino walked in, trench coat unbuttoned, one end of the belt trailing along the tile floor.

"The burn to the back of his calf is four by one and a quarter by two and three-eighths," I dictated to Fielding. "It's dry, contracted, and blistered."

Marino lit a cigarette. "They're raising a stink about him bleeding," he said, and he seemed agitated.

"His rectal temp is one hundred and four," Susan said as she removed the chemical thermometer. "That's at eleven-forty-nine."

"You know why his face was bleeding?" Marino asked.

"One of the guards said a nosebleed," I replied, adding, "We need to turn him over."

"You saw this on the inner aspect of his left arm?" Susan directed my attention to an abrasion.

I examined it through a lens under a strong light. "I don't know. Possibly from one of the restraints."

"There's one on his right arm, too."

I took a look while Marino watched me and smoked. We turned the body, shoving a block under the shoulders. Blood trickled out of the right side of his nose. His head and chin had been shaved to an uneven stubble. I made the Y incision.

"There might be some abrasions here," Susan said, looking at the tongue.

"Take it out." I inserted the thermometer into the liver.

"Jesus," Marino said under his breath.

"Now?" Susan's scalpel was poised.

"No. Photograph the burns around his head. We need to measure those. Then remove the tongue."

"Shit," she complained. "Who used the camera last?"

"Sorry," Fielding said. "There was no film in the drawer. I forgot. By the way, it's your job to keep film in the drawer."

"It would help if you'd tell me when the film drawer's empty."

"Women are supposed to be intuitive. I didn't think I needed to tell you."

"I got the measurement of these burns around his head," Susan reported, ignoring his remark.

"Okay."

Susan gave him the measurements, then started work on the tongue.

Marino backed away from the table. "Jesus," he said again. "That always gets me."

"Liver temp's one hundred and five," I reported to Fielding.

I glanced up at the clock. Waddell had been dead for an hour. He hadn't cooled much. He was big. Electrocution heats you up. The brain temperatures of smaller men I had autopsied were as high as a hundred and ten. Waddell's right calf was at least that, hot to the touch, the muscle in total tetanus.

"A little abrasion at the margin. But nothing big-time," Susan pointed out to me.

"He bite his tongue hard enough to bleed that much?" Marino asked.

"No," I said.

"Well, they're already raising a stink about it." His voice rose. "I thought you'd want to know."

I paused, resting the scalpel on the edge of the table as it suddenly occurred to me. "You were a witness."

"Yeah. I told you I was going to be."

Everybody looked at him.

"Trouble's brewing out there," he said. "I don't want no one leaving this joint alone."

"What sort of trouble?" Susan asked.

"A bunch of religious nuts have been hanging out at Spring Street since this morning. Somehow they got word about his bleeding, and when the ambulance drove off with his body they started marching in this direction like a bunch of zombies."

"Did you see it when he started bleeding?" Fielding asked him.

"Oh, yeah. They juiced him twice. The first time he made this loud hiss, like steam coming out of a radiator, and the blood started pouring out from under his mask. They're saying the chair might have malfunctioned."

Susan started the Stryker saw and no one competed with its loud buzzing as she cut through the skull. I continued examining the organs. Heart was good, coronaries terrific. When the saw stopped, I resumed dictating to Fielding.

"You got the weight?" he asked.

"Heart weighs five-forty, and he's got a single adhesion of the left upper lobe to the aortic arch. Even found four parathyroids, in case you didn't already get that."

"I got it."

I placed the stomach on the cutting board. "It's almost tubular."

"You sure?" Fielding moved closer to inspect. "That's bizarre. A guy this big needs a minimum of four thousand calories a day."

"He wasn't getting it, not lately," I said. "He doesn't have any gastric contents. His stomach is absolutely empty and clean."

"He didn't eat his last meal?" Marino asked me.

"It doesn't appear that he did."

"Do they usually?"

"Yes," I said, "usually."

We were finished by one A.M., and followed the funeral home attendants out to the bay, where the hearse was waiting. As we walked out of the building, darkness throbbed with red and blue lights. Radio static drifted on the cold, damp air, engines rumbled, and beyond the chain-link fence enclosing the parking lot was a ring of fire. Men, women, and children stood silently, faces wavering in candlelight.

The attendants wasted no time sliding Waddell's body into the back of the hearse and slamming the tailgate shut.

Somebody said something I did not get, and suddenly candles showered over the fence like a storm of falling stars and landed softly on the pavement.

"Goddam squirrels!" Marino exclaimed.

Wicks glowed orange and tiny flames dotted the tarmac. The hearse hastily began to back out of the bay. Flashguns were going off. I spotted the Channel 8 news van parked on Main Street. Someone was running along the sidewalk. Uniformed men were stamping out the candles, moving toward the fence, demanding that everyone clear the area.

"We don't want any problems here," an officer said. "Not unless some of you want to spend the night in lockup—"

"Butchers," a woman screamed.

Other voices joined in and hands grabbed the chain-link fence, shaking it.

Marino hurried me to my car.

A chant rose with tribal intensity. *"Butchers, butchers, butchers . . ."*

I fumbled with my keys, dropped them on the floor mat, snatched them up, and managed to find the right one.

"I'm following you home," Marino said.

I turned the heater on high but could not get warm. Twice I checked to make sure my doors were locked. The night took on a surreal quality, a strange asymmetry of light and dark windows, and shadows moved in the corners of my eyes.

We drank Scotch in my kitchen because I was out of bourbon.

"I don't know how you stand this stuff," Marino said rudely.

"Help yourself to whatever else there is in the bar," I told him.

"I'll tough it out."

I wasn't quite sure how to broach the subject, and it was obvious that Marino wasn't going to make it easy for me. He was tense, his face flushed. Strands of gray hair clung to his moist, balding head, and he was chain-smoking.

"Have you ever witnessed an execution before?" I asked.

"Never had a strong urge to."

"But you volunteered this time. So the urge must have been pretty strong."

"I bet if you put some lemon and soda water in this it wouldn't be half bad."

"If you want me to ruin good Scotch, I'll be glad to see what I can do."

He slid the glass toward me and I went to the refrigerator. "I've got bottled Key Lime juice, but no lemon." I searched shelves.

"That's fine."

I dribbled Key Lime juice into his glass, then added the Schweppes. Oblivious to the strange concoction he was sipping, he said, "Maybe you've forgotten, but the Robyn Naismith case was mine. Mine and Sonny Jones's."

"I wasn't around then."

"Oh, yeah. Funny, it seems like you've been here forever. But you know what happened, right?"

I was a deputy chief medical examiner for Dade County when Robyn Naismith was murdered, and I remembered reading about the case, following it in the news, and later seeing a slide presentation about it at a national meeting. The former Miss Virginia was a stunning beauty with a gorgeous alto voice. She was articulate and charismatic before the camera. She was only twenty-seven years old.

The defense claimed that Ronnie Waddell's intent was burglary, and Robyn's misfortune was to walk in on it after returning home from the drugstore. Allegedly, Waddell did not watch television and was unfamiliar with her name or brilliant future when he was ransacking her residence and brutalizing her. He was so hopped up on drugs, the defense argued, that he didn't know what he was doing. The jurors rejected Waddell's temporary insanity plea and recommended the death penalty.

"I know the pressure to catch her killer was incredible," I said to Marino.

"Friggin' unbelievable. We had this great latent print. We had bite marks. We had three guys doing a cold search through the files morning, noon, and night. I got no idea how many hours I put in on that damn case. Then we catch the bastard because he's driving around North Carolina with an expired inspection sticker." He paused, his eyes hard when he added, "Course, Jones wasn't around by then. Too damn bad he missed out on seeing Waddell get his reward."

"Do you blame Waddell for what happened to Sonny Jones?" I asked.

"Hey, what do you think?"

"He was a close friend."

"We worked Homicide together, fished together, was on the same bowling team."

"I know his death was hard for you."

"Yeah, well, the case wore him down. Working all hours, no sleep, never home, and that sure as hell didn't help matters with his wife. He kept telling me he couldn't take it no more and then he stopped telling me anything. One night he decides to eat his gun."

"I'm sorry," I said gently. "But I'm not sure you can blame Waddell for that."

"I had a score to settle."

"And was it settled when you witnessed his execution?"

At first Marino did not reply. He stared across the kitchen, his jaw rigidly set. I watched him smoke and drain his drink.

"Can I refresh that?"

"Yo. Why not."

I got up and did my thing again as I thought about the injustices and losses that had gone into the making of Marino. He had survived a loveless, impoverished childhood in the wrong part of New Jersey, and nursed an abiding distrust of anyone whose lot had been better. Not long ago his wife of thirty years had left him, and he had a son nobody seemed to know anything about. Regardless of his loyalty to law and order and his record of excellent police work, it was not in his genetic code to get along with the brass. It seemed his life's journey had placed him on a hard road. I feared that what he hoped to find at the end was not wisdom or peace but paybacks. Marino was always angry about something.

"Let me ask you this, Doc," he said to me when I returned to the table. "How would you feel if they caught the assholes who killed Mark?"

His question caught me by surprise. I did not want to think about those men.

"Isn't there a part of you that wants to see the bastards hung?" he went on. "Doesn't a part of you want to volunteer for the firing squad so you could pull the trigger yourself?"

Mark died when a bomb placed in a trash can inside London's Victoria Station exploded at the moment he happened to walk past. My shock and grief had catapulted me beyond revenge.

"It's an exercise in futility for me to contemplate punishing a group of terrorists," I said.

Marino stared intensely at me. "That's what's known as one of your famous bullshit answers. You'd give them free autopsies if you could. And you'd want them alive and would cut real slow. I ever tell you what happened to Robyn Naismith's family?"

I reached for my drink.

"Her father was a doctor in northern Virginia, a real fine man," he said. "About six months after the trial, he came down with cancer and a couple months after that was dead. Robyn was the only child. The mother moves to Texas, gets in a car wreck, and spends her days in a wheelchair with nothing but memories. Waddell killed Robyn Naismith's entire family. He poisoned every life he touched."

I thought of Waddell growing up on the farm, images from his meditation drifting through my mind. I envisioned him sitting on porch steps, biting into a tomato that tasted like the sun. I wondered what had gone through his mind the last second of his life. I wondered if he had prayed.

Marino stubbed out a cigarette. He was thinking about leaving.

"Do you know a Detective Trent with Henrico?" I asked.

"Joe Trent. Used to be with K-Nine and got transferred into the detective division after he made sergeant a couple months ago. Sort of a nervous Nellie, but he's all right."

"He called me about a boy—"

He cut me off. "Eddie Heath?"

"I don't know his name."

"A white male about thirteen years old. We're working on it. Lucky's is in the city."

"Lucky's?"

"The convenience store where he was last seen. It's off Chamberlayne Avenue, Northside. What did Trent want?" Marino frowned. "He gotten word that Heath ain't going to pull through and is making an appointment with you in advance?"

"He wants me to look at unusual injuries, possible mutilation."

"Christ. I hate it when it's kids." Marino pushed back his chair and rubbed his temples. "Damn. Every time you get rid of one toad there's another to take his place."

After Marino left, I sat on the hearth in the living room watching coals shift in the fireplace. I was weary and felt a dull, implacable sadness that I did not have the strength to chase away. Mark's death had left a tear in my soul. I had come to realize, incredibly, just how much of my identity had been tied to my love for him.

The last time I saw him was on the day he flew to London, and we managed a quick lunch downtown before he headed to Dulles Airport. What I remembered most clearly about our last hour together was both of us glancing at our watches as storm clouds gathered and rain began to spit against the window beside our booth. He had a nick on his jaw from where he'd cut himself while shaving, and later, when I would see his face in my mind, I would envision that small injury and for some reason be undone by it.

He died in February while the war was ending in the Persian Gulf, and determined to put the pain behind me, I had sold my house and moved to a new neighborhood. What I accomplished was to uproot myself without really going anywhere, and the familiar plants and neighbors that once had given me comfort were gone. Redecorating my new home or redesigning the yard only added to my stress. Everything I did provided distractions for which I had no time, and I could imagine Mark shaking his head.

"For someone so logical . . ." he would smile and say.

"And what would you do?" I would tell him in my thoughts some nights when I could not sleep. "Just what the hell would *you* do if you were still here instead of me?"

Returning to the kitchen, I rinsed out my glass and went into my study to see what awaited me on my answering machine. Several reporters had called, so had my mother and Lucy, my niece. Three other messages were hang ups.

I would have loved an unlisted number but it was not possible. The police, Commonwealth's Attorneys, and the four hundred or so appointed medical examiners statewide had legitimate reasons to reach me after hours. To counter the loss of privacy, I used my answering machine to screen calls, and anyone who left threatening or obscene messages ran the risk of being tracked by Caller ID.

Pressing the review button on the ID box, I began scrolling through the numbers materializing on the narrow screen. When I found the three calls I was looking for, I was perplexed and unsettled. The number was curiously familiar by now. It had been appearing on my screen several times a week of late when the caller would hang up without leaving a message. Once, I had tried dialing the number back to see who answered and had gotten the high-pitched tone of what sounded like a fax machine or a computer modem. For whatever reason, this individual or thing had called my number three times between ten-twenty and eleven P.M., while I was at the morgue waiting for Waddell's body. That didn't make sense. Computerized telephone solicitations should not occur so frequently and at such a late hour, and if one modem trying to dial another was getting me instead, shouldn't someone have figured out by now that his computer was dialing a wrong number?

I woke up several times during the few hours left of the early morning. Every creak or shift of sound in the house made my pulse pick up. Red lights on the burglar alarm's control panel across from the bed glowed ominously, and when I turned or rearranged the covers, motion sensors I did not arm while I was home watched me silently with flashing red eyes. My dreams were strange. At five-thirty I turned on lamps and got dressed.

It was dark out and there was very little traffic as I drove to the office. The parking lot behind the bay was deserted and littered with dozens of small beeswax candles that brought to mind Moravian love feasts and other religious celebrations. But these candles had been used to protest. They had been used as weapons hours before. Upstairs, I fixed coffee and began going through the paperwork Fielding had left for me, curious about the contents of the envelope I'd found in Waddell's back pocket. I was expecting a poem, perhaps another meditation or a letter from his minister.

Instead, I discovered that what Waddell had considered "extremely confidential" and had wanted buried with him were cash register receipts. Inexplicably, five were for tolls; three others were for meals, including a fried chicken dinner ordered at a Shoney's two weeks earlier.

2

Detective Joe Trent would have looked quite youthful were it not for a beard and receding blond hair that was turning gray. He was trim and tall, a crisp trench coat belted tightly around his waist, his shoes perfectly shined. He blinked nervously as we shook hands and introduced ourselves on the sidewalk in front of Henrico Doctor's Emergency Center. I could tell he was upset by Eddie Heath's case.

"You don't mind if we talk out here a minute," he said, his breath turning white. "For privacy reasons."

Shivering, I tucked my elbows close to my sides as a Medflight helicopter made a terrific noise taking off from the helipad on a grassy rise not far from where we stood. The moon was a shaving of ice melting in the slate-gray sky, cars in the parking lots dirty from road salt and frigid winter rains. The early morning was stark and without color, the wind sharp like a slap, and I observed all this more keenly because of the nature of my business here. Had the temperature suddenly risen forty degrees and the sun begun to blaze I do not think I could have felt warm.

"What we got here is real bad, Dr. Scarpetta." He blinked. "I think you'll agree we don't want the details getting out."

"What can you tell me about this boy?" I asked.

"I've talked to his family and several other people who know him. As best I can ascertain, Eddie Heath is just your average kid—likes sports and has a paper route, has never gotten into any trouble with the police. His father works for the phone company and his mother sews for people out of the home. Apparently, last night, Mrs. Heath needed a can of cream of mushroom soup for a casserole she was fixing for dinner and asked Eddie to run over to the Lucky Convenience Store to get it."

"The store is how far from their house?" I asked.

"A couple of blocks, and Eddie's been there any number of times. The people working the counter know him by name."

"He was last seen at what time?"

"Around five-thirty P.M. He was in the store a few minutes and left."

"It would have been dark out," I said.

"Yes, it was." Trent stared off at the helicopter transfigured by distance into a white dragonfly softly thudding through clouds. "At approximately eight-thirty, an officer on routine patrol was checking the back of buildings along Patterson and saw the kid propped up against the Dumpster."

"Do you have photographs?"

"No, ma'am. When the officer realized the boy was alive, his first priority was getting help. We don't have pictures. But I've got a pretty detailed description based on the officer's observations. The boy was nude, and he was propped up, with his legs straight out and arms by his sides and head bent forward. His clothing was in a moderately neat pile on the pavement, along with a small bag containing a can of cream of mushroom soup and a Snickers bar. It was twenty-eight degrees out. We're thinking he may have been left there anywhere from minutes to half an hour before he was found."

An ambulance halted near us. Doors slammed and metal grated as attendants quickly lowered the legs of a stretcher to the ground and wheeled an old man through opening glass doors. We followed and in silence walked through a bright, antiseptic corridor busy with medical personnel and patients dazed by the misfortunes that had brought them here. As we rode the elevator up to the third floor, I wondered what trace evidence had been scrubbed away and tossed in the trash.

"What about his clothes? Was a bullet recovered?" I asked Trent as the elevator doors parted.

"I've got his clothes in my car and will drop them and his PERK off at the lab this afternoon. The bullet's still in his brain. They haven't gone in there yet. I hope like hell they swabbed him good."

The pediatric intensive care unit was at the end of a polished hallway, panes of glass in the double wooden doors covered with friendly dinosaur paper. Inside, rainbows decorated sky blue walls, and animal mobiles were suspended over hydraulic beds in the eight rooms arranged in a semicircle around the nurses' station. Three young women worked behind monitors, one of them typing on a keyboard and another talking on the phone. A slender brunette dressed in a red corduroy jumper and turtleneck sweater identified herself as the head nurse after Trent explained why we were here.

"The attending physician's not in yet," she apologized.

"We just need to look at Eddie's injuries. It won't take long," Trent said. "His family still in there?"

"They stayed with him all night."

We followed her through soft artificial light, past code carts and green tanks of oxygen that would not be parked outside the rooms of little boys and girls were the world the way it ought to be. When we reached Eddie's room, the nurse went inside and shut the door most of the way.

"Just for a few minutes," I overheard her say to the Heaths. "While we do the exam."

"What kind of specialist is it this time?" the father asked in an unsteady voice.

"A doctor who knows a lot about injuries. She's sort of like a police surgeon." The nurse diplomatically refrained from saying I was a medical examiner, or worse, a coroner.

After a pause, the father quietly said, "Oh. This is for evidence."

"Yes. How about some coffee? Maybe something to eat?"

Eddie Heath's parents emerged from the room, both of them considerably overweight, their clothes badly wrinkled from having been slept in. They had the bewildered look of innocent, simple people who have been told the world is about to end, and when they glanced at us with exhausted eyes I wished there were something I could say that would make it not so or at least a little better. Words of comfort died in my throat as the couple slowly walked off.

Eddie Heath did not stir on top of the bed, his head wrapped in bandages, a ventilator breathing air into his lungs while fluids dripped into his veins. His complexion was milky and hairless, the thin membrane of his eyelids a faint bruised blue in the low light. I surmised the color of his hair by his strawberry blond eyebrows. He had not yet emerged from that fragile prepubescent stage when boys are full-lipped and beautiful and sing more sweetly than their sisters. His forearms were slender, the body beneath the sheet small. Only the disproportionately large, still hands tethered by intravenous lines were true to his fledgling gender. He did not look thirteen.

"She needs to see the areas on his shoulder and leg," Trent told the nurse in a low voice.

She got two packets of gloves, one for her and one for me, and we put them on. The boy was naked beneath the sheet, his skin grimy in creases and fingernails dirty. Patients who are unstable cannot be thoroughly bathed.

Trent tensed as the nurse removed the wet-to-dry dressings from the wounds. "Christ," he said under his breath. "It looks even worse than it did last night. Jesus." He shook his head and backed up a step.

If someone had told me that the boy had been attacked by a shark, I might have gone along with it were it not for the neat edges of the wounds, which clearly had been inflicted by a sharp, linear instrument, such as a knife or razor. Sections of flesh the size of elbow patches had been excised from his right shoulder and right inner thigh. Opening my medical bag, I got out a ruler and measured the wounds without touching them, then took photographs.

"See the cuts and scratches at the edges?" Trent pointed. "That's what I was telling you about. It's like he cut some sort of pattern on the skin and then removed the whole thing."

"Did you find any anal tearing?" I asked the nurse.

"When I did a rectal temperature I didn't notice any tears, and no one noticed anything unusual about his mouth or throat when he was intubated. I also checked for old fractures and bruises."

"What about tattoos?"

"Tattoos?" she asked as if she'd never seen a tattoo.

"Tattoos, birthmarks, scars. Anything that someone may have removed for some reason," I said.

"I have no idea," the nurse said dubiously.

"I'll go ask his parents." Trent wiped sweat from his forehead.

"They may have gone to the cafeteria."

"I'll find them," he said as he passed through the doorway.

"What are his doctors saying?" I asked the nurse.

"He's very critical and unresponsive." She stated the obvious without emotion.

"May I see where the bullet went in?" I asked.

She loosened the edges of the bandage around his head and pushed the gauze up until I could see the tiny black hole, charred around the edges. The wound was through his right temple and slightly forward.

"Through the frontal lobe?" I asked.

"Yes."

"They've done an angio?"

"There's no circulation to the brain, due to the swelling. There's no electroencephalic activity, and when we put cold water in his ears there was no caloric activity. It evoked no brain potentials."

She stood on the other side of the bed, gloved hands by her sides and expression dispassionate as she continued to relate the various tests conducted and maneuvers instigated to decrease intracranial pressure. I had paid my dues in ERs and ICUs and knew very well that it is easier to be clinical with a patient who has never been awake. And Eddie Heath would never be awake. His cortex was gone. That which made him human, made him think and feel, was gone and was never coming back. He had been left with vital functions, left with a brain stem. He was a breathing body with a beating heart maintained at the moment by machines.

I began looking for defense injuries. Concentrating on getting out of the way of his lines, I was unaware I was holding his hand until he startled me by squeezing mine. Such reflex movements are not uncommon in people who are cortically dead. It is the equivalent of a baby grabbing your finger, a reflex involving no thought process at all. I gently released his hand and took a deep breath, waiting for the ache in my heart to subside.

"Did you find anything?" the nurse asked.

"It's hard to look with all these lines," I said.

She replaced his dressings and pulled the sheet up to his chin. I took off my gloves and dropped them in the trash as Detective Trent returned, his eyes a little wild.

"No tattoos," he said breathlessly, as if he had sprinted to the cafeteria and back. "No birthmarks or scars, either."

Moments later we were walking to the parking deck. The sun slipped in and out, and tiny snowflakes were blowing. I squinted as I stared into the wind at heavy traffic on Forest Avenue. A number of cars had Christmas wreaths affixed to their grilles.

"I think you'd better prepare for the eventuality of his death," I said.

"If I'd known that, I wouldn't have bothered you to come out. Damn, it's cold."

"You did exactly the right thing. In several days his wounds would have changed."

"They say all of December's going to be like this. Cold as hell and a lot of snow." He stared down at the pavement. "You have kids?"

"I have a niece," I said.

"I've got two boys. One of 'em's thirteen."

I got out my keys. "I'm over here," I said.

Trent nodded, following me. He watched in silence as I unlocked my gray Mercedes. His eyes took in the details of the leather interior as I got in and fastened my seat belt. He looked the car up and down as if appraising a gorgeous woman.

"What about the missing skin?" he asked. "You ever seen anything like that?"

"It's possible we're dealing with someone predisposed to cannibalism," I said.

I returned to the office and checked my mailbox, initialed a stack of lab reports, filled a mug with the liquid tar left in the bottom of the coffeepot, and spoke to no one. Rose appeared so quietly as I seated myself behind my desk that I would not have noticed her immediately had she not placed a newspaper clipping on top of several others centering the blotter.

"You look tired," she said. "What time did you come in this morning? I got here and found coffee made and you had already gone out somewhere."

"Henrico's got a tough one," I said. "A boy who probably will be coming in."

"Eddie Heath."

"Yes," I said, perplexed. "How did you know?"

"He's in the paper, too," Rose replied, and I noticed that she had gotten new glasses that made her patrician face less haughty.

"I like your glasses," I said. "A big improvement over the Ben Franklin frames perched on the end of your nose. What did it say about him?"

"Not much. The article just said that he was found off Patterson and that he had been shot. If my son were still young, no way I'd let him have a paper route."

"Eddie Heath was not delivering papers when he was assaulted."

"Doesn't matter. I wouldn't permit it, not these days. Let's see." She touched a finger to the side of her nose. "Fielding's downstairs doing an autopsy and Susan's off delivering several brains to MCV for consultation. Other than that, nothing happened while you were out except the computer went down."

"Is it still down?"

"I think Margaret's working on it and is almost done," Rose said.

"Good. When it's up again, I need her to do a search for me. Codes to look for would be *cutting, mutilation, cannibalism, bite marks*. Maybe a free-format search for the words *excised, skin, flesh*—a variety of combinations of them. You might try *dismemberment*, too, but I don't think that's what we're really after."

"For what part of the state and what time period?" Rose took notes.

"All of the state for the past five years. I'm particularly interested in cases involving children, but let's not restrict ourselves to that. And ask her to see what the Trauma Registry's got. I spoke with the director at a meeting last month and he seemed more than willing for us to share data."

"You mean you also want to check victims who have survived?"

"If we can, Rose. Let's check everything to see if we find any cases similar to Eddie Heath's."

"I'll tell Margaret now and see if she can get started," my secretary said on her way out.

I began going through the articles she had clipped from a number of morning newspapers. Unsurprisingly, much was being made of Ronnie Waddell's allegedly bleeding from "his eyes, nose, and mouth." The local chapter of Amnesty International was claiming that his execution was no less inhumane that any homicide. A spokesman for the ACLU stated that the electric chair "may have malfunctioned, causing Waddell to suffer terribly," and went on to compare the incident to the execution in Florida in which synthetic sponges used for the first time had resulted in the condemned man's hair catching fire.

Tucking the news stories inside Waddell's file, I tried to anticipate what pugilistic rabbits his attorney, Nicholas Grueman, would pull out of his hat this time. Our confrontations, though infrequent, had become predictable. His true agenda, I was about to believe, was to impeach my professional competence and in general make me feel stupid. But what bothered me most was that Grueman gave no indication that he remembered I had once been his student at Georgetown. To his credit, I had despised my first year of law school, had made my only B, and missed out on *Law Review*. I would never forget Nicholas Grueman as long as I lived, and it did not seem right that he should have forgotten me.

I heard from him on Thursday, not long after I had been informed that Eddie Heath was dead.

"Kay Scarpetta?" Grueman's voice came over the line.

"Yes." I closed my eyes and knew from the pressure behind them that a raging front was rapidly advancing.

"Nicholas Grueman here. I've been looking over Mr. Waddell's provisional autopsy report and have a few questions."

I said nothing.

"I'm talking about Ronnie Joe Waddell."

"What can I help you with?"

"Let's start with his so-called *almost tubular* stomach. An interesting description, by the way. I'm wondering if that's your vernacular or a bona fide medical term? Am I correct in assuming Mr. Waddell wasn't eating?"

"I can't say that he wasn't eating at all. But his stomach had shrunk. It was empty and clean."

"Was it, perhaps, reported to you that he may have been on a hunger strike?"

"No such thing was reported to me." I glanced up at the clock and light stabbed my eyes. I was out of aspirin and had left my decongestant at home.

I heard pages flip.

"It says here that you found abrasions on his arms, the inner aspects of both upper arms," Grueman said.

"That's correct."

"And just what, exactly, is an *inner aspect*?"

"The inside of the arm above the antecubital fossa."

A pause. "The *antecubital fossa*," he said in amazement.

"Well, let me see. I've got my own arm turned palm up and am looking at the inside of my elbow. Or where the arm folds, actually. That would be accurate, wouldn't it? To say that the inner aspect is the side where the arm folds, and the antecubital fossa, therefore, is where the arm folds?"

"That would be accurate."

"Well, well, very good. And to what do you attribute these injuries to the inner aspects of Mr. Waddell's arms?"

"Possibly to restraints," I said testily.

"Restraints?"

"Yes, as in the leather restraints associated with the electric chair."

"You said *possibly*. Possibly restraints?"

"That's what I said."

"Meaning, you can't say with certainty, Dr. Scarpetta?"

"There's very little in this life that one can say with certainty, Mr. Grueman."

"Meaning that it would be reasonable to entertain the possibility that the restraints that caused the abrasions could have been of a different variety? Such as the human variety? Such as marks left by human hands?"

"The abrasions I found are inconsistent with injuries inflicted by human hands," I said.

"And are they consistent with the injuries inflicted by the electric chair, with the restraints associated with it?"

"It is my opinion that they would be."

"Your *opinion*, Dr. Scarpetta?"

"I haven't actually examined the electric chair," I said sharply.

This was followed by a long pause, for which Nicholas Grueman had been famous in the classroom when he wanted a student's obvious inadequacy to hang in the air. I envisioned him hovering over me, hands clasped behind his back, his face expressionless as the clock ticked loudly on the wall. Once I had endured his silent scrutiny for more than two minutes as my eyes raced blindly over pages of the casebook opened before me. And as I sat at my solid walnut desk some twenty years later, a middle-aged chief medical examiner with enough degrees and certificates to paper a wall, I felt my face begin to burn. I felt the old humiliation and rage.

Susan walked into my office as Grueman abruptly ended the encounter with "Good day" and hung up.

"Eddie Heath's body is here." Her surgical gown was untied in back and clean, the expression on her face distracted. "Can he wait until the morning?"

"No," I said. "He can't."

The boy looked smaller on the cold steel table than he had seemed in the bright sheets of his hospital bed. There were no rainbows in this room, no walls or windows decorated with dinosaurs or color to cheer the heart of a child. Eddie Heath had come in naked with IV needles, catheter, and dressings still in place. They seemed sad remnants of what had held him to this world and then disconnected him from it, like string tailing a balloon blowing forlornly through empty air. For the better part of an hour I documented injuries and marks of therapy while Susan took photographs and answered the phone.

We had locked the doors leading into the autopsy suite, and beyond I could hear people getting off the elevator and heading home in the rapidly descending dark. Twice the buzzer sounded in the bay as funeral home attendants arrived to bring a body or take one away. The wounds to Eddie's shoulder and thigh were dry and a dark shiny red.

"God," Susan said, staring. "God, who would do something like that? Look at all the little cuts to the edges, too. It's like somebody cut crisscrosses and then removed the whole area of skin."

"That's precisely what I think was done."

"You think someone carved some sort of pattern?"

"I think someone attempted to eradicate something. And when that didn't work, he removed the skin."

"Eradicate what?"

"Nothing that was already there," I said. "He had no tattoos, birthmarks, or scars in those areas. If something wasn't already there, then perhaps something was added and had to be removed because of the potential evidentiary value."

"Something like bite marks."

"Yes," I said.

The body was not yet fully rigorous and was still slightly warm as I began swabbing any area that a washcloth might have missed. I checked axillas, gluteal folds, behind ears and inside them, and inside the navel. I clipped fingernails into clean white envelopes and looked for fibers and other debris in hair.

Susan continued to glance at me, and I sensed her tension. Finally she asked, "Anything special you're looking for?"

"Dried seminal fluid, for one thing," I said.

"In his axilla?"

"There, in any crease in skin, any orifice, anywhere."

"You don't usually look in all those places."

"I don't usually look for zebras."

"For what?"

"We used to have a saying in medical school. If you hear hoofbeats, look for horses. But in a case like this I know we're looking for zebras," I said.

I began going over every inch of the body with a lens. When I got to his wrists, I slowly turned his hands this way and that, studying them for such a long time that Susan stopped what she was doing. I referred to the diagrams on my clipboard, correlating each mark of therapy with the ones I had drawn.

"Where are his charts?" I glanced around.

"Over here." Susan fetched paperwork from a countertop.

I began flipping through charts, concentrating particularly on emergency room records and the report filled in by the rescue squad. Nowhere did it indicate that Eddie Heath's hands had been bound. I tried to remember what Detective Trent had said to me when describing the scene where the boy's body had been found. Hadn't Trent said that Eddie's hands were by his sides?

"You find something?" Susan finally asked.

"You have to look through the lens to see. There. The undersides of his wrists and here on the left one, to the left of the wrist bone. You see the gummy residue? The traces of adhesive? It looks like smudges of grayish dirt."

"Just barely. And maybe some fibers sticking to it," Susan marveled, her shoulder pressed against mine as she stared through the lens.

"And the skin's smooth," I continued to point out. "Less hair in this area than here and here."

"Because when the tape was removed, hairs would have been pulled out."

"Exactly. We'll take wrist hairs for exemplars. The adhesive and fibers can be matched back to the tape, if the tape is ever recovered. And if the tape that bound him is recovered, it can be matched back to the roll."

"I don't understand." She straightened up and looked at me. "His IV lines were held in place with adhesive tape. You sure that's not the explanation?"

"There are no needle marks on these areas of his wrists that would indicate marks of therapy," I said to her. "And you saw what was taped to him when he came in. Nothing to account for the adhesive here."

"True."

"Let's take photographs and then I'm going to collect this adhesive residue and let Trace see what they find."

"His body was outside next to a Dumpster. Seems like that would be a Trace nightmare."

"It depends on whether this residue on his wrists was in contact with the pavement." I began gently scraping the residue off with a scalpel.

"I don't guess they did a vacuuming out there."

"No, I'm sure they wouldn't have. But I think we can still get sweepings if we ask nicely. It can't hurt to try."

I continued examining Eddie Heath's thin forearms and wrists, looking for contusions or abrasions I might have missed. But I did not find any.

"His ankles look okay," Susan said from the far end of the table. "I don't see any adhesive or areas where the hair is gone. No injuries. It doesn't look like he was taped around his ankles. Just his wrists."

I could recall only a few cases in which a victim's tight bindings had left no mark on skin. Clearly, the strapping tape had been in direct contact with Eddie's skin. He should have moved his hands, wriggled as his discomfort had grown and his circulation had been restricted. But he had not resisted. He had not tugged or squirmed or tried to get away.

I thought of the blood drips on the shoulder of his jacket and the soot and stippling on the collar. I again checked around his mouth, looked at his tongue, and glanced over his charts. If he had been gagged, there was no evidence of it now, no abrasions or bruises, no traces of adhesive. I imagined him propped against the Dumpster, naked and in the bitter cold, his clothing piled by his side, not neatly, not sloppily, but casually from the way it had been described to me. When I tried to sense the emotion of the crime, I did not detect anger, panic, or fear.

"He shot him first, didn't he?" Susan's eyes were alert like those of a wary stranger you pass on a desolate, dark street. "Whoever did this taped his wrists together after he shot him."

"I'm thinking that."

"But that's so weird," she said. "You don't need to bind someone you've just shot in the head."

"We don't know what this individual fantasizes about." The sinus headache had arrived and I had fallen like a city under siege. My eyes were watering; my skull was two sizes too small.

Susan pulled the thick electrical cord down from its reel and plugged in the Stryker saw. She snapped new blades in scalpels and checked the knives on the surgical cart. She disappeared into the X-ray room and returned with Eddie's films, which she fixed to light boxes. She scurried about frenetically and then did something she had never done before. She bumped hard against the surgical cart she had been arranging and sent two quart jars of formalin crashing to the floor.

I ran to her as she jumped back, gasping, waving fumes from her face and sending broken glass skittering across the floor as her feet almost went out from under her.

"Did it get your face?" I grabbed her arm and hurried her toward the locker room.

"I don't think so. No. Oh, God. It's on my feet and legs. I think on my arm, too."

"You're sure it's not in your eyes or mouth?" I helped her strip off her greens.

"I'm sure."

I ducked inside the shower and turned on the water as she practically tore off the rest of her clothes.

I made her stand beneath a blast of tepid water for a very long time as I donned mask, safety glasses, and thick rubber gloves. I soaked up the hazardous chemical with formalin pillows, supplied by the state for biochemical emergencies like this. I swept up glass and tied everything inside double plastic bags. Then I hosed down the floor, washed myself, and changed into fresh greens. Susan eventually emerged from the shower, bright pink and scared.

"Dr. Scarpetta, I'm so sorry," she said.

"My only concern is you. Are you all right?"

"I feel weak and a little dizzy. I can still smell the fumes."

"I'll finish up here," I said. "Why don't you go home."

"I think I'll just rest for a while first. Maybe I'd better go upstairs."

My lab coat was draped over the back of a chair, and I reached inside a pocket and got out my keys. "Here," I said, handing them to her. "You can lie down on the couch in my office. Get on the intercom immediately if the dizziness doesn't go away or you start feeling worse."

She reappeared about an hour later, her winter coat on and buttoned up to her chin.

"How do you feel?" I asked as I sutured the Y incision.

"A little shaky but okay."

She watched me in silence for a moment, then added, "I thought of something while I was upstairs. I don't think you should list me as a witness in this case."

I glanced up at her in surprise. It was routine for anyone present during an autopsy to be listed as a witness on the official report. Susan's request wasn't of great importance, but it was peculiar.

"I didn't participate in the autopsy," she went on. "I mean, I helped with the external exam but wasn't present when you did the post. And I know this is going to be a big case—if they ever catch anyone. If it ever goes to court. And I just think it's better if I'm not listed, since, like I said, I really wasn't present."

"Fine," I said. "I have no problem with that."

She placed my keys on a counter and left.

* * *

Marino was home when I tried him from my car phone as I slowed at a tollbooth about an hour later.

"Do you know the warden at Spring Street?" I asked him.

"Frank Donahue. Where are you?"

"In my car."

"I thought so. Probably half the truckers in Virginia are listening to us on the their CBs."

"They won't hear much."

"I heard about the kid," he said. "You finished with him?"

"Yes. I'll call you from home. There's something you can do for me in the meantime. I need to look over a few things at the pen right away."

"The problem with looking over the pen is it looks back."

"That's why you're going with me," I said.

If nothing else, after two miserable semesters of my former professor's tutelage I had learned to be prepared. So it was on Saturday afternoon that Marino and I were en route to the state penitentiary. Skies were leaden, wind thrashing trees along the roadsides, the universe in a state of cold agitation, as if reflecting my mood.

"You want my private opinion," Marino said to me as we drove, "I think you're letting Grueman jerk you around."

"Not at all."

"Then why is it every time there's an execution and he's involved, you act jerked around?"

"And how would you handle the situation?"

He pushed in the cigarette lighter. "Same way you are. I'd take a damn look at death row and the chair, document everything, and then tell him he's full of shit. Or better yet, tell the press he's full of shit."

In this morning's paper Grueman was quoted as saying

that Waddell had not been receiving proper nourishment and his body bore bruises I could not adequately explain.

"What's the deal, anyway?" Marino went on. "Was he defending these squirrels when you was in law school?"

"No. Several years ago he was asked to run Georgetown's Criminal Justice Clinic. That's when he began taking on death penalty cases pro bono."

"The guy must have a screw loose."

"He's very opposed to capital punishment and has managed to turn whoever he represents into a cause célèbre. Waddell in particular."

"Yo. Saint Nick, the patron saint of dirtbags. Ain't that sweet," Marino said. "Why don't you send him color photos of Eddie Heath and ask if he wants to talk to the boy's family? See how he feels about the pig who committed *that* crime."

"Nothing will change Grueman's opinions."

"He got kids? A wife? Anybody he cares about?"

"It doesn't make any difference, Marino. I don't guess you've got anything new on Eddie."

"No, and neither does Henrico. We've got his clothes and a twenty-two bullet. Maybe the labs will get lucky with the stuff you turned in."

"What about VICAP?" I asked, referring to the FBI's Violent Criminal Apprehension Program, in which Marino and FBI profiler Benton Wesley were regional team partners.

"Trent's working on the forms and will send them off in a couple days," Marino said. "And I alerted Benton about the case last night."

"Was Eddie the type to get into a stranger's car?"

"According to his parents, he wasn't. We're either dealing with a blitz attack or someone who earned the kid's confidence long enough to grab him."

"Does he have brothers and sisters?"

"One of each, both more than ten years older than him. I

think Eddie was an accident," Marino said as the penitentiary came into view.

Years of neglect had faded its stucco veneer to a dirty, diluted shade of Pepto Bismol pink. Windows were dark and covered in thick plastic, tugged and torn by the wind. We took the Belvedere exit, then turned left on Spring Street, a shabby strip of pavement connecting two entities that did not belong on the same map. It continued several blocks past the penitentiary, then simply quit at Gambles Hill, where Ethyl Corporation's white brick headquarters roosted on a rise of perfect lawn like a great white heron at the edge of a landfill.

Drizzle had turned to sleet when we parked and got out of the car. I followed Marino past a Dumpster, then a ramp leading to a loading dock occupied by a number of cats, their insouciance flickering with the wariness of the wild. The main entrance was a single glass door, and stepping inside what purported to be the lobby, we found ourselves behind bars. There were no chairs; the air was frigid and stale. To our right the Communication Center was accessible by a small window, which a sturdy woman in a guard's uniform took her time sliding open.

"Can I help you?"

Marino displayed his badge and laconically explained that we had an appointment with Frank Donahue, the warden. She told us to wait. The window shut again.

"That's Helen the Hun," Marino said to me. "I've been down here more times than I can count and she always acts like she don't know me. But then, I'm not her type. You'll get better acquainted with her in a minute."

Beyond barred gates were a dingy corridor of tan tile and cinder block, and small offices that looked like cages. The view ended with the first block of cells, tiers painted institutional green and spotted with rust. They were empty.

"When will the rest of the inmates be relocated?" I asked.

"By the end of the week."

"Who's left?"

"Some real Virginia gentlemen, the squirrels with segregation status. They're all locked up tight and chained to their beds in C Cell, which is that way." He pointed west. "We won't be walking through there, so don't get antsy. I wouldn't put you through that. Some of these assholes haven't seen a woman in years—and Helen the Hun don't count."

A powerfully built young man dressed in Department of Corrections blues appeared down the corridor and headed our way. He peered at us through bars, his face attractive but hard, with a strong jaw and cold gray eyes. A dark red mustache hid an upper lip that I suspected could turn cruel.

Marino introduced us, adding, "We're here to see the chair."

"Yeah, my name's Roberts and I'm here to give you the royal tour." Keys jingled against iron as he opened the heavy gates. "Donahue's out sick today." The clang of doors shutting behind us echoed off walls. "I'm afraid we got to search you first. If you'll step over there, ma'am."

He began running a scanner over Marino as another barred door opened and "Helen" emerged from the Communication Center. She was an unsmiling woman built like a Baptist church, her shiny Sam Browne belt the only indication she had a waist. Her close-cropped hair was mannishly styled and dyed shoe-polish black, her eyes intense when they briefly met mine. The name tag pinned on a formidable breast read "Grimes."

"Your bag," she ordered.

I handed over my medical bag. She rifled through it, then roughly turned me this way and that as she subjected me to a salvo of probes and pats with the scanner and her hands. In all, the search couldn't have lasted more than twenty seconds, but she managed to acquaint herself with every inch of my flesh, crushing me against her stiffly armored bosom like a wide-bodied spider as thick fingers lingered and she breathed loudly through her mouth. Then she brusquely nodded that I checked out okay as she returned to her lair of cinder block and iron.

Marino and I followed Roberts past bars and more bars, through a series of doors that he unlocked and relocked, the air cold and ringing with the dull chimes of unfriendly metal. He asked us nothing about ourselves and made no references that I would call remotely friendly. His preoccupation seemed to be his role, which this afternoon was tour guide or guard dog, I wasn't sure which.

A right turn and we entered the first cell block, a huge drafty space of green cinder block and broken windows, with four tiers of cells rising to a false roof topped by coils of barbed wire. Sloppily piled along the middle of the brown tile floor were dozens of narrow, plastic-covered mattresses, and scattered about were brooms, mops, and ratty red barber chairs. Leather tennis shoes, blue jeans, and other odd personal effects littered high windowsills, and left inside many of the cells were televisions, books, and footlockers. It appeared that when the inmates had been evacuated they had not been allowed to take all of their possessions with them, perhaps explaining the obscenities scrawled in Magic Marker on the walls.

More doors were unlocked, and we found ourselves outside in the yard, a square of browning grass surrounded by ugly cell blocks. There were no trees. Guard towers rose from each corner of the wall, the men inside wearing heavy coats and holding rifles. We moved quickly and in silence as sleet stung our cheeks. Down several steps, we turned into another opening leading to an iron door more massive than any of the others I had seen.

"The east basement," Roberts said, inserting a key in the lock. "This is the place where no one wants to be."

We stepped inside death row.

Against the east wall were five cells, each furnished with an iron bed and a white porcelain sink and toilet. In the center of the room were a large desk and several chairs where guards sat around the clock when death row was occupied.

"Waddell was in cell two." Roberts pointed. "According to the laws of the Commonwealth, an inmate must be transferred here fifteen days prior to his execution."

"Who had access to him while he was here?" Marino asked.

"Same people who always have access to death row. Legal representatives, the clergy, and members of the death team."

"The death team?" I asked.

"It's made up of Corrections officers and supervisors, the identities of which are confidential. The team becomes involved when an inmate is shipped here from Mecklenburg. They guard him, set up everything from beginning to end."

"Don't sound like a very pleasant assignment," Marino commented.

"It's not an assignment, it's a choice," Roberts replied with the machismo and inscrutability of coaches interviewed after the big game.

"It don't bother you?" Marino asked. "I mean, come on, I saw Waddell go to the chair. It's got to bother you."

"Doesn't bother me in the least. I go home afterward, drink a few beers, go to bed." He reached in the breast pocket of his uniform shirt and pulled out a pack of cigarettes.

"Now, according to Donahue, you want to know everything that happened. So I'm going to walk you through it." He sat on top of the desk, smoking. "On the day of it, December thirteenth, Waddell was allowed a two-hour contact visit with members of his immediate family, which in this case was his mother. We put him in waist chains, leg irons, and cuffs and led him over to the visitors' side around one P.M.

"At five P.M., he ate his last meal. His request was sirloin steak, salad, a baked potato, and pecan pie, which we had prepared for him at Bonanza Steak House. He didn't pick the restaurant. The inmates don't get to do that. And, as is the routine, there were two identical meals ordered. The inmate eats one, a member of the death team eats the other. And this is all to make sure some overly enthusiastic chef doesn't decide to speed up the inmate's journey to the Great Beyond by spicing the food with something extra like arsenic."

"Did Waddell eat his meal?" I asked, thinking about his empty stomach.

"He wasn't real hungry—asked us to save it for him to eat the next day."

"He must have thought Governor Norring was going to pardon him," Marino said.

"I don't know what he thought. I'm just reporting to you what Waddell said when he was served his meal. Afterward, at seven-thirty, personal property officers came to his cell to take an inventory of his property and ask him what he wanted done with it. We're talking about one wristwatch, one ring, various articles of clothing and mail, books, poetry. At eight P.M., he was taken from his cell. His head, face, and right ankle were shaved. He was weighed, showered, and dressed in the clothing he would wear to the chair. Then he was returned to his cell.

"At ten-forty-five, his death warrant was read to him, witnessed by the death team." Roberts got up from the desk. "Then he was led, without restraints, to the adjoining room."

"What was his demeanor at this point?" Marino asked as Roberts unlocked another door and opened it.

"Let's just say that his racial affiliation did not permit him to be white as a sheet. Otherwise, he would've been."

The room was smaller than I had imagined. About six feet from the back wall and centered on the shiny brown cement floor was the chair, a stark, rigid throne of dark polished oak. Thick leather straps were looped around the high slatted back, the two front legs, and the armrests.

"Waddell was seated and the first strap fastened was the chest strap," Roberts continued in the same indifferent tone. "Then the two arm straps, the belly strap, and the straps for the legs." He roughly plucked at each strap as he talked. "It took one minute to strap him in. His face was covered with the leather mask—and I'll show you that in a minute. The helmet was placed on his head, the leg piece attached to his right leg."

I got out my camera, a ruler, and photocopies of Waddell's body diagrams.

"At exactly two minutes past eleven, he received the first current—that's twenty-five hundred volts and six and a half amps. Two amps will kill you, by the way."

The injuries marked on Waddell's body diagrams correlated nicely with the construction of the chair and its restraints.

"The helmet attaches to this." Roberts pointed out a pipe running from the ceiling and ending with a copper wing nut directly over the chair.

I began taking photographs of the chair from every angle.

"And the leg piece attaches to this wing nut here."

The flashbulb going off gave me a strange sensation. I was getting jumpy.

"All this man was, was one big circuit breaker."

"When did he start to bleed?" I asked.

"The minute he was hit the first time, ma'am. And he didn't stop until it was completely over, then a curtain was drawn, blocking him from the view of the witnesses. Three members of the death team undid his shirt and the doc listened with his stethoscope and felt the carotid and pronounced him. Waddell was placed on a gurney and taken into the cooling room, which is where we're headed next."

"Your theory about the chair allegedly malfunctioning?" I said.

"Pure crap. Waddell was six-foot-four, weighed two hundred and fifty-nine pounds. He was cooking long before he sat in the chair, his blood pressure probably out of sight. After he was pronounced, because of the bleeding, the deputy director came over to take a look at him. His eyeballs hadn't popped out. His eardrums hadn't popped out. Waddell had a damn nosebleed, same thing people get when they strain too hard on the toilet."

I silently agreed with him. Waddell's nosebleed was due to the Valsalva maneuver, or an abrupt increase in intrathoracic pressure. Nicholas Grueman would not be pleased with the report I planned to send him.

"What tests had you run to make sure the chair was operating properly?" Marino asked.

"Same ones we always do. First, Virginia Power looks at the equipment and checks it out." He pointed to a large circuit box enclosed in gray steel doors in the wall behind the chair. "Inside this is twenty two-hundred-watt light bulbs attached to plyboard for running tests. We test this during the week before the execution, three times the day of it, and then once more in front of the witnesses after they've assembled."

"Yeah, I remember that," Marino said, staring at the glass-enclosed witness booth no more than fifteen feet away. Inside were twelve black plastic chairs arranged in three neat rows.

"Everything worked like a charm," Roberts said.

"Has it always?" I asked.

"To my knowledge, yes, ma'am."

"And the switch, where is that?"

He directed my attention to a box on the wall to the right of the witness booth. "A key cuts the power on. But the button's in the control room. The warden or a designee turns the key and pushes the button. You want to see that?"

"I think I'd better."

It wasn't much to look at, just a small cubicle directly behind the back wall of the room housing the chair. Inside was a large G.E. box with various dials to raise and lower the voltage, which went as high as three thousand volts. Rows of small lights affirmed that everything was fine or warned that things were not.

"At Greensville, it will all be computerized," Roberts added.

Inside a wooden cupboard were the helmet, leg piece, and two thick cables, which, he explained as he held them up, "attach to the wing nuts above and to one side of the chair, and then to this wing nut on top of the helmet and the one here on the leg piece." He did this without effort, adding, "Just like hooking up a VCR."

The helmet and leg piece were copper riddled with holes, through which cotton string was woven to secure the sponge lining inside. The helmet was surprisingly light, a patina of green tarnish at the edges of the connecting plates. I could not imagine having such a thing placed on top of my head. The black leather mask was nothing more than a wide, crude belt that buckled behind the inmate's head, a small triangle cut in it for the nose. It could have been on display in the Tower of London and I would not have questioned its authenticity.

We passed a transformer with coils leading to the ceiling, and Roberts unlocked another door. We stepped inside another room.

"This is the cooling room," he said. "We wheeled Waddell in here and transferred him to this table."

It was steel, rust showing at the joints.

"We let him cool down for ten minutes, put sandbags on his leg. That's them right there."

The sandbags were stacked on the floor at the foot of the table.

"Ten pounds each. Call it a knee-jerk reaction, but the leg's severely bent. The sandbags straighten it out. And if the burns are bad, like Waddell's were, we dress them with gauze. All done, and we put Waddell back on the stretcher and carried him out the same way you came in. Only we didn't bother with the stairs. No point in anybody getting a hernia. We used the food elevator and carried him out the front door, and loaded him in the ambulance. Then we hauled him into your place, just like we always do after our children ride the Sparky."

Heavy doors slammed. Keys jangled. Locks clicked. Roberts continued talking boisterously as he led us back to the lobby. I barely listened and Marino did not say a word. Sleet mixed with rain beaded grass and walls with ice. The sidewalk was wet, the cold penetrating. I felt queasy. I was desperate to take a long, hot shower and change my clothes.

"Lowlifes like Roberts are just one level above the inmates," Marino said as he started the car. "In fact, some of them aren't any better than the drones they lock up."

Moments later he stopped at a red light. Drops of water on the windshield shimmered like blood, were wiped away and replaced by a thousand more. Ice coated trees like glass.

"You got time for me to show you something?" Marino wiped condensation off the windshield with his coat sleeve.

"Depending on how important it is, I suppose I could make time." I hoped my obvious reluctance would inspire him to take me home instead.

"I want to retrace Eddie Heath's last steps for you." He flipped on the turn signal. "In particular, I think you need to see where his body was found."

The Heaths lived east of Chamberlayne Avenue, or on the wrong side of it, in Marino's words. Their small brick house was but several blocks from a Golden Skillet fried chicken restaurant and the convenience store where Eddie had walked to buy his mother a can of soup. Several cars, large and American, were parked in the Heaths' driveway, and smoke drifted out the chimney and disappeared in the smoky gray sky. Aluminum glinted dully as the front screen door opened and an old woman bundled in a black coat emerged, then paused to speak to someone inside. Clinging to the railing as if the afternoon threatened to pitch her overboard, she made her way down the steps, glancing blankly at the white Ford LTD cruising past.

Had we continued east for another two miles, we would have entered the war zone of the federal housing projects.

"This neighborhood used to be all white," Marino said. "I remember when I first came to Richmond this was a good area to live. Lots of decent, hardworking folks who kept their yards real nice and went to church on Sunday. Times change. Me, I wouldn't let any kid of mine walk around out here after dark. But when you live in a place, you get comfortable. Eddie was comfortable walking around, delivering his papers, and running errands for his mother.

"The night it happened he came out the front door of his crib, cut through to Azalea, then took a right like we're doing as I speak. There's Lucky's on our left, next to the gas station." He pointed out a convenience store with a green horseshoe on the lighted sign. "That corner right over there is a popular hangout for drug drones. They trade crack for cash and fade. We catch the cockroaches, and two days later they're on another corner doing the same thing."

"A possibility Eddie was involved in drugs?" My question would have been somewhat farfetched back in the days when I began my career, but no longer. Juveniles now comprised approximately ten percent of all narcotics trafficking arrests in Virginia.

"No indication of it so far. My gut tells me he wasn't," Marino said.

He pulled into the convenience store's parking lot, and we sat gazing out at advertisements taped to plate glass and lights shining garishly through fog. Customers formed a long line by the counter as the harried clerk worked the cash register without looking up. A young black man in high tops and a leather coat stared insolently at our car as he sauntered out with a quart of beer and dropped change in a pay phone near the front door. A man, red-faced and in paint-spattered jeans, peeled cellophane off a pack of cigarettes as he trotted to his truck.

"I'm betting this is where he met up with his assailant," Marino said.

"How?" I said.

"I think it went down simple as hell. I think he came out of the store and this animal came right up to him and fed him a line to gain his confidence. He said something and Eddie went with him and got in the car."

"His physical findings would certainly support that," I said. "He had no defense injuries, nothing to indicate a struggle. No one inside the convenience store saw him with anyone?"

"No one I've talked to so far. But you see how busy this joint is, and it was dark out. If anybody saw anything, it was probably a customer coming in or returning to his car. I plan to get the media to run something so we can appeal to anyone who might have stopped here between five and six that night. And Crime Stoppers is going to do a segment on it, too."

"Was Eddie streetwise?"

"You get a squirrel who's smooth and even kids who know better can fall for it. I had a case back in New York where a ten-year-old girl walked to the local store to buy a pound of sugar. As she's leaving, this pedophile approaches her and says her father's sent him. He says her mom's just been rushed to the hospital and he's supposed to pick the girl up and take her there. She gets in his car and ends up a statistic." He glanced over at me. "All right, white or black?"

"In which case?"

"Eddie Heath's."

"Based on what you've said, the assailant is white."

Marino backed up and waited for a break in traffic. "No question the MO fits for white. Eddie's old man don't like blacks and Eddie didn't trust them, either, so it's unlikely a black guy gained Eddie's confidence. And if people notice a white boy walking with a white man—even if the boy looks unhappy—they think big brother and little brother or father and son." He turned right, heading west. "Keep going, Doc. What else?"

Marino loved this game. It gave him just as much pleasure when I echoed his thoughts as it did when he believed I was flat-out wrong.

"If the assailant is white, then the next conclusion I'd make is he's not from the projects, despite their close proximity."

"Race aside, why else might you conclude that the perp's not from the projects?"

"The MO again," I said simply. "Shooting someone in the head—even a thirteen-year-old—would not be unheard of in a street killing, but aside from that, nothing fits. Eddie was shot with a twenty-two, not with a nine- or ten-millimeter or large-caliber revolver. He was nude and he was mutilated, suggesting the violence was sexually motivated. As far as we know, he had nothing worth stealing and did not appear to have a life-style that put him at risk."

It was raining hard now, and streets were treacherous with cars moving at imprudent rates of speed with their headlights on. I supposed many people were headed to shopping malls, and it occurred to me that I had done little to prepare for Christmas.

The grocery store on Patterson Avenue was just ahead on

our left. I could not remember its former name, and signs had been removed, leaving nothing but a bare brick shell with a number of windows boarded up. The space it occupied was poorly lit, and I suspected the police would not have bothered to check behind the building at all were there not a row of businesses to the left of it. I counted five of them: pharmacy, shoe repair, dry cleaner, hardware store, and Italian restaurant, all closed and deserted the night Eddie Heath was driven here and left for dead.

"Do you recall when this grocery store went out of business?" I asked.

"About the same time a bunch of other places did. When the war started in the Persian Gulf," Marino said.

He cut through an alleyway, the high beams of his headlights licking brick walls and rocking when the unpaved ground got rough. Behind the store a chain-link fence separated an apron of cracked asphalt from a wooded area stirring darkly in the wind. Through the limbs of bare trees I could see streetlights in the distance and the illuminated sign for a Burger King.

Marino parked, headlights boring into a brown Dumpster cancerous with blistered paint and rust, beads of water running down its sides. Raindrops smacked against glass and drummed the roof, and dispatchers were busy dispatching cars to the scenes of accidents.

Marino pushed his hands against the steering wheel and hunched his shoulders. He massaged the back of his neck. "Christ, I'm getting old," he complained. "I got a rain slicker in the trunk."

"You need it more than I do. I won't melt," I said, opening my door.

Marino fetched his navy blue police raincoat and I turned my collar up to my ears. The rain stung my face and coldly tapped the top of my head. Almost instantly, my ears started getting numb. The Dumpster was near the fence, at the outer limits of the pavement, perhaps twenty yards from the back of the grocery store. I noted that the Dumpster opened from the top, not the side.

"Was the door to the Dumpster open or shut when the police got here?" I asked Marino.

"Shut." The hood of his raincoat made it difficult for him to look at me without turning his upper body. "You notice there's nothing to step up on." He shone a flashlight around the Dumpster. "Also, it was empty. Not a damn thing in it except rust and the carcass of a rat big enough to saddle up and ride."

"Can you lift the door?"

"Only a couple inches. Most of the ones made like this have a latch on either side. If you're tall enough, you can lift the lid a couple inches and slide your hand down along the edge, continuing to raise the lid by bumping the latches in place a little at a time. Eventually you can get it open far enough to stuff a bag of trash inside. Problem is, the latches on this one don't catch. You'd have to open the lid all the way and let it flop over on the other side, and no way you're going to do that unless you climb up on something."

"You're what? Six-one or -two?"

"Yeah. If I can't open the Dumpster, he couldn't either. The favorite theory at the moment is he carried the body out of the car and leaned it up against the Dumpster while he tried to open the door—the same way you put a bag of garbage down for a minute to free your hands. When he can't get the door open, he hauls ass, leaving the kid and his crap right here on the pavement."

"He could have dragged him back there in the woods."

"There's a fence."

"It's not very high, maybe five feet high," I pointed out. "At the very least, he could have left the body *behind* the Dumpster. As it was, if you drove back here, the body was in plain sight."

Marino looked around in silence, shining the flashlight through the chain-link fence. Raindrops streaked through the narrow beam like a million small nails driven down from heaven. I could barely bend my fingers. My hair was soaked and icy water was trickling down my neck. We returned to the car and he switched the heater up high.

"Trent and his guys are all hung up on the Dumpster theory, the location of its door and so on," he said. "My personal opinion is the Dumpster's only role in this is it was a damn easel for the squirrel to prop his work of art against."

I looked out through the rain.

"The point is," he went on in a hard voice, "he didn't bring the kid back here to conceal the body but to make sure it was found. But the guys with Henrico just don't see it. I not only see it, I feel it like something breathing down the back of my neck."

I continued staring out at the Dumpster, the image of Eddie Heath's small body propped against it so vivid it was as if I had been present when he was found. The realization struck me suddenly and hard.

"When was the last time you went through the Robyn Naismith case?" I asked.

"It doesn't matter. I remember everything about it," Marino said, staring straight ahead. "I was waiting to see if it would cross your mind. It hit me the first time I came out here."

3

That night I built a fire and ate vegetable soup in front of it as freezing rain mixed with snow. I had switched off lamps and drawn draperies back from the sliding glass doors. Grass was frosted white, rhododendron leaves curled tight, winter-bare trees backlit by the moon.

The day had drained me, as if a greedy, dark force had sucked the light right out of my being. I felt the invasive hands of a prison guard named Helen, and smelled the stale stench of hovels that once had housed remorseless, hateful men. I remembered holding slides up to lamplight in a hotel bar in New Orleans at the American Academy of Forensic Sciences' annual meeting. Robyn Naismith's homicide was then unsolved, and to discuss what had been done to her as Mardi Gras revelers loudly drifted past had somehow seemed ghastly.

She had been beaten and bullied, and stabbed to death, it was believed, in her living room. But it was Waddell's postmortem acts that had shocked people most, his uncommon and creepy ritual. After she was dead, he undressed her. If he raped her, there was no evidence of it. His preference, it seemed, was to bite and repeatedly penetrate the fleshier parts of her body with a knife. When her friend from work stopped by to check on her, she found Robyn's battered body propped against the television, head drooping forward, arms by her sides, legs straight out, and clothing piled nearby. She looked like a bloody, life-size doll returned to its place after a session of make-believe and play that had turned into a horror.

The court testimony of a psychiatrist was that after Waddell had murdered her, he was overcome by remorse and had sat talking to her body for perhaps hours. A forensic psychologist for the Commonwealth speculated quite the opposite, that Waddell knew Robyn was a television personality and his act of propping her body against the television set was symbolic. He was watching her on TV again and fantasizing. He was returning her to the medium that had brought about their introduction, and this, of course, implied premeditation. The nuances and twists in the endless analyses got only more complicated with time.

The grotesque display of that twenty-seven-year-old anchorwoman's body was Waddell's special signature. Now a little boy was dead ten years later and someone had signed his work—on the eve of Waddell's execution—the same way.

I made coffee, poured it into a thermos, and carried it into my study. Sitting at my desk, I booted up my computer and dialed into the one downtown. I had yet to see the printout of the search Margaret had conducted for me, though I suspected it was one of the reports in the depressingly large stack of paperwork that had been in my box late Friday afternoon. The output file, however, would still be on the hard disk. At the UNIX log-in I typed my user name and password and was greeted by the flashing word *mail*. Margaret, my computer analyst, had sent me a message.

"Check flesh file," it read.

"That's really awful," I muttered, as if Margaret could hear.

Changing to the directory called Chief, where Margaret routinely directed output and copied files I had requested, I brought up the file she had named Flesh.

It was quite large because Margaret had selected from all manners of death and then merged the data with what she had generated from the Trauma Registry. Unsurprisingly, most of the cases the computer had picked up were accidents in which limbs and tissue had been lost in vehicular crashes and misadventures with machines. Four cases were homicides in which the bodies bore bite marks. Two of those victims had been stabbed, the other two strangled. One of the victims was an adult male, two were adult females, and one was a female only six years old. I jotted down case numbers and ICD-9 codes.

Next I began scanning screen after screen of the Trauma Registry's records of victims who had survived long enough to be admitted to a hospital. I expected the information to be a problem, and it was. Hospitals released patient data only after it had been as sterilized and depersonalized as operating rooms. For purposes of confidentiality, names, Social Security numbers, and other identifiers were stripped away. There was no common link as the person traveled through the paperwork labyrinth of rescue squads, emergency rooms, various police departments, and other agencies. The sorry end of the story was that data about a victim might reside in six different agency data bases and never be matched, especially if there had been any entry errors along the way. It was possible, therefore, for me to discover a case that aroused my interest without having much hope of figuring out who the patient was or if he or she had eventually died.

Making a note of Trauma Registry records that might

prove interesting, I exited the file. Finally, I ran a list command to see what old data reports, memos, or notes in my directory I could remove to free up space on the hard disk. That was when I spotted a file I did not understand.

The name of it was tty07. It was only sixteen bytes in size and the date and time were December 16, this past Thursday, at 4:26 in the afternoon. The file's contents was one alarming sentence:

I can't find it.

Reaching for the phone, I started to call Margaret at home and then stopped. The directory Chief and its files were secure. Though anyone could change to my directory, unless he logged in with my user name and password, he should not be able to list the files in Chief or read them. Margaret should be the only person besides me who knew my password. If she had gone into my directory, what was it she could not find and who was she saying this to?

Margaret wouldn't, I thought, staring intensely at that one brief sentence on the screen.

Yet I was unsure, and I thought of my niece. Perhaps Lucy knew UNIX. I glanced at my watch. It was past eight on a Saturday night and in a way I was going to be heartbroken if I found Lucy at home. She should be out on a date or with friends. She wasn't.

"Hi, Aunt Kay." She sounded surprised, reminding me that I had not called in a while.

"How's my favorite niece?"

"I'm your only niece. I'm fine."

"What are you doing at home on a Saturday night?" I asked.

"Finishing a term paper. What are you doing at home on a Saturday night?"

For an instant, I did not know what to say. My seventeen-year-old niece was more adept at putting me in my place than anyone I knew.

"I'm mulling over a computer problem," I finally said.

"Then you've certainly called the right department," said Lucy, who was not given to fits of modesty. "Hold on. Let me move these books and stuff out of the way so I can get to my keyboard."

"It's not a PC problem," I said. "I don't guess you know anything about the operating system called UNIX, do you?"

"I wouldn't call UNIX an operating system, Aunt Kay. It's like calling it the weather when it's really the environment, which is comprised of the weather and all the elements and the edifices. Are you using A-T an' T?"

"Good God, Lucy. I don't know."

"Well, what are you running it on?"

"An NCR mini."

"Then it's A-T an' T."

"I think someone might have broken security," I said.

"It happens. But what makes you think it?"

"I found a strange file in my directory, Lucy. My directory and its files are secure—you shouldn't be able to read anything unless you have my password."

"Wrong. If you have root privileges, you're the superuser and can do anything you want and read anything you want."

"My computer analyst is the only superuser."

"That may be true. But there may be a number of users who have root privileges, users you don't even know about that came with the software. We can check that easily, but first tell me about the strange file. What's it called and what's in it?"

"It's called t-t-y-oh-seven and there's a sentence in it that reads: 'I can't find it.' "

I heard keys clicking.

"What are you doing?" I asked.

"Making notes as we talk. Okay. Let's start with the obvious. A big clue is the file's name, t-t-y-oh-seven. That's a device. In other words, t-t-y-oh-seven is probably somebody's terminal in your office. It's possible it could be a printer, but my guess is that whoever was in your directory decided to send a note to the device called t-t-y-oh-seven. But this person screwed up and instead of sending a note, he created a file."

"When you write a note, aren't you creating a file?" I puzzled.

"Not if you're just sending keystrokes."

"How?"

"Easy. Are you in UNIX now?"

"Yes."

"Type cat redirect t-t-y-q—"

"Wait a minute."

"And don't worry about the slash-dev—"

"Lucy, slow down."

"We're deliberately leaving out the dev directory, which is what I'm betting this person did."

"What comes after cat?"

"Okay. Cat redirect and the device—"

"Please slow down."

"You should have a four-eighty-six chip in that thing, Aunt Kay. Why's it so slow?"

"It's not the damn chip that's slow!"

"Oh, I'm sorry," Lucy said sincerely. "I forgot."

Forgot what?

"Back to the problem," she went on. "I'm assuming you don't have a device called t-t-y-q, by the way. Where are you?"

"I'm still on cat," I said, frustrated. "Then it's redirect . . . Damn. That's the caret pointing right?"

"Yes. Now hit return and your cursor will be bumped down to the next line, which is blank. Then you type the message you want echoed to t-t-y-q's screen."

"See Spot run," I typed.

"Hit return and then do a control C," Lucy said. "Now

you can do an ls minus one and pipe it to p-g and you'll see your file."

I simply typed "ls" and caught a flash of something flying by.

"Here's what I think happened," Lucy resumed. "Someone was in your directory—and we'll get to that in a minute. Maybe they were looking for something in your files and couldn't find whatever it was. So this person sent a message, or tried to, to the device called t-t-y-oh-seven. Only he was in a hurry, and instead of typing cat redirect slash d-e-v slash t-t-y-oh-seven, he left out the dev directory and typed cat redirect t-t-y-oh-seven. So the keystrokes weren't echoed on t-t-y-oh-seven's screen at all. In other words, instead of sending a message to t-t-y-oh-seven, this person unwittingly created a file called t-t-y-oh-seven."

"If the person had typed in the proper command and sent the keystrokes, would the message have been saved?" I asked.

"No. The keystrokes would have appeared on t-t-y-oh-seven's screen, and would have stayed there until the user cleared it. But you would have seen no evidence of this in your directory or anywhere else. There wouldn't be a file."

"Meaning, we don't know how many times somebody might have sent a message from my directory, saying it was done correctly."

"That's right."

"How could someone have been able to read anything in my directory?" I went back to that basic question.

"You're sure no one else might have your password?"

"No one but Margaret."

"She's your computer analyst?"

"That's right."

"She wouldn't have given it to anyone?"

"I can't imagine that she would," I said.

"Okay. You could get in without the password if you have

root privileges," Lucy said. "That's the next thing we'll check. Change to the etc directory and vi the file called Group and look for root group—that's r-o-o-t-g-r-p. See which users are listed after it."

I began to type.

"What do you see?"

"I'm not there yet," I said, unable to keep the impatience out of my voice.

She repeated her instructions slowly.

"I see three log-in names in the root group," I said.

"Good. Write them down. Then colon, q, bang, and you're out of Group."

"Bang?" I asked, mystified.

"An exclamation point. Now you've got to vi the password file—that's p-a-s-s-w-d—and see if any of those log-ins with root privileges maybe don't have a password."

"Lucy." I took my hands off the keyboard.

"It's easy to tell because in the second field you'll see the encrypted form of the user's password, if he has a password. If there's nothing in the second field except two colons, then he's got no password."

"Lucy."

"I'm sorry, Aunt Kay. Am I going too fast again?"

"I'm not a UNIX programmer. You might as well be speaking Swahili."

"You could learn. UNIX is really fun."

"Thank you, but my problem is I don't have time to learn right now. Someone broke into my directory. I keep very confidential documents and data reports in there. Not to mention, if someone is reading my private files, what else is he looking at and who is doing it and why?"

"The who part is easy unless the violator is dialing in by modem from the outside."

"But the note was sent to someone in my office—to a device in my office."

"That doesn't mean that an insider didn't get someone from the outside to break in, Aunt Kay. Maybe the person snooping doesn't know anything about UNIX and needed help to break into your directory, so they got a programmer from the outside."

"This is serious," I said.

"It could be. If nothing else, it sounds to me like your system isn't very secure."

"When's your term paper due?" I asked.

"After the holidays."

"Are you finished?"

"Almost."

"When does Christmas vacation start?"

"It starts Monday."

"How would you like to come up here for a few days and help me out with this?" I asked.

"You're kidding."

"I'm very serious. But don't expect much. I generally don't bother with much in the way of decorations. A few poinsettias and candles in the windows. Now, I *will* cook."

"No tree?"

"Is that a problem?"

"I guess not. Is it snowing?"

"As a matter of fact, it is."

"I've never seen snow. Not in person."

"You'd better let me talk to your mother," I said.

Dorothy, my only sibling, was overly solicitous when she got on the phone several minutes later.

"Are you still working so hard? Kay, you work harder than anyone I've ever met. People are so impressed when I tell them we're sisters. What's the weather like in Richmond?"

"There's a good chance we'll have a white Christmas."

"How special. Lucy ought to see a white Christmas at least

once in her life. I've never seen one. Well, I take that back. There was the Christmas I went skiing out west with Bradley."

I could not remember who Bradley was. My younger sister's boyfriends and husbands were an endless parade I had stopped watching years ago.

"I'd very much like Lucy to spend Christmas with me," I said. "Would that be possible?"

"You can't come to Miami?"

"No, Dorothy. Not this year. I'm in the middle of several very difficult cases and have court scheduled virtually up to Christmas Eve."

"I can't imagine a Christmas without Lucy," she said with great reluctance.

"You've had Christmas without her before. When you went skiing out west with Bradley, for example."

"True. But it was hard," she said, nonplussed. "And every time we've spent a holiday apart, I've vowed to never do it again."

"I understand. Maybe another time," I said, sick to death of my sister's games. I knew she couldn't get Lucy out the door fast enough.

"Actually, I'm on deadline for this newest book and will be spending most of the holiday in front of my computer anyway," she reconsidered quickly. "Maybe Lucy would be better off with you. I won't be much fun. Did I tell you that I now have a Hollywood agent? He's fantastic and knows everybody who's somebody out there. He's negotiating a contract with Disney."

"That's great. I'm sure your books will make terrific movies." Dorothy wrote excellent children's books and had won several prestigious awards. She was simply a failure as a human being.

"Mother's here," my sister said. "She wants to have a word with you. Now listen, it was so good to talk to you. We just don't do it enough. Make sure Lucy eats something besides salads, and I warn you that she'll exercise until it drives you mad. I worry that she's going to start looking masculine."

Before I could say anything, my mother was on the line.

"Why can't you come down here, Katie? It's sunny and you should see the grapefruit."

"I can't do it, Mother. I'm really sorry."

"And now Lucy won't be here, either? Is that what I heard? What am I supposed to do, eat a turkey by myself?"

"Dorothy will be there."

"What? Are you kidding? She'll be with Fred. I can't stand him."

Dorothy had gotten divorced again last summer. I didn't ask who Fred was.

"I think he's Iranian or something. He'll squeeze a penny until it screams and has hair in his ears. I know he's not Catholic, and Dorothy never takes Lucy to church these days. You ask me, that child's going to hell in a hand basket."

"Mother, they can hear you."

"No they can't. I'm in the kitchen by myself staring at a sink full of dirty dishes that I just know Dorothy expects me to do while I'm here. It's just like when she comes to my house, because she hasn't done a thing about dinner and is hoping I'll cook. Does she ever offer to bring anything? Does she care that I'm an old woman and practically a cripple? Maybe you can talk some sense into Lucy."

"In what way is Lucy lacking sense?" I asked.

"She doesn't have any friends except this one girl you have to wonder about. You should see Lucy's bedroom. It looks like something out of a science fiction movie with all these computers and printers and pieces and parts. It's not normal for a teenage girl to live inside her brain all the time like that and not get out with kids her own age. I worry about her just like I used to worry about you."

"I turned out all right," I said.

"Well, you spent far too much time with science books, Katie. You saw what it did to your marriage."

"Mother, I'd like Lucy to fly here tomorrow, if possible. I'll make the reservations from my end and take care of the ticket. Make sure she packs her warmest clothes. Anything she doesn't have, such as a winter coat, we can find here."

"She could probably borrow your clothes. When was the last time you saw her? Last Christmas?"

"I guess it was that long ago."

"Well, let me tell you. She's gotten bosoms since then. And the way she dresses? And did she bother to ask her grandmother's advice before cutting off her beautiful hair? No. Why should she bother telling me that—"

"I've got to call the airlines."

"I wish you were coming here. We could all to be together." Her voice was getting funny. My mother was about to cry.

"I wish I could, too," I said.

Late Sunday morning I drove to the airport along dark, wet roads running through a dazzling world of glass. Ice loosened by the sun slipped from telephone lines, roofs, and trees, shattering to the ground like crystal missiles dropped from the sky. The weather report called for another storm, and I was deeply pleased, despite the inconvenience. I wanted quiet time in front of the fire with my niece. Lucy was growing up.

It did not seem so long ago that she was born. I would never forget her wide, unblinking eyes following my every move in her mother's house, or her bewildering fits of petulance and grief when I failed her in some small way. Lucy's open adoration touched my heart as profoundly as it frightened me. She had caused me to experience a depth of feeling I had not known before.

Talking my way past Security, I waited at the gate, eagerly searching passengers emerging from the boarding bridge. I was looking for a pudgy teenager with long, dark red hair and braces when a striking young woman met my eyes and grinned.

"Lucy," I exclaimed, hugging her. "My God. I almost didn't recognize you."

Her hair was short and deliberately messy, accentuating clear green eyes and good bones I did not know she had. There was not so much as a hint of metal in her mouth, and her thick glasses had been replaced by weightless tortoise-shell frames that gave her the look of a seriously pretty Harvard scholar. But it was the change in her body that astonished me most, for since I had seen her last she had been transformed from a chunky adolescent into a lean, leggy athlete dressed in snug, faded jeans several inches too short, a white blouse, a woven red leather belt, loafers, and no socks. She carried a book satchel, and I caught the sparkle of a delicate gold ankle bracelet. I was fairly certain she was wearing neither makeup nor bra.

"Where's your coat?" I asked as we headed to Baggage.

"It was eighty degrees when I left Miami this morning."

"You'll freeze walking out to the car."

"It's physically impossible for me to freeze while walking to your car unless you're parked in Chicago."

"Perhaps you have a sweater in your suitcase?"

"You ever notice that you talk to me the same way Grans talks to you? By the way, she thinks I look like a 'pet rocker.' That's her malapropism for the month. It's what you get when you cross a pet rock with a punk rocker."

"I've got a couple of ski jackets, corduroys, hats, gloves. You can borrow anything you wish."

She slipped her arm in mine and sniffed my hair. "You're still not smoking."

"I'm still not smoking and I hate being reminded that I'm still not smoking because then I think about smoking."

"You look better and don't stink like cigarettes. And you haven't gotten fat. Geez, this is a dinky airport," said Lucy, whose computer brain had formatting errors in the diplomacy sectors. "Why do they call it Richmond *International*?"

"Because it has flights to Miami."

"Why doesn't Grans ever come see you?"

"She doesn't like to travel and refuses to fly."

"It's safer than driving. Her hip is really getting bad, Aunt Kay."

"I know. I'm going to leave you to get your bags so I can pull the car in front," I said when we got to Baggage. "But first let's see which carousel it is."

"There are only three carousels. I bet I can figure it out."

I left her for the bright, cold air, grateful for a moment alone to think. The changes in my niece had thrown me off guard and I was suddenly more unsure than ever how to treat her. Lucy had never been easy. From day one she had been a prodigious adult intellect ruled by infantile emotions, a volatility accidentally given form when her mother had married Armando. My only advantage had been size and age. Now Lucy was as tall as I was and spoke with the low, calm voice of an equal. She was not going to run to her room and slam the door. She would no longer end a disagreement by screaming that she hated me or was glad I was not her mother. I imagined moods I could not anticipate and arguments I could not win. I had visions of her coolly leaving the house and driving off in my car.

We talked little during the drive, for Lucy seemed fascinated by the winter weather. The world was melting like an ice sculpture as another cold front appeared on the horizon in an ominous band of gray. When we turned into the neighborhood where I had moved since she had visited last, she stared out at expensive homes and lawns, at colonial Christmas decorations and brick sidewalks. A man dressed like an Eskimo was out walking his old, overweight dog, and a black Jaguar gray with road salt sprayed water as it slowly floated past.

"It's Sunday. Where are the children, or aren't there any?" Lucy said as if the observation incriminated me in some way.

"There are a few." I turned on my street.

"No bikes in the yards, no sleds or tree houses. Doesn't anybody ever go outside?"

"This is a very quiet neighborhood."

"Is that why you chose it?"

"In part. It's also quite safe, and hopefully buying a home here will prove to be a good investment."

"Private security?"

"Yes," I said as my uneasiness grew.

She continued staring out at the large homes flowing past. "I bet you can go inside and shut the door and never hear from anyone—never see anyone outside, either, unless they're walking their dog. But you don't have a dog. How many trick-or-treaters did you have on Halloween?"

"Halloween was quiet," I said evasively.

In truth, my doorbell had rung only once, when I was working in my study. I could see in my video monitor the four trick-or-treaters on my porch, and picking up the handset, I started to tell them that I would be right there when I overheard what they were saying to each other.

"No, there isn't a dead body in there," whispered the tiny UVA cheerleader.

"Yes, there is," said Spiderman. "She's on TV all the time because she cuts dead people up and puts them in jars. Dad told me."

I parked inside the garage and said to Lucy, "We'll get you settled in your room and the first order of business after that is for me to build a fire and make a pot of hot chocolate. Then we'll think about lunch."

"I don't drink hot chocolate. Do you have an espresso maker?"

"Indeed I do."

"That would be perfect, especially if you have decaf French roast. Do you know your neighbors?"

"I know who they are. Here, let me get that bag and you take this one so I can unlock the door and deactivate the alarm. Lord, this is heavy."

"Grans insisted I bring grapefruit. They're pretty good but full of seeds." Lucy looked around as she stepped inside my house. "Wow. Skylights. What do you call this style of architecture, besides rich?"

Maybe her disposition would self-correct if I pretended not to notice.

"The guest bedroom is back this way," I said. "I could put you upstairs if you wish, but I thought you'd rather be down here near me."

"Down here is fine. As long as I'm close to the computer."

"It's in my study, which is next door to your room."

"I brought my UNIX notes, books, and a few other things." She paused in front of the sliding glass doors in the living room. "The yard's not as nice as your other one." She said this as if I had let down everyone I had ever known.

"I've got plenty of years to work on my yard. It gives me something to look forward to."

Lucy slowly scanned her surroundings, her eyes finally resting on me. "You've got cameras in your doors, motion sensors, a fence, security gates, and what else? Gun turrets?"

"No gun turrets."

"This is your Fort Apache, isn't it, Aunt Kay? You moved

here because Mark's dead and there's nothing left in the world except bad people."

The comment ambushed me with terrific force, and instantly tears filled my eyes. I went into the guest bedroom and set down her suitcase, then checked towels, soap, and toothpaste in the bath. Returning to the bedroom, I opened the curtains, checked dresser drawers, rearranged the closet, and adjusted the heat while my niece sat on the edge of the bed, following my every move. In several minutes, I was able to meet her eyes again.

"When you unpack, I'll show you a closet you can rummage through for winter things," I said.

"You never saw him the way everybody else did."

"Lucy, we need to talk about something else." I switched on a lamp and made certain the telephone was plugged in.

"You're better off without him," she added with conviction.

"Lucy . . ."

"He wasn't there for you the way he should have been. He never would have been there because that's the way he was. And every time things didn't go right, you changed."

I stood in front of the window and looked out at dormant clematis and roses frozen to trellises.

"Lucy, you need to learn a little gentleness and tact. You can't just say exactly what you think."

"That's a funny thing to hear coming from you. You've always told me how much you hate dishonesty and games."

"People have feelings."

"You're right. Including me," she said.

"Have I somehow hurt your feelings?"

"How do you think I felt?"

"I'm not sure I understand."

"Because you didn't think about me at all. That's why you don't understand."

"I think about you all the time."

"That's like saying you're rich and yet you never give me a dime. What difference does it make to me what you've got hidden away?"

I did not know what to say.

"You don't call me anymore. You haven't come to see me once since he got killed." The hurt in her voice had been saved for a long time. "I wrote you and you didn't write back. Then you called me yesterday and asked me to come visit because you needed something."

"I didn't mean it like that."

"It's the same thing Mom does."

I shut my eyes and leaned my forehead against the cold glass. "You expect too much from me, Lucy. I'm not perfect."

"I don't expect you to be perfect. But I thought you were different."

"I don't know how to defend myself when you make a remark like that."

"You can't defend yourself!"

I watched a gray squirrel hop along the top of the fence bordering the yard. Birds were pecking seeds off the grass.

"Aunt Kay?"

I turned to her and never had I seen her eyes look so dejected.

"Why are men always more important than me?"

"They're not, Lucy," I whispered. "I swear."

My niece wanted tuna salad and *caffè latte* for lunch, and while I sat in front of the fire editing a journal article, she rummaged through my closet and dresser drawers. I tried not to think about another human being touching my clothes, folding something in a way I wouldn't or returning a jacket to the wrong hanger. Lucy had a gift for making me feel like the Tinman rusting in the forest. Was I becoming the rigid, serious adult I would have disliked when I was her age?

"What do you think?" she asked when she emerged from my bedroom at half past one. She was wearing one of my tennis warm-up suits.

"I think you spent a long time to come up with only that. And yes, it fits you fine."

"I found a few other things that are okay, but most of your stuff is too dressy. All these lawyerly suits in midnight blue and black, gray silk with delicate pinstripes, khaki and cashmere, and white blouses. You must have twenty white blouses and just as many ties. You shouldn't wear brown, by the way. And I didn't see much in red, and you'd look good in red, with your blue eyes and grayish blond hair."

"Ash blond," I said.

"Ashes are gray or white. Just look in the fire. We don't wear the same size shoe, not that I'm into Cole-Haan or Ferragamo. I did find a black leather jacket that's really cool. Were you a biker in another life?"

"It's lambskin and you're welcome to borrow it."

"What about your Fendi perfume and pearls? Do you own a pair of jeans?"

"Help yourself." I started to laugh. "And yes, I have a pair of jeans somewhere. Maybe in the garage."

"I want to take you shopping, Aunt Kay."

"I'd have to be crazy."

"Please?"

"Maybe," I said.

"If it's all right, I want to go to your club to work out for a while. I'm stiff from the plane."

"If you'd like to play tennis while you're here, I'll see if Ted has any time to hit with you. My racquets are in the closet to the left. I just switched to a new Wilson. You can hit the ball a hundred miles an hour. You'll love it."

"No, thanks. I'd rather use the StairMaster and weights or go running. Why don't *you* take a lesson from Ted while I work out, and we can go together?"

Dutifully, I reached for the phone and dialed Westwood's pro shop. Ted was booked solid until ten o'clock. I gave Lucy directions and my car keys, and after she left, I read in front of the fire and fell asleep.

When I opened my eyes, I heard coals shift and wind gently touching the pewter wind chimes beyond the sliding glass doors. Snow was drifting down in large, slow flakes, the sky the color of a dusty blackboard. Lights in my yard had come on, the house so silent I was conscious of the clock ticking on the wall. It was shortly after four and Lucy had not returned from the club. I dialed the number for my car phone and no one answered. She had never driven in snow before, I thought anxiously. And I needed to go to the store to pick up fish for dinner. I could call the club and have her paged. I told myself that was ridiculous. Lucy had been gone barely two hours. She was not a child anymore. When it got to be four-thirty, I tried my car phone again. At five I called the club and they could not find her. I began to panic.

"Are you sure she's not on the StairMaster or maybe in the women's locker room taking a shower? Or maybe she stopped by the mixed grill?" I again asked the young woman in the pro shop.

"We've paged her four times, Dr. Scarpetta. And I've gone around looking. I'll check again. If I locate her, I'll have her call you immediately."

"Do you know if she ever showed up at all? She should have gotten there around two."

"Gosh. I just came on at four. I don't know."

I continued calling my car phone.

"The Richmond Cellular customer you have dialed does not answer. . . ."

I tried Marino and he wasn't home or at headquarters. At six o'clock I stood in the kitchen staring out the window. Snow streaked down in the chalky glow of streetlights. My heart beat hard as I paced from room to room and continued calling my car phone. At half past six I had decided to file a missing person report with the police when the telephone rang. Running back to my study, I was reaching for the receiver when I noticed the familiar number eerily materializing on the Caller ID screen. The calls had stopped after the night of Waddell's execution. I had not thought about them since. Bewildered, I froze, waiting for the expected hang up to follow my recorded message. I was shocked when I recognized the voice that began to speak.

"I hate to do this to you, Doc . . ."

Snatching up the receiver, I cleared my throat and said in disbelief, "Marino?"

"Yeah," he said. "I got bad news."

4

Where are you?" I demanded, my eyes riveted to the number on the screen.

"East End, and it's coming down like a bitch," Marino said. "We got a DOA. White female. At a glance appears to be your typical CO suicide, car inside the garage, hose hooked up to the exhaust pipe. But the circumstances are a little weird. I think you better come."

"Where are you placing this call from?" I asked so adamantly that he hesitated. I could feel his surprise.

"The decedent's house. Just got here. That's the other thing. It wasn't secured. The back was unlocked."

I heard the garage door. "Oh, thank God. Marino, hold on," I said, flooded with relief.

Paper bags crackled as the kitchen door shut.

Placing my hand over the receiver, I called out, "Lucy, is that you?"

"No, Frosty the Snowman. You ought to see it coming down out there! It's awesome!"

Reaching for pen and paper, I said to Marino, "The decedent's name and address?"

"Jennifer Deighton. Two-one-seven Ewing."

I did not recognize the name. Ewing was off Williamsburg Road, not too far from the airport in a neighborhood unfamiliar to me.

Lucy walked into my study as I was hanging up the phone. Her face was rosy from the cold, eyes sparkling.

"Where in God's name have you been?" I snapped.

Her smile faded. "Errands."

"Well, we'll discuss this later. I've got to go to a scene."

She shrugged and returned my irritation. "So what else is new?"

"I'm sorry. It's not as if I have control over people dying."

Grabbing coat and gloves, I hurried out to the garage. I started the engine, buckled up, adjusted the heat, and studied my directions before remembering the automatic door opener attached to the visor. It's amazing how quickly an enclosed space will fill with fumes.

"Good God," I said severely to no one but my own distracted self as I quickly opened the garage door.

Poisoning by motor vehicle exhaust is an easy way to die. Young couples necking in the backseat, engine running and heater on, drift off in each other's arms and never wake up. Suicidal individuals turn cars into small gas chambers and leave their problems for others to solve. I had neglected to ask Marino if Jennifer Deighton lived alone.

The snow was already several inches deep, the night lit up by it. There was no traffic in my neighborhood and very little when I got on the downtown expressway. Christmas music played nonstop on the radio as my thoughts flew in a riot of bewilderment and alighted, one by one, on fear. Jennifer Deighton had been calling my number and hanging up, or someone using her telephone had. Now she was dead. The overpass curved above the east end of downtown, where railroad tracks crisscrossed the earth like sutured wounds, and concrete parking decks were higher than many of the buildings. Main Street station hulked out of the milky sky, tile roof frosted white, the clock in its tower a bleary Cyclops eye.

On Williamsburg Road I drove very slowly past a deserted shopping center, and just before the city turned into Henrico County, I found Ewing Avenue. Houses were small, with pickup trucks and old model American cars parked out front. At the 217 address, police cars were in the drive and on both sides of the street. Pulling in behind Marino's Ford, I got out with my medical bag and walked to the end of the unpaved driveway where the single-car garage was lit up like a Christmas crèche. The door was rolled up, police officers gathered inside around a beat-up beige Chevrolet. I found Marino squatting by the back door on the driver's side, studying a section of green garden hose leading from the exhaust pipe through a partially opened window. The interior of the car was filthy with soot, the smell of fumes lingering on the cold, damp air.

"The ignition's still switched on," Marino said to me. "The car ran out of gas."

The dead woman appeared to be in her fifties or early sixties. She was slumped over on her right side behind the steering wheel, the exposed flesh of her neck and hands bright pink. Dried bloody fluid stained the tan upholstery beneath her head. From where I stood, I could not see her face. Opening my medical bag, I got out a chemical thermometer to take the temperature inside the garage, and put on a pair of surgical gloves. I asked a young officer if he could open the car's front doors.

"We were just about to dust," he said.

"I'll wait."

"Johnson, how 'bout dusting the door handles so the doc here can get in the car." He fixed dark Latin eyes on me.

"By the way, I'm Tom Lucero. What we got here is a situation that doesn't completely add up. To begin with, it bothers me there's blood on the front seat."

"There are several possible explanations for that," I said. "One is postmortem purging."

He narrowed his eyes a little.

"When pressure in the lungs forces bloody fluid from the nose and mouth," I explained.

"Oh. Generally, that doesn't happen until the person's started to decompose, right?"

"Generally."

"Based on what we know, this lady's been dead maybe twenty-four hours and it's cold as a morgue fridge in here."

"True," I said. "But if she had her heater running, that in addition to the hot exhaust pouring in would have heated up the inside of the car, and it would have stayed quite warm until the car ran out of gas."

Marino peered through a window opaque with soot and said, "Looks like the heater's pushed all the way to hot."

"Another possibility," I continued, "is that when she became unconscious, she slumped over, striking her face on the steering wheel, the dash, the seat. Her nose could have bled. She could have bitten her tongue or split her lip. I won't know until I examine her."

"Okay, but how about the way she's dressed?" Lucero said. "Strike you as unusual that she'd walk out in the cold, come inside a cold garage, hook up the hose, and get into a cold car with nothing but a gown on?"

The pale blue gown was ankle-length, with long sleeves, and made of what looked like a flimsy synthetic material. There is no dress code for people who commit suicide. It would have been logical for Jennifer Deighton to put on coat and shoes before venturing outside on a frigid winter night. But if she had planned to take her life, she would have known she would not feel the cold long.

The ID officer had finished dusting the car doors. I retrieved the chemical thermometer. It was twenty-nine degrees inside the garage.

"When did you get here?" I asked Lucero.

"Maybe an hour and a half ago. Obviously, it was warmer in here before we opened the door, but not much. The garage isn't heated. Plus, the car hood was cold. I'm guessing the car ran out of gas and the battery went dead a number of hours before we were called."

Car doors opened and I took a series of photographs before going around to the passenger's side to look at her head. I braced myself for a spark of awareness, a detail that might ignite some long-buried memory. But there was not the faintest glimmer. I did not know Jennifer Deighton. I had never seen her before in my life.

Her bleached hair was dark at the roots and tightly wound in small pink curlers, several of which had been displaced. She was grossly overweight, though I could tell from her refined features that she may have been quite pretty in a younger, leaner life. I palpated her head and neck and felt no fractures. I placed the back of my hand against her cheek, then struggled to turn her. She was cold and stiff, the side of her face that had been resting against the seat, pale and blistered from the heat. It did not appear that her body had been moved after death, and the skin did not blanch when pressed. She had been dead at least twelve hours.

It wasn't until I was ready to bag her hands that I noticed something under her right index fingernail. I got out a flashlight for a better look, then retrieved a plastic evidence envelope and a pair of forceps. The tiny fleck of metallic green was embedded in the skin beneath the nail. Christmas glitter, I thought. I also found fibers of a gold tint, and as I studied each of her fingers I found more. Slipping the brown paper bags over her hands and securing them at the wrists with rubber bands, I went around to the other side of the car. I wanted to look at her feet. Her legs were fully rigorous and uncooperative as I pulled them free of the steering wheel and positioned them on the seat. Examining the bottoms of her thick dark socks, I found fibers clinging to the wool that looked similar to the ones I had noticed under her fingernails. Absent was dirt, mud, or grass. An alarm was sounding in the back of my mind.

"Find anything interesting?" Marino asked.

"You found no bedroom slippers or shoes nearby?" I said.

"Nope," Lucero answered. "Like I told you, I thought it unusual she walked out of the house on a cold night with nothing but—"

I interrupted. "We've got a problem. Her socks are too clean."

"Shit," Marino said.

"We need to get her downtown." I backed away from the car.

"I'll tell the squad," Lucero volunteered.

"I want to see the inside of her house," I said to Marino.

"Yeah." He had taken his gloves off and was blowing on his hands. "I want you to see it, too."

While I waited for the squad, I moved about the garage, careful where I stepped and keeping out of the way. There wasn't much to see, just the usual clutter of items needed for the yard and odds and ends that had no other proper storage place. I scanned stacks of old newspapers, wicker baskets, dusty cans of paint, and a rusty charcoal grill that I doubted had been used in years. Sloppily coiled in a corner like a headless green garter snake was the hose from which the segment attached to the exhaust pipe appeared to have been cut. I knelt near the severed end without touching it. The plastic rim did not look sawn but severed at an angle by one hard blow. I spotted a linear cut in the cement floor nearby. Getting to my feet, I surveyed the tools hanging from a pegboard. There was an ax and a maul, both of them rusty and festooned with cobwebs.

The rescue squad was coming in with its stretcher and body pouch.

"Did you find anything inside her house that she might have used to cut the hose?" I asked Lucero.

"No."

Jennifer Deighton did not want to come out of the car, death resisting the hands of life. I moved to the passenger's side to help. Three of us secured her under the arms and waist while an attendant pushed her legs. When she was zipped up and buckled in, they carried her out into the snowy night and I trudged with Lucero along the driveway, sorry that I'd not taken the time to put on boots. We entered the ranch-style brick house through a back door that led into the kitchen.

It looked recently renovated, appliances black, counters and cabinets white, the wallpaper an Oriental pattern of pastel flowers against delicate blue. Heading toward the sound of voices, Lucero and I crossed a narrow hallway with a hardwood floor and stopped at the entrance of a bedroom where Marino and an ID officer were going through dresser drawers. For a long moment, I looked around at the peculiar manifestations of Jennifer Deighton's personality. It was as if her bedroom were a solar cell in which she captured radiant energy and converted it into magic. I thought again of the hang ups I had been getting, my paranoia growing by leaps and bounds.

Walls, curtains, carpet, linens, and wicker furniture were white. Oddly, on the rumpled bed not far from where both pillows were propped against the headboard a crystal pyramid anchored a single blank sheet of white typing paper. On the dresser and beside tabletops were more crystals, with smaller ones suspended from window frames. I could imagine rainbows dancing in the room and light glancing off prismatic glass when the sun poured in.

"Weird, huh?" Lucero asked.

"Was she a psychic of some sort?" I asked.

"Let's put it this way, she had her own business, most of it carried out right there." Lucero moved closer to an answering machine on a table by the bed. The message light was flashing, the number thirty-eight glowing red.

"*Thirty-eight* messages since eight o'clock last night," Lucero added. "I've skipped through a few of 'em. The lady was into horoscopes. Looks like people would call to find out if they were going to have a good day, win the lottery, or be able to pay off their charge cards after Christmas."

Opening the cover of the answering machine, Marino used his pocket knife to flip out the tape, which he sealed inside a plastic evidence envelope. I was interested in several other items on the small bedside table and moved closer to take a look. Next to a notepad and pen was a glass with an inch of clear liquid inside it. I bent close, smelling nothing. Water, I thought. Nearby were two paperback books, Pete Dexter's *Paris Trout* and Jane Roberts's *Seth Speaks*. I saw no other books in the bedroom.

"I'd like to take a look at these," I said to Marino.

"*Paris Trout*," he mused. "What's it about, fishing in France?"

Unfortunately, he was serious.

"They might tell me something about her state of mind before she died," I added.

"No problem. I'll have Documents check them for prints, then hand them over to you. And I think we'd better have Documents take a look at the paper, too," he added, referring to the sheet of blank paper on the bed.

"Right," Lucero said drolly. "Maybe she wrote a suicide note in disappearing ink."

"Come on," Marino said to me. "I want to show you a couple things."

He took me into the living room, where an artificial Christmas tree cowered in a corner, bent from copious gaudy ornaments and strangled by tinsel, lights, and angel hair. Gathered near its base were boxes of candy and cheeses, bubble bath, a glass jar of what looked like spiced tea, and a ceramic unicorn with blazing blue eyes and gilded horn. The gold shag carpet, I suspected, was the origin of the fibers I had noticed on the bottom of Jennifer Deighton's socks and under her fingernails.

Marino slipped a small flashlight from a pocket and squatted.

"Take a look," he said.

I got down beside him as the beam of light illuminated metallic glitter and a bit of slender gold cord in the deep pile of the carpet around the base of the tree.

"When I got here, the first thing I checked was to see if she had any presents under the tree," Marino said, switching the flashlight off. "Obviously, she opened them early. And the wrapping paper and cards got disposed of right over there in the fireplace—it's full of paper ash, some pieces of foil-type paper still unburned. The lady across the street says she noticed smoke coming out of the chimney right before it got dark last night."

"Is this neighbor the one who called the police?" I asked.

"Yeah."

"Why?"

"That I'm not clear on. I got to talk to her."

"When you do, see if you can find out anything about this woman's medical history, if she had psychiatric problems, et cetera. I'd like to know who her physician is."

"I'm going over there in a few minutes. You can come with me and ask her yourself."

I thought of Lucy waiting for me at home as I continued taking in details. In the center of the room, my eyes stopped at four small square indentations in the carpet.

"I noticed that, too," Marino said. "Looks like someone brought a chair in here, probably from the dining room.

There's four chairs around the dining room table. All of 'em have square legs."

"Another thing you might consider doing," I thought out loud, "is checking her VCR. See if she had programmed it to record anything. That might tell us something more about her, too."

"Good idea."

We left the living room, passing through the small dining room with an oak table and four straight-backed chairs. The braided rug on the hardwood floor looked either new or rarely walked on.

"Looks like the room she pretty much lived in was this one," Marino said as we crossed a hallway and entered what clearly was her office.

The room was crammed with the paraphernalia needed to run a small business, including a fax machine, which I investigated immediately. It was turned off, the line connected to it plugged into a single jack in the wall. I looked around some more as my mystification grew. A personal computer, postage machine, various forms, and envelopes crowded a table and the desk. Encyclopedias and books on parapsychology, astrology, zodiac signs, and Eastern and Western religions lined bookcases. I noted several different translations of the Bible and dozens of ledgers with dates written on the spines.

Near the postage machine was a stack of what appeared to be subscription forms, and I picked up one. For three hundred dollars a year, you could call as often as once a day and Jennifer Deighton would spend up to three minutes telling you your horoscope "based on personal details, including the alignment of the planets at the moment of your birth." For an additional two hundred dollars a year, she would throw in "a weekly reading." Upon payment of the fee, the subscriber would receive a card with an identification code that was valid only as long as the annual fee continued to be paid.

"What a lot of horseshit," Marino said to me.

"I'm assuming she lived alone."

"That's the way it's looking so far. A woman alone running a business like this—a damn good way to attract the wrong person."

"Marino, do you know how many telephone lines she has?"

"No. Why?"

I told him about the hang ups I had been getting while he stared hard at me. His jaw muscles began to flex.

"I need to know if her fax machine and phone are on the same line," I concluded.

"Jesus Christ."

"If they are and she happened to have her fax machine turned on the night I dialed back the number that appeared on my Caller ID screen," I went on, "that would explain the tone I heard."

"Jesus friggin' Christ," he said, snatching the portable radio out of his coat pocket. "Why the hell didn't you tell me this before?"

"I didn't want to mention it when others were around."

He moved the radio close to his lips. "Seven-ten." Then he said to me, "If you were worried about hang ups, why didn't you say something weeks ago?"

"I wasn't that worried about them."

"Seven-ten," the dispatcher's voice crackled back.

"Ten-five eight-twenty-one."

The dispatcher sent out a broadcast for 821, the code for the inspector.

"Got a number I need you to dial," Marino said when he and the inspector connected on the air. "You got your cellular phone handy?"

"Ten-fo'."

Marino gave him Jennifer Deighton's number and then turned on the fax machine. Momentarily, it began a series of rings, beeps, and other complaints.

"That answer your question?" Marino asked me.

"It answers one question, but not the most important question," I said.

The name of the neighbor across the street who had notified the police was Myra Clary. I accompanied Marino to her small aluminum-sided house with its plastic Santa lit up on the front lawn and lights strung in the boxwoods. Marino barely had rung the bell when the front door opened and Mrs. Clary invited us in without asking who we were. It occurred to me that she probably had watched our approach from a window.

She showed us into a dismal living room where we found her husband huddled by the electric fire, lap robe over his spindly legs, his vacuous stare fixed on a man lathering up with deodorant soap on television. The pitiful custodial care of the years manifested itself everywhere. Upholstery was threadbare and soiled where human flesh had made repeated contact with it. Wood was cloudy from layers of wax, prints on walls yellowed behind dusty glass. The oily smell of a million meals cooked in the kitchen and eaten on TV trays permeated the air.

Marino explained why we were here as Mrs. Clary moved about nervously, plucking newspapers off the couch, turning down the television, and carrying dirty dinner plates into the kitchen. Her husband did not venture forth from his interior world, his head trembling on its stalklike neck. Parkinson's disease is when the machine shakes violently just before it conks out, as if it knows what is ahead and protests the only way it can.

"Nope, we don't need a thing," Marino said when Mrs. Clary offered us food and drink. "Sit down and try to relax. I know this has been a tough day for you."

"They said she was in her car breathing in those fumes.

Oh, my," she said. "I saw how smoky the window was, looked like the garage had been on fire. I knew the worst right then."

"Who's *they*?" Marino asked.

"The police. After I called, I was watching for them. When they pulled up, I went straight over to see if Jenny was all right."

Mrs. Clary could not sit still in the wing chair across from the couch where Marino and I had settled. Her gray hair had strayed out of the bun on top of her head, face as wrinkled as a dried apple, eyes hungry for information and bright with fear.

"I know you already talked to the police earlier," Marino said, moving the ashtray closer. "But I want you to go through it chapter and verse for us, beginning with when you saw Jennifer Deighton last."

"I saw her the other day—"

Marino interrupted. "Which day?"

"Friday. I remember the phone rang and I went to the kitchen to answer it and saw her through the window. She was pulling into her driveway."

"Did she always park her car in the garage?" I asked.

"She always did."

"What about yesterday?" Marino inquired. "You see her or her car yesterday?"

"No, I didn't. But I went out to get the mail. It was late, tends to be that way this time of year. Three, four o'clock and still no mail. I guess it was close to five-thirty, maybe a little later, when I remembered to check the mailbox again. It was getting dark and I noticed smoke coming out of Jenny's chimney."

"You sure about that?" Marino asked.

She nodded. "Oh, yes. I remember it went through my mind it was a good night for a fire. But fires were always Jimmy's job. He never showed me how, you see. When he was good at something, that was his. So I quit on the fires and had the electric log put in."

Jimmy Clary was looking at her. I wondered if he knew what she was saying.

"I like to cook," she went on. "This time of year I do a lot of baking. I make sugar cakes and give them to the neighbors. Yesterday I wanted to drop one by for Jenny, but I like to call first. It's hard to tell when someone's in, especially when they keep their car in a garage. And you leave a cake on the doormat and one of the dogs around here gets it. So I tried her and got that machine. All day I tried and she didn't answer, and to tell you the truth, I was a little worried."

"Why?" I asked. "Did she have health problems, any sort of problems you were aware of?"

"Bad cholesterol. Way over two hundred's what's she told me once. Plus high blood pressure, which she said ran in the family."

I had not seen any prescription drugs in Jennifer Deighton's house.

"Do you know who her doctor was?" I asked.

"I can't recall. But Jenny believed in natural cures. She told me when she felt poorly she'd meditate."

"Sounds like the two of you were pretty close," Marino said.

Mrs. Clary was plucking at her skirt, hands like hyperactive children. "I'm here all day except when I go to the store." She glanced at her husband, who was staring at the TV again. "Now and then I'd go see her, you know, just being neighborly, maybe to drop by something I'd been cooking."

"Was she a friendly sort?" Marino asked. "She have a lot of visitors?"

"Well, you know she worked out of the house. I think she

handled most of her business over the phone. But occasionally I'd see people going in."

"Anybody you knew?"

"Not that I recall."

"You notice anybody coming by to see her last night?" Marino asked.

"I didn't notice."

"What about when you went out to get your mail and saw the smoke coming out of her chimney? You get any sense she might have had company?"

"I didn't see a car. Nothing to make me think she had company."

Jimmy Clary had drifted off to sleep. He was drooling.

"You said she worked at home," I said. "Do you have any idea what she did?"

Mrs. Clary fixed wide eyes on me. She leaned forward and lowered her voice. "I know what folks said."

"And what was that?" I asked.

She pressed her lips together and shook her head.

"Mrs. Clary," Marino said. "Anything you could tell us might help. I know you want to help."

"There's a Methodist church two blocks away. You can see it. The steeple's lit up at night, has been ever since they built the church three or four years ago."

"I saw the church when I was driving in," Marino replied. "What's that got to do—"

"Well," she cut in, "Jenny moved here, I guess it was early September. And I've never been able to figure it out. The steeple light. You watch when you're driving home. Of course . . ." She paused, her face disappointed. "Maybe it won't do it anymore."

"Do what?" Marino asked.

"Go out and then come back on. The strangest thing I've ever seen. It's lit up one minute, and then you look out your window again and it's dark like the church isn't there. Then next thing you know, you look out again and the steeple's lit up just like it's always been. I've timed it. On for a minute, then off for two, on again for three. Sometimes it will burn for an hour. No pattern to it at all."

"What does this have to do with Jennifer Deighton?" I asked.

"I remember it was not long after she moved in, just weeks before Jimmy had his stroke. It was a cool night so he was building a fire. I was in the kitchen doing dishes and could see the steeple out the window lit up like it always was. And he came in to get himself a drink, and I said, 'You know what the Bible says about being drunk with the Spirit and not with wine.' And he said, 'I'm not drinking wine. I'm drinking bourbon. The Bible's never said a word about bourbon.' Then, right while he was standing there the steeple went dark. It was like the church vanished into thin air. I said, 'There you have it. The Word of the Lord. That's his opinion about you and your bourbon.'

"He laughed like I was the craziest thing, but he never touched another drop. Every night he'd stand in front of the window over the kitchen sink watching. One minute the steeple would be lit up, then it would be dark. I let Jimmy think it was God's doing—anything to keep him off the bottle. The church never behaved like that before Miss Deighton moved across the street."

"Has the light been going on and off lately?" I asked.

"Was still doing it last night. I don't know about now. To tell you the truth, I haven't looked."

"So you're saying that she somehow had an effect on the lights in the church steeple," Marino said mildly.

"I'm saying that more than one person on this street decided about her some time ago."

"Decided what?"

"About her being a witch," Mrs. Clary said.

Her husband had started snoring, making hideous strangling noises that his wife did not seem to notice.

"Sounds to me like your husband there started doing poorly about the time Miss Deighton moved here and the lights started acting funny," Marino said.

She looked startled. "Well, that's so. He had his stroke the end of September."

"You ever think there might be a connection? That maybe Jennifer Deighton had something to do with it, just like you're thinking she had something to do with the church lights?"

"Jimmy didn't take to her." Mrs. Clary was talking faster by the minute.

"You're saying the two of them didn't get along," Marino said.

"Right after she moved in, she came over a couple of times to ask him to help out with a few things around the house, man's work. I remember one time her doorbell was making a terrible buzzing sound inside the house and she appeared on the doorstep, scared she was about to have an electrical fire. So Jimmy went over there. I think her dishwasher flooded once, too, back then. Jimmy's always been real handy." She glanced furtively at her snoring husband.

"You still haven't made it clear why he didn't get along with her," Marino reminded her.

"He said he didn't like going over there," she said. "Didn't like the inside of her house, with all these crystals everywhere. And the phone would ring all the time. But what really gave him the willies was when she told him she read people's fortunes and would do it for him for nothing if he'd keep fixing things around her house. He said, and I remember this like it was yesterday, 'No, thank you, Miss Deighton. Myra's in charge of my future, plans every minute of it.' "

"I wonder if you might know of anybody who had a big enough problem with Jennifer Deighton to wish something bad on her, hurt her in some way," Marino said.

"You think somebody killed her?"

"There's a lot we don't know at this point. We have to check out every possibility."

She crossed her arms under her sagging bosom, hugging herself.

"What about her emotional state?" I inquired. "Did she ever seem depressed to you? Do you know if she had any problems she couldn't seem to cope with, especially of late?"

"I didn't know her that well." She avoided my eyes.

"Did she go to any doctors that you're aware of?"

"I don't know."

"What about next of kin? Did she have family?"

"I have no idea."

"What about her phone?" I then said. "Did she answer it when she was home or did she always let the machine do it?"

"It's been my experience that when she was home, she answered it."

"Which is why you got worried about her earlier today when she wasn't answering the phone when you called," Marino said.

"That's exactly why."

Myra Clary realized too late what she had said.

"That's interesting," Marino commented.

A flush crept up her neck and her hands went still.

Marino asked, "How did you know she was home today?"

She did not answer. Her husband's breath rattled in his chest and he coughed, eyes blinking open.

"I guess I assumed. Because I didn't see her pull out. In her car . . ." Mrs. Clary's voice trailed off.

"Maybe you went over there earlier in the day?" Marino offered, as if trying to be helpful. "To deliver your cake or say hello and thought her car was in the garage?"

She dabbed tears from her eyes. "I was in the kitchen baking all morning and never saw her go out to get the paper or leave in her car. So mid-morning, when I went out, I went over there and rang the bell. She didn't answer. I peeked inside the garage."

"You telling me you saw the windows all smoked up and didn't think something was wrong?" Marino asked.

"I didn't know what it meant, what to do." Her voice went up several octaves. "Lord, Lord. I wish I'd called somebody then. Maybe she was—"

Marino cut in. "I don't know that she was still alive then, that she would have been." He looked pointedly at me.

"When you looked inside the garage, did you hear the car engine running?" I asked Mrs. Clary.

She shook her head and blew her nose.

Marino got up and tucked his notepad back in his coat pocket. He looked dejected, as if Mrs. Clary's spinelessness and lack of veracity deeply disappointed him. By now, there wasn't a role he played that I did not know well.

"I should have called earlier." Myra Clary directed this at me, her voice quavering.

I did not reply. Marino stared at the carpet.

"I don't feel good. I need to go lie down."

Marino slipped a business card out of his wallet and handed it to her. "Anything else comes to mind that you think I ought to know about, you give me a call."

"Yes, sir," she said weakly. "I promise I will."

"You doing the post tonight?" Marino asked me after the front door shut.

Snow was ankle-deep and still coming down.

"In the morning," I said, fishing keys out of my coat pocket. "What do you think?"

"I think her unusual occupation put her at great risk for the wrong sort of person to come along. I also think her apparent isolated existence, as Mrs. Clary described it, and the fact that it appears she opened her Christmas presents early makes suicide an easy assumption. But her clean socks are a major problem."

"You got that right," he said.

Jennifer Deighton's house was lit up, and a flatbed truck with chains on its tires had backed into the driveway. Voices of men working were muted by the snow, and every car on the street was solid white and soft around the edges.

I followed Marino's gaze above the roof of Miss Deighton's house. Several blocks away, the church was etched against the pearl gray sky, the steeple shaped weirdly like a witch's hat. Arches in the arcade stared back at us with mournful, empty eyes when suddenly the light blinked on. It filled spaces and painted surfaces a luminescent ocher, the arcade an unsmiling but gentle face floating in the night.

I glanced over at the Clary house as curtains moved in the kitchen window.

"Jesus, I'm out of here." Marino headed across the street.

"You want me to alert Neils about her car?" I called after him.

"Yeah," he yelled back. "That'd be good."

My house was lit up when I got home and good smells came from the kitchen. A fire blazed and two places had been set on the butler's table in front of it. Dropping my medical bag on the couch, I looked around and listened. From my study across the hall came the faint, rapid clicking of keys.

"Lucy?" I called out, slipping off my gloves and unbuttoning my coat.

"I'm in here." Keys continued to click.

"What have you been cooking?"

"Dinner."

I headed for my study, where I found my niece sitting at my desk staring intensely at the computer monitor. I was stunned when I noticed the pound sign prompt. She was in UNIX. Somehow she had dialed into the computer downtown.

"How did you do that?" I asked. "I didn't tell you the dial-in command, user name, password, or anything."

"You didn't have to tell me. I found the file that told me what the *bat* command is. Plus, you've got some programs in here with your user name and password coded in so you don't get prompted for them. A good shortcut but risky. Your user name is Marley and password is *brain*."

"You're dangerous." I pulled up a chair.

"Who's Marley?" She continued to type.

"We had assigned seating in medical school. Marley Scates sat next to me in labs for two years. He's a neurosurgeon somewhere."

"Were you in love with him?"

"We never dated."

"Was he in love with you?"

"You ask too many questions, Lucy. You can't just ask people anything you want."

"Yes I can. They don't have to answer."

"It's offensive."

"I think I've figured out how someone got into your directory, Aunt Kay. Remember I told you about users that came with the software?"

"Yes."

"There's one called demo that has root privileges but no password assigned to it. My guess is that this is what somebody used and I'll show you what probably happened." Her fingers flew over the keyboard without pause as she talked. "What I'm doing now is going into the system administrator's menu to check out the log-in accounting. We're going to search for a specific user. In this case, root. Now we'll hit g to go and boom. There it is." She ran her finger across a line on the screen.

"On December sixteenth at five-oh-six in the afternoon, someone logged in from a device called t-t-y-fourteen. This person had root privileges and we'll assume is the person who went into your directory. I don't know what he looked at. But twenty minutes later, at five-twenty-six, he tried to send the note 'I can't find it' to t-t-y-oh-seven and inadvertently created a file. He logged out at five-thirty-two, making the total time of the session twenty-six minutes. And it doesn't appear anything was printed, by the way. I took a look at the printer spooler log, which shows files printed. I didn't see anything that caught my attention."

"Let me make sure I've got this straight. Someone tried to send a note from t-t-y-fourteen to t-t-y-oh-seven," I said.

"Yes. And I checked. Both of those devices are terminals."

"How can we determine whose office those terminals are in?" I asked.

"I'm surprised there's not a list somewhere in here. But I haven't found it yet. If all else fails, you can check the cables leading to the terminals. Usually, they're tagged. And if you're interested in my personal opinion, I don't think your computer analyst is the spy. In the first place, she knows your user name and password and would have no need to log in with demo. Also, since I assume the mini is in her office, then I also assume she uses the system terminal."

"She does."

"The device name for your system terminal is t-t-y-b."

"Good."

"Another way to figure out who did this would be to sneak into someone's office when they aren't there but are logged in. All you've got to do is go into UNIX and type 'who am I' and the system will tell you."

She pushed back her chair and got up. "I hope you're hungry. We've got chicken breasts and a chilled wild rice salad made with cashews, peppers, sesame oil. And there's bread. Is your grill in working order?"

"It's after eleven and snowing outside."

"I didn't suggest that we eat outside. I simply would like to cook the chicken on the grill."

"Where did you learn to cook?"

We were walking to the kitchen.

"Not from Mother. Why do you think I was such a little fatso? From eating the junk she bought. Snacks, sodas, and pizza that tastes like cardboard. I have fat cells that will scream for the rest of my life because of Mother. I'll never forgive her."

"We need to talk about this afternoon, Lucy. If you hadn't come home when you did, the police would have been looking for you."

"I worked out for an hour and a half, then took a shower."

"You were gone four and a half hours."

"I had groceries to buy and a few other errands."

"Why didn't you answer the car phone?"

"I assumed it was someone trying to reach you. Plus, I've never used a car phone. I'm not twelve years old, Aunt Kay."

"I know you're not. But you don't live here and have never driven here before. I was worried."

"I'm sorry," she said.

We ate by firelight, both of us sitting on the floor around the butler's table. I had turned off lamps. Flames jumped and shadows danced as if celebrating a magic moment in the lives of my niece and me.

"What do you want for Christmas?" I asked, reaching for my wine.

"Shooting lessons," she said.

5

Lucy stayed up very late working with the computer and I did not hear her stir when I woke up to the alarm early Monday morning. Parting the curtains in my bedroom window, I looked out at powdery flakes swirling in lights burning on the patio. The snow was deep and nothing was moving in my neighborhood. After coffee and a quick scan of the paper, I got dressed and was almost to the door when I turned around. No matter that Lucy was no longer twelve years old, I could not leave without checking on her.

Slipping inside her bedroom, I found her sleeping on her side in a tangle of sheets, the duvet half on the floor. It touched me that she was wearing a sweat suit that she had gotten out of one of my drawers. I had never had another human being wish to sleep in anything of mine, and I straightened the covers, careful not to wake her.

The drive downtown was awful, and I envied workers whose offices were closed because of the snow. Those of us who had not been granted an unexpected holiday crept slowly along the interstate, skating with the slightest tap on the brakes as we peered through streaked windshields that the wipers could not keep clean. I wondered how I would explain to Margaret that my teenage niece thought our computer system was insecure. Who had gotten into my directory, and why had Jennifer Deighton been calling my number and hanging up?

I did not get to the office until half past eight, and when I walked into the morgue, I stopped midway in the corridor, puzzled. Parked at a haphazard angle near the stainless steel refrigerator door was a gurney bearing a body covered by a sheet. Checking the toe tag, I read Jennifer Deighton's name, and I looked around. There was no one inside the office or X-ray room. I opened the door to the autopsy suite and found Susan dressed in scrubs and dialing a number on the phone. She quickly hung up and greeted me with a nervous "Good morning."

"Glad you made it in." I unbuttoned my coat, regarding her curiously.

"Ben gave me a lift," she said, referring to my administrator, who owned a Jeep with four-wheel drive. "So far, we're the only three here."

"No sign of Fielding?"

"He called a few minutes ago and said he couldn't get out of his driveway. I told him we only have one case so far, but if more come in Ben can pick him up."

"Are you aware that our case is parked in the hall?"

She hesitated, blushing. "I was taking her over to X ray when the phone rang. Sorry."

"Have you weighed and measured her yet?"

"No."

"Let's do that first."

She hurried out of the autopsy suite before I could comment further. Secretaries and scientists who worked in the labs upstairs often entered and left the building through the morgue because it was convenient to the parking lot. Maintenance workers were in and out, too. Leaving a body unattended in the middle of a corridor was very poor form and could even jeopardize the case should chain of evidence be questioned in court.

Susan returned pushing the gurney, and we went to work, the stench of decomposing flesh nauseating. I fetched gloves and a plastic apron from a shelf, and clamped various forms in a clipboard. Susan was quiet and tense. When she reached up to the control panel to reset the computerized floor scale, I noticed her hands were shaking. Maybe she was suffering from morning sickness.

"Everything okay?" I asked her.

"Just a little tired."

"You sure?"

"Positive. She weighs one-eighty exactly."

I changed into my greens and Susan and I moved the body into the X-ray room across the hall, transferring it from the gurney to the table. Opening the sheet, I wedged a block under the neck to keep the head from lolling. The flesh of her throat was clean, spared from soot and burns because her chin had been tucked close to her chest while she was inside the car with the engine running. I did not see any obvious injuries, no bruises or broken fingernails. Her nose wasn't fractured. There were no cuts inside her lips and she hadn't bitten her tongue.

Susan took X rays and slipped them into the processor while I went over the front of the body with a lens. I collected a number of barely visible whitish fibers, quite possibly from the sheet or her bed covers, and found others similar to the ones on the bottoms of her socks. She wore no jewelry and was naked beneath her gown. I remembered the rumpled covers on her bed, the pillows propped against the headboard and glass of water on the table. The night of her death she had put curlers in her hair, gotten undressed, and at some point, perhaps, had been reading in bed.

Susan emerged from the developer room and leaned

against the wall, supporting the small of her back with her hands.

"What's the story on this lady?" she asked. "Was she married?"

"It appears she lived alone."

"Did she work?"

"She ran a business out of her home." Something caught my eye.

"What sort of business?"

"Possibly fortune-telling of sorts." The feather was very small and sooty, clinging to Jennifer Deighton's gown in the area of her left hip. Reaching for a small plastic bag, I tried to recall if I'd noticed any feathers around her house. Perhaps the pillows on her bed were filled with feathers.

"Did you find any evidence she was into the occult?"

"Some of her neighbors seemed to think she was a witch," I said.

"Based on what?"

"There's a church near her house. Allegedly, the lights in the steeple starting going on and off after she moved in some months ago."

"You're kidding."

"I saw them go on myself when I was leaving the scene. The steeple was dark. Then suddenly it was lit up."

"Weird."

"It was weird."

"Maybe it's on a timer."

"Unlikely. Lights going on and off all night would not conserve electricity. If it's true they go on and off all night. I saw it happen only once."

Susan did not say anything.

"Possibly there's a short in the wiring." In fact, I thought as I continued to work, I would call the church. They might be unaware of the problem.

"Any strange stuff inside her house?"

"Crystals. Some unusual books."

Silence.

Then Susan said, "I wish you'd told me earlier."

"Pardon?" I glanced up. She was staring uneasily at the body. She looked pale.

"Are you sure you're feeling all right?" I asked.

"I don't like stuff like this."

"Stuff like what?"

"It's like someone having AIDS or something. I ought to be told up front. Especially now."

"It's unlikely this woman has AIDS or—"

"I should have been told. Before I touched her."

"Susan—"

"I went to school with a girl who was a witch."

I stopped what I was doing. Susan was rigid against the wall, hands pressed against her belly.

"Her name was Doreen. She belonged to a coven and our senior year she put a curse on my twin sister, Judy. Judy was killed in a car wreck two weeks before graduation."

Bewildered, I stared at her.

"You know how occult stuff creeps me out! Like that cow's tongue with needles stuck in it that the cops brought in a couple of months ago. The one wrapped up in a list of dead people's names. It was left on a grave."

"It was a prank," I reminded her calmly. "The tongue came from a grocery store, and the names were meaningless, copied from headstones in the cemetery."

"You shouldn't tamper with the satanic, prank or not." Her voice trembled. "I take evil just as seriously as God."

Susan was the daughter of a minister and had abandoned religion long ago. I'd never heard her so much as allude to Satan or mention God unless it was profanely. I'd never known her to be the least bit superstitious or unnerved by anything. She was about to cry.

"Tell you what," I said quietly. "Since it appears I'm going to be short-staffed today, if you'll answer the phones upstairs, I'll take care of things down here."

Her eyes filled with tears, and I immediately went to her.

"It's okay." Putting my arm around her, I walked her out of the room. "Come on," I said gently as she leaned against me, sobbing. "You want Ben to take you home?"

She nodded, whispering, "I'm sorry. I'm sorry."

"All you need is a little rest." I sat her in a chair inside the morgue office and reached for the phone.

Jennifer Deighton had inhaled no carbon monoxide or soot because by the time she had been placed inside her car she was no longer breathing. Her death was a homicide, an obvious one, and throughout the afternoon I impatiently left messages for Marino to call me. Several times I tried to check on Susan but her phone just rang and rang.

"I'm concerned," I said to Ben Stevens. "Susan's not answering her phone. When you drove her home, did she mention that she was planning to go somewhere?"

"She told me she was going to bed."

He was sitting at his desk, going through reams of computer printouts. Rock and roll played quietly from the radio on a bookcase, and he was drinking tangerine-flavored mineral water. Stevens was young, smart, and boyishly good-looking. He worked hard, and played hard in singles bars, so I had been told. I was quite certain his job as my administrator would prove to be a short step on his way to someplace better.

"Maybe she unplugged her phone so she could sleep," he said, turning on his adding machine.

"Maybe that's it."

He launched into an update on our budget woes.

Late afternoon when it was beginning to get dark out, Stevens buzzed my line.

"Susan called. She said she won't be in tomorrow. And I've got a John Deighton on hold. Says he's Jennifer Deighton's brother."

Stevens transferred the call.

"Hello. They said you did my sister's autopsy," a man mumbled. "Uh, Jennifer Deighton's my sister."

"Your name, please?"

"John Deighton. I live in Columbia, South Carolina."

I glanced up as Marino appeared in my office doorway, and motioned for him to take a chair.

"They said she hooked up a hose to her car and killed herself."

"Who said that?" I asked. "And could you speak up, please?"

He hesitated. "I don't remember the name, should've wrote it down but I was too shocked."

The man didn't sound shocked. His voice was so muffled I barely could hear what he was saying.

"Mr. Deighton, I'm very sorry," I said. "But you will have to request any information regarding her death in writing. I will also need, included with your written request, some verification that you are next of kin."

He did not respond.

"Hello?" I asked. "Hello?"

I was answered by a dial tone.

"That's strange," I said to Marino. "Are you familiar with a John Deighton who claims to be Jennifer Deighton's brother?"

"That's who that was? Shit. We're trying to reach him."

"He said someone's already notified him about her death."

"You know where he was calling from?"

"Columbia, South Carolina, supposedly. He hung up on me."

Marino didn't seem interested. "I just came from Vander's office," he said, referring to Neils Vander, the chief fingerprints examiner. "He checked out Jennifer Deighton's car, plus the books that were beside her bed and a poem that was stuck inside one of 'em. As for the sheet of blank paper that was on her bed, he hasn't gotten to that yet."

"Anything so far?"

"He lifted a few. Will run them through the computer if there's a need. Probably most of the prints are hers. Here." He placed a small paper bag on my desk. "Happy reading."

"I think you're going to want those prints run without delay," I said grimly.

A shadow passed over Marino's eyes. He massaged his temples.

"Jennifer Deighton definitely did not commit suicide," I informed him. "Her CO was less than seven percent. She had no soot in her airway. The bright pink tint of her skin was due to exposure to cold, not CO poisoning."

"Christ," he said.

Shuffling through the paperwork in front of me, I handed him a body diagram, then opened an envelope and withdrew Polaroid photographs of Jennifer Deighton's neck.

"As you can see," I went on, "there are no injuries externally."

"What about the blood on the car seat?"

"A postmortem artifact due to purging. She was beginning to decompose. I found no abrasions or contusions, no fingertip bruises. But here"—I showed him a photograph of her neck at autopsy—"she's got irregular hemorrhages in the sternocleidomastoid muscles bilaterally. She's also got a fracture of the right cornua of the hyoid. Her death was caused by asphyxia, due to pressure applied to the neck—"

Marino interrupted, loudly. "You suggesting she got yoked?"

I showed him another photograph. "She's also got some facial petechia, or pinpoint hemorrhages. These findings are consistent with yoking, yes. She's a homicide, and I might suggest that we keep this out of the newspapers as long as possible."

"You know, I didn't need this." He looked up at me with bloodshot eyes. "I got eight uncleared homicides sitting on my desk even as we speak. Henrico don't got shit on Eddie Heath, and the kid's old man calls me almost every day. Not to mention, they're having a damn drug war in Mosby Court. Merry friggin' Christmas. I didn't need this."

"Jennifer Deighton didn't need this either, Marino."

"Keep going. What else did you find?"

"She did have high blood pressure, as her neighbor Mrs. Clary suggested."

"Huh," he said, shifting his eyes away from me. "How could you tell?"

"She had left ventricular hypertrophy, or thickening of the left side of the heart."

"High blood pressure does that?"

"It does. I should find fibrinoid changes in the renal microvasculature or early nephrosclerosis. I suspect the brain will show hypertensive changes, too, in the cerebral arterioles, but I won't be able to say with certainty until I can take a look under the scope."

"You're saying kidney and brain cells get killed off when you got high blood pressure?"

"In a manner of speaking."

"Anything else?"

"Nothing significant."

"What about gastric contents?" Marino asked.

"Meat, some vegetables, partially digested."

"Alcohol or drugs?"

"No alcohol. Drug screens are under way."

"No sign of rape?"

"No injuries or other evidence of sexual assault. I swabbed her for seminal fluid but won't get those reports for a while. Even then, you can't always be sure."

Marino's face was unreadable.

"What are you after?" I finally asked.

"Well, I'm thinking about how this thing was staged. Someone went to a lot of trouble to make us think she gassed herself. But then the lady's dead before he even gets her into her car. What I'm considering is that he didn't mean to whack her inside the house. You know, he applies a choke hold, uses too much force, and she dies. So, maybe he didn't know her health was bad and that's how it happened."

I started shaking my head. "Her high blood pressure has nothing to do with it."

"Explain how she died, then."

"Say the assailant is right-handed, he brought his left arm around the front of her neck and used his right hand to pull the left wrist toward the right." I demonstrated. "This placed pressure eccentrically on her neck, resulting in fracture of the right greater cornua of the hyoid bone. The pressure collapsed her upper airway and put pressure on the carotid arteries. She would have gotten hypoxic, or air hungry. Sometimes pressure on the neck produces bradycardia, a drop in the heart rate, and the victim has an arrhythmia."

"Could you tell from her autopsy if the assailant started using a choke hold that ended up a yoking? If he was just trying to subdue her and used too much force, in other words?"

"I can't tell you that from medical findings."

"But it's possible."

"It's within the realm of possibility."

"Come on, Doc," Marino said, exasperated. "Get off the witness stand for a minute, okay? Somebody else in this office besides you and me?"

No one was. But I was unnerved. Most of my staff had not shown up for work today, and Susan had acted bizarrely. Jennifer Deighton, a stranger, apparently had been trying to call me, then was murdered, and a man who claimed to be her brother had just hung up on me. Not to mention,

Marino's mood was foul. When I felt a loss of control, I became very clinical.

"Look," I said, "he very well may have used a choke hold to subdue her and ended up applying too much force, yoking her by mistake. In fact, I'll even go so far as to suggest that he simply thought he'd knocked her out and didn't know she was dead when he placed her inside her car."

"So we're dealing with a dumb shit."

"I wouldn't conclude that if I were you. But if he gets up tomorrow morning and reads in the paper that Jennifer Deighton was murdered, he may be in for the surprise of his life. He's going to wonder what he did wrong. Which is why I recommended we keep this away from the press."

"I got no problem with that. By the way, just because you didn't know Jennifer Deighton don't mean she didn't know you."

I waited for him to explain.

"I've been thinking about your hang ups. You're on TV, in the papers. Maybe she knew someone was after her, didn't know where to turn, and reached out to you for help. When she got your machine, she was too paranoid to leave a message."

"That's a very depressing thought."

"Almost everything we think in this joint is depressing." He got up from his chair.

"Do me a favor," I said. "Check her house. Tell me if you find any feather pillows, down-filled jackets, feather dusters, anything relating to feathers."

"Why?"

"I found a small feather on her gown."

"Sure. I'll let you know. Are you leaving?"

I glanced past him as I heard the elevator doors open and shut. "Was that Stevens?" I asked.

"Yeah."

"I've got a few more things to do before I go home," I said.

After Marino got on the elevator, I went to a window at the end of the hall that overlooked the parking lot in back. I wanted to make sure Ben Stevens's Jeep was gone. It was, and I watched as Marino emerged from the building, picking his way through crushed snow lit up by street lamps. He trudged to his car and stopped to vigorously shake snow off his feet, like a cat that's stepped in water, before sliding behind the wheel. God forbid that anything should violate the freshened air and Armor All of his inner sanctum. I wondered if he had plans for Christmas and was dismayed that I had not thought to invite him in for dinner. This would be his first Christmas since he and Doris had divorced.

As I made my way back down the empty hall, I ducked into each office along the way to check computer terminals. Unfortunately, no one was logged in, and the only cable tagged with a device number was Fielding's. It was neither tty07 nor tty14. Frustrated, I unlocked Margaret's office and switched on the light.

Typically, it looked as if a fierce wind had blown through, scattering papers across her desk, tipping books over in the bookcase and knocking others on the floor. Stacks of continuous-paper printouts spilled over like accordions, and indecipherable notes and telephone numbers were taped to walls and terminal screens. The minicomputer hummed like an electronic insect and lights danced across banks of modems on a shelf. Sitting in her chair before the system terminal, I slid open a drawer to my right and began rapidly walking my fingers through file tabs. I found several with promising labels such as "users" and "networking," but nothing I perused told me what I needed to know. Looking around as I thought, I noticed a thick bundle of cables that ran up the wall behind the computer and disappeared through the ceiling. Each cable was tagged.

Both tty07 and tty14 were connected directly to the computer. Unplugging tty07 first, I roamed from terminal to terminal to see which had been disconnected as a result. The terminal in Ben Stevens's office was down, then up again when I reconnected the cable. Next I set about to trace tty14, and was perplexed when the unplugging of that cable seemed to illicit no response. Terminals on the desks of my staff continued to work without pause. Then I remembered Susan. Her office was downstairs in the morgue.

Unlocking her door, I noticed two details the instant I walked into her office. There were no personal effects, such as photographs and knickknacks, to be seen, and on a bookshelf over the desk were a number of UNIX, SQL, and WordPerfect reference guides. I vaguely recalled that Susan had signed up for several computer courses last spring. Flipping a switch to turn on her monitor, I tried to log in and was baffled when the system responded. Her terminal was still connected; it could not be tty14. And then I realized something so obvious that I might have laughed were I not horrified.

Back upstairs, I paused in my office doorway, looking in as if someone I had never met worked here. Pooled around the workstation on my desk were lab reports, call sheets, death certificates, and page proofs of a forensic pathology textbook I was editing, and the return bearing my microscope didn't look much better. Against a wall were three tall filing cabinets, and across from them a couch situated far enough away from bookcases that you could easily go around it to reach books on lower shelves. Directly behind my chair was an oak credenza I had found years earlier in the state's surplus warehouse. Its drawers had locks, making it a perfect repository for my pocketbook and active cases that were unusually sensitive. I kept the key under my phone, and I thought again of last Thursday when Susan had broken jars of formalin while I was doing Eddie Heath's autopsy.

I did not know the device number of my terminal, for there had never been occasion when it mattered. Seating myself at my desk and sliding out the keyboard drawer, I tried to log in but my keystrokes were ignored. Disconnecting tty14 had disconnected me.

"Damn," I whispered as my blood ran cold. "Damn!"

I had sent no notes to my administrator's terminal. It was not I who had typed "I can't find it." In fact, when the file was accidentally created late last Thursday afternoon, I was in the morgue. But Susan wasn't. I had given her my keys and told her to lie down on the couch in my office until she recovered from the formalin spill. Was it possible that she not only had broken into my directory but also had gone through files and the paperwork on my desk? Had she attempted to send a note to Ben Stevens because she couldn't find what they were interested in?

One of the trace evidence examiners from upstairs suddenly appeared in my doorway, startling me.

"Hello," he muttered as he looked through paperwork, his lab coat buttoned up to his chin. Pulling out a multiple-page report, he walked in and handed it to me.

"I was getting ready to leave this in your box," he said. "But since you're still here, I'll give it to you in person. I've finished examining the adhesive residue you lifted from Eddie Heath's wrists."

"Building materials?" I asked, scanning the first page of the report.

"That's right. Paint, plaster, wood, cement, asbestos, glass. Typically, we find this sort of debris in burglary cases, often on the suspects' clothing, in their cuffs, pockets, shoes, and so on."

"What about on Eddie Heath's clothes?"

"Some of this same debris was on his clothes."

"And the paints? Tell me about them."

"I found bits of paint from five different origins. Three of them are layered, meaning something was painted and repainted a number of times."

"Are the origins vehicular or residential?" I inquired.

"Only one is vehicular, an acrylic lacquer typically used as a top coat in cars manufactured by General Motors."

It could have come from the vehicle used to abduct Eddie Heath, I thought. And it could have come from anywhere.

"The color?" I inquired.

"Blue."

"Layered?"

"No."

"What about the debris from the area of pavement where the body was found? I asked Marino to get sweepings to you and he said he would."

"Sand, dirt, bits of paving material, plus the miscellaneous debris you might expect around a Dumpster. Glass, paper, ash, pollen, rust, plant material."

"That's different from what you found adhering to the residue on his wrists?"

"Yes. It would appear to me that the tape was applied and removed from his wrists in a location where there's debris from building materials and birds."

"Birds?"

"On the third page of the report," he said. "I found a lot of feather parts."

Lucy was restless and rather irritable when I got home. Clearly, she had not had enough to occupy her during the day, for she had taken it upon herself to rearrange my study. The laser printer had been moved, as had the modem and all of my computer reference guides.

"Why did you do this?" I asked.

She was in my chair, her back to me, and she replied without turning around or slowing her fingers on the keybroad. "It makes more sense this way."

"Lucy, you can't just go into someone else's office and move everything around. How would you feel if I did that to you?"

"There would be no reason to rearrange anything of mine. It's all arranged very sensibly." She stopped typing and swiveled around. "See, now you can reach the printer without getting up from the chair. Your books are right here within reach, and the modem is out of your way completely. You shouldn't set books, coffee cups, and things on top of a modem."

"Have you been in here all day?" I asked.

"Where else would I be? You took the car. I went jogging around your neighborhood. Have you ever tried to run on snow?"

Pulling up a chair, I opened my briefcase and got out the paper bag Marino had given me. "You're saying you need a car."

"I feel stranded."

"Where would you like to go?"

"To your club. I don't know where else. I'd simply like the option. What's in the bag?"

"Books and a poem Marino gave me."

"Since when is he a member of the literati?" She got up and stretched. "I'm going to make a cup of herbal tea. Would you like some?"

"Coffee, please."

"It's bad for you," she said as she left the room.

"Oh, hell," I muttered irritably as I pulled the books and poem out of the bag and red fluorescent powder got all over my hands and clothes.

Neils Vander had done his usual thorough examination, and I had forgotten his passion for his new toy. Several months ago he had acquired an alternate light source and had retired the laser to the scrap heap. The Luma-Lite, with its "state-of-the-art three-hundred-and-fifty-watt high-intensity blue enhanced metal vapor arc lamp," as Vander lovingly described it whenever the subject came up, turned virtually invisible hairs and fibers a burning orange. Semen stains and street drug residues jumped out like solar flares, and best of all, the light could pick up fingerprints that never would have been seen in the past.

Vander had gone the gamut on Jennifer Deighton's paperback novels. They had been placed in the glass tank and exposed to vapors from Super Glue, the cyanoacrylate ester that reacts to the components of perspiration transferred by human skin. Then Vander had dusted the slick covers of the books with the red fluorescent powder that was now all over me. Finally, he had subjected the books to the cool blue scrutiny of the Luma-Lite and purpled pages with Ninhydrin. I hoped he would be rewarded for all of his trouble. My reward was to go into the bathroom and clean up with a wet washcloth.

Flipping through *Paris Trout* was unrevealing. The novel told the story of the heartless murder of a black girl, and if that was significant to Jennifer Deighton's own story, I could not imagine why. *Seth Speaks* was a spooky account of someone supposedly from another life communicating through the author. It did not really surprise me that Miss Deighton, with her otherworldly inclinations, might read such a thing. What interested me most was the poem.

It was typed on a sheet of white paper smudged purple with Ninhydrin and enclosed in a plastic bag:

JENNY

Jenny's kisses many
warmed the copper penny
wedded to her neck
with cotton string.

It was in the spring
  when he had found it
  on the dusty drive
  beside the meadow
  and given it to her.
No words of passion
  spoken.
He loved her
  with a token.
The meadow now is brown
  and overgrown with brambles.
  He is gone.
The coin asleep
  is cold
    down deep
  in a woodland
  wishing pond.

There was no date, no name of the author. The paper was creased from having been folded in quarters. I got up and went into the living room, where Lucy had set coffee and tea on the table and was stirring the fire.

"Aren't you hungry?" she asked.

"As a matter of fact, I am," I said, glancing over the poem again and wondering what it meant. Was "Jenny" Jennifer Deighton? "What would you like to eat?"

"Believe it or not, steak. But only if it's good and the cows haven't been fed a bunch of chemicals," Lucy said. "Is it possible you could bring home a car from work so I could use yours this week?"

"I generally don't bring home the state car unless I'm on call."

"You went to a scene last night when you supposedly weren't on call. You're always on call, Aunt Kay."

"All right," I said. "Why don't we do this. We'll go get the best steak in town. Afterward, we'll stop by the office and I'll drive the wagon home and you can take my car. There's still a little ice on the roads in spots. You have to promise to be extra careful."

"I've never seen your office."

"I'll show it to you if you wish."

"No way. Not at night."

"The dead can't hurt you."

"Yes, they can," Lucy said. "Dad hurt me when he died. He left me to be raised by Mom."

"Let's get our coats."

"Why is it that every time I bring up anything germane to our dysfunctional family, you change the subject?"

I headed to my bedroom for my coat. "Do you want to borrow my black leather jacket?"

"See, you're doing it again," she screamed.

We argued all the way to Ruth's Chris Steak House, and by the time I parked the car I had a headache and was completely disgusted with myself. Lucy had provoked me into raising my voice, and the only other person who could routinely do that was my mother.

"Why are you being so difficult?" I said in her ear as we were shown to a table.

"I want to talk to you and you won't let me," she said.

A waiter instantly appeared for drink orders.

"Dewar's and soda," I said.

"Sparkling water with a twist," Lucy said. "You shouldn't drink and drive."

"I'm having only one. But you're right. I'd be better off not having any. And you're being critical again. How can you expect to have friends if you talk to people this way?"

"I don't expect to have friends." She stared off. "It's others who expect me to have friends. Maybe I don't want any friends because most people bore me."

Despair pressed against my heart. "I think you want friends more than anyone I know, Lucy."

"I'm sure you think that. And you probably also think I should get married in a couple of years."

"Not at all. In fact, I sincerely hope you won't."

"While I was roaming around inside your computer today, I saw the file called 'flesh.' Why do you have a file called that?" my niece asked.

"Because I'm in the middle of a very difficult case."

"The little boy named Eddie Heath? I saw his record in the case file. He was found with no clothes on, next to a Dumpster. Someone had cut out parts of his skin."

"Lucy, you shouldn't read case records," I said as my pager went off. I unclipped it from the waistband of my skirt and glanced at the number.

"Excuse me for a moment," I said, getting up from the table as our drinks arrived.

I found a pay phone. It was almost eight P.M.

"I need to talk to you," said Neils Vander, who was still at the office. "You might want to come down here and bring by Ronnie Waddell's ten print cards."

"Why?"

"We've got an unprecedented problem. I'm about to call Marino, too."

"All right. Tell him to meet me at the morgue in a half hour."

When I returned to the table, Lucy knew by the look on my face that I was about to ruin another evening.

"I'm so sorry," I said.

"Where are we going?"

"To my office, then to the Seaboard Building." I got out my billfold.

"What's in the Seaboard Building?"

"It's where the serology, DNA, and fingerprint labs moved

not so long ago. Marino's going to meet us," I said. "It's been a long time since you've seen him."

"Jerks like him don't change or get better with time."

"Lucy, that's unkind. Marino is not a jerk."

"He was last time I was here."

"You weren't exactly nice to him, either."

"I didn't call him a smartass brat."

"You called him a number of other names, as I recall, and were continually correcting his grammar."

A half hour later, I left Lucy inside the morgue office while I hurried upstairs. Unlocking the credenza, I retrieved Waddell's case file, and no sooner had I boarded the elevator when the buzzer sounded from the bay. Marino was dressed in jeans and a dark blue parka, his balding head warmed by a Richmond Braves baseball cap.

"You two remember each other, don't you?" I said. "Lucy's visiting me for Christmas and is helping out with a computer problem," I explained as we walked out into the cold night air.

The Seaboard Building was across the street from the parking lot behind the morgue and cater-cornered to the front of Main Street Station, where the Health Department's administrative offices had relocated while its former building was being stripped of asbestos. The clock in Main Street Station's tower floated high above us like a hunter's moon, and red lights atop high buildings blinked slow warnings to low-flying planes. Somewhere in the dark, a train lumbered along its tracks, the earth rumbling and creaking like a ship at sea.

Marino walked ahead of us, the tip of his cigarette glowing at intervals. He did not want Lucy here, and I knew she sensed it. When he reached the Seaboard Building, where supplies had been loaded onto boxcars around the time of the Civil War, I rang the bell outside the door. Vander appeared almost immediately to let us in.

He did not greet Marino or ask who Lucy was. If a creature from outer space were to accompany someone he trusted, Vander would not ask any questions or expect to be introduced. We followed him up a flight of stairs to the second floor, where old corridors and offices had been repainted in shades of gunmetal gray and refurnished with cherry-finished desks and bookcases and teal upholstered chairs.

"What are you working on so late?" I asked as we entered the room housing the Automated Fingerprint Identification System, known as AFIS.

"Jennifer Deighton's case," he said.

"Then what do you want with Waddell's ten print cards?" I asked, perplexed.

"I want to be sure it was Waddell you autopsied last week," Vander said bluntly.

"What the hell are you talking about?" Marino looked at him in astonishment.

"I'm getting ready to show you." Vander seated himself before the remote input terminal, which looked like an everyday PC. It was connected by modem to the State Police computer, on which resided a data base of more than six million fingerprints. He hit several keys, activating the laser printer.

"Perfect scores are few and far between, but we got one here." Vander began typing, and a bright white fingerprint filled the screen. "Right index finger, plain whorl." He pointed to the vortex of lines swirling behind glass. "A damn good partial recovered from Jennifer Deighton's house."

"Where in her house?" I asked.

"From a dining room chair. At first I wondered if there was some mistake. But apparently not." Vander continued staring at the screen, then resumed typing as he talked. "The print comes back to Ronnie Joe Waddell."

"That's impossible," I said, shocked.

"You would think so," Vander replied abstractedly.

"Did you find anything in Jennifer Deighton's house that

might indicate she and Waddell were acquainted?" I asked Marino as I opened Waddell's case file.

"No."

"If you've got Waddell's prints from the morgue," Vander said to me, "we'll see how they compare to what's in AFIS."

I pulled out two manila envelopes, and it struck me wrong immediately that both weren't heavy and thick. I felt my face get hot as I opened each and found the expected photographs inside and nothing else. There was no envelope containing Waddell's ten print cards. When I looked up, everybody was looking at me.

"I don't understand this," I said, conscious of Lucy's uneasy stare.

"You don't have his prints?" Marino asked in disbelief.

I rifled through the file again. "They're not here."

"Susan usually does it, right?" he said.

"Yes. Always. She was supposed to make two sets. One for Corrections and one for us. Maybe she gave them to Fielding and he forgot to give them to me."

I got out my address book and reached for the phone. Fielding was home and knew nothing about the fingerprint cards.

"No, I didn't notice her printing him, but I don't notice half of what other people are doing down there," he said. "I just assumed she'd given the cards to you."

Dialing Susan's number next, I tried to remember seeing her get out the spoon and print cards, or rolling Waddell's fingers on the ink pad.

"Do you remember seeing Susan print Waddell?" I asked Marino as Susan's phone continued to ring.

"She didn't do it while I was there. I would have offered to help if she had."

"No answer." I hung up.

"Waddell was cremated," Vander said.

"Yes," I said.

We were silent for a moment.

Then Marino said to Lucy with unnecessary brusqueness, "You mind? We need to talk alone for a minute."

"You can sit in my office," Vander said to her. "Down the hall, last one on the right."

When she was gone, Marino said, "Waddell's supposedly been locked up ten years, and there's no way the print we got from Jennifer Deighton's chair was left ten years ago. She didn't even move into her house on Southside until a few months ago, and the dining room furniture looks brand-new. Plus, there were indentations on the carpet in the living room that make it appear a dining room chair was carried in there, maybe on the night she died. That's why I wanted the chairs dusted to begin with."

"An uncanny possibility," Vander said. "At this moment, we can't prove that the man who was executed last week was Ronnie Joe Waddell."

"Perhaps there is some other explanation for how Waddell's print ended up on a chair in Jennifer Deighton's house," I said. "For example, the penitentiary has a wood shop that makes furniture."

"Unlikely as hell," Marino said. "For one thing, they don't do woodworking or make license plates on death row. And even if they did, most civilians don't end up with prison-made furniture in their house."

"All the same," Vander said to Marino, "it would be interesting if you could track down who and where she bought her dining room set from."

"Don't worry. It's a top priority."

"Waddell's complete past arrest record, including his prints, should all be in one file at the FBI," Vander added. "I'll get a copy of their print card and retrieve the photograph of the thumbprint from Robyn Naismith's case. Where else was Waddell arrested?"

"Nowhere else," Marino said. "The only jurisdiction that will have his records should be Richmond."

"And this print found on a dining room chair is the only one you've identified?" I asked Vander.

"Of course, a number of those lifted came back to Jennifer Deighton," he said. "Particularly on the books by her bed and the folded sheet of paper—the poem. And a couple of unknown partials from her car, as you might expect, maybe left by whoever loaded groceries into her trunk or filled her tank with gas. That's all for now."

"And no luck with Eddie Heath?" I asked.

"There wasn't much to examine. The paper bag, can of soup, candy bar. I tried the Luma-Lite on his shoes and clothes. No luck."

Later, he walked us out through the bay, where locked freezers stored the blood of enough convicted felons to fill a small city, the samples awaiting entry into the Commonwealth's DNA data bank. Parked in front of the door was Jennifer Deighton's car, and it looked more pathetic than I remembered, as if it had gone into a dramatic decline since the murder of its owner. Metal along the sides was creased and dented from being repeatedly struck by other car doors. Paint was rusting in spots and scraped and gouged in others, and the vinyl top was peeling. Lucy paused to peer inside a sooty window.

"Hey, don't touch nothing," Marino said to her.

She looked levelly at him without a word, and all of us went outside.

Lucy drove off in my car and went straight to the house without waiting for Marino or me. When we walked in, she was already in my study with the door shut.

"I can see she's still Miss Congeniality," Marino said.

"You don't win any prizes tonight, either." I opened the fireplace screen and added several logs.

"She'll keep her mouth shut about what we were talking about?"

"Yes," I said wearily. "Of course."

"Yeah, well, I know you trust her, since you're her aunt. But I'm not sure it was a good idea for her to hear all that, Doc."

"I do trust Lucy. She means a lot to me. You mean a lot to me. I hope the two of you will become friends. The bar is open, or I'll be glad to put on a pot of coffee."

"Coffee would be good."

He sat on the edge of the hearth and got out his Swiss Army knife. While I made coffee, he trimmed his nails and tossed the shavings into the fire. I tried Susan's number again, but there was no answer.

"I don't think Susan took his prints," Marino said when I set the coffee tray on the butler's table. "I've been thinking while you were in the kitchen. I know she didn't do it while I was at the morgue that night, and I was there most of the time. So unless it was done right when the body was brought in, forget it."

"It wasn't done then," I said, getting more unnerved. "Corrections was out of there in minutes. The entire scene was very distracting. It was late and everybody was tired. Susan forgot, and I was too busy with what I was doing to notice."

"You hope she forgot."

I reached for my coffee.

"Something's going on with her, based on what you've been telling me. I wouldn't trust her as far as I could throw her," he said.

Right now I didn't.

"We need to talk to Benton," he said.

"You saw Waddell on the table, Marino. You saw him executed. I can't believe we can't say it was him."

"We can't say it. We could compare mug shots and your

morgue photos and still not say it. I hadn't seen him since he got popped more than ten years ago. The guy they walked out to the chair was about eighty pounds heavier. His beard, mustache, and head had been shaved. Sure, there was enough resemblance that I just assumed. But I can't swear it was him."

I recalled Lucy's walking off the plane the other night. She was my niece. I had seen her but a year ago, and still I almost had not recognized her. I knew all too well how unreliable visual identifications can be.

"If someone switched inmates," I said. "And if Waddell is free and someone else was put to death, please tell me why."

Marino spooned more sugar into his coffee.

"A motive, for God's sake. Marino, what would it be?"

He looked up. "I don't know why."

Just then, the door to my study opened and both of us turned as Lucy walked out. She came into the living room and sat on the side of the hearth opposite Marino, who had his back to the fire, elbows on his knees.

"What can you tell me about AFIS?" she asked me as if Marino were not in the room.

"What is it you wish to know?" I said.

"The language. And is it run on a mainframe."

"I don't know the technical details. Why?"

"I can find out if files have been altered."

I felt Marino's eyes on me.

"You can't break into the State Police computer, Lucy."

"I probably could, but I'm not necessarily advocating that. There may be some other way to gain access."

Marino turned to her. "You're saying you could tell if Waddell's records was changed in AFIS?"

"Yes. I'm saying I could tell if his records *were* changed."

Marino's jaw muscles flexed. "Seems to me if someone was slick enough to do it, they'd be slick enough to make sure some computer nerd didn't catch on."

"I'm not a computer nerd. I'm not a nerd of any description."

They fell silent, parked on either end of the hearth like mismatched bookends.

"You can't go into AFIS," I said to Lucy.

She looked impassively at me.

"Not alone," I added. "Not unless there is a safe way to grant you access. And even if there is, I think I'd rather you stay out of it."

"I don't think you'd really rather that. If something was tampered with, you know I'd find out, Aunt Kay."

"The kid's got a god complex." Marino got up from the hearth.

Lucy said to him, "Could you hit the twelve on the clock over there on the wall? If you drew your gun right this minute and took aim?"

"I ain't interested in shooting up your aunt's house in order to prove something to you."

"Could you hit the twelve from where you're standing?"

"You're damn right."

"You're positive."

"Yeah, I'm positive."

"The lieutenant's got a god complex," Lucy said to me.

Marino turned to the fire, but not before I caught a flicker of a smile.

"All Neils Vander has is a workstation and printer," Lucy said. "He's connected to the State Police computer by modem. Has that always been the case?"

"No," I replied. "Before he moved into the new building, there was much more equipment involved."

"Describe it."

"Well, there were several different components. But the actual computer was much like the one Margaret has in her office." Realizing Lucy had not been inside Margaret's office, I added, "A mini."

Firelight cast moving shadows on her face. "I'll bet AFIS

is a mainframe that isn't a mainframe. I'll bet it's a series of minis strung together, all of it connected by UNIX or some other multiuser, multitasking environment. If you got me access to the system, I could probably do it from your terminal here in the house, Aunt Kay."

"I don't want anything traced back to me," I said with feeling.

"Nothing would be traced back to you. I would dial into your computer downtown, then go through a series of gateways, set up a really complicated link. By the time all was said and done, I'd be very hard to track."

Marino headed to the bathroom.

"He acts like he lives here," Lucy said.

"Not quite," I replied.

Several minutes later, I walked Marino out. The crusty snow of the lawn seemed to radiate light, and the air was sharp in my lungs like the first hit of a menthol cigarette.

"I'd love it if you would join Lucy and me for Christmas dinner," I said from the doorway.

He hesitated, looking at his car parked on the street. "That's mighty nice of you, but I can't make it, Doc."

"I wish you did not dislike Lucy so much," I said, hurt.

"I'm tired of her treating me like a dumb shit who was born in a barn."

"Sometimes you act like a dumb shit who was born in a barn. And you haven't tried very hard to earn her respect."

"She's a spoiled Miami brat."

"When she was ten, she was a Miami brat," I said. "But she's never been spoiled. In fact, quite the opposite is true. I want you two to get along. I want that for my Christmas present."

"Who said I was giving you a Christmas present?"

"Of course you are. You're going to give me what I've just requested. And I know exactly how to make it happen."

"How?" he asked suspiciously.

"Lucy wants to learn to shoot and you just told her you could shoot the twelve off a clock. You could give her a lesson or two."

"Forget it," he said.

6

The next three days were typical for the holiday season. No one was in or returning telephone calls. Parking lots had spaces to spare, lunch hours were long, and office errands involved clandestine stops at stores, the bank, and the post office. For all practical purposes, the Commonwealth had shut down before the official holiday began. But Neils Vander was not typical by any standard. He was oblivious to time and place when he called me Christmas Eve morning.

"I'm getting started on an image enhancement over here that I think you might be interested in," he said. "The Jennifer Deighton case."

"I'm on my way," I said.

Heading down the hallway, I almost ran into Ben Stevens as he emerged from the men's room.

"I have a meeting with Vander," I said. "I shouldn't be long, and I've got my paper."

"I was just coming to see you," he said.

Reluctantly, I paused to hear what he had on his mind. I wondered if he detected that it was a struggle for me to act relaxed around him. Lucy continued to monitor our computer from my terminal at home to see if anyone attempted to access my directory again. So far, no one had.

"I had a talk with Susan this morning," Stevens said.

"How is she?"

"She's not coming back to work, Dr. Scarpetta."

I was not surprised, but I was stung that she could not tell me this herself. By now I had tried at least half a dozen times to get hold of her, and either no one answered or her husband did and offered some excuse for why Susan couldn't come to the phone.

"That's it?" I asked him. "She's simply not coming back? Did she give a reason?"

"I think she's having a tougher time with the pregnancy than she thought. I guess the job's just too much right now."

"She'll need to send a letter of resignation," I said, unable to keep the anger from my voice. "And I'll leave it to you to work out the details with Personnel. We'll need to begin looking for a replacement immediately."

"There's a hiring freeze," he reminded me as I walked off.

Outside, snow plowed along roadsides had frozen into mounds of filthy ice impossible to park on or walk across, and the sun burned wanly through portentous clouds. A streetcar carried a small brass band past, and I climbed granite steps gritty with salt as "Joy to the World" moved on. A Forensics police officer let me inside the Seaboard Building, and upstairs I found Vander inside a room bright with color monitors and ultraviolet lights. Seated at the image enhancer's workstation, he was staring intensely at something on the screen as he manipulated a mouse.

"It's not blank," he announced without so much as a "how are you." "Someone wrote something on a piece of paper that was on top of this one, or close to on top of this one. If you look hard, you can barely make out impressions."

Then I began to understand. Centered on the light table to his left was a clean sheet of white paper, and I leaned closer to take a look. The impressions were so faint that I wasn't sure if I was imagining them.

"The sheet of paper found under the crystal on Jennifer Deighton's bed?" I asked, getting excited.

He nodded, moving the mouse some more, adjusting the gray tones.

"Is this live?"

"No. The video camera's already captured the impressions and they're saved on the hard disk. But don't touch the paper. I haven't processed it for prints yet. I'm just getting started, keep your fingers crossed. Come on, come on." He was talking to the enhancer now. "I know the camera saw it fine. You gotta help us out here."

Computerized methods of image enhancement are a lesson in contrasts and conundrums. A camera can differentiate more than two hundred shades of gray, the human eye less than forty. Just because something isn't there doesn't mean it isn't there.

"Thank God with paper you don't have to worry about background noise," Vander went on as he worked. "Speeds things up considerably when you don't have to worry about that. Had a time of it the other day with a bloody print left on a bed sheet. The weave of the fabric, you know. Not so long ago the print would have been worthless. Okay." Another tint of gray washed over the area he was working on. "Now we're getting somewhere. You see it?" He pointed at slender, ghostly shapes on the upper half of the screen.

"Barely."

"What we're trying to enhance here is shadow versus eradicated writing, because nothing was written and erased here. The shadow was produced when oblique light hit the flat surface of this paper and the indentations in it—at least the video camera perceived shadow loud and clear. You and I can't see it without help. Let's try a little more enhancement of the verticals." He moved the mouse. "Darken the horizontals just a tad. Good. It's coming. Two-oh-two, dash. We've got part of a phone number."

I pulled a chair close to him and sat down. "The area code for D.C.," I said.

"I'm making out a four and a three. Or is that an eight?"

I squinted. "I think it's a three."

"That's better. You're right. Definitely a three."

He continued to work for a while and more numbers and words became visible on the screen. Then he sighed and said, "Rats. I can't get the last digit. It's just not there, but look at this before the D.C. area code. 'To' followed by a colon. And right under it is 'from' followed by another colon and another number. Eight-oh-four. That's local. This number's very unclear. A five and maybe a seven, or is that a nine?"

"I think that's going to be Jennifer Deighton's number," I said. "Her fax machine and telephone are on the same line—she had a fax machine in her office, a single-sheet feed that uses ordinary typing paper. It appears she wrote out a fax on top of this sheet of paper. What did she send? A separate document? There's no message here."

"We're not finished yet. We're getting what looks like the date now. An eleven? No, that's a seven. December seventeenth. I'm going to move down."

He moved the mouse and the arrows slid down the screen. Hitting a key, he enlarged the area he wanted to work on, then began painting it with shades of gray. I sat very still while shapes began to slowly materialize out of a literary limbo, curves here, dots there, and *t*'s boldy crossed. Vander worked silently. We barely blinked or breathed. We sat like this for an hour, words gradually getting sharper, one shade of gray contrasting with another, molecule by molecule, bit by bit. He willed them, coaxed them into existence. It was incredible. It was all there.

Exactly one week ago, barely two days before her murder,

Jennifer Deighton had faxed the following message to a number in Washington, D.C.:

> Yes, I'll cooperate, but it's too late, too late, too late. Better you should come here. This is all so wrong!

When I finally looked up from the screen as Vander hit the print button, I was light-headed. My vision was temporarily blurred, adrenaline surging.

"Marino needs to see this immediately. Hopefully, we can figure out whose fax number this is, the Washington number. We've got all but the last digit. How many fax numbers can there be in Washington that are exactly like this except for the last digit?"

"Digits zero through nine." Vander raised his voice above the printer's rat-a-tat-tat. "At the most, there could be only ten. Ten numbers, fax or otherwise, exactly like this one except for the last digit."

He gave me a printout. "I'll clean it up some more and get you a better copy later," he said. "And there's one more thing. I'm not having any luck getting my hands on Ronnie Waddell's print, the photo of the bloody thumbprint recovered from Robyn Naismith's house. Every time I call Archives, I'm told they're still looking for his file."

"Remember what time of year it is. I'll bet there's hardly anybody there," I said, unable to dispel a sense of foreboding.

Back in my office, I got hold of Marino and explained what the image enhancer had discovered.

"Hell, you can forget the phone company," he said. "My contact there's already left for vacation, and nobody else is going to do shit on Christmas Eve."

"There's a chance we can figure out who she sent the fax to on our own," I said.

"I don't know how, short of sending a fax that reads 'Who

are you?' and then hoping you get a fax back that reads 'Hi. I'm Jennifer Deighton's killer.' "

"It depends on if the person has a label programmed into his fax machine," I said.

"A *label*?"

"Your more sophisticated fax machines allow you to program your name or company name into the system. This label will be printed on anything you fax to someone else. But what's more significant is that the label of the person receiving the fax will also appear in the character-display window of the machine sending the fax. In other words, if I send a fax to you, in the character display of my fax machine I'll see 'Richmond Police Department' right above the fax number I've just dialed."

"You got acccess to a fancy fax machine? The one we got in the squad room sucks."

"I've got one here at the office."

"Well, tell me what you find out. I've gotta hit the street."

Quickly, I made up a list of ten telephone numbers, each one beginning with the six digits Vander and I had been able to make out on the sheet of paper found on Jennifer Deighton's bed. I completed each number with a zero, a one, a two, a three, and so on, then began trying them out. Only one of them was answered by an inhuman, high-pitched tone.

The fax machine was located in my computer analyst's office, and Margaret, fortunately, had begun her holiday early, too. I shut her door and sat down at her desk, thinking as the minicomputer hummed and modem lights blinked. Labels worked both ways. If I began a transmission, the label for my office was going to appear in the character-display window of the fax machine I had dialed. I would have to kill the process fast, before the transmission was completed. I hoped that by the time anyone checked the machine to see what was going on, "Office of the Chief Medical Examiner" and our number would have vanished from the window.

Inserting a blank sheet of paper into the tray, I dialed the

Washington number and waited as the transmission began. Nothing materialized in the character-display window. Damn. The fax machine I had dialed did not have a label. So much for that. I killed the process and returned to my office, defeated.

I had just sat down at my desk when the telephone rang.

"Dr. Scarpetta," I answered.

"Nicholas Grueman here. Whatever you just tried to fax, it didn't transmit."

"Excuse me?" I said, stunned.

"I got nothing on this end but a blank sheet of paper with the name of your office stamped on it. Uh, error code zero-zero-one, 'please send again,' it says."

"I see," I said as the hairs on my arms raised.

"Perhaps you were trying to send an amendment to your record? I understand you took a look at the electric chair."

I did not reply.

"Very thorough of you, Dr. Scarpetta. Perhaps you learned something new about those injuries we discussed, the abrasions to the inner aspects of Mr. Waddell's arms? The *antecubital fossas*?"

"Please give me your fax number again," I said quietly.

He recited it for me. The number matched the one on my list.

"Is the fax machine in your office or do you share it with other attorneys, Mr. Grueman?"

"It's right next to my desk. No need to mark anything for my attention. Just send it on—and *do* put a rush on it please, Dr. Scarpetta. I was thinking of going home soon."

I left the office a little later, frustration having driven me out the door. I could not get Marino. There was nothing more I could do. I felt caught in a web of bizarre connections, clueless as to the point in common they shared.

On impulse I pulled into a lot of West Cary where an old man was selling wreaths and Christmas trees. He looked like a lumberjack from a fable as he sat on a stool in the midst of his small forest, the cold air fragrant with evergreen. Perhaps my shunning of the Christmas spirit finally had gotten to me. Or maybe I simply wanted a distraction. At this late date, there wasn't much of a selection, those trees passed over, misshapen or dying, each destined to sit out the season, I suspected, except for the one I chose. It would have been lovely were it not scoliotic. Decorating it proved more an orthopedic challenge than a festive ritual, but with ornaments and strands of lights strategically hung and wire straightening the problem places, it stood proudly in my living room.

"There," I said to Lucy as I stepped back to admire my work. "What do you think?"

"I think it's weird that you suddenly decided to get a tree on Christmas Eve. When was the last time you had one?"

"I suppose when I was married."

"Is that where the ornaments came from?"

"Back then I went to a lot of trouble at Christmas."

"Which is why you don't anymore."

"I'm much busier than I was back then," I said.

Lucy opened the fireplace screen and rearranged logs with the poker. "Did you and Mark ever spend Christmas together?"

"Don't you remember? We came down to see you last Christmas."

"No, you didn't. You came for three days *after* Christmas and flew home on New Year's Day."

"He was with his family on Christmas Day."

"You weren't invited?"

"No."

"Why not?"

"Mark came from an old Boston family. They had certain

ways of doing things. What did you decide about this evening? Did my jacket with the black velvet collar fit?"

"I haven't tried anything. Why do we have to go to all these places?" Lucy said. "I won't know anybody."

"It's not that bad. I simply have to drop off a present to someone who's pregnant and probably not coming back to work. And I need to show the flag at a neighborhood party. I accepted the invitation before I knew you were going to be visiting. You certainly don't have to come with me."

"I'd rather stay here," she said. "I wish I could get started on AFIS."

"Patience," I told her, though I did not feel patient at all.

In the late afternoon, I left another message with the dispatcher and decided that either Marino's pager wasn't working or he was too busy to find a pay phone. Candles glowed in my neighbors' windows, an oblong moon shining high above trees. I played that Christmas music of Pavarotti and the New York Philharmonic, doing what I could to get into the proper frame of mind as I showered and dressed. The party I was to attend did not begin until seven. That gave me enough time to drop off Susan's gift and have a word with her.

She surprised me by answering the phone, and sounded reluctant and tense when I asked if I could drop by.

"Jason's out," she said, as if that mattered somehow. "He went to the mall."

"Well, I have a few things for you," I explained.

"What things?"

"Christmas things. I'm supposed to go to a party, so I won't stay long. Is that all right?"

"I guess. I mean, that's nice."

I had forgotten she lived in Southside, where I rarely went and was inclined to get lost. Traffic was worse than I had feared, the Midlothian Turnpike choked with last-minute shoppers prepared to run you off the road as they ran their Happy Holidays errands. Parking lots swarmed with cars, stores and malls so garishly lit up it was enough to make you blind. Susan's neighborhood was very dark and twice I had to pull over and turn on the interior light to read her directions. After much riding around, I finally found her tiny ranch-style house sandwiched between two others that looked exactly like it.

"Hi," I said, peering at her through leaves of the pink poinsettia in my arms.

She nervously locked the door and showed me to the living room. Pushing books and magazines aside, she set the poinsettia on the coffee table.

"How are you feeling?" I asked.

"Better. Would you like something to drink? Here, let me take your coat."

"Thanks. Nothing to drink. I can't stay but a minute." I handed her a package. "A little something I picked up when I was in San Francisco last summer." I sat on the couch.

"Wow. You really do your shopping early." She avoided my eyes as she curled up in a wing chair. "You want me to open it now?"

"Whatever you'd like."

She carefully sliced through tape with a thumbnail and slipped off the satin ribbon intact. Smoothing the paper into a neat rectangle, as if she planned to reuse it, she placed it in her lap and opened the black box.

"Oh," she said under her breath, unfolding the red silk scarf.

"I thought it would look good with your black coat," I said. "I don't know about you, but I don't like wool against my skin."

"This is beautiful. It's really thoughtful of you, Dr. Scarpetta. I've never had anybody bring me something from San Francisco before."

The expression of her face pricked my heart, and suddenly my surroundings came into sharper focus. Susan was wearing a yellow terry cloth robe, frayed at the cuffs, and a pair of black socks that I suspected belonged to her husband. Furniture was scarred and cheap, upholstery shiny. The artificial Christmas tree near the small TV was scantily decorated and missing several limbs. There were few presents underneath. Propped against a wall was a folded crib that was clearly secondhand.

Susan caught me glancing around and looked ill at ease.

"Everything is so immaculate," I said.

"You know how I am. Obsessive-compulsive."

"Thankfully. If a morgue can look terrific, ours does."

She carefully folded the scarf and returned it to its box. Pulling her robe more tightly around her, she stared silently at the poinsettia.

"Susan," I said gently, "do you want to talk about what's going on?"

She did not look at me.

"It's not like you to get upset as you did the other morning. It's not like you to miss work and then quit without so much as calling me."

She took a deep breath. "I'm really sorry. I just can't seem to handle things too well these days. I really react. Like when I was reminded of Judy."

"I know your sister's death must have been terrible for you."

"We were twins. Not identical. Judy was a lot prettier than me. That was part of the problem. Doreen was jealous of her."

"Doreen was the girl who claimed to be a witch?"

"Yes. I'm sorry. I just don't want to be around anything like that. Especially now."

"It might make you feel better to know that I called the church near Jennifer Deighton's house and was told that the steeple is illuminated with sodium vapor lights that started going bad several months ago. Apparently, no one was aware that the lights hadn't been properly repaired. That seems to be the explanation for why they blink on and off."

"When I was growing up in the church," she said, "there were pentecostals in the congregation who believed in speaking in tongues and casting out demons. I remember this man coming to dinner and talking about his encounter with demons, about lying in bed at night and hearing something breathing in the dark and books flying off shelves and slamming around the room. I was scared to death by stuff like that. I couldn't even see *The Exorcist* when it came out."

"Susan, we have to be objective and clearheaded on the job. We can't let our backgrounds, beliefs, or phobias interfere."

"You didn't grow up the daughter of a minister."

"I grew up Catholic," I said.

"Nothing's the same as growing up the daughter of a fundamentalist minister," she challenged, blinking back tears.

I did not argue.

"I think I've gotten free of old stuff, then it grabs me around the throat," she went on with difficulty. "Like there's this other person inside who messes with me."

"How are you being messed with?"

"Some things have gotten ruined."

I waited for her to elaborate, but she would not. She stared down at her hands, her eyes miserable. "It's just too much pressure," she muttered.

"What is too much pressure, Susan?"

"Work."

"How is it any different than it's ever been?" I assumed she would say that expecting a child made everything different.

"Jason doesn't think it's healthy for me. He's always thought that."

"I see."

"I come home and tell him what my day was like, and he has a real hard time with it. He says, 'Don't you realize how awful this is? There's no way it can be good for you.' He's right. I can't always shake it off anymore. I'm tired of decomposed bodies and people raped, cut up, and shot. I'm tired of dead babies and people killed in their cars. I don't want any more violence." She looked at me, her lower lip trembling. "I don't want any more death."

I thought of how difficult it was going to be to replace her. With someone new, days would be slow, the learning curve long. Worse were the perils of interviewing applicants and screening out the weirdos. Not everyone eager to work in a morgue is the paragon of normalcy. I liked Susan and I felt hurt and deeply troubled. She was not being honest with me.

"Is there anything else you'd like to tell me about?" I asked, my eyes not leaving her.

She glanced at me and I saw fear. "I can't think of anything."

I heard a car door shut.

"Jason's home," she barely said.

Our conversation had ended, and as I got up I said quietly to her, "Please contact me if you need anything, Susan. A reference, or just to talk. You know where I am."

I spoke to her husband only briefly on my way out. He was tall and well built, with curly brown hair and distant eyes. Though he was polite, I could tell he was not pleased to discover me in his house. As I drove across the river, I was shaken by the image that this struggling young couple must have of me. I was the *boss* dressed in a designer suit arriving in her Mercedes to deliver token gifts on Christmas Eve. The alienation of Susan's loyalty touched my deepest insecurities. I was no longer sure of my relationships or how I was perceived. I feared I had failed some test after Mark was killed, as if my reaction to that loss held the answer to a question in the lives of those around me. After all, I was supposed to handle death better than anyone. Dr. Kay Scarpetta, the expert. Instead, I had withdrawn, and I knew others felt the coolness around my edges no matter how friendly or thoughtful I tried to be. My staff no longer confided in me. Now it appeared security in my office had been violated, and Susan had quit.

Taking the Cary Street exit, I turned left into my neighborhood and headed for the home of Bruce Carter, a district court judge. He lived on Sulgrave, several blocks from me, and suddenly I was a child in Miami again, staring at what had seemed mansions to me then. I remembered going door-to-door with a wagon full of citrus fruit, knowing that the elegant hands doling out change belonged to unreachable people who felt pity. I remembered returning home with a pocket full of pennies and smelling the sickness in the bedroom where my father lay dying.

Windsor Farms was quietly rich, with Georgian and Tudor houses neatly arranged along streets with English names, and estates shadowed by trees and surrounded by serpentine brick walls. Private security jealously guarded the privileged, for whom burglar alarms were as common as sprinklers. Unspoken covenants were more intimidating than those in print. You did not offend your neighbors by putting up clotheslines or dropping by unannounced. You did not have to drive a Jaguar, but if your means of transportation was a rusting pickup truck or a morgue wagon, you kept it out of sight inside the garage.

At quarter past seven, I parked behind a long line of cars in front of a white-painted brick house with a slate roof. White lights were caught like tiny stars in boxwoods and spruces, and a fragrant fresh wreath hung on the red front door. Nancy Carter embraced my arrival with a gorgeous smile and arms extended to take my coat. She talked non-stop above the indecipherable language of crowds as light winked off the sequins of her long red gown. The judge's wife was a woman in her fifties refined by money into a work of well-bred art. In her youth, I suspected, she had not been pretty.

"Bruce is somewhere . . ." She glanced about. "The bar's over there."

She directed me to the living room, where the bright holiday attire of guests blended wonderfully with a large vibrant Persian rug that I suspected cost more than the house I had just visited on the other side of the river. I spotted the judge talking to a man I did not know. I scanned faces, recognizing several physicians and attorneys, a lobbyist, and the governor's chief of staff. Somehow I ended up with a Scotch and soda, and a man I had never seen before was touching my arm.

"Dr. Scarpetta? Frank Donahue," he introduced himself loudly. "A Merry Christmas to you."

"And to you," I said.

The warden, who allegedly had been ill the day Marino and I had toured the penitentiary, was small, with coarse features and thick graying hair. He was dressed like a parody of an English toastmaster in bright red tails, a ruffled white dress shirt, and a red bow tie twinkling with tiny electric lights. A glass of straight whiskey tilted perilously in one hand as he offered me the other.

He leaned close to my ear. "I was disappointed I was unable to show you around the day you came to the pen."

"One of your officers took good care of us. Thank you."

"I guess that would have been Roberts."

"I think that was his name."

"Well, it's unfortunate that you had to go to the trouble." His eyes roamed the room and he winked at someone behind me. "A lot of horse crap was what it was. You know, Waddell'd had a couple of nosebleeds in the past, and high blood pressure. Was always complaining about something. Headaches. Insomnia."

I bent my head, straining to hear.

"These guys on death row are consummate con artists. And to be honest, Waddell was one of the worst."

"I wouldn't know," I said, looking up at him.

"That's the trouble, nobody knows. No matter what you say, nobody knows except those of us who are around these guys every day."

"I'm sure."

"Waddell's so-called reformation, him turning into such a sweetheart. Sometime let me tell you about that, Dr. Scarpetta, about the way he used to brag to other inmates about what he did to that poor Naismith girl. Thought he was a real cock of the walk because he *did* a celebrity."

The room was airless and too warm. I could feel his eyes crawl over my body.

"Of course, I don't guess much surprises you, either," he said.

"No, Mr. Donahue. There isn't much that surprises me."

"To be honest, I don't know how you look at what you do every day. Especially this time of year, people killing each other and themselves, like that poor lady who committed suicide in her garage the other night after opening her Christmas presents early."

His remark caught me like an elbow in the ribs. There had been a brief story in the morning paper about Jennifer's Deighton's death, and a police source had been quoted as saying that it appeared she had opened her Christmas presents early. This might imply she had committed suicide, but there had been no statement to that effect.

"Which lady are you referring to?" I asked.

"Don't recall the name." Donahue sipped his drink, his face flushed, eyes bright and constantly moving. "Sad, real sad. Well, you'll have to visit us at our new digs in Greensville one of these days." He smiled broadly, then left me for a bosomy matron in black. He kissed her on the mouth and both of them started laughing.

I went home at the earliest opportunity, to find a fire blazing and my niece stretched out on the couch, reading. I noted several new presents under the tree.

"How was it?" she asked with a yawn.

"You were wise to stay home," I said. "Has Marino called?"

"Nope."

I tried him again, and after four rings he answered irritably.

"I hope I didn't get you too late," I apologized.

"I hope not, either. What's wrong now?"

"A lot of things are wrong. I met your friend Mr. Donahue at a party this evening."

"What a thrill."

"I wasn't impressed, and maybe I'm just paranoid, but I thought it odd he brought up Jennifer Deighton's death."

Silence.

"The other little twist," I went on, "is it appears Jennifer Deighton faxed a note to Nicholas Grueman less than two days before her murder. In it she sounded upset, and I got the impression he wanted to meet with her. She suggested he come to Richmond."

Still Marino said nothing.

"Are you there?" I asked.

"I'm thinking."

"Glad to hear it. But maybe we should think together. Sure I can't change your mind about dinner tomorrow?"

He took a deep breath. "I'd like to, Doc. But I . . ."

A female voice in the background said, "Which drawer's it in?"

Marino evidently placed his hand over the receiver and mumbled something. When he got back to me he cleared his throat.

"I'm sorry," I said. "I didn't know you had company."

"Yeah." He paused.

"I would be delighted if you and your friend would come to dinner tomorrow," I offered.

"The Sheraton's got this buffet. We was going to go to that."

"Well, there's something for you under the tree. If you change your mind, give me a call in the morning."

"I don't believe it. You broke down and got a tree? Bet it's an ugly little sucker."

"The envy of the neighborhood, thank you very much," I said. "Wish your friend a Merry Christmas for me."

7

I woke up the next morning to church bells chiming and draperies glowing with the sun. Though I'd had very little to drink the night before, I felt hung over. Lingering in bed, I fell back to sleep and saw Mark in my dreams.

When I finally got up, the kitchen was fragrant with vanilla and oranges. Lucy was grinding coffee beans.

"You're going to spoil me, and then what will I do? Merry Christmas." I kissed the top of her head, noticing an unusual bag of cereal on the counter. "What's this?"

"Cheshire muesli. A special treat. I brought my own supply. It's best with plain yogurt if you've got it, which you don't. So we'll have to settle for skim milk and bananas. Plus, we have fresh orange juice and decaffeinated French vanilla coffee. I guess we should call Mom and Grans."

While I dialed my mother's number from the kitchen, Lucy went into my study to use that extension. My sister was already at my mother's, and soon the four of us were on the line, my mother complaining at great length about the weather. It was storming fiercely in Miami, she said. Torrential rains accompanied by punishing winds had begun late Christmas Eve, the morning celebrated by a grand illumination of lightning.

"You shouldn't be on the phone during an electrical storm," I said to them. "We'll call back later."

"You're so paranoid, Kay," Dorothy chided. "You look at everything in terms of how it might kill somebody."

"Lucy, tell me about your presents," my mother interjected.

"Grans, we haven't opened them yet."

"Wow. That was really close," Dorothy exclaimed above crackling static. "The lights just flickered."

"Mom, I hope you don't have a file open on your computer," Lucy said. "Because if you do, you probably just lost whatever you were working on."

"Dorothy, did you remember to bring butter?" my mother asked.

"Damn. I knew there was something . . ."

"I must have reminded you three times last night."

"I've told you I can't remember things when you call me while I'm writing, Mother."

"Can you imagine? Christmas Eve and would you go to mass with me? No. You stay home working on that book and then forget to bring the butter."

"I'll go out and get some."

"And just what do you think will be open on Christmas morning?"

"Something will be."

I looked up as Lucy walked into the kitchen.

"I don't believe it," she whispered to me as my mother and sister continued to argue with each other.

After I hung up, Lucy and I went into my living room, where we were returned to a quiet winter morning in Virginia, bare trees still and patches of snow pristine in the shade. I did not think I could ever live in Miami again. The change of seasons was like the phases of the moon, a force that pulled me and shifted my point of view. I needed the full with the new and the nuances in between, days to be short and cold in order to appreciate spring mornings.

Lucy's present from her grandmother was a check for fifty dollars. Dorothy gave money as well, and I felt rather ashamed when Lucy opened the envelope from me and added my check to the others.

"Money seems so impersonal," I apologized.

"It's not impersonal to me because it's what I want. You just bought another meg of memory for my computer." She handed me a small, heavy gift wrapped in red-and-silver paper, and could not suppress her joy when she saw the look on my face as I opened the box and parted layers of tissue paper.

"I thought you could keep your court schedule in it," she said. "It matches your motorcycle jacket."

"Lucy, it's gorgeous." I touched the black lambskin binding of the appointment book and smoothed open its creamy pages. I thought of the Sunday she had come to town, of how late she had stayed out when I'd let her take my car to the club. I bet the sneak had gone shopping.

"And this other present here is just refills for the address section and the next calendar year." She set a smaller gift in my lap as the telephone rang.

Marino wished me a Merry Christmas and said he wanted to drop by with my "present."

"Tell Lucy she'd better dress warmly and not to wear anything tight," he said irritably.

"What are you talking about?" I puzzled.

"No tight jeans or she won't be able to get cartridges in and out of her pockets. You said she wanted to learn how to shoot. Lesson one is this morning before lunch. If she misses class, it's her damn problem. What time are we eating?"

"Between one-thirty and two. I thought you were tied up."

"Yeah, well, I untied myself. I'll be over in about twenty

minutes. Tell the brat it's cold as hell outside. You want to come with us?"

"Not this time. I'll stay here and cook."

Marino's disposition was no more pleasant when he arrived at my door, and he made a great production of checking my spare revolver, a Ruger .38 with rubber grips. Depressing the thumb latch, he pushed open the cylinder and slowly spun it around, peering into each chamber. He pulled back the hammer, looked down the barrel, and then tried the trigger. While Lucy watched him in curious silence, he pontificated on the residue buildup left by the solvent I used and informed me that my Ruger probably had "spurs" that needed filing. Then he drove Lucy away in his Ford.

When they returned several hours later, their faces were rosy from the cold and Lucy proudly sported a blood blister on her trigger finger.

"How did she do?" I asked, drying my hands on my apron.

"Not bad," Marino said, looking past me. "I smell fried chicken."

"No, you don't." I took their coats. "You smell *cotoletta di tacchino alla bolognese.*"

"I did better than 'not bad,' " Lucy said. "I only missed the target twice."

"Just keep dry firing until you stop slapping the trigger. Remember, crawl the hammer back."

"I've got more soot on me than Santa after he's come down the chimney," Lucy said cheerfully. "I'm going to take a shower."

In the kitchen I poured coffee as Marino inspected a counter crowded with Marsala, fresh-grated Parmesan, prosciutto, white truffles, sautéed turkey fillets, and other assorted ingredients that were going into our meal. We went into the living room, where the fire was blazing.

"What you did was very kind," I said. "I appreciate it more than you'll ever know."

"One lesson's not enough. Maybe I can work with her a couple more times before she goes back to Florida."

"Thank you, Marino. I hope you didn't go to a lot of bother and sacrifice to change your plans."

"It was no big deal," he said curtly.

"Apparently, you decided against dinner at the Sheraton," I probed. "Your friend could have joined us."

"Something came up."

"Does she have a name?"

"Tanda."

"That's an interesting name."

Marino's face was turning crimson.

"What's Tanda like?" I asked.

"You want to know the truth, she ain't worth talking about." Abruptly, he got up and headed down the hall to the bathroom.

I'd always been careful not to quiz Marino about his personal life unless he invited me to do so. But I could not resist this time.

"How did you and Tanda meet?" I asked when he returned.

"The FOP dance."

"I think it's terrific that you're getting out and meeting new people."

"It sucks, if you really want to know. I haven't dated nobody in more than thirty years. It's like Rip Van Wrinkle waking up in another century. Women are different from what they used to be."

"How so?" I tried not to smile. Clearly, Marino did not think any of this was amusing.

"They're not simple anymore."

"Simple?"

"Yeah, like Doris. What we had wasn't complicated. Then after thirty years she suddenly splits and I have to start over. I go to this friggin' dance at the FOP because some of the guys talk me into it. I'm minding my own business when Tanda comes up to my table. Two beers later, she asks me for my phone number, if you can believe that."

"Did you give it to her?"

"I say, 'Hey, if you want to get together, you give me your number. I'll do the calling.' She asks me which zoo I escaped from, then invites me bowling. That's how it started. How it ended is her telling me she rear-ended somebody a couple weeks back and was charged with reckless driving. She wanted me to fix it."

"I'm sorry." I fetched his present from under the tree and handed it to him. "I don't know if this will help your social life or not."

He unwrapped a pair of Christmas-red suspenders and compatible silk tie.

"That's mighty nice, Doc. Geez." Getting up, he muttered in disgust, "Damn water pills," and headed to the bathroom again. Several minutes later, he returned to the hearth.

"When was your last checkup?" I asked.

"A couple weeks ago."

"And?"

"And what do you think?" he said.

"You have high blood pressure, that's what I think."

"No shit."

"What, specifically, did your doctor tell you?" I asked.

"It's one-fifty over one-ten, and my damn prostrate's enlarged. So I'm taking these water pills. Up and down all the time feeling like I gotta go and half the time I can't. If things don't get better, he says he's gonna turp me."

A *turp* was a transurethral resection of the prostate. That wasn't serious, though it wasn't much fun. Marino's blood pressure worried me. He was a prime candidate for a stroke or a heart attack.

"Plus, my ankles swell," he went on. "My feet hurt and I

get these damn headaches. I've gotta quit smoking, give up coffee, lose forty pounds, cut down on stress."

"Yes, you've got to do all of those things," I said firmly. "And it doesn't look to me like you're doing any of them."

"We're only talking about changing my whole life. And you're one to talk."

"I don't have high blood pressure and I quit smoking exactly two months and five days ago. Not to mention, if I lost forty pounds I wouldn't be here."

He glared into the fire.

"Listen," I said. "Why don't we work on this together? We'll both cut back on coffee and get into exercise routines."

"I can just see you doing aerobics," he said sourly.

"I'll play tennis. You can do aerobics."

"Anybody so much as waves a pair of tights near me, they're dead."

"You're not being very cooperative, Marino."

He impatiently changed the subject. "You got a copy of the fax you told me about?"

I went to my study and returned with my briefcase. Snapping it open, I handed him the printout of the message Vander had discovered with the image enhancer.

"This was on the blank sheet of paper we found on Jennifer Deighton's bed, right?" he asked.

"That's correct."

"I still can't figure out why she had a blank sheet of paper on her bed with a crystal on top of it. What were they doing there?"

"I don't know," I said. "What about the messages on her answering machine? Anything?"

"We're still running them down. We've got a lot of people to interview." He slipped a pack of Marlboros out of his shirt pocket and blew out a loud breath of air. "Damn." He slapped the pack on top of the coffee table. "You're going to nag me every time I light up one of these now, aren't you?"

"No, I'll just stare at it. But I won't say a word."

"You remember that interview of you that was on PBS a couple months back?"

"Vaguely."

"Jennifer Deighton taped it. The tape was in her VCR and we started playing it and there you were."

"What?" I asked, amazed.

"Of course, you weren't the only thing featured on that particular program. There was also some crap about an archaeology dig and a Hollywood movie they filmed around here."

"Why would she tape me?"

"It's just another piece that's not fitting with anything else yet. Except the calls made from her phone—the hang ups. It looks like Deighton was thinking about you before she was whacked."

"What else have you found out about her?"

"I gotta smoke. You want me to go outside?"

"Of course not."

"It gets weirder," he said. "While going through her office, we came across a divorce decree. Appears she was married in 1961, got divorced two years later, and changed her name back to Deighton. Then she moved from Florida to Richmond. The name of her ex is Willie Travers, and he's one of these health nut types—you know, into *whole* health. Hell, I can't think of the name."

"Holistic medicine?"

"That's it. Still lives in Florida, Fort Myers Beach. I got him on the phone. Hard as hell to get much out of him, but I managed to find out a few things. He says he and Miss Deighton continued feeling friendly toward each other after they split and, in fact, continued seeing each other."

"He came up here?"

"Travers said she'd go down there to see him, in Florida. They'd get together, as he put it, 'for old times' sake.' Last time she was down there was this past November, around Thanksgiving. I also pried out of him a little bit about Deighton's brother and sister. The sister's a lot younger, married, lives out West. The brother's the eldest, in his mid-fifties, and manages a grocery store. He had throat cancer a couple years back and his voice box was cut out."

"Wait a minute," I said.

"Yeah. You know what that sounds like. You'd know it if you heard it. No way the guy who called you at the office was John Deighton. It was somebody else who had personal reasons for being interested in Jennifer Deighton's autopsy findings. He knew enough to get the name right. He knew enough to get it straight that he's supposed to be from Columbia, South Carolina. But he didn't know about the real John Deighton's health problems, didn't know he should sound like he's talking through a machine."

"Does Travers know his ex-wife's death is a homicide?" I asked.

"I told him the medical examiner is still running tests."

"And he was in Florida when she died?"

"Allegedly. I'd like to know where your friend Nicholas Grueman was when she died."

"He has never been a friend," I said. "How will you approach him?"

"I won't for a while. You only get one shot with someone like Grueman. How old is he?"

"Somewhere in his sixties," I said.

"He a big guy?"

"I haven't seen him since I was in law school." I got up to stir the fire. "Back then Grueman's build was trim bordering on thin. I would describe his height as average."

Marino did not say anything.

"Jennifer Deighton weighed one-eighty," I reminded him. "It appears her killer yoked her and then carried her body out to her car."

"All right. So maybe Grueman had help. You want a far-out scenario? Try this one on for size. Grueman represented Ronnie Waddell, who wasn't exactly a pencil-neck. Or maybe we should say, *isn't* exactly a pencil-neck. Waddell's print was found inside Jennifer Deighton's house. Maybe Grueman did go to see her and he didn't go alone."

I stared into the fire.

"By the way, I didn't see nothing in Jennifer Deighton's house that could have been the source of the feather you found," he added. "You asked me to check."

Just then, his pager sounded. Snapping it off his belt, he squinted at the narrow screen.

"Damn," he complained, heading into the kitchen to use the phone.

"What's going . . . *What*?" I heard him say. "Oh, Christ. You sure?" He was silent for a moment. He sounded very tense when he said, "Don't bother. I'm standing fifteen feet from her."

Marino ran a red light at West Cary and Windsor Way, and headed east. Grille lights flashed and scanner lights danced in the white Ford LTD. Ten-codes crackled over the radio as I envisioned Susan curled up in the wing chair, her terry cloth robe pulled tightly around her to ward off a chill that had nothing to do with the temperature in the room. I remembered the expression on her face shifting constantly like clouds, her eyes revealing no secrets to me.

I was shivering and could not seem to catch my breath. My heart beat hard in my throat. Police had found Susan's car in an alleyway off Strawberry Street. She was in the driver's seat, dead. It was unknown what she had been doing in that part of town or what might have motivated her assailant.

"What else did she say when you talked with her last night?" Marino asked.

Nothing significant would come to mind. "She was tense," I said. "Something was bothering her."

"What? You got any guesses?"

"I don't know what." My hands shook as I fumbled with my medical bag and checked the contents again. Camera, gloves, and everything else were accounted for. I remembered Susan once saying that if anyone tried to abduct or rape her, they'd have to kill her first.

There had been a number of late afternoons when it was just the two of us cleaning up and filling out paperwork. We had had many personal conversations about being a woman and loving men, and what it would be like to be a mother. Once we had talked about death and Susan confessed she was afraid of it.

"I'm not talking about hell, either, the fire and brimstone my father preaches about—I'm not afraid of that," she said adamantly. "I'm just afraid of this being all there is."

"This isn't all there is," I said.

"How do you know?"

"Something's gone. You look at their faces and you can tell. Their energy has departed. The spirit didn't die. Just the body did."

"But how do you know?" she asked again.

Easing up on the accelerator, Marino turned onto Strawberry Street. I glanced in my side mirror. Another police car was behind us, light bar flashing red and blue. We passed restaurants and a small grocery store. Nothing was open, and the few cars out pulled over to let us pass. Near the Strawberry Street Café, the narrow street was lined with cruisers and unmarked units, and an ambulance was blocking the entrance of an alleyway. Two television trucks had parked a little farther down. Reporters moved restlessly along the perimeter cordoned off in yellow tape. Marino parked and our doors opened at the same time. Instantly, cameras pointed our way.

I watched where Marino stepped and was right behind him. Shutters whirred, film advanced, and microphones were raised. Marino's long strides did not pause and he did not answer anyone. I averted my face. Rounding the ambulance, we ducked under the tape. The old burgundy Toyota was parked head-in midway along a narrow stretch of cobblestone covered with churned-up, dirty snow. Ugly brick walls pressed in from either side and blocked out the low sun's slanted rays. Police were taking photographs, talking, and looking around. Water slowly dripped from roofs and rusting fire escapes. The smell of garbage wafted on the damp, stirring air.

It barely registered that the young Latin-looking officer talking on a portable radio was someone I had recently met. Tom Lucero watched us as he mumbled something and got off the air. From where I stood, all I could see through the Toyota's open driver's door was a left hip and arm. A shock went through me as I recognized the black wool coat, the brush-gold wedding band, and black plastic watch. Wedged between the windshield and the dash was her red medical examiner's plate.

"Tags come back to Jason Story. I guess that's her husband," Lucero said to Marino. "She's got identification on her in her purse. The name on the driver's license is Susan Dawson Story, a twenty-eight-year-old white female."

"What about money?"

"Eleven dollars in her billfold and a couple of credit cards. Nothing so far to suggest robbery. You recognize her?"

Marino leaned forward to get a better look. His jaw muscles bunched. "Yeah. I recognize her. This how the car was found?"

"We opened the driver's door. That's it," Lucero said, stuffing the portable radio in a pocket.

"The engine was off, doors unlocked?"

"They were. Like I told you on the phone, Fritz spotted the car while on routine patrol. Uh, around fifteen hundred hours, and he noticed the M.E.'s tag in the window." He glanced at me. "If you go around to the passenger's side and look in, you can see blood in the area of her right ear. Someone did a real neat job."

Marino backed away and scanned the messy snow. "Don't look like we'll have much luck with footprints."

"You got that right. It's melting like ice cream. Was when we got here."

"Any cartridge cases?"

"Zip."

"Her family know?"

"Not yet. I thought you might want to handle this one," Lucero said.

"Just make damn sure who she is and where she worked don't leak out to the media before the family knows. Jesus." Marino turned his attention to me. "What do you want to do here?"

"I don't want to touch anything inside the car," I muttered, surveying the surroundings as I got out my camera. I was alert and thinking clearly but my hands would not stop shaking. "Give me a minute to look, then let's get her on a stretcher."

"You guys ready for the doc?" Marino asked Lucero.

"We're ready."

Susan was dressed in faded blue jeans and scuffed lace-up boots, her black wool coat buttoned to her chin. My heart constricted as I noticed the red silk scarf peeking out of her collar. She wore sunglasses and leaned back in the driver's seat as if she had gotten comfortable and dozed off. On the light gray upholstery behind her neck was a reddish stain. I moved around to the other side of the car and saw the blood Lucero had mentioned. As I began taking photographs, I paused, then leaned closer to her face, detecting the faint fragrance of a distinctive masculine cologne. Her seat belt, I noted, was unfastened.

I did not touch her head until the squad had arrived and Susan's body was on a stretcher inside the back of an ambulance. I climbed in and spent several minutes looking for bullet wounds. I found one in the right temple, another in the hollow at the back of the neck, just below the hairline. I ran my gloved fingers through her chestnut hair, looking for more blood and not finding it.

Marino climbed into the back of the ambulance. "How many times was she shot?" he asked me.

"I've found two entrances. No exits, though I can feel one bullet beneath the skin over her left temporal bone."

He glanced tensely at his watch. "The Dawsons don't live too far from here. In Glenburnie."

"The Dawsons?" I peeled off my gloves.

"Her parents. I've got to talk to them. Now. Before some toad leaks something and they end up hearing about this on the damn radio or TV. I'll get a marked unit to take you home."

"No," I said. "I'll go with you. I think I should."

Streetlights were coming on as we drove away. Marino stared hard at the road, his face dangerously red.

"Damn!" he blurted, pounding his fist on the steering wheel. "Goddam! Shooting her in the head. *Shooting a pregnant woman.*"

I stared out the side window, my shattered thoughts filled with fragmented images and distortion.

I cleared my throat. "Has her husband been located?"

"No answer at their crib. Maybe he's with her parents. God, I hate this job. Christ, I don't want to do this. Merry friggin' Christmas. I knock on your door and you're screwed because I'm going to tell you something that will ruin your life."

"You have not ruined anybody's life."

"Yeah, well, get ready, 'cause I'm about to."

He turned onto Albemarle. Supercans had been rolled to the edge of the street and were surrounded by leaf bags bulging with Christmas trash. Windows glowed warmly, multicolored tree lights filling some of them. A young father was pulling his small son along the sidewalk on a fishtailing sled. They smiled and waved at us as we passed. Glenburnie was the neighborhood of middle-class families, of young professionals, single, married, and gay. In the warm months, people sat on their porches and cooked out in their yards. They had parties and hailed each other from the street.

The Dawsons' modest house was Tudor style, comfortably weathered with neatly pruned evergreens in front. Windows upstairs and down were lit up, an old station wagon parked by the curb.

The bell was answered by a woman's voice on the other side of the door. "Who is it?"

"Mrs. Dawson?"

"Yes?"

"Detective Marino, Richmond P.D. I need to talk with you," he said loudly, holding his badge up to the peephole.

Locks clicked free as my pulse raced. During my various medical rotations, I had experienced patients screaming in pain as they begged me not to let them die. I had reassured them falsely, "You're going to be just fine," as they died gripping my hand. I had said "I'm sorry" to loved ones desperate in small, airless rooms where even chaplains felt lost. But I had never delivered death to someone's door on Christmas Day.

The only resemblance I could see between Mrs. Dawson and her daughter was the strong curve of their jaws. Mrs. Dawson was sharp-featured, with short, frosted hair. She could not have weighed more than a hundred pounds and reminded me of a frightened bird. When Marino introduced me, panic filled her eyes.

"What's happened?" she barely said.

"I'm afraid I have very bad news for you, Mrs. Dawson," Marino said. "It's your daughter, Susan. I'm afraid she's been killed."

Small feet sounded in a nearby room, and a little girl appeared in a doorway to the right of us. She stopped and regarded us with wide blue eyes.

"Hailey, where's Grandpa?" Mrs. Dawson's voice quavered, her face ashen now.

"Upstairs." Hailey was a tiny tomboy in blue jeans and leather sneakers that looked brand-new. Her blond hair shone like gold and she wore glasses to straighten a lazy left eye. I guessed she was, at the most, eight.

"You go tell him to come downstairs," Mrs. Dawson said. "And you and Charlie stay up there until I come get you."

The child hesitated in the doorway, inserting two fingers into her mouth. She stared warily at Marino and me.

"Hailey, go on now!"

Hailey left with an abrupt burst of energy.

We sat in the kitchen with Susan's mother. Her back did not touch the chair. She did not weep until her husband walked in minutes later.

"Oh, Mack," she said in a weak voice. *"Oh, Mack."* She began to sob.

He put his arm around her, pulling her close. His face blanched and he pressed his lips together as Marino explained what had happened.

"Yes, I know where Strawberry Street is," Susan's father said. "I don't know why she would have gone there. To my knowledge, it's not an area where she normally went. Nothing would have been open today. I don't know."

"Do you know where her husband, Jason Story, is?" Marino asked.

"He's here."

"Here?" Marino glanced around.

"Upstairs, asleep. Jason's not feeling well."

"The children are whose?"

"Tom and Marie's. Tom's our son. They're visiting for the holidays and left early this afternoon. For Tidewater. To visit friends. They should be home anytime." He reached for his wife's hand. "Millie, these people have a lot of questions to ask. You'd better get Jason."

"I tell you what," Marino said. "I'd rather talk to him alone for a minute. Maybe you could take me to him?"

Mrs. Dawson nodded, hiding her face in her hands.

"I think you best check on Charlie and Hailey," her husband said to her. "See if you can get your sister on the phone. Maybe she can come."

His pale blue eyes followed his wife and Marino out of the kitchen. Susan's father was tall, with fine bones, his dark brown hair thick, with very little gray. His gestures were economical, his emotions well contained. Susan had gotten her looks from him and perhaps her disposition.

"Her car is old. She has nothing of value to steal, and I know she would not have been involved. Not in drugs or anything." He searched my face.

"We don't know why this happened, Reverend Dawson."

"She was pregnant," he said, the words catching in his throat. "How could anyone?"

"I don't know," I said. "I don't know how."

He coughed. "She did not own a gun."

For a moment, I did not know what he meant. Then I realized, and reassured him, "No. The police did not find a gun. There's no evidence she did this to herself."

"The police? You aren't the police?"

"No. I'm the chief medical examiner. Kay Scarpetta."

He stared numbly at me.

"Your daughter worked for me."

"Oh. Of course. I'm sorry."

"I don't know how to comfort you," I said with difficulty.

"I haven't begun to deal with this myself. But I'm going to do everything possible to find out what happened. I want you to know that."

"Susan spoke of you. She always wanted to be a doctor." He averted his gaze, blinking back tears.

"I saw her last night. Briefly, at her home." I hesitated, reluctant to probe the soft places of their lives. "Susan seemed troubled. And she has not been herself at work of late."

He swallowed, fingers laced tightly on top of the table. His knuckles were white.

"We need to pray. Would you pray with me, Dr. Scarpetta?" He held out his hand. "Please."

As his fingers wrapped firmly around mine, I could not help but think of Susan's obvious disregard for her father and distrust for what he represented. Fundamentalists frightened me, too. I felt anxious shutting my eyes and holding hands with the Reverend Mack Dawson as he thanked God for a mercy I saw no evidence of and claimed promises too late for God to keep. Opening my eyes, I withdrew my hand. For an uneasy moment I feared that Susan's father sensed my skepticism and would question my beliefs. But the fate of my soul was not foremost on his mind.

A loud voice sounded from upstairs, a muffled protest I could not make out. A chair scraped across the floor. The telephone rang and rang, and the voice rose again in a primal outcry of rage and pain. Dawson closed his eyes. He muttered something under his breath that seemed rather strange. I thought he said, "Stay in your room."

"Jason has been here the entire time," he said. I could see his pulse pounding in his temples. "I realize he can speak for himself. But I just want you to know this from me."

"You mentioned he's not feeling well."

"He woke up with a cold, the beginning of one. Susan took his temperature after lunch and encouraged him to go to bed. He would never hurt . . . Well." He coughed again. "I know the police have to ask, have to consider domestic situations. But that's not the case here."

"Reverend Dawson, what time did Susan leave the house today, and where did she say she was going?"

"She left after dinner, after Jason went to bed. I think that would have been around one-thirty or two. She said she was going over to a friend's house."

"Which friend?"

He stared past me. "A friend she went to high school with. Dianne Lee."

"Where does Dianne live?"

"Northside, near the seminary."

"Susan's car was found off Strawberry Street, not in Northside."

"I suppose if somebody . . . She could have ended up anywhere."

"It would be helpful to know if she ever made it to Dianne's house, and whose idea the visit was," I said.

He got up and started opening kitchen drawers. It took him three tries to find the telephone directory. His hands trembled as he turned pages and dialed a number. Clearing his throat several times, he asked to speak to Dianne.

"I see. What was that?" He listened for a moment. "No, no." His voice shook. "Things are not all right."

I sat quietly as he explained, and I imagined him many years earlier praying and talking on the phone as he dealt with the death of his other daughter, Judy. When he returned to the table, he confirmed what I feared. Susan had not visited her friend that afternoon, nor had there been any plan for her to do so. Her friend was not in town.

"She's with her husband's family in North Carolina," Susan's father said. "She's been there several days. Why would Susan lie? She didn't have to. I've always told her no matter what, she didn't have to lie."

"It would seem she did not want anyone to know where she was going or who she was going to see. I know that raises unhappy speculations, but we need to face them," I said gently.

He stared down at his hands.

"Were she and Jason getting along all right?"

"I don't know." He fought to regain his composure. "Dear Lord, not again." Again he whispered curiously. "Go to your room. Please go." Then he looked up at me with bloodshot eyes. "She had a twin sister. Judy died when they were in high school."

"In a car accident, yes. Susan told me. I'm so sorry."

"She's never gotten over it. She blamed God. She blamed me."

"I did not get that impression," I said. "If she blamed anyone, it seemed to be a girl named Doreen."

Dawson slipped out a handkerchief and quietly blew his nose. "Who?" he asked.

"The girl in high school who allegedly was a witch."

He shook his head.

"She supposedly put a curse on Judy?" But it was pointless to explain further. I could tell that Dawson did not know what I was talking about. We both turned as Hailey walked into the kitchen. She was cradling a baseball glove, her eyes frightened.

"What have you got there, darling?" I asked, trying to smile.

She came close to me. I could smell the new leather. The glove was tied with string, a softball in the sweet spot like a large pearl inside an oyster.

"Aunt Susan gave it to me," she said in a small voice. "You got to break it in. I have to put it under my mattress. Aunt Susan says I have to for a week."

Her grandfather reached for her and lifted her onto his lap. He buried his nose in her hair, holding her tight. "I need for you to go to your room for a little while, sugar. Will you do that for me so I can take care of things? Just for a while?"

She nodded, her eyes not leaving me.

"What are Grandma and Charlie doing?"

"Don't know." She slid off his lap and reluctantly left us.

"You said that before," I said to him.

He looked lost.

"You told her to go to her room," I said. "I heard you say that earlier, mutter something about going to your room. Who were you talking to?"

He dropped his eyes. "The child is self. Self feels intensely, cries, cannot control emotions. Sometimes it is best to send self to his room as I just did Hailey. To hold together. A trick I learned. When I was a boy I learned, had to; my father did not react well if I cried."

"It is all right to cry, Reverend Dawson."

His eyes filled with tears. I heard Marino's footsteps on the stairs. Then he strode into the kitchen and Dawson said the phrase again, in anguish, under his breath.

Marino looked at him, baffled. "I think your son's home," he said.

Susan's father began to weep uncontrollably as car doors slammed shut out front in the wintry darkness and laughter sounded from the porch.

Christmas dinner went into the trash, the evening spent pacing about the house and talking on the phone while Lucy stayed inside my study with the door shut. Arrangements had to be made. Susan's homicide had thrown the office into a state of crisis. Her case would have to be sealed, photographs kept away from those who had known her. The police would have to go through her office and her locker. They would want to interview members of my staff.

"I can't be down there," Fielding, my deputy chief, told me over the phone.

"I realize that," I said, a lump forming in my throat. "I neither expect nor want anyone down there."

"And you?"

"I have to be."

"Christ. I can't believe this has happened. I just can't believe it."

Dr. Wright, my deputy chief in Norfolk, kindly agreed to drive to Richmond early the next morning. Because it was Sunday, no one else was in the building except for Vander, who had come to assist with the Luma-Lite. Had I been emotionally capable of doing Susan's autopsy, I would have refused. The worst thing I could do for her was to jeopardize her case by having the defense question the objectivity and judgment of an expert witness who also happened to be her boss. So I sat at a desk in the morgue while Wright worked. From time to time he commented to me above the clatter of steel instruments and running water as I stared at the cinder-block wall. I did not touch any of her paperwork or label a single test tube. I did not turn around to look.

Once I asked him, "Did you smell anything on her or her clothes? A cologne of some sort?"

He stopped what he was doing and I heard him walk several steps. "Yes. Definitely around the collar of her coat and on the scarf."

"Does it smell like men's cologne to you?"

"Hmm. I think so. Yes, I'd say the fragrance is masculine. Perhaps her husband wears cologne?" Wright was near retirement age, a balding, potbellied man with a West Virginian accent. He was a very capable forensic pathologist and knew exactly what I was contemplating.

"Good question," I said. "I'll ask Marino to check it. But her husband was ill yesterday and went to bed after lunch. That doesn't mean he didn't have on cologne. It doesn't mean her brother or father didn't have on cologne that got on her collar when they hugged her."

"This looks small-caliber. No exit wounds."

I closed my eyes and listened.

"The wound in her right temple is three-sixteenths of an inch with half an inch of smoke—an incomplete pattern. A little bit of stippling and some powder but most will be lost in her hair. There's some powder in the temporalis muscle. Nothing much in bone or dura."

"Trajectory?" I asked.

"The bullet goes through the posterior aspect of the right frontal lobe, travels across anterior to basal ganglia and strikes the left temporal bone, and gets hung up in muscle under the skin. And we're talking about a plain lead bullet, uh, copper coated but not jacketed."

"And it didn't fragment?" I asked.

"No. Then we've got this second wound here at the nape of the neck. Black, burned abraded margin with muzzle mark. A little laceration about one-sixteenth of an inch at the edges. Lots of powder in the occipital muscles."

"Tight contact?"

"Yes. Looks to me like he pressed the barrel hard against her neck. The bullet enters at the junction of the foramen magnum and C-one and takes out the cervical-medullary junction. Travels right up into the pons."

"What about the angle?" I asked.

"It's angled up quite a bit. I'd say that if she was sitting in the car at the time she received this wound, she was slumped forward or had her head bowed."

"That's not the way she was found," I said. "She was leaning back in the seat."

"Then I guess he positioned her that way," Wright commented. "After he shot her. And I'd say that this shot that went through the pons was fired last. I would speculate she was already incapacitated, maybe slumped over when she was shot the second time."

At intervals I could handle it, as if we were not referring to anyone I knew. Then a tremor would go through me, tears fighting to break free. Twice I had to walk outside and stand in the parking lot in the cold. When he got to the ten-week-old fetus in her womb, a girl, I retreated to my office upstairs. According to Virginia law, the unborn child was not a person and therefore could not have been murdered because you cannot murder a nonperson.

"Two for the price of one," Marino said bitterly over the phone later in the day.

"I know," I said, digging a bottle of aspirin out of my pocketbook.

"In court the damn jurors won't be told she was pregnant. It won't be admissible, don't count he murdered a pregnant woman."

"I know," I said again. "Wright's about done. Nothing significant turned up during her external exam. No trace to speak of, nothing that jumped out. What's going on at your end?"

"Susan was definitely going through something," Marino said.

"Problems with her husband?"

"According to him, her problem was with you. He claims you were doing weird shit like calling her a lot at home, hassling her. And sometimes she'd come home from work acting half crazy, like she was scared shitless about something."

"Susan and I did not have a problem." I swallowed three aspirin with a mouthful of cold coffee.

"I'm just telling you what the guy's saying. Other thing is—and I think you'll find this interesting—looks like we got us another feather. Not that I'm saying it links Deighton and this one, Doc, or that I'm necessarily thinking that way. But damn. Maybe we're dealing with some squirrel who wears down-filled gloves, a jacket. I don't know. It's just not typical. Only other time I've ever found feathers was when this drone broke into a crib by smashing out a window and cut his down jacket on broken glass."

My head hurt so much I felt sick to my stomach.

"What we found in Susan's car is real small—a little piece of white down," he went on. "It was clinging to the upholstery of the passenger's door. On the inside, near the floor, a couple inches below the armrest."

"Can you get that to me?" I asked.

"Yeah. What are you going to do?"

"Call Benton."

"I've been trying, dammit. I think he and the wife went out of town."

"I need to ask him if Minor Downey can help us."

"You talking about a person or a fabric softener?"

"Minor Downey with hairs and fibers at the FBI labs. His specialty is feather analysis."

"And his name's *Downey*, it really is?" Marino was incredulous.

"It really is," I said.

8

The telephone rang for a long time at the FBI's Behavioral Science Unit, located in the subterranean reaches of the Academy at Quantico. I could envision its bleak, confusing hallways and offices cluttered with the mementos of polished warriors like Benton Wesley, who had gone skiing, I was told.

"In fact, I'm the only one here at the moment," said the courteous agent who answered the phone.

"This is Dr. Kay Scarpetta and it's urgent that I reach him."

Benton Wesley returned my call almost immediately.

"Benton, where are you?" I raised my voice above terrible static.

"In my car," he said. "Connie and I spent Christmas with her family in Charlottesville. We're just west of there on our way to Hot Springs. I heard about what happened to Susan Story. God, I'm sorry. I was going to call you tonight."

"You're breaking up. I almost can't hear you."

"Hold on."

I waited impatiently for a good minute. Then he was back.

"That's better. We were in a low area. Listen, what do you need from me?"

"I need the Bureau's help with analysis of some feathers."

"No problem. I'll call Downey."

"I need to talk," I said with great reluctance, for I knew I was putting him on the spot. "I don't feel it can wait."

"Hold on."

This time the pause was not due to static. He was conferring with his wife.

"Do you ski?" His voice came back.

"It depends on who you ask."

"Connie and I are on our way to the Homestead for a couple of days. We could talk there. Can you get away?"

"I'll move heaven and earth to, and I'll bring Lucy."

"That's good. She and Connie can pal around while you and I talk. I'll see about your room when we check in. Can you bring something for me to look at?"

"Yes."

"Including whatever you've got on the Robyn Naismith case. Let's cover every base and every imagined one."

"Thank you, Benton," I said gratefully. "And please thank Connie."

I decided to leave the office immediately, and offered little explanation.

"It will be good for you," Rose said, jotting down the Homestead's number. She did not understand that my intention was not to unwind at a five-star resort. For an instant, her eyes were bright with tears as I told her to let Marino know where I was so he could contact me immediately if there were any new developments in Susan's case.

"Please don't release my whereabouts to anyone else," I added.

"Three reporters have called in the last twenty minutes," she said. "Including the *Washington Post.*"

"I'm not discussing Susan's case right now. Tell them the

usual, that we're waiting on lab results. Just tell them I'm out of town and unavailable."

I was haunted by images as I drove west toward the mountains. I pictured Susan in her baggy scrubs, and the faces of her mother and father as Marino told them their daughter was dead.

"Are you feeling okay?" Lucy asked. She had been looking at me every other minute since we left my house.

"I'm just preoccupied," I replied, concentrating on the road. "You're going to love skiing. I have a feeling you'll be good at it."

She silently gazed out the windshield. The sky was a washed-out denim blue, mountains rising in the distance dusted with snow.

"I'm sorry about this," I added. "It seems that every time you visit, something happens and I can't give you my full attention."

"I don't need your full attention."

"Someday you'll understand."

"Maybe I'm the same way about my work. In fact, maybe I learned from you. I'll probably be successful like you, too."

My spirit felt as heavy as lead. I was grateful that I was wearing sunglasses. I did not want Lucy to see my eyes.

"I know you love me. That's what counts. I know my mother doesn't love me," my niece said.

"Dorothy loves you as much as she is able to love anyone."

"You're absolutely right. As much as she is able to, which isn't much because I'm not a man. She only loves men."

"No, Lucy. Your mother doesn't really love men. They are a symptom of her obsessive quest of finding somebody who will make her whole. She doesn't understand that she has to make herself whole."

"The only thing 'whole' in the equation is she picks assholes every time."

"I agree that her batting average hasn't been good."

"I'm not going to live like that. I don't want to be anything like her."

"You aren't," I said.

"I read in the brochure they have skeet shooting where we're going."

"They have all sorts of things."

"Did you bring one of the revolvers?"

"You don't shoot skeet with a revolver, Lucy."

"You do if you're from Miami."

"If you don't stop yawning, you're going to get me started."

"Why didn't you bring a gun?" she persisted.

The Ruger was in my suitcase, but I did not intend to tell her that. "Why are you so worried about whether I brought a gun?" I asked.

"I want to be good at it. So good I can shoot the twelve off the clock every time I try," she said sleepily.

My heart ached as she rolled up her jacket and used it as a pillow. She lay next to me, the top of her head touching my thigh as she slept. She did not know how strongly tempted I was to send her back to Miami this minute. But I could tell she sensed my fear.

The Homestead was situated on fifteen thousand acres of forest and streams in the Allegheny Mountains, the main section of the hotel dark red brick with white-pillared colonnades. The white cupola had a clock on each of its four sides that always agreed on the time and could be read for miles, and tennis courts and golf greens were solid white with snow.

"You're in luck," I said to Lucy as gracious men in gray uniforms stepped our way. "The ski conditions are going to be terrific."

Benton Wesley had accomplished what he had promised, and we found a reservation waiting for us when we got to the front desk. He had booked a double room with glass doors opening onto a balcony overlooking the casino, and on top of a table were flowers from Connie and him. "Meet us on the slopes," the card read. "We scheduled a lesson for Lucy at three-thirty."

"We've got to hurry," I said to Lucy as we flung open suitcases. "You've got your first ski lesson in exactly forty minutes. Try these." I tossed her a pair of red ski pants, which were followed by jacket, socks, mittens, and sweater flying through the air and landing on her bed. "Don't forget your butt pack. Anything else you need we'll have to get later."

"I don't have any ski glasses," she said, pulling a bright blue turtleneck over her head. "I'll go snow-blind."

"You can use my goggles. The sun will be going down soon anyway."

By the time we caught the shuttle to the slopes, rented equipment for Lucy, and connected her with the instructor at the rope tow, it was twenty-nine minutes past three. Skiers were brilliant spots of color moving downhill, and it was only when they got close that they turned into people. I leaned forward in my boots, skis firmly wedged against the slope as I scanned lines and lifts, my hand shielding my eyes. The sun was nearing the top of trees, the snow dazzled by its touch, but shadows were spreading and the temperature was dropping quickly.

I spotted the man and woman simply because their parallel skiing was so graceful, poles lifted like feathers and barely flicking snow as they soared and turned like birds. I recognized Benton Wesley's silver hair and raised my hand. Glancing back at Connie and yelling something I could not hear, he pushed off and schussed downhill like a knife, skis so close together I doubted you could fit a piece of paper between them.

When he stopped in a spray of snow and pushed back his goggles, it suddenly occurred to me that if I did not know him I would have been watching him anyway. Black ski pants hugged well-muscled legs I had never known were beneath the trousers of his conservative suits, and the jacket he wore reminded me of a Key West sunset. His face and eyes were brightened by the cold, making his sharp features more striking than formidable. Connie eased to a stop beside him.

"It's wonderful that you're here," Wesley said, and I could never see him or hear his voice without being reminded of Mark. They had been colleagues and best friends. They could have passed for brothers.

"Where's Lucy?" Connie asked.

"Conquering the rope tow even as we speak." I pointed.

"I hope you didn't mind my signing her up for a lesson."

"Mind? I can't thank you enough for being so thoughtful. She's having the time of her life."

"I think I'll stand right here and watch her for a while," Connie said. "Then I'll be ready for something hot to drink and I have a feeling Lucy will be, too. Ben, you look like you haven't had enough."

Wesley said to me, "You up for a few quick runs?"

We exchanged remarks about nonessential matters as we moved through the line, and then were silent when the lift swung around and seated us. Wesley lowered the bar as the cable slowly pulled us toward the mountaintop. The air was numbing and deliciously clean, and filled with the quiet sounds of skis swishing and dully slapping hard-packed snow. Snow from snow machines drifted like smoke through the woods between slopes.

"I talked to Downey," he said. "He'll see you at headquarters just as soon as you can get there."

"That's good news," I said. "Benton, what have you been told?"

"Marino and I have talked several times. It appears you have several cases going on right now that aren't connected by evidence, necessarily, but by a peculiar coincidence in timing."

"I think we're dealing with more than coincidence. You know about Ronnie Waddell's print turning up in Jennifer Deighton's house."

"Yes." He stared off at a stand of evergreens backlit by the setting sun. "As I've told Marino, I'm hoping there's a logical explanation for how Waddell's print got there."

"The logical explanation may very well be that he was, at some point, inside her house."

"Then we're dealing with a situation so bizarre as to defy description, Kay. A death row convict is out on the street killing again. And we're supposed to assume someone else took his place in the chair on the night of December thirteenth. I doubt there would have been many volunteers."

"You wouldn't think so," I said.

"What do you know about Waddell's criminal history?"

"Very little."

"I interviewed him years ago, in Mecklenburg."

I glanced over at him with interest.

"I'll preface my next remarks by saying that he was not particularly cooperative in that he would not discuss Robyn Naismith's murder. He claimed that if he killed her, he didn't remember it. Not that this is unusual. Most of the violent offenders I have interviewed either claim to have poor recall, or they deny that they committed the crimes. I had a copy of Waddell's Assessment Protocol faxed to me before you got here. We'll go over it after dinner."

"Benton, I'm already glad I'm here."

He stared straight ahead, our shoulders barely touching. The slope beneath us got steeper as we rode in silence for a while. Then he said, "How are you, Kay?"

"Better. There are still moments."

"I know. There will always be moments. But fewer of them, I hope. Days, perhaps, where you don't feel it."

"Yes," I said. "There are days when I don't."

"We've got a very good lead on the group responsible. We think we know who placed the bomb."

We raised the tips of our skis and leaned forward as the lift eased us out like baby birds nudged from the nest. My legs were stiff and cold from the ride, and trails in the shade were treacherous with ice. Wesley's long white skis vanished against the snow and caught light at the same time. He danced down the slope in dazzling puffs of diamond dust, pausing every now and then to look back. I waved him on by barely lifting a pole as I made languid parallel turns and floated over moguls. Halfway into the run I was limber and warm, thoughts flying free.

When I returned to my room as it was getting dark, I discovered Marino had left a message that he would be at headquarters until five-thirty and for me to call ASAP.

"What's going on?" I said when he answered.

"Nothing that's going to make you sleep better. For starters, Jason Story's badmouthing you to anyone who will stand still long enough to listen—including reporters."

"His rage has to go somewhere," I said, my mood darkening again.

"Well, what he's doing ain't good, but it also ain't the worst of our problems. We can't locate ten print cards for Waddell."

"Not *anywhere*?"

"You got it. We've checked his files at Richmond P.D., the State Police, and the FBI. That's every jurisdiction that should have them. No cards. Then I contacted Donahue at the pen to see if I could track down Waddell's personal effects, such as books, letters, hairbrush, toothbrush—anything that might be a source for latent prints. And guess what? Donahue says the only things Waddell's mother wanted were his watch and ring. Everything else Corrections destroyed."

I sat heavily on the edge of the bed.

"And I saved the best for last, Doc. Firearms hit paydirt and you ain't going to believe it. The bullets recovered from Eddie Heath and Susan Story was fired from the same gun, a twenty-two."

"Dear God," I said.

Downstairs in the Homestead Club, a band was playing jazz, but the audience was small and the music was not too loud to talk over. Connie had taken Lucy to a movie, leaving Wesley and me at a table in a deserted corner of the dance floor. Both of us were sipping cognac. He did not seem as physically tired as I was, but tension had returned to his face.

Reaching behind him, he took another candle from an unoccupied table and set it by two others he had claimed. The light was unsteady but adequate, and though we did not get long stares from guests, we did get glances. I supposed it seemed a strange place to work, but the lobby and dining room were not private enough, and Wesley was much too circumspect to suggest we meet in his room or mine.

"There would seem to be a number of conflicting elements here," he said. "But human behavior is not set in stone. Waddell was in prison for ten years. We don't know how he might have changed. I would categorize Eddie Heath's murder as a sexually motivated homicide while, at first glance, Susan Story's homicide appears to be an execution, a hit."

"As if two different perpetrators are involved," I said, toying with my cognac.

He leaned forward, idly flipping through Robyn Naismith's case file. "It's interesting," he said, without looking up. "You hear so much about modus operandi, about the offender's signature. He always selects this type of victim or chooses this sort of location and prefers knives, and so on. But, in fact, this isn't always the case. Nor is the emotion of the crime always obvious. I said that Susan Story's homicide, *at first glance*, does not appear to be sexually motivated. But the more I've thought about it, the more I believe there is a sexual component. I think this killer is into piquerism."

"Robyn Naismith was stabbed multiple times," I said.

"Yes. I'd say that what was done to her is a textbook example. There was no evidence of rape—not that this means it didn't occur. But no semen. The repeated plunging of the knife in her abdomen, buttocks, and breasts was a substitute for penile penetration. Obvious piquerism. Biting is less obvious, not at all related to any oral components of the sexual act, it is my opinion, but again, a substitute for penile penetration. Teeth sinking into flesh, cannibalism, like John Joubert did to the newspaper delivery boys he murdered in Nebraska. Then we have bullets. You would not associate shootings with piquerism unless you thought about it for a moment. Then the dynamics, in some instances, become clear. Something penetrating flesh. That was the Son of Sam's thing."

"There's no evidence of piquerism in Jennifer Deighton's death."

"True. This goes back to what I was saying. There isn't always a clear pattern. Certainly, we're not talking about a clear pattern here, but there is one element that the murders of Eddie Heath, Jennifer Deighton, and Susan Story have in common. I would classify the crimes as organized."

"Not as organized with Jennifer Deighton," I pointed out. "It appears the killer attempted to disguise her death as a suicide and failed. Or perhaps he did not intend to kill her at all and got carried away with a choke hold."

"Her death before she was placed inside her car probably wasn't the plan," Wesley agreed. "But the fact is, it appears there *was* a plan. And the garden hose hooked up to the exhaust pipe was severed with a sharp tool that was never recovered. Either the killer brought his own tool or weapon to the scene, or he disposed of whatever it was he found at her house and used. That's organized behavior. But before we go too far with this, let me remind you that we don't have a twenty-two bullet or other piece of evidence that might link Jennifer Deighton's homicide with the homicides of the Heath boy and Susan."

"I think we do, Benton. Ronnie Waddell's print was recovered from a dining room chair inside Jennifer Deighton's house."

"We don't know that it was Ronnie Waddell who pumped slugs into the other two."

"Eddie Heath's body was positioned in a manner reminiscent of Robyn Naismith's case. The boy was attacked the night Ronnie Waddell was to be executed. Don't you think there's some weird thread here?"

"Let's put it this way," he said. "I don't want to think it."

"Neither of us wants to. Benton, what's your gut feeling?"

He motioned for the waitress to bring more cognac, candlelight illuminating the clean lines of his left cheekbone and chin.

"My gut feeling? Okay. I have a very bad gut feeling about all of this," he said. "I believe Ronnie Waddell is the common denominator, but I don't know what that means. A latent print recently found at a scene was identified as his, yet we can't locate his ten print cards or anything else that might effect a positive identification. He also wasn't printed at the morgue, and the person who allegedly forgot to do so has since been murdered with the same gun used on Eddie Heath. Waddell's legal counsel, Nick Grueman, apparently knew Jennifer Deighton, and in fact, it appears she faxed a message to Grueman days before she was murdered. Finally, yes, there is a subtle and peculiar similarity between Eddie

Heath's and Robyn Naismith's deaths. Frankly, I can't help but wonder if the attack on Heath wasn't, for some reason, intended to be symbolic."

He waited until our drinks had been set before us, then opened a manila envelope that was attached to Robyn Naismith's case. That small act triggered something I had not thought of before.

"I had to get her photographs from Archives," I said.

Wesley glanced at me as he slipped on his glasses.

"In cases this old, the paper records have been reduced to microfilm, the printouts of which are in the file you've got. The original documents are destroyed, but we keep the original photos. They go to Archives."

"Which is what? A room in your building?"

"No, Benton. A warehouse near the state library—the same warehouse where the Bureau of Forensic Science stores evidence from its old cases."

"Vander still hasn't found the photograph of the bloody thumbprint Waddell left inside Robyn Naismith's house?"

"No," I said as Wesley met my eyes. We both knew that Vander was never going to find it.

"Christ," he said. "Who retrieved Robyn Naismith's photos for you?"

"My administrator," I replied. "Ben Stevens. He made a trip to Archives a week or so before Waddell's execution."

"Why?"

"During the final stages of the appeals process, there are always a lot of questions asked and I like to have ready access to the case or cases involved. So a trip to Archives is routine. What's a little different in the instance we're talking about is I didn't have to ask Stevens to get the photos from Archives. He volunteered."

"And that's unusual?"

"In retrospect, I must admit that it is."

"The implication," Wesley said, "is that your administrator may have volunteered because what he was really interested in was Waddell's file—or more specifically, the photograph of the bloody thumbprint that's supposed to be inside it."

"All I can say with certainty is if Stevens wanted to tamper with a file in Archives, he couldn't do so unless he had legitimate reason for visiting Archives. If, for example, it came back to me that he had been there when none of the medical examiners had made a request, it would look odd."

I went on to tell Wesley about the breach of security in my office computer, explaining that the two terminals involved were assigned to me and Stevens. While I talked, Wesley took notes. When I fell silent, he looked up at me.

"It doesn't sound as if they found what they were looking for," he said.

"My suspicion is that they didn't."

"That brings us around to the obvious question. What were they looking for?"

I slowly swirled my cognac. In the candlelight it was liquid amber, and each sip deliciously burned going down.

"Maybe something pertaining to Eddie Heath's death. I was looking for any other cases in which victims may have had bite marks or cannibalistic-type injuries, and had a file in my directory. Beyond that, I can't imagine what anyone might have been looking for."

"Do you ever keep intradepartmental memos in your directory?"

"In word processing, a subdirectory."

"Same password to access those documents?"

"Yes."

"And in word processing you would store autopsy reports and other documents pertaining to cases?"

"I would. But at the time my directory was broken into there wasn't anything sensitive on file that I can think of."

"But whoever broke in didn't necessarily know that."

"Obviously not," I said.

"What about Ronnie Waddell's autopsy report, Kay? When your directory was broken into, was his report in the computer?"

"It would have been. He was executed Monday, December thirteenth. The break-in occurred late on the afternoon of Thursday, December sixteenth, while I was doing Eddie Heath's post and Susan was upstairs in my office, supposedly resting on the couch after the formalin spill."

"Perplexing." He frowned. "Assuming Susan is the one who went into your directory, why would she be interested in Waddell's autopsy report—if that's what this is all about? She was *present* during his autopsy. What could she have read in your report that she wouldn't have already known?"

"Nothing I can think of."

"Well, let me rephrase that. What pertaining to his autopsy would she not have learned from being present the night his body was brought to the morgue? Or maybe I'd better say the night *a body* was brought to the morgue, since we're no longer so sure this individual was Waddell," he added grimly.

"She wouldn't have had access to lab reports," I said. "But the lab work wouldn't have been completed by the time my directory was broken into. Tox and HIV screens, for example, take weeks."

"And Susan would have known that."

"Certainly."

"So would your administrator."

"Absolutely."

"There must be something else," he said.

There was, but as it came to mind I could not imagine the significance. "Waddell—or whoever the inmate was—had an envelope in the back pocket of his jeans that he wanted buried with him. Fielding wouldn't have opened this envelope until he had gone upstairs with his paperwork after the post."

"So Susan couldn't have known what was inside the envelope while she was in the morgue that night?" Wesley asked with interest.

"That's right. She couldn't have."

"And was there anything of significance inside this envelope?"

"There was nothing inside but several receipts for food and tolls."

Wesley frowned. "Receipts," he repeated. "What in God's name would he have been doing with those? Do you have them here?"

"They're in his file." I got out the photocopies. "The dates are all the same, November thirtieth."

"Which should have been about the time Waddell was transported from Mecklenburg to Richmond."

"That's right. He was transported fifteen days before his execution," I said.

"We need to run down the codes on these receipts, see what locations we get. This may be important. Very important, in light of what we're contemplating."

"That Waddell is alive?"

"Yes. That somehow a switch was made and he was released. Maybe the man who went to the chair wanted these receipts in his pocket when he died because he was trying to tell us something."

"Where would he have gotten them?"

"Perhaps during the transport from Mecklenburg to Richmond, which would have been an ideal time to pull something," Wesley replied. "Maybe two men were transported, Waddell and someone else."

"You're suggesting they stopped for food?"

"Guards aren't supposed to stop for anything while transporting a death row inmate. But if some conspiracy were involved, anything could have happened. Maybe they stopped and got take-out food, and it was during this interval that Waddell was freed. Then the other inmate was taken on to

Richmond and put in Waddell's cell. Think about it. How would any of the guards or anybody else at Spring Street have any way of knowing the inmate brought in wasn't Waddell?"

"He might say he wasn't, but that doesn't mean that anyone would have listened."

"I suspect they wouldn't have listened."

"What about Waddell's mother?" I asked. "Supposedly, she had a contact visit with him hours before the execution. Certainly, she would know if the inmate she saw was not her son."

"We need to verify that the contact visit occurred. But whether it did or didn't, it would have been to Mrs. Waddell's benefit to go along with any scheme. I don't imagine she wanted her son to die."

"Then you're convinced that the wrong man was executed," I said reluctantly, for there were few theories, at the moment, that I more wanted to disprove.

His answer was to open the envelope containing Robyn Naismith's photographs and slide out a thick stack of color prints that would continue to shock me no matter how many times I looked at them. He slowly shuffled through the pictorial history of her terrible death.

Then he said, "When we consider the three homicides that have just occurred, Waddell doesn't profile right."

"What are you saying, Benton? That after ten years in prison his personality changed?"

"All I can say to you is that I've heard of organized killers decompensating, flying apart. They begin to make mistakes. Bundy, for example. Toward the end he became frenzied. But what you generally don't see is a disorganized individual swinging the other way, the psychotic person becoming methodical, rational—becoming organized."

When Wesley alluded to the Bundys and Son of Sams in the world, he did so theoretically, impersonally, as if his analyses and theories were formulated from secondary sources.

He did not brag. He did not name-drop or assume the role of one who knew these criminals personally. His demeanor, therefore, was deliberately misleading.

He had, in fact, spent long, intimate hours with the likes of Theodore Bundy, David Berkowitz, Sirhan Sirhan, Richard Speck, and Charles Manson, in addition to the lesser-known black holes who had sucked light from the planet Earth. I remembered Marino telling me once that when Wesley returned from some of these pilgrimages into maximum-security penitentiaries, he would look pale and drained. It almost made him physically ill to absorb the poison of these men and endure the attachments they inevitably formed to him. Some of the worst sadists in recent history regularly wrote letters to him, sent Christmas cards, and inquired after his family. It was no small wonder that Wesley seemed like a man with a heavy burden and so often was silent. In exchange for information, he did the one thing that not one of us wants to do. He allowed the monster to connect with him.

"Was it determined that Waddell was psychotic?" I asked.

"It was determined that he was sane when he murdered Robyn Naismith." Wesley pulled out a photograph and slid it across the table to me. "But frankly, I don't think he was."

The photograph was the one I remembered most vividly, and as I studied it I could not imagine an unsuspecting soul walking in on such a scene.

Robyn Naismith's living room did not have much furniture, just several barrel chairs with dark green cushions and a chocolate-brown leather couch. A small Bakhara rug was in the middle of the parquet floor, the walls wide planks stained to look like cherry or mahogany. A console television was against the wall directly across from the front door, affording whoever entered a full frontal view of Ronnie Joe Waddell's horrible artistry.

What Robyn's friend had seen the instant she unlocked

the door and pushed it open as she called out Robyn's name was a nude body sitting on the floor, back propped against the TV, skin so streaked and smeared with dried blood that the exact nature of the injuries could not be determined until later at the morgue. In the photograph, coagulating blood pooled around Robyn's buttocks looked like red-tinted tar, and tossed nearby were several bloody towels. The weapon was never found, though police did determine that a German-made stainless steel steak knife was missing from a set hanging in the kitchen, and the characteristics of the blade were consistent with her wounds.

Opening Eddie Heath's file folder, Wesley withdrew a scene diagram drawn by the Henrico County police officer who had discovered the critically wounded boy behind the vacant grocery store. Wesley placed the diagram next to the photograph of Robyn Naismith. For a moment, neither of us spoke as our eyes went back and forth from one to the other. The similarities were more pronounced that I had imagined, the positions of their bodies virtually identical, from their hands by their sides to their loosely piled clothing near their bare feet.

"I have to admit, it's eerie as hell," Wesley remarked. "It's almost as if Eddie Heath's scene is a mirror image of this one." He touched the photograph of Robyn Naismith. "Bodies positioned like rag dolls, propped against boxlike objects. A big console TV. A brown Dumpster." Spreading more photographs on the table like playing cards, he drew another from the deck. This one was a close-up of her body at the morgue, the ragged tangential circles of human bite marks apparent on her left breast and left inner thigh.

"Again, a striking similarity," he said. "Bite marks here and here corresponding closely with the areas of missing flesh on Eddie Heath's shoulder and thigh. In other words"—he slipped off his glasses and looked up at me—"Eddie Heath was probably bitten, the flesh excised to eradicate evidence."

"Then his killer is at least somewhat familiar with forensic evidence," I said.

"Almost any felon who has spent time in prison is familiar with forensic evidence. If Waddell didn't know about bitemark identification when he murdered Robyn Naismith, he would know about it now."

"You're talking like he's the killer again," I pointed out. "A moment ago you said he doesn't profile right."

"Ten years ago, he didn't profile right. That's all I'm asserting."

"You've got his Assessment Protocol. Can we talk about it?"

"Of course."

The Protocol was actually a forty-page FBI questionnaire filled in during a face-to-face prison interview with a violent offender.

"Flip through this yourself," Wesley said, sliding Waddell's Protocol in front of me. "I'd like to hear your thoughts without further input from me."

Wesley's interview of Ronnie Joe Waddell had taken place six years ago at death row in Mecklenburg County. The Protocol began with the expected descriptive data. Waddell's demeanor, emotional state, mannerisms, and style of conversation indicated that he was agitated and confused. Then, when Wesley had given him opportunity to ask questions, Waddell asked only one: "I saw little white flakes when we passed a window. Is it snowing or are they ashes from the incinerator?"

The date on the Protocol, I noted, was August.

Questions about how the murder might have been prevented went nowhere. Would Waddell have killed his victim in a populated area? Would he have killed her if witnesses had been present? Would anything have stopped him from killing her? Did he think that capital punishment was a deterrent? Waddell said he could not remember killing "the lady on TV." He did not know what would have stopped him from committing an act he could not recall. His only memory was of being "sticky." He said it was like waking up from a wet dream. The stickiness Ronnie Waddell experienced was not semen. It was Robyn Naismith's blood.

"His problem list sounds rather mundane," I thought out loud. "Headaches, extreme shyness, marked daydreaming, and leaving home at the age of nineteen. I don't see anything here that one might consider the usual red flags. No cruelty to animals, fire setting, assaults, et cetera."

"Keep going," Wesley said.

I scanned several more pages. "Drugs and alcohol," I said.

"If he hadn't been locked up, he would have died a junkie or gotten shot on the street," Wesley said. "And what's interesting is the substance abuse did not begin until early adulthood. I remember Waddell told me he had never tasted alcohol until he was twenty and away from home."

"He was raised on a farm?"

"In Suffolk. A fairly big farm that grew peanuts, corn, soybeans. His entire family lived on it and worked for the owners. There were four children, Ronnie Joe the youngest. Their mother was very religious and took the children to church every Sunday. No alcohol, swearing, or cigarettes. His background was very sheltered. He'd really never been off the farm until his father died and Ronnie decided to leave. He took the bus to Richmond and had little trouble getting work because of his physical strength. Breaking up asphalt with a jackhammer, lifting heavy loads, that sort of thing. My theory is he could not handle temptation when he was finally faced with it. First it was beer and wine, then marijuana. Within a year he was into cocaine and heroin, buying and selling, and stealing whatever he could get his hands on.

"When I asked him how many criminal acts he had committed that he had never been arrested for, he said he couldn't count them. He said he was doing burglaries, breaking into cars—property crimes, in other words. Then he broke into Robyn Naismith's house and she had the misfortune of coming home while he was there."

"He wasn't described as violent, Benton," I pointed out.

"Yes. He never profiled as your typical violent offender. The defense claimed that he was made temporarily insane by drugs and alcohol. To be honest, I think this was the case. Not long before he murdered Robyn Naismith he had started getting into PCP. It is quite possible that when Waddell encountered Robyn Naismith he was completely deranged and later had little or no recollection of what he did to her."

"Do you remember what he stole, if anything?" I asked. "I wonder if there was clear evidence when he broke into her house that his intent was to commit burglary."

"The place was ransacked. We know jewelry was missing. The medicine cabinet was cleaned out and her billfold was empty. It's hard to know what else was stolen because she lived alone."

"No significant relationship?"

"A fascinating point." Wesley stared off at an old couple dancing soporifically to the husky tones of a saxophone. "Semen stains were recovered from a bed sheet and the mattress cover. The stain on the sheet had to be fresh unless Robyn didn't change her bed linens very often, and we know that Waddell was not the origin of the stains. They didn't match his blood type."

"No one who knew her ever made reference to a lover?"

"No one ever did. Obviously, there was keen interest in who this person was, and since he never contacted the police, it was suspected that she had been having an affair, possibly with one of her married colleagues or sources."

"Maybe she was," I said. "But he wasn't her killer."

"No. Ronnie Joe Waddell was her killer. Let's take a look."

I opened Waddell's file and showed Wesley the photographs of the executed inmate I had autopsied on the night of December thirteenth. "Can you tell if this is the man you interviewed six years ago?"

Wesley impassively studied the photographs, going through them one by one. He looked at close-ups of the face and back of the head, and glanced over shots of the upper body and hands. He detached a mug shot from Waddell's Assessment Protocol and began comparing as I looked on.

"I see a resemblance," I said.

"That's about as much as we can say," Wesley replied. "The mug shot's ten years old. Waddell had a beard and mustache, was very muscular but lean. His face was lean. This guy"—he pointed to one of the morgue photographs—"is shaven and much heavier. His face is much fuller. I can't say these are the same man, based on these photos."

I couldn't confirm it, either. In fact, I could think of old pictures of me that no one else would recognize.

"Do you have any suggestions about how we're going to resolve this problem?" I asked Wesley.

"I'll toss out a few things," he said, stacking the photographs and straightening the edges against the tabletop. "Your old friend Nick Grueman's some kind of player in all this, and I've been thinking about the best way to deal with him without tipping our hand. If Marino or I talk to him, he'll know instantly that something's up."

I knew where this was going and I tried to interrupt, but Wesley would not let me. "Marino's mentioned your difficulties with Grueman, that he calls and in general jerks you around. And then, of course, there is the past, your years at Georgetown. Maybe you should talk with him."

"I don't want to talk with him, Benton."

"He may have photographs of Waddell, letters, other documents. Something with Waddell's prints. Or maybe there's something he might say in the course of conversation that would be revealing. The point is, you have access to him, if you wish, through your normal activities, when the rest of us don't. And you're going to D.C. anyway to see Downey."

"No," I said.

"It's just a thought." He looked away from me and motioned for the waitress to bring the check. "How long will Lucy be visiting you?" he asked.

"She doesn't have to be back at school until January seventh."

"I remember she's pretty good with computers."

"She's more than pretty good."

Wesley smiled a little. "So Marino's told me. He says she thinks she can help with AFIS."

"I'm sure she'd like to try." I suddenly felt protective again, and torn. I wanted to send her back to Miami, and yet I didn't.

"You may or may not remember, but Michele works for the Department of Criminal Justice Services, which assists the State Police in running AFIS," Wesley said.

"I should think that might worry you a little right now." I finished my brandy.

"There isn't a day of my life that I don't worry," he said.

The next morning a light snow began to fall as Lucy and I dressed in ski clothes that could be spotted from here to the Eiger.

"I look like a traffic cone," she said, staring at her blaze orange reflection in the mirror.

"That's right. If you get lost on a trail, it won't be hard to find you." I swallowed vitamins and two aspirin with sparkling water from the minibar.

My niece eyed my outfit, which was almost as electric as hers, and shook her head. "For someone so conservative, you certainly dress like a neon peacock for sports."

"I try not to be a stick-in-the-mud all of the time. Are you hungry?"

"Starved."

"Benton's supposed to meet us in the dining room at eight-thirty. We can go down now if you don't want to wait."

"I'm ready. Isn't Connie going to eat with us?"

"We're going to meet her on the slopes. Benton wants to talk shop first."

"I would think it must bother her to be left out," Lucy said. "Whenever he talks with anyone, it seems she isn't invited."

I locked the room door and we headed down the quiet corridor.

"I suspect Connie doesn't wish to be involved," I said in a low voice. "For her to know every detail of her husband's work would only be a burden for her."

"So he talks to you instead."

"About cases, yes."

"About work. And work is what matters most to both of you."

"Work certainly seems to dominate our lives."

"Are you and Mr. Wesley about to have an affair?"

"We're about to have breakfast." I smiled.

The Homestead's buffet was typically overwhelming. Long cloth-covered tables were laden with Virginia-cured bacon and ham, every concoction of eggs imaginable, pastries, breads, and griddle cakes. Lucy seemed immune to the temptations, and headed straight for the cereals and fresh fruit. Shamed into good behavior by her example and by my recent lecture to Marino about his health, I avoided everything I wanted, including coffee.

"People are staring at you, Aunt Kay," Lucy said under her breath.

I assumed the attention was due to our vibrant attire until

I opened the morning's *Washington Post* and was shocked to discover myself on the front page. The headline read, "MURDER IN THE MORGUE," the story a lengthy account of Susan's homicide, which was accompanied by a prominently placed photograph of me arriving at the scene and looking very tense. Clearly, the reporter's major source was Susan's distraught husband, Jason, whose information painted a picture of his wife leaving her job under peculiar, if not suspicious, circumstances less than a week before her violent death.

It was asserted, for example, that Susan recently confronted me when I attempted to list her as a witness in the case of a murdered young boy, even though she had not been present during his autopsy. When Susan became ill and stayed out of work "after a formalin spill," I called her home with such frequency that she was afraid to answer the phone, then I "showed up on her doorstep the night before her murder" with a poinsettia and vague offers of favors.

"I walked into my house after Christmas shopping and there was the Chief Medical Examiner inside my living room," Susan's husband was quoted. "She [Dr. Scarpetta] left right away, and as soon as the door shut Susan started crying. She was terrified of something but wouldn't tell me what."

As unsettling as I found Jason Story's public disparagement of me, worse was the revelation of Susan's recent financial transactions. Supposedly, two weeks before her death she paid off more than three thousand dollars in credit card bills after having deposited thirty-five hundred dollars into her checking account. The sudden windfall could not be explained. Her husband had been laid off from his sales job during the fall and Susan earned less than twenty thousand dollars a year.

"Mr. Wesley's here," Lucy said, taking the paper from me.

Wesley was dressed in black ski pants and turtleneck, a

bright red jacket tucked under his arm. I could tell by the expression on his face, the firm set of his jaw, that he was aware of the news.

"Did the *Post* try to talk to you?" He pulled out a chair. "I can't believe they ran this damn thing without giving you a chance for comment."

"A reporter from the *Post* called as I was leaving the office yesterday," I replied. "He wanted to question me about Susan's homicide and I chose not to talk to him. I guess that was my chance."

"So you didn't know anything, had no forewarning about the slant of this thing."

"I was in the dark until I picked up the paper."

"It's all over the news, Kay." He met my eyes. "I heard it on television this morning. Marino called. The press in Richmond is having a field day. The implication is that Susan's murder may be connected to the medical examiner's office—that you may be involved and have suddenly left town."

"That's insane."

"How much of the article is true?" he asked.

"The facts have been completely distorted. I did call Susan's house when she didn't show up at work. I wanted to make certain she was all right, and then I needed to find out if she remembered printing Waddell at the morgue. I did go see her on Christmas Eve to give her a gift and the poinsettia. I suppose my promise of favors was when she told me she was quitting and I said for her to let me know if she needed a reference, or if there was anything I could do for her."

"What about this business of her not wanting to be listed as a witness in Eddie Heath's case?"

"That was the afternoon she broke several jars of formalin and retreated upstairs to my office. It's routine to list autopsy assistants or techs as witnesses when they assist in the posts. In this instance, Susan was present for only the external examination and was adamant about not wanting her name on Eddie Heath's autopsy report. I thought her request and demeanor were weird, but there was no confrontation."

"This article makes it look as if you were paying her off," Lucy said. "That's what I would wonder if I read this and didn't know."

"I certainly wasn't paying her off, but it sounds as if someone was," I said.

"It's all making a little more sense," Wesley said. "If this bit about her financial picture is accurate, then Susan had gotten a substantial sum of money, meaning she must have supplied a service to someone. Around this same time your computer was broken into and Susan's personality changed. She became nervous and unreliable. She avoided you as much as she could. I think she couldn't face you, Kay, because she knew she was betraying you."

I nodded, struggling for composure. Susan had gotten into something she did not know how to get out of, and it occurred to me that this might be the real explanation for why she fled from Eddie Heath's post and then from Jennifer Deighton's. Her emotional outbursts had nothing to do with witchcraft or feeling dizzy after being exposed to formalin fumes. She was panicking. She did not want to witness either case.

"Interesting," Wesley said when I voiced my theory. "If you ask what of value did Susan Story have to sell, the answer is information. If she didn't witness the posts, she had no information. And whoever was buying this information from her is quite likely the person she was going to meet on Christmas Day."

"What information would be so important that someone would be willing to pay thousands of dollars for it and then murder a pregnant woman?" Lucy asked bluntly.

We did not know, but we had a guess. The common denominator, once again, seemed to be Ronnie Joe Waddell.

"Susan didn't forget to print Waddell or whoever it was that was executed," I said. "She deliberately didn't print him."

"That's the way it looks," Wesley agreed. "Someone else asked her to conveniently forget to print him. Or to lose his cards in the event that you or another member of your staff printed him."

I thought of Ben Stevens. The bastard.

"And this brings us back to what you and I concluded last night, Kay," Wesley went on. "We need to go back to the night Waddell was supposed to have been executed and determine who it was they strapped in the chair. And a place to start is AFIS. What we want to know is if and what records were tampered with." He was talking to Lucy now. "I've got it set up for you to go through the journal tapes, if you're willing."

"I'm willing," Lucy said. "When do you want me to start?"

"You can start as soon as you want because the first step will involve only the telephone. You need to call Michele. She's a systems analyst for Department of Criminal Justice Services and works out of the State Police headquarters. She's involved with AFIS and will go into detail with you about how everything works. Then she'll begin mounting the journal tapes so you can access them."

"She doesn't mind my doing this?" Lucy asked warily.

"On the contrary. She's thrilled. The journal tapes are nothing more than audit logs, a record of changes made to the AFIS data base. They're not readable, in other words. I think Michele called them 'hex dumps,' if that means anything to you."

"Hexadecimal, or base sixteen. Hieroglyphics, in other words," Lucy said. "It means that I'll have to decipher the data and write a program that will look for anything that's gone against the identification numbers of the records you're interested in."

"Can you do it?" Wesley asked.

"Once I figure out the code and record layout. Why doesn't the analyst you know do it herself?"

"We want to be as discreet as possible. It would attract notice if Michele suddenly abandoned her normal duties and started wading through journal tapes ten hours a day. You can work invisibly from your aunt's home computer by dialing in on a diagnostic line."

"As long as when Lucy dials in it can't be traced back to my residence," I said.

"It won't be," Wesley said.

"And no one is likely to notice that someone from the outside is dialing into the State Police computer and wading through the tapes?" I asked.

"Michele says she can maneuver it so there's no problem." Unzipping a pocket of his ski jacket, Wesley slipped out a card and gave it to Lucy. "Here are her work and home phone numbers."

"How do you know you can trust her?" Lucy asked. "If tampering has gone on, how do you know she's not involved?"

"Michele has never been good at lying. From the time she was a little girl she would stare down at her feet and turn as red as Rudolf's nose."

"You knew her when she was a little girl?" Lucy looked baffled.

"And before," Wesley said. "She's my eldest daughter."

9

After much debate, we came up with what seemed a reasonable plan. Lucy would stay at the Homestead with the Wesleys until Wednesday, allowing me a brief period to grapple with my problems without worrying about her welfare. After breakfast, I drove off in a gentle snow that by the time I reached Richmond had turned to rain.

By late afternoon, I had been to the office and the labs. I had conferred with Fielding and several of the forensic scientists, and had avoided Ben Stevens. I returned not a single reporter's call and ignored my electronic mail, for if the health commissioner had sent me a communication, I did not want to know what it said. At half past four I was filling my car with gas at an Exxon station on Grove Avenue when a white Ford LTD pulled in behind me. I watched Marino get out, hitch up his trousers, and head to the men's room. When he returned a moment later, he covertly glanced around as if worried that someone might have observed his trip to the toilet. Then he strolled over to me.

"I saw you as I was driving past," he said, jamming his hands into the pockets of his blue blazer.

"Where's your coat?" I began cleaning the front windshield.

"In the car. It gets in my way." He hunched his shoulders against the cold, raw air. "If you ain't thinking about stopping these rumors, then you'd better start thinking about it."

I irritably returned the squeegee to its container of cleaning solution. "And just what do you suggest I do, Marino? Call Jason Story and tell him I'm sorry his wife and unborn child are dead but I would certainly appreciate it if he would vent his grief and rage elsewhere?"

"Doc, he blames you."

"After reading his quotes in the *Post*, I suspect any number of people are blaming me. He's managed to portray me as a Machiavellian bitch."

"You hungry?"

"No."

"Well, you look hungry."

I looked at him as if he'd lost his mind.

"And if something looks a certain way to me, it's my duty to check it out. So I'm giving you a choice, Doc. I can get us some Nabs and sodas from the machines over there, and we can stand out here freezing our asses off and inhaling fumes while we prevent other poor bastards from using the self-service pumps. Or we can zip over to Phil's. I'm buying either way."

Ten minutes later we were sitting in a corner booth perusing glossy illustrated menus offering everything from spaghetti to fried fish. Marino faced the dark-tinted front door and I had a perfect view of the rest rooms. He was smoking, as were most of the people around us, and I was reminded that it is hell to quit. He actually could not have selected a more ideal restaurant, considering the circumstances. Philip's Continental Lounge was an old, neighborhood establishment where patrons who had known each other all their lives continued to meet regularly for hearty food and bottled beer. The typical customer was good-natured and gregarious, and unlikely to recognize me or care unless my picture regularly appeared in the sports section of the newspaper.

"It's like this," Marino said as he closed his menu. "Jason Story believes Susan would still be alive if she'd had another job. And he's probably right. Plus, he's a loser—one of these self-centered assholes who believes everything is everybody else's fault. The truth is, he's probably more to blame for Susan's death than anyone."

"You're not suggesting that *he* killed her?"

The waitress appeared and we ordered. Grilled chicken and rice for Marino and a kosher chili dog for me, plus two diet sodas.

"I'm not suggesting that Jason shot his wife," Marino said quietly. "But he set her up for getting involved in whatever it was that precipitated her homicide. Paying the bills was Susan's responsibility, and she was under big-time financial stress."

"Unsurprisingly," I said. "Her husband had just lost his job."

"It's too bad he didn't lose his high dollar taste. We're talking Polo shirts and Britches of Georgetown slacks and silk ties. A couple weeks after he gets laid off, the jerk goes out and buys seven hundred bucks' worth of ski equipment and then heads off to Wintergreen for the weekend. Before that it was a two-hundred-dollar leather jacket and a four-hundred-dollar bicycle. So Susan's down at the morgue working like a dog and then coming home to face bills her salary won't put a dent in."

"I had no idea," I said, pained by a sudden vision of Susan sitting at her desk. Her daily ritual was to spend her lunch hour in her office, and on occasion I would join her there to chat. I remembered her generic-brand corn chips and the sale stickers on her sodas. I don't think she ever ate or drank anything she had not brought from home.

"Jason's spending habits," Marino went on, "leads to the

shit he's causing you. He's badmouthing you like hell to anybody who will listen because you're a doctor–lawyer–Indian chief who drives a Mercedes and lives in a big house in Windsor Farms. I think the dumbass believes if he can somehow blame you for what happened to his wife, maybe he can get a little compensation."

"He can try until he's blue in the face."

"And he will."

Our diet drinks arrived, and I changed the subject. "I'm meeting with Downey in the morning."

Marino's eyes wandered to the television over the bar.

"Lucy's getting started on AFIS. And then I've got to do something about Ben Stevens."

"What you ought to do is get rid of him."

"Do you have any idea how difficult it is to fire a state employee?"

"They say it's easier to fire Jesus Christ," Marino said. "Unless the employee is appointed and got a grade off the charts, like you. You still ought to find some way to run the bastard off."

"Have you talked to him?"

"Oh, yeah. According to him, you're arrogant, ambitious, and strange. A real pain in the ass to work for."

"He actually said something like that?" I asked in disbelief.

"That was the drift."

"I hope someone is checking into his finances. I'd be interested to know if he's made any large deposits lately. Susan didn't get into trouble alone."

"I agree with you. I think Stevens knows a lot and is covering his tracks like crazy. By the way, I checked with Susan's bank. One of the tellers remembers her making the thirty-five-hundred-dollar deposit in *cash.* Twenties, fifties, and hundred-dollar bills that she was carrying in her purse."

"What did Stevens have to say about Susan?"

"He's saying that he really didn't know her, but that it

was his impression there was some problem between you and her. In other words, he's reinforcing what's been in the news."

Our food arrived, and it was all I could do to swallow a single bite because I was so angry.

"And what about Fielding?" I said. "Does he think I'm horrible to work for?"

Marino stared off again. "He says you're very driven and he's never been able to figure you out."

"I didn't hire him to figure me out, and compared to him, I am certainly driven. Fielding is disenchanted with forensic medicine and has been for several years. He expends most of his energy in the gym."

"Doc"—Marino met my eyes—"you are driven compared to *anyone*, and most people can't figure you out. You don't exactly walk around with your heart on your sleeve. In fact, you can come across as someone who don't have feelings. You're so damn hard to read that to others who don't know you, it sometimes appears that nothing gets to you. Other cops, lawyers, they ask me about you. They want to know what you're really like, how you can do what you do every day—what the deal is. They see you as somebody who don't get close to anyone."

"And what do you tell them when they ask?" I said.

"I don't tell them a damn thing."

"Are you finished psychoanalyzing me yet, Marino?"

He lit a cigarette. "Look, I'm going to say something to you, and you ain't gonna like it. You've always been this reserved, professional lady—someone real slow to let anybody in, but once the person's there, he's there. He's got a damn friend for life and you'd do anything for him. But you've been different this past year. You've had about a hundred walls up ever since Mark got killed. For those of us around you, it's like being in a room that was once seventy degrees and suddenly the temperature's down to about fifty-five. I don't think you're even aware of it.

"So nobody's feeling all that attached to you right now. Maybe they even resent you a little bit because they feel ignored or snubbed by you. Maybe they never liked you anyway. Maybe they're just indifferent. The thing about people is, whether you're sitting on a throne or a hot seat, they're going to use your position to their advantage. And if there's no bond between you and them, that just makes it all the easier for them to try to get what they want without giving a rat's ass about what happens to you. And that's where you are. There's a lot of people who've been waiting for years to see you bleed."

"I don't intend to bleed." I pushed my plate away.

"Doc"—he blew out smoke—"you're already bleeding. And common sense tells me that if you're swimming with sharks and start bleeding, you ought to get the hell out of the water."

"Might we converse without speaking in clichés, at least for a minute or two?"

"Hey. I can say it in Portuguese or Chinese and you're not going to listen to me."

"If you speak Portuguese or Chinese, I promise I'll listen. In fact, if you ever decide to speak English I promise I'll listen."

"Comments like that don't win you any fans. That's just what I'm talking about."

"I said it with a smile."

"I've seen you cut open bodies with a smile."

"Never. I always use a scalpel."

"Sometimes there isn't a difference between the two. I've seen your smile make defense attorneys bleed."

"If I'm such a dreadful person, why are we friends?"

"Because I've got more walls up than you do. The fact is, there's a squirrel in every tree and the water's full of sharks. All of them want a piece of us."

"Marino, you're paranoid."

"You're damn right, which is why I wish you'd lay low for a while, Doc. Really," he said.

"I can't."

"You want to know the truth, it's going to start looking like a conflict of interests for you to have anything to do with these cases. It's going to make you come off looking worse."

I said, "Susan is dead. Eddie Heath is dead. Jennifer Deighton is dead. There is corruption in my office, and we aren't certain who went to the electric chair the other week. You're suggesting I just walk away until everything somehow magically self-corrects?"

Marino reached for the salt but I got it first. "Nope. But you can have all the pepper you want," I said, sliding the pepper shaker closer.

"This health crap is going to kill me," he warned. "Because one of these days I'm going to get so pissed I'm going to do everything at once. Five cigarettes going, a bourbon in one hand and a cup of coffee in the other, steak, baked potato loaded with butter, sour cream, salt. And then I'm going to blow every circuit in the box."

"No, you're not going to do any of those things," I said. "You're going to be kind to yourself and live at least as long as I do."

We were silent for a while, picking at our food.

"Doc, no offense, but just what do you think you're going to find out about damn feather parts?"

"Hopefully, their origin."

"I can save you the trouble. They came from birds," he said.

I left Marino at close to seven P.M. and returned downtown. The temperature had risen above forty, the night dark and lashing out in fits of rain violent enough to stop traffic. Sodium vapor lamps were pollen-yellow smudges behind the morgue, where the bay door was shut, every parking space vacant. Inside the building, my pulse quickened as I followed the brightly lit corridor past the autopsy suite to Susan's small office.

As I unlocked the door, I did not know what I expected to find, but I was drawn to her filing cabinet and desk drawers, to every book and old telephone message. Everything looked the same as it had before she died. Marino was quite skilled at going through someone's private space without disturbing the natural disorder of things. The telephone was still askew on the right corner of the desk, the cord twisted like a corkscrew. Scissors and two pencils with broken points were on the green paper blotter, her lab coat draped over the back of her chair. A reminder of a doctor's appointment was still taped to her computer monitor, and as I stared at the shy curves and gentle slant of her neat script, I trembled inside. Where had she gone adrift? Was it when she married Jason Story? Or was her destruction set up much earlier than that, when she was the young daughter of a scrupulous minister, the twin left behind when her sister was killed?

Sitting in her chair, I rolled it closer to the filing cabinet and began slipping out one file after another and glancing through the contents. Most of what I perused was brochures and other printed information pertaining to surgical supplies and miscellaneous items used in the morgue. Nothing struck me as curious until I discovered that she had saved virtually every memo she had ever gotten from Fielding, but not one from Ben Stevens or me, when I knew that both of us had sent her plenty. Further searching through drawers and bookshelves produced no files for Stevens or me, and that's when I concluded that someone had taken them.

My first thought was that Marino might have carried them off. Then something else occurred to me with a jolt, and I hurried upstairs. Unlocking the door to my office, I went straight to the file drawer where I kept mundane administrative paperwork such as telephone call sheets, memos, printouts of electronic mail communications I had received, and drafts of budget proposals and long-term plans. Frantically, I rifled through folders and drawers. The thick file I was looking for was simply labeled "Memos," and in it were copies of every memo I had sent to my staff and various other agency personnel over the past several years. I searched Rose's office and carefully checked my office again. The file was gone.

"You son of a bitch," I said under my breath as I headed furiously down the hall. "You goddam son of a bitch."

Ben Stevens's office was impeccably neat and so carefully appointed that it looked like a display in a discount furniture store. His desk was a Williamsburg reproduction with bright brass pulls and a mahogany veneer, and he had brass floor lamps with dark green shades. The floor was covered with a machine-made Persian rug, the walls arranged with large prints of alpine skiers and men on thundering horses swinging polo sticks and sailors racing through snarling seas. I began by pulling Susan's personnel file. The expected job description, résumé, and other documents were inside. Absent were several memos of commendation I had written since hiring her and had added to her file myself. I began opening desk drawers, and discovered in one of them a brown vinyl kit containing toothbrush, toothpaste, razor, shaving cream, and a small bottle of cologne.

Perhaps it was the barely perceptible shift of air when the door was silently pulled open wider, or perhaps I simply sensed a presence the way an animal would. I happened to look up to find Ben Stevens standing in the doorway as I sat at his desk screwing the cap back on a bottle of Red cologne. For a long, icy moment, our eyes held and neither of us spoke. I did not feel fear. I did not feel the least bit concerned by what he had caught me doing. I felt rage.

"You're keeping unusually late hours, Ben." Zipping up his toilet kit, I returned it to its drawer. I laced my fingers on top of the blotter, my movements, my speech, deliberate and slow.

"The thing I've always liked about working after hours is there is no one else around," I said. "No distractions. No risk of someone walking in and interrupting whatever it is you are doing. No eyes or ears. Not a sound, except on rare occasion when the security guard happens to wander through. And we all know that doesn't happen often unless his attention is solicited, because he hates coming into the morgue at any time. I've never known a security guard who didn't hate that. Same goes for the cleaning crew. They won't even go downstairs, and they do as little up here as they can get away with. But that point is moot, isn't it? It's close to nine o'clock. The cleaning crew is always gone by seven-thirty.

"What intrigues me is that I did not guess before now. It never crossed my mind. Maybe that is a sad comment about how preoccupied I've been. You told the police you did not know Susan personally, yet you frequently gave her rides to and from work, such as on the snowy morning I autopsied Jennifer Deighton. I remember that Susan was very distracted on that occasion. She left the body in the middle of the corridor, and she was dialing a number on the phone and quickly hung up when I walked into the autopsy suite. I doubt she was placing a business call at seven-thirty in the morning on a day when most people weren't going to venture out of their homes because of the weather. And there was no one in the office to call—no one had gotten in yet, except you. If she were dialing your number, why would her impulse be to hide that from me? Unless you were more than her direct supervisor.

"Of course, your relationship with me is equally intriguing. We seem to get along fine, then suddenly you claim that I am the worst boss in Christendom. It makes me wonder if Jason Story is the only person talking to reporters. It's amazing, this persona I suddenly have. This image. The tyrant. The neurotic. The person who is somehow responsible for the violent death of my morgue supervisior. Susan and I had a very cordial working relationship, and until recently, Ben, so did we. But it's my word against yours, especially now, since any scrap of paper that might document what I'm saying has conveniently disappeared. And my prediction is that you have already leaked to someone that important personnel files and memorandums have vanished from the office, thus implying that I'm the one who took them. When files and memos disappear, you can say anything you want about the contents of them, can't you?"

"I don't know what you're talking about," Ben Stevens said. He moved away from the doorway but did not come close to the desk or take a chair. His face was flushed, his eyes hard with hate. "I don't know anything about any missing files or memos, but if it's true, then I can't hide that fact from the authorities, just as I can't hide the fact that I happened to stop by the office tonight to get something I'd left and discovered you rummaging through my desk."

"What did you leave, Ben?"

"I don't have to answer your questions."

"Actually, you do. You work for me, and if you come into the building late at night and I happen to know about it, I have the right to question you."

"Go ahead and put me on leave. Try to fire me. That will certainly look good for you right now."

"You are a squid, Ben."

His eyes widened and he wet his lips.

"Your efforts to sabotage me are just a lot of ink you're squirting into the water because you're panicking and want to divert attention from yourself. Did you kill Susan?"

"You're losing your goddam mind." His voice shook.

"She left her house early afternoon on Christmas Day, allegedly to meet a girlfriend. In truth, the person she was meeting was you, wasn't it? Did you know that when she was dead in her car, her coat collar and scarf smelled like men's cologne, like the Red cologne you keep in your desk so you can freshen up before you hit the bars in the Slip after work?"

"I don't know what you're talking about."

"Who was paying her?"

"Maybe you were."

"That's ridiculous," I said calmly. "You and Susan were involved in some money-making scheme, and my guess is that you are the one who initially got her involved because you knew her vulnerabilities. She probably had confided in you. You knew how to convince her to go along, and Lord knows you could use the money. Your bar tabs alone have got to blow your budget. Partying is very expensive, and I know what you get paid."

"You don't know anything."

"Ben." I lowered my voice. "Get out of it. Stop while there's still time. Tell me who's behind this."

He would not look me in the eye.

"The stakes are too high when people start dying. Do you think if you killed Susan that you'll get away with it?"

He said nothing.

"If someone else killed her, do you think you're immune, that the same thing can't happen to you?"

"You're threatening me."

"Nonsense."

"You can't prove that the cologne you smelled on Susan was mine. There's no test for something like that. You can't put a *smell* in a test tube; you can't save it," he said.

"I'm going to ask you to leave now, Ben."

He turned and walked out of his office. When I heard the elevator doors shut, I went down the hall and peered out a window overlooking the parking lot in back. I did not venture out to my car until Stevens had driven away.

* * *

The FBI Building is a concrete fortification at 9th Street and Pennsylvania Avenue in the heart of D.C., and when I arrived the following morning, it was in the wake of at least a hundred noisy schoolchildren. They brought to mind Lucy at their age as they stomped up steps, dashed to benches, and flocked restlessly about huge shrubs and potted trees. Lucy would have loved touring the laboratories, and I suddenly missed her intensely.

The babble of shrill young voices faded as if carried away from me by the wind, my step brisk and directed, for I had been here enough times to know the way. Heading toward the center of the building, I passed the courtyard, then a restricted parking area and a guard before reaching the single glass door. Inside was a lobby of tan furniture, mirrors, and flags. A photograph of the president smiled from one wall, while posted on another was a hit parade of the ten most wanted fugitives in the land.

At the escort desk, I presented my driver's license to a young agent whose demeanor was as grim as his gray suit.

"I'm Dr. Kay Scarpetta, Chief Medical Examiner of Virginia."

"Who are you here to see?"

I told him.

He compared me to my photograph, ascertained that I was not armed, placed a phone call, and gave me a badge. Unlike the Academy at Quantico, Headquarters had an ambience that seemed to starch the soul and stiffen the spine.

I had never met Special Agent Minor Downey, though the irony of his name had conjured up unfair images. He would be an effete, frail man with pale blond hair covering every inch of his body except for his head. His eyes would be weak, his skin rarely touched by the sun, and of course he would drift in and out of places and never draw attention to himself. Naturally, I was wrong. When a fit man in shirtsleeves appeared and looked straight at me, I got up from my chair.

"You must be Mr. Downey," I said.

"Dr. Scarpetta." He shook my hand. "Please call me Minor."

He was at the most forty, and attractive in a scholarly sort of way, with his rimless glasses, neatly clipped brown hair, and maroon-and-navy-striped tie. He exuded a prepossession and intellectual intensity immediately noticeable to anyone who has suffered through arduous years of postgraduate education, for I could not recall a professor from Georgetown or Johns Hopkins who did not commune with the uncommon and find it impossible to connect with pedestrian human beings.

"Why feathers?" I asked as we boarded the elevator.

"I have a friend who's an ornithologist at the Smithsonian's Museum of Natural History," he said. "When government aviation officials started getting her help with bird strikes, I got interested. You see, birds get ingested by aircraft engines and when you're going through the wreckage on the ground, you find these feather parts and want to figure out which bird caused the problem. In other words, whatever got sucked in was chewed up pretty good. A sea gull can crash a B-1 bomber, and you lose one engine to a bird strike with a wide-bodied plane full of people and you've got a problem. Or take the case of the loon that went through the windshield of a Lear jet and decapitated the pilot. So that's part of what I do. I work on bird ingestions. We test turbines and blades by throwing in chickens. You know, can the plane survive one chicken or two?

"But birds figure into all sorts of things. Pigeon down in poop on the bottom of a suspect's shoes—was the suspect in the alleyway where the body was found or not? Or the guy who stole a Double Yellow Amazon during the course of a burglary, and we find down pieces in the back of his car that are identified as coming from a Double Yellow Amazon. Or the down feather recovered from the body of a woman who was raped and murdered. She was found in a Panasonic stereo speaker box in a Dumpster. The down looked like a small white mallard feather to me, same type of feather in the down comforter on the suspect's bed. That case was made with a feather and two hairs."

The third floor was a city block of laboratories where examiners analyzed the explosives, paint chips, pollens, tools, tires, and debris used in crimes or collected from scenes. Gas chromatography detectors, microspectrophotometers, and mainframes ran morning, noon, and night, and reference collections filled rooms with automotive paint types, duct tapes, and plastics. I followed Downey through white hallways past the DNA analysis labs, then into the Hairs and Fibers Unit where he worked. His office also functioned as a laboratory, with dark wood furniture and bookcases sharing space with countertops and microscopes. Walls and carpet were beige, and crayon drawings tacked to a bulletin board told me this internationally respected feather expert was a father.

Opening a manila envelope, I withdrew three smaller envelopes made of transparent plastic. Two contained the feathers collected from Jennifer Deighton's and Susan Story's homicides, while a third contained a slide of the gummy residue from Eddie Heath's wrists.

"This is the best one, it seems," I said, pointing out the feather I had recovered from Jennifer Deighton's nightgown.

He took it out of its envelope and said, "This is down—a breast or back feather. It's got a nice tuft on it. Good. The more feather you've got, the better." Using forceps, he stripped several of the branchlike projections or "barbs" from both sides of the shaft and, stationing himself at the stereoscopic microscope, placed them on a thin film of xylene that he had dropped on a slide. This served to separate the tiny structures, or float them out, and when he was satisfied that each barb was pristinely fanned, he touched a corner of green blotting paper to the xylene to absorb it. He added the mounting medium Flo-Texx, then a coverslip, and placed the slide under the comparison microscope, which was connected to a video camera.

"I'll start off by telling you that the feathers of all birds have basically the same structure," he said. "You've got a central shaft, barbs, which in turn branch into hairlike barbules, and you've got a broadened base, at the top of which is a pore called the superior umbilicus. The barbs are the filaments that result in the feather's *feathery* appearance, and when they're magnified you'll find they're actually like minifeathers coming out of the shaft." He turned on the monitor. "Here's a barb."

"It looks like a fern," I said.

"In many instances, yes. Now we're going to magnify it some more so we can get a good look at the barbules, for it is the features of the barbules that allow for an identification. Specifically, what we're most interested in are the nodes."

"Let me see if I've got this straight," I said. "Nodes are features of barbules, barbules are features of barbs, barbs are features of feathers, and feathers are features of birds."

"Right. And each family of birds has its own peculiar feather structure."

What I saw on the monitor's screen looked, unremarkably, like a stick figure depiction of a weed or an insect leg. Lines were connected in segments by three-dimensional triangular structures that Downey said were the nodes.

"It's the size, shape, number, and pigmentation of nodes and their placement along the barbule that are key," he patiently explained. "For example, with starlike nodes you're dealing with pigeons, ringlike nodes are chickens and turkeys, enlarged flanges with prenodal swelling are cuckoos. These"—he pointed to the screen—"are clearly triangular, so right away I know your feather is either duck or goose. Not that this should come as any great surprise. The typical origin of feathers collected in burglaries, rapes, and homicides are pillows, comforters, vests, jackets, gloves. And generally the filler in these items comprises chopped feathers and down from ducks and geese, and in cheap stuff, chickens.

"But we can definitely rule out chickens here. And I'm about to decide that your feather did not come from a goose, either."

"Why?" I asked.

"Well, the distinction would be easy if we had a whole feather. Down is tough. But based on what I'm seeing here, there are, on average, just too few nodes. Plus, they aren't located throughout the barbule but are more distal, or located more toward the end of the barbule. And that's a characteristic of ducks."

He opened a cabinet and slid out several drawers of slides.

"Let's see. I've got about sixty slides of ducks. To be on the safe side I'm going to run through all of them, eliminating as I go."

One by one he placed slides under the comparison microscope, which is basically two compound microcopes combined into one binocular unit. On the video monitor was a circular field of light divided down the middle by a fine line, the known feather specimen on one side of the line and the one we hoped to identify on the other. Rapidly, we scanned mallard, Muscovy, harlequin, scoter, ruddy, and American widgeon, and then dozens more. Downey did not have to look long at any one of them to know that the duck we sought was being elusive.

"Am I just imagining it, or is this one more delicate than the others?" I said of the feather in question.

"You're not imagining it. It's more delicate, more streamlined. See how the triangular structures don't flare out quite as much?"

"Okay. Now that you've pointed it out."

"And this is giving us an important hint about the bird.

That's what's fascinating. Nature really does have a reason for things, and I'm suspicious that in this case the reason is insulation. The purpose of down is to trap air, and the finer the barbules, the more streamlined or tapered the nodes, and the more distal the location of the nodes, the more efficient the down is going to be at trapping air. When air's trapped or dead, it's like being in a small, insulated room with no ventilation. You're going to be warm."

He placed another slide on the microscope's stage, and this time I could see that we were close. The barbules were delicate, the nodes tapered and distally located.

"What have we got?" I asked.

"I've saved the prime suspects for last." He looked pleased. "Sea ducks. And top in the lineup are the eiders. Let's bump the magnification up to four hundred." He switched the objective lens, adjusted the focus, and off we went through several more slides. "Not the king or the spectacle. And I don't think it's the stellar because of the brownish pigmentation at the base of the node. Your feather doesn't have that, see?"

"I see."

"So we'll try the common eider. Okay. There's consistency in pigmentation," he said, staring intensely at the screen. "And, let's see, an average of two nodes located distally along the barbules. Plus, the streamlining for extra good insulating quality—and that's important if you're swimming around in the Arctic Ocean. I think this is it, the *Somateria mollissima*, typically found in Iceland, Norway, Alaska, and the Siberian shores. I'll run another check with SEM," he added, referring to scanning electron microscopy.

"To scan for what?"

"Salt crystals."

"Of course," I said, fascinated. "Because eider ducks are saltwater birds."

"Exactly. And interesting ones at that, a noteworthy example of exploitation. In Iceland and Norway, their breeding colonies are protected from predators and other disruptions so that people can collect the down with which the female lines her nest and covers her eggs. The down is then cleaned and sold to manufacturers."

"Manufacturers of what?"

"Typically, sleeping bags and comforters." As he talked, he was mounting several downy barbs from the feather found inside Susan Story's car.

"Jennifer Deighton had nothing like that in her house," I said. "Nothing filled with feathers at all."

"Then we're probably dealing with a secondary or tertiary transfer in which the feather got transferred to the killer who in turn transferred it to his victim. You know, this is very interesting."

The specimen was on the monitor now.

"Eider duck again," I said.

"I think so. Let's try the slide. This is from the boy?"

"Yes," I said. "From an adhesive residue on Eddie Heath's wrists."

"I'll be damned."

The microscopic debris showed up on the monitor as a fascinating variety of colors, shapes, fibers, and the familiar barbules and triangular nodes.

"Well, that puts a pretty big hole in my personal theory," Downey said. "If we're talking about three homicides that occurred at different locations and at different times."

"That's what we're talking about."

"If just one of these feathers was eider duck, then I'd be tempted to consider the possibility that it was a contaminant. You know, you see these labels that say one hundred percent acrylic and it turns out to be ninety percent acrylic and ten percent nylon. Labels lie. If the run before your acrylic sweater, for example, was a lot of nylon jackets, then the very first sweaters that come off afterward will have nylon contaminants. As you run more sweaters through, the contaminant is dissipated."

"In other words," I said, "if somebody is wearing a down-filled jacket or owns a comforter that got eider contaminants in it when it was manufactured, then the probability is almost nonexistent that this individual's jacket or comforter would be leaking only the eiderdown contaminants."

"Precisely. So we'll assume the item in question is filled with pure eiderdown, and that is extremely curious. Usually what I'm going to see in cases that come through here are your Kmart-variety jackets, gloves, or comforters filled with chicken feathers or maybe goose. Eider is a specialty item, a very exclusive shop item. A vest, jacket, comforter, or sleeping bag filled with eiderdown is going to have very low leakage, be very well made—and prohibitively expensive."

"Have you ever had eiderdown submitted as evidence before?"

"This is the first."

"Why is it so valuable?"

"The insulating qualities I've already described. But aesthetic appeal also has a lot to do with it. The common eider's down is snow-white. Most down is dingy."

"And if I purchased a specialty item filled with eiderdown, would I be aware that it's filled with this snow-white down or would the label simply say 'duck down'?"

"I'm quite sure you'd be aware of it," he said. "The label would probably say something like 'one hundred percent eiderdown.' There would have to be something that would justify the price."

"Can you run a computer check on down distributors?"

"Sure. But to state the obvious, no distributor is going to be able to tell you the eiderdown you've collected is theirs, not without the accompanying garment or item. Unfortunately, a feather isn't enough."

"I don't know," I said. "It might be."

By noon I had walked two blocks to where I had parked my car, and was inside with the heater blasting. I was so close to New Jersey Avenue that I felt like the tide being pulled by the moon. I fastened my seat belt, fiddled with the radio, and twice reached for the phone and changed my mind. It was crazy to even consider contacting Nicholas Grueman.

He won't be in anyway, I thought, reaching for the phone again and dialing.

"Grueman," the voice said.

"This is Dr. Scarpetta." I raised my voice above the heater's fan.

"Well, hello. I was just reading about you the other day. You sound like you're calling from a car phone."

"That's because I am. I happen to be in Washington."

"I'm truly flattered that you would think of me while you're passing through my humble town."

"There is nothing humble about your town, Mr. Grueman, and there is nothing social about this call. I thought you and I should discuss Ronnie Joe Waddell."

"I see. How far are you from the Law Center?"

"Ten minutes."

"I haven't eaten lunch and I don't suppose you have, either. Does it suit you if I have sandwiches sent in?"

"That would be fine," I said.

The Law Center was located some thirty-five blocks from the university's main campus, and I remembered my dismay many years before when I realized that my education would not include walking the old, shaded streets of the Heights and attending classes in fine eighteenth-century brick buildings. Instead, I was to spend three long years in a brand-new facility devoid of charm in a noisy, frantic section of D.C. My disappointment, however, did not last long. There was a certain excitement, not to mention convenience, in studying law in the shadow of the U.S. Capitol. But perhaps more significant was that I had not been a student long when I met Mark.

What I remembered most about my early encounters with Mark James during the first semester of our first year was his physical effect on me. At first I found the very sight of him unsettling, though I had no idea why. Then, as we became acquainted, his presence sent adrenaline charging through my blood. My heart would gallop and I would suddenly find myself acutely aware of his every gesture, no matter how common. For weeks, our conversations were entranced as they stretched into the early-morning hours. Our words were not elements of speech as much as they were notes to some secret inevitable crescendo, which happened one night with the dazzling unpredictability and force of an accident.

Since those days, the Law Center's physical plant had significantly grown and changed. The Criminal Justice Clinic was on the fourth floor, and when I got off the elevator there was no one in sight and offices I passed looked unoccupied. It was, after all, still the holidays, and only the relentless or desperate would be inclined to work. The door to room 418 was open, the secretary's desk vacant, the door to Grueman's inner office ajar.

Not wanting to startle him, I called out his name as I approached his door. He did not answer.

"Hello, Mr. Grueman? Are you here?" I tried again as I pushed his door open farther.

His desk was inches deep in clutter that pooled around a computer, and case files and transcripts were stacked on the floor along the base of the crowded bookcases. Left of his desk was a table bearing a printer and a fax machine that was busily sending something to someone. As I stood quietly staring around, the telephone rang three times and then stopped. Blinds were drawn in the window behind the desk, perhaps to reduce the glare on the computer screen, and leaning against the sill was a scarred and battered brown leather briefcase.

"Sorry about that." A voice behind me nearly sent me out of my shoes. "I stepped out for just a moment and was hoping I'd get back before you arrived."

Nicholas Grueman did not offer me his hand or a personal greeting of any kind. His preoccupation seemed to be returning to his chair, which he did very slowly and with the aid of a silver-topped cane.

"I would offer you coffee, but none is made when Evelyn isn't here," he said, seating himself in his judge's chair. "But the deli that will be delivering lunch shortly is bringing something to drink. I hope you can wait, and please take a chair, Dr. Scarpetta. It makes me nervous when a woman is looking down on me."

I pulled a chair closer to his desk and was amazed to realize that in the flesh Grueman was not the monster I recalled from my student days. For one thing, he seemed to have shrunk, though I suspected the more likely explanation was that I had inflated him to Mount Rushmore proportions in my imagination. I saw him now as a slight, white-haired man whose face had been carved by the years into a compelling caricature. He still wore bow ties and vests and smoked a pipe, and when he looked at me, his gray eyes were as capable of dissection as any scalpel. But I did not find them cold. They were simply unrevealing, as were mine most of the time.

"Why are you limping?" I boldly asked him.

"Gout. The disease of despots," he said without a smile.

"It acts up from time to time, and please spare me any good advice or remedies. You doctors drive me to distraction with your unsolicited opinions on every subject from malfunctioning electric chairs to the food and drink I should exclude from my miserable diet."

"The electric chair did not malfunction," I said. "Not in the case I'm sure you're alluding to."

"You cannot possibly know what I am alluding to, and it seems to me that during your brief tenure here I had to admonish you more than once about your great facility for making assumptions. I regret that you did not listen to me. You are still making assumptions, though in this instance your assumption was, in fact, correct."

"Mr. Grueman, I am flattered that you remember me as a student, but I did not come here to reminisce about the wretched hours I spent in your classroom. Nor am I here to engage, again, in the mental martial arts you seem to thrive on. For the record, I will tell you that you have the distinction of being the most misogynistic and arrogant professor I encountered during my thirty-some years of formal education. And I must thank you for schooling me so well in the art of dealing with bastards, for the world is full of them and I must deal with them every day."

"I'm sure you do deal with them every day, and I haven't decided yet whether you're good at it."

"I'm not interested in your opinion on that subject. I would like you to tell me more about Ronnie Joe Waddell."

"What would you like to know beyond the obvious fact that the ultimate outcome was incorrect? How would you like politics to determine whether you are put to death, Dr. Scarpetta? Why, just look at what's happening to you now. Isn't your recent bad press politically motivated, at least in part? Every party involved has his own agenda, something to gain from disparaging you publicly. It has nothing to do with fairness or truth. So just imagine what it would be like if these same people possessed the power to deprive you of your liberty or even of your life.

"Ronnie was torn to pieces by a system that is irrational and unfair. It made no difference what earlier precedents were applied or whether claims were addressed on direct or collateral review. It made no difference what issue I raised because in this instance in your lovely Commonwealth, habeas did not serve as a deterrent designed to ensure that state trial and appellate judges conscientiously sought to conduct their proceedings in a manner consistent with established constitutional principles. God forbid that there should have been the slightest interest in constitutional violations on furthering the evolution of our thinking in some area of the law. In the three years that I fought for Ronnie, I might as well have been dancing a jig."

"What constitutional violations are you referring to?" I asked.

"How much time do you have? But let's begin with the prosecution's obvious use of peremptory challenges in a racially discriminatory manner. Ronnie's rights under the equal protection clause were violated from hell to breakfast, and prosecutorial misconduct blatantly infringed his Sixth Amendment right to a jury drawn from a fair cross section of the community. I don't suppose you saw Ronnie's trial or even know much about it since it was more than nine years ago and you were not in Virginia. The local publicity was overwhelming, and yet there was no change of venue. The jury was comprised of eight women and four men. Six of the women and two of the men were white. The four black jurors were a car salesman, a bank teller, a nurse, and a college professor. The professions of the white jurors ranged from a retired railroad switchman who still called blacks 'niggers' to a rich housewife whose only exposure to blacks was when she watched the news and saw that another one of them had shot someone in the projects. The demographics of the jury made it impossible for Ronnie to be sentenced fairly."

"And you're saying that such a constitutional impropriety or any other in Waddell's case was politically motivated? What possible political motivation could there have been for putting Ronnie Waddell to death?"

Grueman suddenly glanced toward the door. "Unless my ears deceive me, I believe lunch has arrived."

I heard rapid footsteps and paper crinkle, then a voice called out, "Yo, Nick. You in here?"

"Come on in, Joe," Grueman said without getting up from his desk.

An energetic young black man in blue jeans and tennis shoes appeared and placed two bags in front of Grueman.

"This one's got the drinks, and in here we got two sailor sandwiches, potato salad, and pickles. That's fifteen-forty."

"Keep the change. And look, Joe, I appreciate it. Don't they ever give you a vacation?"

"People don't quit eating, man. Gotta run."

Grueman distributed the food and napkins while I desperately tried to figure out what to do. I was finding myself increasingly swayed by his demeanor and words, for there was nothing shifty about him, nothing that struck me as condescending or insincere.

"What political motivation?" I asked him again as I unwrapped my sandwich.

He popped open a ginger ale and removed the top from his container of potato salad. "Several weeks ago I thought I might just get an answer to that question," he said. "But then the person who could have helped me was suddenly found dead inside her car. And I'm quite certain you know who I'm talking about, Dr. Scarpetta. Jennifer Deighton is one of your cases, and although it has yet to be publicly stated that her death is a suicide, that is what one has been led to believe. I find the timing of her death rather remarkable, if not chilling."

"Am I to understand that you knew Jennifer Deighton?" I asked as blandly as possible.

"Yes and no. I'd never met her, and our telephone conversations, what few we had, were very brief. You see, I never contacted her until after Ronnie was dead."

"From which I am also to understand that she knew Waddell."

Grueman took a bite of his sandwich and reached for his ginger ale. "She and Ronnie definitely knew each," he said. "As you must know, Miss Deighton had a horoscope service, was into parapsychology and that sort of thing. Well, eight years ago, when Ronnie was on death row in Mecklenburg, he happened to see an advertisement for her services in some magazine. He wrote to her, initially in hopes that she could look into her crystal ball, so to speak, and tell him his future. Specifically, I think he wanted to know if he was going to die in the electric chair, and this is not an uncommon phenomenon—inmates writing psychics, palm readers, and asking about their futures, or contacting the clergy and asking for prayers. What was a little more unusual in Ronnie's case was that he and Miss Deighton apparently began an intimate correspondence that lasted until several months before his death. Then her letters to him suddenly stopped."

"Are you considering that her letters to him might have been intercepted?"

"There is no question about that. When I talked to Jennifer Deighton on the telephone, she claimed that she had continued to write to Ronnie. She also said that she had received no letters from him over the past several months, and I'm very suspicious that this is because his letters were intercepted as well."

"Why did you wait to contact her until after the execution?" I puzzled.

"I did not know about her before then. Ronnie said nothing about her to me until our last conversation, which was, perhaps, the strangest conversation I've ever had with any inmate I've represented." Grueman toyed with his sandwich and then pushed it away from him. He reached for his pipe. "I'm not sure if you're aware of this, Dr. Scarpetta, but Ronnie quit on me."

"I have no idea what you mean."

"The last time I talked with Ronnie was one week before he was to be transported from Mecklenburg to Richmond. At that time, he stated that he knew he was going to be executed and that nothing I did was going to make a difference. He said that what was going to happen to him had been set into motion since the beginning and he had accepted the inevitability of his death. He said that he was looking foward to dying and preferred that I cease pursuing federal habeas corpus relief. Then he requested that I not call him or come see him again."

"But he didn't fire you."

Grueman shot flame into the bowl of his briar pipe and sucked on the stem. "No, he did not. He simply refused to see me or talk to me on the phone."

"It would seem that this alone would have warranted a stay of execution pending a competency determination," I said.

"I tried that. I tried citing everything from *Hays* versus *Murphy* to the Lord's Prayer. The court rendered the brilliant decision that Ronnie had not asked to be executed. He'd simply stated that he looked forward to death, and the petition was denied."

"If you had no contact with Waddell in the several weeks before his execution, then how did you learn of Jennifer Deighton?"

"During my last conversation with Ronnie he made three last requests of me. The first was that I see to it that a meditation he had written was published in the newspaper days before his death. He gave this to me and I worked it out with the *Richmond Times-Dispatch*."

"I read it," I said.

"His second request—and I quote—was 'Don't let nothing happen to my friend.' And I asked him what friend he referred to, and he said, and again I quote, 'If you're a good man, look out for her. She never hurt no one.' He gave me her name and asked me not to contact her until after his death. Then I was to call and tell her how much she had meant to him. Well, of course I did not abide by that wish to the letter. I tried to contact her immediately because I knew I was losing Ronnie and I felt that something was terribly wrong. My hope was that this friend might be able to help. If they had corresponded with each other, for example, then maybe she could enlighten me."

"And did you reach her?" I asked, recalling Marino's telling me that Jennifer Deighton had been in Florida for two weeks around Thanksgiving.

"No one ever answered the phone," Grueman replied. "I tried on and off for several weeks, and then, to be frank, because of timing and health fortuities relating to the pace of litigation, the holidays, and a god-awful ambush of gout, my attention was diverted. I did not think to call Jennifer Deighton again until Ronnie was dead and I needed to contact her and convey, per Ronnie's request, that she had meant a lot to him, et cetera."

"When you had attempted to reach her earlier," I said, "did you leave messages on her answering machine?"

"It wasn't turned on. Which makes sense, in retrospect. She didn't need to return from vacation to face five hundred messages from people who can't make a decision until their horoscopes have been read. And if she left a message on her machine saying that she was out of town for two weeks, that would have been a perfect invitation for burglars."

"Then what happened when you finally reached her?"

"That was when she divulged that they had corresponded for eight years and that they loved each other. She claimed that the *truth would never be known.* I asked her what she meant but she would not tell me and got off the phone. Finally, I wrote her a letter imploring her to speak with me."

"When did you write this letter?" I asked.

"Let me see. The day after the execution. I suppose that would have been December fourteenth."

"And did she respond?"

"She did, by fax, interestingly enough. I did not know she had a fax machine, but my fax number was on my stationery. I have a copy of her fax if you would like to see it."

He shuffled through thick file folders and other paperwork on his desk. Finding the file he was looking for, he flipped through it and withdrew the fax, which I recognized instantly. "Yes, I'll cooperate," it read, "but it's too late, too late, too late. Better you should come here. This is all so wrong!" I wondered how Grueman would react if he knew that her communication with him had been recreated through image enhancement in Neils Vander's laboratory.

"Do you know what she meant? What was too late and what was so wrong?" I asked.

"Obviously, it was too late to do anything to stop Ronnie's execution since that had already occurred four days earlier. I'm not certain what she thought was so wrong, Dr. Scarpetta. You see, I have sensed for quite some time that there was something malignant about Ronnie's case. He and I never developed much of a rapport and that alone is odd. Generally, you get very close. I'm the only advocate in a system that wants you dead—the only one working for you in a system that doesn't work for you. But Ronnie was so aloof with his first attorney that this individual decided the case was hopeless and quit. Later, when I took on the case, Ronnie was just as distant. It was extraordinarily frustrating. Just when I would think he was beginning to trust me, a wall would go up. He would suddenly retreat into silence and literally begin to perspire."

"Did he seem frightened?"

"Frightened, depressed, sometimes angry."

"Are you suggesting that there was some conspiracy involved in his case and he might have told his friend about it, perhaps in one of his earlier letters to her?"

"I don't know what Jenny Deighton knew, but I suspect she knew something."

"Did Waddell refer to her as 'Jenny'?"

Grueman reached for his lighter again. "Yes."

"Did he ever mention to you a novel called *Paris Trout*? '

"That's interesting"—he looked surprised. "I haven't thought of this in quite some time, but during one of my early sessions with Ronnie several years ago, we talked about books and his poetry. He liked to read, and suggested I should read *Paris Trout*. I told him I had already read the novel, but was curious as to why he would recommend it. He said, very quietly, 'Because that's the way it works, Mr. Grueman. And there's no way you're gonna change nothing.' At the time I interpreted this to mean that he was a southern black pitted against the white man's system, and no federal habeas remedy or any other magic I might invoke during the judicial review process was going to alter his fate."

"Is this still your interpretation?"

He stared thoughtfully through a cloud of fragrant smoke. "I believe so. Why are you interested in Ronnie's recommended reading list?" He met my eyes.

"Jennifer Deighton had a copy of *Paris Trout* by her bed. Inside it was a poem that I suspect Waddell wrote for her. It's not important. I was just curious."

"But it is important or you wouldn't have inquired about it. What you're contemplating is that perhaps Ronnie recommended the novel to her for the same reason that he recommended it to me. The story, in his mind, was somehow his story. And that leads us back to the question of how much he had divulged to Miss Deighton. In other words, what secret of his did she carry with her to the grave?"

"What do you think it was, Mr. Grueman?"

"I think a very nasty indiscretion has been covered up, and for some reason Ronnie was privy to it. Maybe this relates to what goes on behind bars, that is, corruption within the prison system. I don't know but I wish I did."

"But why hide anything when you're facing death? Why not just go ahead and take your chances and talk?"

"That would be the rational thing to do, now, wouldn't it? And now that I have so patiently and generously answered your probing questions, Dr. Scarpetta, perhaps you can better understand why I have been more than a little concerned about any abuse Ronnie may have received prior to his execution. You can understand better, perhaps, my passionate opposition to capital punishment, which is cruel and unusual. You don't have to have bruises or abrasions or bleed from your nose to make it so."

"There was no evidence of physical abuse," I said. "Nor did we find drugs present. You have gotten my report."

"You are being evasive," Grueman said, knocking tobacco out of his pipe. "You are here today because you want something from me. I have given you a lot through a dialogue that I did not have to engage in. But I have been willing because I am forever in pursuit of fairness and truth, despite how I may appear to you. And there is another reason. A former student of mine is in trouble."

"If you are referring to me, then let me remind you of your own dictum. Don't make assumptions."

"I don't believe I am."

"Then I must convey acute curiosity over this sudden charitable attitude you're allegedly displaying toward a former student. In fact, Mr. Grueman, the word *charity* has never entered my mind in connection with you."

"Perhaps, then, you don't know the true meaning of the word. An act or feeling of goodwill, giving alms to the needy. Charity is giving to someone what he needs versus what you want to give him. I have always given you what you need. I gave you what you needed while you were my student, and I'm giving you what you need today, though the acts are expressed very differently because the needs are very different.

"Now I am an old man, Dr. Scarpetta, and perhaps you think I don't remember much about your days at Georgetown. But you might be surprised to hear that I remember you vividly because you were one of the most promising students I ever taught. What you did not need from me was strokes and applause. The danger for you was not that you would lose faith in yourself and your excellent mind but that you would lose yourself, period. Do you think when you looked exhausted and distracted in my class that I did not know the reason? Do you think I was unaware of your complete preoccupation with Mark James, who was mediocre by your standards, by the way? And if I appeared angry with you and very hard on you, it was because I *wanted to get your attention.* I wanted you to *get mad.* I wanted you to feel alive in the law instead of feeling only in love. I feared you would throw away a magnificent opportunity because your hormones and emotions were in overdrive. You see, we wake up one day to regret such decisions. We wake up in an empty bed with an empty day stretching before us and nothing to look forward to but empty weeks, months, and years. I was determined that you would not waste your gifts and give away your power."

I stared at him in astonishment as my face began to burn.

"I have never been sincere in my insults and lack of chivalry toward you," he went on with the same quiet intensity and precision that made him frightening in the courtroom. "These are tactics. We lawyers are famous for our tactics. They are the slices and spins we put on the ball, the angles and speed we use to bring about a certain necessary effect. At the foundation of all that I am is a sincere and passionate desire to make my students tough and pray that they make a difference in this botched-up world we live in. And I feel no disappointment in you. You are, perhaps, one of my brightest stars."

"Why are you saying all this to me?" I asked.

"Because at this time in your life, you need to know it. You are in trouble, as I've already stated. You are simply too proud to admit it."

I was silent, my thoughts engaged in a fierce debate.

"I will help you if you will allow it."

If he was telling me the truth, then it was vital that I respond in kind. I glanced toward his open door and imagined how easy it would be for anyone to walk in here. I imagined how easy it would be for someone to confront him as he hobbled to his car.

"If these incriminating stories continue to be printed in the newspaper, for example, it would behoove you to develop a few strategies—"

I interrupted him. "Mr. Grueman, when was the last time you saw Ronnie Joe Waddell?"

He paused and stared up at the ceiling. "The last time I was in his physical presence would have been at least a year ago. Typically, most of our conversations were over the phone. I would have been with him in the end had he permitted it, as I've already mentioned."

"Then you never saw him or spoke with him when he was supposedly at Spring Street awaiting execution."

"*Supposedly?* That's a curious choice of words, Dr. Scarpetta."

"We can't prove it was Waddell who was executed the night of December thirteenth."

"Certainly you're not serious." He looked amazed.

I explained all that had transpired, including that Jennifer Deighton was a homicide and Waddell's fingerprint had turned up on a dining room chair inside her home. I told him about Eddie Heath and Susan Story, and the evidence that someone had tampered with AFIS. When I was finished, Grueman was sitting very still, his eyes riveted on me.

"My Lord," he muttered.

"Your letter to Jennifer Deighton never turned up," I went on. "The police found neither that nor her original fax to you when they searched her house. Maybe someone took them. Maybe her killer burned them in her fireplace the night of her death. Or maybe she disposed of them herself because she was afraid. I do believe she was killed because of something she knew."

"And this would be why Susan Story was killed, too? Because she knew something?"

"Certainly that's possible," I said. "My point is that so far two people linked to Ronnie Waddell have been murdered. In terms of someone who might know a lot about Waddell, you would be considered high on the list."

"So you think I may be next," he said with a wry smile. "You know, perhaps my biggest grievance against the Almighty is that the difference between life and death should so often turn on timing. I consider myself forewarned, Dr.

Scarpetta. But I am not foolish enough to think that if someone intends to shoot me I can successfully elude him."

"You could at least try," I said. "You could at least take precautions."

"And I shall."

"Maybe you and your wife could go on a vacation, get out of town for a while."

"Beverly has been dead for three years," he said.

"I'm very sorry, Mr. Grueman."

"She had not been well for many years—in fact, not for most of the years we were together. Now that I have no one to depend on me, I have given myself up to my proclivities. I am an incurable workaholic who wants to change the world."

"I suspect that if anyone could come close to changing it, you could."

"That is an opinion not based on any sort of fact, but I appreciate it nonetheless. And I also want to express to you my great sadness over Mark's death. I did not know him well when he was here, but he seemed to be a decent-enough fellow."

"Thank you." I got up and put on my coat. It took me a moment to find my car keys.

He got up, too. "What do we do next, Dr. Scarpetta?"

"I don't suppose you have any letters or other items from Ronnie Waddell that might be worth processing for his latent prints?"

"I have no letters, and any documents that he might have signed would have been handled by a number of people. You're welcome to try."

"I'll let you know if we have no other alternative. But there is one final thing I've been meaning to ask." We paused in the doorway. Grueman was leaning on his cane. "You mentioned that during your last conversation with Waddell, he made three last requests. One was to publish his meditation, another to call Jennifer Deighton. What was the third?"

"He wanted me to invite Norring to the execution."

"And did you?"

"Well, of course," Grueman said. "And your fine governor didn't even have the manners to RSVP."

10

It was late afternoon, and Richmond's skyline was in view when I called Rose.

"Dr. Scarpetta, where are you?" My secretary sounded frantic. "Are you in your car?"

"Yes. I'm about five minutes from downtown."

"Well, keep driving. Don't come here right now."

"What?"

"Lieutenant Marino's trying to reach you. He said if I talk to you to tell you to call him before you do anything. He said it's very, very urgent."

"Rose, what on earth are you talking about?"

"Have you been listening to the news? Did you read the afternoon paper?"

"I've been in D.C. all day. What news?"

"Frank Donahue was found dead early this afternoon."

"The prison warden? That Frank Donahue?"

"Yes."

My hands tensed on the wheel as I stared hard at the road. "What happened?"

"He was shot. He was found in his car a couple of hours ago. It's just like Susan."

"I'm on my way," I said, gliding into the left lane and accelerating.

"I really wouldn't. Fielding's already started on him. Please call Marino. You need to read the evening paper. They know about the bullets."

"They?" I said.

"Reporters. They know about the bullets linking Eddie Heath's and Susan's cases."

I called Marino's pager and told him I was on my way home. When I pulled into my garage, I went straight to the front stoop and retrieved the evening paper.

A photograph of Frank Donahue smiled above the fold. The headline read, "STATE PENITENTIARY WARDEN SLAIN." Below this was a second story featuring the photograph of another state official—me. That story's lead was that the bullets recovered from the bodies of the Heath boy and Susan had been fired from the same gun, and a number of bizarre connections seemed to link both homicides to me. In addition to the same intimations that had run in the *Post* was information much more sinister.

My fingerprints, I was stunned to read, had been recovered from an envelope containing cash that the police had found inside Susan Story's house. I had demonstrated an "unusual interest" in Eddie Heath's case by appearing at Henrico Doctor's Hospital, prior to his death, to examine his wounds. Later I had performed his autopsy, and it was at this time that Susan refused to witness his case and supposedly fled from the morgue. When she was murdered less than two weeks later, I responded to the scene, appeared unannounced at the home of her parents directly afterward to ask them questions, and insisted on being present during the autopsy.

I was not directly assigned a motive for malevolence toward anyone, but the one implied in Susan's case was as infuriating as it was amazing. I may have been making major mistakes on the job. I had neglected to print Ronnie Joe

Waddell when his body came to the morgue after his execution. I recently had left the body of a homicide victim in the middle of a corridor, virtually in front of an elevator used by numerous people who worked in the building, thus seriously compromising the chain of evidence. I was described as aloof and unpredictable, with colleagues observing that my personality had begun to change after the death of my lover, Mark James. Perhaps Susan, who had worked by my side daily, had possessed knowledge that could ruin me professionally. Perhaps I had been paying for her silence.

"My fingerprints?" I said to Marino the instant he appeared at my door. "What the hell is this business about fingerprints belonging to me?"

"Easy, Doc."

"I might just file suit this time. This has gone too far."

"I don't think you want to be filing anything right now." He got out his cigarettes as he followed me to the kitchen, where the evening paper was spread out on the table.

"Ben Stevens is behind this."

"Doc, I think what you want to do is listen to what I've got to say."

"He's got to be the source of the leak about the bullets—"

"Doc. Goddam it, shut up."

I sat down.

"My ass is in the fire, too," he said. "I'm working the cases with you, and now suddenly you've become an element. Yes, we did find an envelope in Susan's house. It was in a dresser drawer under some clothes. There were three one-hundred-dollar bills inside it. Vander processed the envelope and several latents popped up. Two of them are yours. Your prints, like mine and those of a lot of other investigators, are in AFIS for exclusionary purposes, in case we ever do a dumbshit thing like leave our prints at a scene."

"I did not leave prints at any scene. There's a logical explanation for this. There has to be. Maybe the envelope was one I touched at some point at the office or the morgue, and Susan took it home."

"It's definitely not an office envelope," Marino said. "It's about twice as wide as a legal-size envelope and made of stiff, shiny black paper. There's no writing on it."

I looked at him in disbelief as it dawned on me. "The scarf I gave her."

"What scarf?"

"Susan's Christmas present from me was a red silk scarf I bought in San Francisco. What you're describing is the envelope it was in, a glossy black envelope made of cardboard or stiff paper. The flap closed with a small gold seal. I wrapped the present myself. Of course my prints would be on it."

"So what about the three hundred dollars?" he said, avoiding my eyes.

"I don't know anything about any money."

"I'm saying, why was it in the envelope you gave her?"

"Maybe because she wanted to hide her cash in something. The envelope was handy. Maybe she didn't want to throw it away. I don't know. I had no control over what she did with something I gave her."

"Did anybody see you give her the scarf?" he asked.

"No. Her husband wasn't home when she opened my gift."

"Yeah, well, the only gift from you anyone seemed to know about was a pink poinsettia. Don't sound like Susan said a word about you giving her a scarf."

"For God's sake, she was wearing the scarf when she was shot, Marino."

"That don't tell us where it came from."

"You're about to move into the accusatory stage," I snapped.

"I'm not accusing you of nothing. Don't you get it? This is the way it goes, goddam it. You want me to baby you and pat your hand so some other cop can bust in here and broadside you with questions like this?"

He got up and began pacing the kitchen, staring at the floor, his hands in his pockets.

"Tell me about Donahue," I said quietly.

"He was shot in his ride, probably early this morning. According to his wife, he left the house around six-fifteen. Around one-thirty this afternoon, his Thunderbird was found parked at Deep Water Terminal with him in it."

"I read that much in the paper."

"Look. The less we talk about it, the better."

"Why? Are reporters going to imply that I killed him, too?"

"Where was you at six-fifteen this morning, Doc?"

"I was getting ready to leave my house and drive to Washington."

"You got any witnesses that will verify you couldn't have been cruising around Deep Water Terminal? It's not very far from the Medical Examiner's Office, you know. Maybe two minutes."

"That's absurd."

"Get used to it. This is just the beginning. Wait until Patterson sinks his teeth into you."

Before Roy Patterson had run for Commonwealth Attorney, he had been one of the city's more combative, egotistical criminal lawyers. Back then he had never appreciated what I had to say, since in the majority of cases, medical examiner testimony does not cause jurors to think more kindly of the defendant.

"I ever told you how much Patterson hates your guts?" Marino went on. "You embarrassed him when he was a defense attorney. You sat there cool as a cat in your sharp suits and made him look like an idiot."

"He made himself look like an idiot. All I did was answer his questions."

"Not to mention, your old boyfriend Bill Boltz was one of his closest pals, and I don't even need to go into that."

"I wish you wouldn't."

"I just know Patterson's going to go after you. Shit, I bet he's a happy man right now."

"Marino, you're red as a beet. For God's sake, don't go stroking out on me."

"Let's get back to this scarf you said you gave to Susan."

"I *said* I gave to Susan?"

"What was the name of the store in San Francisco that sold it to you?" he asked.

"It wasn't a store."

He glanced sharply at me as he continued to pace.

"It was a street market. Lots of booths and stalls selling art, handmade things. Like Covent Garden," I explained.

"You got a receipt?"

"I would have had no reason to save it."

"So you don't know the name of the booth or whatever. So there's no way to verify that you bought a scarf from some artist type who uses these glossy black envelopes."

"I can't verify it."

He paced some more and I stared out the window. Clouds drifted past an oblong moon, and the dark shapes of trees moved in the wind. I got up to close the blinds.

Marino stopped pacing. "Doc, I'm going to need to go through your financial records."

I did not say anything.

"I've got to verify that you haven't made any large withdrawals of cash in recent months."

I remained silent.

"Doc, you haven't, have you?"

I got up from the table, my pulse pounding.

"You can talk to my attorney," I said.

After Marino left, I went upstairs to the cedar closet where I stored my private papers and began collecting bank statements, tax returns, and various accounting records. I thought of all the defense attorneys in Richmond who would probably be delighted if I were locked up or exiled for the rest of my days.

I was sitting in the kitchen making notes on a legal pad when my doorbell rang. I let Benton Wesley and Lucy in, and I knew instantly by their silence that it was unnecessary to tell them what was going on.

"Where's Connie?" I asked wearily.

"She's going to stay through the New Year with her family in Charlottesville."

"I'm going back to your study, Aunt Kay," Lucy said without hugging me or smiling. She left with her suitcase.

"Marino wants to go through my financial records," I said to Wesley as he followed me into the living room. "Ben Stevens is setting me up. Personnel files and copies of memos are missing from the office, and he's hoping it will appear that I took them. And Roy Patterson, according to Marino, is a happy man these days. That's the update of the hour."

"Where do you keep the Scotch?"

"I keep the good stuff in the hutch over there. Glasses are in the bar."

"I don't want to drink your good stuff."

"Well, I do." I began building a fire.

"I called your deputy chief as I was driving in. Firearms has already taken a look at the slugs that were in Donahue's brain. Winchester one-fifty-grain lead, unjacketed, twenty-two-caliber. Two of them. One went in his left cheek and traveled up through the skull, the other was a tight contact at the nape of his neck."

"Fired from the same weapon that killed the other two?"

"Yes. Do you want ice?"

"Please." I closed the screen and returned the poker to its stand. "I don't suppose any feathers were recovered from the scene or from Donahue's body."

"Not that I know of. It's clear that his assailant was standing outside the car and shot him through the open driver's window. That doesn't mean this individual wasn't inside with him earlier, but I don't think so. My guess is Donahue was supposed to meet someone at Deep Water Terminal in the parking lot. When this person arrived, Donahue rolled down his window and that was it. Did you have any luck with Downey?" He handed me my drink and settled on the couch.

"It appears that the origin of the feathers and feather particles recovered from the three other cases is common eider duck."

"A sea duck?" Wesley frowned. "The down is used in what, ski jackets, gloves?"

"Rarely. Eiderdown is extremely expensive. Your average person is not going to own anything filled with it."

I proceeded to inform Wesley of the events of the day, sparing no details as I confessed that I had spent several hours with Nicholas Grueman and did not believe he was even remotely involved in anything sinister.

"I'm glad you went to see him," Wesley said. "I was hoping you would."

"Are you surprised by how it turned out?"

"No. It makes sense the way it turned out. Grueman's predicament is somewhat similar to your own. He gets a fax from Jennifer Deighton and it looks suspicious, just as it looks suspicious that your prints were found on an envelope in Susan's dresser drawer. When violence hits close to you, you get splashed. You get dirty."

"I'm more than splashed. I feel as if I'm about to drown."

"At the moment, it seems that way. Maybe you ought to be talking to Grueman about that."

I did not reply.

"I'd want him on my side."

"I wasn't aware that you knew him."

Ice rattled quietly as Wesley sipped his drink. Brass on the hearth gleamed in the firelight. Wood popped, sending sparks swarming up the chimney.

"I know about Grueman," he said. "I know that he graduated number one from Harvard Law School, was the editor of the *Law Review,* and was offered a teaching position there but turned it down. That broke his heart. But his wife, Beverly, did not want to move from the D.C. area. Apparently, she had a lot of problems, not the least of which was a young daughter from a first marriage who was institutionalized at Saint Elizabeths at the time Grueman and Beverly met. He moved to D.C. The daughter died several years later."

"You've been running a background check on him," I said.

"Sort of."

"Since when?"

"Since I learned he had received a fax from Jennifer Deighton. By all accounts, it appears he's Mr. Clean, but someone still had to talk to him."

"That's not the only reason you suggested it to me, is it?"

"An important reason but not the only one. I thought you should go back there."

I took a deep breath. "Thank you, Benton. You are a good man with the best of intentions."

He lifted his glass to his lips and stared into the fire.

"Please don't interfere," I added.

"It's not my style."

"Of course it is. You're a pro at it. If you want to quietly steer, propel, or unplug someone from behind the scenes, you know how to do it. You know how to throw up so many obstacles and blow out so many bridges that someone like me would be lucky to find her way home."

"Marino and I are very involved in all this, Kay. Richmond P.D.'s involved. The Bureau's involved. Either we've got a psychopath out there who should have been executed or we've got somebody else who seems intent on making us think someone is out there who should have been executed."

"Marino doesn't want me involved at all," I said.

"He's in an impossible situation. He's the chief homicide investigator for the city and a member of a Bureau VICAP team, yet he's your colleague and friend. He's supposed to find out everything he can about you and what's gone on in your office. Yet his inclination is to protect you. Try to put yourself in his position."

"I will. But he needs to put himself in mine."

"That's only fair."

"The way he talks, Benton, you would think half the world has a vendetta against me and would love to see me go up in flames."

"Maybe not half the world, but there are people other than Ben Stevens who are standing around with boxes of matches and gasoline."

"Who else?"

"I can't give you names because I don't know. And I'm not going to claim that ruining you professionally is the major mission for whoever is behind all this. But I suspect it's on the agenda, if for no other reason than that the cases would be severely compromised if it appears that all evidence routed through your office is tainted. Not to mention, without you, the Commonwealth loses one of its most potent expert witnesses." He met my eyes. "You need to consider what your testimony would be worth right now. If you took the stand this minute, would you be helping or hurting Eddie Heath?"

The remark cut to the bone.

"Right this minute, I would not be helping him much. But if I default, how much will that help him or anyone?"

"That's a good question. Marino doesn't want you hurt further, Kay."

"Then perhaps you can impress upon him that the only reasonable response to such an unreasonable situation is for me to allow him to do his job while he allows me to do mine."

"Can I refresh that?" Getting up, he returned with the bottle. We didn't bother with ice.

"Benton, let's talk about the killer. In light of what's happened to Donahue, what are you thinking now?"

He set down the bottle and stirred the fire. For a moment, he stood before the fireplace, his back to me, hands in his pockets. Then he sat on the edge of the hearth, his forearms on his knees. Wesley was more restless than I had seen him in a very long time.

"If you want to know the truth, Kay, this animal scares the hell out of me."

"How is he different from other killers you have pursued?"

"I think he started out with one set of rules and then decided to change them."

"His rules or someone else's?"

"I think the rules were not his at first. Whoever was behind the conspiracy to free Waddell first made the decisions. But this guy's got his own rules now. Or maybe it would be better to say that there are no rules now. He's cunning and he's careful. So far, he's in control."

"What about motive?" I asked.

"That's hard. Maybe it would be better for me to phrase it in terms of mission or assignment. I suspect there's some method to his madness, but the madness is what turns him on. He gets off on playing with people's minds. Waddell was locked up for ten years, then suddenly the nightmare of his original crime is revisited. On the night of his execution, a boy is murdered in a sexually sadistic fashion that is reminiscent of Robyn Naismith's case. Other people start dying, and all of them are in some way connected to Waddell. Jennifer Deighton was his friend. Susan, it appears, was involved, at least tangentially, in whatever this conspiracy is. Frank Donahue was the prison warden and would have supervised the execution that occurred on the night of December thirteenth. And what is this doing to everybody else, to the other players?"

"I should think that anyone who has had any association with Ronnie Waddell, either legitimately or otherwise, would feel very threatened," I replied.

"Right. If a cop killer is on the loose and you are a cop, you know you may be next. I could walk out your door tonight and this guy's waiting in the shadows to gun me down. He could be out in his car somewhere, looking for Marino or trying to find my house. He could be fantasizing about taking out Grueman."

"Or me."

Wesley got up and began rearranging the fire again.

"Do you think it would be wise for me to send Lucy back to Miami?" I asked.

"Christ, Kay, I don't know what to tell you. She doesn't want to go home. That comes across loud and clear. You might feel better if she returned to Miami tonight. For that matter, I might feel better if you went with her. In fact, everybody—you, Marino, Grueman, Vander, Connie, Michele, me—would probably feel better if *all* of us left town. But then who would be left?"

"He would," I said. "Whoever he is."

Wesley glanced at his watch and set his glass on the coffee table. "None of us should interfere with each other," he said. "We can't afford to."

"Benton, I have to clear my name."

"It is exactly what I would do. Where do you want to start?"

"With a feather."

"Please explain."

"It's possible that this killer went out and bought some specialty item filled with eiderdown, but I'd say there's a good chance he stole it."

"That's a plausible theory."

"We can't trace the item unless we have its label or some other piece to trace back to a manufacturer, but there may be another way. Maybe something could appear in the newspaper."

"I don't think we want the killer to know he's leaking feathers everywhere. He's sure to get rid of the item in question."

"I agree. But that doesn't preclude your getting one of your journalist sources to run some trumped-up little feature about the eider duck and its prized down, and how items filled with it are so expensive that they've become a hot commodity for thieves. Maybe this could be tied in with the ski season or something."

"What? In hopes someone out there will call and say that his car was broken into and his down-filled jacket was stolen?"

"Yes. If the reporter quotes some detective who supposedly has been assigned to the thefts, this gives readers someone they can call. You know, people read a story and say, 'The same thing happened to me.' Their impulse is to help. They want to feel important. So they pick up the phone."

"I'll have to give it some thought."

"Admittedly, it's a long shot."

We began walking to the door.

"I spoke briefly with Michele before leaving the Homestead," Wesley said. "She and Lucy have already been conferring. Michele says your niece is rather frightening."

"She's been a holy terror since the day she was born."

He smiled. "Michele didn't mean it like that. She says that Lucy's intellect is frightening."

"Sometimes I worry that it's too much wattage for such a fragile vessel."

"I'm not certain she's all that fragile. Remember, I just spent the better part of two days with her. I'm very impressed with Lucy on many fronts."

"Don't you go trying to recruit her for the Bureau."

"I'll wait until she finishes college. That will take her, what? All of a year?"

Lucy did not emerge from my study until Wesley had driven off and I was carrying our glasses into the kitchen.

"Did you enjoy yourself?" I asked her.

"Sure."

"Well, I hear you got along famously with the Wesleys." I turned off the faucet and sat at the table where I'd left my legal pad.

"They're nice people."

"Rumor has it they think you're nice, too."

She opened the refrigerator door and idly stared inside. "Why was Pete here earlier?"

It seemed odd to hear Marino referred to by his first name. I supposed he and Lucy had moved from a state of cold war to détente when he had taken her shooting.

"What makes you think he was here?" I asked.

"I smelled cigarettes when I came in the house. I assume he was here unless you're smoking again." She shut the refrigerator door and came over to the table.

"I'm not smoking again, and Marino was here briefly."

"What did he want?"

"He wanted to ask me a lot of questions," I said.

"About what?"

"Why do you need to know the details?"

Her eyes moved from my face to the stack of financial files to the legal pad filled with my indecipherable penmanship. "It doesn't matter why since you obviously don't want to tell me."

"It's complicated, Lucy."

"You always say something's complicated when you want to shut me out," she said as she turned and walked away.

I felt as if my world were falling apart, the people in it scattering like dry seeds in the wind. When I watched parents with their children, I marveled over the gracefulness of their interactions and secretly feared I lacked an instinct that couldn't be learned.

I found my niece in my study sitting before the computer. Columns of numbers combined with letters of the alphabet were on the screen, and embedded here and there were fragments of what I assumed were data. She was making computations with a pencil on graph paper, and did not look up as I moved next to her.

"Lucy, your mother has had many men in and out of your house, and I am well aware of how that has made you feel. But this is not your house and I am not your mother. It is not necessary for you to feel threatened by my male colleagues and friends. It is not necessary for you to constantly be looking for evidence that some man was here, and it is unfounded for you to be suspicious of my relationship with Marino or Wesley or anyone else."

She did not respond.

I placed my hand on her shoulder. "I may not be the constant presence in your life that I wish I could be, but you are very important to me."

Erasing a number and brushing rubber particles off the paper, she said, "Are you going to get charged with a crime?"

"Of course not. I haven't committed any crimes." I leaned closer to the monitor.

"What you're looking at is a hex dump," she said.

"You were right. It's hieroglyphics."

Placing her fingers on the keyboard, Lucy began moving the cursor as she explained, "What I'm doing here is trying to get the exact position of the SID number. That's the State Identification Number, which is the unique identifier. Every person in the system has a SID number, including you, since your prints are in AFIS, too. In a fourth-generation language, like SQL, I could actually query by a column name. But in hexadecimal the language is technical and mathematical.

There are no column names, only positions in the record layout. In other words, if I wanted to go to Miami, in SQL I would simply tell the computer I want to go to Miami. But in hexadecimal, I would have to say that I want to go to a position that is this many degrees north of the equator and this many degrees east of the prime meridian.

"So to extend the geographical analogy, I'm figuring out the longitude and latitude of the SID number and also of the number that indicates the record type. Then I can write a program to search for any SID number where the record is a type two, which means a deletion, or a type three, which is an update. I'll run this program through each journal tape."

"You're assuming that if a record has been tampered with, then what was changed was the SID?" I asked.

"Let's just say it would be a whole lot easier to tamper with the SID number than it would be to mess with the actual fingerprint images on the optical disk record. And that's really all you've got in AFIS—the SID number and the corresponding prints. The person's name, history, and other personal information are in his CCH, or Computerized Criminal History, which resides on CCRE, or the Central Criminal Records Exchange."

"As I understand it, the records in CCRE are matched to the prints in AFIS by the SID numbers," I said.

"Exactly."

Lucy was still working when I went to bed. I fell right to sleep, only to awaken at two A.M. I did not drift off again until five, and my alarm roused me less than an hour later. I drove downtown in the dark and listened as one of the local radio announcers gave a news update. He reported that police had questioned me, and I had refused to disclose information pertaining to my financial records. He went on to remind everyone that Susan Story had deposited thirty-five hundred dollars in her checking account just weeks before her murder.

When I got to the office, I had barely taken off my coat when Marino called.

"The damn major can't keep his mouth shut," he said right off.

"Obviously."

"Shit, I'm sorry."

"It's not your fault. I know you have to report to him."

Marino hesitated. "I need to ask you about your guns. You don't own a twenty-two, right?"

"You know all about my handguns. I have a Ruger and a Smith and Wesson. And if you pass that along to Major Cunningham, I'm sure I'll hear about it on the radio within the hour."

"Doc, he wants them submitted to the firearms lab."

For an instant, I thought Marino was joking.

"He thinks you should be willing to submit them for examination," he added. "He thinks it's a good idea to show right away that the bullets recovered from Susan, the Heath kid, and Donahue couldn't have been fired from your guns."

"Did you tell the major that the revolvers I have are *thirty-eights*?" I asked, incensed.

"Yes."

"And he knows that *twenty-two* slugs were recovered from the bodies?"

"Yeah. I went round and round with him about it."

"Well, ask him for me if he knows of an adapter that would make it possible to use twenty-two rim-fire cartridges in a thirty-eight revolver. If he does, tell him he ought to present a paper on it at the next American Academy of Forensic Sciences meeting."

"I really don't think you want me to tell him that."

"This is nothing but politics, publicity ploys. It's not even rational."

Marino did not comment.

"Look," I said evenly, "I have broken no laws. I am not

submitting my financial records, firearms, or anything else to anyone until I have been appropriately advised. I understand that you must do your job, and I want you to do your job. What I want is to be left alone so I can do mine. I have three cases downstairs and Fielding's off to court."

But I was not to be left alone, and this was made clear when Marino and I concluded our conversation and Rose appeared in my office. Her face was pale, her eyes frightened.

"The governor wants to see you," she said.

"When?" I asked as my heart skipped.

"At nine."

It was already eight-forty.

"Rose, what does he want?"

"The person who called didn't say."

Fetching my coat and umbrella, I walked out into a winter rain that was just beginning to freeze. As I hurried along 14th Street, I tried to recall the last time I had spoken to Governor Joe Norring and decided it was almost a year ago at a black-tie reception at the Virginia Museum. He was Republican, Episcopalian, and held a law degree from UVA. I was Italian, Catholic, born in Miami, and schooled in the North. In my heart I was a Democrat.

The Capitol resides on Shockhoe Hill and is surrounded by an ornamental iron fence erected in the early nineteenth century to keep out trespassing cattle. The white brick building Jefferson designed is typical of his architecture, a pure symmetry of cornices and unfluted columns with Ionic capitals inspired by a Roman temple. Benches line the granite steps leading up through the grounds, and as freezing rain fell relentlessly I thought of my annual spring resolution to take a lunch hour away from my desk and sit here in the sun. But I had yet to do it. Countless days of my life had been lost to artificial light and windowless, confined spaces that defied any architectural rubric.

Inside the Capitol, I found a ladies' room and attempted

to bolster my confidence by making repairs. Despite my efforts with lipstick and brush, the mirror had nothing reassuring to say. Bedraggled and unsettled, I took the elevator to the top of the Rotunda, where previous governors gaze sternly from oil portraits three floors above Houdon's marble statue of George Washington. Midway along the south wall, journalists milled about with notepads. cameras, and microphones. It did not occur to me that I was their quarry until, as I approached, video cameras were mounted on shoulders, microphones were drawn like swords, and shutters began clicking with the rapidity of automatic weapons.

"Why won't you disclose your finances?"

"Dr. Scarpetta . . ."

"Did you give money to Susan Story?"

"What kind of handgun do you own?"

"Doctor . . ."

"Is it true that personnel records have disappeared from your office?"

They chummed the water with their accusations and questions as I fixed my attention straight ahead, my thoughts paralyzed. Microphones jabbed at my chin, bodies brushed against me, and lights flashed in my eyes. It seemed to take forever to reach the heavy mahogany door and escape into the genteel stillness behind it.

"Good morning," said the receptionist from her fine wood fortress beneath a portrait of John Tyler.

Across the room, at a desk before a window, a plainclothes Executive Protection Unit officer glanced at me, his face inscrutable.

"How did the press know about this?" I asked the receptionist.

"Pardon?" She was an older woman, dressed in tweed.

"How did they know I was meeting with the governor this morning?"

"I'm sorry. I wouldn't know."

I settled on a pale blue love seat. Walls were papered in the same pale blue; the furniture was antique, with chair seats covered in needlepoint depicting the state seal. Ten minutes slowly passed. A door opened and a young man I recognized as Norring's press secretary stepped inside and smiled at me.

"Dr. Scarpetta, the governor will see you now." He was slight of build, blond, and dressed in a navy suit and yellow suspenders.

"I apologize for making you wait. Unbelievable weather we're having. And I understand it's supposed to drop into the teens tonight. The streets will be glass in the morning."

He ushered me through one well-appointed office after another, where secretaries concentrated behind computer screens and aides moved about silently and with purpose. Knocking lightly on a formidable door, he turned the brass knob and stepped aside, chivalrously touching my back as I preceded him into the private space of the most powerful man in Virginia. Governor Norring did not get up from his padded leather chair behind his uncluttered burled walnut desk. Two chairs were arranged across from him and I was shown to one while he continued perusing a document.

"Would you like something to drink?" the press secretary asked me.

"No, thank you."

He left, softly shutting the door.

The governor placed the document on the desk and leaned back in his chair. He was a distinguished-looking man with just enough irregularity of his features to cause one to take him seriously, and he was impossible to miss when he walked into a room. Like George Washington, who was six foot two in a day of short men, Norring was well above average height, his hair thick and dark at an age when men are balding or going gray.

"Doctor, I've been wondering if there might be a way to

extinguish this fire of controversy before it's completely out of control." He spoke with the soothing cadences of Virginian conversation.

"Governor Norring, I certainly hope there is."

"Then please help me understand why you are not cooperating with the police."

"I wish to seek the advice of an attorney, and have not had a chance to do so. I don't view this as a lack of cooperation."

"It certainly is your right not to incriminate yourself," he said slowly. "But the very suggestion of your invoking the Fifth only darkens the cloud of suspicion surrounding you. I'm certain you must be aware of that."

"I'm aware that I will probably be criticized no matter what I do right now. It is reasonable and prudent for me to protect myself."

"Were you making payments to your morgue supervisor, Susan Story?"

"No, sir, I was not. I have done nothing wrong."

"Dr. Scarpetta." He leaned forward in his chair and laced his fingers on top of the desk. "It is my understanding that you are unwilling to cooperate by turning over any records that might substantiate these claims you've made."

"I have not been informed that I am a suspect in any crime, nor have I received Miranda warnings. I have waived no rights. I have had no opportunity to seek counsel. At this moment, it is not my intention to open the files of my professional and personal life to the police or anyone else."

"Then, in summary, you are refusing to make full disclosure," he said.

When a state official is accused of conflict of interests or any other manner of unethical behavior, there are only two defenses, full disclosure or resignation. The latter yawned before me like an abyss. It was clear that the governor's intention was to maneuver me over the edge.

"You are a forensic pathologist of national stature and the Chief Medical Examiner of this Commonwealth," he went on. "You've enjoyed a very distinguished career and an impeccable reputation in the law enforcement community. But in the matter before us, you are showing poor judgment. You are not being meticulous about avoiding any appearance of impropriety."

"I have been meticulous, Governor, and I have done nothing wrong," I repeated. "The facts will bear this out, but I will not discuss the matter further until I speak with an attorney. And I will not make full disclosure unless it is through him and before a judge in a sealed hearing."

"A sealed hearing?" His eyes narrowed.

"Certain details of my personal life affect individuals besides me."

"Who? Husband, children, lover? It is my understanding you have none of these, that you live alone and are—to use the cliché—wedded to your work. Just who might you be protecting?"

"Governor Norring, you are baiting me."

"No, ma'am. I'm simply looking for anything to corroborate your claims. You say you are concerned with protecting others, and I'm inquiring as to who these *others* might be. Certainly not patients. Your patients are deceased."

"I do not feel that you are being fair or impartial," I said, and I knew I sounded cold. "Nothing about this meeting was fair from the outset. I'm given twenty minutes' notice to be here and am not told the agenda—"

He interrupted. "Why, Doctor, I should think you might have guessed the agenda."

"Just as I should have guessed that our meeting was a public event."

"I understand the press came out in force." His expression did not change.

"I'd like to know how this occurred," I said heatedly.

"If you're asking if this office notified the press of our meeting, I'm telling you that we did not."

I did not respond.

"Doctor, I'm not certain you understand that as public servants we must operate by a different set of rules. In a sense, we are not allowed private lives. Or perhaps it would be better to say that if our ethics or judgment are questioned, the public has a right to examine, in some instances, the most private aspects of our existences. Whenever I am about to undertake a certain activity or even write a check, I have to ask myself if what I am doing will hold up under the most intense scrutiny."

I noticed that he scarcely used his hands when he talked, and that the fabric and design of his suit and tie were a lesson in understated extravagance. My attention darted here and there as he continued his admonition, and I knew that nothing I might do or say would save me in the end. Though I had been appointed by the health commissioner, I would not have been offered the job, nor could I last long in it without the support of the governor. The quickest way to lose that was to cause him embarrassment or conflict, which I had already accomplished. He had the power to force my resignation. I had the power to buy myself a little time by threatening to embarrass him more.

"Doctor, perhaps you would like to tell me what you would do if you were in my position?"

Beyond the window rain was mixed with sleet, and buildings in the banking district were bleak against a dreary, pewter sky. I stared at Norring in silence, then quietly spoke. "Governor Norring, I would like to think that I would not summon the chief medical examiner to my office to gratuitously insult her, both professionally and personally, and then demand of her that she surrender the rights guaranteed to every person by the Constitution.

"Further, I would like to think that I would accept this

person's innocence until she had been proven guilty, and would not compromise her ethics and the Hippocratic oath she had sworn to uphold by demanding that she open confidential files to public scrutiny when doing so might do harm to herself and to others. I would like to think, Governor Norring, that I would not give an individual who has served the Commonwealth faithfully no choice but to resign for cause."

The governor absently picked up a silver fountain pen as he considered my words. For me to resign for cause after meeting with him would imply to all of the reporters waiting beyond his office door that I had quit because Norring had asked me to do something that I considered unethical.

"I have no interest in your resigning at this moment," he said coldly. "In fact, I would not accept your resignation. I am a fair man, Dr. Scarpetta, and, I hope, a wise one. And wisdom dictates that I cannot have someone performing legal autopsies on the victims of homicide when this individual, herself, is being implicated in homicide or as an accessory to it. Therefore, I think it best to relieve you with pay until this matter is resolved." He reached for the phone. "John, would you be so kind as to show the chief medical examiner out?"

Almost instantly, the smiling press secretary appeared.

As I emerged from the governor's offices, I was accosted from every direction. Flashguns went off in my eyes, and it seemed that everyone was shouting. The lead news item the rest of the day and the following morning was that the governor had temporarily relieved me of my duties until I could clear my name. An editorial conjectured that Norring had shown himself to be a gentleman, and if I were a lady I would offer to step down.

11

Friday I stayed home in front of the fire, continuing the tedious and frustrating job of making notes to myself as I attempted to document my every move over the past few weeks. Unfortunately, I was in my car driving home from the office at the time the police believed Eddie Heath was abducted from the convenience store. When Susan was murdered, I was home alone, for Marino had taken Lucy shooting. I was also by myself the early morning that Frank Donahue was shot. I had no witnesses to testify to my activities during the three murders.

Motive and modus operandi would be significantly more difficult to sell. It is very uncommon for a woman to kill execution style, and there could be no motive at all in Eddie Heath's slaying unless I were a closet sexual sadist.

I was deep in thought when Lucy called out, "I've got something."

She was seated before the computer, the chair swiveled around to one side, her feet propped up on an ottoman. In her lap were numerous sheets of paper, and to the right of the keyboard was my Smith and Wesson thirty-eight.

"Why do you have my revolver in here?" I asked uneasily.

"Pete told me to dry-fire it whenever I have a chance. So I've been practicing while running my program through the journal tapes."

I picked up the revolver, pushed the thumb latch, and checked the chambers, just to be sure.

"Though I've still got a few tapes to run through, I think I've already gotten a hit on what we're looking for," she said.

I felt a surge of optimism as I pulled up a chair.

"The journal tape for December ninth shows three interesting TUs."

"TUs?" I asked.

"Tenprint Updates," Lucy explained. "We're talking about three records. One was completely dropped or deleted. The SID number of another was altered. Then we have a third record which was a new entry made around the same time the other two were deleted or changed. I logged into CCRE and ran the SID numbers of both the altered record and the new record entered. The altered record comes back to Ronnie Joe Waddell."

"What about the new record?" I said.

"That's spooky. There's no criminal history. I entered the SID number five times and it kept coming back to 'no record found.' Do you understand the significance?"

"Without a history in CCRE, we have no way of knowing who this person is."

Lucy nodded. "Right. You've got someone's prints and SID number in AFIS, but there's no name or other personal identifiers to match him up with. And that would indicate to me that somebody dropped this person's record from CCRE. In other words, CCRE has been tampered with, too."

"Let's go back to Ronnie Waddell," I said. "Can you reconstruct what was done to his record?"

"I've got a theory. First, you need to know that the SID number is a unique identifier and has a unique index, meaning the system won't allow you to enter a duplicate value. So if, for example, I wanted to switch SID numbers with you, I'd have to delete your record first. Then, after I've changed my SID number to yours, I'd reenter your record, giving you my old SID number."

"And that's what you think happened?" I asked.

"Such a transaction would explain the TUs I've found in the journal tape for December ninth."

Four days before Waddell's execution, I thought.

"There's more," Lucy said. "On December sixteenth, Waddell's record was deleted from AFIS."

"How can that be?" I asked, baffled. "A print from Jennifer Deighton's house came back to Waddell when Vander ran it through AFIS a little over a week ago."

"AFIS crashed on December sixteenth at ten-fifty-six A.M., exactly ninety-eight minutes after Waddell's record was deleted," Lucy replied. "The data base was restored with the journal tapes, but you've got to keep in mind that a backup is done only once a day, late in the afternoon. Therefore, any changes made to the data base the morning of December sixteenth hadn't been backed up yet when the system crashed. When the data base was restored, so was Waddell's record."

"You mean someone tampered with Waddell's SID number four days before his execution? Then three days after his execution, someone deleted his record from AFIS?"

"That's the way it looks to me. What I can't figure is why the person didn't just delete his record in the first place. Why go to all the trouble to change the SID number, only to turn around and delete his entire record?"

Neils Vander had a simple answer to that when I called him moments later.

"It's not unusual for an inmate's prints to be deleted from AFIS after he's dead," Vander said. "In fact, the only reason we wouldn't delete a deceased inmate's records would be if it were possible his prints might turn up in any unsolved cases. But Waddell had been in prison for nine, ten years—he'd been out of commission too long to make it worthwhile to keep his prints on line."

"Then the deletion of his record on December sixteenth would have been routine," I said.

"Absolutely. But it would not have been routine to delete his record on December ninth, when Lucy believes his SID number was altered, because Waddell was still alive then."

"Neils, what do you think this is all about?"

"When you change somebody's SID number, Kay, in effect you have changed his identity. I may get a hit on his prints, but when I enter the corresponding SID number in CCRE, it's not his history I'm going to get. I'll either get no history at all, or the history of somebody else."

"You got a hit on a print left at Jennifer Deighton's house," I said. "You entered the corresponding SID number in CCRE and it came back to Ronnie Waddell. Yet we now have reason to believe his original SID number was changed. We really don't know who left the print on her dining room chair, do we?"

"No. And it's becoming clear that someone has gone to a lot of trouble to make sure we can't verify who that person might be. I can't prove it's not Waddell. I can't prove that it is."

Images flashed in my mind as he spoke.

"In order to verify that Waddell did not leave that print on Jennifer Deighton's chair, I need an old print of his that I can trust, one that I know couldn't have been tampered with. But I just don't know where else to look."

I envisioned dark paneling and hardwood floors, and dried blood the color of garnets.

"Her house," I muttered.

"Whose house?" Vander puzzled.

"Robyn Naismith's house," I said.

* * *

Ten years previously, when Robyn Naismith's house was processed by the police, they would not have arrived with laser or Luma-Lite. There was no such thing as DNA printing then. There was no automated fingerprint system in Virginia, no computerized means to enhance a bloody partial print left on a wall or anywhere else. Though new technology generally is irrelevant in cases that have long been closed, there are exceptions. I believed Robyn Naismith's murder was one of them.

If we could spray her house with chemicals, it was possible we could literally resurrect the scene. Blood clots, drips, drops, spatters, stains, and screams bright red. It seeps into crevices and cracks, and sneaks under cushions and floors. Though it may disappear with washing and fade with the years, it never completely goes away. Like the writing that wasn't there on the sheet of paper found on Jennifer Deighton's bed, there was blood invisible to the naked eye inside the rooms where Robyn Naismith had been accosted and killed. Unaided by technology, police had found one bloody print during the original investigation of the crime. Maybe Waddell had left more. Maybe they were still there.

Neils Vander, Benton Wesley, and I drove west toward the University of Richmond, a splendid collection of Georgian buildings surrounding a lake between Three Chopt and River roads. It was from here that Robyn Naismith had graduated with honors many years before, and her love of the area had been such that she had later bought her first home two blocks from the campus.

Her former small brick house with its mansard roof was set on a half-acre lot. I was not surprised that the site should have been ideal for a burglar. The yard was dense with trees, the back of the house dwarfed by three gigantic magnolias that completely blocked the sun. I doubted the neighbors on either side could have seen or heard anything at Robyn Naismith's house, had they been home. The morning Robyn was murdered, her neighbors were at work.

Due to the circumstances that had placed the house on the market ten years ago, the price had been low for the neighborhood. We'd discovered the university had decided to buy it for faculty housing, and had kept much of what was left inside it. Robyn had been unmarried, an only child, and her parents in northern Virginia did not want her furnishings. I suspected they could not bear to live with or even look at them. Professor Sam Potter, a bachelor who taught German, had been renting the house from his employer since its purchase.

As we gathered camera equipment, containers of chemicals, and other items from the trunk, the back door opened. An unwholesome-looking man greeted us with an uninspired good-morning.

"You need a hand with that?" Sam Potter came down the steps, sweeping his long, receding black hair out of his eyes and smoking a cigarette. He was short and pudgy, his hips wide like a woman's.

"If you want to get the box here," Vander said.

Potter dropped the cigarette to the ground and didn't bother stamping it out. We followed him up the steps and into a small kitchen with old avocado-green appliances and dozens of dirty dishes. He led us through the dining room, with laundry piled on the table, then into the living room at the front of the house. I set down what I was carrying and tried not to register my shock as I recognized the console television connected to a cable outlet in the wall, the draperies, the brown leather couch, the parquet floor, now scuffed and as dull as mud. Books and papers were scattered everywhere, and Potter began to talk as he carelessly collected them.

"As you can see, I'm not domestically inclined," he said,

his German accent distinct. "I will stick these things on the dining room table for now. There," he said when he returned. "Anything else you would like me to move?" He slipped a pack of Camels from the breast pocket of his white shirt and dug a book of matches from his faded denim jeans. A pocket watch was attached to a belt loop by a leather thong, and I noticed a number of things as he slid it out to glance at the time and then lit the cigarette. His hands trembled, his fingers were swollen, and broken blood vessels covered his cheekbones and nose. He had not bothered to empty ashtrays, but he had collected bottles and glasses and had been careful to carry out the trash.

"This is fine. You don't need to move anything else," Wesley said. "If we do, we'll put it back."

"And you said this chemical you're using won't damage anything and isn't toxic to humans?"

"No, it's not hazardous. It will leave a grainy residue—similar to when salt water dries," I said to him. "We'll do our best to clean up."

"I really don't want to be here while you do this," Potter said, taking a nervous drag on the cigarette. "Can you give me an approximation of how much time it will require?"

"Hopefully, no more than two hours." Wesley was looking around the room, and though his face was completely devoid of expression, I could imagine what was going through his mind.

I took off my coat and didn't know where to put it, while Vander opened a box of film.

"Should you finish before I get back, please shut the door and make sure it's locked. I don't have an alarm to worry about." Potter went back out through the kitchen, and when he started his car it sounded like a diesel bus.

"It's a shame, really," Vander said as he lifted two bottles of chemicals from a box. "This could be a very nice house. But inside it's not much better than a lot of slums I've seen.

Did you notice the scrambled eggs in the skillet on the stove? What more do you want to pick up here?" He squatted on the floor. "I don't want to mix this up until we're ready."

"I'd say we need to move as much out of here as we can. You've got the pictures, Kay?" Wesley said.

I got out Robyn Naismith's scene photographs. "You've noticed that our professor friend is living with her furniture," I said.

"Well, then we'll leave it here," Vander said as if it were common for furniture from a ten-year-old murder scene to still be in place. "But the rug's got to go. I can tell that didn't come with the house."

"How?" Wesley stared down at the blue-and-red braided rug beneath his feet. It was filthy and curling up at the edges.

"If you lift up the edge, you can see that the parquet is just as dull and scratched underneath as it is everywhere else. The rug hasn't been here long. Besides, it doesn't look very well made. I doubt it would have lasted all this time."

Spreading several photographs on the floor, I turned them this way and that until the perspectives were right and we could tell what needed to be moved. What furnishings were original to the room had been rearranged. As much as it was possible to do so, we began to re-create the scene of Robyn's death.

"Okay, the ficus tree goes over there," I said like a stage director. "Right, but slide the couch back about two more feet, Neils. And that way just a little bit more. The tree was maybe four inches from the left armrest. A little closer. That's good."

"No, it's not. The branches are over the couch."

"The tree's a little bigger now."

"I can't believe it's still alive. I'm surprised anything could live around Professor Potter except maybe bacteria or fungi."

"And the rug goes?" Wesley took off his jacket.

"Yes. She had a small runner by the front door and another small Oriental under the coffee table. Most of the floor was bare."

He got down on his hands and knees and began to roll up the rug.

I went over to the television and studied the VCR on top and the cable connection leading into the wall.

"This has got to go against the wall opposite the couch and the front door. Either of you gentlemen good with VCRs and cable connections?"

"No," they answered simultaneously.

"Then I'm left to my own devices. Here goes."

I disconnected the cable and the VCR, unplugged the TV, and carefully slid it across the bare, dusty floor. Referring to the photographs again, I moved it a few more feet until it was directly opposite the front door. Next I surveyed the walls. Potter apparently collected art and was fond of an artist whose name I could not quite make out, but it looked French. The sketches were charcoal studies of the female form with lots of curves, pink splotches, and triangles. One by one they all came down and I propped them against the walls in the dining room. By this point, the room was almost bare and I was itching from the dust.

Wesley wiped his forehead on the back of his arm. "Are we about ready?" He looked at me.

"I think so. Of course, not everything is here. She had three barrel chairs right over there." I pointed.

"They're in the bedrooms," Vander said. "Two in one bedroom and one in the other. Do you want me to bring them out?"

"Might as well."

He and Wesley carried in the chairs.

"She had a painting on that wall over there, and another one to the right of the door leading into the dining room,"

I pointed out. "A still life and an English landscape. So Potter couldn't live with her art but didn't seem to have a problem with anything else."

"We need to go around the house and close all blinds, shades, and curtains," Vander said. "If any light is still coming through, then tear off a section of this paper"—he pointed to a roll of heavy brown paper on the floor—"and tape it over the window."

For the next fifteen minutes, the house was filled with the sounds of footsteps, venetian blinds rattling, and scissors slicing through paper. Occasionally somebody swore loudly when the paper had been cut too short or the tape stuck to nothing but itself. I stayed in the living room and covered the glass in the front door and in the two windows facing the street. When the three of us reconvened and turned out the lights, the house was pitch-black. I could not even see my hand in front of my face.

"Perfect," Vander said as the overhead light went back on.

Putting on gloves, he set bottles of distilled water, chemicals, and two plastic spray bottles on the coffee table. "Here's the way we're going to work this," he said. "Dr. Scarpetta, you can spray while I videotape, and if an area reacts, just keep spraying it until I tell you to move on."

"What do you want me to do?" Wesley asked.

"Keep out of the way."

"What's in this stuff?" he asked as Vander unscrewed the caps from bottles of dry chemicals.

"You don't really want to know," I replied.

"I'm a big boy. You can tell me."

"The reagent's a mixture of sodium perborate, which Neils is mixing with distilled water, and three-aminophthalhydrazide and sodium carbonate," I said, getting a packet of gloves out of my pocketbook.

"And you're certain it will work on blood this old?" Wesley asked.

"Actually, aged and decomposed blood reacts better with luminol than do fresh bloodstains because the more oxidized the blood, the better. As blood ages, it becomes more strongly oxidized."

"I don't think any of the wood in here is salt treated, do you?" Vander looked around.

"I shouldn't think so." I explained to Wesley, "The biggest problem with luminol is false positives. A number of things react with it, such as copper and nickel, and the copper salts in salt-treated wood."

"It also likes rust, household bleach, iodine, and formalin," Vander added. "Plus, the peroxidases found in bananas, watermelon, citrus fruit, a number of vegetables. Also horseradish."

Wesley looked at me with a smile.

Vander opened an envelope and removed two squares of filter paper that were stained with dried, diluted blood. Then he added mixture A to B and told Wesley to hit the lights. A couple of quick sprays, and a bluish white neon glow appeared on the coffee table. It began to fade almost as quickly as it had appeared.

"Here," Vander said to me.

I felt the spray bottle touch my arm, and took hold of it. A tiny red light went on as Vander depressed the power button on the video camera; then the night-vision lamp burned white and looked wherever he did like a luminescent eye.

"Where are you?" Vander's voice sounded to my left.

"I'm in the center of the room. I can feel the edge of the coffee table against my leg," I said, as if we were children playing in the dark.

"I'm way the hell out of the way." Wesley's voice carried from the direction of the dining room.

Vander's white light slowly moved toward me. I reached out and touched his shoulder. "Ready?"

"I'm recording. Start and just keep going until I tell you to stop."

I began spraying the floor around us, my finger nonstop on the trigger as a mist floated over me and shapes and geometrical configurations materialized around my feet. For an instant, it was like speeding through the dark over the illuminated grid of a city far below. Old blood trapped in the crevices of the parquet emitted a blue-white glow. I sprayed and sprayed, without having any real sense of where I was in relation to anything else, and saw footprints all over the room. I bumped against the ficus tree and dim white streaks appeared on the planter that held it. To my right smeared handprints flashed on the wall.

"Lights," Vander said.

Wesley turned on the overhead light and Vander mounted a thirty-five-millimeter camera on a tripod to keep it still. The only light available would be the fluorescence of the luminol, and the film would need a long exposure time to capture it. I retrieved a full bottle of luminol and, when the lights were out again, resumed spraying the smeared handprints on the wall while the camera captured the eerie images on film. Then we moved on. Lazy, wide swipes appeared on paneling and parquet, and the stitching on the leather couch was a neon hatch line incompletely tracing the square shapes of the cushions.

"Can you lift them out of the way?" Vander asked.

One by one I slid the cushions onto the floor and sprayed down the couch's frame. The spaces between the cushions glowed. On the backrest appeared more swipes and smears, and on the ceiling appeared a constellation of small, bright stars. It was on the old television that we got our first pyrophoric display of false positives, as metal around the dials and screen lit up and cable connecters turned the blue-white of thin milk. There was nothing remarkable about the TV, only a few smudges that might be blood, but the floor directly in front of it, where Robyn's body had been found, went crazy. The blood was so pervasive that I could see the edges of the parquet's inlays and the direction of the wood fibers constituting the grain. A drag mark feathered out several feet from the densest concentration of luminescence, and nearby was a curious pattern of tangential rings made by an object with a circumference slightly smaller than a basketball.

The search did not end in the living room. We began to follow footprints. At intervals we were forced to turn on lights, mix more luminol, and move clutter out of the way, particularly in the linguistic landfill that once had been Robyn's bedroom and now was where Professor Potter lived. The floor was several inches deep in research papers, journal articles, exams, and scores of books written in German, French, and Italian. Clothes were strewn about and draped over things so haphazardly it was as if a whirlwind had kicked up in the closet and created a vortex in the center of the room. We picked up as best we could, creating stacks and piles on the unmade double bed. Then we followed Waddell's bloody path.

It led me into the bathroom, with Vander at my heels. Shoe prints and smudges were scattered about the floor, and the same circular patterns that we had found in the living room fluoresced by the side of the bathtub. When I began spraying the walls, halfway up and on either side of the toilet, two huge handprints suddenly appeared. The video camera's light floated closer.

Then Vander's voice said excitedly, "Flip on the light."

Potter's powder room was, to say the least, as disreputably maintained as the rest of his domain. Vander almost had his nose to the wall as he scrutinized the area where the prints had appeared.

"Can you see them?"

"Umm. Maybe barely." He cocked his head to one side, then the other, squinting. "This is fantastic. You see, the wallpaper is this deep blue design, so nothing much is going to show to the naked eye. And it's plasticized or vinyl—a good surface for prints, in other words."

"Jesus," said Wesley, who was standing in the doorway of the bathroom. "The damn toilet doesn't look like it's been cleaned since he moved in. Hell, it's not even flushed."

"Even if he did mop up or wipe down the walls from time to time, you really can't get rid of every trace of blood," I said to Vander. "On a linoleum floor like this, for example, a residue gets down in the pebbly surface, and luminol is going to bring it up."

"Are you saying that if we sprayed down this place again in another ten years, the blood would still be here?" Wesley was amazed.

"The only way you could eradicate most of the blood would be to repaint everything, repaper the walls, refinish the floors, and pitch the furniture," Vander said. "If you want to get rid of absolutely every trace, you'd have to tear down the house and start over."

Wesley looked at his watch. "We've been here three and a half hours."

"Here's what I suggest we do," I said. "Benton, you and I can begin restoring the rooms to their normal state of chaos, and Neils, we'll leave you to do what you need to do."

"Fine. I'll get the Luma-Lite set up in here, and keep your fingers crossed that it can enhance the ridge detail."

We returned to the living room. While Vander carried the portable Luma-Lite and camera equipment back to the bath, Wesley and I looked around at the couch, the old TV, and the dusty, scarred floor, both of us somewhat dazed. With the lights on there was not so much as the slightest trace of the horror we had seen in the dark. On this sunny winter's afternoon, we had crawled back in time and witnessed what Ronnie Joe Waddell had done.

Wesley stood very still near the paper-covered window. "I'm afraid to sit anywhere or lean up against anything. Christ. There's blood all over this goddam house."

As I looked around, I pictured fading white in the blackness, my eyes traveling slowly from the couch, across the floor, and stopping at the TV. The couch's cushions were still on the floor where I had left them, and I squatted to take a closer look. The blood that had seeped into the brown stitching was not visible now, nor were the streaks and smears on the brown leather backrest. But a careful examination revealed something that was important but not necessarily surprising. On the side of one of the seat cushions that had been flush against the backrest I found a linear cut that was, at most, three-quarters of an inch long.

"Benton, was Waddell left-handed, by chance?"

"It seems to me he was."

"They thought he stabbed and beat her on the floor near the TV because there was so much blood around her body," I said, "but he didn't. He killed her on the couch. I think I need to go outside. If this place weren't such a sewer, I'd be tempted to pinch one of the professor's cigarettes."

"You've been good for too long," Wesley said. "An unfiltered Camel would land you on your ass. Go on and get some fresh air. I'll start cleaning up."

I left the house to the sound of paper being ripped down from the windows.

That night began the most peculiar New Year's Eve in memory for Benton Wesley, Lucy, and me. I wouldn't go so far as to say the holiday was all that odd for Neils Vander. I had talked to him at seven P.M., and he was still in his lab, but that was fairly normal for a man whose raison d'être would cease to exist were the fingerprints of two individuals ever found to be the same.

Vander had edited the scene videocassette tapes to a VCR and turned copies over to me late that afternoon. For the better part of the early evening, Wesley and I had been stationed in front of my television, taking notes and making diagrams as we slowly went through the footage. Lucy, meanwhile, was working on dinner, and came into the living room only briefly from time to time to catch a glimpse. The luminescent images on the dark screen did not seem to disturb her. At a glance, the uninitiated could not possibly know what they meant.

By eight-thirty, Wesley and I had gone through the tapes and completed our notes. We believed we had charted the course of Robyn Naismith's killer from the moment she walked into her house to Waddell's exit through the kitchen door. It was the first time in my career I had retrospectively worked the scene of a homicide that had been solved for years. But the scenario that emerged was important for one very good reason. It demonstrated, at least to our satisfaction, that what Wesley had told me at the Homestead was correct. Ronnie Joe Waddell did not fit the profile of the monster we were now tracking.

The latent smudges, smears, spatters, and spurts that we had followed were as close to an instant replay as I had ever seen in the reconstruction of a crime. Though the courts might consider much of what we determined was opinion, it did not matter. Waddell's personality did, and we felt pretty certain that we had captured it.

Because the blood we had found in other areas of the house clearly had been tracked and transferred by Waddell, it was realistic to say that his assault of Robyn Naismith was restricted to the living room, where she died. The kitchen and front doors were equipped with deadbolt locks that could not be opened without a key. Since Waddell had entered the house through a window and left through the kitchen door, it had been surmised that when Robyn returned from the store, she had come in through the kitchen. Perhaps she had not bothered to relock the door, but more likely she had not had time. It had been conjectured that while Waddell was ransacking her belongings, he heard her drive up and park behind the house. He went into the kitchen and got a steak knife from the stainless steel set hanging on a wall. When she unlocked the door, he was waiting. Chances are, he simply grabbed her first and forced her through the open doorway that led into the living room. He may have talked to her for a while. He may have demanded money. He may have been with her only moments before the confrontation became physical.

Robyn had been dressed and sitting or supine on the end of the couch near the ficus tree when Waddell struck the first blow with the knife. The blood spatters that had appeared on the backrest of the couch, the planter, and the dark paneling nearby were consistent with an arterial spurt, caused when an artery is severed. The resulting spatter pattern is reminiscent of an electrocardiogram tracing due to fluctuations of arterial blood pressure, and one has no blood pressure unless he or she is alive.

So we knew that Robyn was alive and on the couch when she was first assaulted. But it was unlikely she was still breathing when Waddell removed her clothing, which upon later examination revealed a single three-quarters-of-an-inch cut in the front of the bloodstained blouse where the knife had been plunged into her chest and moved back and forth to completely transect her aorta. Since she was stabbed many more times than that, and bitten, it was safe to conclude that most of Waddell's frenzied, piqueristic attack on her had occurred postmortem.

Then this man, who later would claim he did not remember killing "the lady on TV," suddenly woke up, in a sense.

He got off her body and had second thoughts about what he had done. The absence of drag marks near the couch suggested that Waddell carried the body from the couch and laid it on the floor on the other side of the room. He dragged it into an upright position and propped it against the TV. Then he set about to clean up. The ring marks that glowed on the floor, I believed, were left by the bottom of a bucket that he carried back and forth from the body to the bathtub down the hall. Each time he returned to the living room to mop up more blood with towels, or perhaps to check on his victim as he continued raiding her belongings and drinking her booze, he again bloodied the bottom of his shoes. This explained the profusion of shoe prints wandering peripatetically throughout her house. The activities themselves explained something else. Waddell's postoffense behavior was inconsistent with that of someone who felt no remorse.

"Here he is, this uneducated farm boy who's living in the big city," Wesley explained. "He's stealing to support a drug habit that's rotting his brain. First marijuana, then heroin, coke, and finally PCP. And one morning he suddenly comes to and finds himself brutalizing the corpse of a stranger."

Logs shifted in the fire as we stared at big handprints glowing as white as chalk on the dark television screen.

"The police never found vomit in the toilet or around it," I said.

"He probably cleaned that up, too. Thank God he didn't wipe down the wall above the john. You don't lean against a wall like that unless you're commode-hugging sick."

"The prints are fairly high above the back of the toilet," I observed. "I think he vomited, and when he stood up got dizzy, lurched forward, and raised his hands just in time to prevent his head from slamming into the wall. What do you think? Remorse or was he just stoned out of his mind?"

Wesley looked at me. "Let's consider what he did with the body. He sat it upright, tried to clean it with towels, and left the clothes in a moderately neat stack on the floor near her ankles. Now, you can look at that two ways. He was lewdly displaying the body and thereby showing contempt. Or he was demonstrating what he considered caring. Personally, I think it was the latter."

"And the way Eddie Heath's body was displayed?"

"That feels different. The positioning of the boy mirrors the positioning of the woman, but something's missing."

Even as he spoke, I suddenly realized what it was. "A *mirror* image," I said to Wesley in amazement. "A mirror reflects things backward or in reverse."

He looked curiously at me.

"Remember when we were comparing Robyn Naismith's scene photographs with the diagram depicting the position of Eddie Heath's body?"

"I remember vividly."

"You said that what was done to the boy—from the bite marks to the way his body was propped against a boxy object to his clothing being left in a tidy pile nearby—was a mirror image of what had been done to Robyn. But the bite marks on Robyn's inner thigh and above her breast were on the left side of her body. While Eddie's injuries—what we believe are eradicated bite marks—were on the *right*. His right shoulder and right inner thigh."

"Okay." Wesley still looked perplexed.

"The photograph that Eddie's scene most closely resembles is the one of her nude body propped against the big console TV."

"True."

"What I'm suggesting is that maybe Eddie's killer saw the same photograph of Robyn that we did. But his perspective is based on his own body's left and right. And his right would have been Robyn's left, and his left would have been her right, because in the photograph she's facing whoever is looking on."

"That's not a pleasant thought," Wesley said as the telephone rang.

"Aunt Kay?" Lucy called out from the kitchen. "It's Mr. Vander."

"We got a confirmation," Vander's voice came over the line.

"Waddell did leave the print in Jennifer Deighton's house?" I asked.

"No, that's just it. He definitely did not."

12

Over the next few days, I retained Nicholas Grueman, delivering to him my financial records and other information he requested, the health commissioner summoned me to his office to suggest that I resign, and the publicity would not end. But I knew much that I had not known even a week before.

It was Ronnie Joe Waddell who died in the electric chair the night of December 13. Yet his identity remained alive and was wreaking havoc in the city. As best as could be determined, prior to Waddell's death his SID number in AFIS had been swapped with another's. Then the other person's SID number was dropped completely from the Central Computerized Records Exchange, or CCRE. This meant there was a violent offender at large who had no need of gloves when he committed his crimes. When his prints were run through AFIS, they would come back as a dead man's every time. We knew this nefarious individual left a wake of feathers and flecks of paint, but we could surmise almost nothing about him until January 3 of the new year.

On that morning, the *Richmond Times-Dispatch* ran a

planted story about highly prized eiderdown and its appeal to thieves. At one-fourteen P.M., Officer Tom Lucero, head of the fictitious investigation, received his third call of the day.

"Hi. My name's Hilton Sullivan," the voice said loudly.

"What can I do for you, sir?" Lucero's deep voice asked.

"It's about the cases you're investigating. The eiderdown clothes and things that are supposedly hot with thieves. There was this article about it in the paper this morning. It said you're the detective."

"Right."

"Well, it really pisses me off that the cops are *so* stupid." He got louder. "It said in the paper that since Thanksgiving this and that have been stolen from stores, cars, and homes in the greater Richmond metropolitan area. You know, comforters, a sleeping bag, three ski jackets, blah, blah, blah. And the reporter quoted several people."

"What is your point, Mr. Sullivan?"

"Well, obviously the reporter got the victims' names from the cops. In other words, from you."

"It's public information."

"I don't really give a shit about that. I just want to know how come you didn't mention *this victim*, yours truly? You don't even remember my name, do you?"

"I'm sorry, sir, but I can't say that I do."

"Figures. Some fucking asshole breaks into my condo and wipes me out, and other than smearing black powder everywhere—on a day when I was dressed in white cashmere, I might add—the cops don't do a thing. I'm one of your fucking cases."

"When was your condo broken into?"

"Don't you remember? I'm the one who raised such a stink about my down vest. If it wasn't for me, you guys would never have even heard of eiderdown! When I told the cop that among other things my vest had been taken and it

had cost me five hundred bucks *on sale,* you know what he said?"

"I have no idea, sir."

"He said, 'What's it stuffed with, cocaine?' And I said, 'No, *Sherlock.* Eider duck down.' And he looked around nervous as hell and dropped his hand close to his nine-mil. The dumb-shit really thought there was some other person in my place named *Eider* and I'd just yelled at this person to *duck down,* like I was going to pull a gun or something. At that point I just left and—"

Wesley switched off the tape recorder.

We sat in my kitchen. Lucy was working out at my club again.

"The B-and-E this Hilton Sullivan's talking about was in fact reported by him on Saturday, December eleventh. Apparently, he'd been out of town, and when he returned to his condo that Saturday afternoon, he discoverd that he'd been burglarized," Wesley explained.

"Where is his condo located?" I asked.

"Downtown on West Franklin, an old brick building with condos that start at a hundred grand. Sullivan lives on the first floor. The perpetrator got in through an unsecured window."

"No alarm system?"

"No."

"What was stolen?"

"Jewelry, money, and a twenty-two revolver. Of course, that doesn't necessarily mean that Sullivan's revolver is the one that was used to kill Eddie Heath, Susan, and Donahue. But I think we're going to find that it is, because there's no question that our guy did the B-and-E."

"Prints were recovered?"

"A number of them. The city had them, and you know

how their backlog is. With all the homicides, B-and-Es aren't a top priority. In this instance, the latents had been processed and were just sitting. Pete intercepted them right after Lucero got the call. Vander's already run them through the system. He got a hit in exactly three seconds."

"Waddell again."

Wesley nodded.

"How far is Sullivan's condo from Spring Street?"

"Within walking distance. I think we know where our guy escaped from."

"You're checking out recent releases?"

"Oh, sure. But we're not going to find him in a stack of paper on somebody's desk. The warden was too careful for that. Unfortunately, he's also dead. I think he sent this inmate back out on the street, and the first thing he did was burglarize a condominium and probably find himself a set of wheels."

"Why would Donahue free an inmate?"

"My theory is that the warden needed some dirty work done. So he selected an inmate to be his personal operative and set the animal loose. But Donahue made a slight tactical error. He picked the wrong guy, because the person who's committing these killings is not going to be controlled by anyone. My suspicion, Kay, is that Donahue never intended for anyone to die, and when Jennifer Deighton turned up dead, he freaked."

"He was probably the one who called my office and identified himself as John Deighton."

"Could very well be. The point is that Donahue's intention was to have Jennifer Deighton's house ransacked because someone was looking for something—perhaps communications from Waddell. But a simple burglary isn't enough fun. The warden's little pet likes to hurt people."

I thought of the indentations in the carpet of Jennifer

Deighton's living room, the injuries to her neck, and the fingerprint recovered from her dining room chair.

"He may have sat her in the middle of her living room and stood behind her with his arm yoked around her neck while he interrogated her."

"He may have done that to get her to tell him where things were. But he was being sadistic. Possibly forcing her to open her Christmas presents was also sadistic," said Wesley.

"Would someone like this go to the trouble to disguise her death as a suicide by placing her body in her car?" I asked.

"He might. This guy's been in the system. He's not interested in getting caught, and it's probably a challenge to see who he can fool. He eradicated bite marks from Eddie Heath's body. If he ransacked Jennifer Deighton's house, he left no evidence. The only evidence he left in Susan's case was two twenty-two slugs and a feather. Not to mention, the guy altered his fingerprints."

"You think that was his idea?"

"It was probably something that the warden cooked up, and swapping records with Waddell may simply have been a matter of convenience. Waddell was about to be executed. If I wanted to trade an inmate's prints with someone, I'd choose Waddell's. Either the inmate's latents are going to come back to someone who is dead or—and this is more likely—eventually the dead person's records will be purged from the State Police computers, so if my little helper is messy and leaves prints somewhere, they aren't going to be identified at all."

I stared at him, dumbfounded.

"What?" Surprise flickered in his eyes.

"Benton, do you realize what we're saying? We're sitting here talking about computer records that were altered before Waddell died. We're talking about a burglary and the murder of a little boy that were committed before Waddell was dead. In other words, the warden's operative, as you call him, was released before Waddell was executed."

"I don't believe there can be a question about that."

"Then the assumption was that Waddell was going to die," I pointed out.

"Christ." Wesley flinched. "How could anyone be certain? The governor can intervene literally at the last minute."

"Apparently, someone knew that the governor wasn't going to."

"And the only person who could know that with certainty is the governor," he finished the thought for me.

I got up and stood before the kitchen window. A male cardinal pecked sunflower seeds from the feeder and flew off in a splash of bloodred.

"Why?" I asked without turning around. "Why would the governor have a special interest in Waddell?"

"I don't know."

"If it's true, he won't want the killer caught. When people get caught, they talk."

Wesley was silent.

"Nobody involved will want this person caught. And nobody involved will want me on the scene. It will be much better if I resign or am fired—if the cases are screwed up as much as possible. Patterson is tight with Norring."

"Kay, we've got two things we don't know yet. One is motive. The other is the killer's own agenda. This guy is doing his own thing, beginning with Eddie Heath."

I turned around and faced him. "I think he began with Robyn Naismith. I believe this monster has studied her crime scene photographs, and either consciously or subconsciously re-created one of them when he assaulted Eddie Heath and propped his body against a Dumpster."

"That could very well be," Wesley said, staring off. "But

how could an inmate get access to Robyn Naismith's scene photographs? Those would not be in Waddell's prison jacket."

"This may be just one more thing that Ben Stevens helped with. Remember, I told you that he was the one who got the photos from Archives. He could have had copies made. The question is *why* would the photos be relevant? Why would Donahue or someone else even ask for them?"

"Because the inmate wanted them. Maybe he demanded them. Maybe they were a reward for special services."

"That is sickening," I said with quiet anger.

"Exactly." Wesley met my eyes. "This goes back to the killer's agenda, his needs and desires. It is very possible that he'd heard a lot about Robyn's case. He may have known a lot about Waddell, and it would excite him to think about what Waddell had done to his victim. The photographs would be a turn-on to someone who has a very active and aggressive fantasy life that is devoted to violent, sexualized thought. It is not farfetched to suppose that this person incorporated the scene photographs—one or more of them—into his fantasies. And then suddenly he's free, and he sees a young boy walking in the dark to a convenience store. The fantasy becomes real. He acts it out."

"He re-created Robyn Naismith's death scene?"

"Yes."

"What do you suppose his fantasy is now?"

"Being hunted."

"By us?"

"By people like us. I'm afraid he might imagine that he is smarter than everybody else and no one can stop him. He fantasizes about games he can play and murders he might commit that would reinforce these images he entertains. And for him, fantasy is not a substitute for action but a preparation for it."

"Donahue could not have orchestrated releasing a monster like this, altering records, or anything else without help," I said.

"No. I'm sure he got key people to cooperate, like someone at State Police headquarters, maybe a records person with the city and even the Bureau. People can be bought if you have something on them. And they can be bought with cash."

"Like Susan."

"I don't think Susan was the key person. I'm more inclined to suspect that Ben Stevens was. He's out in the bars. Drinks, parties. Did you know he's into a little recreational coke when he can get it?"

"Nothing would surprise me anymore."

"I've got a few guys who have been asking a lot of questions. Your administrator has a life-style he can't afford. And when you screw with drugs, you end up screwing with bad people. Stevens's vices would have made him an easy mark for a dirtbag like Donahue. Donahue probably had one of his henchmen make a point of running into Stevens in a bar and they start talking. Next thing, Stevens has just been offered a way to make some pretty decent change."

"What way, exactly?"

"My guess is to make sure Waddell wasn't printed at the morgue, and to make sure the photograph of his bloody thumbprint disappeared from Archives. That was probably just the beginning."

"And he enlisted Susan."

"Who wasn't willing but had major financial problems of her own."

"So who do you think was making the payoffs?"

"They were probably handled by the same person who originally made Stevens's acquaintance and sucked him into this. One of Donahue's guys, maybe one of his guards."

I remembered the guard named Roberts who had given

Marino and me the tour. I remembered how cold his eyes were.

"Saying the contact is a guard," I said, "then who was this guard meeting with? Susan or Stevens?"

"My guess is with Stevens. Stevens wasn't going to trust Susan with a lot of cash. He's going to want to shave his share off the top because dishonest people believe everybody is dishonest."

"He meets the contact and gets the cash," I said. "Then Ben would meet with Susan to give her a cut?"

"That's probably what the scenario was Christmas Day when she left her parents' house ostensibly to visit a friend. She was going to meet Stevens, only the killer got to her first."

I thought of the cologne I smelled on her collar and her scarf, and I remembered Stevens's demeanor when I'd confronted him in his office the night I was looking through his desk.

"No," I said. "That's not how it went."

Wesley just looked at me.

"Stevens has several qualities that would set Susan up for what happened," I said. "He doesn't care about anyone but himself. And he's a coward. When things get hot, he's not going to stick his neck out. His first impulse is to let someone else take the fall."

"Like he's doing in your case by badmouthing you and stealing files."

"A perfect example," I said.

"Susan deposited the thirty-five hundred dollars in early December, a couple of weeks before Jennifer Deighton's death."

"That's right."

"All right, Kay. Let's go back a bit. Susan or Stevens or both of them tried to break into your computer days after Waddell's execution. We've speculated that they were looking for something in the autopsy report that Susan could not have observed firsthand during the post."

"The envelope he wanted buried with him."

"I'm still stumped over that. The codes on the receipts do not confirm what we'd speculated about earlier—that the restaurants and tollbooths are located between Richmond and Mecklenburg, and that the receipts were from the transport that brought Waddell from Mecklenburg to Richmond fifteen days prior to his execution. Though the dates on the receipts are consistent with the time frame, the locations are not. The codes come back to the stretch of I-95 between here and Petersburg."

"You know, Benton, it very well may be that the explanation for the receipts is so simple that we've completely overlooked it," I said.

"I'm all ears."

"Whenever you go anywhere for the Bureau, I imagine you have the same routine I do when traveling for the state. You document every expense and save every receipt. If you travel often, you tend to wait until you can combine several trips on one reimbursement voucher to cut down on the paperwork. Meanwhile, you're keeping your receipts somewhere."

"All that makes good sense in terms of explaining the receipts in question," Wesley said. "Someone on the prison staff, for example, had to go to Petersburg. But how did the receipts then turn up in Waddell's back pocket?"

I thought of the envelope with its urgent plea that it accompany Waddell to the grave. Then I recalled a detail that was as poignant as it was mundane. On the afternoon of Waddell's execution, his mother had been allowed a two-hour visit with him.

"Benton, have you talked to Ronnie Waddell's mother?"

"Pete went to see her in Suffolk several days ago. She's not feeling particularly friendly or cooperative toward people like us. In her eyes, we're the ones who sent her son to the chair."

"So she didn't reveal anything significant about Waddell's demeanor when she visited him the afternoon of his execution?"

"Based on what little she said, he was very quiet and frightened. One interesting point, though. Pete asked her what had happened to Waddell's personal effects. She said that Corrections gave her his watch and ring and explained that he had donated his books, poetry, and so on to the N-double-A-C-P."

"She didn't question that?" I asked.

"No. She seemed to think it made sense for Waddell to do that."

"Why?"

"She doesn't read or write. What's important is that she was lied to, as were we when Vander tried to track down personal effects in hopes of getting latent prints. And the origin of these lies most likely was Donahue."

"Waddell knew something," I said. "For Donahue to want every scrap of paper that Waddell had written on and every letter ever sent to him, then there must be something that Waddell knew that certain people don't want anyone else to know."

Wesley was silent.

Then he said, "What did you say is the name of the cologne Stevens wears?"

"Red."

"And you're fairly certain this is what you smelled on Susan's coat and scarf?"

"I wouldn't swear to it in court, but the fragrance is quite distinctive."

"I think it's time for Pete and me to have a little prayer meeting with your administrator."

"Good. And I think I can help get him in the proper frame of mind if you'll give me until noon tomorrow."

"What are you going to do?"

"Probably make him a very nervous man," I said.

* * *

I was working at the kitchen table early that evening when I heard Lucy drive into the garage, and I got up to greet her. She was dressed in a navy blue warm-up suit and one of my ski jackets, and was carrying a gym bag.

"I'm dirty," she said, pulling away from my hug, but not before I smelled gun smoke in her hair. Glancing down at her hands, I saw enough gunshot residues on the right one to make a trace element analyst ecstatic.

"Whoa," I said as she started to walk off. "Where is it?"

"Where's what?" she asked innocently.

"The gun."

Reluctantly, she withdrew my Smith and Wesson from her jacket pocket.

"I wasn't aware you had a license for carrying a concealed weapon," I said, taking the revolver from her and making sure it was unloaded.

"I don't need one if I'm carrying it concealed in my own house. Before that I had it on the car seat in plain view."

"That's good but not good enough," I said quietly. "Come on."

Wordlessly, she followed me to the kitchen table, and we sat down.

"You said you were going to Westwood to work out," I said.

"I know that's what I said."

"Where have you been, Lucy?"

"The Firing Line on Midlothian Turnpike. It's an indoor range."

"I know what it is. How many times have you done this?"

"Four times." She looked me straight in the eye.

"My God, Lucy."

"Well, what am I supposed to do? Pete's not going to take me anymore."

"Lieutenant Marino is very, very busy right now," I said,

and the remark sounded so patronizing that I was embarrassed. "You're aware of the problems," I added.

"Sure I am. Right now he's got to stay away. And if he stays away from you, he stays away from me. So he's out on the street because there's some maniac on the loose who's killing people like your morgue supervisor and the prison warden. At least Pete can take care of himself. Me? I've been shown how to shoot one lousy time. Gee, thanks a lot. That's like giving me one tennis lesson and then entering me in Wimbledon."

"You're overreacting."

"No. The problem is you're underreacting."

"Lucy . . ."

"How would you feel if I told you that every time I come visit you, I never stop thinking about that night?"

I knew exactly which night she meant, though over the years we had managed to go on as if nothing had happened.

"I would not feel good if I knew you were upset by anything that has to do with me," I said.

"*Anything?* What happened was just *anything*?"

"Of course it wasn't just anything."

"Sometimes I wake up at night because I dream a gun is going off. Then I listen to the awful silence and remember lying there, staring into the dark. I was so scared I couldn't move, and I wet my bed. And there were sirens and red lights flashing, and neighbors coming out on their porches and looking out their windows. And you wouldn't let me see it when they carried him out, and you wouldn't let me go upstairs. I wish I had, because imagining it has been worse."

"That man is dead, Lucy. He can't hurt anyone now."

"There are others just as bad, maybe worse than him."

"I'm not going to tell you there aren't."

"What are you doing about it, then?"

"I spend my every waking moment picking up the pieces

of the lives destroyed by evil people. What more do you want me to do?"

"If you let something happen to you, I promise I will hate you," my niece said.

"If something happens to me, I don't suppose it will matter who hates me. But I wouldn't want you to hate anyone because of what it would do to you."

"Well, I will hate you. I swear."

"I want you to promise me, Lucy, that you won't lie to me again."

She did not say a word.

"I don't ever want you to feel that you need to hide anything from me," I said.

"If I'd told you I wanted to go to the range, would you have let me?"

"Not without Lieutenant Marino or me."

"Aunt Kay, what if Pete can't catch him?"

"Lieutenant Marino is not the only person on the case," I said, not answering her question, because I did not know how to answer it.

"Well, I feel sorry for Pete."

"Why?"

"He has to stop whoever this person is, and he can't even talk to you."

"I imagine he's taking things in stride, Lucy. He's a pro."

"That's not what Michele says."

I glanced over at her.

"I was talking to her this morning. She says that Pete came by the house the other night to see her father. She said that Pete looks awful—his face was as red as a fire truck and he was in a horrible mood. Mr. Wesley tried to get him to go to the doctor or take some time off, but no way."

I felt miserable. I wanted to call Marino immediately, but I knew it wasn't wise. I changed the subject.

"What else have you and Michele been talking about? Anything new with the State Police computers?"

"Nothing good. We've tried everything we can think of to figure out who Waddell's SID number was switched with. But any records marked for deletion were overwritten long ago on the hard disk. And whoever is responsible for the tampering was swift enough to do full system backups after the records were altered, meaning we can't run SID numbers against an earlier version of CCRE and see who pops up. Generally, you have at least one backup that's three to six months old. But not so in this case."

"Sounds like an inside job to me."

I thought how natural it seemed to be home with Lucy. She no longer was a guest or an irascible little girl. "We need to call your mother and Grans," I said.

"Do we have to tonight?"

"No. But we do need to talk about your returning to Miami."

"Classes don't start until the seventh, and it won't make any difference if I miss the first few days."

"School is very important."

"It's also very easy."

"Then you should do something on your own to make it harder."

"Missing classes will make it harder," she said.

The next morning I called Rose at eight-thirty, when I knew a staff meeting was in progress across the hall, meaning that Ben Stevens was occupied and would not know I was on the line.

"How are things?" I asked my secretary.

"Awful. Dr. Wyatt couldn't get here from the Roanoke office because they got snow in the mountains and the roads are bad. So yesterday Fielding had four cases with no one to help him. Plus, he was due in court and then got called to a scene. Have you talked to him?"

"We touch base when the poor man has a moment to get to the phone. This might be a good time for us to track down a few of our former fellows and see if one of them might consider coming here to help us hang on for a while. Jansen's doing private path in Charlottesville. You want to try him and see if he wants to give me a call?"

"Certainly. That's a fine idea."

"Tell me about Stevens," I said.

"He hasn't been here very much. He signs out in such an abbreviated, vague fashion that no one is ever sure where he's gone. I'm suspicious he's looking for another job."

"Remind him not to ask me for a recommendation."

"I wish you'd give him a great one so someone else would take him off our hands."

"I need for you to call the DNA lab and get Donna to do me a favor. She should have a lab request for the analysis of the fetal tissue from Susan's case."

Rose was silent. I could feel her getting upset.

"I'm sorry to bring this up," I said gently.

She took a deep breath. "When did you request the analysis?"

"The request was actually made by Dr. Wright, since he did the post. He would have his copy of the lab request at the Norfolk office, along with the case."

"You don't want me to call Norfolk and have them make a copy for us?"

"No. This can't wait, and I don't want anyone to know that I've requested a copy. I want it to appear that our office inadvertently got a copy. That's why I want you to deal directly with Donna. Ask her to pull the lab request immediately and I want you to pick it up in person."

"Then what?"

"Then put it in the box up front where all the other copies of lab requests and reports are left for sorting."

"You're sure about this?"

"Absolutely," I said.

I hung up and retrieved a telephone directory, which I was flipping through when Lucy walked into the kitchen. She was barefoot and still wearing the sweat suit she had slept in. Groggily wishing me a good morning, she began rummaging in the refrigerator as I ran my finger down a column of names. There were maybe forty listings for the name Grimes, but no Helens. Of course, when Marino had referred to the guard as Helen the Hun, he was being snide. Maybe Helen wasn't her real name at all. I noted that there were three listings with the initial H., two for the first name and one for a middle name.

"What are you doing?" Lucy asked, setting a glass of orange juice on the table and pulling out a chair.

"I'm trying to track down someone," I said, reaching for the phone.

I had no luck with any of the Grimeses I called.

"Maybe she's married," Lucy suggested.

"I don't think so." I called Directory Assistance and got the listing for the new penitentiary in Greensville.

"What makes you think she isn't?"

"Intuition." I dialed. "I'm trying to reach Helen Grimes," I said to the woman who answered.

"Are you referring to an inmate?"

"No. To one of your guards."

"Hold, please."

I was transferred.

"Watkins," a male voice mumbled.

"Helen Grimes, please," I said.

"Who?"

"Officer Helen Grimes."

"Oh. She don't work here anymore."

"Could you please tell me where I could reach her, Mr. Watkins? It's very important."

"Hold on." The phone clunked against wood. In the background, Randy Travis was singing.

Minutes later, the man returned. "We're not allowed to give out information like that, ma'am."

"That's fine, Mr. Watkins. If you give me your first name, I'll just send all this to you and you can forward it to her."

A pause. "All *what*?"

"This order she placed. I was calling to see if she wanted it mailed fourth-class or sent ground."

"What order?" He didn't sound happy.

"The set of encyclopedias she ordered. There are six boxes weighing eighteen pounds each."

"Well, you can't be sending no 'cyclopedias here."

"Then what do you suggest I do with them, Mr. Watkins? She's already made the down payment and your business address was the one she gave us."

"Shhhhooo. Hold on."

I heard paper rustle; then keys clicked on a keyboard.

"Look," the man said quickly. "The best I can do is give you a P.O. box. You just send the stuff there. Don't be sending nothing to me."

He gave me the address and abruptly hung up. The post office where Helen Grimes received her mail was in Goochland County. Next I called a bailiff I was friendly with at the Goochland courthouse. Within the hour he had looked up Helen Grimes's home address in court records, but her telephone number was unlisted. At eleven A.M., I gathered my pocketbook and coat, and found Lucy in my study.

"I've got to go out for a few hours," I said.

"You lied to whoever you were talking to on the phone." She stared into the computer screen. "You don't have any *encyclopedias* to deliver to anyone."

"You're absolutely right. I did lie."

"So sometimes it's okay to lie and sometimes it's not."

"It's never really okay, Lucy."

I left her in my chair, modem lights winking and various computer manuals open and scattered over my desk and on the floor. On the screen the cursor pulsed rapidly. I waited until I was well out of sight before slipping my Ruger into my pocketbook. Though I was licensed to carry a concealed weapon, I rarely did. Setting the alarm, I left the house through the garage and drove west until Cary Street put me on River Road. The sky was marbled varying shades of gray. I was expecting Nicholas Grueman to call any day. A bomb ticked silently in the records I had given him, and I did not look forward to what he was going to say.

Helen Grimes lived on a muddy road just west of the North Pole restaurant, and on the border of a farm. Her house looked like a small barn, with few trees on its tiny parcel of land, and window boxes clumped with dead shoots that I guessed once had been geraniums. There was no sign in front to announce who lived inside, but the old Chrysler pulled up close to the porch announced that at least somebody did.

When Helen Grimes opened her door, I could tell by her blank expression that I was about as foreign to her as my German car. Dressed in jeans and an untucked denim shirt, she planted her hands on her substantial hips and did not budge from the doorway. She seemed unbothered by the cold or who I said I was, and it wasn't until I reminded her of my visit to the penitentiary that recognition flickered in her small, probing eyes.

"Who told you where I live?" Her cheeks were flushed, and I wondered if she might hit me.

"Your address is in the court records for Goochland County."

"You shouldn't have looked for it. How would you like it if I dug up your home address?"

"If you needed my help as much as I need yours, I wouldn't mind, Helen," I said.

She just looked at me. I noticed that her hair was damp, an earlobe smudged with black dye.

"The man you worked for was murdered," I said. "Someone who worked for me was murdered. And there are others. I'm sure you've been keeping up with some of what is going on. There is reason to suspect that the person who is doing this was an inmate at Spring Street—someone who was released, perhaps around the time that Ronnie Joe Waddell was executed."

"I don't know anything about anybody being released." Her eyes drifted to the empty street behind me.

"Would you know anything about an inmate who disappeared? Someone, perhaps, who wasn't legitimately released? It seems that with the job you had you would have known who entered the penitentiary and who left."

"Nobody disappeared that I heard of."

"Why don't you work there anymore?" I asked.

"Health reasons."

I heard what sounded like a cupboard door shut from somewhere inside the space she guarded.

I kept trying. "Do you remember when Ronnie Waddell's mother came to the penitentiary to visit him on the afternoon of his execution?"

"I was there when she came in."

"You would have searched her and anything she had with her. Am I correct?"

"Yes."

"What I'm trying to determine is if Mrs. Waddell might have brought anything to give her son. I realize that visiting rules prohibit people from bringing in items for the inmates—"

"You can get permission. She got it."

"Mrs. Waddell got permission to give something to her son?"

"Helen, you're letting all the heat out," a voice sounded sweetly from behind her.

Intense blue eyes suddenly fixed on me like gun sights in the space between Helen Grimes's meaty left shoulder and the door frame. I caught a flash of a pale cheek and aquiline nose before the space was empty again. The lock rattled and the door was quietly shut behind the erstwhile prison guard. She leaned up against it, staring at me. I repeated my question.

"She did bring something for Ronnie, and it wasn't much. I called the warden for permission."

"You called Frank Donahue?"

She nodded.

"And he granted permission?"

"Like I said, it wasn't much, what she brought for him."

"Helen, what was it?"

"A picture of Jesus about the size of a postcard, and something was wrote on the back. I don't remember exactly. Something like 'I will be with you in paradise,' only the spelling was wrong. Paradise was spelled like 'pair of dice,' all run together," Helen Grimes said without a trace of a smile.

"And that was it?" I asked. "This was what she wanted to give her son before he died?"

"I told you that was it. Now, I need to go in, and I don't want you coming here again." She put her hand on the doorknob as the first few drops of rain slowly slipped from the sky and left wet spots the size of nickels on the cement stoop.

When Wesley arrived at my house later in the day, he wore a black leather pilot's jacket, a dark blue cap, and a trace of a smile.

"What's happening?" I asked as we retreated to the

kitchen, which by now had become such a common meeting place for us that he always took the same chair.

"We didn't break Stevens, but I think we put a pretty big crack in him. Your having the lab request left where he would find it did the trick. He's got good reason to fear the results of DNA testing done on fetal tissue from Susan Story's case."

"He and Susan were having an affair," I said, and it was odd that I did not object to Susan's morals. I was disappointed in her taste.

"Stevens admitted to the affair and denied everything else."

"Such as having any idea where Susan got thirty-five hundred dollars?" I said.

"He denies knowing anything about that. But we're not finished with him. A snitch of Marino's says he saw a black Jeep with a vanity plate in the area where Susan was shot and about the time we think it happened. Ben Stevens drives a black Jeep with the vanity plate '1 4 Me.' "

"Stevens didn't kill her, Benton," I said.

"No, he didn't. I think what happened is Stevens got spooked when whoever he was dealing with wanted information about Jennifer Deighton's case."

"The implication would have been pretty clear," I agreed. "Stevens knew that Jennifer Deighton was murdered."

"And coward that he is, he decides that when it is time for the next payoff, he'll let Susan handle it. Then he'll meet her directly afterward to get his share."

"By which time she's already been killed."

Wesley nodded. "I think whoever was sent to meet her shot her and kept the money. Later—maybe mere minutes later—Stevens appears in the designated spot, the alleyway off Strawberry Street."

"What you're describing is consistent with her position in the car," I said. "Originally, she had to have been slumped forward in order for the assailant to have shot her in the nape of the neck. But when she was found, she was leaning back in the seat."

"Stevens moved her."

"When he first approached the car, he wouldn't have immediately known what was wrong with her. He couldn't see her face if she were slumped forward against the steering wheel. He leaned her back in the seat."

"And then ran like hell."

"And if he'd just splashed on some of his cologne before heading out to meet her, then he would have cologne on his hands. When he leaned her back in the seat, his hands would have been in contact with her coat—probably in the area of her shoulders. That's what I smelled at the scene."

"We'll break him eventually."

"There are more important things to do, Benton," I said, and I told him about my visit with Helen Grimes and what she had said about Mrs. Waddell's last visit with her son.

"My theory," I went on, "is that Ronnie Waddell wanted the picture of Jesus buried with him, and that this may have been his last request. He puts it in an envelope and writes on it 'Urgent, extremely confidential,' and so on."

"He couldn't have done this without Donahue's permission," Wesley said. "According to protocol, the inmate's last request must be communicated to the warden."

"Right, and no matter what Donahue's been told, he's going to be too paranoid to let Waddell's body be carried off with a sealed envelope in a pocket. So he grants Waddell's request, then devises a way to see what's inside the envelope without a hassle or a stink. He decides to switch envelopes after Waddell is dead, and instructs one of his thugs to take care of it. And this is where the receipts come in."

"I was hoping you'd get around to that," Wesley said.

"I think the person made a little mistake. Let's say he's got a white envelope on his desk, and inside it are receipts from a recent trip to Petersburg. Let's say he gets a similar white envelope, tucks something innocuous inside it, and then writes the same thing on the front that Waddell had written on the envelope he wanted buried with him."

"Only the guard writes this on the wrong envelope."

"Yes. He writes it on the one containing the receipts."

"And he's going to discover this later when he looks for his receipts and finds the innocuous something inside the envelope instead."

"Precisely," I said. "And that's where Susan fits in. If I were the guard who made this mistake, I'd be very worried. The burning question for me would be whether one of the medical examiners opened that envelope in the morgue, or if the envelope was left sealed. If I, this guard, also happened to be the contact for Ben Stevens, the person forking over cash in exchange for making sure Waddell's body wasn't printed at the morgue, for example, then I'd know exactly where to turn."

"You'd contact Stevens and tell him to find out if the envelope was opened. And if so, whether its contents made anybody suspicious or inclined to go around asking questions. It's called tripping over your paranoia and ending up with many more problems than you would have had if you'd just been cool. But it would seem Stevens could have answered that question easily."

"Not so," I said. "He could ask Susan, but she didn't witness the opening of the envelope. Fielding opened it upstairs, photocopied the contents, and sent the original out with Waddell's other personal effects."

"Stevens couldn't have just pulled the case and looked at the photocopy?"

"Not unless he broke the lock on my credenza," I said.

"Then, in his mind, the only other alternative was the computer."

"Unless he asked Fielding or me. He would know better

than that. Neither of us would have divulged a confidential detail like that to him or Susan or anyone else."

"Does he know enough about computers to break into your directory?"

"Not to my knowledge, but Susan had taken several courses and had UNIX books in her office."

The telephone rang and I let Lucy answer it. When she came into the kitchen, her eyes were uneasy.

"It's your lawyer, Aunt Kay."

She moved the kitchen phone within reach, and I picked it up without moving from my chair. Nicholas Grueman wasted no words on a greeting but went straight to his point.

"Dr. Scarpetta, on November twelfth you wrote a money market account check to the tune of *ten thousand dollars cash.* And I find no records in any of your bank statements that might indicate this money was deposited in any of your various accounts."

"I didn't deposit the money."

"You walked out of the bank with ten thousand dollars cash?"

"No, I did not. I wrote the check at Signet Bank, downtown, and with it purchased a cashier's check in British sterling."

"To whom was the cashier's check made out?" my former professor asked as Benton Wesley stared tensely at me.

"Mr. Grueman, the transaction was of a private nature and in no way has any bearing on my profession."

"Come now, Dr. Scarpetta. *You know* that's not good enough."

I took a deep breath.

"Certainly, you know we're going to be asked about this. Certainly, you must realize it doesn't look good that within weeks of your morgue assistant's depositing an unexplained amount of cash, you wrote a check for a large amount of cash."

I shut my eyes and ran my fingers through my hair as Wesley got up from the table and came around behind me.

"Kay"—I felt Wesley's hands on my shoulders—"for God's sake, you've got to tell him."

13

Had Grueman never been a practitioner of the law, I would not have entrusted my welfare to him. But before teaching he had been a litigator of renown, and he had done civil rights work and prosecuted mobsters for the Justice Department during the Robert Kennedy era. Now he represented clients who had no money and were condemned to die. I appreciated Grueman's seriousness and needed his cynicism.

He was not interested in trying to negotiate or protest my innocence. He refused to present the slightest shred of evidence to Marino or anyone. He told no one of the ten-thousand-dollar check, which was, he said, the worst piece of evidence against me. I was reminded of what he had taught his students on the first day of criminal law: *Just say no. Just say no. Just say no.* My former professor abided by these rules to the letter, and frustrated Roy Patterson's every effort.

Then on Thursday, January 6, Patterson called me at home and requested that I come downtown to his office to talk.

"I'm sure we can clear all this up," he said amicably. "I just need to ask you a few questions."

The implication was that if I cooperated, then something worse might be derailed, and I marveled that Patterson would consider, for even a moment, that such a shopworn maneuver would work with me. When the Commonwealth's Attorney wants to chat, he's on a fishing expedition that does not involve letting anything go. The same is true of the police. In good Gruemanian fashion, I told Patterson no, and the next morning was subpoenaed to appear before the special grand jury on January 20. This was followed by a subpoena duces tecum for my financial records. First Grueman claimed the Fifth, then filed a motion to quash the subpoena. A week later, we had no choice but to comply unless I wished to be held in contempt of court. About this same time, Governor Norring appointed Fielding acting chief medical examiner of Virginia.

"There's another TV van. I just saw it go by," Lucy said from the dining room, where she stood staring out the window.

"Come on in and eat lunch," I called out to her from the kitchen. "Your soup is getting cold."

Silence.

Then, "Aunt Kay?" She sounded excited.

"What is it?"

"You'll never guess who just pulled up."

From the window over the sink, I watched the white Ford LTD park in front. The driver's door opened, and Marino climbed out. He hitched up his trousers and adjusted his tie, his eyes taking in everything around him. As I watched him follow the sidewalk to my porch, I was so powerfully touched that it startled me.

"I'm not sure if I should be glad to see you or not," I said when I opened the door.

"Hey, don't worry. I'm not here to arrest you, Doc."

"Please come in."

"Hi, Pete," Lucy said cheerfully.

"Aren't you supposed to be in school or something?"

"No."

"What? Down there in South America they give you January off?"

"That's right. Because of the bad weather," my niece said. "When it drops below seventy degrees, everything shuts down."

Marino smiled. He looked about the worst I had ever seen him.

Moments later I had built a fire in the living room, and Lucy had left to run errands.

"How have you been?" I asked.

"Are you going to make me smoke outside?"

I slid an ashtray closer to him.

"Marino, you have suitcases under your eyes, your face is flushed, and it's not warm enough in here for you to be perspiring."

"I can tell you've missed me." He pulled a dingy handkerchief from his back pocket and mopped his brow. Then he lit a cigarette and stared into the fire. "Patterson's being an asshole, Doc. He wants to scorch you."

"Let him try."

"He will, and you'd better be ready."

"He has no case against me, Marino."

"He has a fingerprint found on an envelope inside Susan's house."

"I can explain that."

"But you can't prove it, and then there's his little trump card. And I swear I shouldn't be telling you this, but I'm going to."

"What trump card?"

"You remember Tom Lucero?"

"I know who he is," I said. "I don't know him."

"Well, he can be a charmer and he's a pretty damn good cop, to be honest. Turns out he's been snooping around Signet Bank and talked up one of the tellers until she slipped him information about you. Now, he wasn't supposed to ask and she wasn't supposed to tell. But she told him she remembered you writing a big check for cash sometime before Thanksgiving. According to her, it was for ten grand."

I stared stonily at him.

"I mean, you can't really blame Lucero. He's just doing his job. But Patterson knows what to look for as he rummages through your financial records. He's going to hammer you hard when you get before the special grand jury."

I did not say a word.

"Doc." He leaned forward and met my eyes. "Don't you think you ought to talk about it?"

"No."

Getting up, he went to the fireplace and nudged the curtain open far enough to flick the cigarette inside.

"Shit, Doc," he said quietly. "I don't want you indicted."

"I shouldn't drink coffee and I know you shouldn't, but I feel like having something. Do you like hot chocolate?"

"I'll drink some coffee."

I got up to fix it. My thoughts buzzed sluggishly like a housefly in the fall. My rage had nowhere to go. I made a pot of decaf and hoped Marino would not know the difference.

"How is your blood pressure?" I asked him.

"You want to know the truth? Some days, if I was a kettle I'd be whistling."

"I don't know what I'm going to do with you."

He perched on the edge of the hearth. The fire sounded like the wind, and reflected flames danced in brass.

"For one thing," I went on, "you probably shouldn't even be here. I don't want you having any problems."

"Hey, fuck the CA, the city, the governor, and all of them," he said with sudden anger.

"Marino, we can't give in. Someone knows who this killer is. Have you talked to the officer who showed us around the penitentiary? Officer Roberts?"

"Yo. The conversation went exactly nowhere."

"Well, I didn't fare a whole lot better with your friend Helen Grimes."

"That must've been a treat."

"Are you aware that she no longer works for the pen?"

"She never did any *work* there that I know of. Helen the Hun was lazy as hell, unless she was patting down one of the lady guests. Then she got industrious. Donahue liked her, don't ask me why. After he got whacked, she got reassigned to guard tower duty in Greensville and suddenly developed a knee problem or something."

"I have a feeling she knows a lot more than she let on," I said. "Especially if she and Donahue were friendly with each other."

Marino sipped his coffee and looked out the sliding glass doors. The ground was frosted white, and snowflakes seemed to be falling faster. I thought of the snowy night I was summoned to Jennifer Deighton's house, and images flashed in my mind of an overweight woman in curlers sitting in a chair in the middle of her living room. If the killer had interrogated her, he had done so for a reason. What was it he had been sent to find?

"Do you think the killer was after letters when he appeared at Jennifer Deighton's house?" I asked Marino.

"I think he was after something that had to do with Waddell. Letters, poems. Things he may have mailed to her over the years."

"Do you think this person found what he was looking for?"

"Let's just put it this way, he may have looked around, but he was so tidy we couldn't tell."

"Well, I don't think he found a thing," I said.

Marino looked skeptically at me as he lit another cigarette. "Based on what?"

"Based on the scene. She was in her nightgown and curlers. It appears she had been reading in bed. That doesn't sound like someone who is expecting company."

"I'll go along with that."

"Then someone appears at her door and she must have let him in, because there was no sign of forcible entry and no sign of a struggle. I think what may have happened next is this person demanded that she turn over to him whatever it was he was looking for, and she wouldn't. He gets angry, gets a chair from the dining room, and sets it in the middle of her living room. He sits her in it and basically tortures her. He asks questions, and when she doesn't tell him what he wants to hear he tightens the choke hold. This goes on until it goes too far. He carries her out and puts her in her car."

"If he was going in and out of the kitchen, that might explain why that door was unlocked when we arrived," Marino considered.

"It might. In summary, I don't think he intended for her to die when she did, and after he tried to disguise her death he probably didn't hang around very long. Maybe he got scared, or maybe he simply lost interest in his assignment. I doubt he rummaged through her house at all, and I also doubt that he would have found anything if he had."

"We sure as hell didn't," Marino said.

"Jennifer Deighton was paranoid," I said. "She indicated to Grueman in the fax she sent him that there was something wrong about what was being done to Waddell. Apparently, she'd seen me on the news and had even tried to contact me, but continued to hang up when she got my machine."

"Are you thinking she might have had papers or something that would tell us what the hell this is all about?"

"If she had," I said, "then she was probably sufficiently frightened to get them out of her house."

"And stash them where?"

"I don't know, but maybe her ex-husband would. Didn't she visit him for two weeks the end of November?"

"Yeah." Marino looked interested. "As a matter of fact, she did."

Willie Travers had an energetic, pleasant voice over the phone when I finally reached him at the Pink Shell resort in Fort Myers Beach, Florida. But he was vague and noncommittal when I began to ask questions.

"Mr. Travers, what can I do to make you trust me?" I finally asked in despair.

"Come down here."

"That's going to be very difficult at present."

"I'd have to see you."

"Excuse me?"

"That's the way I am. If I can see you, I can read you and know if you're okay. Jenny was the same way."

"So if I come down to Fort Myers Beach and let you *read* me, you will help me?"

"Depends on what I pick up."

I made airline reservations for six-fifty the following morning. Lucy and I would fly to Miami. I would leave her with Dorothy and drive to Fort Myers Beach, where there was a very good chance I would spend a night wondering if I'd lost my mind. Chances were overwhelming that Jennifer Deighton's holistic health nut of an ex would turn out to be a great big waste of time.

Saturday, the snow had stopped when I got up at four A.M. and went into Lucy's bedroom to wake her. For a moment I listened to her breathe, then lightly touched her shoulder and whispered her name in the dark. She stirred and sat straight up. On the plane, she slept to Charlotte, then wallowed in one of her unbearable moods the rest of the way to Miami.

"I'd rather take a cab," she said, staring out the window.

"You can't take a cab, Lucy. Your mother and her friend will be looking for you."

"Good. Let them drive around the airport all day. Why can't I come with you?"

"You need to go home, and I need to drive straight to Fort Myers Beach, and then I'm going to fly from there back to Richmond. Trust me. It wouldn't be any fun."

"Being with Mother and her latest idiot isn't any fun, either."

"You don't know he's an idiot. You've never met him. Why don't you give him a chance?"

"I wish Mother would get AIDS."

"Lucy, don't say such a thing."

"She deserves it. I don't understand how she can sleep with every dickhead who takes her out to dinner and a movie. I don't understand how she can be your sister."

"Lower your voice," I whispered.

"If she missed me so much, she'd want to pick me up herself. She wouldn't want someone else around."

"That's not necessarily true," I told her. "When you fall in love someday, you'll understand better."

"What makes you think I've never been in love?" She looked furiously at me.

"Because if you had been, you would know that being in love brings out both the best and the worst in us. One day we're generous and sensitive to a fault, and the next we're not fit to shoot. Our lives become lessons in extremes."

"I wish Mother would hurry up and go through menopause."

Mid-afternoon, as I drove the Tamiami Trail in and out of

the shade, I patched up the holes guilt had chewed into my conscience. Whenever I dealt with my family, I felt irritated and annoyed. Whenever I refused to deal with them, I felt the same way I had as a child, when I learned the art of running away without leaving home. In a sense, I had become my father after he died. I was the rational one who made A's and knew how to cook and handle money. I was the one who rarely cried and whose reaction to the volatility in my disintegrating home was to cool down and disperse like a vapor. Consequently, my mother and sister accused me of indifference, and I grew up harboring a secret shame that what they said was true.

I arrived in Fort Myers Beach with the air-conditioning on and the visor down to shield the sun. Water met the sky in a continuum of vibrant blue, and palms were bright green feathers atop trunks as sturdy as ostrich legs. The Pink Shell resort was the color of its name. It backed up to Estero Bay and threw its front balconies open wide to the Gulf of Mexico. Willie Travers lived in one of the cottages, but I was not due to meet him until eight P.M. Checking into a one-bedroom apartment, I literally left a trail of clothes on the floor as I snatched off my winter suit and grabbed shorts and a tennis shirt out of my bag. I was out the door and on the beach in seven minutes.

I did not know how many miles I walked, for I lost track of time, and each stretch of sand and water looked magnificently the same. I watched bobbing pelicans throw their heads back as they downed fish like shots of bourbon, and I deftly stepped around the flaccid blue balloons of beached Portuguese men-of-war. Most people I passed were old. Occasionally, the high-pitched voice of a child lifted above the roar of waves like a bit of bright paper carried by the wind. I picked up sand dollars worn smooth by the surf and leached shells reminiscent of peppermints sucked thin. I thought of Lucy and missed her again.

When most of the beach was in shade, I returned to my room. Showering and changing, I got in my car and cruised Estero Boulevard until hunger guided me like a divining rod into the parking lot of the Skipper's Galley. I ate red snapper and drank white wine while the horizon faded to a dusky blue. Soon boat lights drifted low in the darkness and I could not see the water.

By the time I found cottage 182 near the bait shop and fishing pier, I was as relaxed as I had been in a long time. When Willie Travers opened the door, it seemed we had been friends forever.

"The first order of business is refreshment. Surely you haven't eaten," he said.

I regretfully told him I had.

"Then you'll simply have to eat again."

"But I couldn't."

"I will prove you wrong within the hour. The fare is very light. Grouper grilled in butter and Key Lime juice with a generous sprinkling of fresh ground pepper. And we have seven-grain bread I make from scratch that you'll never forget as long as you live. Let's see. Oh, yes. Marinated slaw and Mexican beer."

He said all this as he popped the caps off two bottles of Dos Equis. Jennifer Deighton's former husband had to be close to eighty years old, his face as ruined by the sun as cracked mud, but the blue eyes set in it were as vital as a young man's. He smiled a lot as he talked, and was beef jerky lean. His hair reminded me of white tennis ball fuzz.

"How did you come to live here?" I asked, looking around at mounted fish on the walls and rugged furnishings.

"A couple of years ago I decided to retire and fish, so I worked out a deal with the Pink Shell. I'd run their bait shop if they'd let me rent one of the cottages at a reasonable rate."

"What was your profession before you retired?"

"Same as it is now." He smiled. "I practice holistic medicine, and you never really retire from that any more than you retire from religion. The difference is, now I work with people I want to work with, and I no longer have an office in town."

"Your definition of holistic medicine?"

"I treat the whole person, plain and simple. The point is to get people in balance." He looked appraisingly at me, set his beer down, and came over to the captain's chair where I sat. "Would you mind standing up?"

I was in a mood to be agreeable.

"Now hold out one of your arms. I don't care which one, but hold it straight out so it's parallel to the floor. That's fine. Now I'm going to ask you a question and then as you answer I'm going to try to push your arm down while you resist. Do you view yourself as the family hero?"

"No." My arm instantly yielded to his pressure and lowered like a drawbridge.

"Well, you do view yourself as the family hero. That tells me you're pretty damn hard on yourself and have been from the word *go*. All right. Now let's put your arm up again and I'm going to ask you another question. Are you good at what you do?"

"Yes."

"I'm pushing down as hard as I can and your arm is steel. So you are good at what you do."

He returned to the couch and I sat back down.

"I must admit that my medical teaching makes me somewhat skeptical," I said with a smile.

"Well, it shouldn't, because the principles are no different from what you deal with every day. Bottom line? The body doesn't lie. No matter what you tell yourself, your energy level responds to what is actually true. If your head says you aren't the family hero or you love yourself when that's not how you feel, your energy gets weak. Is this making any sense?"

"Yes."

"One of the reasons Jenny came down here once or twice a year was so I could balance her. And when she was here last, around Thanksgiving, she was so out of whack I had to work with her several hours every day."

"Did she tell you what was wrong?"

"A lot of things were wrong. She'd just moved and didn't like her neighbors, especially the ones across the street."

"The Clarys," I said.

"I suppose that was the name. The woman was a busybody and the man was a flirt until he had a stroke. Plus, Jenny's horoscope readings had gotten out of hand and were wearing her out."

"What was your opinion of this business she ran?"

"Jenny had a gift but she was spreading it too thin."

"Would you label her a psychic?"

"Nope. I wouldn't label Jenny—wouldn't even begin to try. She was into a lot of things."

I suddenly remembered the blank sheet of paper anchored by the crystal on her bed and asked Travers if he might know what that meant, or if it meant anything.

"It meant she was concentrating."

"Concentrating?" I puzzled. "On what?"

"When Jenny wanted to meditate, she would get a white sheet of paper and put a crystal on top of it. Then she would sit very still and slowly turn the crystal around and around, watching light from the facets move on the paper. That did for her what staring at the water does for me."

"Was anything else bothering her when she came to see you, Mr. Travers?"

"Call me Willie. Yes, and you know what I'm about to say. She was upset about this convict who was waiting to be executed, Ronnie Waddell. Jenny and Ronnie had been writing to each other for many years, and she just couldn't deal with the thought of him being put to death."

"Do you know if Waddell ever revealed anything to her that could have placed her in jeopardy?"

"Well, he gave her something that did."

I reached for my beer without taking my eyes off him.

"When she came down here at Thanksgiving, she brought all of the letters he had written and anything else he had sent her over the years. She wanted me to keep them down here for her."

"Why?"

"So they would be safe."

"She was worried about somebody trying to get them from her?"

"All I know is, she was spooked. She told me that during the first week of this past November, Waddell called her collect and said he was ready to die and didn't want to fight it anymore. Apparently, he was convinced nothing could save him, and he asked her to go to the farm in Suffolk and get his belongings from his mother. He said he wanted Jenny to have them, and not to worry, that his mother would understand."

"What were those belongings?" I asked.

"Just one thing." He got up. "I'm not real sure of the significance—and I'm not sure I want to be sure. So I'm going to turn it over to you, Dr. Scarpetta. You can take it on back to Virginia. Share it with the police. Do with it what you want."

"Why are you suddenly being helpful?" I asked. "Why not weeks ago?"

"Nobody bothered to come see me," he said loudly from another room. "I told you when you called that I don't deal with people over the phone."

When he returned, he set a black Hartmann briefcase at my feet. The brass lock had been pried open and the leather was scarred.

"Fact is, you'd be doing me a big favor to get this out of my life," Willie Travers said, and I could tell he meant it. "The very thought of it makes my energy bad."

The scores of letters Ronnie Waddell had written Jennifer Deighton from death row were neatly bundled in rubber bands and sorted chronologically. I skimmed through few in my hotel room that night, because their importance all but disappeared in the light of other items I found.

Inside the briefcase were legal pads filled with handwritten notes that made little sense, for they referred to cases and dilemmas of the Commonwealth from more than ten years ago. There were pens and pencils, a map of Virginia, a tin of Sucrets throat lozenges, a Vick's inhaler, and a tube of Chapstick. Still in its yellow box was an EpiPen, a .3-milligram epinephrine auto-injector routinely kept by people fatally allegeric to bee stings or some foods. The prescription label was typed with the patient's name, the date, and the information that the EpiPen was one of five refills. Clearly, Waddell had stolen the briefcase from Robyn Naismith's house on the fateful morning he murdered her. It may be that he had no idea who it belonged to until he carried it off and broke the lock. Waddell discovered he had savaged a local celebrity whose lover, Joe Norring, was then the attorney general of Virginia.

"Waddell never had a chance," I said. "Not that he necessarily deserved clemency in light of the severity of his crime. But from the moment he was arrested, Norring was a worried man. He knew he had left his briefcase at Robyn's house, and he knew it had not been recovered by the police."

Why he had left his briefcase at Robyn's house was not

clear, unless he'd simply forgotten it on a night that neither of them could know was her last.

"I can't even begin to imagine Norring's reaction when he heard," I said.

Wesley glanced at me over the rim of his glasses as he continued perusing paperwork. "I don't think we can imagine it. It was bad enough he had to worry about the world discovering he was having an affair, but his connection with Robyn would have instantly made him the prime suspect in her murder."

"In a way," Marino said, "he was lucky as hell Waddell took the briefcase."

"I'm sure in his mind he was unlucky either way he looked at it," I said. "If the briefcase had turned up at the scene, he was in trouble. If the briefcase was stolen, as it was, then Norring had to worry about it turning up somewhere."

Marino got the coffeepot and refilled everyone's cup. "Somebody must have done something to ensure Waddell's silence."

"Maybe." Wesley reached for the cream. "Then again, maybe Waddell never opened his mouth. My guess is he feared from the beginning that what he had stumbled upon only made matters worse for him. The briefcase could be used as a weapon, but who would it destroy? Norring or Waddell? Was Waddell going to trust the system enough to badmouth the AG? Was he going to trust the system enough years later to badmouth the governor—the only man who could spare his life?"

"So Waddell remained silent, knowing that his mother would protect what he had hidden on the farm until he was ready for someone else to have it," I said.

"Norring had ten damn years to find his briefcase," Marino said. "Why did he wait so long to start looking?"

"I suspect Norring has had Waddell watched from the beginning," Wesley said, "and that this surveillance was stepped up considerably over the past few months. The closer Waddell got to the execution, the less he had to lose, and the more likely he was to start talking. It's possible someone was monitoring his phone conversation when he called Jennifer Deighton in November. And it's possible that when word got to Norring, he panicked."

"He should have," Marino said. "I personally searched through all of Waddell's belongings when we was working the case. The guy had next to nothing, and if anything belonging to him was back on the farm, we never found it."

"And Norring would have known that," I said.

"Hell, yes," Marino said. "So he's going to know there's something strange about *belongings* from the farm being given to this friend of Waddell's. Norring starts seeing that damn briefcase in his nightmares again, and to make matters worse, he can't have someone just barge into Jennifer Deighton's house while Waddell's still alive. If something happens to her, there's no telling what Waddell will do. And the worst possibility would be if he started singing to Grueman."

"Benton," I said, "would you happen to know why Norring was carrying epinephrine? What is he allergic to?"

"Apparently, to shellfish. Apparently, he keeps EpiPens all over the place."

While they continued to talk, I checked the lasagna in the oven and opened a bottle of Kendall-Jackson. The case against Norring would take a very long time, if it could be proven at all, and I thought I understood, to a degree, how Waddell must have felt.

It wasn't until close to eleven P.M. that I called Nicholas Grueman at home.

"I'm finished in Virginia," I said. "As long as Norring is in office, he'll make sure I won't be. They've taken my life, goddamn it, but I'm not giving them my soul. I plan to take the Fifth every time."

"Then you will certainly be indicted."

"Considering the bastards I'm up against, I think that's a certainty anyway."

"My, my, Dr. Scarpetta. Have you forgotten the bastard representing you? I don't know where you spent your weekend, but I spent mine in London."

I felt the blood drain from my face.

"Now, there's no guaranteeing that we can slide this around Patterson," said this man I used to think I hated, "but I'm going to move heaven and earth to get Charlie Hale on the stand."

14

January 20 was as windy as March but much colder, and the sun was blinding as I drove east on Broad Street toward the John Marshall courthouse.

"Now I will tell you something else you already know," Nicholas Grueman said. "The press is going to be churning up the water like bluefish on a feeding frenzy. You fly too low, you lose a leg. We'll walk side by side, eyes cast down, and don't turn and look at anyone no matter who it is or what he says."

"We're not going to find a parking place," I said, turning left on 9th. "I knew this would happen."

"Slow down. That good woman right there on the side is doing something. Wonderful. She's leaving, if she can ever get the wheels turned enough."

A horn blared behind me.

I glanced at my watch, then turned to Grueman like an athlete awaiting last-minute instruction from the coach. He wore a long navy blue cashmere coat and black leather gloves, his silver-topped cane leaning against the seat and a battle-scarred briefcase in his lap.

"Now remember," he said. "Your friend Mr. Patterson decides who's going in and who isn't, so we've got to depend on the jurors to intervene, and that's going to be up to you. You've got to connect with them, Kay. You've got to make friends with ten or eleven strangers the instant you walk into that room. No matter what they want to chat with you about, don't put up a wall. Be accessible."

"I understand," I said.

"We're going for broke. A deal?"

"A deal."

"Good luck, Doctor." He smiled and patted my arm.

Inside the courthouse, we were stopped by a deputy with a scanner. He went through my pocketbook and briefcase as he had a hundred times before when I had come to testify as an expert witness. But this time he said nothing to me and avoided my eyes. Grueman's cane set off the scanner, and he was the paragon of patience and courtesy as he explained that the silver top and tip would not come off, and that there truly was nothing concealed inside the dark wood shaft.

"What does he think I have here, a blowgun?" he remarked as we boarded the elevator.

The instant the doors opened on the third floor, reporters descended with the predicted predatory vigor. My counselor moved quickly for a man with gout, his strides punctuated by taps of his cane. I felt surprisingly detached and out of focus until we were inside the nearly deserted courtroom, where Benton Wesley sat in a corner with a slight young man I knew was Charlie Hale. The right side of his face was a road map of fine pink scars. When he stood and self-consciously slipped his right hand into his jacket pocket, I saw that he was missing several fingers. Dressed in an ill-fitting somber suit and tie, he glanced around while I preoccupied myself with the mechanics of being seated and sorting through my briefcase. I could not speak to him, and the three men had the presence of mind to pretend they did not notice that I was upset.

"Let's talk for a minute about what they have," Grueman said. "I believe we can count on Jason Story testifying, and Officer Lucero. And, of course, Marino. I don't know who else Patterson will include in this Star Chamber proceeding of his."

"For the record," Wesley said, looking at me, "I have spoken to Patterson. I've told him he doesn't have a case and I'll testify to that at the trial."

"We're assuming there will be no trial," Grueman said. "And when you go in, I want you to make sure the jurors know that you talked to Patterson and told him he has no case but he insisted on going forward. Whenever he asks a question and you respond by addressing an issue that you have already addressed with him in private, I want you to say so. 'As I told you in your office,' or 'As I clearly stated when we spoke whenever it was,' et cetera, et cetera.

"It is important that the jurors know that you are not only an FBI special agent, but that you are the chief of the Behavioral Science Unit at Quantico, the purpose of which is to analyze violent crime and develop psychological profiles of the perpetrators. You may wish to state that Dr. Scarpetta in no way, shape, or form fits the profile of the perpetrator of the crime in question, and in fact, that you find the thought absurd. It is also important that you impress upon the jurors that you were Mark James's mentor and closest friend. Volunteer whatever you can because you can rest assured that Patterson isn't going to ask. Make it clear to the jurors that Charlie Hale *is here.*"

"What if they do not request me?" Charlie Hale asked.

"Then our hands are tied," Grueman replied. "As I explained when we talked in London, this is the prosecutor's show. Dr. Scarpetta has no right to present any evidence, so we have to get at least one of the jurors to invite us in through the back door."

"That's quite something," Hale said.

"You have the copies of the deposit slip and the fees you have paid?"

"Yes, sir."

"Very good. Don't wait to be asked. Just put them on the table as you're talking. And the status of your wife is the same since we spoke?"

"Yes, sir. As I told you, she's had the in vitro fertilization. So far, so good."

"Remember to get that in if you can," Grueman said.

Several minutes later, I was summoned to the jury room.

"Of course. He wants you first." Grueman got up with me. "Then he'll call in your detractors so he can leave a bad taste in the jurors' mouths." He went as far as the door. "I will be right here when you need me."

Nodding, I went inside and took the empty chair at the head of the table. Patterson was out of the room, and I knew this was one of his gambits. He wanted me to endure the silent scrutiny of these ten strangers who held my welfare in their hands. I met the gazes of all and even exchanged smiles with a few. A serious young woman wearing bright red lipstick decided not to wait for the Commonwealth's Attorney.

"What made you decide to deal with dead people instead of the living?" she asked. "It seems a strange thing for a doctor to choose."

"It is my intense concern for the living that makes me study the dead," I said. "What we learn from the dead is for the benefit of the living, and justice is for those left behind."

"Don't it get to you?" inquired an old man with big, rough

hands. The expression on his face was so sincere that he seemed in pain.

"Of course it does."

"How many years did you have to go to school after you graduated from high school?" asked a heavyset black woman.

"Seventeen years, if you include residencies and the year I was a fellow."

"Lord have mercy."

"Where all did you go?"

"To school, you mean?" I said to the thin young man wearing glasses.

"Yes, ma'am."

"Saint Michael's, Our Lady of Lourdes Academy, Cornell, Johns Hopkins, Georgetown."

"Was your daddy a doctor?"

"My father owned a small grocery store in Miami."

"Well, I'd hate to be the one paying for all that schooling."

Several of the jurors laughed softly.

"I was fortunate enough to receive scholarships," I said. "Beginning with high school."

"I have an uncle who works at the Twilight Funeral Home in Norfolk," said someone else.

"Oh, come on, Barry. There really isn't a funeral home called that."

"I kid you not."

"That's nothing. We got one in Fayetteville owned by the Stiff family. Guess what it's called."

"No way."

"You're not from around here."

"I'm a native of Miami," I replied.

"Then the name Scarpetta's Spanish?"

"Actually, it's Italian."

"That's interesting. I thought all Italians was dark."

"My ancestors are from Verona in northern Italy, where a sizable segment of the population shares blood with the Savoyards, Austrians, and Swiss," I patiently explained. "Many of us are blue-eyed and blond."

"Boy, I bet you can cook."

"It's one of my favorite pastimes."

"Dr. Scarpetta, I'm not real clear on your position," said a well-dressed man who looked about my age. "Are you the chief medical examiner for Richmond?"

"For the Commonwealth. We have four district offices. Central Office here in Richmond, Tidewater in Norfolk, Western in Roanoke, and the Northern Office in Alexandria."

"So the chief just happens to be located here in Richmond?"

"Yes. That seems to make the most sense, since the medical examiner system is part of state government and Richmond is where the legislature meets," I replied as the door opened and Roy Patterson walked in.

He was a broad-shouldered, good-looking black man with close-shorn hair that was going gray. His dark blue suit was double-breasted, and his initials were embroidered on the cuffs of his pale yellow shirt. He was known for his ties, and this one looked hand painted. He greeted the jurors and was tepid toward me.

I discovered that the woman wearing the bright red lipstick was the foreman. She cleared her throat and informed me that I did not have to testify, and that anything I said could be used against me.

"I understand," I said, and I was sworn in.

Patterson hovered about my chair and offered a minimum of information about who I was, and elaborated on the power of my position and the ease with which this power could be abused.

"And who would there be to witness it?" he asked. "On many occasions there was no one to observe Dr. Scarpetta at work except for the person who was by her side virtually every day. Susan Story. You can't hear testimony from her because she and her unborn child are dead, ladies and gentlemen. But there are others you will hear from today. And they will paint for you a chilling portrait of a cold, ambitious woman, an empire builder who was making grievous mistakes on the job. First, she paid for Susan Story's silence. Then she killed for it.

"And when you hear tales of the *perfect crime,* who better able to carry it off than someone who is an expert in solving crimes? An expert would know that if you plan to shoot someone inside a vehicle, it would behoove you to choose a low-caliber weapon so you don't run the risk of bullets ricocheting. An expert would leave no telling evidence at the scene, not even spent shells. An expert would not use her own revolver—the gun or guns that friends and colleagues know she possesses. She would use something that could not be traced back to her.

"Why, she might even *borrow* a revolver from the lab, because, ladies and gentlemen, every year the courts routinely confiscate hundreds of firearms used in the commission of crimes, and some of these weapons are donated to the state firearms lab. For all we know, the twenty-two revolver that was put against the back of Susan Story's skull is, as we speak, hanging on a pegboard in the firearms lab or downstairs in the range the examiners use for test fires and where Dr. Scarpetta routinely practices shooting. And by the way, she is good enough to qualify for any police department in America. And she has killed before, though to give her credit, in the instance I'm referring to her actions were ruled to be self-defense."

I stared down at my hands folded on top of the table as the court reporter played her silent keys and Patterson went on. His rhetoric was always eloquent, though he usually did not know when to quit. When he asked me to explain the fingerprints recovered from the envelope found in Susan's dresser, he made such a big production of pointing out how unbelievable my explanation was that I suspected the reaction of some was to wonder why what I'd said *couldn't* be true. Then he got to the money.

"Is it not true, Dr. Scarpetta, that on November twelfth you appeared at the downtown branch of Signet Bank and made out a check for *cash* for the sum of ten thousand dollars?"

"That is true."

Patterson hesitated for an instant, his surprise visible. He had counted on my taking the Fifth.

"And is it true that on this occasion you did not deposit the money in any of your various accounts?"

"That is also true," I said.

"So several weeks before your morgue supervisor inexplicably deposited thirty-five hundred dollars into her checking account, you walked out of Signet Bank with ten thousand dollars cash on your person?"

"No, sir, I did not. In my financial records you should have found a copy of a cashier's check made out to the sum of seven thousand, three hundred and eighteen pounds sterling. I have my copy here." I got it out of my briefcase.

Patterson barely glanced at it as he asked the court reporter to tag it as evidence.

"Now, this is very interesting," he said. "You purchased a cashier's check made out to someone named Charles Hale. Was this some creative scheme of yours to disguise payoffs you were making to your morgue supervisor and perhaps to others? Did this individual named Charles Hale turn around and convert pounds back into dollars and route the cash elsewhere—perhaps to Susan Story?"

"No," I said. "And I never delivered the check to Charles Hale."

"You didn't?" He looked confused. "Then what did you do with it?"

"I gave it to Benton Wesley, and he saw to it that the check was delivered to Charles Hale. Benton Wesley—"

He cut me off. "The story just gets more preposterous."

"Mr. Patterson . . ."

"Who is Charles Hale?"

"I would like to finish my previous statement," I said.

"Who is Charles Hale?"

"I'd like to hear what she was trying to say," said a man in a plaid blazer.

"Please," Patterson said with a cold smile.

"I gave the cashier's check to Benton Wesley. He is a special agent for the FBI, a suspect profiler at the Behavioral Science Unit in Quantico."

A woman timidly raised her hand. "Is he the one I've read about in the papers? The one they call in when there are these awful murders like the ones in Gainesville?"

"He is the one," I said. "He is a colleague of mine. He was also the best friend of a friend of mine, Mark James, who also was a special agent for the FBI."

"Dr. Scarpetta, let's get the record straight here," Patterson said impatiently. "Mark James was more than a, quote, *friend* of yours."

"Are you asking me a question, Mr. Patterson?"

"Aside from the obvious conflict of interest involved in the chief medical examiner's sleeping with an FBI agent, the subject is nongermane. So I won't ask—"

I interrupted him. "My relationship with Mark James began in law school. There was no conflict of interest, and for the record, I object to the Commonwealth's Attorney's reference to whom I allegedly was sleeping with."

The court reporter typed on.

My hands were clasped so tightly my knuckles were white.

Patterson asked again, "Who is Charles Hale and why would you give him the equivalent of ten thousand dollars?"

Pink scars flashed in my mind, and I envisioned two fingers attached to a stump shiny with scar tissue.

"He was a ticket agent at Victoria Station in London," I said.

"Was?"

"He was on Monday, February eighteenth, when the bomb went off."

No one told me. I heard reporters on the news all day and had no idea until my phone rang on February 19 at two-forty-one A.M. It was six-forty-one in the morning in London, and Mark had been dead for almost a day. I was so stunned as Benton Wesley tried to explain, that none of it made any sense.

"That was yesterday, I read about that yesterday. You mean it happened again?"

"The bombing happened yesterday morning during rush hour. But I just found out about Mark. Our legal attaché in London just notified me."

"You're sure? You're absolutely sure?"

"Jesus, I'm sorry, Kay."

"They've identified him with certainty?"

"With certainty."

"You're sure. I mean . . ."

"Kay. I'm at home. I can be there in an hour."

"No, no."

I was shivering all over but could not cry. I wandered through my house, moaning quietly and wringing my hands.

"But you did not know this Charles Hale prior to his being injured in the bombing, Dr. Scarpetta. Why would you give him ten thousand dollars?" Patterson dabbed his forehead with a handkerchief.

"He and his wife have wanted children and could not have them."

"And how would you know such an intimate detail about strangers?"

"Benton Wesley told me, and I responded by suggesting Bourne Hall, the leading research facility for in vitro fertilization. IVF is not covered by national health insurance."

"But you said the bombing was way back in February. You just wrote the check in November."

"I did not know about the Hales' problem until this past fall, when the FBI had a photo spread for Mr. Hale to look at and somehow learned of his difficulties. I'd told Benton long ago to let me know if there was ever anything I could do for Mr. Hale."

"Then you took it upon yourself to finance in vitro fertilization for strangers?" Patterson asked as if I'd just told him that I believed in leprechauns.

"Yes."

"Are you a *saint*, Dr. Scarpetta?"

"No."

"Then please explain your motivation."

"Charles Hale tried to help Mark."

"Tried to help him?" Patterson was pacing. "Tried to help him buy a ticket or catch a train or find the men's room? Just what is it that you mean?"

"Mark was conscious briefly, and Charles Hale was seriously injured on the ground next to him. He tried to move rubble off Mark. He talked to him, took off his jacket, and wrapped it around . . . He, uh, tried to stop the hemorrhaging. He did everything he could. There was nothing that would have saved him, but he wasn't alone. I am so grateful for that. Now there will be a new life in the world, and I am thankful I could do something in return. It helps. There is at least some meaning. No. I'm not a saint. The need was mine, too. When I helped the Hales, I was helping me."

The room was so quiet it was as if it were empty.

The woman wearing red lipstick leaned forward a little to get Patterson's attention.

"I expect Charlie Hale is way over there in England. But I wonder if we could subpoena Benton Wesley?"

"It's not necessary to subpoena either one of them," I answered. "Both of them are here."

When the foreman informed Patterson that the special grand jury had refused to indict, I was not there to see it. Nor was I present when Grueman was told. As soon as I had finished testifying, I had begun frantically looking for Marino.

"I saw him come out of the men's room maybe a half hour ago," said a uniformed officer I found smoking a cigarette by a water fountain.

"Can you try him on your radio?" I asked.

Shrugging, he unfastened his radio from his belt and asked the dispatcher to raise Marino. Marino did not respond.

I took the stairs and broke into a trot when I got outside. When I was in my car, I locked the doors and started the engine. I grabbed the phone and tried headquarters, which was directly across the street from the courthouse. While a detective in the squad room told me that Marino wasn't in, I drove through the lot in back looking for his white Ford LTD. It wasn't there. Then I pulled into an empty reserved place and called Neils Vander.

"You remember the burglary on Franklin—the prints you recently ran that matched up with Waddell?" I asked.

"The burglary in which the eiderdown vest was stolen?"

"That's the one."

"I remember it."

"Was the complainant's ten print card turned in for exclusionary purposes?"

"No, I didn't have that. Just the latents recovered from the scene."

"Thank you, Neils."

Next I called the dispatcher.

"Can you tell me if Lieutenant Marino is marked on?" I asked.

She came back to me. "He is marked on."

"Listen, please see if you can raise him and find out where he is. Tell him this is Dr. Scarpetta and it's urgent."

Maybe a minute later the dispatcher's voice came over the line. "He's at the city pumps."

"Tell him I'm two minutes from there and on my way."

The gas pumps used by the city police were located on a bleak patch of asphalt surrounded by a chain-link fence. Filling up was strictly self-service. There was no attendant, no rest room or vending machines, and the only way you were going to clean your windshield was if you brought your own paper towels and Windex. Marino was tucking his gas card in the side pouch where he always kept it when I pulled up next to him. He got out and came around to my window.

"I just heard the news on the radio." He couldn't contain his smile. "Where's Grueman? I want to shake his hand."

"I left him at the courthouse with Wesley. What happened?" I suddenly felt light-headed.

"You don't know?" he asked, incredulous. "Shit, Doc. They cut you loose, that's what happened. I can think of maybe two times in my career that a special grand jury hasn't returned with a true bill."

I took a deep breath and shook my head. "I guess I should be dancing a jig. But I don't feel like it."

"I probably wouldn't, either."

"Marino, what was the name of that man who claimed his eiderdown vest was stolen?"

"Sullivan. Hilton Sullivan. Why?"

"During my testimony, Patterson made the outrageous accusation that I might have used a revolver from the firearms lab to shoot Susan. In other words, there is always a risk involved if you use your own weapon because if it's checked and it's proven that it fired the bullets, then you've got a lot of explaining to do."

"What's this got to do with Sullivan?"

"When did he move into his condo?"

"I don't know."

"If I were going to kill someone with my Ruger, it would be pretty clever of me to report it stolen to the police before I commit any crimes. Then if for some reason the gun is ever recovered—if, for example, the heat is on and I decide to toss it—the cops might trace the serial number back to me, but I can prove through the burglary report I filed that the gun was not in my possession at the time of the crime."

"Are you suggesting Sullivan falsified a report? That he staged the burglary?"

"I'm suggesting you consider that," I said. "It's convenient that he has no burglar alarm and left a window unlocked. It's convenient that he was obnoxious with the cops. I'm sure they were delighted to see him leave and weren't about to go the extra mile and get his fingerprints for exclusionary purposes. Especially since he was dressed in white and bitching about the dusting powder everywhere. My point is, how do you know that the prints in Sullivan's condo weren't left by Sullivan? He lives there. His prints would be all over the place."

"In AFIS they matched up with Waddell."

"Exactly."

"If that's the case, then why would Sullivan call the police in response to that story about eiderdown we planted in the paper?"

"As Benton said, this guy loves to play games. He loves to jerk people around. He skates on the edge for kicks."

"Shit. Let me use your phone."

He came around to the passenger's side and got in. Dialing

Directory Assistance, he got the number of the building where Sullivan lived. When the superintendent was on the line, Marino asked him how long ago Hilton Sullivan had purchased his condominium.

"Well, then, who does?" Marino asked. He scribbled something on a notepad. "What's the number and what street does it face? Okay. What about his car? Yeah, if you've got it."

When Marino hung up, he looked at me. "Christ, the squirrel doesn't own the condo at all. It's owned by some businessman who rents it, and Sullivan started renting it the friggin' first week in December. He paid the deposit on the sixth, to be exact." He opened the car door, adding, "And he drives a dark blue Chevy van. An old one with no windows."

Marino followed me back to headquarters and we left my car in his parking place. We shot across Broad Street, heading toward Franklin.

"Let's hope the manager hasn't alerted him." Marino raised his voice above the roar of the engine.

He slowed down and parked in front of an eight-story brick building.

"His condo's in back," he explained, looking around. "So he shouldn't be able to see us." He reached under the seat and got out his nine-millimeter to back up the .357 in the holster under his left arm. Tucking the pistol in the back of his trousers and an extra clip in his pocket, he opened his door.

"If you're expecting a war, I'll be glad to stay in the car," I said.

"If a war starts, I'll toss you my three-fifty-seven and a couple speed loaders, and you damn better be as good a shot as Patterson's been saying you are. Stay behind me at all times." At the top of the steps, he rang the bell. "He's probably not going to be here."

Momentarily, the lock clicked free and the door opened.

An elderly man with bushy gray eyebrows identified himself as the building superintendent Marino had spoken to earlier on the phone.

"Do you know if he's in?" Marino asked.

"I have no idea."

"We're going to go up and check."

"You won't be going up because he's on this floor." The superintendent pointed east. "Just follow that corridor and take the first left. It's a corner apartment at the very end. Number seventeen."

The building possessed a quiet but tired luxuriousness, reminiscent of old hotels that no one particularly wants to stay in anymore because the rooms are too small and the decor is too dark and a little frayed. I noted cigarette burns in the deep red carpet, and the stain on the paneling was almost black. Hilton Sullivan's corner apartment was announced by a small brass 17. There was no peephole, and when Marino knocked, we heard footsteps.

"Who is it?" a voice asked.

"Maintenance," Marino said. "Here to change the filter in your heater."

The door opened, and the instant I saw the piercing blue eyes in the space and they saw me, my breath caught. Hilton Sullivan tried to slam shut the door, but Marino's foot was wedged against the jamb.

"Get to the side!" Marino shouted at me as he snatched out his revolver and leaned as far away from the door's opening as he could.

I darted up the corridor as he suddenly kicked the door open wide and it slammed against the wall inside. Revolver ready, he went in, and I waited in dread for a scuffle or gunfire. Minutes went by. Then I heard Marino saying something on his portable radio. He reappeared, sweating, his face an angry red.

"I dont fucking believe it. He went out the window like

a damn jackrabbit and there's not a sign of him. Goddamn son of a bitch. His van's sitting right out there in the lot in back. He's off on foot somewhere. I've sent out an alert to units in the area." He wiped his face on his sleeve and struggled to catch his breath.

"I thought he was a woman," I said numbly.

"Huh?" Marino stared at me.

"When I went to see Helen Grimes, he was inside her house. He looked out the door once while we were talking on the porch. I thought it was a woman."

"Sullivan was at Helen the Hun's house?" Marino said loudly.

"I'm sure of it."

"Jesus Christ. That don't make a damn bit of sense."

But it did make sense when we began looking around Sullivan's apartment. It was elegantly furnished with antiques and fine rugs, which Marino said belonged to the owner, not to Sullivan, according to the superintendent. Jazz drifted from the bedroom, where we found Hilton Sullivan's blue down jacket on the bed next to a beige corduroy shirt and a pair of faded jeans, neatly folded. His running shoes and socks were on the rug. On the mahogany dresser were a green cap and a pair of sunglasses, and a loosely folded blue uniform shirt that still had Helen Grimes's nameplate pinned above the breast pocket. Beneath it was a large envelope of photographs that Marino went through while I silently looked on.

"Holy shit," Marino muttered every other minute.

In more than a dozen of them, Hilton Sullivan was nude and in poses of bondage, and Helen Grimes was his sadistic guard. One favorite scenario seemed to be Sullivan sitting in a chair while she played the role of interrogator, yoking him from behind or inflicting other punishments. He was an exquisitely pretty blond young man, with a lean body that I suspected was surprisingly strong. Certainly, he was agile.

We found a photograph of Robyn Naismith's bloody body propped against the television in her living room, and another one of her on a steel table in the morgue. But what unnerved me more than any of this was Sullivan's face. It was absolutely devoid of expression, his eyes cold the way I imagined they would be when he killed.

"Maybe we know why Donahue liked him so much," Marino said, sliding the photographs back inside their envelope. "Someone was taking these pictures. Donahue's wife told me the warden's hobby was photography."

"Helen Grimes must know who Hilton Sullivan really is," I said as sirens wailed.

Marino peered out the window. "Good. Lucero's here."

I examined the down vest on the bed and discovered a downy white feather protruding from a minute tear in a seam.

More engines sounded. Car doors slammed shut.

"We're out of here," Marino said when Lucero arrived. "Make sure you impound his blue van." He turned to me. "Doc? You remember how to get to Helen Grimes's crib?"

"Yes."

"Let's go talk at her."

Helen Grimes did not have much to say.

When we got to her house some forty-five minutes later, we found the front door unlocked and went inside. The heat was turned up as high as it would go, and I could have been anywhere in the world and recognized the smell.

"Holy God," Marino said when he walked into the bedroom.

Her headless body was in uniform and sitting in a chair against the wall. It wasn't until three days later that the farmer across the road found the rest of her. He didn't know why anyone would have left a bowling bag in one of his fields. But he wished he had never opened it.

EPILOGUE

The yard behind my mother's Miami house was half in the shade and half in the gentle sun, and hibiscus grew in a riot of red on either side of the back screen door. Her Key Lime tree by the fence was heavy with fruit when virtually all others in the neighborhood were barren or dead. It was a fact I failed to understand, for I had not known it was possible to criticize plants into good health. I thought you had to talk nicely to them.

"Katie?" my mother called from the kitchen window. I heard water drumming into the sink. There was no point in answering.

Lucy knocked out my queen with a castle. "You know," I said, "I really hate playing chess with you."

"Then why do you keep asking me?"

"*Me* asking *you*? You force me, and one game is never enough."

"That's because I keep giving you another chance. But you blow it every time."

We were sitting across from each other at the patio table. The ice in our lemonades had melted and I felt a little sunburned.

"Katie? Will you and Lucy go out after a while and get the wine?" my mother said from the window.

I could see the shape of her head and the round outline of her face. Cupboard doors opened and shut; then the telephone sounded its high-pitched ring. It was for me, and my mother simply handed the cordless phone out the door.

"It's Benton," the familiar voice said. "I see from the papers that the weather's great down there. It's raining here and a lovely forty-five degrees."

"Don't make me homesick."

"Kay, we think we've got an ID. And by the way, someone went to a lot of trouble. Fake identifications—good ones. He was able to walk into a gun store, and rent a condo, with no questions asked."

"Where'd he get his money?"

"Family. He's probably had some stashed. Anyway, after going through prison records and talking to a lot of people, it seems that Hilton Sullivan is an alias for a thirty-one-year-old male named Temple Brooks Gault from Albany, Georgia. His father owns a pecan plantation and there's a lot of money. Gault's typical in some ways—preoccupied with guns, knives, martial arts, violent pornography. He's antisocial, et cetera."

"In what ways is he atypical?" I asked.

"His pattern would indicate that he's completely unpredictable. He doesn't really fit any profile, Kay. This guy's off the charts. If something strikes his fancy, he just does it. He's consummately narcissistic and vain—his hair, for example. He highlights it himself. We found the bleach, rinses, and so on in his apartment. Some of his inconsistencies are, well, weird."

"Such as?"

"He was driving this beat-up old van that was once owned by a housepainter. Doesn't appear Gault ever washed it or bothered to clean it out, not even after he murdered Eddie

Heath inside the thing. We've got some pretty promising trace, by the way, and blood that's consistent with Eddie's type. That's disorganized. Yet Gault also apparently eradicated bite marks and had his fingerprints changed. That's as organized as hell."

"Benton, what is his history?"

"A manslaughter conviction. Two and a half years ago he got angry with a man in a bar and kicked him in the head. This was in Abingdon, Virginia. Gault, by the way, has a black belt in karate."

"Any new developments on locating him?" I watched Lucy set up the chessboard.

"None. But for all of us involved in the cases, I'll say what I've said before. This guy's absolutely without fear. He's very much guided by impulse and is, therefore, troublesome to second-guess."

"I understand."

"Just make sure you exercise the appropriate precautions at all times."

There were no appropriate precautions against someone like this, I thought.

"All of us need to be alert."

"I understand," I said again.

"Donahue had no idea what he unleashed. Or better put, Norring didn't. Though I don't believe our good governor handpicked this dirtbag. He just wanted his damn briefcase and probably gave Donahue the necessary funds and told him to take care of it. We're not going to get any hard time for Norring. He's been too careful and too many people aren't around to talk." He paused, adding, "Of course, there's your attorney and me."

"What do you mean?"

"I've been clear—in a subtle way, of course—that it would be a damn shame if something got leaked about the briefcase stolen from Robyn Naismith's house. Grueman had a little tête-à-tête with him, too, and reports that Norring looked a little queasy when it was mentioned that it must have been a harrowing experience when he drove himself to the ER the might before Robyn's death."

By checking old newspaper clips and talking to contacts in various ERs around the city, I had discovered that the night before Robyn's murder, Norring had been treated at Henrico Doctor's emergency room after administering epinephrine to himself by injection in his left thigh. Apparently, he had suffered a severe allergic reaction to Chinese food, cartons for which I recalled from police reports had been found in Robyn Naismith's trash. My theory was that shrimp or some other shellfish had inadvertently gotten mixed in with spring rolls or something else he and Robyn had eaten for dinner. He had begun to go into anaphylactic shock, had used one of his EpiPens—perhaps one he'd kept at Robyn's house—and then had driven himself to the hospital. In his great distress, he had left without his briefcase.

"I just want Norring as far away from me as possible," I said.

"Well, it seems he's been suffering health problems of late and has decided it would be wise to resign and look for something less stressful in the private sector. Perhaps on the West Coast. I'm quite certain he won't bother you. Ben Stevens won't bother you. For one thing, he—like Norring—is too busy looking over his shoulder for Gault. Let's see. Last I heard, Stevens was in Detroit. Did you know?"

"Did you threaten him, too?"

"Kay, I never threaten anyone."

"Benton, you're one of the most threatening people I've ever met."

"Does that mean you won't work with me?"

Lucy was drumming her fingers on top of the table and leaning her cheek against her fist.

"Work with you?" I asked.

"That's really why I'm calling, and I know you'll need to think about it. But we'd like you to come on board as a consultant to the Behavioral Science Unit. We're just talking a couple of days a month—as a rule. Of course, there will be times when things get a little crazy. You'll review the medical and forensic details of cases to assist us in working up the profiles. Your interpretations would be very useful. And besides, you probably know that Dr. Elsevier, who has been serving as our consulting forensic pathologist for the past five years, is retiring as of June one."

Lucy poured her lemonade on the grass, got up, and began stretching.

"Benton, I'll have to think about it. For one thing, my office is still in shambles. Give me a little time to hire a new morgue supervisor and administrator and get things back on track. When do you need to know?"

"By March?"

"Fair enough. Lucy says hello."

When I hung up, Lucy looked defiantly at me. "Why do you say something like that when it isn't true? I didn't say hello to him."

"But you desperately wanted to." I got up. "I could tell."

"Katie!" My mother was in the window again. "You really should come in. You've been outside all afternoon. Did you remember to put on sun block?"

"We're in the *shade,* Grans," Lucy called out. "Remember this *huge* ficus tree back here?"

"What time did your mother say she was coming over?" my mother asked her granddaughter.

"As soon as she and what's-his-name finish screwing, they'll be here."

My mother's face disappeared from the window and water drummed in the sink again.

"Lucy!" I whispered.

She yawned and wandered to the edge of the yard to catch an elusive ray of sun. Turning her face to it, she closed her eyes.

"You're going to do it, aren't you, Aunt Kay?" she said.

"Do what?"

"Whatever Mr. Wesley was asking you to do."

I began putting the chess game back in its box.

"Your silence is a very loud answer," my niece said. "I know you. You're going to do it."

"Come on," I said. "Let's go get the wine."

"Only if I get to drink some."

"Only if you're not driving anywhere tonight."

She slipped her arm around my waist and we went inside the house.

THE BODY FARM

To Senator Orrin Hatch of Utah
for his tireless fight against crime

They that go down to the sea in ships, that do business in great waters; These see the works of the Lord, and his wonders in the deep.

Psalm 107:23–24

1

On the sixteenth of October, shadowy deer crept to the edge of dark woods beyond my window as the sun peeked over the cover of the night. Plumbing above and below me groaned, and one by one other rooms went bright as sharp tattoos from ranges I could not see riddled the dawn. I had gone to sleep and gotten up to the sound of gunfire.

It is a noise that never stops in Quantico, Virginia, where the FBI Academy is an island surrounded by Marines. Several days a month I stayed on the Academy's security floor, where no one could call me unless I wanted them to or follow me after too many beers in the Boardroom.

Unlike the Spartan dormitory rooms occupied by new agents and visiting police, in my suite were TV, kitchen, telephone, and a bathroom I did not have to share. Smoking and alcohol were not allowed, but I suspected that the spies and protected witnesses typically sequestered here obeyed the rules about as well as I did.

As coffee heated in the microwave, I opened my briefcase to retrieve a file that had been waiting for me when I had checked in last night. I had not reviewed it yet for I could not bring myself to wrap my mind around such a thing, to take such a thing to bed. In that way I had changed.

Since medical school, I had been accustomed to exposing myself to any trauma at any hour. I had worked around the clock in emergency rooms and performed autopsies alone in the morgue until dawn. Sleep had always been a brief export to some dark, vacant place I rarely later recalled. Then gradually over the years something perniciously shifted. I began to dread working late at night, and was prone to bad dreams when terrible images from my life popped up in the slot machine of my unconscious.

Emily Steiner was eleven, her dawning sexuality a blush on her slight body, when she wrote in her diary two Sundays before, on October 1:

> Oh, Im' so happy! Its almost 1 in the morning and Mom doesnt know Im' writing in my dairy because Im' in bed with the flash light. We went to the cover dish supper at the church and Wren was there! I could tell he noticed me. Then he gave me a fireball! I saved it while he wasnt looking. Its in my secret box. This afternoon we have youth group and he wants me to meet him early and not tell anyone!!!

At three-thirty that afternoon, Emily left her house in Black Mountain, just east of Asheville, and began the two-mile walk to the church. After the meeting, other children recalled seeing her leave alone as the sun slipped below the foothills at six P.M. She veered off the main road, guitar case in hand, and took a shortcut around a small lake. Investigators believed it was during this walk she encountered the man who hours later would steal her life. Perhaps she stopped to talk to him. Perhaps she was unaware of his presence in the gathering shadows as she hurried home.

In Black Mountain, a western North Carolina town of seven thousand people, local police had worked very few homicides or sexual assaults of children. They had never worked a case that was both. They had never thought about Temple Brooks Gault of Albany, Georgia, though his face smiled from Ten Most Wanted lists posted across the land. Notorious criminals and their crimes had never been a concern in this picturesque part of the world known for Thomas Wolfe and Billy Graham.

I did not understand what would have drawn Gault there or to a frail child named Emily who was lonely for her father and a boy named Wren. But when Gault had gone on his murderous spree in Richmond two years before, his choices had seemed just as devoid of rationality. In fact, they still did not make sense.

Leaving my suite, I passed through sun-filled glass corridors as memories of Gault's bloody career in Richmond seemed to darken the morning. Once he had been within my reach. I literally could have touched him, for a flicker, before he had fled through a window and was gone. I had not been armed on that occasion, and it was not my business to go around shooting people anyway. But I had not been able to shake the chill of doubt that had settled over my spirit back then. I had not stopped wondering what more I could have done.

Wine has never known a good year at the Academy, and I regretted drinking several glasses of it in the Boardroom the night before. My morning run along J. Edgar Hoover Road was worse than usual.

Oh, God, I thought. *I'm not going to make it.*

Marines were setting up camouflage canvas chairs and telescopes on roadsides overlooking ranges. I felt bold male eyes as I slowly jogged past, and knew the gold Department of Justice crest on my navy T-shirt was duly noted. The soldiers probably assumed I was a female agent or visiting cop, and it disturbed me to imagine my niece running this same route. I wished Lucy had picked another place to intern. Clearly, I had influenced her life, and very little frightened me quite as much as that did. It had become my habit to worry about her during workouts when I was in agony and aware of growing old.

HRT, the Bureau's Hostage Rescue Team, was out on maneuvers, helicopter blades dully batting air. A pickup truck hauling shot-up doors roared past, followed by another caravan of soldiers. Turning around, I began the one-and-a-half-mile stretch back to the Academy, which could have passed for a modern tan brick hotel were it not for its rooftops of antennas and location out in the middle of a wooded nowhere.

When at last I reached the guard booth, I veered around tire shredders and lifted my hand in a weary salute to the officer behind glass. Breathless and sweating, I was contemplating walking the rest of the way in when I sensed a car slowing at my rear.

"You trying to commit suicide or something?" Captain Pete Marino said loudly across the Armor-Alled front seat of his silver Crown Victoria. Radio antennas bobbed like fishing rods, and despite countless lectures from me, he wasn't wearing his seat belt.

"There are easier ways than this," I said through his open passenger's window. "Not fastening your seat belt, for example."

"Never know when I might have to bail out of my ride in a hurry."

"If you get in a wreck, you'll certainly bail out in a hurry," I said. "Probably through the windshield."

An experienced homicide detective in Richmond, where both of us were headquartered, Marino recently had been promoted and assigned to the First Precinct, the bloodiest section of the city. He had been involved with the FBI's Violent Criminal Apprehension Program, or VICAP, for years.

In his early fifties, he was a casualty of concentrated doses of tainted human nature, bad diet, and drink, his face etched by hardship and fringed with thinning gray hair. Marino was overweight, out of shape, and not known for a sweet disposition. I knew he was here for the Steiner consultation, but wondered about the luggage in his backseat.

"Are you staying for a while?" I asked.

"Benton signed me up for Street Survival."

"You and who else?" I asked, for the purpose of Street Survival was not to train individuals but task forces.

"Me and my precinct's entry team."

"Please don't tell me part of your new job description is kicking in doors."

"One of the pleasures of being promoted is finding your ass back in uniform and out on the street. In case you haven't noticed, Doc, they ain't using Saturday Night Specials out there anymore."

"Thank you for the tip," I said dryly. "Be sure to wear thick clothing."

"Huh?" His eyes, blacked out by sunglasses, scanned mirrors as other cars crept past.

"Paint bullets hurt."

"I don't plan on getting hit."

"I don't know anyone who plans on it."

"When did you get in?" he asked me.

"Last night."

Marino slid a pack of cigarettes from his visor. "You been told much?"

"I've looked at a few things. Apparently the detectives from North Carolina are bringing in most of the case records this morning."

"It's Gault. It's gotta be."

"Certainly there are parallels," I said cautiously.

Knocking out a Marlboro, he clamped it between his lips. "I'm going to nail that goddam son of a bitch if I have to go to hell to find him."

"If you find out he's in hell, I wish you'd just leave him there," I said. "Are you free for lunch?"

"As long as you're buying."

"I always buy." I stated a fact.

"And you always should." He slipped the car into drive. "You're a goddam doctor."

I trotted and walked to the track, cut across it and let myself into the back of the gym. Inside the locker room three young, fit women in various stages of nudity glanced at me as I walked in.

"Good morning, ma'am," they said in unison, instantly identifying themselves. Drug Enforcement Administration agents were notorious around the Academy for their annoyingly chivalrous greetings.

I self-consciously began taking off wet clothes, having never grown accustomed to the rather male militaristic attitude here, where women did not think twice about chatting or showing off their bruises with nothing on but the lights. Clutching a towel tightly, I hurried to the showers. I had just turned on the water when a pair of familiar green eyes peeked around the plastic curtain, startling me. The soap shot out of my hands and skidded across the tile floor, stopping near my niece's muddy Nikes.

"Lucy, can we chat *after* I get out?" I yanked the curtain shut.

"Geez, Len just about killed me this morning," she said happily as she booted the soap back into the stall. "It was great. Next time we run the Yellow Brick Road I'll ask him if you can come."

"No, thank you." I massaged shampoo into my hair. "I have no desire for torn ligaments and broken bones."

"Well, you really should run it once, Aunt Kay. It's a rite of passage up here."

"Not for me it isn't."

Lucy was silent for a moment, then uncertain when she said, "I need to ask you something."

Rinsing my hair and pushing it out of my eyes, I gathered

the curtain and looked out. My niece was standing back from the stall, filthy and sweaty from head to toe, blood smudging her gray FBI T-shirt. At twenty-one, she was about to graduate from the University of Virginia, her face honed into a beautiful sharpness, her short auburn hair brightened by the sun. I remembered when her hair was long and red, when she wore braces and was fat.

"They want me to come back after graduation," she said. "Mr. Wesley's written a proposal and there's a good chance the Feds will approve."

"What's your question?" Ambivalence kicked in hard again.

"I just wondered what you thought about it."

"You know there's a hiring freeze."

Lucy looked closely at me, trying to read information I did not want her to have.

"I couldn't be a new agent straight out of college anyway," she said. "The point is to get me into ERF now, maybe through a grant. As for what I'll do after that"—she shrugged—"who knows?"

ERF was the Bureau's recently built Engineering Research Facility, an austere complex on the same grounds as the Academy. The workings within were classified, and it chagrined me a little that I was the chief medical examiner of Virginia, the consulting forensic pathologist for the Bureau's Investigative Support Unit, and had never been cleared to enter hallways my young niece passed through every day.

Lucy took off her running shoes and shorts, and pulled her shirt and sports bra over her head.

"We'll continue this conversation later," I said as I stepped out of the shower and she stepped in.

"Ouch!" she complained as spray hit her injuries.

"Use lots of soap and water. How did you do that to your hand?"

"I slipped coming down a bank and the rope got me."

"We really should put some alcohol on that."

"No way."

"What time will you leave ERF?"

"I don't know. Depends."

"I'll see you before I head back to Richmond," I promised as I returned to the lockers and began drying my hair.

Scarcely a minute later, Lucy, not given to modesty either, trotted past me wearing nothing but the Breitling watch I'd given her for her birthday.

"Shit!" she said under her breath as she began yanking on her clothes. "You wouldn't believe everything I've got to do today. Repartition the hard disk, reload the whole thing because I keep running out of space, allocate more, change a bunch of files. I just hope we don't have any more hardware problems." She complained on unconvincingly. Lucy loved every minute of what she did every day.

"I saw Marino when I was out running. He's up for the week," I said.

"Ask him if he wants to do some shooting." She tossed her running shoes inside her locker and shut the door with an enthusiastic clang.

"I have a feeling he'll be doing plenty of that." My words followed her out as half a dozen more DEA agents walked in, dressed in black.

"Good morning, ma'am." Laces whipped against leather as they took off their boots.

By the time I was dressed and had dropped my gym bag back in my room, it was quarter past nine and I was late.

Leaving through two sets of security doors, I hurried down three flights of stairs, boarded the elevator in the gun-cleaning room, and descended sixty feet into the Academy's lower level, where I routinely waded through hell. Inside the conference room, nine police investigators, FBI profilers, and a VICAP analyst sat at a long oak table. I pulled out a chair next to Marino as comments caromed around the room.

"This guy knows a hell of a lot about forensic evidence."

"And anybody who's served time does."

"What's important is he's extremely comfortable with this type of behavior."

"That suggests to me he's *never* served time."

I added my file to other case material going around the room and whispered to one of the profilers that I wanted a photocopy of Emily Steiner's diary.

"Yeah, well, I disagree," Marino said. "The fact someone's done time don't mean he fears he's going to do time again."

"Most people would fear it—you know, the proverbial cat on the hot stove."

"Gault ain't most people. He likes hot stoves."

I was passed a stack of laser prints of the Steiners' ranch-style house. In back, a first-floor window had been pried open, and through it the assailant had entered a small laundry room of white linoleum and blue-checked walls.

"If we consider the neighborhood, the family, the victim herself, then Gault's getting bolder."

I followed a carpeted hallway into the master bedroom, where the decor was pastel prints of tiny bouquets of violets and loose flying balloons. I counted six pillows on the canopied bed and several more on a closet shelf.

"We're talking about a real small window of vulnerability here."

The bedroom with its little girl decor belonged to Emily's mother, Denesa. According to her police statement, she had awakened at gunpoint around two A.M.

"He may be taunting us."

"It wouldn't be the first time."

Mrs. Steiner described her attacker as of medium height and build. Because he was wearing gloves, a mask, long pants, and a jacket, she was uncertain about race. He gagged and bound her with blaze orange duct tape and put her in the closet. Then he went down the hall to Emily's room, where he snatched her from her bed and disappeared with her in the dark early morning.

"I think we should be careful about getting too hung up on this guy. On Gault."

"Good point. We need to keep an open mind."

I interrupted. "The mother's bed is made?"

The counterpunctal conversation stopped.

A middle-aged investigator with a dissipated, florid face said, "Affirmative," as his shrewd gray eyes alighted, like an insect, on my ash-blond hair, my lips, the gray cravat peeking out of the open collar of my gray-and-white-striped blouse. His gaze continued its surveillance, traveling down to my hands, where he glanced at my gold Intaglio seal ring and the finger that bore no sign of a wedding band.

"I'm Dr. Scarpetta," I said, introducing myself to him without a trace of warmth as he stared at my chest.

"Max Ferguson, State Bureau of Investigation, Asheville."

"And I'm Lieutenant Hershel Mote, Black Mountain Police." A man crisply dressed in khaki and old enough to retire leaned across the table to offer a big calloused hand. "Sure is a pleasure, Doc. I've heard right much about ya."

"Apparently"—Ferguson addressed the group—"Mrs. Steiner made her bed before the police arrived."

"Why?" I inquired.

"Modesty, maybe," offered Liz Myre, the only woman profiler in the unit. "She's already had one stranger in her bedroom. Now she's got cops coming in."

"How was she dressed when the police got there?" I asked.

Ferguson glanced over a report. "A zip-up pink robe and socks."

"This was what she had worn to bed?" a familiar voice sounded behind me.

Unit Chief Benton Wesley shut the conference room door as he briefly met my eyes. Tall and trim, with sharp features and silver hair, he was dressed in a single-breasted dark suit and was loaded down with paperwork and carousels of slides. No one spoke as he briskly took his chair at the head of the table and jotted several notes with a Mont Blanc pen.

Wesley repeated, without looking up, "Do we know if this was the way she was dressed when the assault took place? Or did she put on the robe after the fact?"

"I'd call it more a gown than a robe," Mote spoke up. "Flannel material, long sleeves, down to her ankles, zipper up the front."

"She didn't have on nothing under it except panties," Ferguson offered.

"I won't ask you how you know that," Marino said.

"Panty line, no bra. The state pays me to be observant. The Feds, for the record"—he looked around the table—"don't pay me for shit."

"Nobody should pay for your shit unless you eat gold," Marino said.

Ferguson got out a pack of cigarettes. "Anybody mind if I smoke?"

"I mind."

"Yeah, me, too."

"Kay." Wesley slid a thick manila envelope my way. "Autopsy reports, more photos."

"Laser prints?" I asked, and I was not keen on them, for like dot matrix images, they are satisfactory only from a distance.

"Nope. The real McCoy."

"Good."

"We're looking for offender traits and strategies?" Wesley glanced around the table as several people nodded. "And we have a viable suspect. Or I'm assuming we're assuming we do."

"No question in my mind," Marino said.

"Let's go through the crime scene, then the victimology," Wesley went on as he began perusing paperwork. "And I think it's best we keep the names of known offenders out of the mix for the moment." He surveyed us over his reading glasses. "Do we have a map?"

Ferguson passed out photocopies. "The victim's house and the church are marked. So is the path we think she took around the lake on her way home from the church meeting."

Emily Steiner could have passed for eight or nine with her tiny fragile face and form. When her most recent school photograph had been taken last spring, she had worn a buttoned-up kelly green sweater; her flaxen hair was parted on one side and held in place with a barrette shaped like a parrot.

To our knowledge, no other photographs were taken of her until the clear Saturday morning of October 7, when an old man arrived at Lake Tomahawk to enjoy a little fishing. As he set up a lawn chair on a muddy ledge close to the water, he noticed a small pink sock protruding from nearby brush. The sock, he realized, was attached to a foot.

"We proceeded down the path," Ferguson was saying, and he was showing slides now, the shadow of his ballpoint pen pointing on the screen, "and located the body here."

"And that's how far from the church and her house?"

"About a mile from either one, if you drive. A little less than that as a crow flies."

"And the path around the lake would be as a crow flies?"

"Pretty much."

Ferguson resumed. "She's lying with her head in a northernly direction. We have a sock partially on the left foot, a sock on the other. We have a watch. We have a necklace. She was wearing blue flannel pajamas and panties, and to this day they have not been found. This is a close-up of the injury to the rear of her skull."

The shadow of the pen moved, and above us through thick walls muffled gunshots sounded from the indoor range.

Emily Steiner's body was nude. Upon close inspection by the Buncombe County medical examiner, it was determined that she had been sexually assaulted, and large dark shiny patches on her inner thighs, upper chest, and shoulder were areas of missing flesh. She also had been gagged and bound with blaze orange duct tape, her cause of death a single small-caliber gunshot wound to the back of the head.

Ferguson showed slide after slide, and as images of the girl's pale body in the rushes flashed in the dark, there was silence. No investigator I'd ever met had ever gotten used to maimed and murdered children.

"Do we know the weather conditions in Black Mountain from October one through the seventh?" I asked.

"Overcast. Low forties at night, upper fifties during the day," Ferguson replied. "Mostly."

"Mostly?" I looked at him.

"On the average," he enunciated slowly as the lights went back on. "You know, you add the temperatures together and divide by the number of days."

"Agent Ferguson, any significant fluctuation matters," I said with a dispassion that belied my growing dislike of this man. "Even one day of unusually high temperatures, for example, would alter the condition of the body."

Wesley began a new page of notes. When he paused, he looked at me. "Dr. Scarpetta, if she was killed shortly after she was abducted, how decomposed should she have been when she was found on October seventh?"

"Under the conditions described, I would expect her to be moderately decomposed," I said. "I also would expect insect activity, possibly other postmortem damage, depending on how accessible the body was to carnivores."

"In other words, she should be in a lot worse shape than this"—he tapped photographs—"if she'd been dead six days."

"More decomposed than this, yes."

Perspiration glistened at Wesley's hairline and had dampened the collar of his starched white shirt. Veins were prominent in his forehead and neck.

"I'm right surprised no dogs got to her."

"Well, now, Max, I'm not. This ain't the city, with mangy strays everywhere. We keep our dogs penned in or on a leash."

Marino indulged in his dreadful habit of picking apart his Styrofoam coffee cup.

Her body was so pale it was almost gray, with greenish discoloration in the right lower quadrant. Fingertips were dry, the skin receding from the nails. There was slippage of her hair and the skin of her feet. I saw no evidence of defense injuries, no cuts, bruises, or broken nails that might indicate a struggle.

"The trees and other vegetation would have shielded her from the sun," I commented as vague shadows drifted over my thoughts. "And it doesn't appear that her wounds bled out much, if at all, otherwise I would expect more predator activity."

"We're assuming she was killed somewhere else," Wesley interpolated. "Absence of blood, missing clothing, location of the body, and so on would indicate she was molested and shot elsewhere, then dumped. Can you tell if the missing flesh was done postmortem?"

"At or around the time of death," I replied.

"To remove bite marks again?"

"I can't tell you that from what I have here."

"In your opinion, are the injuries similar to Eddie Heath's?" Wesley referred to the thirteen-year-old boy Temple Gault had murdered in Richmond.

"Yes." I opened another envelope and withdrew a stack of autopsy photographs bound in rubber bands. "In both cases we have skin excised from shoulder, upper inner thigh. And Eddie Heath was shot in the head, his body dumped."

"It also strikes me that despite the gender differences, the body types of the girl and boy are similar. Heath was small, prepubescent. The Steiner girl is very small, almost prepubescent."

I pointed out, "A difference worth noting is that there are no crisscrosses, no shallow cuts at the margins of the Steiner girl's wounds."

Marino explained to the North Carolina officers, "In the Heath case, we think Gault first tried to eradicate bite marks by slicing through them with a knife. Then he figures that's not doing the job so he removes pieces of skin about the size of my shirt pocket. This time, with the little girl he's snatched, maybe he just cuts out the bite marks and is done with it."

"You know, I *really* am uncomfortable with these assumptions. We can't assume it's Gault."

"It's been almost two years, Liz. I doubt Gault got born again or has been working for the Red Cross."

"You don't know that he hasn't. Bundy worked in a crisis center."

"And God talked to the Son of Sam."

"I can assure you God told Berkowitz nothing," Wesley said flatly.

"My point is that maybe Gault—if it's Gault—just cut out the bite marks this time."

"Well, it's true. Like in anything else, these guys get better with practice."

"Lord, I hope this guy don't get any better." Mote dabbed his upper lip with a folded handkerchief.

"Are we about ready to profile this thing?" Wesley glanced around the table. "Would you go for white male?"

"It's a predominantly white neighborhood."

"Absolutely."

"Age?"

"He's logical and that adds years on."

"I agree. I don't think we're talking about a youthful offender here."

"I'd start with twenties. Maybe late twenties."

"I'd go with late twenties to mid-thirties."

"He's very organized. His weapon of choice, for example,

is one he brought with him versus something he found at the scene. And it doesn't look as if he had any trouble controlling his victim."

"According to family members and friends, Emily wouldn't have been hard to control. She was shy, easily frightened."

"Plus, she had a history of being sick, in and out of doctors' offices. She was accustomed to being compliant with adults. In other words, she pretty much did what she was told."

"Not always." Wesley's face was expressionless as he perused the pages of the dead girl's diary. "She didn't want her mother to know she was up at one A.M., in bed with a flashlight. Nor does it appear she planned to tell her mother she was going to the church meeting early that Sunday afternoon. Do we know if this boy, Wren, showed up early as planned?"

"He didn't show until the meeting started at five."

"What about Emily's relationships with other boys?"

"She had typical eleven-year-old relationships. Do you love me? Circle yes or no."

"What's wrong with that?" Marino asked, and everybody laughed.

I continued arranging photographs in front of me like tarot cards as my uneasiness grew. The gunshot wound to the back of the head had entered the right parietal-temporal region of the skull, lacerating the dura and a branch of the middle meningeal artery. Yet there was no contusion, no subdural or epidural hematomas. Nor was there vital reaction to injuries of the genitalia.

"How many hotels are there in your area?"

"I reckon around ten. Now a couple are bed-and-breakfast places, homes where you can get a room."

"Have you been keeping up with registered guests?"

"To tell you the truth, we hadn't thought about that."

"If Gault's in town, he's got to be staying somewhere."

Her laboratory reports were equally perplexing: vitreous

sodium level elevated to 180, potassium 58 milliequivalents per liter.

"Max, let's start with the Travel-Eze. In fact, if you'll do it, I'll hit the Acorn and Apple Blossom. Might want to try the Mountaineer, too, though that's a little farther down the road."

"Gault's most likely to stay in a place where he has maximum anonymity. He's not going to want the staff noticing his coming and going."

"Well, he's not going to have a whole lot of choice. We don't have nothing all that big."

"Probably not the Red Rocker or Blackberry Inn."

"I wouldn't think so, but we'll check 'em out anyway."

"What about Asheville? They must have a few large hotels."

"They got all kinds of things since they passed liquor by the drink."

"You thinking he took the girl to his room and killed her there?"

"No. Absolutely not."

"You can't hold a little kid hostage like that somewhere and not have someone notice. Like housekeeping, room service."

"That's why it would surprise me if Gault's staying in a hotel. The cops started looking for Emily right after she was kidnapped. It was all over the news."

The autopsy had been performed by Dr. James Jenrette, the medical examiner who had been called to the scene. A hospital pathologist in Asheville, Jenrette was under contract with the state to perform forensic autopsies on the rare occasion such a need might arise in the cloistered foothills of western North Carolina. His summary that "some findings were unexplained by the gunshot wound to the head" was simply not enough. I slipped off my glasses and rubbed the bridge of my nose as Benton Wesley spoke.

"What about tourist cabins, rental properties in your area?"

"Yes, sir," Mote answered. "Lots and lots of them." He

turned to Ferguson. "Max, I reckon we'd better check them, too. Get a list, see who's been renting what."

I knew Wesley sensed my troubled mood when he said, "Dr. Scarpetta? You look like you have something to add."

"I'm perplexed by the absence of vital reaction to any of her injuries," I said. "And though the condition of her body suggests she has been dead only several days, her electrolytes don't fit her physical findings. . . ."

"Her what?" Mote's expression went blank.

"Her sodium is high, and since sodium stays fairly stable after death, we can conclude that her sodium was high at the time of her death."

"What does that mean?"

"It could mean she was profoundly dehydrated," I said. "And by the way, she was underweight for her age. Do we know anything about a possible eating disorder? Had she been sick? Vomiting? Diarrhea? A history of taking diuretics?" I scanned the faces around the table.

When no one replied, Ferguson said, "I'll run it by the mother. I gotta talk to her anyway when I get back."

"Her potassium is elevated," I went on. "And this also needs to be explained, because vitreous potassium becomes elevated incrementally and predictably after death as cell walls leak and release it."

"Vitreous?" Mote asked.

"The fluid of the eye is very reliable for testing because it's isolated, protected, and therefore less subject to contamination, putrefaction," I answered. "The point is, her potassium level suggests she's been dead longer than her other findings indicate."

"How long?" Wesley asked.

"Six or seven days."

"Could there be any other explanation for this?"

"Exposure to extreme heat that would have escalated decomposition," I replied.

"Well, that's not going to be it."

"Or an error," I added.

"Can you check it out?"

I nodded.

"Doc Jenrette thinks the bullet in her brain killed her instantly," Ferguson announced. "Seems to me you get killed instantly and there's not going to be any vital reaction."

"The problem," I explained, "is this injury to her brain should not have been instantly fatal."

"How long could she have survived with it?" Mote wanted to know.

"Hours," I replied.

"Other possibilities?" Wesley said to me.

"*Commotio cerebri*. It's like an electrical short circuit—you get a bang on the head, die instantly, and we can't find much if any injury." I paused. "Or it could be that *all* of her injuries are postmortem, including the gunshot wound."

Everybody let that sink in for a moment.

Marino's coffee cup was a small pile of Styrofoam snow, the ashtray in front of him littered with wadded gum wrappers.

He said, "You find anything to indicate maybe she was smothered first?"

I told him I had not.

He began clicking his ballpoint pen open and shut. "Let's talk about her family some more. What do we know about the father besides he's deceased?"

"He was a teacher at Broad River Christian Academy in Swannanoa."

"Same place Emily went?"

"Nope. She went to the public elementary school in Black Mountain. Her daddy died about a year ago," Mote added.

"I noticed that," I said. "His name was Charles?"

Mote nodded.

"What was his cause of death?" I asked.

"I'm not sure. But it was natural."

Ferguson added, "He had a heart condition."

Wesley got up and moved to the whiteboard.

"Okay." He uncapped a black Magic Marker and began writing. "Let's go over the details. Victim's from a middle-class family, white, age eleven, last seen by her peers around six o'clock in the afternoon of October 1 when she walked home alone from a church meeting. On this occasion, she took a shortcut, a path that follows the shore of Lake Tomahawk, a small man-made lake.

"If you look at your map, you'll see there is a clubhouse on the north end of the lake and a public pool, both of which are open only in the summer. Over here you've got tennis courts and a picnic area that are available year-round. According to the mother, Emily arrived home shortly after six-thirty. She went straight to her room and practiced guitar until dinner."

"Did Mrs. Steiner say what Emily ate that night?" I asked the group.

"She told me they had macaroni and cheese and salad," Ferguson said.

"At what time?" According to the autopsy report, Emily's stomach contents consisted of a small amount of brownish fluid.

"Around seven-thirty in the evening is what she told me."

"That would have been digested by the time she was kidnapped at two in the morning?"

"Yes," I said. "It would have cleared her stomach long before then."

"It could be that she wasn't given much in the way of food and water while held in captivity."

"Thus accounting for her high sodium, her possible dehydration?" Wesley asked me.

"That's certainly possible."

He wrote some more. "There's no alarm system in the house, no dog."

"Do we know if anything was stolen?"

"Maybe some clothes."

"Whose?"

"Maybe the mother's. While she was taped up in the closet, she thought she heard him opening drawers."

"If so, he was right tidy. She also said she couldn't tell if anything was missing or disturbed."

"What did the father teach? Did we get to that?"

"Bible."

"Broad River's one of these fundamentalist places. The kids start the day singing 'Sin Shall Not Have Dominion Over Me.'"

"No kidding."

"I'm serious as a heart attack."

"Jesus."

"Yeah, they talk about Him a lot, too."

"Maybe they could do something with my grandson."

"Shit, Hershel, nobody could do nothing with your grandson because you spoil him rotten. How many minibikes he's got now? Three?"

I spoke again. "I'd like to know more about Emily's family. I assume they are religious."

"Very much so."

"Any other siblings?"

Lieutenant Mote took a deep, weary breath. "That's what's really sad about this one. There was a baby some years back, a crib death."

"Was this also in Black Mountain?" I asked.

"No, ma'am. It was before the Steiners moved to the area. They're from California. You know, we got folks from all over."

Ferguson added, "A lot of foreigners head to our hills to retire, vacation, attend religious conventions. Shit, if I had a nickel for every Baptist I wouldn't be sitting here."

I glanced at Marino. His anger was as palpable as heat, his face boiled red. "Just the kind of place Gault would get off on. The folks there read all the big stories about the son of a bitch in *People* magazine, *The National Enquirer, Parade.* But it never enters no one's mind the squirrel might come to town. To them he's Frankenstein. He don't really exist."

"Don't forget they did that TV movie on him, too," Mote spoke again.

"When was that?" Ferguson scowled.

"Last summer, Captain Marino told me. I don't recollect the actor's name, but he's been in a lot of those Termination movies. Isn't that right?"

Marino didn't care. His private posse was thundering through the air. "I think the son of a bitch's still there." He pushed his chair back and added another wad of gum to the ashtray.

"Anything's possible," Wesley said matter-of-factly.

"Well." Mote cleared his throat. "Whatever you boys want to do to help out would be mighty appreciated."

Wesley glanced at his watch. "Pete, you want to cut the lights again? I thought we'd run through these earlier cases, show our two visitors from North Carolina how Gault spent his time in Virginia."

For the next hour horrors flashed in the dark like disjointed scenes from some of my very worst dreams. Ferguson and Mote never took their wide eyes off the screen. They did not say a word. I did not see them blink.

2

Beyond windows in the Boardroom plump groundhogs sunned themselves on the grass as I ate salad and Marino scraped the last trace of the fried chicken special off his plate.

The sky was faded denim blue, trees hinting of how brightly they would burn when fall reached its peak. In a way I envied Marino. The physical demands of his week would almost seem a relief compared to what waited for me, perched darkly over me, like a huge insatiable bird.

"Lucy's hoping you'll find time to do some shooting with her while you're here," I said.

"Depends on if her manners have improved." Marino pushed his tray away.

"Funny, that's what she usually says about you."

He knocked a cigarette out of his pack. "You mind?"

"It doesn't matter because you're going to smoke it anyway."

"You never give a fella any credit, Doc." The cigarette wagged as he talked. "It's not like I haven't cut back." He fired up his lighter. "Tell the truth. You think about smoking every minute."

"You're right. Not a minute goes by that I don't wonder how I stood doing anything so unpleasant and antisocial."

"Bullshit. You miss it like hell. Right now you wish you was me." He exhaled a stream of smoke and gazed out the window. "One day this entire joint's going to end up a sinkhole because of these friggin' groundhogs."

"Why would Gault have gone to western North Carolina?" I asked.

"Why the hell would he go anywhere?" Marino's eyes got hard. "You ask any question about that son of a bitch and the answer's the same. *Because he felt like it.* And he ain't gonna stop with the Steiner girl. Some other little kid—some woman, man, hell, it don't matter—is going to be in the wrong place at the wrong time when Gault gets another itch."

"And you really think he's still there?"

He tapped an ash. "Yeah, I really think he is."

"Why?"

"Because the fun's just begun," he said as Benton Wesley walked in. "The greatest goddam show on earth and he's sitting back watching, laughing his ass off as the Black Mountain cops run around in circles trying to figure out what the hell to do. They average one homicide a year there, by the way."

I watched Wesley head for the salad bar. He ladled soup into a bowl, placed crackers on his tray, and dropped several dollars in a paper plate set out for customers when the cashier wasn't around. He did not indicate that he had seen us, but I knew he had a gift for taking in the smallest details of his surroundings while seeming in a fog.

"Some of Emily Steiner's physical findings make we wonder if her body was refrigerated," I said to Marino as Wesley headed toward us.

"Right. I'm sure it was. At the hospital morgue." Marino gave me an odd look.

"Sounds like I'm missing something important," Wesley said as he pulled out a chair and sat down.

"I'm contemplating that Emily Steiner's body was refrigerated before it was left at the lake," I said.

"Based on what?" A gold Department of Justice cuff link peeked out of his coat sleeve as he reached for the pepper shaker.

"Her skin was doughy and dry," I answered. "She was well preserved and virtually unmolested by insects or animals."

"That pretty much shoots down the idea of Gault staying in some tourist trap motel," Marino said. "He sure as hell didn't stash the body in his minibar."

Wesley, always meticulous, spooned clam chowder away from him and raised it to his lips without spilling a drop.

"What's been turned in for trace?" I asked.

"Her jewelry and socks," Wesley replied. "And the duct tape, which unfortunately was removed before being checked for prints. It was pretty cut up at the morgue."

"Christ," Marino muttered.

"But it's distinctive enough to hold promise. In fact, I can't say I've ever seen blaze orange duct tape before." He was looking at me.

"I certainly haven't," I said. "Do your labs know anything about it yet?"

"Nothing yet except there's a pattern of grease streaks, meaning the edges of the roll the tape came from are streaked with grease. For whatever that's worth."

"What else do the labs have?" I asked.

Wesley said, "Swabs, soil from under the body, the sheet and pouch used to transport her from the lake."

My frustration grew as he continued to talk. I wondered what had been missed. I wondered what microscopic witnesses had been silenced forever.

"I'd like copies of her photographs and reports, and lab results as they come in," I said.

"Whatever's ours is yours," Wesley replied. "The labs will contact you directly."

"We got to get time of death straight," Marino said. "It ain't adding up."

"It's very important we sort that out," Wesley concurred. "Can you do some more checking?"

"I'll do what I can," I said.

"I'm supposed to be in Hogan's Alley." Marino got up from the table as he glanced at his watch. "In fact, I guess they've started without me."

"I hope you plan to change your clothes first," Wesley said to him. "Wear a sweatshirt with a hood."

"Yo. So I get dropped by heat exhaustion."

"Better than getting dropped by nine-millimeter paint bullets," Wesley said. "They hurt like hell."

"What? You two been discussing this or something?"

We watched him leave. He buttoned his blazer over his big belly, smoothed his wispy hair, rearranged his trousers as he walked. Marino had a habit of self-consciously grooming himself like a cat whenever he made an entrance or an exit.

Wesley stared at the dirty ashtray where Marino had been sitting. He turned his eyes to me, and I thought they seemed uncommonly dark, his mouth set as if it had never known how to smile.

"You've got to do something about him," he said.

"I wish I had that power, Benton."

"You're the only one who comes close to having that power."

"That's frightening."

"What's frightening is how red his face got during the consultation. He's not doing a goddam thing he's supposed to do. Fried foods, cigarettes, booze." Wesley glanced away. "Since Doris left he's gone to hell."

"I've seen some improvement," I said.

"Brief remissions." He met my eyes again. "In the main he's killing himself."

In the main, Marino was and had been all of his life. And I did not know what to do about it.

"When are you going back to Richmond?" he asked, and I wondered what went on behind his walls. I wondered about his wife.

"That depends," I answered. "I was hoping to spend a little time with Lucy."

"She's told you we want her back?"

I stared out at sunlit grass and leaves stirring in the wind. "She's thrilled," I said.

"You're not."

"No."

"I understand. You don't want Lucy to share your reality, Kay." His face softened almost imperceptibly. "I suppose it should relieve me that in one department, at least, you are not completely rational or objective."

I was not completely rational or objective in more than one department, and Wesley knew this all too well.

"I'm not even certain what she's doing over there," I said. "How would you feel if it were one of your children?"

"The same way I always feel when it's my children. I don't want them in law enforcement or the military. I don't want them familiar with guns. And yet I want them involved in all of these things."

"Because you know what's out there," I said, my eyes again on his and lingering longer than they should.

He crumpled his napkin and placed it on his tray. "Lucy likes what she's doing. So do we."

"I'm glad to hear it."

"She's remarkable. The software she's helping us develop for VICAP is going to change everything. We're not talking about that much time before it's possible for us to track these animals around the globe. Can you imagine if Gault had murdered the Steiner girl in Australia? Do you think we'd know?"

"Chances are we wouldn't," I said. "Certainly not this soon. But we don't know it's Gault who killed her."

"What we do know is that time is more lives." He reached for my tray and stacked it on top of his.

Both of us got up from the table.

"I think we should drop in on your niece," he said.

"I don't think I'm cleared."

"You're not. But give me a little time and I'll bet I can remedy that."

"I would love it."

"Let's see, it's one o'clock now. How about meeting me back here at four-thirty?" he said as we walked out of the Boardroom.

"How's Lucy getting along in Washington, by the way?" He referred to the least-sought-after dormitory, with its tiny beds and towels too small to cover anything that mattered. "I'm sorry we couldn't have offered her more privacy."

"Don't be. It's good for her to have a roommate and suitemates, not that she necessarily gets along with them."

"Geniuses don't always work and play well with others."

"The only thing she ever flunked on her report card," I said.

I spent the next several hours on the phone, unsuccessfully trying to reach Dr. Jenrette, who apparently had taken the day off to play golf.

My office in Richmond, I was pleased to hear, was under control, the day's cases thus far requiring only views, which were external examinations with body fluids drawn. Blessedly, there had been no homicides from the night before, and my two court cases for the rest of the week had both settled. At the appointed time and place, Wesley and I met.

"Put this on." He handed me a special visitor's pass, which I clipped to my jacket pocket next to my faculty name tag.

"No problems?" I asked.

"It was a stretch, but I managed to pull it off."

"I'm relieved to know I passed the background check," I said ironically.

"Well, just barely."

"Thanks a lot."

He paused, then lightly touched my back as I preceded him through a doorway.

"I don't need to tell you, Kay, that nothing you see or hear at ERF leaves the building."

"You're right, Benton. You don't need to tell me."

Outside the Boardroom, the PX was packed with National Academy students in red shirts browsing at everything imaginable emblazoned with "FBI." Fit men and women politely passed us on steps as they headed to class, not a single blue shirt to be found in the color-coded crowd, for there had been no new agent classes in over a year.

We followed a long corridor to the lobby, where a digital sign above the front desk reminded guests to keep visitor's passes properly displayed. Beyond the front doors, distant gunfire peppered the perfect afternoon.

The Engineering Research Facility was three beige concrete-and-glass pods with large bay doors and high chain-link fences. Rows of parked cars bore testament to a population I never saw, for ERF seemed to swallow its employees and send them away at moments when the rest of us were unconscious.

At the front door, Wesley paused by a sensor module with a numeric keypad that was attached to the wall. He inserted his right thumb over a reading lens, which scanned his print as the data display instructed him to type in his Personal Identification Number. The biometric lock was released with a faint click.

"Obviously, you've been here before," I commented as he held the door for me.

"Many times," he said.

I was left to wonder what business typically brought him here as we followed a beige-carpeted corridor, softly lit and silent, and more than twice the length of a football field. We passed laboratories where scientists in somber suits and lab coats were busily engaged in activities I knew nothing of and could not identify at a glance. Men and women worked in cubicles and over countertops scattered with tools, hardware, video displays, and strange devices. Behind windowless double doors a power saw whined through wood.

At an elevator, Wesley's fingerprint was required again before we could access the rarefied quiet where Lucy spent her days. The second floor was, in essence, an air-conditioned cranium enclosing an artificial brain. Walls and carpet were muted gray, space precisely partitioned like an ice cube tray. Each cubicle contained two modular desks with sleek computers, laser printers, and piles of paper. Lucy was easy to spot. She was the only analyst wearing FBI fatigues.

Her back was to us as she talked into a telephone headset, one hand manipulating a stylus over a computerized message pad, the other typing on a keyboard. If I had not known better, I might have thought she was composing music.

"No, no," she said. "One long beep followed by two short ones and we're probably talking about a malfunction with the monitor, maybe the board containing the video chips."

She swiveled around in her chair when her peripheral vision picked us up.

"Yes, it's a huge difference if it's just one short beep," she explained to the person on the line. "Now we're talking about a problem in a system board. Listen, Dave, can I get back with you?"

I noticed a biometric scanner on her desk, half buried beneath paper. On the floor and filling a shelf overhead were formidable programming manuals, boxes of diskettes and tapes, stacks of computer and software magazines, and a variety of pale blue bound publications stamped with the Department of Justice seal.

"I thought I'd show your aunt what you're up to," Wesley said.

Lucy slipped off the headset, and if she was happy to see us I could not tell.

"Right now I'm up to my ears in problems," she said. "We're getting errors on a couple four-eighty-six machines." She added for my benefit, "We're using PCs to develop the Crime Artificial Intelligence Network known as CAIN."

"*CAIN?*" I marveled. "That's a rather ironic acronym for a system designed to track violent criminals."

Wesley said, "I suppose you could look at it as the ultimate act of contrition on the part of the world's first murderer. Or maybe it simply takes one to know one."

"Basically," Lucy went on, "our ambition is for CAIN to be an automated system that models the real world as much as possible."

"In other words," I said, "it's supposed to think and act the way we do."

"Exactly." She resumed typing. "The crime analysis report you're accustomed to is right here."

Appearing on the screen were queries from the familiar fifteen-page form I had been filling out for years whenever a body was unidentified or the victim of an offender who probably had murdered before and would again.

"It's been condensed a little." Lucy brought up more pages.

"The form's never really been the problem," I pointed out. "It's getting the investigator to complete the darn thing and send it in."

"Now they'll have choices," Wesley said. "They can have a dumb terminal in their precinct that will allow them to sit down and fill in the form on-line. Or for the true Luddite, we have paper—a bubble form or the original one, which can be sent off as usual or faxed."

"We're also working with handwriting recognition technology," Lucy went on. "Computerized message pads can be used while the investigator's in his car, the squad room, waiting around for court. And anything we get on paper—handwritten or otherwise—can be scanned into the system.

"The interactive part comes when CAIN gets a hit or needs

supplementary information. He'll actually communicate with the investigator by modem, or by leaving messages in voice or by electronic mail."

"The potential's enormous," Wesley said to me.

I knew the real reason he had brought me here. This cubicle felt far removed from inner-city field offices, bank robberies, and drug busts. Wesley wanted me to believe if Lucy worked for the Bureau, she would be safe. Yet I knew better, for I understood the ambushes of the mind.

The clean pages my young niece was showing me in her pristine computer would soon carry names and physical descriptions that would make violence real. She would build a data base that would become a landfill of body parts, tortures, weapons and wounds. And one day she would hear the silent screams. She would imagine the faces of victims in crowds she passed.

"I assume what you're applying to police investigators will also have meaning for us," I said to Wesley.

"It goes without saying that medical examiners will be part of the network."

Lucy showed us more screens and elaborated on other marvels in words difficult even for me. Computers were the modern Babel, I had decided. The higher technology reached, the greater the confusion of tongues.

"That's the thing about Structure Query Language," she was explaining. "It's more declarative than navigational, meaning the user specifies *what* he wants accessed from the data base instead of *how* he wants it accessed."

I had begun watching a woman walking in our direction. She was tall, with a graceful but strong stride, a long lab coat flowing around her knees as she slowly stirred a paintbrush in a small aluminum can.

"Have we decided what we're going to run this on eventually?" Wesley continued chatting with my niece. "A mainframe?"

"Actually, the trend is toward downsized client/data base server environments. You know, minis, LANs. Everything gets smaller."

The woman turned into our cubicle, and when she looked up, her eyes went straight to mine and held for a piercing instant before shifting away.

"Was there a meeting scheduled that I didn't know about?" she said with a cool smile as she set the can on her desk. I got the distinct impression she was displeased by the intrusion.

"Carrie, we'll have to take care of our project a little later. Sorry," Lucy said. She added, "I assume you've met Benton Wesley. This is Dr. Kay Scarpetta, my aunt. And this is Carrie Grethen."

"A pleasure to meet you," Carrie Grethen said to me, and I was bothered by her eyes.

I watched her slide into her chair and absently smooth her dark brown hair, which was long and pinned back in an old-fashioned French twist. I guessed she was in her mid-thirties, her smooth skin, dark eyes, and cleanly sculpted features giving her face a patrician beauty both remarkable and rare.

As she opened a file drawer, I noted how orderly her work space was compared to my niece's, for Lucy was too far gone into her esoteric world to give much thought to where to store a book or stack paper. Despite her ancient intellect, she was very much the college kid who chewed gum and lived with clutter.

Wesley spoke. "Lucy? Why don't you show your aunt around?"

"Sure." She seemed reluctant as she exited a screen and got up.

"So, Carrie, tell me exactly what you do here," I heard him say as we walked away.

Lucy glanced back in their direction, and I was startled by the emotion flickering in her eyes.

"What you see in this section is pretty self-explanatory," she said, distracted and quite tense. "Just people and workstations."

"All of them working on VICAP?"

"There's only three of us involved with CAIN. Most of what's done up here is tactical"—she glanced back again. "You know, tactical in the sense of using computers to get a piece of equipment to operate better. Like various electronic collection devices and some of the robots Crisis Response and HRT use."

Her mind was definitely elsewhere as she led me to the far end of the floor, where there was a room secured by another biometric lock.

"Only a few of us are cleared to go in here," she said, scanning her thumb and entering her Personal Identification Number. The gunmetal-gray door opened onto a refrigerated space neatly arranged with workstations, monitors, and scores of modems with blinking lights stacked on shelves. Bundled cables running out the backs of equipment disappeared beneath the raised floor, and monitors swirling with bright blue loops and whorls boldly proclaimed "CAIN." The artificial light, like the air, was clean and cold.

"This is where all fingerprint data are stored," Lucy told me.

"From the locks?" I looked around.

"From the scanners you see everywhere for physical access control and data security."

"And is this sophisticated lock system an ERF invention?"

"We're enhancing and troubleshooting it here. In fact, right now I'm in the middle of a research project pertaining to it. There's a lot to do."

She bent over a monitor and adjusted the brightness of the screen.

"Eventually we'll also be storing fingerprint data from out in the field when cops arrest somebody and use electronic scanning to capture live fingerprints," she went on. "The offender's prints will go straight into CAIN, and if he's committed other crimes from which latent prints were recovered and scanned into the system, we'll get a hit in seconds."

"I assume this will somehow be linked to automated fingerprint identification systems around the country."

"Around the country and hopefully around the world. The point is to have all roads lead here."

"Is Carrie also assigned to CAIN?"

Lucy seemed taken aback. "Yes."

"So she's one of the three people."

"That's right."

When Lucy offered nothing further, I explained, "She struck me as unusual."

"I suppose you could say that about everybody here," my niece answered.

"Where is she from?" I persisted, for I had taken an instant dislike to Carrie Grethen. I did not know why.

"Washington State."

"Is she nice?" I asked.

"She's very good at what she does."

"That doesn't quite answer my question." I smiled.

"I try not to get into the personalities of this place. Why are you so curious?" Defensiveness crept into her tone.

"I'm curious because she made me curious," I simply said.

"Aunt Kay, I wish you'd stop being so protective. Besides, it's inevitable in light of what you do professionally that you're going to think the worst about everyone."

"I see. I suppose it's also inevitable, in light of what I do professionally, that I'm going to think everyone is dead," I said dryly.

"That's ludicrous," my niece said.

"I was simply hoping you'd met some nice people here."

"I would appreciate it if you would also quit worrying about whether I have friends."

"Lucy, I'm not trying to interfere with your life. All I ask is that you're careful."

"No, that isn't all you ask. You *are* interfering."

"It is not my intention," I said, and Lucy could make me angrier than anyone I knew.

"Yes, it is. You really don't want me here."

I regretted my next words even as I said them. "Of course I do. I'm the one who got you this damn internship."

She just stared at me.

"Lucy, I'm sorry. Let's not argue. Please." I lowered my voice and placed my hand on her arm.

She pulled away. "I've got to go check on something."

To my amazement, she abruptly walked off, leaving me alone in a high-security room as arid and chilly as our encounter had become. Colors eddied on video displays, and lights and digital numbers glowed red and green as my thoughts buzzed dully like the pervasive white noise. Lucy was the only child of my irresponsible only sister, Dorothy, and I had no children of my own. But my love for my niece could not be explained by just that.

I understood her secret shame born of abandonment and isolation, and wore her same suit of sorrow beneath my polished armor. When I tended to her wounds, I was tending to my own. This was something I could not tell her. I left, making certain the door was locked behind me, and it did not escape Wesley's notice when I returned from my tour without my guide. Nor did Lucy reappear in time to say good-bye.

"What happened?" Wesley asked as we walked back to the Academy.

"I'm afraid we got into another one of our disagreements," I replied.

He glanced over at me. "Someday get me to tell you about my disagreements with Michele."

"If there's a course in being a mother or an aunt, I think I need to enroll. In fact, I wish I had enrolled a long time ago.

All I did was ask her if she'd made any friends here and she got angry."

"What's your worry?"

"She's a loner."

He looked puzzled. "You've alluded to this before. But to be honest, she doesn't impress me as a loner at all."

"What do you mean?"

We stopped to let several cars pass. The sun was low and warm against the back of my neck, and he had taken off his suit jacket and draped it over his arm.

He gently touched my elbow when it was safe to cross. "I was at the Globe and Laurel several nights ago and Lucy was there with a friend. In fact, it may have been Carrie Grethen, but I'm really not sure. But they seemed to be having a pretty good time."

My surprise couldn't have been much more acute had Wesley just told me Lucy had hijacked a plane.

"And she's been up in the Boardroom a number of late nights. You see one side of your niece, Kay. What's always a shock to parents or parental figures is that there's another side they don't see."

"The side you're talking about is completely foreign to me," I said, and I did not feel relieved. The idea that there were elements of Lucy I did not know was only more disconcerting.

We walked in silence for a moment, and when we reached the lobby I quietly asked, "Benton, is she drinking?"

"She's old enough."

"I realize that," I said.

I was about to ask him more when my heavy preoccupations were aborted by the simple, swift action of his reaching around and snapping his pager off his belt. He held it up and frowned at the number in the display.

"Come on down to the unit," he said, "and let's see what this is about."

3

Lieutenant Hershel Mote could not keep the note of near hysteria out of his voice when Wesley returned his telephone call at twenty-nine minutes past six P.M.

"You're where?" Wesley asked him again on the speaker phone.

"In the kitchen."

"Lieutenant Mote, take it easy. Tell me exactly where you are."

"I'm in SBI Agent Max Ferguson's kitchen. I can't believe this. I've never seen nothing like this."

"Is there anybody else there?"

"It's just me here alone. Except for what's upstairs, like I told you. I've called the coroner and the dispatcher's seeing who he can raise."

"Take it easy, Lieutenant," Wesley said again with his usual unflappability.

I could hear Mote's heavy breathing.

I said to him, "Lieutenant Mote? This is Dr. Scarpetta. I want you to leave everything exactly the way you found it."

"Oh, Lordy," he blurted. "I done cut him down. . . ."

"It's okay. . . ."

"When I walked in I . . . Lord have mercy, I couldn't just leave him like that."

"It's all right," I reassured him. "But it's very important that nobody touches him now."

"What about the coroner?"

"Not even him."

Wesley's eyes were on me. "We're heading out. You'll see us no later than twenty-two hundred hours. In the meantime, you sit tight."

"Yes, sir. I'm just going to sit right in this chair till my chest stops hurting."

"When did this start?" I wanted to know.

"When I got here and found him. I started having these pains in my chest."

"Have you ever had them before?"

"Not that I recollect. Not like this."

"Describe where they are," I said with growing alarm.

"Right in the middle."

"Has the pain gone to your arms or neck?"

"No, ma'am."

"Any dizziness or sweating?"

"I'm sweating a bit."

"Does it hurt when you cough?"

"I've not been coughing. So I don't reckon I can say."

"Have you ever had any heart disease or high blood pressure?"

"Not that I know of."

"And you smoke?"

"I'm doing it now."

"Lieutenant Mote, I want you to listen to me carefully. I want you to put out your cigarette and try to calm down. I'm very concerned because you've had a terrible shock, you're a smoker, and that's a setup for a coronary. You're down there and I'm up here. I want you to call an ambulance right now."

"The pain's settling down a little. And the coroner should be here any minute. He's a doctor."

"That would be Dr. Jenrette?" Wesley inquired.

"He's all we got 'round here."

"I don't want you fooling around with chest pains, Lieutenant Mote," I said firmly.

"No, ma'am, I won't."

Wesley wrote down addresses and phone numbers. He hung up and made another call.

"Is Pete Marino still running around out there?" he asked whoever had answered the phone. "Tell him we've got an urgent situation. He's to grab an overnight bag and meet us over at HRT as fast as he can get there. I'll explain when I see him."

"Look, I'd like Katz in on this one," I said as Wesley got up from his desk. "We're going to want to fume everything we can for prints, in the event things aren't the way they appear."

"Good idea."

"I doubt he'd be at The Body Farm this late. You might want to try his pager."

"Fine. I'll see if I can track him down," he said of my forensic scientist colleague from Knoxville.

When I got to the lobby fifteen minutes later, Wesley was already there, a tote bag slung over his shoulder. I had had just enough time in my room to exchange pumps for more sensible shoes, and to grab other necessities, including my medical bag.

"Dr. Katz is leaving Knoxville now," Wesley told me. "He'll meet us at the scene."

Night was settling beneath a distant slivered moon, and trees stirring in the wind sounded like rain. Wesley and I followed the drive in front of Jefferson and crossed a road dividing the Academy complex from acres of field offices and firing ranges. Closest to us, in the demilitarized zone of barbecues and picnic tables shaded by trees, I spotted a familiar figure so out of context that for an instant I thought I was mistaken. Then I recalled Lucy once mentioning to me that she sometimes wandered out here alone after dinner to think, and my heart lifted at the chance of making amends with her.

"Benton," I said, "I'll be right back."

The faint sound of conversation drifted toward me as I neared the edge of the woods, and I wondered, bizarrely, if my niece were talking to herself. Lucy was perched on top of a picnic table, and as I drew closer I was about to call her name when I saw she was speaking to someone seated below her on the bench. They were so close to each other their silhouettes were one, and I froze in the darkness of a tall, dense pine.

"That's because you always do that," Lucy was saying in a wounded tone I knew well.

"No, it's because you always assume I'm doing that." The woman's voice was soothing.

"Well, then, don't give me cause."

"Lucy, can't we get past this? *Please.*"

"Let me have one of those."

"I wish you wouldn't start."

"I'm not starting. I just want a puff."

I heard the spurt of a match striking, and a small flame penetrated the darkness. For an instant, my niece's profile was illuminated as she leaned closer to her friend, whose face I could not see. The tip of the cigarette glowed as they passed it back and forth. I silently turned and walked away.

Wesley resumed his long strides when I got back to him. "Someone you know?" he asked.

"I thought it was," I said.

We walked without speaking past empty ranges with rows of target frames and steel silhouettes eternally standing at attention. Beyond, a control tower rose over a building constructed completely of tires, where HRT, the Bureau's Green Berets, practiced maneuvers with live ammunition. A white-and-blue

Bell JetRanger waited on the nearby grass like a sleeping insect, its pilot standing outside with Marino.

"We all here?" the pilot asked as we approached.

"Yes. Thanks, Whit," Wesley said.

Whit, a perfect specimen of male fitness in a black flight suit, opened the helicopter's doors to help us board. We strapped ourselves in, Marino and I in back, Wesley up front, and put on headsets as blades began to turn, the jet engine warming.

Minutes later, the dark earth was suddenly far beneath our feet as we rose above the horizon, air vents open and cabin lights off. Our transmitted voices blurted on and off in our ears as the helicopter sped south toward a tiny mountain town where another person was dead.

"He couldn't have been home long," Marino said. "We know . . . ?"

"He wasn't." Wesley's voice cut in from the copilot's seat. "He left Quantico right after the consultation. Flew out of National at one."

"We know what time his plane got to Asheville?"

"Around four-thirty. He could have been back to his house by five."

"In Black Mountain?"

"Right."

I spoke. "Mote found him at six."

"Jesus." Marino turned to me. "Ferguson must've started beating off the minute he hit—"

The pilot cut in, "We got music if anybody wants it."

"Sure."

"What flavor?"

"Classical."

"Shit, Benton."

"You're outvoted, Pete."

"Ferguson hadn't been home long. That much is clear no matter who or what's to blame," I resumed our jerky conversation as Berlioz began in the background.

"Looks like an accident. Like autoeroticism gone bad. But we don't know."

Marino nudged me. "Got any aspirins?"

I dug in my pocketbook in the dark, then got a mini Maglite out of my medical bag and rooted around some more. Marino muttered profanities when I motioned I could not help him, and I realized he was still in the sweatpants, hooded sweatshirt, and lace-up boots he had been wearing at Hogan's Alley. He looked like a harddrinking coach for some bush-league team, and I could not resist shining the light over incriminating red paint stains on his upper back and left shoulder. Marino had gotten shot.

"Yeah, well, you ought to see the other guys," his voice abruptly sounded in my ears. "Yo, Benton. Got any aspirins?"

"Airsick?"

"Having too much fun for that," said Marino, who hated to fly.

The weather was in our favor as we chopped a path through the clear night at around a hundred and five knots. Cars below us glided like bright-eyed waterbugs as the lights of civilization flickered like small fires in the trees. The vibrating darkness might have soothed me to sleep were my nerves not running hot. My mind would not stay still as images clashed and questions screamed.

I envisioned Lucy's face, the lovely curve of her jaw and cheek as she leaned into the flame cupped by her girlfriend's hands. Their impassioned voices sounded in my memory, and I did not know why I was stunned. I did not know why it should matter. I wondered how much Wesley was aware. My niece had been interning at Quantico since fall semester had begun. He had seen her quite a lot more than I had.

There was not a breath of wind until we got into the mountains, and for a while the earth was a pitch-black plain.

"Going up to forty-five hundred feet," our pilot's voice sounded in our headsets. "Everybody all right back there?"

"I don't guess you can smoke in here," Marino said.

At ten past nine, the inky sky was pricked with stars, the Blue Ridge a black ocean swelling without motion or sound. We followed deep shadows of woods, smoothly turning with the pitch of blades toward a brick building that I suspected was a school. Around a corner, we found a football field with police lights flashing and flares burning copper in an unnecessary illumination of our landing zone. And the Nightsun's thirty million peak candlepower blazed down from our belly as we made our descent. At the fifty-yard line, Whit settled us softly like a bird.

"'Home of the War Horses,'" Wesley read from bunting draped along the fence. "Hope they're having a better season than we are."

Marino gazed out his window as the blades slowed down. "I haven't seen a high school football game since I was in one."

"I didn't know you played football," I remarked.

"Yo. Number twelve."

"What position?"

"Tight end."

"That figures," I said.

"This is actually Swannanoa," Whit announced. "Black Mountain's just east."

We were met by two uniformed officers from the Black Mountain Police. They looked too young to drive or carry guns, their faces pale and peculiar as they tried not to stare. It was as if we had arrived by spacecraft in a blaze of gyrating lights and unearthly quiet. They did not know what to make of us or what was happening in their town, and it was with very little conversation that they drove us away.

Moments later, we parked along a narrow street throbbing with engines and emergency lights. I counted three cruisers in addition to ours, one ambulance, two fire trucks, two unmarked cars, and a Cadillac.

"Great," Marino muttered as he shut the car door. "Everybody and his cousin Abner's here."

Crime-scene tape ran from the front porch posts to shrubbery, fanning out on either side of the beige two-story aluminum-sided house. A Ford Bronco was parked in the gravel drive ahead of an unmarked Skylark with police antennas and lights.

"The cars are Ferguson's?" Wesley asked as we mounted concrete steps.

"The ones in the drive, yes, sir," the officer replied. "That window up in the corner's where he's at."

I was dismayed when Lieutenant Hershel Mote suddenly appeared in the front doorway. Obviously, he had not followed my advice.

"How are you feeling?" I asked him.

"I'm holding on." He looked so relieved to see us I almost expected a hug. But his face was gray. Sweat ringed the collar of his denim shirt and shone on his brow and neck. He reeked of stale cigarettes.

We hesitated in the foyer, our backs to stairs that led to the second floor.

"What's been done?" Wesley asked.

"Doc Jenrette took pictures, lots of 'em, but he didn't touch nothing, just like you said. He's outside talking to the squad if you need him."

"There's a lot of cars out there," Marino said. "Where is everybody?"

"A couple of the boys are in the kitchen. And one or two's poking around the yard and in the woods out back."

"But they haven't been upstairs?"

Mote let out a deep breath. "Well, now, I'm not going to stand here and lie to you. They did go on up and look. But nobody's messed with anything, I can promise you that. The Doc's the only one who got close."

He started up the stairs. "Max is . . . he's . . . Well, goddam." He stopped and looked back at us, his eyes bright with tears.

"I'm not clear on how you discovered him," Marino said.

We resumed climbing steps as Mote struggled for composure. The floor was covered in the same dark red carpet I had seen downstairs, the heavily varnished pine paneling the color of honey.

He cleared his throat. "About six this evening I stopped by to see if Max wanted to go out for some supper. When he didn't come to the door, I figured he was in the shower or something and came on in."

"Were you aware of anything that might have indicated he had a history of this type of activity?" Wesley delicately asked.

"No, sir," Mote said with feeling. "I can't imagine it. I sure don't understand. . . . Well, I've heard tell of people rigging up weird things. I can't say I know what it's for."

"The point of using a noose while masturbating is to place pressure on the carotids," I explained. "This constricts the flow of oxygen and blood to the brain, which supposedly enhances orgasm."

"Also known as going while you're coming," Marino remarked with his typical subtlety.

Mote did not accompany us as we moved forward to a lighted doorway at the end of the hall.

SBI Agent Max Ferguson had a manly, modest bedroom with pine chests of drawers and a rack filled with shotguns and rifles over a rolltop desk. His pistol, wallet, credentials, and a box of Rough Rider condoms were on the table by the quilt-covered bed, the suit I'd seen him wearing in Quantico this morning neatly draped over a chair, shoes and socks nearby.

A wooden bar stool stood between the bathroom and closet, inches from where his body was covered with a colorful crocheted afghan. Overhead, a severed nylon cord dangled from an eye hook screwed into the wooden ceiling. I got gloves and a thermometer out of my medical bag. Marino swore under his breath as I pulled the afghan back from what must have been

Ferguson's worst nightmare. I doubted he would have feared a bullet half as much.

He was on his back, the size-D cups of a long-line black brassiere stuffed with socks that smelled faintly of musk. The pair of black nylon panties he had put on before he died had been pulled down around his hairy knees, and a condom still clung limply to his penis. Magazines nearby revealed his predilection for women in bondage with spectacularly augmented breasts and nipples the size of saucers.

I examined the nylon noose tightly angled around the towel padding his neck. The cord, old and fuzzy, had been severed just above the eighth turn of a perfect hangman's knot. His eyes were almost shut, his tongue protruding.

"Is this consistent with him sitting on the stool?" Marino looked up at the segment of rope attached to the ceiling.

"Yes," I said.

"So he was beating off and slipped?"

"Or he may have lost consciousness and then slipped," I answered.

Marino moved to the window and leaned over a tumbler of amber liquid on the sill. "Bourbon," he announced. "Straight or close to it."

The rectal temperature was 91 degrees, consistent with what I would have expected had Ferguson been dead approximately five hours in this room, his body covered. Rigor mortis had started in the small muscles. The condom was a studded affair with a large reservoir that was dry, and I went over to the bed to take a look at the box. One condom was missing, and when I stepped into the master bathroom I found the purple foil wrapper in the wicker trash basket.

"That's interesting," I said as Marino opened dresser drawers.

"What is?"

"I guess I assumed he would have put on the condom while he was rigged up."

"Makes sense to me."

"Then wouldn't you expect the wrapper to be near his body?" I picked it out of the trash, touching as little of it as possible, and placed it inside a plastic bag.

When Marino didn't respond, I added, "Well, I guess it all depends on when he pulled down his panties. Maybe he did that before he put the noose around his neck."

I walked back into the bedroom. Marino was squatting by a chest of drawers, staring at the body, a mixture of incredulity and disgust on his face.

"And I always thought the worst thing that could happen is you croak on the john," he said.

I looked up at the eye bolt in the ceiling. There was no way to tell how long it had been there. I started to ask Marino if he had found any other pornography when we were startled by a heavy thud in the hallway.

"What the hell . . . ?" Marino exclaimed.

He was out the door, and I was right behind him.

Lieutenant Mote had collapsed near the stairs. He was facedown and motionless on the carpet. When I knelt beside him and turned him over, he was already blue.

"He's in cardiac arrest! Get the squad!" I pulled Mote's jaw forward to make sure his airway was unobstructed.

Marino's feet thundered down the stairs as I placed my fingers on Mote's carotid and felt no pulse. I thumped his chest but his heart would not answer. I began CPR, compressing his chest once, twice, three times, four, then tilted his head back and blew once into his mouth. His chest rose, and one-two-three-four I blew again.

I maintained a rhythm of sixty compressions per minute as sweat rolled down my temples and my own pulse roared. My arms ached and were becoming as unwilling as stone when I began the third minute and the noise of paramedics and police swelled up from the stairs. Someone gripped my elbow and guided me out of the way as many pairs of gloved hands slapped on leads, hung a bottle of IV fluid, and started a line. Voices barked orders and announced every activity in the loud dispassion of rescue efforts and emergency rooms.

As I leaned against the wall and tried to catch my breath, I noticed a short, fair young man incongruously dressed for golf watching the activity from the landing. After several glances in my direction, he approached me shyly.

"Dr. Scarpetta?"

His earnest face was sunburned below his brow, which obviously had been spared by a cap. It occurred to me that he probably belonged to the Cadillac parked out front.

"Yes?"

"James Jenrette," he said, confirming my suspicions. "Are you all right?" He withdrew a neatly folded handkerchief and offered it to me.

"I'm doing okay, and I'm very glad you're here," I said sincerely, for I could not turn over my latest patient to someone who was not an M.D. "Can I entrust Lieutenant Mote to your care?" My arms trembled as I wiped my face and neck.

"Absolutely. I'll go with him to the hospital." Jenrette next handed me his card. "If you have any other questions tonight, just page me."

"You'll be posting Ferguson in the morning?" I asked.

"Yes. You're welcome to assist. Then we'll talk about all this." He looked down the hall.

"I'll be there. Thank you." I managed a smile.

Jenrette followed the stretcher out, and I returned to the bedroom at the end of the hall. From the window, I watched lights pulse blood red on the street below as Mote was placed inside the ambulance. I wondered if he would live. I sensed the presence of Ferguson in his flaccid condom and stiff brassiere, and none of it seemed real.

The tailgate slammed. Sirens whelped as if in protest before they began to scream. I was not aware that Marino had walked into the room until he touched my arm.

"Katz is downstairs," he informed me.

I slowly turned around. "We'll need another squad," I said.

4

It had long been a theoretical possibility that latent fingerprints could be left on human skin. But the likelihood of recovering them had been so remote as to discourage most of us from trying.

Skin is a difficult surface, for it is plastic and porous, and its moisture, hairs, and oils interfere. On the uncommon occasion that a print is successfully transferred from assailant to victim, the ridge detail is far too fragile to survive much time or exposure to the elements.

Dr. Thomas Katz was a master forensic scientist who had maniacally pursued this elusive evidence for most of his career. He also was an expert in time of death, which he researched just as diligently with ways and means that were not commonly known to the hoi polloi. His laboratory was called The Body Farm, and I had been there many times.

He was a small man with prepossessed blue eyes, a great shock of white hair, and a face amazingly benevolent for the atrocities he had seen. When I met him at the top of the stairs, he was carrying a box window fan, a tool chest, and what looked like a section of vacuum cleaner hose with several odd attachments. Marino was behind him with the rest of what Katz called his "Cyanoacrylate Blowing Contraption," a double-decker aluminum box fitted with a hot plate and a computer fan. He had spent hundreds of hours in his East Tennessee garage perfecting this rather simple mechanical implement.

"Where are we heading?" Katz asked me.

"The room at the end of the hall." I relieved him of the window fan. "How was your trip?"

"More traffic than I bargained for. Tell me what all's been done to the body."

"He was cut down and covered with a wool afghan. I have not examined him."

"I promise not to delay you too much. It's a lot easier now that I'm not bothering with a tent."

"What do you mean, *a tent*?" Marino frowned as we entered the bedroom.

"I used to put a plastic tent over the body and do the fuming inside it. But too much vapor and the skin gets too frosted. Dr. Scarpetta, you can set the fan in that window." Katz looked around. "I might have to use a pan of water. It's a bit dry in here."

I gave him as much history as we had at this point.

"Do you have any reason to think this is something other than an accidental autoerotic asphyxiation?" he asked.

"Other than the circumstances," I replied, "no."

"He was working that little Steiner girl's case."

"That's what we mean by circumstances," Marino said.

"Lord, if that hasn't been in the news all over."

"We were in Quantico this morning meeting about that case," I added.

"And he comes straight home and then this." Katz looked thoughtfully at the body. "You know, we found a prostitute in a Dumpster the other week and got a good outline of a hand on her ankle. She'd been dead four or five days."

"Kay?" Wesley stepped into the doorway. "May I see you for a minute?"

"And you used this thing on her?" Marino's voice followed us into the hall.

"I did. She had painted fingernails, and as it turns out, they're real good, too."

"For what?"

"Prints."

"Where does this go?"

"Doesn't matter much. I'm going to fume the entire room. I'm afraid it's going to mess up the place."

"I don't think he's gonna complain."

Downstairs in the kitchen, I noticed a chair by the phone where I supposed Mote had sat for hours waiting for us to arrive. Nearby on the floor was a glass of water and an ashtray crammed with cigarette butts.

"Take a look," said Wesley, who was accustomed to searching for odd evidence in odd places.

He had filled the double sink with foods he had gotten out of the freezer. I moved closer to him as he opened the folds of a small, flat package wrapped in white freezer paper. Inside were shrunken pieces of frozen flesh, dry at the edges and reminiscent of yellowed waxy parchment.

"Any chance I'm thinking the wrong thing?" Wesley's tone was grim.

"Good God, Benton," I said, stunned.

"They were in the freezer on top of these other things. Ground beef, pork chops, pizza." He nudged packages with a gloved finger. "I was hoping you'd tell me it's chicken skin. Maybe something he uses for fish bait or who knows what."

"There are no feather holes, and the hair is fine like human hair."

He was silent.

"We need to pack this in dry ice and fly it back with us," I said.

"That won't be tonight."

"The sooner we can get immunological testing done, the sooner we can confirm it's human. DNA will confirm identity."

He returned the package to the freezer. "We need to check for prints."

"I'll put the tissue in plastic and we'll submit the freezer paper to the labs," I said.

"Good."

We climbed the stairs. My pulse would not slow down. At the end of the hallway, Marino and Katz stood outside the shut door. They had threaded a hose through the hole where the doorknob had been, the contraption humming as it pumped Super Glue vapors into Ferguson's bedroom.

Wesley had yet to mention the obvious, so finally I did. "Benton, I didn't see any bite marks or anything else someone may have tried to eradicate."

"I know," he said.

"We're almost done," Katz told us when we got to them. "A room this size and you can get by with less than a hundred drops of Super Glue."

"Pete," Wesley said, "we've got an unexpected problem."

"I thought we'd already reached our quota for the day," he said, staring blandly at the hose pumping poison beyond the door.

"That should do it," said Katz, who was typically impervious to the moods of those around him. "All I got to do now is clear out the fumes with the fan. That will take a minute or two."

He opened the door and we backed away. The overpowering smell didn't seem to bother him in the least.

"He probably gets high off the stuff," Marino muttered as Katz walked into the room.

"Ferguson's got what appears to be human skin in his freezer." Wesley went straight to the point.

"You want to run that one by me again?" Marino said, startled.

"I don't know what we're dealing with here," Wesley added as the window fan inside the room began to whir. "But we got one detective dead with incriminating evidence found with his frozen hamburgers and pizza. We got another detective with a heart attack. We've got a murdered eleven-year-old girl."

"Goddam," Marino said, his face turning red.

"I hope you brought enough clothes to stay for a while," Wesley added to both of us.

"Goddam," Marino said again. "That son of a bitch."

He looked straight at me and I knew exactly what he was thinking. A part of me hoped he was wrong. But if Gault wasn't playing his usual malignant games, I wasn't certain the alternative was better.

"Does this house have a basement?" I asked.

"Yes," Wesley answered.

"What about a big refrigerator?" I asked.

"I haven't seen one. But I haven't been in the basement."

Inside the bedroom, Katz turned off the window fan. He motioned to us that it was all right to come in.

"Man, try getting this shit off," Marino said as he looked around.

Super Glue dries white and is as stubborn as cement. Every surface in the room was lightly frosted with it, including Ferguson's body. With flashlight angled, Katz sidelighted smudges on walls, furniture, windowsills, and the guns over the desk. But it was just one he found that brought him to his knees.

"It's the nylon," our friendly mad scientist said with pure delight as he knelt by the body and leaned close to Ferguson's pulled-down panties. "You know, it's a good surface for prints because of the tight weave. He's got some kind of perfume on."

He slipped the plastic sheath off his Magna brush, and the

bristles fell open like a sea anemone. Unscrewing the lid from a jar of Delta Orange magnetic powder, Katz dusted a very good latent print that someone had left on the dead detective's shiny black nylon panties. Partial prints had materialized around Ferguson's neck, and Katz used contrasting black powder on them. But there wasn't enough ridge detail to matter. The strange frost everywhere I looked made the room seem cold.

"Of course, this print on his panties is probably his own," Katz mused as he continued to work. "From when he pulled them down. He might have had something on his hands. The condom's probably lubricated, for example, and if some of that transferred to his fingers, he could have left a good print. You're going to want to take these?" He referred to the panties.

"I'm afraid so," I said.

He nodded. "That's all right. Pictures will do." He got out his camera. "But I'd like the panties when you're finished with them. As long as you don't use scissors, the print will hold up fine. That's the good thing about Super Glue. Can't get it off with dynamite."

"How much more do you need to do here tonight?" Wesley said to me, and I could tell he was anxious to leave.

"I want to look for anything that might not survive the body's transport, and take care of what you found in the freezer," I said. "Plus we need to check the basement."

He nodded and said to Marino, "While we take care of these things, how about your being in charge of securing this place?"

Marino didn't seem thrilled with the assignment.

"Tell them we'll need security around the clock," Wesley added firmly.

"Problem is, they don't got enough uniforms in this town to do anything around the clock," Marino said sourly as he walked off. "The damn bastard's just wiped out half the police department."

Katz looked up and spoke, his Magna brush posed midair. "Seems like you're pretty certain who you're looking for."

"Nothing's certain," Wesley said.

"Thomas, I'm going to have to ask for another favor," I said to my dedicated colleague. "I need you and Dr. Shade to run an experiment for me at The Farm."

"Dr. Shade?" Wesley said.

"Lyall Shade is an anthropologist at the University of Tennessee," I explained.

"When do we start?" Katz loaded a new roll of film into his camera.

"Immediately, if possible. It will take a week."

"Fresh bodies or old?"

"Fresh."

"That really is the guy's name?" Wesley went on.

It was Katz who answered as he took a photograph. "Sure is. Spelled L-Y-A-L-L. Goes all the way back to his great-grandfather, a surgeon in the Civil War."

5

Max Ferguson's basement was accessible by concrete steps in back of his house, and I could tell by dead leaves drifted against them that no one had been here for a while. But I could be no more exact than that, for fall had peaked in the mountains. Even as Wesley tried the door, leaves spiraled down without a sound as if the stars were shedding ashes.

"I'm going to have to break the glass," he said, jiggling the knob some more as I held a flashlight.

Reaching inside his jacket, he withdrew the Sig Sauer nine-millimeter pistol from its shoulder holster and sharply tapped the butt against a large pane in the center of the door. The noise of glass shattering startled me even though I was prepared for it, and I half expected police to rapidly materialize from the dark. But no footfall or human voice was carried on the wind, and I imagined the existentialist terror Emily Steiner must have felt before she died. No matter where that might have been, no one had heard her smallest cry, no one had come to save her.

Tiny glass teeth left in the mullion sparkled as Wesley

carefully put his arm through the opening and found the inside knob.

"Damn," he said, pushing against the door. "The latch bolt must be rusted."

Working his arm in farther to get a better grip, he was straining against the stubborn lock when suddenly it gave. The door flew open with such force that Wesley spilled into the opening, knocking the flashlight out of my hand. It bounced, rolled, and was extinguished by concrete as I was hit by a wall of cold, foul air. In complete darkness, I heard broken glass scrape as Wesley moved.

"Are you all right?" I blindly inched forward, hands held out in front of me. *"Benton?"*

"Jesus." He sounded shaky as he got to his feet.

"Are you okay?"

"Damn, I can't believe this." His voice moved farther away from me.

Glass crunched as he groped along the wall, and what sounded like an empty paint bucket clanged dully as he knocked it with his foot. I squinted when a naked bulb went on overhead, my eyes adjusting to a vision of Benton Wesley dirty and dripping blood.

"Let me see." I gently took hold of his left wrist as he scanned our surroundings, rather dazed. "Benton, we need to get you to a hospital," I said as I examined multiple lacerations on his palm. "You've got glass embedded in several of these cuts, and you're going to need stitches."

"You're a doctor." The handkerchief he wrapped around his hand instantly turned red.

"You need a hospital," I repeated as I noticed blood spreading darkly through the torn fabric of his left trouser leg.

"I hate hospitals." Behind his stoicism, pain smoldered in his eyes like fever. "Let's look around and get out of this hole. I promise not to bleed to death in the meantime."

I wondered where the hell Marino was.

It did not appear that SBI Agent Ferguson had entered his basement in years. Nor did I see any reason why he should have unless he had a penchant for dust, cobwebs, rusting garden tools, and rotting carpet. Water stained the concrete floor and cinderblock walls, and body parts of crickets told me that legions had lived and died down here. As we wandered corner to corner, we saw nothing to make us suspicious that Emily Steiner had ever been a visitor.

"I've seen enough," said Wesley, whose bright red trail on the dusty floor had come full circle.

"Benton, we've got to do something about your bleeding."

"What do you suggest?"

"Look that way for a moment." I directed him to turn his back to me.

He did not question why as he complied, and I quickly stepped out of my shoes and hiked up my skirt. In seconds, I had my panty hose off.

"Okay. Let me have your arm," I told him next.

I tucked it snugly between my elbow and side as any physician in similar circumstances might. But as I wrapped the panty hose around his injured hand, I could feel his eyes on me. I became intensely aware of his breath touching my hair as his arm touched my breast, and a heat so palpable I feared he felt it, too, spread up my neck. Amazed and completely flustered, I quickly finished my improvised dressing of his wounds and backed away.

"That should hold you until we can get to a place where I can do something more serious." I avoided his eyes.

"Thank you, Kay."

"I suppose I should ask where we're going next," I went on in a bland tone that belied my agitation. "Unless you're planning on our sleeping in the helicopter."

"I put Pete in charge of accommodations."

"You do live dangerously."

"Usually not this dangerously." He flipped off the light and made no attempt to relock the basement door.

The moon was a gold coin cut in half, the sky around it midnight blue, and through branches of far-off trees peeked the lights of Ferguson's neighbors. I wondered if any of them knew he was dead. On the street, we found Marino in the front seat of a Black Mountain Police cruiser, smoking a cigarette, a map spread open in his lap. The interior light was on, the young officer behind the wheel no more relaxed than he had seemed hours earlier when he had picked us up at the football field.

"What the hell happened to you?" Marino said to Wesley. "You decide to punch out a window?"

"More or less," Wesley replied.

Marino's eyes wandered from Wesley's panty-hose bandage to my bare legs. "Well, well, now ain't that something," he muttered. "I wish they'd taught that when I was taking CPR."

"Where are our bags?" I ignored him.

"They're in the trunk, ma'am," said the officer.

"Officer T. C. Baird here's going to be a Good Samaritan and drop us by the Travel-Eze, where yours truly's already taken care of reservations," Marino went on in the same irritating tone. "Three deluxe rooms at thirty-nine ninety-nine a pop. I got us a discount because we're cops."

"I'm not a cop." I looked hard at him.

Marino flicked his cigarette butt out the window. "Take it easy, Doc. On a good day, you could pass for one."

"On a good day, so can you," I answered him.

"I think I've just been insulted."

"No, I'm the one who's just been insulted. You know better than to misrepresent me for discounts or any other reason," I said, for I was an appointed government official bound by very clear rules. Marino knew damn well that I could not afford the slightest compromise of scrupulosity, for I had enemies. I had many of them.

Wesley opened the cruiser's back door. "After you," he

quietly said to me. Of Officer Baird he asked, "Do we know anything further about Mote?"

"He's in intensive care, sir."

"What about his condition?"

"It doesn't sound too good, sir. Not at this time."

Wesley climbed in next to me, delicately resting his bandaged hand on his thigh. He said, "Pete, we've got a lot of people to talk to around here."

"Yeah, well, while you two was playing doctor in the basement, I was already working on that." Marino held up a notepad and flipped through pages scribbled with illegible notes.

"Are we ready to go?" Baird asked.

"More than ready," Wesley answered, and he was losing patience with Marino, too.

The interior light went off and the car moved forward. For a while, Marino, Wesley, and I talked as if the young officer wasn't there as we passed over unfamiliar dark streets, cool mountain air blowing through barely opened windows. We sketched out our strategy for tomorrow morning. I would assist Dr. Jenrette with the autopsy of Max Ferguson while Marino talked to Emily Steiner's mother. Wesley would fly back to Quantico with the tissue from Ferguson's freezer, and the results of these activities would determine what we did next.

It was almost two A.M. when we spotted the Travel-Eze Motel ahead of us on U.S. 70, its sign neon yellow against the rolling dark horizon. I couldn't have been happier had our quarters been a Four Seasons, until we were informed at the registration desk that the restaurant had closed, room service had ended, and there was no bar. In fact, the clerk advised in his North Carolina accent, at this hour we would be better off looking forward to breakfast instead of looking back at the dinner we had missed.

"You got to be kidding," Marino said, thunder gathering in

his face. "If I don't get something to eat my gut's going to turn inside out."

"I'm mighty sorry, sir." The clerk was but a boy with rosy cheeks and hair almost as yellow as the motel's sign. "But the good news is there's vending machines on each floor." He pointed. "And a Mr. Zip no more'n a mile from here."

"Our ride just left." Marino glared at him. "What? I'm supposed to walk a mile at this hour to some joint called *Mr. Zip*?"

The clerk's smile froze, fear shining in his eyes like tiny candles as he looked to Wesley and me for reassurance. But we were too worn out to be much help. When Wesley rested his bloody panty-hose wrapped hand on the counter, the lad's expression turned to horror.

"Sir! Do you need a doctor?" His voice went up an octave and cracked.

"Just my room key will be fine," Wesley replied.

The clerk turned around and nervously lifted three keys from their consecutive hooks, dropping two of them to the carpet. He stooped to pick them up and dropped one of them again. At last, he presented them to us, the room numbers stamped on the attached plastic medallions big enough to read at twenty paces.

"You ever heard of security in this joint?" Marino said as if he had hated the boy since birth. "You're supposed to write the room number on a piece of paper which you *privately* slip to the guest so every drone can't see where he keeps the wife and Rolex. In case you ain't keeping up with the news, you had a murder real close to here just a couple weeks back."

In speechless bewilderment the clerk watched Marino next hold up his key as if it were a piece of incriminating evidence.

"No minibar key? Meaning forget having a drink in the room at this hour, too?" Marino raised his voice some more. "Never mind. I don't want no more bad news."

As we followed a sidewalk to the middle of the small

motel, TV screens flickered blue and shadows moved behind filmy curtains over plate-glass windows. Alternating red and green doors reminded me of the plastic hotels and homes of Monopoly as we climbed stairs to the second floor and found our rooms. Mine was neatly made and cozy, the television bolted to the wall, water glasses and ice bucket wrapped in sanitary plastic.

Marino repaired to his quarters without bidding us good-night, shutting his door just a little too hard.

"What the hell's eating him?" Wesley asked as he followed me into my room.

I did not want to talk about Marino, and pulling a chair close to one of the double beds, I said, "Before I do anything we need to clean you up."

"Not without painkiller."

Wesley went out to fill the ice bucket and removed a fifth of Dewar's from his tote bag. He fixed drinks while I spread a towel on the bed and arranged it with forceps, packets of Betadine, and 5-O nylon sutures.

"This is going to hurt, isn't it." He looked at me as he took a big swallow of Scotch.

I put on my glasses and replied, "It's going to hurt like hell. Follow me." I headed into the bathroom.

For the next several minutes, we stood side by side at the sink while I washed his wounds with warm soapy water. I was as gentle as possible and he did not complain, but I could feel him flinch in the small muscles of his hand. When I glanced at his face in the mirror, he was perspiring and pale. He had five gaping lacerations in his palm.

"You're just lucky you missed your radial artery," I said.

"I can't tell you how lucky I feel."

Looking at his knee, I added, "Sit here." I lowered the toilet lid.

"Do you want me to take my pants off?"

"Either that or we cut them."

He sat down. "They're ruined anyway."

With a scalpel, I sliced through the fine wool fabric of his left trouser leg while he sat very still, his leg fully extended. The cut on his knee was deep, and I shaved around it and washed it thoroughly, placing towels on the floor to blot bloody water dripping everywhere. As I led Wesley back into the bedroom, he limped over to the bottle of Scotch and refilled his glass.

"And by the way," I told him, "I appreciate the thought, but I don't drink before surgery."

"I guess I should be grateful," he answered.

"Yes, you should be."

He seated himself on the bed, and I took the chair, moving it close. I tore open foil packets of Betadine and began to swipe his wounds.

"Jesus," he said under his breath. "What is that, battery acid?"

"It's a topical antibacterial iodine."

"You keep that in your medical bag?"

"Yes."

"I didn't realize first aid was an option for most of your patients."

"Sadly, it isn't. But I never know when I might need it." I reached for the forceps. "Or when someone else at a scene might—like you." I withdrew a sliver of glass and placed it on the towel. "I know this may come as a great shock to you, Special Agent Wesley, but I started out my career with living patients."

"And when did they start dying on you?"

"Immediately."

He tensed as I extracted a very small sliver.

"Hold still," I said.

"So what's Marino's problem? He's been a total ass lately."

I placed two more slivers of glass on the towel and stanched the bleeding with gauze. "You'd better take another swallow of your drink."

"Why?"

"I've gotten all of the glass."

"So you're finished and we're celebrating." He sounded the most relieved I had ever heard him.

"Not quite." I leaned close to his hand, satisfied that I had not missed anything. Then I opened a suture packet.

"Without Novocain?" he protested.

"As few stitches as you need to close these cuts, numbing you would hurt as much as the needle," I calmly explained, gripping the needle with the forceps.

"I'd still prefer Novocain."

"Well, I don't have any. It might be better if you don't look. Would you like me to turn on the TV?"

Wesley stoically stared away from me as he answered between clenched teeth, "Just get it over with."

He did not utter a protest while I worked, but as I touched his hand and leg I could feel him tremble. He took a deep breath and began to relax when I dressed his wounds with Neosporin and gauze.

"You're a good patient." I patted his shoulder as I got up.

"Not according to my wife."

I could not remember the last time he had referred to Connie by name. On the rare occasion he mentioned her at all, it was a fleeting allusion to a force he seemed conscious of, like gravity.

"Let's sit outside and finish our drinks," he said.

The balcony beyond my room door was a public one that stretched the entire length of the second floor. At this hour the few guests who might have been awake were too far away to hear our conversation. Wesley arranged two plastic chairs close together. We had no table between us, so he set our drinks and bottle of Scotch on the floor.

"Do you want more ice?" he asked.

"This is fine."

He had turned off lamps inside the room, and beyond us the

barely discernible shapes of trees began to move in concert the longer I stared at them. Headlights were small and sporadic along the distant highway.

"On a scale of one to ten, how awful would you rank this day?" he spoke quietly in the dark.

I hesitated, for I had known many awful days in my career. "I suppose I'd give it a seven."

"Assuming ten's the worst."

"I have yet to have a ten."

"What would that be?" I felt him look at me.

"I'm not sure," I said, superstitious that naming the worst might somehow manifest it.

He fell silent and I wondered if he was thinking about the man who had been my lover and his best friend. When Mark had been killed in London several years before, I had believed there could be no pain worse than that. Now I feared I was wrong.

Wesley said, "You never answered my question, Kay."

"I told you I wasn't sure."

"Not that question. I'm talking about Marino now. I asked you what his problem is."

"I think he's very unhappy," I answered.

"He's always been unhappy."

"I said *very*."

He waited.

"Marino doesn't like change," I added.

"His promotion?"

"That and what's going on with me."

"Which is?" Wesley poured more Scotch into our glasses, his arm brushing against me.

"My position with your unit is a significant change."

He did not agree or disagree but waited for me to say more.

"I think he somehow perceives that I've shifted my alliances." I realized I was getting only more vague. "And that is unsettling. Unsettling for Marino, I mean."

Still, Wesley offered no opinion, ice cubes softly rattling as he sipped his drink. We both knew very well what part of Marino's problem was, but it was nothing that Wesley and I had done. Rather, it was something Marino sensed.

"It's my opinion that Marino's very frustrated with his personal life," Wesley said. "He's lonely."

"I believe both of those things are true," I said.

"You know, he was with Doris for thirty-some years and then suddenly finds himself single again. He's clueless, has no idea how to go about it."

"Nor has he ever really dealt with her leaving. It's stored up. Waiting to be ignited by something unrelated."

"I've worried about that. I've worried about what that something unrelated might be."

"He still misses her. I believe he still loves her," I said, and the hour and the alcohol made me feel sad for Marino. I rarely could stay angry with him long.

Wesley shifted his position in his chair. "I guess that would be a ten. At least for me."

"To have Connie leave you?" I looked over at him.

"To lose someone you're in love with. To lose a child you're at war with. To not have closure." He stared straight ahead, his sharp profile softly backlit by the moon. "Maybe I'm kidding myself, but I think I could take almost anything as long as there's resolution, an ending, so I can be free of the past."

"We are never free of that."

"I agree that we aren't entirely." He continued staring ahead when he next said, "Marino has feelings for you that he can't handle, Kay. I think he always has."

"They're best left unacknowledged."

"That sounds somewhat cold."

"I don't mean it coldly," I said. "I would never want him to feel rejected."

"What makes you assume he doesn't already feel that way?"

"I'm not assuming he doesn't." I sighed. "In fact, I'm fairly certain he's feeling pretty frustrated these days."

"Actually, *jealous* is the word that comes to mind."

"Of you."

"Has he ever tried to ask you out?" Wesley went on as if he had not heard what I just said.

"He took me to the Policeman's Ball."

"Umm. That's pretty serious."

"Benton, let's not joke about him."

"I wasn't joking," he said gently. "I care very much about his feelings and I know you do." He paused. "In fact, I understand his feelings very well."

"I understand them, too."

Wesley set down his drink.

"I guess I should go in and try to get at least a couple hours' sleep," I decided without moving.

He reached over and placed his good hand on my wrist, his fingers cool from holding his glass. "Whit will fly me out of here when the sun is up."

I wanted to take his hand in mine. I wanted to touch his face.

"I'm sorry to leave you."

"All I need is a car," I said as my heart beat harder.

"I wonder where you rent one around here. The airport, maybe?"

"I guess that's why you're an FBI agent. You can figure out things like that."

His fingers worked their way down to my hand and he began to stroke it with his thumb. I had always known our path one day would lead to this. When he had asked me to serve as his consultant at Quantico, I had been aware of the danger. I could have said no.

"Are you in much pain?" I asked him.

"I will be in the morning, because I'm going to have a hangover."

"It is the morning."

I leaned back and shut my eyes as he touched my hair. I felt his face move closer as he traced the contours of my throat with his fingers, then his lips. He touched me as if he had always wanted to, while darkness swept in from the far reaches of my brain and light danced across my blood. Our kisses were stolen like fire. I knew I had found the unforgivable sin I had never been able to name, but did not care.

We left our clothes where they landed and went to bed. We were tender with his wounds but not deterred by them, and made love until dawn began to catch around the horizon's edge. Afterward I sat on the porch watching the sun spill over the mountains, coloring the leaves. I imagined his helicopter lifting and turning like a dancer in air.

6

In the center of downtown, across the street from the Exxon station, was Black Mountain Chevrolet, where Officer Baird delivered Marino and me at 7:45 A.M.

Apparently, the local police had been spreading word throughout the business community that the "Feds" had arrived and were staying "under cover" at the Travel-Eze. Though I did not feel quite the celebrity, neither did I feel anonymous when we drove off in a new silver Caprice while it seemed that everyone who had ever thought of working for the dealership stood outside the showroom and watched.

"I heard some guy call you *Quincy*," Marino said as he opened a steak biscuit from Hardee's.

"I've been called worse. Do you have any idea how much sodium and fat you're ingesting right now?"

"Yeah. About one third of what I'm going to ingest. I got three biscuits here, and I plan to eat every damn one of them. In case you've got a problem with your short-term memory, I missed dinner last night."

"You don't need to be rude."

"When I miss food and sleep, I get rude."

I did not volunteer that I had gotten less sleep than Marino, but I suspected he knew. He would not look me in the eye this morning, and I sensed that beneath his irritability he was very depressed.

"I didn't sleep worth a damn," he went on. "The acoustics in that joint suck."

I pulled down the visor as if that somehow would alleviate my discomfort, then turned the radio on and switched stations until I landed on Bonnie Raitt. Marino's rental car was being equipped with a police radio and scanner and would not be ready until the end of the day. I was to drop him off at Denesa Steiner's house and someone would pick him up later. I drove while he ate and gave directions.

"Slow down," he said, looking at a map. "This should be Laurel coming up on our left. Okay, you're going to want to hang a right at the next one."

We turned again to discover a lake directly ahead of us that was no bigger than a football field and the color of moss. Its picnic areas and tennis courts were deserted, and it did not appear that the neatly maintained clubhouse was currently in use. The shore was lined with trees beginning to brown with the wane of fall, and I imagined a little girl with guitar case in hand heading home in the deepening shadows. I imagined an old man fishing on a morning like this and his shock at what he found in the brush.

"I want to come out here later and walk around," I said.

"Turn here," Marino said. "Her house is at the next corner."

"Where is Emily buried?"

"About two miles over that way." He pointed east. "In the church cemetery."

"This is the church where her meeting was?"

"Third Presbyterian. If you view the lake area as being sort of like the Washington Mall, you got the church at one end and the Steiner crib at the other with about two miles in between."

I recognized the ranch-style house from the photographs

I had reviewed at Quantico yesterday morning. It seemed smaller, as so many edifices do when you finally see them in life. Situated on a rise far back from the street, it was nestled on a lot thick with rhododendrons, laurels, sourwoods, and pines.

The gravel sidewalk and front porch had been recently swept, and clustered at the edge of the driveway were bulging bags of leaves. Denesa Steiner owned a green Infiniti sedan that was new and expensive, and this rather surprised me. I caught a glimpse of her arm in a long black sleeve holding the screen door for Marino as I drove away.

The morgue in Asheville Memorial Hospital was not unlike most I had seen. Located in the lowest level, it was a small bleak room of tile and stainless steel with but one autopsy table that Dr. Jenrette had rolled close to a sink. He was making the Y incision on Ferguson's body when I arrived at shortly after nine. As blood became exposed to air, I detected the sickening sweet odor of alcohol.

"Good morning, Dr. Scarpetta," Jenrette said, and he seemed pleased to see me. "Greens and gloves are in the cabinet over there."

I thanked him, though I would not need them, for the young doctor would not need me. I expected this autopsy to be all about finding nothing, and as I looked closely at Ferguson's neck, I got my first validation. The reddish pressure marks I had observed late last night were gone, and we would find no deep injury to underlying tissue and muscle. As I watched Jenrette work, I was humbly reminded that pathology is never a substitute for investigation. In fact, were we not privy to the circumstances, we would have no idea why Ferguson had died, except that he had not been shot, stabbed, or beaten, nor had he succumbed to some disease.

"I guess you noticed the way the socks smell that he had stuffed in his bra," Jenrette said as he worked. "I'm wondering if you found anything to correspond with that, like a bottle of perfume, some sort of cologne?"

He lifted out the block of organs. Ferguson had a mildly fatty liver.

"No, we didn't," I replied. "And I might add that fragrances are generally used in scenarios like this when there's more than one person involved."

Jenrette glanced up at me. "Why?"

"Why bother if you're alone?"

"I guess that makes sense." He emptied the stomach contents into a carton. "Just a little bit of brownish fluid," he added. "Maybe a few nutlike particles. You say he flew back to Asheville not long before he was found?"

"That's right."

"So maybe he ate peanuts on the plane. And drank. His STAT alcohol's point one-four."

"He probably also drank when he got home," I said, recalling the glass of bourbon in the bedroom.

"Now, when you talk about there being more than one person in some of these situations, is this gay or straight?"

"Often gay," I said. "But the pornography is a big clue."

"He was looking at nude women."

"The magazines found near his body featured nude women," I restated his remark, for we had no way of knowing what Ferguson had been looking at. We knew only what we had found. "It's also important that we didn't see any other pornography or sexual paraphernalia in his house," I added.

"I guess I would assume there would be more of it," Jenrette said as he plugged in the Stryker's saw.

"Usually, these guys keep trunkloads of it," I said. "They never throw it out. Frankly, it bothers me quite a lot that we found only four magazines, all of them current issues."

"It's like he was really new at this."

"There are many factors that suggest he was inexperienced," I replied. "But mostly what I'm seeing is inconsistency."

"Such as?" He incised the scalp behind the ears, folding it down to expose the skull, and the face suddenly collapsed into a sad, slack mask.

"Just as we found no bottle of perfume to account for the fragrance he had on, we found no women's clothing in the house except what he had on," I said. "There was only one condom missing from the box. The rope was old, and we found nothing, including other rope, that might be the origin of it. He was cautious enough to wrap a towel around his neck, yet he tied a knot that's extremely dangerous."

"As the name suggests," said Jenrette.

"Yes. A hangman's knot pulls very smoothly and won't let go," I said. "Not exactly what you want to use when you're intoxicated and perched on top of a varnished bar stool, which you're more likely to fall off of than a chair, by the way."

"I wouldn't think many people would know how to tie a hangman's knot," Jenrette mused.

"The question is, did Ferguson have reason to know?" I said.

"I guess he could have looked it up in a book."

"We found no books about knot tying, no nautical-type books or anything like that in his house."

"Would it be hard to tie a hangman's knot? If there were instructions, let's say?"

"It wouldn't be impossible, but it would take a little practice."

"Why would someone be interested in a knot like that? Wouldn't a slip knot be easier?"

"A hangman's knot is morbid, ominous. It's neat, precise. I don't know." I added, "How is Lieutenant Mote?"

"Stable, but he'll be in the ICU for a while."

Dr. Jenrette turned on the Stryker's saw. We were silent as he removed the skull cap. He did not speak again until he had removed the brain and was examining the neck.

"You know, I don't see a thing. No hemorrhage to the strap

muscles, hyoid's intact, no fractures of superior horns of the thyroid cartilage. The spine's not fractured, but I don't guess that happens except in judicial hangings."

"Not unless you're obese, with arthritic changes of the cervical vertebrae, and get accidentally suspended in a weird way," I said.

"You want to look?"

I pulled on gloves and moved a light closer.

"Dr. Scarpetta, how do we know he was alive when he was hanged?"

"We can't really know that with certainty," I said. "Unless we find another cause of death."

"Like poisoning."

"That's about the only thing I can think of at this point. But if that's the case, it had to be something that worked very fast. We do know he hadn't been home long before Mote found him dead. So the odds are against the bizarre and in favor of his death being caused by asphyxia due to hanging."

"What about manner?"

"Pending," I suggested.

When Ferguson's organs had been sectioned and returned to him in a plastic bag placed inside his chest cavity, I helped Jenrette clean up. We hosed down the table and floor while a morgue assistant rolled Ferguson's body away and tucked it into the refrigerator. We rinsed syringes and instruments as we chatted some more about what was happening in an area of the world that initially had attracted the young doctor because it was safe.

He told me he had wished to start a family in a place where people still believed in God and the sanctity of life. He wanted his children in church and on athletic fields. He wanted them untainted by drugs, immorality, and violence on TV.

"Thing is, Dr. Scarpetta," he went on, "there really isn't any place left. Not even here. In the past week I've worked an eleven-year-old girl who was sexually molested and murdered.

And now a State Bureau of Investigation agent dressed in drag. Last month I got a kid from Oteen who overdosed on cocaine. She was only seventeen. Then there are the drunk drivers. I get them and the people they smash into all the time."

"Dr. Jenrette?"

"You can call me Jim," he said, and he looked depressed as he began to collect paperwork from a countertop.

"How old are your children?" I asked.

"Well, my wife and I keep trying." He cleared his throat and averted his eyes, but not before I saw his pain. "How about you? You got children?"

"I'm divorced and have a niece who's like my own," I said. "She's a senior at UVA and currently doing an internship at Quantico."

"You must be mighty proud of her."

"I am," I replied, my mood shadowed again by images and voices, by secret fears about Lucy's life.

"Now I know you want to talk to me some more about Emily Steiner, and I've still got her brain here if you want to see it."

"I very much do."

It is not uncommon for pathologists to fix brains in a ten percent solution of formaldehyde called formalin. The chemical process preserves and firms tissue. It makes further studies possible, especially in cases involving trauma to this most incredible and least understood of all human organs.

The procedure was sadly utilitarian to the point of indignity, should one choose to view it like that. Jenrette went to a sink and retrieved from beneath it a plastic bucket labeled with Emily Steiner's name and case number. The instant Jenrette removed her brain from its formalin bath and placed it on a cutting board, I knew the gross examination would tell me only more loudly that something was very wrong with this case.

"There's absolutely no vital reaction," I marveled, fumes from the formalin burning my eyes.

Jenrette threaded a probe through the bullet track.

"There's no hemorrhage, no swelling. Yet the bullet didn't pass through the pons. It didn't pass through the basal ganglia or any other area that's vital." I looked up at him. "This is not an immediately lethal wound."

"I can't argue that one."

"We should look for another cause of death."

"I sure wish you'd tell me what, Dr. Scarpetta. I've got tox testing going on. But unless that turns up something significant, there's nothing I can think of that could account for her death. Nothing but the gunshot to her head."

"I'd like to look at a tissue section of her lungs," I said.

"Come on to my office."

I was considering that the girl might have been drowned, but as I sat over Jenrette's microscope moments later moving around a slide of lung tissue, questions remained unanswered.

"If she drowned," I explained to him as I worked, "the alveoli should be dilated. There should be edema fluid in the alveolar spaces with disproportionate autolytic change of the respiratory epithelium." I adjusted the focus again. "In other words, if her lungs had been contaminated by fresh water, they should have begun decomposing more rapidly than other tissues. But they didn't."

"What about smothering or strangulation?" he asked.

"The hyoid was intact. There were no petechial hemorrhages."

"That's right."

"And more importantly," I pointed out, "if someone tries to smother or strangle you, you're going to fight like hell. Yet there are no nose or lip injuries, no defense injuries whatsoever."

He handed me a thick case file. "This is everything," he said.

While he dictated Max Ferguson's case, I reviewed every report, laboratory request, and call sheet pertaining to Emily Steiner's murder. Her mother, Denesa, had called Dr. Jenrette's office anywhere from one to five times daily since Emily's body had been found. I found this rather remarkable.

"The decedent was received inside a black plastic pouch sealed by the Black Mountain Police. The seal number is 445337 and the seal is intact—"

"Dr. Jenrette?" I interrupted.

He removed his foot from the pedal of the dictating machine. "You can call me Jim," he said again.

"It seems her mother has called you with unusual frequency."

"Some of it is us playing telephone tag. But yes." He slipped off his glasses and rubbed his eyes. "She's called a lot."

"Why?"

"Mostly she's just terribly distraught, Dr. Scarpetta. She wants to make sure her daughter didn't suffer."

"And what did you tell her?"

"I told her with a gunshot wound like that, it's probable she didn't. I mean, she would have been unconscious . . . uh, probably was when the other things were done."

He paused for a moment. Both of us knew that Emily Steiner had suffered. She had felt raw terror. At some point she must have known she was going to die.

"And that's it?" I asked. "She's called this many times to find out if her daughter suffered?"

"Well, no. She's had questions and information. Nothing of particular relevance." He smiled sadly. "I think she just needs someone to talk to. She's a sweet lady who's lost everyone in her life. I can't tell you how badly I feel for her and how much I pray they catch the horrible monster who did this. That Gault monster I've read about. The world will never be safe as long as he's in it."

"The world will never be safe, Dr. Jenrette. But I can't tell you how much we want to catch him, too. Catch Gault. Catch anybody who does something like this," I said as I opened a thick envelope of glossy eight-by-ten photographs.

Only one was unfamiliar, and I studied it intensely for a long time as Dr. Jenrette's unemphatic voice went on. I did not know what I was seeing because I had never seen anything quite like this, and my emotional response was a combination of excitement and fear. The photograph showed Emily Steiner's left buttock, where there was an irregular brownish blotch on the skin no bigger than a bottle cap.

"The visceral pleura shows scattered petechiae along the interlobar fissures—"

"What is this?" I interrupted Dr. Jenrette's dictation again.

He put down the microphone as I came around to his side of the desk and placed the photograph in front of him. I pointed out the mark on Emily's skin as I smelled Old Spice and thought of my ex-husband, Tony, who had always worn too much of it.

"This mark on her buttock is not covered in your report," I added.

"I don't know what that is," he said without a trace of defensiveness. He simply sounded tired. "I just assumed it was some sort of postmortem artifact."

"I don't know of any artifact that looks like that. Did you resect it?"

"No."

"Her body was on something that left that mark." I returned to my chair, sat down, and leaned against the edge of his desk. "It could be important."

"Yes, if that's the case, I could see how it might be important," he replied, looking increasingly dejected.

"She's not been in the ground long." I spoke quietly but with feeling.

He stared uneasily at me.

"She's never going to be in better shape than she is now," I went on. "I really think we ought to take another look at her."

He did not blink as he wet his lips.

"Dr. Jenrette," I said, "let's get her up *now*."

* * *

Dr. Jenrette flipped through cards in his Rolodex and reached for the phone. I watched him dial.

"Hello, Dr. James Jenrette here," he said to whoever answered. "I wonder if Judge Begley might be in?"

The Honorable Hal Begley said he would see us in his chambers in half an hour. I drove while Jenrette gave directions, and I parked on College Street with plenty of time to spare.

The Buncombe County Courthouse was an old dark brick building that I suspected had been the tallest edifice downtown until not too many years before. Its thirteen stories were topped by the jail, and as I looked up at barred windows against a bright blue sky, I thought of Richmond's overcrowded jail, spread out over acres, with coils of razor wire the only view. I believed it would not be long before cities like Asheville would need more cells as violence continued to become so alarmingly common. "Judge Begley's not known for his patience," Dr. Jenrette warned me as we climbed marble steps inside the old courthouse. "I can promise he's not going to like your plan."

I knew that Dr. Jenrette did not like my plan, either, for no forensic pathologist wants a peer digging up his work. Dr. Jenrette and I both knew that implicit in all of this was that he had not done a good job.

"Listen," I said as he headed down a corridor on the third floor, "I don't like the plan, either. I don't like exhumations. I wish there were another way."

"I guess I just wish I had more experience in the kinds of cases you see every day," he added.

"I don't see cases like this every day," I said, touched by his humility. "Thank God, I don't."

"Well, I'd be lying to you, Dr. Scarpetta, if I said that it wasn't real hard on me when I got called to that little girl's scene. Maybe I should have spent a little more time."

"I think Buncombe County is extremely lucky to have you," I said sincerely as we opened the judge's outer office door. "I wish I had more doctors like you in Virginia. I'd hire you."

He knew I meant it and smiled as a secretary as old as any woman I'd ever met who was still employed peered up at us through thick glasses. She used an electric typewriter instead of a computer, and I surmised from the numerous gray steel cabinets lining walls that filing was her forte. Sunlight seeped wanly through barely opened venetian blinds, a galaxy of dust suspended in the air. I smelled Rose Milk as she rubbed a dollop of moisturizing cream into her bony hands.

"Judge Begley's expecting you," she said before we introduced ourselves. "You can just go on in. That door there." She pointed to a shut door across from the one we had just come through. "Now just so you know, court's adjourned for lunch and he's due back at exactly one."

"Thank you," I said. "We'll try not to keep him long."

"Won't make any difference if you try."

Dr. Jenrette's shy knock on the judge's thick oak door was answered by a distracted "Come in!" from the other side. We found His Honor behind a partner's desk, suit jacket off as he sat erectly in an old red leather chair. He was a gaunt, bearded man nearing sixty, and as he glanced over notes in a legal pad, I made a number of telling assessments about him. The orderliness of his desk told me that he was busy and quite capable, and his unfashionable tie and soft-soled shoes bespoke someone who did not give a damn how people like me assessed him.

"Why do you want to violate the sepulchre?" he asked in slow Southern cadences that belied a quick mind as he turned a page in a legal pad.

"After going over Dr. Jenrette's reports," I replied, "we agree some questions were not answered by the first examination of Emily Steiner's body."

"I know of Dr. Jenrette but don't believe I know you," Judge Begley said to me as he placed the legal pad on the desk.

"I'm Dr. Kay Scarpetta, the chief medical examiner of Virginia."

"I was told you had something to do with the FBI."

"Yes, sir. I am the consulting forensic pathologist for the Investigative Support Unit."

"Is that like the Behavioral Science Unit?"

"One and the same. The Bureau changed the name several years ago."

"You're talking about the folks who do the profiling of these serial killers and other aberrant criminals who until recently we didn't have to worry about in these parts." He watched me closely, lacing his fingers in his lap.

"That's what we do," I said.

"Your Honor," Dr. Jenrette said. "The Black Mountain Police has requested the assistance of the FBI. There's some fear that the man who murdered the Steiner girl is the same man who killed a number of people in Virginia."

"I'm aware of that, Dr. Jenrette, since you were so kind as to explain some of this when you called earlier. However, the only item on the agenda right now is your wish for me to grant you the right to dig up this little girl.

"Before I let you do something as upsetting and disrespectful as that, you're going to have to give me a powerfully good reason. And I do wish the two of you would sit down and make yourselves comfortable. That's why I have chairs on that side of my desk."

"She has a mark on her skin," I said as I seated myself.

"What sort of mark?" He eyed me with interest as Dr. Jenrette slipped a photograph out of an envelope and set it on the judge's blotter.

"You can see it in the photograph," Jenrette said.

The judge's eyes dropped to the photograph, his face unreadable.

"We don't know what the mark is," I explained. "But it may tell us where the body lay. It may be some type of injury."

He picked up the photograph, squinting as he examined it more closely. "Aren't there studies of photographs you can do? Seems to me there's all sorts of scientific things they do these days."

"There are," I answered. "But the problem is, by the time we finish conducting any studies, the body will be in such poor condition that we'll no longer be able to tell anything from it if we still need to exhume it. The longer the interval gets, the harder it is to distinguish between an injury or other significant mark on the body and artifacts due to decomposition."

"There are a lot of details about this case that make it very odd, Your Honor," Dr. Jenrette said. "We just need all the help we can get."

"I understand the SBI agent working the case was found hanged yesterday. I saw that in the morning paper."

"Yes, sir," Dr. Jenrette said.

"Are there odd details about his death, too?"

"There are," I replied.

"I hope you're not going to come back here a week from now and want to dig him up."

"I can't imagine that," I said.

"This little girl has a mama. And just how do you think she's going to feel about what you've got in mind?"

Neither Dr. Jenrette nor I replied. Leather creaked as the judge shifted in his chair. He glanced past us at a clock on the wall.

"See, that's my biggest problem with what you're asking," he went on. "I'm thinking about this poor woman, about what all she's been through. I have no interest whatsoever in putting her through anything else."

"We wouldn't ask if we didn't think it was important to the investigation of her daughter's death," I said. "And I know Mrs. Steiner must want justice, Your Honor."

"You go get her mama and bring her to me," Judge Begley said as he got up from his chair.

"Excuse me?" Dr. Jenrette looked bewildered.

"I want her mama brought to me," the judge repeated.

"I should be freed up by two-thirty. I'll expect to see you back here."

"What if she won't come?" Dr. Jenrette asked, and both of us got up.

"Can't say I'd blame her a bit."

"You don't need her permission," I said with calm I did not feel.

"No, ma'am, I don't," said the judge as he opened the door.

7

Dr. Jenrette was kind enough to let me use his office while he disappeared into the hospital labs, and for the next several hours I was on the phone.

The most important task, ironically, turned out to be the easiest. Marino had no trouble convincing Denesa Steiner to accompany him to the judge's chambers that afternoon. More difficult was figuring out how to get them there, since Marino still did not have a car.

"What's the holdup?" I asked.

"The friggin' scanner they put in don't work," he said irritably.

"Can't you do without that?"

"They don't seem to think so."

I glanced at my watch. "Maybe I'd better come get you."

"Yeah, well, I'd rather get there myself. She's got a pretty decent ride. In fact, there are some who say an Infiniti's better than a Benz."

"That's moot, since I'm driving a Chevrolet at the moment."

"She said her father-in-law used to have a Benz a lot like yours and you ought to think of switching to an Infiniti or Legend."

I was silent.

"Just food for thought."

"Just get here," I said shortly.

"Yeah, I will."

"Fine."

We hung up without good-byes, and as I sat at Dr. Jenrette's cluttered desk I felt exhausted and betrayed. I had been through Marino's bad times with Doris. I had supported him as he had begun venturing forth into the fast, frightening world of dating. In return, he had always telegraphed judgments about my personal life without benefit of having been asked.

He had been negative about my ex-husband, and very critical of my former lover, Mark. He rarely had anything nice to say about Lucy or the way I dealt with her, and he did not like my friends. Most of all, I felt his cold stare on my relationship with Wesley. I felt Marino's jealous rage.

He was not at Begley's office when Dr. Jenrette and I returned at half past two. As minutes crept by inside the judge's chambers, my anger grew.

"Tell me where you were born, Dr. Scarpetta," the judge said to me from the other side of his immaculate desk.

"Miami," I replied.

"You certainly don't talk like a Southerner. I would have placed you up north somewhere."

"I was educated in the North."

"It might surprise you to know that I was, too," he said.

"Why did you settle here?" Dr. Jenrette asked him.

"I'm sure for some of the very same reasons that you did."

"But you're from here," I said.

"Going back three generations. My great-grandfather was born in a log cabin around here. He was a teacher. That was on my mother's side. On my father's side we had mostly moonshiners until about halfway into this century. Then we had preachers. I believe that might be them now."

Marino opened the door, and his face peeked in before his

feet did. Denesa Steiner was behind him, and though I would never accuse Marino of chivalry, he was unusually attentive and gentle with this rather peculiarly put together woman whose dead daughter was our reason for gathering. The judge rose, and out of habit so did I, as Mrs. Steiner regarded each of us with curious sadness.

"I'm Dr. Scarpetta." I offered my hand and found hers cool and soft. "I'm terribly sorry about this, Mrs. Steiner."

"I'm Dr. Jenrette. We've talked on the phone."

"Won't you be seated," the judge said to her very kindly.

Marino moved two chairs close together, directing her to one while he took the other. Mrs. Steiner was in her mid- to late thirties and dressed entirely in black. Her skirt was full and below her knees, a sweater buttoned to her chin. She wore no makeup, her only jewelry a plain gold wedding ring. She looked the part of a spinster missionary, yet the longer I studied her, the more I saw what her puritanical grooming could not hide.

She was beautiful, with smooth pale skin and a generous mouth, and curly hair the color of honey. Her nose was patrician, her cheekbones high, and beneath the folds of her horrible clothes hid a voluptuously well formed body. Nor had her attributes successfully eluded anything male and breathing in the room. Marino, in particular, could not take his eyes off her.

"Mrs. Steiner," the judge began, "the reason I wanted you to come here this afternoon is these doctors have made a request I wanted you to hear. And let me say right off how much I appreciate your coming. From all accounts, you've shown nothing but courage and decency during these unspeakably trying hours, and I have no intention whatsoever of adding to your burdens unnecessarily."

"Thank you, sir," she said quietly, her tapered, pale hands clasped tightly in her lap.

"Now, these doctors have found a few things in the photographs taken after little Emily died. The things they've found are mysterious and they want to take another look at her."

"How can they do that?" she asked innocently in a voice steady and sweet, and not indigenous to North Carolina.

"Well, they want to exhume her," the judge replied.

Mrs. Steiner did not look upset but baffled, and my heart ached for her as she fought back tears.

"Before I say yes or no to their request," Begley went on, "I want to see how you might feel about this."

"You want to dig her up?" She looked at Dr. Jenrette, then me.

"Yes," I answered her. "We would like to examine her again immediately."

"I don't understand what you might find this time that you didn't find before." Her voice trembled.

"Maybe nothing that will matter," I said. "But there are a few details I noticed in photographs that I'd like to get a closer look at, Mrs. Steiner. These mysterious things might help us catch whoever did this to Emily."

"Do you want to help us snatch the SOB who killed your baby?" the judge asked.

She nodded vigorously as she wept, and Marino spoke with fury. "You help us, and I promise we're going to nail the goddam bastard."

"I'm sorry to put you through this," said Dr. Jenrette, who would forever be convinced he had failed.

"Then may we proceed?" Begley leaned forward in his chair as if poised to spring, for like everyone in his chambers, he felt this woman's horrible loss. He felt her abject vulnerability in a manner that I was convinced would forever change the way he viewed offenders with hard luck stories and excuses who approached his bench.

Denesa Steiner nodded again because she could not speak. Then Marino helped her out of the room, leaving Jenrette and me.

"Dawn will come early and there are plans to make," Begley said.

"We need to coordinate a lot of people," I concurred.

"Which funeral home buried her?" Begley asked Jenrette.

"Wilbur's."

"That's in Black Mountain?"

"Yes, Your Honor."

"The name of the funeral director?" The judge was taking notes.

"Lucias Ray."

"What about the detective working this case?"

"He's in the hospital."

"Oh, that's right." Judge Begley looked up and sighed.

I was not sure why I went straight there, except that I had said I would, and I was mad at Marino. I was irrationally offended by, of all things, his allusion to my Mercedes, which he had unfavorably compared to an Infiniti.

It wasn't that his comment was right or wrong, but that its intent was to cause irritation and insult. I would not have asked Marino to go with me now had I believed in Loch Ness monsters, creatures from lagoons, and the living dead. I would have refused had he begged, despite my secret fear of water snakes. Actually, of all snakes great and small.

There was enough light left when I reached Lake Tomahawk to retrace what I had been told were Emily's last steps. Parking by a picnic area, I followed the shoreline with my eyes as I wondered why a little girl would walk out here as night began to fall. I recalled how fearful I had been of the canals when I was growing up in Miami. Every log was an alligator and cruel people loitered along the isolated shores.

As I got out of my car, I wondered why Emily had not been afraid. I wondered if there might be some other explanation for why she had chosen this route.

The map Ferguson had passed around during the consultation at Quantico indicated that on the early evening of October 1, Emily had left the church and veered off the street at the point where I was standing. She had passed picnic tables and turned right on a dirt trail that appeared to have been worn by foot traffic rather than cleared, for the path was well defined in some spots and imperceptible in others as it followed the shore through woods and weeds.

I briskly passed riotous clumps of tall grasses and brush as the shadow of mountain ranges deepened over water and the wind picked up, carrying the sharp promise of winter. Dead leaves crackled beneath my shoes as I drew upon the clearing marked on the map with a tiny outline of a body. By now, it had gotten quite dark.

I dug inside my handbag for my flashlight, only to recall that it was broken and still inside Ferguson's basement. I found one book of matches left from my smoking days, and it was half empty.

"Damn," I exclaimed under my breath as I began to feel fear.

I slipped out my .38 and tucked it in a side pocket of my jacket, my hand loose around its grips as I stared at the muddy ledge at the water's edge where Emily Steiner's body had been found. Shadows compared to photographs I recalled indicated that surrounding brush had recently been cut back, but any other evidence of recent activity had been gently covered by nature and the night. Leaves were deep. I rearranged them with my feet to look for what I suspected the local police might not.

I had worked enough violent crimes in my career to have learned one very important truth. A crime scene has a life of its own. It remembers trauma in soil, insects altered by body fluids, and plants trampled by feet. It loses its privacy just as any witness does, for no stone is left undisturbed, and the curious do not stop coming just because there are no further questions to ask.

It is common for people to continue visiting a scene long after there is a reason. They take souvenirs and photographs. They leave letters, cards, and flowers. They come in secret and leave that way, for it is shameful to stare just because you cannot help it. It seems a violation of something sacred even to leave a rose.

I found no flowers in this spot as I swept leaves out of the way. But my toe did strike several small, hard objects that dropped me to my hands and knees, eyes straining. After much rooting around, I recovered what appeared to be four gumballs still in plastic wrappers. It was not until I held them close to a lighted match that I realized the candies were jawbreakers, or Fireballs, as Emily had called them in her diary. I got up, breathing hard.

Furtively, I glanced around, listening to every sound. The noise of my feet crashing through leaves seemed horrendously loud as I followed a path that I now could not see at all. Stars were out, the half moon my only guide, my matches long since spent. I knew from the map that I was not far from the Steiners' street, and it was closer to pick my way there than attempt returning to my car.

I was perspiring beneath my coat and terrified of tripping, for in addition to not having a flashlight, I also had failed to bring my portable phone. It occurred to me that I would not want any of my colleagues to see me now, and if I injured myself, I might have to lie about how it happened.

Ten minutes into this awful journey, bushes grabbed my legs and destroyed my hose. I stubbed my toe on a root and stepped in mud up to my ankles. When a branch stung my face, barely missing my eye, I stood still, panting and frustrated to the point of tears. To my right, between the street and me, was a dense expanse of woods. To my left was the water.

"Shit," I said rather loudly.

Following the shore was the lesser danger, and as I continued I actually got somewhat more adept at it. My eyes adapted better to moonlight. I became more surefooted and intuitive, and could sense from shifts in dampness and temperature of air when I was nearing dryer ground or mud or straying too far from the path. It was as if I were instantly evolving into a nocturnal creature in order to keep my species alive.

Then, suddenly, streetlights were ahead as I reached the end of the lake opposite where I had parked. Here the woods had been cleared for tennis courts and a parking lot, and as Emily had done several weeks before, I veered off the path and momentarily was on pavement again. As I walked along her street, I realized I was trembling.

I remembered the Steiner house was two down on the left, and as I got closer to it I wasn't certain what I would say to Emily's mother. I had no desire to tell her where I had been or why, for the last thing she needed was more upset. But I knew no one else in this area and could not imagine knocking on a stranger's door to use the phone.

No matter how hospitable anyone in Black Mountain might be, I would be asked why I looked as if I had been lost in a wilderness. It was possible someone might even find me frightening, especially if I had to explain what I did for a profession. As it turned out, my fears were invalidated by an unexpected knight who suddenly rode out of the dark and nearly ran me down.

I got to the Steiners' driveway as Marino was backing out of it in a new midnight-blue Chevrolet. As I waved at him in the beam of his headlights, I could see the blank expression on his face as he abruptly hit the brakes. His mood shifted from incredulity to rage.

"God damn sonofabitch, you practically gave me a heart attack. I coulda run you over."

I fastened my shoulder harness and locked the door.

"What the fuck're you doing out here? Shit!"

"I'm glad you finally got your car and that the scanner works. And I very much need a very strong Scotch and I'm not sure where one finds anything like that around here," I said as my teeth began to chatter. "How do you turn the heat on?"

Marino lit a cigarette, and I wanted one of those, too. But there were some vows I would never break. He turned the heat on high.

"Jesus. You look like you've been mud wrestling," he said, and I couldn't remember when I had seen him so rattled. "What the hell've you been doing? I mean, are you okay?"

"My car's parked by the clubhouse."

"What clubhouse?"

"On the lake."

"The lake? What? You've been *out there* after dark? Have you lost your friggin' mind?"

"What I've lost is my flashlight, and I didn't remember that until it was a little late." As I spoke, I slipped my .38 out of my coat pocket and returned it to my handbag, a move that Marino did not miss. His mood worsened.

"You know, I don't know what the fuck's your problem. I think you're losing it, Doc. I think it's all caught up with you and you're getting goofy as a shithouse rat. Maybe you're going through the change."

"If I were going through 'the change' or anything else so personal and so none-of-your-business, you can rest assured I would not discuss it with you. If for no other reason than your vast male dullness or sensitivity of a fence post—which may or may not be gender related, I have to add, to be fair. Because I wouldn't want to assume that all men are like you. If I did, I know I would give them up entirely."

"Maybe you should."

"Maybe I will!"

"Good! Then you can be just like your bratty niece! Hey. Don't think it ain't obvious which way she swings."

"And that is yet one more thing that isn't your goddam business," I said furiously. "I can't believe you're stooping so low as to stereotype Lucy, to dehumanize her just because she doesn't make the exact choices you would."

"Oh yeah? Well maybe the problem is that she does makes the exact same choices I would. I date women."

"You don't know the first thing about women," I said, and it occurred to me that the car was an oven and I had no idea where we were going. I flipped the heat down and glared out my window.

"I know enough about women to know you'd drive anybody crazy. And I can't believe you were out walking around the lake after dark. *By yourself.* So just what the hell would you have done if *he* was out there, too?"

"Which he?"

"Goddam I'm hungry. I saw a steakhouse on Tunnel Road when I was up this way earlier. I hope they're still open."

"Marino, it's only six forty-five."

"Why did you go out there?" he asked again, and both of us were calming down.

"Someone left candy on the ground where her body was discovered. Fireballs." When he made no reply, I added, "The same candy she mentioned in her diary."

"I don't remember that."

"The boy she had a crush on. I think his name was Wren. She wrote that she had seen him at a church supper and he gave her a Fireball. She saved it in her secret box."

"They never found it."

"Found what?"

"Whatever this secret box was. Denesa couldn't find it either. So maybe Wren left the Fireballs at the lake."

"We need to talk to him," I said. "It would appear that you and Mrs. Steiner are developing a good rapport."

"Nothing like this should ever have happened to someone like her."

"Nothing like this should ever happen to anyone."

"I see a Western Sizzler."

"No, thank you."

"How about Bonanza?" He flipped on his turn signal.

"Absolutely not."

Marino surveyed brightly lighted restaurants lining Tunnel Road as he smoked another cigarette. "Doc, no offense, but you've got an attitude."

"Marino, don't bother with the 'no offense' preamble. All it does is telegraph that I'm about to be offended."

"I know there's a Peddler around here. I saw it in the Yellow Pages."

"Why were you looking up restaurants in the Yellow Pages?" I puzzled, for I'd always known him to shop for restaurants the same way he did for food. He cruised without a list and took what was easy, cheap, and filling.

"I wanted to see what was in the area in case I wanted something nice. How about calling so I know how to get there?"

I reached for the car phone and thought of Denesa Steiner, for I was not who Marino had hoped he would be taking to the Peddler this night.

"Marino," I told him quietly. "Please be careful."

"Don't start in about red meat again."

"That's not what worries me most," I said.

8

The cemetery behind Third Presbyterian Church was a rolling field of polished granite headstones behind a chain link fence choked with trees.

When I arrived at 6:15, dawn bruised the horizon and I could see my breath. Ground spiders had put up their webbed awnings to begin the business of the day, and I respectfully stepped around them as Marino and I walked through wet grass toward Emily Steiner's grave.

She was buried in a corner close to woods where the lawn was pleasantly mingled with cornflowers, clover, and Queen Anne's lace. Her monument was a small marble angel, and to find it we simply followed the scraping noise of shovels digging dirt. A truck with a winch had been left running at the site, and its headlights illuminated the progress of two leathery old men in overalls. Shovels glinted, the surrounding grass bleached of color, and I smelled damp earth as it fell from steel blades to a mound at the foot of the grave.

Marino turned on his flashlight, and the tombstone stood in sad relief against the morning, wings folded back and head bent in prayer. The epitaph carved in its base read:

There is no other in the World—
Mine was the only one

"Jeez. Got any idea what that means?" Marino said close to my ear.

"Maybe we can ask him," I replied as I watched the approach of a startlingly large man with thick white hair.

His long dark overcoat flowed around his ankles as he walked, giving the eerie impression from a distance that he was several inches off the ground. When he got to us, I saw he had a Black Watch scarf wrapped around his neck, black leather gloves on his huge hands, and rubbers pulled over his shoes. He was close to seven feet tall, with a torso the size of a barrel.

"I'm Lucias Ray," he said, and enthusiastically shook our hands as we introduced ourselves.

"We were wondering about the significance of the epitaph," I said.

"Mrs. Steiner sure did love her little girl. It's just pitiful," the funeral director said in a thick drawl that sounded more Georgian than North Carolinian. "We have a whole book of verses you can look through when you're deciding on what to have inscribed."

"Then Emily's mother got this from your book?" I asked.

"Well, to tell you the truth, no. I believe she said it's Emily Dickinson."

The grave diggers had put down their shovels, and it was light enough now for me to see their faces, wet with sweat and as furrowed as a farmer's fields. Heavy chain clanked as they unwound it from the winch's drum. Then one of the men stepped down into the grave. He secured the chain to hooks on the sides of the concrete vault as Ray went on to tell us that more people had shown up for Emily Steiner's funeral than he had ever heard of around here.

"They were outside the church, on the lawn, and it took close to two hours for all of them to walk past the casket to pay their respects."

"Did you have an open casket?" Marino asked in surprise.

"No, sir." Ray watched his men. "Now, Mrs. Steiner wanted to, but I wouldn't hear of it. I told her she was distraught and would thank me later for saying no. Why, her little girl wasn't in any kind of shape for a thing like that. I knew a lot of folks would show up just to stare. Course, a lot of rubberneckers showed up anyway, seeing as how there was so much in the news."

The winch strained loudly and the truck's diesel engine throbbed as the vault was slowly lifted from the earth. Soil rained down in chunks as the concrete burial chamber rocked higher in the air with each turn of the crank, and one of the men stood by like a member of a ground crew to direct with his hands.

At almost the precise moment the vault was free of its grave and lowered to the grass, we were invaded by television crews with cameras mounted and reporters and photographers. They swarmed around the gaping wound in the earth and the vault so stained with red clay that it almost looked bloody.

"Why are you exhuming Emily Steiner?" one of them called out.

"Is it true the police have a suspect?" yelled another.

"Dr. Scarpetta?"

"Why has the FBI been called in?"

"Dr. Scarpetta?" A woman pushed a microphone close to my face. "It sounds like you're second-guessing the Buncombe County medical examiner."

"Why are you desecrating this little girl's grave?"

And above the fray Marino suddenly bellowed as if he had been wounded, "Get the fuck out of here now! You're interfering with an investigation! You hear me, goddam it?" He stomped his feet. "Leave now!"

The reporters froze with shocked faces. They stared at him

with open mouths as he continued to rail against them, complexion crimson, blood vessels bulging in his neck.

"The only one desecrating anything around here is you assholes! And if you don't leave right now, I'm gonna start breaking cameras and anything else in my reach, including your goddam ugly heads!"

"Marino," I said, and I placed my hand on his arm. He was so tense he had turned to iron.

"All my goddam career I've been dealing with you assholes and I've had it! You hear me! I've goddam had it, you bunch of motherfuckin-sonofabitch BLOODSUCKIN' PARASITES!"

"Marino!" I pulled him by the wrist as fear electrified every nerve in my body. Never had I seen him in such a rage. *Dear Lord,* I thought. *Don't let him shoot anyone.*

I got in front of him to make him look at me, but his eyes danced wildly above my head. "Marino, listen to me! They're leaving. Please calm down. Marino, take it easy. Look, every last one of them is leaving right now. See them? You've certainly made your point. They're almost running."

The journalists were gone as suddenly as they had appeared, like some phantom band of marauders that had materialized and vanished in the mist. Marino stared across the empty expanse of gently rolling lawn with its sprigs of plastic flowers and perfect rows of gray markers. The clarion sound of steel striking steel rang out again and again. With hammer and chisel the diggers broke the vault's coal tar seal, then lowered the lid to the earth as Marino hurried into the woods. We pretended not to notice the hideous grunts and groans and gagging sounds coming from mountain laurels as he vomited.

"Do you still have a bottle of each of the fluids you used for embalming?" I asked Lucias Ray, whose reaction to the advancing troops of media and Marino's outburst seemed more quizzical than bothered.

"I may have half a bottle left of what I used on her," he said.

"I'll need chemical controls for toxicology," I explained.

"It's just formaldehyde and methanol with a trace of lanoline oil—as common as chicken soup. Now, I did use a lower concentration because of her small size. Your detective friend sure don't look too good," he added as Marino emerged from the woods. "You know, the flu's going around."

"I don't think he has the flu," I said. "How did the reporters find out we were here?"

"Now, you got me on that one. But you know how folks are." He paused to spit. "Always someone who's got to run his yap."

Emily's steel casket was painted as white as the Queen Anne's lace that had grown around her plot, and the diggers did not need the winch to lift it out of the vault and gently lower it to the grass. The casket was small like the body inside it. Lucias Ray slipped a radio out of a coat pocket and spoke into it.

"You can come on now," he said.

"Ten-four," a voice came back.

"No more reporters, I sure hope like heck?"

"They're all gone."

A shiny black hearse glided through the cemetery's entrance and drove half in the woods and half on the grass, miraculously dodging graves and trees. A fat man wearing a trench coat and porkpie hat got out to open the tailgate, and the diggers slid the casket inside while Marino watched from a distance, mopping his face with a handkerchief.

"You and I need to talk." I had moved close and spoke quietly to him as the hearse went on its way.

"I don't need nothing right now." His face was pale.

"I've got to meet Dr. Jenrette at the morgue. Are you coming?"

"No," he said. "I'm going on back to the Travel-Eze. I'm gonna drink beer until I puke again, then I'm gonna switch to bourbon. And after that I'm gonna call Wesley's ass and ask him when the shit we can get out of this armpit town, because I tell you, I don't have another decent shirt here and I just ruined this one. I don't even have a tie."

"Marino, go lie down."

"I'm living out of a bag this big," he went on, holding his hands not too far apart.

"Take Advil, drink as much water as you can hold, and eat some toast. I'll check on you when we finish at the hospital. If Benton calls, tell him I'll have my portable phone with me or he can call my pager."

"He's got those numbers?"

"Yes," I said.

Marino glanced at me over his handkerchief as he mopped his face again. I saw the hurt in his eyes before it slipped back behind its walls.

9

Dr. Jenrette was doing paperwork in the morgue when I arrived as the hearse did shortly before ten. He smiled nervously at me as I took off my suit jacket and put a plastic apron over my clothes.

"Would you have a guess as to how the press found out about the exhumation?" I asked, unfolding a surgical gown.

He looked startled. "What happened?"

"About a dozen reporters showed up at the cemetery."

"That's a real shame."

"We need to make sure nothing more gets out," I said, tying the gown in back and doing my best to sound patient. "What happens here needs to remain here, Dr. Jenrette."

He said nothing.

"I know I am a visitor and I wouldn't blame you if you resented the hell out of my presence. So please don't think I'm insensitive to the situation or indifferent to your authority. But you can rest assured that whoever murdered this little girl keeps up with the news. Whenever something gets leaked, *he* finds out about it, too."

Dr. Jenrette, pleasant person that he was, did not look the

least bit offended as he listened carefully. "I'm just trying to think of who all knew," he said. "The problem is by the time word got around that could have been a lot of people."

"Let's make sure word doesn't get around about anything we might find in here today," I said as I heard our case arrive.

Lucias Ray walked in first, the man in the porkpie hat right behind him pulling the church cart bearing the white casket. They maneuvered their cargo through the doorway and parked close to the autopsy table. Ray slipped a metal crank out of his coat pocket and inserted it in a small hole at the casket's head. He began cranking loose the seal as if he were starting a Model-T.

"That should do it," he said, dropping the crank back into his pocket. "Hope you don't mind my waiting around to check on my work. It's an opportunity I don't usually get, since we're not in the habit of digging up people after we bury 'em."

He started to open the lid, and if Dr. Jenrette hadn't placed his hands on top of it to stop him, I would have.

"Ordinarily that wouldn't be a problem, Lucias," Dr. Jenrette said. "But it's really not a good idea for anyone else to be here right now."

"I think that's being a might bit touchy." Ray's smile got tight. "It's not like I haven't seen this child before. Why I know her inside and out better than her own mama."

"Lucias, we need you to go on now so Dr. Scarpetta and I can get this done," Dr. Jenrette spoke in his same sad soft tone. "I'll call you when we're finished."

"Dr. Scarpetta"—Ray fixed his eyes on me—"I must say it does appear folks are a little less friendly since the Feds came to town."

"This is a homicide investigation, Mr. Ray," I said. "Perhaps it would be best not to take things personally since nothing has been intended that way."

"Come on, Billy Joe," the funeral director said to the man in the porkpie hat. "Let's go get something to eat."

They went out. Dr. Jenrette locked the door.

"I'm sorry," he said, pulling on gloves. "Lucias can be overbearing sometimes, but he really is a good person."

I was suspicious we would find that Emily had not been properly embalmed or had been buried in a fashion that did not reflect what her mother had paid. But when Jenrette and I opened the casket's lid, I saw nothing that immediately struck me as out of order. The white satin lining had been folded over her body, and on top of it I found a package wrapped in white tissue paper and pink ribbon. I started taking photographs.

"Did Ray mention anything about this?" I handed the package to Jenrette.

"No." He looked perplexed as he turned it this way and that.

The smell of embalming fluid wafted up strongly as I opened the lining. Beneath it Emily Steiner was well preserved in a long-sleeve, high-collar dress of pale blue velveteen, her braided hair in bows of the same material. A fuzzy whitish mold typically found on bodies that have been exhumed covered her face like a mask and had started on the tops of her hands, which were on her waist, clasped around a white New Testament. She wore white knee socks and black patent leather shoes. Nothing she had been dressed in looked new.

I took more photographs; then Jenrette and I lifted her out of the casket and placed her on top of the stainless steel table, where we began to undress her. Beneath her sweet, little girl clothes hid the awful secret of her death, for people who die gracefully do not bear the wounds she had.

Any honest forensic pathologist will admit that autopsy artifacts are ghastly. There is nothing quite like the Y incision in any premortem surgical procedure, for it looks like its name. The scalpel goes from each clavicle to sternum, runs the length of the torso, and ends at the pubis after a small detour around the navel. The incision made from ear to ear at the back of the head before sawing open the skull is not attractive, either.

Of course, injuries to the dead do not heal. They can only be covered with high lacy collars and strategically coiffed hair. With heavy makeup from the funeral home and a wide seam running the length of her small body, Emily looked like a sad rag doll stripped of its frilly clothes and abandoned by its heartless owner.

Water drummed into a steel sink as Dr. Jenrette and I scrubbed away mold, makeup, and the flesh-colored putty filling the gunshot wound to the back of the head and the areas of the thighs, upper chest, and shoulders where skin had been excised by her killer. We removed eye caps beneath eyelids and took out sutures. Our eyes watered and noses began to run as sharp fumes rose from the chest cavity. Organs were breaded with embalming powder, and we quickly lifted them out and rinsed some more. I checked the neck, finding nothing that my colleague hadn't already documented. Then I wedged a long thin chisel between molars to open the mouth.

"It's stubborn," I said in frustration. "We're going to have to cut the masseters. I want to look at the tongue in its anatomical position before getting at it through the posterior pharynx. But I don't know. We may not be able to."

Dr. Jenrette fitted a new blade into his scalpel. "What are we looking for?"

"I want to make certain she didn't bite her tongue."

Minutes later I discovered that she had.

"She's got marks right there at the margin," I pointed out. "Can you get a measurement?"

"An eighth of an inch by a quarter."

"And the hemorrhages are about a quarter of an inch deep. It looks like she might have bitten herself more than once. What do you think?"

"It looks to me like maybe she did."

"So we know she had a seizure associated with her terminal episode."

"The head injury could do that," he said, fetching the camera.

"It could, but then why doesn't the brain show that she survived long enough to have a seizure?"

"I guess we've got the same unanswered question."

"Yes," I said. "It's still very confusing."

When we turned the body, I absorbed myself in studying the peculiar mark that was the point of this grim exercise as the forensic photographer arrived and set up his equipment. For the better part of the afternoon we took rolls of infrared, ultraviolet, color, high-contrast, and black-and-white film, with many special filters and lenses.

Then I went into my medical bag and got out half a dozen black rings made of acrylonitrile-butadiene-styrene plastic, or more simply, the material that commonly composes pipes used for water and sewage lines. Every year or two I got a forensic dentist I knew to cut the three-eighth-inch-thick rings with a band saw and sand them smooth for me. Fortunately, it wasn't often I needed to pull such an odd trick out of my bag, for rarely was it necessary to remove a human bite mark or other impression from the body of someone murdered.

Deciding on a ring three inches in diameter, I used a machinist's die punch to stamp Emily Steiner's case number and location markers on each side. Skin, like a painter's canvas, is on a stretch, and in order to support the exact anatomical configuration of the mark on Emily's left buttock during and after its removal, I needed to provide a stable matrix.

"Have you got Super Glue?" I asked Dr. Jenrette.

"Sure." He brought me a tube.

"Keep taking photographs of every step, if you don't mind," I instructed the photographer, a slight Japanese man who never stood still.

Positioning the ring over the mark, I fixed it to the skin with the glue and further secured it with sutures. Next I dissected the tissue around the ring and placed it *en bloc* in formalin. All the while I tried to figure out what the mark meant. It was an irregular circle incompletely filled with a strange brownish discoloration that I believed was the imprint of a pattern. But I could not make out what, no matter how many Polaroids we looked at from how many different angles.

We did not think about the package wrapped in white tissue paper until the photographer had left and Dr. Jenrette and I had notified the funeral home that we were ready for their return.

"What do we do about this?" Dr. Jenrette asked.

"We have to open it."

He spread dry towels on a cart and set the gift on top of them. Carefully slicing the paper with a scalpel, he exposed an old box from a pair of size-six women's loafers. He cut through many layers of Scotch tape and removed the top.

"Oh my," he said under his breath as he stared in bewilderment at what someone had intended for a little girl's grave.

Shrouded in two sealed freezer bags inside the box was a dead kitten that could not have been but a few months old. It was as stiff as plyboard when I lifted it out, its delicate ribs protruding. The cat was a female, black with white feet, and she wore no collar. I saw no evidence of what had killed her until I took her into the X-ray room, and a little later was mounting her films on a light box.

"Her cervical spine is fractured," I said as a chill pricked up the hair on the back of my neck.

Dr. Jenrette frowned as he moved closer to the light box. "It looks like the spine's been moved out of the usual position here." He touched the film with a knuckle. "That's weird. It's displaced laterally? I don't think that could happen if she got hit by a car."

"She wasn't hit by a car," I told him. "Her head's been twisted clockwise by ninety degrees."

I found Marino eating a cheeseburger in his room when I returned to the Travel-Eze at almost seven P.M. His gun, wallet, and car keys were on top of one bed and he was on the other, shoes and socks scattered across the floor as if he had walked out of them. I could tell he had probably gotten back here not too long before I did. His eyes followed me as I went to the television and turned it off.

"Come on," I said. "We have to go out."

The "gospel truth" according to Lucias Ray was that Denesa Steiner had placed the package in Emily's casket. He had simply assumed that beneath the gift wrapping was a favorite toy or doll.

"When did she do this?" Marino asked as we walked briskly through the motel's parking lot.

"Right before the funeral," I replied. "Have you got your car keys?"

"Yeah."

"Then why don't you drive."

I had a nasty headache I blamed on formalin fumes and lack of food and sleep.

"Have you heard from Benton?" I asked as casually as possible.

"There should have been a bunch of messages at the desk for you."

"I came straight to your room. And how would you know if I had a lot of messages?"

"The clerk tried to give 'em to me. He figured between the two of us I look like the doctor."

"That's because you look like a man." I rubbed my temples.

"It's mighty white of you to notice."

"Marino, I wish you wouldn't talk like such a racist, because I really don't think you are one."

"How do you like my ride?"

His car was a maroon Chevrolet Caprice, fully loaded with flashing lights, a radio, telephone, scanner. It had even come equipped with a mounted video camera and a Winchester stainless steel Marine twelve-gauge shotgun. Pump action, it held seven rounds and was the same model the FBI used.

"My God," I said in disbelief as I got into the car. "Since when do they need riot guns in Black Mountain, North Carolina?"

"Since now." He cranked the engine.

"Did you request all this?"

"Nope."

"Would you like to explain to me how a ten-person police force can be better equipped than the DEA?"

"Because maybe the people who live around here really understand what community policing's all about. This community's got a bad problem right now, and what's happening is area merchants and concerned citizens are donating shit to help. Like the cars, phones, the shotgun. One of the cops told me some old lady called up just this morning and wanted to know if the federal agents that had come to town to help would like to have Sunday dinner with her."

"Well, that's very nice," I said, baffled.

"Plus, the town council's thinking about making the police department bigger, and I have a suspicion that helps explain some things."

"What things?"

"Black Mountain's gonna need a new chief."

"What happened to the old one?"

"Mote was about as close to a chief as they had."

"I'm still not clear on where you're going with this."

"Hey, maybe where I'm going is right here in this town, Doc. They're looking for an experienced chief and treating me like I'm 007 or something. It don't take a rocket scientist to figure it out."

"Marino, what in God's name is going on with you?" I asked very calmly.

He lit a cigarette. "What? First you don't think I look like a doctor? Now I don't look like a chief, either? I guess to you I don't look like nothing but a Dogtown slob who still talks like he's eating spaghetti with the mob back in Jersey and only takes out women in tight sweaters who tease their hair."

He blew out smoke furiously. "Hey, just because I like to bowl don't mean I'm some tattooed redneck. And just because I didn't go to all these Ivy League schools like you did don't mean I'm a dumb shit."

"Are you finished?"

"And another thing," he railed on, "there's a lot of really good places to fish around here. They got Bee Tree and Lake James, and except for Montreat and Biltmore, the real estate's pretty cheap. Maybe I'm just sick as shit of drones shooting drones and serial killers costing more to keep alive in the pen than I friggin' get paid to lock their asses up. *If* the assholes even stay in the pen, and that's the biggest 'if' of all."

We had been parked in the Steiner driveway for five minutes now. I stared out at the house lit up wondering if she knew we were here and why.

"Now are you finished?" I asked him.

"No, I ain't finished. I'm just sick of talking."

"In the first place, I didn't go to Ivy League schools. . . ."

"Well, what do you call Johns Hopkins and Georgetown?"

"Marino, goddam it, shut up."

He glared out the windshield and lit another cigarette.

"I was a poor Italian brought up in a poor Italian neighborhood just like you were," I said. "The difference is that I was in Miami and you were in New Jersey. I've never pretended to be better than you, nor have I ever called you stupid. In fact, you're anything but stupid, even if you butcher the English language and have never been to the opera.

"My list of complaints about you all go back to one thing. You're stubborn, and when you're at your worst, you're bigoted and intolerant. In other words, you act toward others the way you suspect they're acting toward you."

Marino jerked up the door handle. "Not only do I not got

time for a lecture from you, I ain't interested in one." He threw down his cigarette and stamped it out.

We walked in silence to Denesa Steiner's front door, and I had a feeling when she opened it she could sense Marino and I had been fighting. He would not look my way or acknowledge me in any way as she led us to a living room that was unnervingly familiar because I had seen photographs of it before. The decor was country, with an abundance of ruffles, plump pillows, hanging plants, and macramé. Behind glass doors, a gas fire glowed, and numerous clocks did not argue time. Mrs. Steiner was in the midst of watching an old Bob Hope movie on cable.

She seemed very tired as she turned off the television and sat in a rocking chair. "This hasn't been a very good day," she said.

"Well, now, Denesa, there's no way it could have been." Marino sat in a wing chair and gave her his full attention.

"Did you come here to tell me what you found?" she asked, and I realized she was referring to the exhumation.

"We still have a lot of tests to conduct," I told her.

"Then you didn't find anything that will catch that man." She spoke with quiet despair. "Doctors always talk about tests when they don't know anything. I've learned that much after all I've been through."

"These things take time, Mrs. Steiner."

"Listen," Marino said to her. "I really am sorry to bother you, Denesa, but we've got to ask you a few more questions. The Doc here wants to ask you some."

She looked at me and rocked.

"Mrs. Steiner, there was a gift-wrapped package in Emily's casket that the funeral director says you wanted buried with her," I said.

"Oh, you're talking about Socks," she said matter-of-factly.

"Socks?" I asked.

"She was a stray kitten who started coming around here.

I guess that would have been a month or so ago. And of course Emily was such a sensitive thing she started feeding it and that was it. She did love that little cat." She smiled as her eyes teared up.

"She called her Socks because she was pure black except for these perfect white paws." She held out her hands, splaying her fingers. "It looked like she had socks on."

"How did Socks die?" I carefully asked.

"I don't really know." She pulled tissues from a pocket and dabbed her eyes. "I found her one morning out in front. This was right after Emily . . . I just assumed the poor little thing died of a broken heart." She covered her mouth with the tissues and sobbed.

"I'm going to get you something to drink." Marino got up and left the room.

His obvious familiarity with both the house and its owner struck me as extremely unusual, and my uneasiness grew.

"Mrs. Steiner," I said gently, leaning forward on the couch. "Emily's kitten did not die of a broken heart. It died of a broken neck."

She lowered her hands and took a deep, shaky breath. Her eyes were red-rimmed and wide as they fixed on me. "What do you mean?"

"The cat died violently."

"Well, I guess it got hit by a car. That's such a pity. I told Emily I was afraid of that."

"It wasn't hit by a car."

"Do you suppose one of the dogs around here got it?"

"No," I said as Marino returned with what looked like a glass of white wine. "The kitten was killed by a person. Deliberately."

"How could you know such a thing as that?" She looked terrified, and her hands trembled as she took the wine and set it on the table next to her chair.

"There were physical findings that make it clear the cat's neck was wrung," I continued to explain very calmly. "And I know it's awful for you to hear details like this, Mrs. Steiner, but you must know the truth if you are to help us find the person responsible."

"You got any idea who might have done something like that to your little girl's kitten?" Marino sat back down and leaned forward again, forearms resting on his knees, as if he wanted to assure her that she could depend on and feel safe with him.

She silently struggled for composure. Reaching for her wine, she took several unsteady sips. "I do know I've gotten some calls." She took a deep breath. "You know, my fingernails are blue. I'm such a wreck." She held out a hand. "I can't settle down. I can't sleep. I don't know what to do." She dissolved into tears again.

"Denesa, it's all right," Marino said kindly. "You just take your time. We're not going anywhere. Now tell me about the phone calls."

She wiped her eyes and went on. "It's been men mostly. Maybe one woman who said if I'd kept my eye on my little girl like a good mother, this wouldn't have . . . But one sounded young, like a boy playing pranks. He said something. You know. Like he'd seen Emily riding her bike. This was after . . . So it couldn't have been. But this other one, he was older. He said he wasn't finished." She drank more wine.

"He wasn't finished?" I asked. "Did he say anything else?"

"I don't remember." She shut her eyes.

"When was this?" Marino asked.

"Right after she was found. Found by the lake." She reached for her wine again and knocked it over.

"I'll get that." Marino abruptly got up. "I need to smoke."

"Do you know what he meant?" I asked her.

"I knew he was referring to what happened. To who did this to her. I felt he was saying it wasn't the end of bad things. And I guess it was a day later I found Socks."

"Captain, maybe you could fix me some toast with peanut

butter or cheese. I feel like my blood sugar's getting low," said Mrs. Steiner, who seemed oblivious to the glass on its side and the puddle of wine on the table by her chair.

He left the room again.

"When the man broke into your house and abducted your daughter," I said, "did he speak to you at all?"

"He said if I didn't do exactly what he said, he'd kill me."

"So you heard his voice."

She nodded as she rocked, her eyes not leaving me.

"Did it sound like the voice on the phone that you were just telling us about?"

"I don't know. It might have. But it's hard to say."

"Mrs. Steiner . . . ?"

"You can call me Denesa." Her stare was intense.

"What else do you remember about him, the man who came into your house and taped you up?"

"You're wondering if he might be that man in Virginia who killed the little boy."

I said nothing.

"I remember seeing pictures of the little boy and his family in *People* magazine. I remember thinking back then how awful it was, that I couldn't imagine being his mother. It was bad enough when Mary Jo died. I never thought I'd get past that."

"Is Mary Jo the child you lost to SIDS?"

Interest sparked beneath her dark pain, as if she were impressed or curious that I would know this detail. "She died in my bed. I woke up and she was next to Chuck, dead."

"Chuck was your husband?"

"At first I was afraid he might have accidentally rolled on top of her during the night and smothered her. But they said no. They said it was SIDS."

"How old was Mary Jo?" I asked.

"She'd just had her first birthday." She blinked back tears.

"Had Emily been born yet?"

"She came a year later, and I just knew the same thing was going to happen to her. She was so colicky. So frail. And the doctors were afraid she might have apnea, so I had to constantly check on her in her sleep. To make sure she was breathing. I remember walking around like a zombie because I never had a night's sleep. Up and down all night, night after night. Living with that horrible fear."

She closed her eyes for a moment and rocked, brow furrowed by grief, hands clenching armrests.

It occurred to me that Marino did not want to hear me question Mrs. Steiner because of his anger, and that was why he was out of the room so much. I knew then his emotions had wrestled him into the ropes. I feared he would no longer be effective in this case.

Mrs. Steiner opened her eyes and they went straight to mine. "He's killed a lot of people and now he's here," she said.

"Who?" I was confused by what I had been thinking.

"Temple Gault."

"We don't know for a fact he's here," I said.

"I know he is."

"How do you know that?"

"Because of what was done to my Emily. It's the same thing." A tear slid down her cheek. "You know, I guess I should be afraid he'll get me next. But I don't care. What do I have left?"

"I'm very sorry," I said as kindly as I could. "Can you tell me anything more about that Sunday? The Sunday of October first?"

"We went to church in the morning like we always did. And Sunday school. We ate lunch, then Emily was in her room. She was practicing guitar some of the time. I didn't see her much, really." She stared the wide stare of remembering.

"Do you recall her leaving the house early for her youth group meeting?"

"She came into the kitchen. I was making banana bread. She

said she had to go early to practice guitar and I gave her some change for the collection like I always did."

"What about when she came home?"

"We ate." She was not blinking. "She was unhappy. And wanted Socks in the house and I said no."

"What makes you think she was unhappy?"

"She was difficult. You know how children can get when they're in moods. Then she was in her room awhile and went to bed."

"Tell me about her eating habits," I said, recalling that Ferguson had intended to ask Mrs. Steiner this after he returned from Quantico. I supposed he'd never had the chance.

"She was picky. Finicky."

"Did she finish her dinner Sunday night after her meeting?"

"That was part of what we got into a fuss about. She was just pushing her food around. Pouting." Her voice caught. "It was always a struggle. . . . It was always hard for me to get her to eat."

"Did she have a problem with diarrhea or nausea?"

Her eyes focused on me. "She was sick a lot."

"Sick can mean a lot of different things, Mrs. Steiner," I said patiently. "Did she have frequent diarrhea or nausea?"

"Yes. I already told Max Ferguson that." Tears flowed freely again. "And I don't understand why I have to keep answering these same questions. It just opens up things. Opens up wounds."

"I'm sorry," I said with a gentleness that belied my surprise. When had she told Ferguson this? Did he call her after he left Quantico? If so, she must have been one of the last people to talk to him before he died.

"This didn't happen to her because she was sickly," Mrs. Steiner said, crying harder. "It seems people should be asking questions that would help catch *him*."

"Mrs. Steiner—and I know this is difficult—but where were you living when Mary Jo died?"

"Oh God, please help me."

She buried her face in her hands. I watched her try to compose herself, shoulders heaving as she wept. I sat numbly as she got still, little by little, her feet, her arms, her hands. She slowly lifted her eyes to me. Through their bleariness gleamed a strange cold light that oddly made me think of the lake at night, of water so dark it seemed another element. And I felt fretful the way I did in my dreams.

She spoke in a low voice. "What I want to know, Dr. Scarpetta, is do you know that man?"

"What man?" I asked, and then Marino walked back in with a peanut butter and jelly sandwich on toast, a dish towel, and a bottle of chablis.

"The man who killed the little boy. Did you ever talk to Temple Gault?" she asked as Marino set her glass upright and refilled it, and placed the sandwich nearby.

"Here, let me help with that." I took the dish towel from him and wiped up spilled wine.

"Tell me what he looks like." She shut her eyes again.

I saw Gault in my mind, his piercing eyes and light blond hair. He was sharp featured, small and quick. But it was the eyes. I would never forget them. I knew he could slit a throat without flinching. I knew he had killed all of them with that same blue stare.

"Excuse me," I said, realizing Mrs. Steiner was still talking to me.

"Why did you let him get away?" she repeated her question as if it were an accusation, and began crying again.

Marino told her to get some rest, that we were leaving. When we got into the car, his mood was horrible.

"Gault killed her cat," he said.

"We don't know that for a fact."

"I ain't interested in hearing you talk like a lawyer right now."

"I am a lawyer," I said.

"Oh yeah. Excuse me for forgetting you got that degree, too. It just slips my mind that you *really are* a doctor-lawyer-Indian chief."

"Do you know if Ferguson called Mrs. Steiner after he left Quantico?"

"Hell, no, I don't know."

"He mentioned in the consultation he intended to ask her several medical questions. Based on what Mrs. Steiner said to me, it sounds like he did, meaning he must have talked to her shortly before his death."

"So maybe he called her as soon as he got home from the airport."

"And then he goes straight upstairs and puts a noose around his neck?"

"No, Doc. He goes straight upstairs to beat off. Maybe talking to her on the phone put him in the mood."

That was possible.

"Marino, what's the last name of the little boy Emily liked? I know his first name was Wren."

"Why?"

"I want to go see him."

"In case you don't know much about kids, it's almost nine o'clock on a school night."

"Marino," I said evenly, "answer my question."

"I know he don't live too far from the Steiners' crib." He pulled off on the side of the road and turned on his interior light. "His last name's Maxwell."

"I want to go to his house."

He flipped through his notepad, then glanced over at me. Behind his tired eyes I saw more than resentment. Marino was in terrific pain.

The Maxwells lived in a modern log cabin that was probably prefabricated and had been built on a wooded lot in view of the lake.

We pulled into a gravel drive lit by floodlights the color of pollen. It was cool enough for rhododendron leaves to begin to curl, and our breath turned to smoke as we waited on the porch for someone to answer the bell. When the door opened, we faced a young, lean man with a thin face and black-rimmed glasses. He was dressed in a dark wool robe and slippers. I wondered if anyone stayed up past ten o'clock in this town.

"I'm Captain Marino and this is Dr. Scarpetta," Marino said in a serious police tone that would fill any citizen with dread. "We're working with the local authorities on the Emily Steiner case."

"You're the ones from out of town," the man said.

"Are you Mr. Maxwell?" Marino asked.

"Lee Maxwell. Please come in. I guess you want to talk about Wren."

We entered the house as an overweight woman in a pink sweatsuit came downstairs. She looked at us as if she knew exactly why we were there.

"He's up in his room. I was reading to him," she said.

"I wonder if I might speak to him," I said in as nonthreatening a voice as possible, for I could tell the Maxwells were upset.

"I can get him," the father said.

"I'd rather go on up, if I might," I said.

Mrs. Maxwell absently fiddled with a seam coming loose on a cuff of her sweatshirt. She was wearing small silver earrings shaped like crosses that matched a necklace she had on.

"Maybe while the doc does that," Marino spoke up, "I can talk to the two of you?"

"That policeman who died already talked to Wren," said the father.

"I know." Marino spoke in a manner that told them he didn't care who had talked to their son. "We promise not to take up too much of your time," he added.

"Well, all right," Mrs. Maxwell said to me.

I followed her slow, heavy progress up uncarpeted stairs to

a second floor that had few rooms but was so well lit my eyes hurt. There didn't seem to be a corner inside or out of the Maxwells' property that wasn't flooded with light. We walked into Wren's bedroom and the boy was in pajamas and standing in the middle of the floor. He stared at us as if we'd caught him in the middle of something we weren't supposed to see.

"Why aren't you in bed, son?" Mrs. Maxwell sounded more weary than stern.

"I was thirsty."

"Would you like me to get you another glass of water?"

"No, that's okay."

I could see why Emily would have found Wren Maxwell cute. He had been growing in height faster than his muscles could keep up, and his sunny blond hair wouldn't stay out of his dark blue eyes. Lanky and shaggy, with a perfect complexion and mouth, he had chewed his fingernails to the quick. He wore several bracelets of woven rawhide that could not be taken off without cutting, and they somehow told me he was very popular in school, especially with girls, whom I expected he treated quite rudely.

"Wren, this is Dr."—she looked at me—"I'm sorry, but you're going to have say your last name again."

"I'm Dr. Scarpetta." I smiled at Wren, whose expression turned to bewilderment.

"I'm not sick," he quickly said.

"She's not that kind of doctor," Mrs. Maxwell told her son.

"What kind are you?" By now his curiosity had overcome his shyness.

"Well, she's a doctor sort of like Lucias Ray is one."

"He ain't a doctor." Wren scowled at his mother. "He's an undertaker."

"Now you go on and get in bed, son, so you don't catch cold. Dr. Scarletti, you can pull up that chair and I'll be downstairs."

"Her name's *Scarpetta,*" the boy fired at his mother, who was already out the door.

He climbed into his twin bed and covered himself with a wool blanket the color of bubble gum. I noticed the baseball theme of the curtains drawn across his window, and the silhouettes of trophies behind them. On pine walls were posters of several sports heroes, and I recognized none of them except Michael Jordan, who was typically airborne in Nikes like some magnificent god. I pulled a chair close to the bed and suddenly felt old.

"What sport do you play?" I asked him.

"I play for the Yellow Jackets," he answered brightly, for he had found a co-conspirator in his quest to stay up past bedtime.

"The Yellow Jackets?"

"That's my Little League team. You know, we beat everybody around here. I'm surprised you haven't heard of us."

"I'm certain I would have heard of your team if I lived here, Wren. But I don't."

He regarded me as if I were some exotic creature behind glass in the zoo. "I play basketball, too. I can dribble between my legs. I bet you can't do that."

"You're absolutely right. I can't. I'd like you to tell me about your friendship with Emily Steiner."

His eyes dropped to his hands, which were nervously fiddling with the edge of the blanket.

"Had you known her a long time?" I continued.

"I've seen her around. We're in the same youth group at church." He looked at me. "Plus, we're both in the sixth grade but we have different homeroom teachers. I have Mrs. Winters."

"Did you get to know Emily right after her family moved here?"

"I guess so. They came from California. Mom says they have earthshakes out there because the people don't believe in Jesus."

"It seems Emily liked you a great deal," I said. "In fact,

I'd say she had a big crush on you. Were you aware of that?"

He nodded, eyes cast down again.

"Wren, can you tell me about the last time you saw her?"

"It was at church. She came in with her guitar because it was her turn."

"Her turn for what?"

"For music. Usually Owen or Phil plays the piano, but sometimes Emily would play guitar. She wasn't very good."

"Were you supposed to meet her at church that afternoon?"

Color mounted his cheeks and he sucked in his lower lip to keep it from trembling.

"It's all right, Wren. You didn't do anything wrong."

"I asked her to meet me there early," he quietly said.

"What was her reaction?"

"She said she would but not to tell anybody."

"Why did you want her to meet you early?" I continued to probe.

"I wanted to see if she would."

"Why?"

Now his face was very red and he was working hard to hold back tears. "I don't know," he barely said.

"Wren, tell me what happened."

"I rode my bike to the church just to see if she was there."

"What time would this have been?"

"I don't know. But it was at least an hour before the meeting was supposed to start," he said. "And I saw her through the window. She was inside sitting on the floor practicing guitar."

"Then what?"

"I left and came back with Paul and Will at five. They live over there." He pointed.

"Did you say anything to Emily?" I asked.

Tears spilled down his cheeks, and he impatiently wiped them away. "I didn't say nothing. She kept staring at me but

I pretended not to see her. She was upset. Jack asked her what was wrong."

"Who's Jack?"

"The youth leader. He goes to Montreat Anderson College. He's real fat and's got a beard."

"What was her reply when Jack asked what was wrong?"

"She said she felt like she was getting the flu. Then she left."

"How long before the meeting was over?"

"When I was getting the basket off the top of the piano. 'Cause it was my turn to take up the collection."

"This would have been at the very end of the meeting?"

"That's when she ran out. She took the shortcut." He bit his lower lip and gripped the blanket so hard that the small bones of his hands were clearly defined.

"How do you know she took a shortcut?" I asked.

He looked up at me and sniffed loudly. I handed him several tissues, and he blew his nose.

"Wren," I persisted, "did you actually *see* Emily take the shortcut?"

"No, ma'am," he meekly said.

"Did anybody see her take the shortcut?"

He shrugged.

"Then why do you think she took it?"

"Everybody says so," he replied simply.

"Just as everybody has said where her body was found?" I was gentle. When he did not respond, I added more forcefully, "And you know exactly where that is, don't you, Wren?"

"Yes, ma'am," he said almost in a whisper.

"Will you tell me about that place?"

Still staring at his hands, he answered, "It's just this place where lots of colored people fish. There's a bunch of weeds and slime, and huge bullfrogs and snakes hanging out of the trees, and that's where she was. A colored man found her, and all she had on was her socks, and it scared him so bad he turned white as you are. After that Dad put in all the lights."

"Lights?"

"He put all these lights in the trees and everywhere. It makes it harder for me to sleep, and then Mom gets mad."

"Was it your father who told you about the place at the lake?"

Wren shook his head.

"Then who did?" I asked.

"Creed."

"Creed?"

"He's one of the janitors at school. He makes toothpicks, and we buy them for a dollar. Ten for a dollar. He soaks them in peppermint and cinnamon. I like the cinnamon best 'cause they're real hot like Fireballs. Sometimes I trade him candy when I run out of lunch money. But you can't tell anybody." He looked worried.

"What does Creed look like?" I asked as a quiet alarm began to sound in the back of my brain.

"I don't know," Wren said. "He's a greaser 'cause he's always wearing white socks with boots. I guess he's pretty old." He sighed.

"Do you know his last name?"

Wren shook his head.

"Has he always worked at your school?"

He shook his head again. "He took Albert's place. Albert got sick from smoking, and they had to cut his lung out."

"Wren," I asked, "did Creed and Emily know each other?"

He was talking faster and faster. "We used to make her mad by saying Creed was her boyfriend 'cause one time he gave her some flowers he picked. And he would give her candy 'cause she didn't like toothpicks. You know, a lot of girls would rather have candy than toothpicks."

"Yes," I answered with a grim smile, "I suspect a lot of girls would."

The last thing I asked Wren was if he had visited the place at the lake where Emily's body had been found. He claimed he had not.

"I believe him," I said to Marino as we drove away from the Maxwells' well-lit house.

"Not me. I think he's lying his little ass off so his old man don't whip the shit out of him." He turned down the heat. "This ride heats up better than any one I've ever had. All it's missing is heaters in the seats like you got in your Benz."

"The way he described the scene at the lake," I went on, "tells me he's never been there. I don't think he left the candy there, Marino."

"Then who did?"

"What do you know about a custodian named Creed?"

"Not a damn thing."

"Well," I said, "I think you'd better find him. And I'll tell you something else. I don't think Emily took the shortcut around the lake on her way home from the church."

"Shit," he complained. "I hate it when you get like this. Just when pieces start to fall in place you shake the hell out of them like a damn puzzle in a box."

"Marino, I took the path around the lake myself. There's no way an eleven-year-old girl—or anybody else, for that matter—would do that when it's getting dark. And it would have been almost completely dark by six P.M., which was the time Emily headed home."

"Then she lied to her mother," Marino said.

"It would appear so. But why?"

"Maybe because Emily was up to something."

"Such as?"

"I don't know. You got any Scotch in the room? I mean, there's no point in asking if you got bourbon."

"You're right," I said. "I don't have bourbon."

I found five messages awaiting me when I returned to the

Travel-Eze. Three were from Benton Wesley. The Bureau was sending the helicopter to pick me up at dawn.

When I got hold of Wesley he cryptically said, "Among other things, we've got rather a crisis situation with your niece. We're bringing you straight back to Quantico."

"What's happened?" I asked as my stomach closed like a fist. "Is Lucy all right?"

"Kay, this is not a secured line."

"But is she all right?"

"Physically," he said, "she's fine."

10

The next morning I woke up to mist and could not see the mountains. My return north was postponed until afternoon, and I went out for a run in the brisk, moist air.

I wended my way through neighborhoods of cozy homes and modest cars, smiling as a miniature collie behind a chain link fence raced from one border of the yard to another, barking frantically at falling leaves. The owner emerged from the house as I went past.

"Now, Shooter, hush up!"

The woman wore a quilted robe, fuzzy slippers, and curlers, and didn't seem to mind a bit walking outside like that. She picked up the newspaper and smacked it against her palm as she yelled some more. I imagined that prior to Emily Steiner's death, the only crime anyone worried about in this part of the world was a neighbor stealing your newspaper or stringing toilet paper through your trees.

Cicadas were sawing the same scratchy tune they had played last night, and locust, sweet peas, and morning glories were wet with dew. By eleven, a cold rain had begun to fall, and I felt as if I were at sea surrounded by brooding waters. I imagined the sun was a porthole, and if I could look through it to the other side I might find an end to this gray day.

It was half past two before the weather improved enough for me to leave. I was instructed that the helicopter could not land at the high school because the Warhorses and majorettes would be in the midst of practice. Instead, Whit and I were to meet at a grassy field inside the rugged stone double-arched gate of a tiny town called Montreat, which was as Presbyterian as predestination and but a few miles from the Travel-Eze.

The Black Mountain Police arrived with me before Whit appeared, and I sat in a cruiser parked on a dirt road, watching children play flag football. Boys ran after girls and girls ran after boys as everybody pursued the small glory of snatching a red rag from an opposing player's waistband. Young voices carried on a wind that sometimes caught the ball and passed it through the fingers of trees huddled at borders, and whenever it spiraled out of bounds into briars or the street, everybody paused. Equality was sent to the bench as girls waited for boys. When the ball was retrieved, play went on as usual.

I was sorry to interrupt this innocent frolicking when the distinctive chopping noise became audible. The children froze into a tableau of wonderment as the Bell JetRanger lowered itself with a roaring wind to the center of the field. I boarded and waved good-bye as we rose above trees.

The sun settled into the horizon like Apollo lying down to sleep, and then the sky was as thick as octopus ink. I saw no stars when we arrived at the Academy. Benton Wesley, who had been kept informed of our progress by radio, was waiting when we landed. The instant I climbed out of the helicopter, he had my arm and was leading me away.

"Come on," he said. "It's good to see you, Kay," he added under his breath, and the pressure of his fingers on my arm unsettled me more.

"The fingerprint recovered from Ferguson's panties was left by Denesa Steiner."

"What?"

He propelled me swiftly through the dark. "And the ABO grouping of the tissue we found in his freezer is O-positive. Emily Steiner was O-positive. We're still waiting for DNA, but it appears Ferguson stole the lingerie from the Steiner home when he broke in to abduct Emily."

"You mean, when *someone* broke in and abducted Emily."

"That's right. Gault could be playing games."

"Benton, for God's sake, what crisis? Where's Lucy?"

"I imagine she's in her dorm room," he replied as we walked into the lobby of Jefferson.

I squinted in the light and was not cheered by a digital sign behind the information desk announcing WELCOME TO THE FBI ACADEMY. I did not feel welcome this night.

"What did she do?" I persisted as he used a magnetized card to unlock a set of glass doors with Department of Justice and National Academy seals.

"Wait until we get downstairs," he said.

"How's your hand? And your knee?" I remembered.

"Much better since I went to a doctor."

"Thanks," I said dryly.

"I'm referring to you. You're the only doctor I've been to recently."

"I might as well clean your stitches while I'm here."

"That won't be necessary."

"I need hydrogen peroxide and cotton swabs. Don't worry." I smelled Hoppes as we walked through the gun-cleaning room. "It shouldn't hurt very much."

We took the elevator to the lower level, where the Investigative Support Unit was the fire in the belly of the FBI. Wesley reigned over eleven other profilers, and at this hour, every one of them had left for the day. I had always liked the space where Wesley worked, for he was a man of sentiment and understatement, and one could not possibly know this without knowing him.

While most people in law enforcement filled walls and shelves with commendations and souvenirs from their war against base human nature, Wesley chose paintings, and he had several very fine ones. My favorite was an expansive landscape by Valoy Eaton, who I believed was as good as Remington and one day would cost as much. I had several Eaton oil paintings in my home, and what was odd was that Wesley and I had discovered the Utahan artist independent of each other.

This is not to say that Wesley did not have his occasional exotic trophy, but he displayed only those that held meaning. The Viennese white police cap, the bearskin cap from a Cold Stream Guard, and silver gaucho spurs from Argentina, for example, had nothing to do with serial killers or any other atrocity Wesley worked as a matter of course. They were gifts from well-traveled friends like me. In fact, Wesley had many mementos of our relationship because when words failed I spoke in symbols. So he had an Italian scabbard, a pistol with scrimshawed ivory grips, and a Mont Blanc pen that he kept in a pocket over his heart.

"Talk to me," I said, taking a chair. "What else is going on? You look awful."

"I feel awful." He loosened his tie and ran his fingers through his hair. "Kay"—he looked at me—"I don't know how to tell you this. Christ!"

"Just say it," I said very quietly as my blood went cold.

"It appears that Lucy broke into ERF, that she violated security."

"How could she break in?" I asked incredulously. "She has clearance to be there, Benton."

"She does not have clearance to be there at three o'clock in the morning, which was when her thumbprint was scanned into the biometric lock system."

I stared at him in disbelief.

"And your niece certainly does not have clearance to go into classified files pertaining to classified projects being worked on over there."

"What projects?" I dared to ask.

"It appears she went into files pertaining to electro-optics, thermal imaging, video and audio enhancement. And she apparently printed programs from the electronic version of case management that she's been working on for us."

"You mean from CAIN?"

"Yes, that's right."

"What *wasn't* gotten into?" I asked, stunned.

"Well, that's really the point. She got into virtually everything, meaning it's difficult for us to know what she was really after and for whom."

"Are the devices the engineers are working on really so secret?"

"Some of them are, and all of the techniques are, from a security standpoint. We don't want it known that we use this device in this situation and use something else in another."

"She couldn't have," I said.

"We know she did. The question is why."

"All right, then, why?" I blinked back tears.

"Money. That would be my guess."

"That's ridiculous. If she needs money she knows she can come to me."

"Kay"—Wesley leaned forward and folded his hands on top of his desk—"do you have any idea how valuable some of this information is?"

I did not reply.

"Imagine, for example, if ERF developed a surveillance device that could filter out background noise so we could be privy to virtually any conversation of interest to us anywhere in the world. Imagine who out there would love to know the details of our rapid prototyping or tactical satellite systems, or for that matter, the artificial intelligence software Lucy is developing. . . ."

I held up my hand to stop him. "Enough," I said as I took a deep, shaky breath.

"Then you tell me why," Wesley said. "You know Lucy better than I do."

"I'm no longer so sure I know her at all. And I don't know how she could do such a thing, Benton."

He paused, staring off for a moment before meeting my eyes again. "You've indicated to me that you're worried about her drinking. Can you elaborate on that?"

"My guess is she drinks like she does everything else—in extreme. Lucy is either very good or very bad, and alcohol is just one example." I knew even as I said the words I was darkening Wesley's suspicions.

"I see," he said. "Is there alcoholism in her family?"

"I'm beginning to think there's alcoholism in everybody's family," I said bitterly. "But yes. Her father was an alcoholic."

"This would be your brother-in-law?"

"He was very briefly. As you know, Dorothy's been married four times."

"Are you aware that there have been nights when Lucy didn't return to her dormitory room?"

"I know nothing about that. Was she in her bed the night of the break-in? She has suitemates and a roommate."

"She could have snuck out when everyone was asleep. So we don't know. Are you and your niece getting along well?" he then asked.

"Not especially."

"Kay, could she have done something like this to punish you?"

"No," I said, and I was getting angry with him. "And what I'm not interested in at the moment is your using me to *profile* my niece."

"Kay"—his voice softened—"I don't want this to be true any more than you do. I'm the one who recommended her to ERF. I'm the one who's been working on our hiring her after she graduates from UVA. Do you think I'm feeling very good?"

"There must be some other way this could have happened."

He slowly shook his head. "Even if someone had discovered Lucy's PIN, they still couldn't have gotten in because the biometric system would also require a scan of her actual finger."

"Then she wanted to be caught," I replied. "Lucy more than anyone would know that if she went into classified automated files, she would leave log-in and log-out times, activity logs, and other tracks."

"I agree. She would know this better than anyone. And that's why I'm more interested in possible motive. In other words, what was she trying to prove? Who was she trying to hurt?"

"Benton," I said. "What will happen?"

"OPR will conduct an official investigation," he answered, referring to the Bureau's Office of Professional Responsibility, which was the equivalent of a police department's Internal Affairs.

"If she's guilty?"

"It depends on whether we can prove she stole anything. If she did, she's committed a felony."

"And if she didn't?"

"Again, it depends on what OPR finds. But I think it's safe to say that at the very least Lucy has violated our security codes and no longer has a future with the FBI," he said.

My mouth was so dry I almost couldn't talk. "She will be devastated."

Wesley's eyes were shadowed by fatigue and disappointment. I knew how much he liked my niece.

"In the meantime," he went on in the same flat tone he used when reviewing cases, "she can't stay at Quantico. She's already been told to pack her things. Maybe she can stay in Richmond with you until our investigation is concluded."

"Of course, but you know I won't be there all the time."

"We're not placing her under house arrest, Kay," he said,

and his eyes got warmer for an instant. Very briefly I caught a glimpse of what stirred silently in his cool, dark waters.

He got up.

"I'll drive her to Richmond tonight." I got up, too.

"I hope you're all right," he said, and I knew what he meant, and I knew I could not think about that now.

"Thank you," I replied, and impulses fired crazily between neurons, as if a fierce battle were being fought in my mind.

Lucy was stripping her bed when I found her in her room not much later, and she turned her back to me when I walked in.

"What can I help you with?" I asked.

She stuffed sheets into a pillowcase. "Nothing," she said. "I've got it under control."

Her quarters were plainly furnished with institutional twin beds, desks, and chairs of oak veneer. By Yuppie apartment standards, the rooms in Washington dormitory were dreary, but if viewed as barracks they weren't half bad. I wondered where Lucy's suitemates and roommate were and if they had any idea what had happened.

"If you'll just check the wardrobe to make sure I've gotten everything," Lucy said. "It's the one on the right. And check the drawers."

"Everything is empty unless the coat hangers are yours. These nice padded ones."

"They're Mother's."

"Then I assume you want them."

"Nope. Leave them for the next idiot who ends up in this pit."

"Lucy," I said, "it's not the Bureau's fault."

"It's not fair." She knelt on her suitcase to fasten the clasps. "Whatever happened to innocent until proven guilty?"

"Legally, you are innocent until proven guilty. But until this breach of security is sorted out, you can't blame the Academy for not wanting you to continue working in classified areas.

Besides, you haven't been arrested. You've simply been asked to go on leave for a while."

She turned to face me, her eyes exhausted and red. "For a while means forever."

As I questioned her closely in the car, she vacillated from pitiful tears to volatile flares that scorched everything within reach. Then she fell asleep, and I knew nothing more than I had before. As a cold rain began to fall, I turned on fog lamps and followed the trail of bright red taillights streaking the blacktop ahead. At unwelcome intervals rain and clouds gathered densely in dips and turns, making it almost impossible to see. But instead of pulling over and waiting for the weather to pass, I shifted to a lower gear and drove on in my machine of burled walnut, soft leather, and steel.

I still wasn't certain why I had bought my charcoal Mercedes 500E, except that after Mark died, it had seemed important to drive something new. It might have been the memories, for we had loved and fought with each other desperately in my previous car. Or perhaps it was simply that life got harder as I got older and I needed more power to get by.

I heard Lucy stir as I turned into Windsor Farms, the old Richmond neighborhood where I lived amid stately Georgian and Tudor homes not far from the banks of the James. My headlights caught tiny reflectors on ankles of an unfamiliar boy riding a bicycle just ahead, and I passed a couple I did not recognize who were holding hands and walking their dog. Gum trees had dropped another load of prickly seeds over my yard, several rolled newspapers were on the porch, and the supercans were still parked by the street. It did not require long absences for me to feel like an outsider and for my house to look like no one was home.

While Lucy carried in luggage, I started the gas logs in the living room and put on a pot of Darjeeling tea. For a while I sat alone in front of the fire, listening to the sounds of my niece as she got settled, took a shower, and in general took her time. We were about to have a discussion that filled both of us with dread.

"Are you hungry?" I asked when I heard her walk in.

"No. Do you have any beer?"

I hesitated, then replied, "In the refrigerator in the bar."

I listened a little longer without turning around, because when I looked at Lucy I saw her the way I wanted her to be. Sipping tea, I mustered up the strength to face this frighteningly beautiful and brilliant woman with whom I shared snippets of genetic code. After all these years, it was time we met.

She came to the fire and sat on the floor, leaning against the stone hearth as she drank Icehouse beer out of the bottle. She had helped herself to a boldly colorful warm-up suit I wore on the infrequent occasions when I played tennis these days, and her feet were bare, her wet hair combed back. I realized that if I didn't know her and she walked past, I would turn to look again, and this wasn't solely due to her fine figure and face. One sensed the facility with which Lucy spoke, walked, and in the smallest ways guided her body and her eyes. She made everything seem easy, which was partially why she did not have many friends.

"Lucy," I began, "help me understand."

"I've been fucked," she said, taking a swallow of beer.

"If that's true, then how?"

"What do you mean 'if'?" She stared hard at me, her eyes filling with tears. "How can you think for even a minute . . . Oh, shit. What's the point?" She looked away.

"I can't help you if you don't tell me the truth," I said, getting up as I decided that I wasn't hungry, either. I went to the bar and poured Scotch over crushed ice.

"Let's start with the facts," I suggested as I returned to my chair. "We know someone entered ERF at around three A.M. on this past Tuesday. We know your PIN was used and your thumb was scanned. It is further documented by the system that this person—again, who has your PIN and print—went into numerous files. The log-out time was at precisely four thirty-eight A.M."

"I've been set up and sabotaged," Lucy said.

"Where were you while all this was going on?"

"I was asleep." She angrily gulped down the rest of her beer and got up for another one.

I sipped my Scotch slowly because it was not possible to drink a Dewar's Mist fast. "It has been alleged that there have been nights when your bed was empty," I quietly said.

"And you know what? It's nobody's business."

"Well, it is, and you know that. Were you in your bed the night of the break-in?"

"It's my business what *bed* I'm in, when, and where, and nobody else's," she said.

We were silent as I thought of Lucy sitting on top of the picnic table in the dark, her face illuminated by the match cupped in another woman's hands. I heard her speaking to her friend and understood the emotions carrying her words, for I knew the language of intimacy well. I knew when love was in someone's voice, and I knew when it was not.

"Exactly where were you when ERF was broken into?" I asked her again. "Or should I ask you instead who you were with?"

"I don't ask you who you're with."

"You would if it might save me from being in a lot of trouble."

"My private life is irrelevant," she went on.

"No, I think it is rejection you fear," I said.

"I don't know what you're talking about."

"I saw you in the picnic area the other night. You were with a friend."

She looked away. "So now you're spying on me, too." Her voice trembled. "Well, don't waste any sermons on me, and you can forget Catholic guilt because I don't believe in Catholic guilt."

"Lucy, I'm not judging you," I said, but in a way I was. "Help me understand."

"You imply I'm unnatural or abnormal, otherwise I would not need understanding. I would simply be accepted without a second thought."

"Can your friend vouch for your whereabouts at three o'clock Tuesday morning?" I asked.

"No," she answered.

"I see" was all I said, and my acceptance of her position was a concession that the girl I knew was gone. I did not know this Lucy, and I wondered what I had done wrong.

"What are you going to do now?" she asked me as the evening tensely wore on.

"I've got this case in North Carolina. I have a feeling I'm going to be there a lot for a while," I said.

"What about your office here?"

"Fielding's holding down the fort. I do have court in the morning, I think. In fact, I need to call Rose to verify the time."

"What kind of case?"

"A homicide."

"I figured that much. Can I come with you?"

"If you'd like."

"Well, maybe I'll just go back to Charlottesville."

"And do what?" I asked.

Lucy looked frightened. "I don't know. I don't know how I'd get there, either."

"You're welcome to my car when I'm not using it. Or you could go to Miami until the semester's over, then back to UVA."

She downed the last mouthful of beer and got up, her eyes bright with tears again. "Go ahead and admit it, Aunt Kay. You think I did it, don't you?"

"Lucy," I said honestly, "I don't know what to think. You and the evidence are saying two different things."

"I have never doubted you." She looked at me as if I had broken her heart.

"You're welcome to stay here through Christmas," I said.

11

The member of the North Richmond Gang on trial the next morning wore a double-breasted navy suit and an Italian silk tie with a perfect Windsor knot. His white shirt looked crisp; he was cleanly shaven and minus his earring.

Trial lawyer Tod Coldwell had dressed his client well because he knew that jurors have an exceedingly difficult time resisting the notion that what you see is what you get. Of course, I believed that axiom, too, which was why I introduced into evidence as many color photographs from the victim's autopsy as possible. It was safe to say that Coldwell, who drove a red Ferrari, did not like me much.

"Isn't it true, Mrs. Scarpetta," Coldwell pontificated in court this cool autumn day, "that people under the influence of cocaine can become very violent and even demonstrate superhuman strength?"

"Certainly cocaine can cause the user to become delusional and excited," I continued directing my answers to the jury. "Superhuman strength, as you call it, is often associated with cocaine or PCP—which is a horse tranquilizer."

"And the victim had both cocaine and benzoylecgonine

in his blood," Coldwell went on as if I had just agreed with him.

"Yes, he did."

"Mrs. Scarpetta, I wonder if you would explain to the jury what that means?"

"I would first like to explain to the jury that I am a medical doctor with a law degree. I have a specialty in pathology and a subspecialty in forensic pathology, as you've already stipulated, Mr. Coldwell. Therefore, I would appreciate being addressed as Dr. Scarpetta instead of Mrs. Scarpetta."

"Yes, ma'am."

"Would you please repeat the question?"

"Would you explain to the jury what it means if someone has cocaine"—he glanced at his notes—"and benzoylecgonine in his blood?"

"Benzoylecgonine is the metabolite of cocaine. To say that someone had both on board means some of the cocaine the victim had taken had already metabolized and some had not," I replied, aware of Lucy in a back corner, her face partially hidden by a column. She looked miserable.

"Which would indicate he was a chronic abuser, especially since he had many old needle tracks. And this may also suggest that when my client was confronted by him on the night of July third, my client had a very excited, agitated, and violent person on his hands, and had no choice but to defend himself." Coldwell was pacing, his dapper client watching me like a twitchy cat.

"Mr. Coldwell," I said, "the victim—Jonah Jones—was shot sixteen times with a Tec-Nine nine-millimeter gun that holds thirty-six rounds. Seven of those shots were to his back, and three of them were close or contact shots to the back of Mr. Jones's head.

"In my opinion, this is inconsistent with a shooting in which the shooter was defending himself, especially since Mr. Jones had a blood alcohol of point two-nine, which is almost three times the legal limit in Virginia. In other words, the victim's motor skills and judgment were substantially impaired when he was assaulted. Frankly, I'm amazed that Mr. Jones could even stand up."

Coldwell swung around to face Judge Poe, who had been nicknamed "the Raven" for as long as I had been in Richmond. He was weary to his ancient soul of drug dealers killing each other, of children carrying guns to school and shooting each other on the bus.

"Your Honor," Coldwell said dramatically, "I would ask that Mrs. Scarpetta's last statement be struck from the record since it is both speculative and inflammatory, and without a doubt beyond her area of expertise."

"Well, now, I don't know that what the doctor has to say is beyond her expertise, Mr. Coldwell, and she's already asked you politely to refer to her properly as *Dr.* Scarpetta, and I'm losing patience with your antics and ploys. . . ."

"But, Your Honor—"

"The fact is that I've had Dr. Scarpetta in my courtroom on many occasions and I'm well aware of her level of expertise," the judge went on in his Southern way of speaking that reminded me of pulling warm taffy.

"Your Honor . . . ?"

"Seems to me she deals with this sort of thing every day. . . ."

"Your Honor?"

"Mr. Coldwell," the Raven thundered, his balding pate turning red, "if you interrupt me one more goddam time I'm going to hold you in contempt of court and let you spend a few nights in the goddam city jail! Are we clear?"

"Yes, sir."

Lucy was craning her neck to see, and every juror was alert.

"I'm going to allow the record to reflect exactly what Dr. Scarpetta said," the judge went on.

"No further questions," Coldwell said tersely.

Judge Poe concluded with a violent bang of the gavel that woke up an old woman toward the back who had been fast asleep beneath a black straw hat for most of the morning. Startled, she sat straight up and blurted, "Who is it?" Then she remembered where she was and began to cry.

"It's all right, Mama," I heard another woman say as we adjourned for lunch.

Before leaving downtown, I stopped by the Health Department's Division of Vital Records, where an old friend and colleague of mine was the state registrar. In Virginia, one could not legally be born or buried without Gloria Loving's signature, and though she was as local as shad roe, she knew her counterpart in every state in the union. Over the years, I had relied on Gloria many times to verify that people had been on this planet or had not, that they had been married, divorced, or were adopted.

I was told she was on her lunch break in the Madison Building cafeteria. At quarter past one, I found Gloria alone at a table, eating vanilla yogurt and canned fruit cocktail. Mostly, she was reading a thick paperback thriller that was a *New York Times* bestseller, according to the cover.

"If I had to eat lunches like yours, I wouldn't bother," I said, pulling out a chair.

She looked up at me, her blank expression followed by joy. "Goodness gracious! Why, my Lord. What on earth are you doing here, Kay?"

"I work across the street, in case you've forgotten."

Delighted, she laughed. "Can I get you a coffee? Honey, you look tired."

Gloria Loving's name had defined her at birth, and she had grown up true to her calling. She was a big, generous woman of some fifty years who deeply cared about every certificate that crossed her desk. Records were more than paper and nosology codes to her, and she would hire, fire, or blast General Assembly in the name of one. It did not matter whose.

"No coffee, thanks," I said.

"Well, I heard you didn't work across the street anymore."

"I love the way people resign me when I've not been here for a couple of weeks. I'm a consultant with the FBI now. I'm in and out a lot."

"In and out of North Carolina, I guess, based on what I've been following in the news. Even Dan Rather was talking about the Steiner girl's case the other night. It was on CNN, too. Lord, it's cold in here."

I looked around at the bleak state government cafeteria where few people seemed thrilled with their lives. Many were huddled over trays, jackets and sweaters buttoned to their chins.

"They've got all the thermostats reset to sixty degrees to conserve energy, if that isn't the joke of all time," Gloria went on. "We have *steam heat* that comes out of the Medical College of Virginia, so cutting the thermostats doesn't save one watt of electricity."

"It feels colder in here than sixty degrees," I commented.

"That's because it's fifty-three, which is about what it is outside."

"You're welcome to come across the street and use my office," I said with a sly smile.

"Well, now, that's got to be the warmest spot in town. What can I do to help you, Kay?"

"I need to track down a SIDS that allegedly occurred in California around twelve years ago. The infant's name is Mary Jo Steiner, the parents' names Denesa and Charles."

She made the connection immediately but was too professional to probe. "Do you know Denesa Steiner's maiden name?"

"No."

"Where in California?"

"I don't know that, either," I said.

"Any possibility you can find out? The more information, the better."

"I'd rather you try running what I've got. If that fails, I'll see what else I can find out."

"You said an *alleged* SIDS. There's some suspicion that maybe it wasn't a SIDS? I need to know in case it might have been coded another way."

"Supposedly, the child was a year old when she died. And that bothers me considerably. As you know, the peak age for SIDS is three to four months old. Over six months old, and SIDS is unlikely. After a year, you're almost always talking about some other subtle form of sudden death. So yes, the death could have been coded a different way."

She played with her tea bag. "If this was Idaho, I'd just call Jane and she could run the nosology code for SIDS and have an answer for me in ninety seconds. But California's got thirty-two million people. It's one of the hardest states. It might take a special run. Come on, I'll walk you out. That will be my exercise for the day."

"Is the registrar in Sacramento?" We followed a depressing corridor busy with desperate citizens in need of social services.

"Yes. I'm going to call him as soon as I go back upstairs."

"I assume you know him, then."

"Oh, sure." She laughed. "There are only fifty of us. We have no one to talk to but each other."

That night I took Lucy to La Petite France, where I surrendered to Chef Paul, who sentenced us to languid hours of fruit-marinated lamb kabobs and a bottle of 1986 Château Gruaud Larose. I promised her *crema di cioccolata eletta* when we got home, a lovely chocolate mousse with pistachio and marsala that I kept in the freezer for culinary emergencies.

But before that we drove to Shocko Bottom and walked along cobblestones beneath lamplight in a part of the city that not so long ago I would not have ventured near. We were close to the river, and the sky was midnight blue with stars flung wide. I thought of Benton and then I thought of Marino for very different reasons.

"Aunt Kay," Lucy said as we entered Chetti's for cappuccino, "can I get a lawyer?"

"For what purpose?" I asked, although I knew.

"Even if the FBI can't prove what they're saying I did, they'll still slam me for the rest of my life." Pain could not hide behind her steady voice.

"Tell me what you want."

"A big gun."

"I'll find you one," I said.

I did not return to North Carolina on Monday as I had planned but flew to Washington instead. There were rounds to make at FBI headquarters, but more than anything I needed to see an old friend.

Senator Frank Lord and I had attended the same Catholic high school in Miami, although not at the same time. He was quite a lot older than I, and our friendship did not begin until I was working for the Dade County Medical Examiner's Office and he was the district attorney. When he became governor, then senator, I was long gone from the southern city of my birth. He and I did not become reconnected until he was appointed chairman of the Senate Judiciary Committee.

Lord had asked me to be an adviser as he fought to pass the most formidable crime bill in the history of the nation, and I had solicited his help, too. Unbeknownst to Lucy, he had been her patron saint, for without his intervention, she probably would not have been granted either permission or academic credit for her internship this fall. I wasn't certain how to tell him the news.

At almost noon, I waited for him on a polished cotton couch in a parlor with rich red walls and Persian rugs and a splendid crystal chandelier. Outside, voices carried along the marble corridor, and an occasional tourist peeked through the doorway in hopes of catching a glimpse of a politician or some other important person inside the Senate dining room. Lord arrived on time and full of energy, and gave me a quick, stiff hug. He was a kind, unassuming man shy about showing affection.

"I got lipstick on your face." I wiped a smudge off his jaw.

"Oh, you should leave it so my colleagues have something to talk about."

"I suspect they have plenty to talk about anyway."

"Kay, it's wonderful to see you," he said, escorting me into the dining room.

"You may not think it's so wonderful," I said.

"Of course I will."

We picked a table before a stained-glass window of George Washington on a horse, and I did not look at the menu because it never changed. Senator Lord was a distinguished man with thick gray hair and deep blue eyes. He was quite tall and lean, and had a penchant for elegant silk ties and old-fashioned finery such as vests, cuff links, pocket watches and stickpins.

"What brings you to D.C.?" he asked, placing his linen napkin in his lap.

"I have evidence to discuss at the FBI labs," I said.

He nodded. "You're working on that awful case in North Carolina."

"Yes."

"That psycho must be stopped. Do you think he's there?"

"I don't know."

"Because I'm just wondering why he would be," Lord went on. "It would seem he would have moved on to another place where he could lay low for a while. Well, I suppose logic has little to do with the decisions these evil people make."

"Frank," I said, "Lucy's in a lot of trouble."

"I can tell something's wrong," he said matter-of-factly. "I see it in your face."

He listened to me for half an hour as I told him everything, and I was so grateful for his patience. I knew he had to vote several times that day and that many people wanted slivers of his time.

"You're a good man," I said with feeling. "And I have let you down. I asked you for a favor, which is something I almost never do, and the situation has ended in disgrace."

"Did she do it?" he asked, and he had scarcely touched his grilled vegetables.

"I don't know," I replied. "The evidence is incriminating." I cleared my throat. "She says she didn't do it."

"Has she always told you the truth?"

"I thought so. But I've also been discovering of late that there are many important facets to her that she has not told me."

"Have you asked?"

"She's made it clear that some things aren't my business. And I shouldn't judge."

"If you're afraid of being judgmental, Kay, then you probably already are. And Lucy would sense this no matter what you say or don't say."

"I've never enjoyed being the one who criticizes and corrects her," I said, depressed. "But her mother, Dorothy, who is my only sibling, is too male dependent and self-centered to deal with the reality of a daughter."

"And now Lucy is in trouble, and you are wondering how much of it is your fault."

"I'm not conscious of wondering that."

"We rarely are conscious of those primitive anxieties that creep out from under reason. And the only way to banish them is to turn on all the lights. Do you think you're strong enough to do that?"

"Yes."

"Let me remind you that if you ask, you also must be able to live with the answers."

"I know."

"Let's just suppose for a moment that Lucy's innocent," said Senator Lord.

"Then what?" I asked.

"If Lucy didn't violate security, obviously someone else did. My question is why?"

"My question is *how,*" I said.

He gestured for the waitress to bring coffee. "What we really must determine is motive. And what would Lucy's motive be? What would anybody's motive be?"

Money was the easy answer, but I did not think that was it and told him so.

"Money is power, Kay, and everything is about power. We fallen creatures can never get enough of it."

"Yes, the forbidden fruit."

"Of course. All crime stems from it," he said.

"Every day that tragic truth is carried in on a stretcher," I agreed.

"Which tells you what about the problem at hand?" He stirred sugar into his coffee.

"It tells me motive."

"Well, of course. Power, that's it. Please, what would you like me to do?" my old friend asked.

"Lucy will not be charged with any crime unless it is proven that she stole from ERF. But as we speak, her future is ruined—at least in terms of a career in law enforcement or any other one that might involve a background investigation."

"Have they proven that she was the one who got in at three in the morning?"

"They have as much proof as they need, Frank. And that's the problem. I'm not certain how hard they'll work to clear her name, if she is innocent."

"If?"

"I'm trying to keep an open mind." I reached for my coffee and decided that the last thing I needed was more physical stimulation. My heart was racing and I could not keep my hands still.

"I can talk to the director," Lord said.

"All I want is someone behind the scenes making sure this

thing is thoroughly investigated. With Lucy gone, they may not think it matters, especially since there is so much else to cope with. And she's just a college student, for God's sake. So why should they care?"

"I would hope the Bureau would care more than that," he said, his mouth grim.

"I understand bureaucracies. I've worked in them all my life."

"As have I."

"Then you must be clear on what I'm saying."

"I am."

"They want her in Richmond with me until next semester," I said.

"Then that is their verdict." He reached for his coffee again.

"Exactly. And that's easy for them, but what about my niece? She's only twenty-one years old. Her dream has just blown up midflight. What is she supposed to do? Go back to UVA after Christmas and pretend nothing went wrong?"

"Listen." He touched my arm with a tenderness that always made me wish he were my father. "I will do what I can without the impropriety of meddling with an administrative problem. Trust me on that front?"

"I do."

"In the meantime, if you don't mind a little personal advice?" He motioned for the waitress as he glanced at his watch. "Well, I'm late." He looked back at me. "Your biggest problem is a domestic one."

"I disagree," I said with feeling.

"You can disagree all you like." He smiled at the waitress as she gave him the check. "You're the closest thing to a mother Lucy has ever had. How are you going to help her through this?"

"I thought I was doing that today."

"And I thought you were doing this because you wanted to

see me. Excuse me?" He motioned for the waitress. "I don't think this is our check. We didn't have four entrées."

"Let me see. Oh, my. Oh, I sure am sorry, Senator Lord. It's the table there."

"In that case, make Senator Kennedy pay both tabs. His and mine." He handed her both bills. "He won't object. He believes in tax and spend."

The waitress was a big woman in a black dress and white apron, and hair stiffened into a black pageboy. She smiled and suddenly felt fine about her mistake. "Yes, sir! I sure will tell the senator that."

"And you tell him to add on a generous tip, Missouri," he said as she walked off. "You tell him I said so."

Missouri Rivers wasn't a day younger than seventy, and since she'd left Raleigh decades ago on a northbound train, she had seen senators feast and fast, resign and get reelected, fall in love and fall from glory. She knew when to interrupt and get on with the business of serving food, and when to refill tea or simply disappear. She knew the secrets of the heart hidden so well in this lovely room, for the true measure of a human being is the way he treated people like her when no one was observing. She loved Senator Lord. I knew that from the soft light in her eyes when she looked at him or heard his name.

"I'm just encouraging you to spend some time with Lucy," he continued. "And don't get caught up in slaying other people's dragons, especially her dragons."

"I don't believe she can slay this dragon alone."

"My point is that Lucy doesn't need to know from you we had this conversation today. She doesn't need to know from you that I will pick up the phone on her behalf as soon as I return to my office. If anybody tells her anything, let it be me."

"Agreed," I said.

A little later I caught a taxi outside the Russell Building and found Benton Wesley where he said he would be at precisely two-fifteen. He was sitting on a bench in the amphitheater outside FBI headquarters, and though he seemed engrossed in a novel, he sensed me long before I was about to call his name. A group taking a tour paid no attention to us as they walked past, and Wesley closed his book and slipped it into the pocket of his coat as he got up.

"How was your trip?" he asked.

"By the time I get to and from National, it takes as long to fly as it does to drive."

"You flew?" He held the door to the lobby for me.

"I'm letting Lucy use my car."

He slipped off his sunglasses and got each of us a visitor's pass. "You know the director of the crime labs, Jack Cartwright?"

"We've met."

"We're going to his office for a quick and dirty briefing," he said. "Then there's a place I want to take you."

"Where might that be?"

"A place that's difficult to go to."

"Benton, if you're going to be cryptic, then I'll have no choice but to retaliate by speaking Latin."

"And you know how much I hate it when you do that."

We inserted our visitor's passes into a turnstile and followed a long corridor to an elevator. Every time I came to headquarters I was reminded of how much I did not like the place. People rarely gave me eye contact or smiled, and it seemed everything and everyone hid behind various shades of white and gray. Endless corridors connected a labyrinth of laboratories that I could never find when left to my own devices, and worse, people who worked here did not seem to know how to get anywhere, either.

Jack Cartwright had an office with a view, and sunlight filled his windows, reminding me of the splendid days I missed when I was working hard and worried.

"Benton, Kay, good afternoon." Cartwright shook our hands.

"Please have a seat. And this is George Kilby and Seth Richards from the labs. Have you met?"

"No. How do you do?" I said to Kilby and Richards, who were young, serious, and soberly attired.

"Would anybody like coffee?"

Nobody did, and Cartwright seemed eager to get on with our business. He was an attractive man whose formidable desk bore testimony to the way he got things done. Every document, envelope, and telephone message was in its proper place, and on top of a legal pad was an old silver Parker fountain pen that only a purist would use. I noticed he had plants in his windows and photographs of his wife and daughters on the sills. Outside sunlight winked on windshields as cars moved in congested herds, and vendors hawked T-shirts, ice cream, and drinks.

"We've been working on the Steiner case," Cartwright began, "and there are a number of interesting developments so far. I will start with what is probably most important, and that's the typing of the skin found in the freezer.

"Although our DNA analysis is not finished, we can tell you with certainty that the tissue is human and the ABO grouping is O-positive. As I'm sure you know, the victim, Emily Steiner, was also O-positive. And the size and shape of the tissue are consistent with her wounds."

"I'm wondering if you've been able to determine what sort of cutting instrument was used to excise the tissue," I said, taking notes.

"A sharp cutting instrument with a single edge."

"Which could be just about any type of knife," Wesley said.

Cartwright went on. "You can see where the point penetrated the flesh first as the assailant began to cut. So we're talking about a knife with a point and a single edge. That's as much as we can narrow it down. And by the way"—he looked at Wesley—"we've found no human blood on any of the knives you had sent in. Uh, the things from the Ferguson house."

Wesley nodded, his face impervious as he listened.

"Okay, trace evidence," Cartwright resumed. "And this is where it begins to get interesting. We have some unusual microscopic material that came from Emily Steiner's body and hair, and also from the bottoms of her shoes. We've got several blue acrylic fibers consistent with the blanket from her bed, plus green cotton fibers consistent with the green corduroy coat she wore to the youth group meeting at her church.

"There are some other wool fibers that we don't know the origin of. Plus we found dust mites, which could have come from anywhere. But what couldn't have come from anywhere is this."

Cartwright swiveled around in his chair and turned on a video display on the credenza behind him. The screen was filled with four different sections of some sort of cellular material that brought to mind honeycomb, only this had peculiar areas stained amber.

"What you're looking at," Cartwright told us, "are sections of a plant called *Sambucus simpsonii,* which is simply a woody shrub indigenous to the coastal plains and lagoons of southern Florida. What's fascinating are these dark spots right here." He pointed to the stained areas. "George"—he looked at one of the young scientists—"this is your bailiwick."

"Those are tannin sacs." George Kilby moved closer to us, joining the discussion. "You can see them especially well here on this radial section."

"What exactly is a tannin sac?" Wesley wanted to know.

"It's a vessel that transports material up and down the plant's stem."

"What sort of material?"

"Generally waste products that result from cellular activities. And just so you know, what you're looking at here is the pith. That's the part of the plant that has these tannin sacs."

"Then you're saying that the trace evidence in this case is pith?" I asked.

Special Agent George Kilby nodded. "That's right. The

commercial name is pithwood, even though technically there really is no such thing."

"What is pithwood used for?" Wesley asked.

It was Cartwright who answered, "It's often used to hold small mechanical parts or pieces of jewelry. For example, a jeweler might stick a small earring or watch gear into a pith button so it doesn't roll off the table or get brushed off by his sleeve. These days, most people just use Styrofoam."

"Was there much of this pithwood trace on her body?" I asked.

"There was a fair amount of it, mostly in the bloody areas, which was where most of her trace was."

"If someone wanted pithwood," Wesley said, "where would he get it?"

"The Everglades, if you wanted to cut down the shrub yourself," Kilby replied. "Otherwise you'd order it."

"From where?"

"I know there's a company in Silver Spring, Maryland."

Wesley looked at me. "Guess we need to find out who repairs jewelry in Black Mountain."

I said to him, "I'd be surprised if they even have a jeweler in Black Mountain."

Cartwright spoke again. "In addition to the trace evidence already mentioned, we found microscopic pieces of insects. Beetles, crickets, and roaches—nothing peculiar, really. And there were flecks of white and black paint, neither of them automotive. Plus, she had sawdust in her hair."

"From what kind of wood?" I asked.

"Mostly walnut, but we did also identify mahogany." Cartwright looked at Wesley, who was looking out the window. "The skin you found in the freezer didn't have any of this same material on it, but her wounds did."

"Meaning those injuries were inflicted before her body came in contact with wherever it was that it picked up this trace?" Wesley said.

"You could assume that," I said. "But whoever excised the skin and saved it may have rinsed it off. It would have been bloody."

"What about the inside of a vehicle?" Wesley went on. "Such as a trunk?"

"It's a possibility," Kilby said.

I knew the direction Wesley's thoughts were heading. Gault had murdered thirteen-year-old Eddie Heath inside a beat-up used van that had been rife with a baffling variety of trace evidence. Succinctly put, Mr. Gault, the psychopathic son of a wealthy pecan plantation owner in Georgia, derived intense pleasure from leaving evidence that seemed to make no sense.

"About the blaze orange duct tape," Cartwright said, finally getting around to that subject. "Am I correct in saying a roll of it has yet to show up?"

"We haven't found anything like that," Wesley replied.

Special Agent Richards looked through pages of notes as Cartwright said to him, "Well, let's get on with that, because I personally think it's going to be the most important thing we've got in this case."

Richards began talking in earnest, for like every devout forensic scientist I had met, he had a passion for his specialty. The FBI's reference library of duct tapes contained more than a hundred types for the purpose of identification when duct tape was involved in the commission of a crime. In fact, malevolent use of the silvery stuff was so common that I honestly could not pass by a roll of it in hardware or grocery stores without household thoughts turning into remembered horrors.

I had collected body parts of people blown up by bombs made with duct tape. I had removed it from the bound victims of sadistic killers and from bodies weighted with cinder blocks and dumped into rivers and lakes. I could not count the times I had peeled it from the mouths of people who were not allowed to scream until they were wheeled into my morgue. For it was only there the body could speak freely. It was only there someone cared about every awful thing that had been done.

"I've never seen duct tape like this before," Richards was saying. "And due to its high yarn count I can also say with confidence that whoever bought the tape did not get it from a store."

"How can you be so sure of that?" Wesley asked.

"This is industrial grade, with a yarn count of sixty-two warp and a fifty-six woof, versus your typical economy grade of twenty/ten that you might pick up at Walmart or Safeway for a couple of bucks. The industrial grade can cost as much as ten bucks a roll."

"Do you know where the tape was manufactured?" I asked.

"Shuford Mills of Hickory, North Carolina. They're one of the biggest duct tape manufacturers in the country. Their best-known brand is Shurtape."

"Hickory is only sixty miles or so east of Black Mountain," I said.

"Have you talked to anyone at Shuford Mills?" Wesley asked Richards.

"Yes. They're still trying to track down information for me. But this much we already know. The blaze orange tape was a specialty item that Shuford Mills manufactured solely for a private label customer in the late eighties."

"What is a private label customer?" I asked.

"Someone who wants a special tape and orders maybe a minimum of five hundred cases of it. So there could be hundreds of tapes out there we're never going to see, unless it turns up like this blaze orange tape did."

"Can you give me an example of what sort of person might design his own duct tape?" I inquired further.

"I know some stock car racers do," Richards replied. "For example, the duct tape Richard Petty has made for his pit crew is red and blue, while Daryl Waltrip's is yellow. Shuford Mills also had a contractor some years back who was sick of his workers walking off the job with his expensive tape. So he had his own bright purple tape made. You know, you got purple tape repairing your ductwork at home or fixing the leak in your kid's wading pool, and it's pretty obvious you stole it."

"Could that be the purpose of the blaze orange tape? To prevent workers from stealing it?" I asked.

"Possibly," said Richards. "And by the way, it's also flame retardant."

"Is that unusual?" Wesley asked.

"Very much so," Richards replied. "I associate flame-retardant duct tapes with aircraft and submarines, neither of which would have any need of a tape that's blaze orange, or at least I wouldn't think so."

"Why would anyone need a tape that is blaze orange?" I asked.

"The million-dollar question," Cartright said. "When I think of blaze orange, I think of hunting and traffic cones."

"Let's get back to the killer taping up Mrs. Steiner and her daughter," Wesley suggested. "What else can you tell us about the mechanics of that?"

"We found traces of what appears to be furniture varnish on some of the tape ends," Richards said. "Also, the sequence the tape was torn from the roll is inconsistent with the sequence it was applied to the mother's wrists and ankles. All this means is that the assailant tore off as many segments of tape as he thought he would need, and probably stuck them to the edge of a piece of furniture. When he began binding Mrs. Steiner, the tape was ready and waiting for him to use, one piece at a time."

"Only he got them out of order," Wesley said.

"Yes," said Richards. "I have them numbered according to the sequence they were used to bind the mother and her daughter. Would you like to look?"

We said that we would.

Wesley and I spent the rest of the afternoon in the Materials

Analysis Unit, with its gas chromatographs, mass spectrometers, differential scanning calorimeters, and other intimidating instruments for determining materials and melting points. I parked myself near a portable explosive detector while Richards went on about the weird duct tape used to bind Emily and her mother.

He explained that when he had used hot blowing air to open the tape receipted to him by the Black Mountain police, he counted seventeen pieces ranging from eight to nineteen inches in length. Mounting them on sheets of thick transparent vinyl, he had numbered the segments two different ways—to show the sequence the tape had been torn from the roll and the sequence the assailant had used when he taped his victims.

"The sequence of the tape used on the mother is completely out of whack," he was saying. "This piece here should have been first. Instead, it was last. And since this one was torn from the roll second, it should have been used second instead of fifth.

"The little girl, on the other hand, was taped in sequence. Seven pieces were used, and they went around her wrists in the order they were torn from the roll."

"She would have been easier to control," Wesley remarked.

"One would think so," I said, and then I asked Richards, "Did you find any of the varnish-type residue on the tape recovered from her body?"

"No," he replied.

"That's interesting," I said, and the detail bothered me.

We saved the dirty streaks on the tape for last. They had been identified as hydrocarbons, which is just a highbrow name for grease. So this didn't guide us a bit one way or another because unfortunately grease is grease. The grease on the tape could have come from a car. It could have come from a Mack truck in Arizona.

12

Wesley and I went on to the Red Sage at half past four, which was early for drinks. But neither of us felt very good.

It was hard for me to meet his eyes now that we were alone again, and I wanted him to bring up what had happened between us the other night. I did not want to believe I was the only one who thought it mattered.

"They have microbrewery beer on tap," Wesley said as I studied the menu. "It's quite good, if you're a beer drinker."

"Not unless I've worked out for two hours in the middle of summer and am very thirsty and craving pizza," I said, a little stung that he didn't seem to know this detail about me. "In fact, I really don't like beer and never have. I only drink it when there's absolutely nothing else, and even then I can't say it tastes good."

"Well, there's no point in getting angry about it."

"I'm certainly not angry."

"You sound angry. And you won't look at me."

"I'm fine."

"I study people for a living and I'm telling you that you're not fine."

"You study psychopaths for a living," I said. "You don't study female chief medical examiners who reside on the right side of the law and simply want to relax after an intense, long day of thinking about murdered children."

"It's very hard to get into this restaurant."

"I can see why. Thank you for going to a lot of trouble."

"I had to use my influence."

"I'm sure you did."

"We'll have wine with dinner. I'm surprised they have Opus One. Maybe that will make you feel better."

"It's overpriced and styled after a Bordeaux, which is a little heavy for sipping, and I wasn't aware we were dining here. I've got a plane to catch in less than two hours. I think I'll just have a glass of Cabernet."

"Whatever you'd like."

I did not know what I liked or wanted at the moment.

"I'm heading back to Asheville tomorrow," Wesley went on. "If you want to stay over tonight, we could go together."

"Why are you going back there?"

"Our assistance was requested before Ferguson ended up dead and Mote had a heart attack. Trust me, the Black Mountain police are sincere in their appreciation and panic. I've made it clear to them that we will do what we can to help. If it turns out that I need to bring in other agents, I will."

Wesley had a habit of always getting the waiter's name and addressing him by it throughout the meal. Our waiter's name was Stan, and it was Stan this and Stan that as Wesley and he discussed wines and specials. It was really the only dopey thing Wesley did, his sole quirky mannerism, and as I witnessed it this evening it irritated the hell out of me.

"You know, it doesn't make the waiter feel he has a relationship with you, Benton. In fact, it seems just a little patronizing, like the sort of thing a radio personality would do."

"What does?" He was without a clue.

"Calling him by name. Repeatedly doing it, I mean."

He stared at me.

"Well, I'm not trying to be critical," I went on, making matters worse. "I'm just mentioning it as a friend because no one else would, and you should know. A friend would be that honest, I'm saying. A *true* one would."

"Are you quite finished?" he asked.

"Quite." I forced a little smile.

"Now, then, do you want to tell me what's really bothering you, or should I just bravely hazard a guess?"

"There is absolutely nothing bothering me," I said as I began to cry.

"My God, Kay." He offered me his napkin.

"I have my own." I wiped my eyes.

"This is about the other night, isn't it?"

"Maybe you should tell me which other night you mean. Maybe you have *other nights* on a regular basis."

Wesley tried to suppress his laughter, but he could not. For several minutes neither of us could talk because he was laughing and I was caught between crying and laughing.

Stan the waiter returned with drinks, and I took several swallows of mine before speaking again.

"Listen," I finally said. "I'm sorry. But I'm tired, this case is horrible to deal with, Marino and I aren't getting along, and Lucy's in trouble."

"That's enough to push anyone to tears," Wesley said, and I could tell it bothered him that I hadn't added him to my list of things wrong. It perversely pleased me that it bothered him.

"And yes, I'm concerned about what happened in North Carolina," I added.

"Do you regret it?"

"What good does it do to say that I do or I don't?"

"It would do me good for you to say that you don't."

"I can't say that," I said.

"Then you do regret it."

"No, I don't."

"Then you don't regret it."

"Dammit, Benton, leave it be."

"I'm not going to," he said. "I was there, too."

"Excuse me?" I puzzled.

"The night it happened? Remember? Actually it was very early in the morning. What we did took two. I was there. You weren't the only person there who had to think about it for days. Why don't you ask me whether I regret it?"

"No," I said. "You're the one who's married."

"If I committed adultery, so did you. *It takes two,*" he said again.

"My plane leaves in an hour. I've got to go."

"You should have thought about that before starting this conversation. You can't just walk out in the middle of something like this."

"Certainly I can."

"Kay?" He looked into my eyes and lowered his voice. He reached across the table and took my hand.

I got a room in the Willard that night. Wesley and I talked a very long time and resolved matters sufficiently for us to rationalize our repeating the same sin. When we got off the elevator in the lobby early the next morning, we were very low key and polite with one another, as if we had only just met but had a lot in common. We shared a taxi to National Airport and got a flight to Charlotte, where I spent an hour with Lucy on the phone. "Yes," I said. "I am finding someone and have in fact already started on that," I told her in the USAir Club.

"I need to do something now," she said again.

"Please try to be patient."

"No. I know who's doing this to me and I'm going to do something about it."

"Who?" I asked, alarmed.

"When it's time, it will be known."

"Lucy, who did what to you? Please tell me what you're talking about."

"I can't right now. There's something I must do first. When are you coming home?"

"I don't know. I'll call you from Asheville as soon as I get a feel for what's going on."

"So it's okay for me to use your car?"

"Of course."

"You won't be using it for at least a couple days, right?"

"I don't think so. But what is it you're contemplating?" I was getting increasingly unsettled.

"I might need to go up to Quantico, and if I do and spend the night I wanted to make sure you wouldn't mind."

"No, I don't mind," I said. "As long as you're careful, Lucy, that's what matters to me."

Wesley and I boarded a prop plane that made too much noise for us to talk in the air. So he slept while I sat quietly with my eyes shut as sunlight filled the window and turned the inside of my eyelids red. I let my thoughts wander wherever they would, and many images came to me from corners I had forgotten. I saw my father and the white gold ring he wore on his left hand where a wedding band would have been, but he had lost his at the beach and could not afford another one.

My father had never been to college, and I remembered his high school ring was set with a red stone that I wished were a ruby because we were so poor. I thought we could sell it and have a better life, and I remembered my disappointment when my father finally told me that his ring wasn't worth the gasoline it would take to drive to South Miami. There was something about the way he said this that made me know he had never really lost his wedding ring.

He had sold it when he did not know what else to do, but to tell Mother was to destroy her. It had been many years since I had thought about this, and I supposed my mother still had his ring somewhere, unless she had buried it with him, and maybe she had. I could not recall, since I was only twelve when he had died.

As I drifted in and out of places, I saw silent scenes of people who simply appeared without invitation. It was very odd. I did not know why it mattered, for example, that Sister Martha, my third-grade teacher, was suddenly writing with chalk on the board or a girl named Jennifer was walking out a door as hail bounced on the churchyard like a million small white marbles.

These people from my past slipped in and vanished as I almost slept, and a sorrow welled up that made me aware of Wesley's arm. We were touching slightly. When I focused on the exact point of contact between us, I could smell the wool of his jacket warming in the sun and imagine long fingers of elegant hands that brought to mind pianos and fountain pens and brandy snifters by the fire.

I think it was precisely then I knew I was in love with Benton Wesley. Because I had lost every man I had loved before him, I did not open my eyes until the flight attendant asked us to put our seats in the upright position because we were about to land.

"Is someone meeting us?" I asked him as if this were all that had been on my mind during our hour in the air.

He looked at me for a long moment. His eyes were the color of bottled beer when light hit them a certain way. Then the shadow of deep preoccupations returned them to hazel flecked with gold, and when his thoughts were more than even he could bear, he simply looked away.

"I suppose we're returning to the Travel-Eze," I next asked as he collected his briefcase and unbuckled his seat belt before we had been signaled that we could. The flight attendant pretended not to notice, because Wesley sent out his own signals that made most people slightly afraid.

"You talked to Lucy a long time in Charlotte," he said.

"Yes." We rolled past a wind sock having a deflated day.

"Well?" His eyes filled with light again as he turned toward the sun.

"Well, she thinks she knows who's behind what's happened to her."

"What do you mean, *who's behind* it?" He frowned.

"I think the meaning's apparent," I said. "It's not apparent only if you assume nobody is behind anything because Lucy is guilty."

"Her thumb was scanned at three in the morning, Kay."

"That much is clear."

"And what is also clear is that her thumb couldn't have been scanned without her thumb being physically present, without her hand, arm, and the rest of her being physically present at the time the computer says she was."

"I'm very aware of how it looks," I said.

He put on sunglasses and we got up. "And I'm reminding you of how it looks," he said in my ear as he followed me down the aisle.

We could have moved out of the Travel-Eze for more luxurious quarters in Asheville. But where we stayed did not seem important to anyone by the time we met Marino at the Coach House restaurant, which was famous for reasons that were not exactly clear.

I got a peculiar feeling immediately when the Black Mountain officer who had collected us at the airport let us off in the restaurant parking lot and silently drove away. Marino's state-of-the-art Chevrolet was near the door, and he was inside alone at a corner table, facing the cash register, as everyone tries to do if he's ever been touched by the law.

He did not get up when we walked in, but watched us dispassionately as he stirred a tall glass of iced tea. I had the uncanny sensation that he, the Marino I had worked with for years, the well-meaning, street-smart hater of potentates and protocol, was granting us an audience. Wesley's cool caution told me that he knew something was very off center, too. For one thing, Marino had on a dark suit that clearly was new.

"Pete," Wesley said, taking a chair.

"Hello," I said, taking another chair.

"They got really good chicken fried steak here," Marino said, not looking at either of us. "They got chef salads, if you don't want nothing that heavy," he added, apparently for my benefit.

The waitress was pouring water, handing out menus, and rattling off specials before anyone had a chance to say another word. By the time she went on her way with our apathetic orders, the tension at our table was almost unbearable.

"We have quite a lot of forensic information that I think you'll find interesting," Wesley began. "But first, why don't you fill us in?"

Marino, who looked the unhappiest I'd ever seen him, reached for his iced tea and then set it back down without taking a sip. He patted his pocket for his cigarettes before picking them up from the table. He did not talk until he was smoking, and it frightened me that he would not give us his eyes. He was so distant it was as if we had never known him, and whenever I had seen this in the past with someone I had worked with, I knew what it meant. Marino was in trouble. He had slammed shut the windows leading into his soul because he did not want us to see what was there.

"The big thing going down right now," Marino began as he exhaled smoke and nervously tapped an ash, "is the janitor at Emily Steiner's school. Uh, the subject's name is Creed Lindsey, white male, thirty-four, works as a janitor at the elementary school, has for the past two years.

"Prior to that he was a janitor at the Black Mountain public library, and before that did the same damn thing for an elementary school in Weaverville. And I might add that at the school in Weaverville during the time the subject was there, they had a hit-and-run of a ten-year-old boy. There was suspicion that Lindsey was involved. . . ."

"Hold on," Wesley said.

"A hit-and-run?" I asked. "What do you mean he was involved?"

"Wait," Wesley said. "Wait, wait, wait. Have you talked to Creed Lindsey?" He looked at Marino, who met his gaze but fleetingly.

"That's what I'm leading to. The drone's disappeared. The minute he got the word we wanted to talk to him—and I'll be damned if I know who opened his fat mouth, but someone did—he split. He ain't showed up at work and he ain't been back to his crib."

He lit another cigarette. When the waitress was suddenly at his elbow with more tea, he nodded her way as if he'd been here many times before and always tipped well.

"Tell me about the hit-and-run," I said.

"Four years ago this November, a ten-year-old kid's riding his bike and gets slammed by some asshole who's over the center line coming around a curve. The kid's DOA, and all the cops ever get is there's a white pickup truck driving at a high rate of speed in the area around the time the accident occurred. And they get white paint off the kid's jeans.

"Meanwhile, Creed Lindsey's got an old white pickup, a Ford. He's known to drive the same road where the accident occurred, and he's known to hit the package store on payday, which coincidentally was exactly when the kid got hit."

Marino's eyes never stopped moving as he talked on and on. Wesley and I were getting increasingly restless.

"So when the cops want to question him, boom, he's gone," Marino continued. "Don't come back to the area for five damn weeks—says he was visiting a sick relative or some bullshit like that. By then, the friggin' truck's as blue as a robin's egg. Everybody knows the son of a bitch did it, but they got no proof."

"Okay." Wesley's voice commanded that Marino stop. "That's very interesting, and maybe this janitor was involved in the hit-and-run. But where are you going with this?"

"Seems like that ought to be pretty obvious."

"Well, it's not, Pete. Help me out here."

"Lindsey likes kids, plain and simple. He takes jobs that put him in contact with kids."

"It sounds to me like he takes the jobs he has because he's unskilled at anything but sweeping floors."

"Shit. He could do that at the grocery store, the old folks' home, or something. Every place he's worked is full of kids."

"Okay. Let's just go with that. So he sweeps floors in places where children are. Then what?" Wesley studied Marino, who clearly had a theory he was not to be dissuaded from.

"Then he kills his first kid four years ago, and I'm sure as hell not saying he meant to do it. But he does, and he lies, and he's guilty as hell and gets totally screwed up because of this terrible secret he carries. That's how other things get started in people."

"Other things?" Wesley asked very smoothly. "What other things, Pete?"

"He's feeling guilty about kids. He's looking at 'em every goddam day and wanting to reach out, be forgiven, get close, undo it, shit. I don't know.

"But next thing his emotions get carried away and now he's watching this little girl. He gets sweet on her, wants to reach out. Maybe he spots her the night she's walking home from the church. Maybe he even talks to her. But hell, ain't no problem to figure out where she lives. It's a friggin' small town. He's into it now."

He took a swallow of tea and lit another cigarette as he talked on.

"He snatches her because if he can keep her with him for a while, he can make her understand that he never meant to hurt no one, that he's good. He wants her to be his friend. He wants to be loved because if she'll love him, she'll undo the terrible thing he did back then. But it don't go down like that. See, she's not cooperating. She's terrified. And bottom line is when what goes down don't fit the fantasy, he freaks and kills her. And now, goddam it, he's done it again. Two kids killed."

Wesley started to speak, but our food was arriving on a big brown tray.

The waitress, an older woman with thick, tired legs, was slow serving us. She wanted everything to please the important man from out of town who was wearing a new navy blue suit.

The waitress said many yes sirs and seemed very pleased when I thanked her for my salad, which I did not plan to eat. I had lost any appetite I might have had before we arrived at the Coach House, which was famous for something, I felt quite sure. But I could not look at julienne strips of ham, turkey, and cheddar cheese, and especially not sliced boiled eggs. In fact, I felt sick.

"Would there be anything else?"

"No, thank you."

"This looks real good, Dot. You mind bringing a little more butter?"

"Yes, sir, it will be coming right up. And what about you, ma'am? Can I get you some more dressing maybe?"

"Oh, no, thank you. This is perfect the way it is."

"Why, thank you. You folks are mighty nice, and we sure appreciate your visiting. You know, we have a buffet every Sunday after church."

"We'll remember that." Wesley smiled at her.

I knew I was going to leave her at least five dollars, if only she would forgive me for not touching my food.

Wesley was trying to think what to say to Marino, and I had never before been witness to anything between them quite like this.

"I guess I'm wondering if you've completely abandoned your original theory," Wesley said.

"Which theory?" Marino tried to cut into his fried steak with a fork, and when that didn't work, he reached for the pepper and A.1. sauce.

"Temple Gault," Wesley said. "It would appear that you aren't looking for him anymore."

"I didn't say nothing like that."

"Marino," I said, "what about this hit-and-run business?"

He raised his hand and motioned for the waitress. "Dot, I guess I'm going to need a sharp knife. The hit-and-run is important because this guy's got a history of violence. The local people are real antsy about him because of that and also because he paid a lot of attention to Emily Steiner. So I'm just letting you know that's what's going down."

"How would that theory explain the human skin in Ferguson's freezer?" I asked. "And by the way, the blood type is the same as Emily's. We're still waiting on DNA."

"Wouldn't explain it worth a damn."

Dot returned with a serrated knife, and Marino thanked her. He sawed into his fried steak. Wesley nibbled broiled flounder, staring down at his plate for long intervals while his VICAP partner talked.

"Listen, for all we know, Ferguson did the kid. And sure, we can't rule out the possibility Gault's in town, and I'm not saying we should."

"What more do we know about Ferguson?" Wesley asked. "And are you aware that the print lifted from the panties he was wearing comes back to Denesa Steiner?"

"That's because the panties was stolen from her house the night the squirrel busted in and snatched her kid. Remember? She said while she was in the closet she thought she heard him going through her drawers, and later was suspicious he took some of her clothing."

"That and the skin in his freezer certainly cause me to want to look very hard at this guy," Wesley said. "Is there any possibility he'd had contact with Emily in the past?"

I interjected, "Because of his profession, he certainly would have had reason to know about the cases in Virginia, about Eddie Heath. He could have tried to make the Steiner murder mimic something else. Or maybe he got the idea from what happened in Virginia."

"Ferguson was squirrelly," Marino said, sawing off another piece of meat. "That much I can tell you, but nobody around here seemed to know a whole hell of a lot."

"How long did he work for the SBI?" I asked.

"Going on ten years. Before that he was a state trooper, and before that he was in the army."

"He was divorced?" Wesley asked.

"You mean there's somebody who ain't?"

Wesley was quiet.

"Divorced twice. Got an ex-wife in Tennessee and one in Enka. Four kids all grown and living the hell all over the place."

"What does his family have to say about him?" I asked.

"You know, it's not like I've been here for six months." Marino reached for the A.1. sauce again. "I can only talk to so many people in one day, and that's only if I'm lucky enough to get them the first or second time I call. And seeing's how you two haven't been here and all of this has been dumped in my lap, I hope you won't take it personal if I say that there's only so much goddam time in a day."

"Pete, we understand that," Wesley said in his most reasonable tone. "And that's why we're here. We are well aware there is a lot of investigating to do. Maybe even more than I originally thought, because nothing's fitting together right. It seems this case is going in at least three different directions and I'm not seeing many connections, except that I really want to look hard at Ferguson. We do have forensic evidence that points at him. The skin in his freezer. Denesa Steiner's lingerie."

"They got good cherry cobbler here," Marino said, looking

for the waitress. She was standing just outside the kitchen door watching him, waiting for his slightest signal.

"How many times have you eaten here?" I asked him.

"I got to eat somewhere, isn't that right, Dot?" He raised his voice as our ever-vigilant waitress appeared.

Wesley and I ordered coffee.

"Why, honey, wasn't your salad all right?" She was sincerely distressed.

"It was fine," I assured her. "I'm just not as hungry as I thought."

"You want me to wrap that up for you?"

"No, thank you."

When she moved on, Wesley got around to telling Marino what we knew about the forensic evidence. We talked for a while about the pithwood and the duct tape, and by the time Marino's cobbler had been served and eaten and he had started smoking again, we had pretty much exhausted the conversation. Marino had no more idea what the blaze orange flame-retardant duct tape or pithwood meant than we did.

"Damn," he said again. "That's just strange as shit. I haven't come across a thing that would fit with any of that."

"Well," said Wesley, whose attention was beginning to drift, "the tape is so unusual that someone around here has to have seen it before. If it's from around here. And if it isn't, I'm confident we'll track it down." He pushed back his chair.

"I'll take care of this." I picked up the bill.

"They don't take American Express here," Marino said.

"It's one-fifty now." Wesley got up. "Let's meet back at the hotel at six and work out a plan."

"I hate to remind you," I said to him. "But it's a motel, not a hotel, and at the moment you and I don't have a car."

"I'll drop you at the Travel-Eze. Your car should already be there waiting. And Benton, we can find you one, too, if you think you're gonna need it," Marino said as if he were Black Mountain's new chief of police, or perhaps the mayor.

"I don't know what I'm going to need right now," he said.

13

Detective Mote had been moved to a private room and was in stable but guarded condition when I went to see him later that day. Not knowing my way around town very well, I'd resorted to the hospital gift shop, where they had but a very small selection of flower arrangements to choose from behind refrigerated glass.

"Detective Mote?" I hesitated in his doorway.

He was propped up in bed dozing, the TV on loud.

"Hi," I said a little louder.

He opened his eyes and for an instant had no idea who I was. Then he remembered and smiled as if he'd been dreaming of me for days.

"Well, Lord have mercy, Dr. Scarpetta. Now I never would've thought you'd still be hanging 'round here."

"I'm sorry about the flowers. They didn't have much to choose from downstairs." I carried in a pitiful bunch of mums and daisies in a thick green vase. "How about if I just put them right here?"

I set the arrangement on the dresser, and felt sad that his only other flowers were more pathetic than mine.

"There's a chair right there if you can sit for a minute."

"How are you feeling?" I asked.

He was pale and thinner, and his eyes looked weak as he stared out the window at a lovely fall day.

"Well, I'm just trying to go with the flow, like they say," he said. "It's hard to know what's around the corner, but I'm thinking about fishing and the woodworking I like to do. You know, I've been wanting for years to build a little cabin someplace. And I like to whittle walking sticks from basswood."

"Detective Mote," I said hesitantly, for I did not want to upset him, "has anyone from your department come to visit?"

"Why sure," he answered as he continued staring out at a stunning blue sky. "A couple fellas have dropped by or else called."

"How do you feel about what's going on in the Steiner investigation?"

"Not too good."

"Why?"

"Well, I'm not there, for one thing. For another, it seems like everybody's riding off in his own direction. I'm worried about it some."

"You've been involved in the case from the start," I said. "You must have known Max Ferguson pretty well."

"I guess not as well as I thought."

"Are you aware that he's a suspect?"

"I know it. I know all about it."

The sun through the window made his eyes so pale they seemed made of water. He blinked several times and dabbed tears caused by bright light or emotion.

He talked some more. "I also know they're looking hard at Creed Lindsey, and you know it's sort of a shame for either of 'em."

"In what way?" I asked.

"Well, now, Dr. Scarpetta, Max ain't exactly here to defend himself."

"No, he isn't," I agreed.

"And Creed couldn't begin to know how to defend himself, even if he was here."

"Where is he?"

"I hear he's run off someplace, not that it's the first time. He done the same thing when that little boy was run over and killed. Everybody thought Creed was guiltier than sin. So he disappeared and turned up again like a bad penny. Now and again he just goes off to what they used to call Colored Town and drinks himself into a hole."

"Where does he live?"

"Off Montreat Road, up there in Rainbow Mountain."

"I'm afraid I'm not familiar with where that is."

"When you get to the Montreat gate, it's the road going up the mountain to the right. Used to be only mountain folk up there, what you'd probably call hillbillies. But during the last twenty years a lot of them has gone on to other places or passed on and folk like Creed's moved in."

He paused for a minute, his expression distant and thoughtful. "You can see his place from down below on the road. He's got an old washing machine on the porch and pitches most his trash out the back door into the woods." He sighed. "The plain fact is, Creed wasn't gifted with smarts."

"Meaning?"

"Meaning he's scared of what he don't understand, and he can't understand something like what's going on around here."

"Meaning you also don't think he's involved in the Steiner girl's death," I said.

Detective Mote closed his eyes as the monitor over his bed registered a steady pulse of 66. He looked very tired. "No ma'am, I don't for a minute. But there's a reason he's running, you ask me, and I can't get that out of my mind."

"You said he was scared. That seems reason enough."

"I just have this feeling there's something else. But I guess there's no point in my stewing over it. Not a darn thing I can do. Not unless all of 'em want to line up outside my door and let me ask 'em whatever I want, and that sure isn't likely to happen."

I did not want to ask him about Marino, but I felt I must. "What about Captain Marino? Have you heard much from him?"

Mote looked straight at me. "He came on in the other day with a fifth of Wild Turkey. It's in my closet over there." He raised an arm off the covers and pointed.

We both sat silently for a moment.

"I know I'm not supposed to be drinking," he added.

"I want you to listen to your doctors, Lieutenant Mote. You've got to live with this, and that means not doing any of those things that got you into trouble."

"I know I got to quit smoking."

"It can be done. I never thought I could."

"You still miss it?"

"I don't miss the way it made me feel."

"I don't like the way any bad habit makes me feel, but that's got nothing to do with it."

I smiled. "Yes, I miss it. But it does get easier."

"I told Pete I don't want to see him ending up in here like me, Dr. Scarpetta. But he's a hardhead."

I was unsettled by the memory of Mote turning blue on the floor as I tried to save his life, and I believed it was simply a matter of time before Marino suffered a similar experience. I thought of the fried steak lunch, his new clothes and car and strange behavior. It almost seemed he had decided he did not want to know me anymore, and the only way to bring that about was to change into someone I did not recognize.

"Certainly Marino has gotten very involved. The case is terribly consuming," I lamely said.

"Mrs. Steiner can't think of much else, not that I blame her a bit. If it was me, I reckon I'd put everything I got into it, too."

"What has she put into it?" I said.

"She's got a lot of money," Mote said.

"I wondered about that." I thought of her car.

"She's done a lot to help in this investigation."

"Help?" I asked. "In what way, exactly?"

"Cars. Like the one Pete's driving, for example. Someone's got to pay for all that."

"I thought those things were donated by area merchants."

"Now, I will have to say that what Mrs. Steiner's done has inspired others to pitch in. She's got this whole area thinking about this case and feeling for her, and not a soul wants someone else's child to suffer the same thing.

"It's really like nothing I've ever seen in my twenty-two years of police work. But then, I have to say I've never seen a case like this to begin with."

"Did she actually pay for the car I'm driving?" It required great restraint on my part not to raise my voice or seem anything but calm.

"She donated both cars and some other businesspeople have kicked in the other things. Lights, radios, scanners."

"Detective Mote," I said, "how much money has Mrs. Steiner given to your department?"

"I reckon close to fifty."

"Fifty?" I looked at him in disbelief. "Fifty thousand dollars?"

"That's right."

"And no one has a problem with that?"

"Far as I'm concerned, it's no different than the power company donating a car to us some years back because there's a transformer they want us to keep an eye on. And the Quick Stops and 7-Elevens give us coffee so we'll come in all hours. It's all about people helping us to help them. It works fine as long as nobody tries to take advantage."

His eyes were steady on me, his hands still on top of the covers. "I guess in a big city like Richmond you got more rules."

"Any gift to the Richmond Police Department that is over twenty-five hundred dollars has to be approved by an O and R," I said.

"I don't know what that is."

"An Ordinance and Resolution, which has to be brought before the city council."

"Sounds mighty complicated."

"And it should be, for obvious reasons."

"Well, sure," Mote said, and mainly he just sounded weary and worn down by the revelation that his body was not to be trusted anymore.

"Can you tell me just what this fifty thousand dollars is to be used for, besides acquiring several additional cars?" I asked.

"We need a chief of police. I was pretty much the whole enchilada, and it don't look too good for me at this point, to be honest. And even if I can go back to some sort of light duty, it's time the town has someone with experience in charge. Things aren't the way they used to be."

"I see," I commented, and the reality of what was happening was clarifying in a very disturbing way. "I should let you get some rest."

"I'm mighty glad you came by."

He squeezed my hand so hard I was in pain, and I sensed a deep despair he probably could not have explained were he completely conscious of it. To almost die is to know that one day you will, and to never again feel the same about anything.

Before I returned to the Travel-Eze, I drove to the Montreat gate, went through it, and turned around. I went back out the other side as I tried to think what to do. There was very little traffic, and when I pulled off on the shoulder and stopped for a bit, people passing me probably assumed I was but one more tourist who was lost or looking for Billy Graham's house. From where I was parked, I had a perfect view of Creed Lindsey's neighborhood. In fact, I could see his house and its old boxy white washing machine on the porch.

Rainbow Mountain must have been named on an October afternoon like this one. Leaves were varying intensities of red, orange, and yellow that were fiery in the sun and rich in the shade, and shadows crept deeper into clefts and valleys as the sun settled lower. In another hour light would be gone. I might not have decided to drive up that dirt road had I not detected wisps of smoke drifting from Creed's leaning stone chimney.

Pulling back out on the pavement, I crossed to the other side and turned onto a dirt road that was narrow and rutted. Red dust boiled up from the rear of my car as I climbed closer to a neighborhood that was about as unwelcoming as any I had ever seen. It appeared that the road went to the top of the mountain and quit. Scattered along it were a series of old humpbacked trailers and dilapidated homes built of unpainted boards or logs. Some had tar paper roofs while others were tin, and the few vehicles I saw were old pickup trucks and a station wagon painted a strange crème de menthe green.

Creed Lindsey's place had an empty patch of dirt beneath trees where I could tell he usually parked, and I pulled in and cut the engine. For a time, I sat looking at his shack and its dilapidated, slanting porch. It seemed a light might have been on inside, or it could have been the way the window caught the low sun. As I thought about this man who sold red-hot toothpicks to children and had picked wildflowers for Emily as he swept floors and emptied trash at their school, I debated the wisdom of what I was doing.

My original intention, after all, had been to see where Creed Lindsey lived in relation to the Presbyterian church and Lake Tomahawk. Now that certain questions were answered, I had other ones. I could not just drive away from a fire on a hearth in a home where no one was supposed to be. I could not stop thinking about what Mote had said, and of course there were the Fireballs I had found. They really were the main reason I had to talk to this man called Creed.

I knocked on the door for a long time, thinking I heard someone move around inside, and feeling watched. But no one came to let me in, and my verbal salutations went unanswered. The window to my left was dusty and had no screen. On the other side I could see a margin of dark wood flooring and part of a wooden chair illuminated by a small lamp on a table.

Though I reasoned that a lamp on did not mean anyone was home, I smelled wood smoke and thought the stack of kindling on the porch was piled high and freshly split. I knocked again and the wooden door felt loose beneath my knuckles, as if it wouldn't take much to kick it in.

"Hello?" I called. "Is anybody home?"

I was answered by the sound of trees shaken by gusts of wind. The air was chilled in the shade and I detected the faint odor of things rotting, mildewing, and falling apart. In the woods on either side of this one- or two-room shack with its rusting roof and bent TV antenna was the trash of many years blessedly covered in part by leaves. Mostly I saw disintegrating paper, plastic milk jugs, and cola bottles that had been lying out there long enough for labels to be bleached.

So I concluded that the lord of the manor had forsaken his unseemly way of pitching garbage out the door, since none of it looked recent. As I was momentarily lost in this observation, I became aware of a presence behind me. I felt eyes on my back so palpably that hair raised on my arms as I slowly turned around.

The girl was a strange apparition on the road near the rear bumper of my car. She stood as motionless as a deer staring at me in the gathering dusk, dull brown hair limp around her narrow pale face, eyes slightly crossed. She held herself very still. I sensed in her long, lanky limbs that she would bound out of sight if I made any movement or sound the least bit startling. For the longest time, she continued to stare and I looked right back as if I accepted the necessity of this strange encounter. When she shifted her stance a little and seemed to breathe and blink again, I dared to speak.

"I wonder if you can help me," I said gently without fear.

She slipped bare hands in the pockets of a dark wool coat that was several sizes too small. She wore wrinkled khaki pants rolled up at the ankles, and scuffed tan leather boots. I thought she was in her early teens, but it was hard to say.

"I'm from out of town," I tried again, "and it's very important that I locate Creed Lindsey. The man who lives here, or at least I think he lives in this house. Can you help me?"

"Whadyou want thar fer?" Her voice was high-pitched and reminded me of banjo strings. I knew I would have a hard time understanding a word of what she might have to say.

"I need him to help me," I said very slowly.

She moved several steps closer, her eyes never leaving mine. They were pale and crossed like a Siamese cat's.

"I know he thinks there are people looking for him," I went on with deadly calm. "But I'm not one of them. I'm not one of them at all. I'm not here to cause him harm in any way."

"What's thar name?"

"My name is Dr. Kay Scarpetta," I answered her.

She stared harder at me as if I had just told her the most curious secret. It occurred to me that if she knew what a doctor was, she might never have encountered one who was a woman.

"Do you know what a medical doctor is?" I asked her.

She stared at my car as if it contradicted what I had just said.

"There are some doctors who help the police when people get hurt. That's what I do," I said. "I'm helping the police here. That's why I have a car like this. The police are letting me drive it while I'm here because I'm not from these parts. I'm from Richmond, Virginia."

My voice trailed off as she looked silently at my car, and I had the disheartening feeling that I had said too much and all was lost. I would never find Creed Lindsey. It had been incredibly foolish to imagine for even a moment that I could communicate with a people I did not know and could not begin to understand.

I was about to decide to return to my car and drive away when the girl suddenly approached. I was startled when she took my hand and without a word tugged me toward my car. She pointed through the window at my black medical bag on the passenger's seat.

"That's my medical bag," I said. "Do you want me to get it?"

"Yes, get thar," she said.

Opening the door, I did. I wondered if she was merely curious, but then she was pulling me out onto the unpaved street where I had first seen her. Wordlessly, she led me up the hill, her hand rough and dry like corn husks as it continued to grasp mine firmly and with purpose.

"Would you tell me your name?" I asked as we climbed at a brisk pace.

"Deborah."

Her teeth were bad, and she was gaunt and old before her time, typical in the cases of chronic malnutrition that I often saw in a society where food was not always the answer. I expected that Deborah's family, like many I encountered in inner cities, subsisted on all the high empty calories that food stamps could buy.

"Deborah what?" I asked as we neared a tiny slab house. It appeared to have been built of trimmings from a sawmill and covered with tar paper, portions of which were supposed to look like brick.

"Deborah Washburn."

I followed her up rickety wooden steps leading to a weathered porch with nothing on it but firewood and a faded turquoise glider. She opened a door that hadn't seen paint in too long to remember its color, and pulled me inside, where the reason for this mission became instantly clear.

Two tiny faces too old for their very young years looked up from a bare mattress on the floor where a man sat bleeding into rags in his lap as he tried to sew up a cut on his right thumb. On the floor nearby was a glass jar half filled with a clear liquid that I doubted was water, and he had managed to get a stitch or two in with a regular needle and thread. For a moment, we regarded each other in the glare of an overhead bare light bulb.

"Thar's a doctor," Deborah said to him.

He stared at me some more as blood dripped from his thumb, and I guessed he was in his late twenties or early thirties. His hair was long and black and in his eyes, his skin sickly pale, as if it had never seen the sun. Tall and thick through the middle, he stunk of old grease, sweat, and alcohol.

"Where'd you get her from?" the man asked the child.

The other children stared vacantly at the TV, which as best I could see was the only electrical object in the house besides the one light bulb.

"Thar was looking for thar," Deborah said to him, and I realized with amazement that she used *thar* for every pronoun, and that the man must be Creed Lindsey.

"Why'd you bring her?" He didn't seem particularly upset or afraid.

"Thar hurt."

"How did you cut yourself?" I asked him as I opened my bag.

"On my knife."

I looked closely. He had raised a substantial flap of skin.

"Stitching's not going to be the best thing to do here," I said, and I got out topical antiseptic, Steristrips and Benzoin-glue. "When did you do this?"

"This afternoon. I come in and tried to pry the lid off a can."

"Do you remember the last time you had a tetanus shot?"

"Naw."

"You should go get one tomorrow. I'd do it but I don't have anything like that with me."

He watched me as I looked around for paper towels. The kitchen was nothing but a woodstove, and water came from a pump in the sink. Rinsing my hands and shaking them dry as best I could, I knelt by him on the mattress and took hold of his hand. It was callused and muscular, with dirty, torn nails.

"This is going to hurt a little," I said. "And I don't have anything to help with pain, so if you've got something, go ahead." I looked at the jar of clear fluid.

He looked down at it, too, then reached for it with his good hand. He took a swallow and the white lightning or corn liquor or whatever the hell it was brought tears to his eyes. I waited until he took another swallow before cleaning his wound and holding the flap in place with glue and paper tapes. When I was finished he was relaxed. I wrapped his thumb with gauze and wished I had an Ace bandage.

"Where's your mother?" I said to Deborah as I put wrappers and the needle inside my bag, since I didn't see a trash can.

"Thar's at thar Burger Hut."

"Is that where she works?"

She nodded as one of her siblings got up to change channels.

"Are you Creed Lindsey?" I matter-of-factly asked my patient.

"Why're you asking?" He spoke with the same twang, and I did not think he was as mentally slow as Lieutenant Mote had indicated.

"I need to speak to him."

"What for?"

"Because I don't think he had anything to do with what happened to Emily Steiner. But I think he knows something that might help us find who did."

He reached for the jar of liquor. "What would he know?"

"I guess I'd like to ask him that," I said. "I suspect he liked Emily and feels real upset about what happened. And I also suspect that when he feels upset he gets away from people like he's doing now, especially if he thinks he might be in any sort of trouble."

He stared down at the jar, slowly swirling its contents.

"He never did nothing to her that night."

"That night?" I asked. "Do you mean the night she disappeared?"

"He saw her walking with her guitar and slowed his truck to say hi. But he didn't do nothing. He didn't give her a ride or nothing."

"Did he ask to give her a ride?"

"He wouldn't have 'cause he'd know she wouldn't have a-taken it."

"Why wouldn't she have?"

"She don't like him. She don't like Creed even though he gives her presents." His lower lip trembled.

"I hear he was very nice to her. I hear he gave her flowers at school. And candy."

"He never gave her no candy 'cause she wouldn't have a-taken it."

"She wouldn't take it?"

"She wouldn't. Not even the kind she liked. I seen her take it from others."

"Fireballs?"

"Wren Maxwell trades 'em to me for the toothpicks and I seen him give the candy to her."

"Was she by herself when she was walking home that night with her guitar?"

"She was."

"Where?"

"On the road. About a mile from the church."

"Then she wasn't walking on the path that goes around the lake?"

"She was on the road. It was dark."

"Where were the other children from her youth group?"

"They was way behind her, the ones I saw. I didn't see but three or four. She was walking fast and crying. I slowed down when I seen she was crying. But she kept walking and I went on. I kept her in sight for a while 'cause I was afeared something was wrong."

"Why did you think that?"

"She was crying."

"Did you watch her until she got to her house?"

"Yeah."

"You know where her house is?"

"I know where."

"Then what happened?" I asked, and I knew very well why the police were looking for him. I could understand their suspicions and knew they would grow only darker if they heard what he was telling me.

"I seen her go in the house."

"Did she see you?"

"Naw. Some of the time I didn't have my headlights on."

Dear God, I thought. "Creed, do you understand why the police are concerned?"

He swirled the liquor some more, and his eyes turned in a little and were an unusual mixture of brown and green.

"I didn't do nothing to her," he said, and I believed him.

"You were just keeping your eye on her because you saw she was upset," I said. "And you liked her."

"I saw she was upset, I did." He took a sip from the jar.

"Do you know where she was found? Where the fisherman found her?"

"I know of it."

"You've been to the spot."

He did not answer.

"You visited the spot and left her candy. After she was dead."

"A lot of folks has been there. They go to look. But her kin don't go."

"Her kin? Do you mean her mother?"

"She don't go."

"Has anyone seen you go there?"

"Naw."

"You left candy in that place. A present for her."

His lip was trembling again and his eyes watered. "I left her Fireballs." When he said "fire" it sounded like "far."

"Why in that place? Why not on her grave?"

"I didn't want no one to see me."

"Why?"

He stared at the jar and did not need to say it. I knew why. I could imagine the names the schoolchildren called him as he pushed his broom up and down halls. I could imagine the smirks and laughter, the terrible teasing that ensued if it seemed Creed Lindsey got sweet on anyone. And he had been sweet on Emily Steiner and she had been sweet on Wren.

It was very dark when I went out, and Deborah followed me like a silent cat as I returned to my car. My heart physically ached, as if I had pulled muscles in my chest. I wanted to give her money but I knew I should not.

"You make him be careful with that hand and keep it clean," I said to her as I opened the door to my Chevrolet. "And you need to get him to a doctor. Do you have a doctor here?"

She shook her head.

"You get your mother to find him one. Someone at the Burger Hut can tell her. Will you do that?"

She looked at me and took my hand.

"Deborah, you can call me at the Travel-Eze. I don't have the number, but it's in the phone book. Here's my card so you can remember my name."

"Thar don't have a phone," she said, watching me intently as she held on to my hand.

"I know you don't. But if you needed to call, you could find a pay phone, couldn't you?"

She nodded.

A car was coming up the hill.

"Thar's thar mother."

"How old are you, Deborah?"

"Eleven."

"Do you go to the public school here in Black Mountain?" I asked, shocked to think she was Emily's age.

She nodded again.

"Did you know Emily Steiner?"

"Thar was ahead of thar."

"You weren't in the same grade?"

"No." She let go of my hand.

The car, an ancient heap of a Ford with a headlight out, rumbled past, and I caught a glimpse of the woman looking our way. I would never forget the weariness of that flaccid face with its sunken mouth and hair in a net. Deborah loped after her mother, and I shut my door.

I took a long hot bath when I got back to the motel and thought about getting something to eat. But when I looked at the room service menu I found myself staring mindlessly and decided instead to read for a while. The telephone startled me awake at half past ten.

"Yes?"

"Kay?" It was Wesley. "I need to talk to you. It's very important."

"I'll come to your room."

I went straight there and knocked on the door. "It's Kay," I said.

"Hold on." His voice sounded from the other side.

A pause, and the door opened. His face confirmed that something was terribly wrong.

"What is it?" I walked in.

"It's Lucy."

He shut the door, and I judged by the desk that he had spent most of the afternoon on the phone. Notes were scattered everywhere. His tie was on the bed, his shirt untucked.

"She's been in an accident," he said.

"What?" My blood went cold.

He shut the door and was very distracted.

"Is she all right?" I could not think.

"It happened earlier this evening on Ninety-five just north of Richmond. She'd apparently been at Quantico and went out to eat and then drove back. She ate at the Outback. You know, the Australian steakhouse in northern Virginia? We know she stopped in Hanover at the gun store—at Green Top—and it was after she left there that she had the accident." He paced as he talked.

"Benton, *is she all right*?" I could not move.

"She's at MCV. It was pretty bad, Kay."

"Oh my God."

"Apparently she ran off the road at the Atlee/Elmont exit and overcorrected. When the tags came back to you, the state police called your office from the scene and the service got Fielding to track you down. He called me because he didn't want you to get the news over the phone. Well, the point is, since he's a medical examiner he was afraid of what your first reaction would be if he started to tell you that Lucy had just been in an accident—"

"Benton!"

"I'm sorry." He put his hands on my shoulders. "Jesus. I'm not good at this when it's . . . Well, when it's you. She's got some cuts and a concussion. It's a damn miracle she's alive. The car flipped several times. Your car. It's totaled. They had to cut her out of it and Medflight her in. To be honest, they thought by the look of the wreck that it wasn't survivable. It's just unbelievable she's okay."

I closed my eyes and sat on the edge of the bed. "Was she drinking?" I asked.

"Yes."

"Tell me the rest of it."

"She's been charged with driving under the influence. They took her blood alcohol at the hospital and it's high. I'm not sure how high."

"And no one else was hurt?"

"No other car was involved."

"Thank God."

He sat next to me and rubbed my neck. "It's a wonder she made it as far as she did without incident. She'd had a lot to drink when she was out to dinner, I guess." He put his arm around me and pulled me close. "I've already booked a flight for you."

"What was she doing at Green Top?"

"She purchased a gun. A Sig Sauer P230. They found it in the car."

"I have to get back to Richmond now."

"There isn't anything until early in the morning, Kay. It can wait until then."

"I'm cold," I said.

He got his suit jacket and put it over my shoulders. I began to shiver. The terror I'd felt when I saw Wesley's face and felt the tension in his tone brought back the night when he had called about Mark.

I had known the instant I'd heard Wesley's voice on the line that his news was very bad, and then he had begun to explain about the bombing in London, about Mark being in the train station walking past at the very moment it happened, and it had nothing to do with him, wasn't directed at him, but he was dead. Grief was like a seizure that shook me like a storm. It left me spent in a way I had never known before, not even when my father had died. I could not react back then, when I was young, when my mother was weeping and everything seemed lost.

"It will be all right," Wesley said, and now he was up pouring me a drink.

"What else do you know about it?"

"Nothing else, Kay. Here, this will help." He handed me a Scotch straight up.

Had there been a cigarette in the room, I would have put it between my lips and lit it. I would have ended my abstinence and forgotten my resolve just like that.

"Do you know who her doctor is? Where are the cuts? Did the air bags deploy?"

He began kneading my neck again and did not answer my questions because he had already made it clear he knew nothing more. I drank the Scotch quickly because I needed to feel it.

"I will go in the morning, then," I said.

His fingers worked their way up into my hair and felt wonderful.

My eyes were shut as I began to talk to him about my afternoon. I told him about my visit in the hospital with Lieutenant Mote. I told him about the people on Rainbow Mountain, about the girl who knew no pronouns and Creed, who knew that Emily Steiner had not taken the shortcut around the lake after her youth group meeting at the church.

"It's so sad, because I could see it as he was telling me," I went on, thinking of her diary. "She was supposed to meet Wren early and of course he did not show. Then he ignored her completely, so she didn't wait until the meeting was over. She ran ahead of everyone else.

"She hurried off because she was hurt and humiliated and didn't want anyone to know. Creed just happened to be out in his truck and saw her, and wanted to make sure she got home okay because he could tell she was upset. He liked her from afar just as she liked Wren from afar. And now she's horribly dead. It seems this is all about people loving people who don't love them back. It's about hurt getting passed on."

"Murder is always about that, really."

"Where's Marino?"

"I don't know."

"What he's doing is all wrong. He knows better than this."

"I think he's gotten involved with Denesa Steiner."

"I know he has."

"I can see how it would happen. He's lonely, had no luck with women, and in fact hasn't even had a clue about women since Doris left. Denesa Steiner's devastated, needy, appeals to his bruised male ego."

"Apparently, she has a lot of money."

"Yes."

"How did that happen? I thought her late husband taught school."

"I understand his family had a lot of money. They made it in oil or something out west. You're going to have to pass on the details of your encounter with Creed Lindsey. It's not going to look good for him."

I knew that.

"I can imagine how you feel about it, Kay. But I'm not even sure I'm comfortable with what you've told me. It bothers me that he followed her in his truck and had his headlights off. It bothers me that he knew where she lived and had been so aware of her at school. It bothers me a great deal that he visited the spot where her body was found and left the candy."

"Why was the skin in Ferguson's freezer? How does Creed Lindsey fit with that?"

"Either Ferguson put the skin in there or someone else did. It's as simple as that. And I don't think Ferguson did it."

"Why not?"

"He doesn't profile right. And you know that, too."

"And Gault?"

Wesley did not answer.

I looked up at him, for I had learned to feel his silence. I could follow it like the cool walls of a cave. "You're not telling me something," I said.

"We've just gotten a call from London. We think he's killed again, this time there."

I shut my eyes. "Dear God, no."

"This time a boy. Fourteen. Killed within the past few days."

"Same MO as Eddie Heath?"

"Eradicated bite marks. Gunshot to the head, body displayed. Close enough."

"That doesn't mean Gault wasn't in Black Mountain," I said as my doubts grew.

"At this moment we can't say it doesn't mean that. Gault could be anywhere. But I don't know about him anymore. There are many similarities between the Eddie Heath and Emily Steiner cases. But there are many differences."

"There are differences because this case is different," I said. "And I don't think Creed Lindsey put the skin in Ferguson's freezer."

"Listen, we don't know why that was there. We don't know that someone didn't leave it on his doorstep and Ferguson found it the minute he got home from the airport. He put it in the freezer like any good investigator would, and didn't live long enough to tell anyone."

"You're suggesting Creed waited until Ferguson got home and then delivered it?"

"I'm suggesting the police are going to consider Creed left it."

"Why would he do that?"

"Remorse."

"Whereas Gault would do it to jerk us around."

"Absolutely."

I was silent for a moment. Then I said, "If Creed did all this, then how do you explain Denesa Steiner's print on the panties Ferguson was wearing?"

"If he had a fetish about wearing women's clothing when he did his autoerotic thing, he could have stolen them. He was in and out of her house while he was working Emily's case. He could have taken lingerie from her very easily. And wearing something of hers while he masturbated added to the fantasy."

"Is that really what you think?"

"I really don't know what I think. I'm throwing these things out at you because I know what's going to happen. I know what Marino will think. Creed Lindsey is a suspect. In fact, what he told you about following Emily Steiner gives us probable cause to search his house and truck. If we find anything, and if Mrs. Steiner thinks he looks or sounds like the man who broke into her house that night, Creed's going to be charged with capital murder."

"What about the forensic evidence?" I said. "Have the labs come back with anything more?"

Wesley got up and tucked his shirttail in as he talked. "We've traced the blaze orange duct tape to Attica Correctional Facility in New York. Apparently, some prison administrator got tired of duct tape walking off and decided to have some specially made that would be less convenient to steal.

"So he picked blaze orange, which was also the color of the clothes the inmates wore. Since the tape was used inside the penitentiary to repair things like mattresses, for example, it was essential that it be flame-retardant. Shuford Mills made one run of the stuff—I think around eight hundred cases—back in 1986."

"That's very weird."

"As for the trace evidence on the adhesive of the strips used to bind Denesa Steiner, the residue is a varnish that's consistent with the varnish on the dresser in her bedroom. And that's pretty much what you would expect, since he bound her in her bedroom. So that information is relatively useless."

"Gault was never incarcerated at Attica, was he?" I asked.

Wesley was putting on his tie in front of the mirror. "No. But that wouldn't preclude his getting hold of the tape in another way. Someone could have given it to him. He did have a close friendship with the warden when the state pen was in Richmond—the warden he later murdered. I suppose it's worth checking that out, in the event some of the tape somehow ended up there."

"Are we going somewhere?" I asked as he slipped a fresh handkerchief into his back pocket and his pistol into a holster on his belt.

"I'm taking you out to dinner."

"What if I don't want to go?"

"You will."

"You're awfully sure of yourself."

He leaned over and kissed me as he removed his jacket from my shoulders. "I don't want you by yourself right now." He put the jacket on and looked very handsome in his precise, somber way.

We found a big brightly lit truck stop that featured everything from T-bones to a Chinese buffet. I ate egg drop soup and steamed rice because I did not feel well. Men in denim and boots heaped ribs and pork and shrimp in thick orange sauces on their plates and stared at us as if we were from Oz. My fortune cookie warned of fair-weather friends while Wesley's promised marriage.

Marino was waiting for us at the motel when we got back at shortly after midnight. I told him what I knew and he was not happy about it.

"I wish you hadn't gone up there," he said. We were in Wesley's room. "It's not your place to be interviewing people."

"I am authorized to investigate any violent death fully and to ask any questions I wish. It's ridiculous for you to even say such a thing, Marino. You and I have worked together for years."

"We're a team, Pete," Wesley said. "That's what the unit's all about. It's why we're here. Listen, I don't mean to be a hardass, but I can't let you smoke in my room."

He put his pack and lighter back into his pocket. "Denesa's told me Emily used to complain about Creed."

"She knows the police are looking for him?" Wesley asked.

"She's not in town," he evasively replied.

"Where is she?"

"She's got a sick sister in Maryland and went up there for a few days. My point is, Creed gave Emily the creeps."

I envisioned Creed on the mattress sewing up his thumb. I saw his crooked stare and pasty face, and I was not surprised that he might have frightened a little girl.

"A lot of questions still aren't answered," I said.

"Yeah, well, a lot of questions have been answered," Marino countered.

"To think that Creed Lindsey did this doesn't make sense," I said.

"It's making more sense every day."

"I wonder if he has a television in his house," Wesley said.

I thought for a minute. "Certainly, people don't have much up there, but they seem to have TVs."

"Creed could have learned all about Eddie Heath from television. Several of these true crime and news shows did segments on the case."

"Shit, stuff about that case was all over the friggin' universe," Marino said.

"I'm going to bed," I said.

"Well, don't let me hold you up." Marino glared at both of us as he got up from his chair. "I sure wouldn't want to do that."

"I've about had enough of your insinuations," I said as my anger boiled up.

"I sure as hell ain't insinuating. I'm just calling 'em as I see 'em."

"Let's not get into this," Wesley calmly said.

"Let's do." I was tired and stressed and fueled by Scotch. "Let's just do it right here in this room, the three of us together. Since this is all about the three of us."

"It sure as hell isn't," Marino said. "There's only one relationship in this room, and I'm not part of it. My opinion of it's my own business, and I have a right to it."

"Your opinion is self-righteous and wrongheaded," I said, furious. "You're acting like a thirteen-year-old with a crush."

"If that ain't just the biggest load of bullshit I ever heard." Marino's face was dark.

"You're so damn possessive and jealous you're making me crazy."

"In your dreams."

"You've got to stop this, Marino. You're destroying our relationship."

"I wasn't aware we had one."

"Of course we do."

"It's late," Wesley warned. "Everybody's under a lot of stress. We're tired. Kay, now is not a good time for this."

"Now is all we've got," I said. "Marino, goddam it, I care about you, but you're pushing me away. You're getting into things here that are scaring me to death. I'm not sure you even see what you're doing."

"Well, let me tell you something." Marino looked as if he hated me. "I don't think you're in a position to say I'm into anything. In the first place, you don't know shit. And in the second, at least I'm not screwing anybody who's married."

"Pete, that's enough," Wesley snapped.

"You're damn right it is." Marino stormed out of the room, slamming the door so hard I was certain it could be heard throughout the entire motel.

"Dear God," I said. "This is just awful."

"Kay, you spurned him, and that's why he's out of his mind."

"I did not spurn him."

Wesley was walking around, agitated. "I knew he was attached to you. All these years I've known he really cares about you. I just had no idea it went this deep. *I had absolutely no idea."*

I did not know what to say.

"The guy's not stupid. I suppose it was just a matter of time before he figured some things out. But I had no way of knowing it would affect him this way."

"I'm going to bed," I said again.

I slept for a while, and then I was wide awake. I stared into the dark, thinking about Marino and what I was doing. I was having an affair and did not feel concerned about it, and I did not understand that. Marino knew I was having an affair, and he was jealous beyond reason. I could never be romantically interested in him. I would have to tell him, but I could not imagine the occasion when such a conversation might occur.

I got up at four and sat out on the porch in the cold, looking at the stars. The Big Dipper was almost directly overhead, and I remembered Lucy as a toddler worrying that it would pour water on her if she stood under it very long. I remembered her perfect bones and skin, and incredible green eyes. I remembered the way she had looked at Carrie Grethen and believed that was part of what went wrong.

14

Lucy was not in a private room, and I walked right past her at first because she did not look like anyone I knew. Her hair, stiff with blood, was dark red and standing up, her eyes black-and-blue. She was propped up in bed in a drug-induced stage that was neither here nor there. I got close to her and took her hand.

"Lucy?"

She barely opened her eyes. "Hi," she said groggily.

"How are you feeling?"

"Not too bad. I'm sorry, Aunt Kay. How did you get here?"

"I rented a car."

"What kind?"

"A Lincoln."

"Bet you got one with air bags on both sides." She smiled wanly.

"Lucy, what happened?"

"All I remember is going to the restaurant. Then someone was sewing up my head in the emergency room."

"You have a concussion."

"They think I hit the top of my head on the roof when the car was flipping. I feel so bad about your car." Her eyes filled with tears.

"Don't worry about the car. That's not important. Do you remember anything at all about the accident?"

She shook her head and reached for a tissue.

"Do you remember anything about dinner at the Outback or your visit to Green Top?"

"How did you know? Oh, well." She drifted for a moment, eyelids heavy. "I went to the restaurant about four."

"Who did you meet?"

"Just a friend. I left at seven to come back here."

"You had a lot to drink," I said.

"I didn't think I had that much. I don't know why I ran off the road, but I think something happened."

"What do you mean?"

"I don't know. I can't remember, but it seems like something happened."

"What about the gun store? Do you remember stopping there?"

"I don't remember leaving."

"You bought a .380 semiautomatic pistol, Lucy. Do you remember that?"

"I know that's why I went there."

"So you go to a gun shop when you've been drinking. Can you tell me what was in your mind?"

"I didn't want to be staying at your house without protection. Pete recommended the gun."

"Marino did?" I asked, shocked.

"I called him the other day. He said to get a Sig and said he always uses Green Top in Hanover."

"He's in North Carolina," I said.

"I don't know where he was. I called his pager and he called me back."

"I have guns. Why didn't you ask me?"

"I want my own and I'm old enough now." She could not keep her eyes open much longer.

I found her doctor on the floor and caught up with him for a moment before I left. He was very young and talked to me as if I were a worried aunt or mother who did not know the difference between a kidney and a spleen. When he rather abruptly explained to me that a concussion was basically a bruised brain resulting from a severe blow, I did not say a word or change the expression on my face. He blushed when a medical student, who happened to be one of my advisees, passed us in the hall and greeted me by name.

I left the hospital and went to my office, where I had not been for more than a week. My desk looked rather much as I feared it would, and I spent the next few hours trying to clear it while I tried to track down the state police officer who worked Lucy's accident. I left a message, then called Gloria Loving at Vital Records.

"Any luck?" I asked.

"I can't believe I'm getting to talk to you twice in one week. Are you across the street again?"

"I am." I couldn't help but smile.

"No luck so far, Kay," she said. "We haven't found any record in California of a Mary Jo Steiner who died of SIDS. We're trying to code the death several other ways. Is it possible you could get a date and place of death?"

"I'll see what I can do," I said.

I thought of calling Denesa Steiner and ended up just staring at the phone. I was about to do it when State Police Officer Reed, whom I had been trying to reach, returned my call.

"I wonder if you could fax me your report," I said to him.

"Actually, Hanover's got a lot of that."

"I thought the accident occurred on Ninety-five," I said, for the interstate was state police jurisdiction, no matter the locale.

"Officer Sinclair rolled up just as I did, so he gave me a hand.

When the tags came back to you, I thought it was important to check that out."

Oddly, it had not crossed my mind before this moment that tags coming back to me would have created quite a stir.

"What is Officer Sinclair's first name?" I asked.

"His initials are A. D., I believe."

I was very fortunate that Officer Andrew D. Sinclair was in his office when I called him next. He told me Lucy was involved in a single-car accident that occurred while she was driving at a high rate of speed southbound on Ninety-five just north of the Henrico County line.

"How high a rate of speed?" I asked him.

"Seventy miles per hour."

"What about skid marks?"

"We found one thirty-two feet long where it appears she tapped her brakes and then went off the road."

"Why would she tap her brakes?"

"She was traveling at a high rate of speed and under the influence, ma'am. Could be she drifted off to sleep and suddenly was on somebody's bumper."

"Officer Sinclair, you need a skid mark of three hundred and twenty-nine feet to calculate that someone was driving seventy miles an hour. You have a thirty-two-foot skid mark here. I don't see how you can possibly calculate that she was driving seventy miles an hour."

"The speed limit on that stretch is sixty-five" was all he had to say.

"What was her blood alcohol?"

"Point one-two."

"I wonder if you could fax me your diagrams and report as soon as possible and tell me where my car was towed."

"It's at Covey's Texaco in Hanover. Off Route One. It's totaled, ma'am. If you can give me your fax number, I'll get you those reports right away."

I had them within the hour, and by using an overlay to

interpret the codes I determined that Sinclair basically assumed Lucy was drunk and fell asleep at the wheel. When she suddenly awoke and tapped her brakes, she went into a skid, lost control of the car, left the pavement, and overcorrected. This resulted in her jerking back onto the road and flipping across two lanes of traffic before crashing upside down into a tree.

I had serious problems with his assumptions and one important detail. My Mercedes had antilock brakes. When Lucy hit the brakes she should not have gone into the sort of skid Officer Sinclair had described.

I left my office and went downstairs to the morgue. My deputy chief, Fielding, and two young female forensic pathologists I had hired last year had cases on the three stainless steel tables. The sharp noise of steel against steel rose above the background thunder of water drumming into sinks, air blowing, and generators humming. The huge stainless steel refrigerator door opened with a loud suck as one of the morgue assistants rolled out another body.

"Dr. Scarpetta, can you look at this?" Dr. Wheat was a woman from Topeka. Her intelligent gray eyes peered out at me from behind a plastic face shield speckled with blood.

I went to her table.

"Does this look like soot in the wound?" She pointed a bloody gloved finger at a bullet wound to the back of the neck.

I bent close. "It's got burned edges, so maybe it's searing. Was there clothing?"

"He didn't have a shirt on. It happened in his residence."

"Well, this is an ambiguous one. We need to get a microscopic."

"Entrance or exit?" Fielding asked as he studied a wound from his own case. "Let me get your vote while you're here."

"Entrance," I said.

"Me, too. Are you going to be around?"

"In and out."

"In and out of town or in and out of here?"

"Both. I've got my Skypager."

"It's going all right?" he asked, his formidable biceps bunching as he cut through ribs.

"It's a nightmare, really," I said.

It took half an hour to get to the Texaco gas station with the twenty-four-hour towing service that had taken care of my car. I spotted my Mercedes in a corner near a chain link fence, and the sight of its destruction tightened my stomach. I got weak in the knees.

The front end was crumpled up against the windshield, the driver's side gaping like a toothless mouth. Hydraulic tools had forced open the doors, which had been removed along with the center post. My heart beat hard as I got close, and I jumped when a deep drawl sounded behind me.

"May I help ya?"

I turned to face a grizzled old man wearing a faded red cap with PURINA over the bill.

"This is my car," I told him.

"I sure as hell hope you wasn't the one driving it."

I noticed the tires were not flat and both air bags had deployed.

"It sure is a shame." He shook his head as he stared at my hideously mangled Mercedes-Benz. "Believe this is the first one of these I've seen. A 500E. Now, one of the boys here knows Mercedes and tells me Porsche helped design the engine in this one and there aren't but so many around. What is it? A '93? I don't reckon your husband got it around here."

I noticed that the left taillight was shattered, and near it was a scrape that was smudged with what appeared to be greenish paint. I bent over to get a closer look as my nerves began to tensely hum.

The man talked on. "Course, with as few miles as you had on it, it's more'n likely a '94. If you don't mind my asking, about how much would one like this cost? About fifty?"

"Did you tow this in?" I straightened up, my eyes darting over details that were sending off alarms, one right after another.

"Toby brought it in last night. I don't guess you'd know the horsepower."

"Was it *exactly* like this at the scene?"

The man looked slightly befuddled.

"For example," I went on, "the phone's off the hook."

"I guess so when a car's been flipping and slams into a tree."

"And the sunscreen's up."

He leaned over and peered in at the back windshield. He scratched his neck. "I just figured it was dark because the glass is tinted. I didn't notice the screen was up. You wouldn't think someone'd put it up at night."

I carefully leaned inside to look at the rearview mirror. It had been flipped up to reduce the glare of headlights from the rear. I got keys out of my pocketbook and sat sidesaddle on the driver's seat.

"Now I wouldn't be doing that if I was you. That metal's like bunches of knives in there. And there's an awful lot of blood on the seats and ever'where."

I hung up the car phone and turned on the ignition. The phone sounded its tone to tell me it was working, and red lights went on warning me not to run down the battery. The radio and the CD player were off. Headlights and fog lamps were on. I picked up the phone and hit redial. It began to ring and a woman's voice answered.

"Nine-one-one."

I hung up, my pulse pounding in my neck as chills raced up to the roots of my hair. I looked around at red spatters on the dark gray leather, on the dash and console, and all over the inside of the roof. They were too red and thick. Here and there bits of angel hair pasta were cemented to the interior of my car.

I got out a metal fingernail file and scraped off greenish paint from the damage to the rear. Folding the paint flecks into a tissue, next I tried to pry off the damaged taillight unit. When I couldn't, I got the man to fetch a screwdriver.

"It's a '92," I said as I rapidly walked away, leaving him staring after me with an open mouth. "Three hundred and fifteen horsepower. It cost eighty thousand dollars. There are only six hundred in this country—*were*. I bought it at McGeorge in Richmond. I don't have a husband." I was breathing hard as I got in the Lincoln. "It's not blood inside it, goddam it. Goddam it. Goddam it!" I muttered on as I slammed the door shut and started the engine.

Tires squealed as I shot out into the highway and raced back to 95 South. Just past the Atlee/Elmont exit I slowed down and pulled off the road. I kept as far off the pavement as I could, and when cars and trucks roared past I was hit by walls of wind.

Sinclair's report stated that my Mercedes had left the pavement approximately eighty feet north of the eighty-six-mile marker. I was at least two hundred feet north of that when I spotted a yaw mark not far from broken taillight glass in the right lane. The mark, which was a sideways scuff about two feet long, was about ten feet from a set of straight skid marks that were approximately thirty feet long. I darted in and out of traffic, collecting glass.

I started walking again, and it was approximately another hundred feet before I got to marks on pavement that Sinclair had diagrammed in his report. My heart skipped another beat as I stared, stunned, at black rubber streaks left by my Pirelli tires the night before last. They were not skids at all, but acceleration marks made when tires spin abruptly straight ahead, as I had done when leaving the Texaco station moments earlier.

It was just after she had made these marks that Lucy had lost control and had gone off the road. I saw her tire impressions in the dirt, the smear of rubber when she overcorrected and a tire caught the pavement's edge. I surveyed deep gashes in the road made when the car flipped, the gouge in the tree in the median, and bits of metal and plastic scattered everywhere.

I drove back to Richmond not sure what to do or whom to call. Then I thought of Investigator McKee with the state police. We had worked many traffic fatality scenes together and spent many hours in my office moving Matchbox cars on my desk until we believed we had reconstructed what had led to a crash. I left a message with his office, and he returned my call shortly after I got home.

"I didn't ask Sinclair if he got casts of the tire impressions where she left the road, but I can't imagine he would have," I said, after explaining a little of what was going on.

"No, he wouldn't have," McKee concurred. "I heard a lot about it, Dr. Scarpetta. There was a lot of talk. And the thing was, what Reed first noticed when he responded to the scene was your low number tag."

"I talked to Reed briefly. He wasn't very involved."

"Right. Under ordinary circumstances, when the Hanover officer . . . uh, Sinclair, rolled up, Reed would have told him things were under control and done all the diagrams and measurements himself. But he sees this low three-digit tag and bells go off. He knows the car belongs to somebody important in government.

"Sinclair gets to do his thing while Reed gets on the radio and the phone, calls for a supervisor, runs the tag ASAP. Bingo. The car comes back to you, and now his first thought is it's you inside. So you can imagine how it was out there."

"A circus."

"You got it. Turns out Sinclair just got out of the academy. Your wreck was his second."

"Even if it was his twentieth, I can see how he might have made a mistake. There was no reason for him to look for skid marks two hundred feet up from where Lucy went off the road."

"And you're certain it was a yaw mark you saw?"

"Absolutely. You make those casts, and you're going to find the impression on the shoulder's going to match the impression back there on the road. The only way that yaw mark or scuff could have been left was if an outside force caused the car to suddenly change direction."

"And then acceleration marks two hundred or so feet later," he thought out loud. "Lucy gets hit from the rear, taps her brakes, and keeps on going. Seconds later she suddenly accelerates and loses control."

"Probably about the same time she dialed Nine-one-one," I said.

"I'll check with the cellular phone company and get the exact time of that call. Then we'll find it on the tape."

"Someone was on her bumper with their high beams on, and she flipped on the night mirror, and finally resorted to putting up the rear sunscreen to block out the glare. She didn't have the radio or CD player on because she was concentrating hard. She was wide awake and scared because someone's on top of her.

"This person finally hits her from the rear and Lucy applies the brakes," I continued to reconstruct what I believed had happened. "She drives on, and realizes the person is gaining on her again. Panicking, Lucy floors it and loses control. All of this would have taken place in seconds."

"If what you found out there is right, it sure could have happened exactly like that."

"Will you look into it?"

"You bet. What about the paint?"

"I'll turn it, the taillight unit, and everything else in to the labs and ask them to put a rush on it."

"Put my name on the paperwork. Have them call me with the results right away."

* * *

It was five o'clock and dark out when I got off the phone in my upstairs office. I looked around dazed, and felt like a stranger in my house. Hunger gnawing my stomach was followed by nausea, and I drank Mylanta from the bottle and rummaged in the medicine cabinet for Zantac. My ulcer had vanished during the summer, but unlike former lovers, it always came back.

Both phone lines rang and were answered by voice mail. I heard the fax machine as I soaked in the tub and sipped wine on top of medicine. I had so much to do. I knew my sister, Dorothy, would want to come immediately. She always rose to crisis occasions because it fed her need for drama. She would use it for research. No doubt, in her next children's book, one of her characters would deal with an auto wreck. Critics again would rave about the sensitivity and wisdom of Dorothy, who mothered people she imagined much better than she did her only daughter.

The fax, I found, was Dorothy's flight schedule. She was arriving late tomorrow afternoon and would stay with Lucy in my home.

"She won't be in the hospital long, will she?" she asked, when I called her minutes later.

"I imagine I'll be bringing her here in the afternoon," I said.

"She must look terrible."

"Most people do after automobile accidents."

"But is any of it *permanent*?" She almost whispered. "She won't be disfigured, will she?"

"No, Dorothy. She won't be disfigured. How aware have you been of her drinking?"

"Now how would I know anything about that? She's up there near you in school and never seems to want to come home. And when she does she certainly doesn't confide in me or her grandmother. I would think if anyone were aware, you should have been."

"If she's convicted of DUI, the courts could order her into treatment," I said as patiently as possible.

Silence.

Then, "My God."

I went on, "Even if they don't, it would be a good idea for two reasons. The most obvious is that she needs to deal with the problem. Second, the judge may look upon her case with more sympathy if she volunteers to get some help."

"Well, I'm just going to leave all that up to you. You're the doctor-lawyer in the family. But I know my little girl. She's not going to want to do it. I can't imagine her going off to some mental ward where they don't have computers. She'd never be able to face anyone again."

"She will not be going off to a *mental ward*, and there is nothing the least bit shameful about being treated for alcohol or drug abuse. What's shameful is to let it go on to ruin your life."

"I've always stopped at three glasses of wine."

"There are many types of addictions," I said. "Yours happens to be to men."

"Oh, Kay." She laughed. "That's quite something coming from you. By the way, are you seeing anyone?"

15

Senator Frank Lord heard a rumor that I had been in a wreck and called me before the sun was up the next morning.

"No," I told him as I sat half dressed on the edge of my bed. "Lucy was driving my car."

"Oh, dear!"

"She's doing fine, Frank. I'll be bringing her home this afternoon."

"Apparently one of the papers up here printed that it was you who had wrecked and there was a suspicion alcohol was a factor."

"Lucy was trapped in the car for a while. No doubt some policeman made an assumption when the tags came back to me, and this ended up being relayed to a reporter on deadline." I thought of Officer Sinclair. He would get my vote for such a blunder.

"Kay, can I do anything to help?"

"Do you have any further clues as to what might have happened at ERF?"

"There are some interesting developments. Have you heard Lucy mention someone named Carrie Grethen?"

"They're co-workers. I've met her."

"Apparently she's connected to a spy shop, one of these places that sells high-tech surveillance devices."

"You aren't serious."

"Afraid so."

"Well, I can certainly see why she would have been interested in getting a job at ERF, and it stuns me that the Bureau would have hired her with that in her background."

"No one knew. Apparently, it's her boyfriend who owns the shop. The only reason we know she's a frequent visitor is she's been under surveillance."

"She dates a man?"

"Excuse me?"

"The owner of the spy shop is a man?"

"Yes."

"Who says it is her boyfriend?"

"Apparently she did when questioned after being seen in the shop."

"Can you tell me more about both of them?"

"Not much at present, but I have the shop's address, if you want to hold on a minute. Let me dig it out."

"What about her home address or the boyfriend's home address?"

"I'm afraid I don't have those."

"Whatever information you can give me, then."

I looked around for a pencil and wrote as my mind raced. The name of the shop was Eye Spy, and it was in the Springfield Mall, just off I-95. If I left now, I could be there by mid-morning and back in time to bring Lucy home from the hospital.

"Just so you know," Senator Lord was saying, "Miss Grethen has been dismissed from ERF because of the spy shop connection, which she obviously omitted divulging during her application process. But at this point, there's no evidence whatsoever she was involved in the break-in."

"She certainly had motive," I said, holding my anger in check.

"ERF is a Santa's workshop for someone who sells espionage equipment." I paused, thinking. "Do you know when she was hired by the Bureau, and did she apply for the job or did ERF recruit her?"

"Let's see. It's in my notes here. It just says here that she submitted an application last April and started mid-August."

"Mid-August was about the same time Lucy started. What did Carrie do before that?"

"It seems her entire career has been in computers. Hardware, software, programming. And engineering, which was partly why the Bureau was interested in her. She's very creative and ambitious, and unfortunately, dishonest. Several people recently interviewed have begun to paint a portrait of a woman who has been lying and cheating her way to the top for years."

"Frank, she applied for the job at ERF so she could spy for the spy shop," I said. "She may also be one of these people who hates the FBI."

"Both scenarios are possible," he agreed. "It's a matter of finding proof. Even if we can, unless there is evidence she took something, she can't be prosecuted."

"Lucy mentioned to me before all this happened that she was involved in some research pertaining to the biometric lock system at ERF. Do you know anything about that?"

"I'm not aware of any research projects of that nature."

"But would you necessarily know if there was one?"

"There's a good chance I would. I've been given quite a lot of detailed information pertaining to ongoing classified projects at Quantico—because of the crime bill, the money I've been trying to appropriate for the Bureau."

"Well, it's strange that Lucy would say she was involved in a project that doesn't seem to exist," I said.

"Sadly, that detail might only make her situation look more incriminating."

I knew he was right. As suspicious as Carrie Grethen appeared, the case against Lucy was still stronger.

"Frank," I went on, "do you happen to know what types of cars Carrie Grethen and her boyfriend drive?"

"Certainly, we can get that information. Why are you interested?"

"I have reason to believe Lucy's wreck was no accident and she may still be in serious danger."

He paused. "Would it be a good idea to keep her on the Academy's security floor for a while?"

"Ordinarily, that would be the perfect place," I said. "But I don't think she needs to be anywhere near the Academy right now."

"I see. Well, that makes sense. There are other places if you need me to intervene."

"I think I have a place."

"I'm off to Florida tomorrow, but you've got my numbers there."

"More fund-raisers?" I knew he was exhausted, for the election was little more than a week away.

"That, too. And the usual brush fires. NOW's picketing, and my opponent remains very busy painting me as the woman hater with horns and a pointed tail."

"You've done more for women than anyone I know," I said. "Especially this one right here."

I finished getting dressed and by seven-thirty was drinking my first cup of coffee on the road in my rental car. The weather was gloomy and cold, and I noticed very little of what I passed as I drove north.

A biometric lock system, like any lock system, would have to be *picked* were someone to bypass it. Some locks truly did require nothing more than a credit card, while others could be dismantled or released with various tools, such as Slim Jims. But a lock system that scanned fingerprints could not be violated by such simple mechanical means. As I contemplated the break-in at ERF and how someone might have accomplished this, several thoughts drifted through my mind.

Lucy's print had been scanned into the system at approximately three o'clock in the morning, and that was only possible if her finger had been present—or a facsimile of her finger had been present. I recalled from International Association of Identification meetings I had attended over the years that many notorious criminals had made many creative attempts at altering their fingerprints.

The ruthless gangster John Dillinger had dropped acid on his cores and deltas, while the lesser-known Roscoe Pitts had surgically removed his prints from the first knuckle up. These methods and others had failed, and the gentlemen would have been better served had they stayed painlessly with the prints God had given them. Their altered latents simply went into the FBI's Mutilated File, which, frankly, was far easier to search. Not to mention, burned and mangled fingers look a little fishy if you happen to be a suspect.

But what came to mind most vividly was a case years ago of an especially resourceful burglar whose brother worked in a funeral home. The burglar, who had been imprisoned many times, attempted to give himself a pair of gloves that would leave someone else's prints. This he accomplished by repeatedly dipping a dead man's hands into liquid rubber, forming layer after layer until the "gloves" could be pulled off.

The plan did not work well for at least two reasons. The burglar had neglected to knock air bubbles out with each layer of rubber, and this made for rather odd latent prints recovered at the next mansion he hit. He also had not bothered to research the individual whose prints he stole. Had he done so, he would have learned that the decedent was a convicted felon who had died peacefully while out on parole.

I thought of my visit to ERF on a sunny afternoon that now seemed years ago. I had sensed that Carrie Grethen was not pleased to find Wesley and me in her office when she walked in stirring a viscous substance, which, in retrospect, could have been liquid silicone or rubber. It was during this visit that Lucy mentioned the biometric lock research she was "in the middle of." Maybe what she had said was literally true. Maybe Carrie had intended at that moment to make a rubber cast of Lucy's thumb.

If my theory about what Carrie had done was accurate, I knew it could be proven. I wondered why none of us had thought before to ask a very simple question. Did the print scanned into the biometric lock system *physically match* Lucy's, or were we simply taking the computer's word for it?"

"Well, I would assume so," Benton Wesley said to me when I got him on the car phone.

"Of course you would assume it. Everyone would assume it. But if someone made a cast of Lucy's thumb and scanned it into the system, the print should be a *reversal* of the corresponding one on her ten-print card on file with the Bureau. A mirror image, in other words."

Wesley paused, then sounded surprised. "Damn. But wouldn't the scanner have detected the print was backward and rejected it?"

"Very few scanners could distinguish between a print and an inversion of that same print. But a fingerprint examiner could," I said. "The print scanned into the biometric lock system should still be digitally stored in the data base."

"If Carrie Grethen did this, don't you think she would have eradicated the print from the data base?"

"I doubt it," I replied. "She's not a fingerprint examiner. It's unlikely she would realize that every time a latent print is left, it's reversed. And it matches a ten-print card only because those prints are reversed as well. Now if you made a cast of a digit and left a latent print with it, you would actually have a reversal of a reversal."

"So a latent made with this rubber thumb would be a reversal of the same latent made with the person's actual thumb."

"Precisely."

"Christ, I'm not good with things like this."

"Don't worry about it, Benton. I know it's confusing, but take my word for it."

"I always do, and it sounds like we need to get a hard copy of the print in question."

"Absolutely, and right away. There's something else I want to ask you. Were you aware of a research project pertaining to ERF's biometic lock system?"

"A research project conducted by the Bureau?"

"Yes."

"No. I'm not aware of any project like that."

"That's what I thought. Thank you, Benton."

Both of us paused, waiting for a personal word from the other. But I did not know what else to say. So much was inside me.

"Be careful," he told me, and we said good-bye.

I found the spy shop not more than a half hour later in a huge shopping mall teaming with cars and people. Eye Spy was inside near Ralph Lauren and Crabtree & Evelyn. It was a small shop with a window display of the finest that legal espionage had to offer. I hesitated a safe distance away until a customer at the register moved, allowing me to see who was working at the counter. An older, overweight man was ringing up an order, and I could not believe he could be Carrie Grethen's lover. No doubt this detail was yet one more of her lies.

When the customer left, there was only one other, a young man in a leather jacket perusing a showcase of voice-activated tape recorders and portable voice stress analyzers. The fat man behind the counter wore thick glasses and gold chains, and looked like he always had a deal for someone.

"Excuse me," I said as quietly as possible. "I'm looking for Carrie Grethen."

"She went out for coffee, should be back in a minute." He studied my face. "Can I help you with something?"

"I'll look around until she returns," I said.

"Sure."

I had just gotten interested in a special attaché case that included a hidden tape recorder, wire tap alerts, telephone descrambler, and night vision devices, when Carrie Grethen walked in. She stopped when she saw me, and for an unnerving instant I thought she might fling her cup of coffee in my face. Her eyes drove through mine like two steel nails.

"I need a word with you," I said.

"I'm afraid this is not a good time." She tried to smile, to sound civil, because now there were four customers in this very small store.

"Of course it's a good time," I said, holding her gaze.

"Jerry?" She looked at the fat man. "Can you handle things for a few minutes?"

He stared hard at me like a dog ready to lunge.

"I promise I won't be long," she reassured him.

"Yeah, sure," he said with the distrust of the dishonest.

I followed her out of the store and we found an empty bench near a fountain.

"I heard about Lucy's accident and I'm sorry about that. I hope she's all right," Carrie said coldly as she sipped her coffee.

"You don't care in the least how Lucy is," I said. "And there's no point in wasting any of your charm on me because I have you figured out. I *know* what you did."

"You don't know anything." She smiled her frosty smile, and the air was filled with the sounds of water.

"I know you made a cast of Lucy's thumb in rubber, and figuring out her Personal Identification Number was simple since you were with each other so much. All you had to do was be observant and note the code she punched in. This was how you accessed the biometric lock system the early morning you violated ERF."

"My, don't you have an active imagination?" She laughed

and her eyes got harder. "And I might advise you to be very careful making accusations like that."

"I'm not interested in your advice, Miss Grethen. I'm interested only in giving you a warning. It will soon be proven that Lucy did not break into ERF. You were smart but not smart enough, and you made one fatal oversight."

She was silent, but I could see her mind racing behind her icy facade. Her curiosity was desperate.

"I don't know what you're talking about," she said with self-confidence that was beginning to waver.

"You may be good with computers, but you are not a forensic scientist. The case against you is very simple." I put forth my theory with the certitude of any good lawyer who knows how to play the game. "You asked Lucy to assist you in a so-called research project involving the biometric lock system at ERF."

"Research project? There is no research project," she said hatefully.

"And that's the point, Miss Grethen. There is no research project. You lied to her so you could get her to let you make a cast of her thumb in liquid rubber."

She laughed shortly. "My goodness. You've been watching too much James Bond. You don't really think anyone would believe—"

I cut her off. "This rubber thumb you made was then used to get into the lock system so you and whoever else could commit what amounts to industrial espionage. But you made *one mistake.*"

Her face was livid.

"Would you like to hear what that mistake was?"

Still, she said nothing, but she wanted to know. I could feel her paranoia radiating like heat.

"You see, Miss Grethen," I went on in the same reasonable tone. "When you make a cast of a finger, the print impression on it is actually a reversal or mirror image of the original one. So the print of your rubber thumb was an inversion of Lucy's print. *In other words, it was backward.* And an examination of the print that was scanned into the system at three in the morning will show this quite clearly."

She swallowed hard, and what she said next validated all that I conjectured. "You can't prove it was me who did that."

"Oh, we will prove it. But there's a more important bit of information for you to go away with this day." I leaned closer. I could smell her coffee breath. "You took advantage of my niece's feelings for you. You took advantage of her youth and naïveté and decency."

I leaned so close I was in her face. "Don't you ever come near Lucy again. Don't you ever speak to her. Don't you ever call her again. Don't you ever *think* about her."

My hand in my coat pocket gripped my .38. I almost wanted her to make me use it.

"And if I find out you were the one who ran her off the road," I went on in a quiet voice that rang like cold surgical steel, "I will personally track you down. You will be haunted by me the rest of your wretched life. I will always be there when you come up for parole. I will tell parole board after parole board and governor after governor that you are a character disorder who is a menace to society. Do you understand?"

"Go to hell," she said.

"I will never go to hell," I said. "But you are already there."

She abruptly got up, and her angry strides carried her back into the spy shop. I watched a man follow her in and begin to speak to her as I sat on the bench, my heart beating hard. I did not know why he made me pause. There was something about the sharpness of his profile at a glance, the V-shape of his lean, strong back, and the unnatural blackness of his slicked hair. Dressed in a splendid midnight-blue silk suit, he carried what looked like an alligator skin briefcase. I was about to walk away when he turned toward me, and for an electric instance our eyes met. His were piercing blue.

I did not run. I was like a squirrel in the middle of a road that starts to dash this way and that only to end up where it began. I began walking as fast as I could, then began to run, and the sound of water falling was like feet falling as I imagined him in pursuit. I did not go to a pay phone because I was afraid to stop. I thought my heart would burst as it hammered harder and harder.

I sprinted through the parking lot, my hands shaking as I unlocked my car. I did not reach for the phone until I was moving fast and did not see him.

"Benton! Oh my God!"

"Kay? Jesus, what is it?" His alarmed voice crackled horribly over the phone, for northern Virginia is notorious for too much cellular traffic.

"Gault!" I breathlessly exclaimed as I slammed on my brakes just before rear-ending a Toyota. "I saw Gault!"

"You saw Gault? Where?"

"In Eye Spy."

"In what? What did you say?"

"The shop Carrie Grethen works in. The one she's been connected to. He was there, Benton! I saw him walk in as I was leaving, and he started talking to her, and then he saw me and I ran."

"Slow down, Kay!" Wesley's voice was tense. I couldn't recall him ever sounding this tense. "Where are you now?"

"I'm on I-95 South. I'm fine."

"Just keep driving, for God's sake. Don't stop for anything. Do you think he saw you get into your car?"

"I don't think so. Shit, I don't know!"

"Kay," he said with authority. "Calm down." He spoke slowly. "I want you to calm down. I don't want you getting into an accident. I'm going to make calls. We'll find him."

But I knew we wouldn't. I knew by the time the first agent or cop got the first call, Gault would be gone. He had recognized me. I had seen it in his cold blue stare. He would know exactly what I would do the minute I could, and he would disappear again.

"I thought you said he was in England," I stupidly said.

"I said we believe he was," Wesley said.

"Don't you see, Benton?" I went on because my mind would not stop. Connections were being made left and right. "He's involved in this. He's involved in what happened at ERF. *It may be he's the one who sent Carrie Grethen, who got her to do what she did. His spy."*

Wesley was silent as this sank in. It was a thought so terrible that he did not want to think it.

His voice began to break up. I knew he was getting frantic, too, because conversations like this one should not be conducted over a car phone. "To get what?" he crackled. "What would he want to get into there?"

I knew. I knew exactly what. "CAIN," I said as the line went dead.

16

I got back to Richmond and did not sense Gault's malignant shadow at my heels. He had other agendas and demons to fight, and had not chosen to come after me, I believed. Even so, I reset the alarm the moment I entered my house. I went nowhere, not even to the bathroom, without my gun.

At shortly after two P.M., I drove to MCV, and Lucy traveled by wheelchair to my car. She insisted on wheeling herself despite my insistence that I propel her prudently, as a loving aunt would. She would have none of my help. But as soon as we got home she succumbed to my attentions and I tucked her in bed, where she sat up dozing.

I put on a pot of Zuppa di Aglio Fresco, a fresh garlic soup popular in the hills of Brisighella, where it has been fed to babies and the elderly for many years. That and ravioli filled with sweet squash and chestnuts would do the trick, and it lifted my mood when a fire was blazing in the living room and wonderful aromas filled the air. It was true that when I went long periods without cooking, it felt as if no one lived in my lovely home or cared. It almost seemed my house got sad.

Later, beneath a sky threatening rain, I drove to the airport to meet my sister's plane. I had not seen her for a while, and she was not the same. She never was from visit to visit, for Dorothy was acutely insecure, which was why she could be so mean, and she had a habit of changing her hair and dress regularly.

This late afternoon as I stood at the USAir gate, I scanned faces of passengers coming off the jetway, leaving myself open for anything familiar. I recognized her by her nose and the dimple in her chin, since neither was easily altered. She wore her hair black and close to her head like a leather helmet, her eyes behind large glasses, a bright red scarf thrown around her neck. Fashionably thin in jodhpurs and lace-up boots, she strode straight to me and kissed my cheek.

"Kay, it's so wonderful to see you. *You look tired.*"

"How's Mother?"

"Her hip, you know. What are you driving?"

"A rental car."

"Well, the first thing that went through my mind was your being without your Mercedes. I couldn't possibly imagine being without mine."

Dorothy had a 190E that she had gotten while dating a Miami cop. The car had been confiscated from a drug dealer and was sold at auction for a pittance. It was dark blue with spoilers and custom pinstripes.

"Do you have luggage?" I asked.

"Just this. How fast was she driving?"

"Lucy doesn't remember anything."

"You can't imagine how I felt when the phone rang. My God. My heart literally stopped."

It was raining and I had not brought an umbrella.

"No one can relate unless they've experienced the same thing. That moment. That simply awful moment when you don't know exactly what's happened, but you can tell the news is bad about someone you love. I hope you're not parked too far from here. Maybe it's best if I just wait."

"I'll have to leave the lot, pay, then come back around." I could see my car from where we stood on the sidewalk. "It will take ten or fifteen minutes."

"That's perfectly all right. Don't you worry about me. I'll just stand inside and watch for you. I need to use the ladies' room. It must be so nice not to have to worry about some things anymore."

She did not elaborate until she was in the car and we were on our way.

"Do you take hormones?"

"For what?" It was raining very hard, large drops hammering the roof like a stampeding herd of small animals.

"The change." Dorothy pulled a plastic bag out of her purse and began nibbling on a gingersnap.

"What change?"

"You know. Hot flashes, moods. I know a woman who started getting them the minute she turned forty. The mind's a powerful thing."

I turned on the radio.

"We were offered some dreadful snack, and you know how I get when I don't eat." She ate another gingersnap. "Only twenty-five calories and I allow myself eight a day, so we'll need to stop and get some. And apples, of course. You're so lucky. You don't seem to have to worry about your weight at all, but then I imagine if I did what you do I probably wouldn't have much of an appetite, either."

"Dorothy, there's a treatment center in Rhode Island that I want to talk to you about."

She sighed. "I'm worried sick about Lucy."

"It's a four-week program."

"I just don't know if I could stand the thought of her being all the way up there, locked up like that." She ate another cookie.

"Well, you're going to have to stand it, Dorothy. This is very serious."

"I doubt she'll go. You know how stubborn she can be." She thought for a minute. "Well, maybe it would be a good thing." She sighed again. "Maybe while she's there they can fix a few other things."

"What other things, Dorothy?"

"I might as well tell you that I don't know what to do about her. I just don't understand what went wrong, Kay." She began to cry. "With all due respect, you can't imagine what it's like to have a child turn out this way. Bent like a twig. I don't know what happened. Certainly, it's not from any example set at home. I'll take the blame for some things, but not for this."

I turned the radio off and looked over at her. "What *are* you talking about?" I was struck again by how much I disliked my sister. It made no sense to me that she was my sister, for I failed to find anything in common between us except our mother and memories of once living in the same house.

"I can't believe you haven't wondered about it, or maybe to you it somehow seems normal." Her emotions gathered momentum as our encounter tumbled farther downhill. "And I'd be less than honest if I didn't tell you I've worried about your influence in that department, Kay, not that I'm judging because certainly your personal life is your own business and some things you can't help." She blew her nose as tears flowed and rain fell hard. "Damn! This is so difficult."

"Dorothy, for God's sake. *What on earth are you taking about?*"

"She watches every goddam thing you do. If you brush your teeth a certain way, you can rest assured she's going to do the same thing. And for the record I've been very understanding when not everybody would. Aunt Kay this and Aunt Kay that. All these years."

"Dorothy . . ."

"Not once have I complained or tried to pry her away from your bosom, so to speak. I've always just wanted what's best for her, and so I indulged her little case of hero worship."

"Dorothy . . ."

"You have no idea of the sacrifice." She blew her nose loudly. "It wasn't like it wasn't bad enough that I was always being compared to you in school, and putting up with Mother's comments because you were always so fucking *perfect* at everything.

"I mean, goddam. Cooking, fixing things, taking care of the car, paying the bills. You were just a regular man of the house when we were growing up. And then you became my daughter's *father*—if that doesn't take the cake."

"Dorothy!"

But she would not stop.

"And I can't compete with that. I certainly can't be her *father*. I will concede that you're more of a man than I am. Oh yes. You win the hell out of that one hands down, *Dr. Scarpetta, Esquire*. I mean, shit. It's so unfair, and then you get the tits in the family to boot. *The man in the family gets the big tits!*"

"Dorothy, shut up."

"No, I won't and you can't make me," she whispered furiously.

We were back in our small room with the small bed we shared, where we learned to hate each other quietly while Father was dying. We were at the kitchen table silently eating macaroni again while he dominated our lives from his sickbed down the hall. Now we were about to walk into my house where Lucy was hurt, and I marveled that Dorothy did not recognize a script that was as old and predictable as we were.

"Just what exactly are you trying to blame me for?" I said as I opened the garage door.

"Let's put it this way. Lucy's not dating is not something she got from me. That's for damn sure."

I switched off the engine and looked at her.

"Nobody appreciates and enjoys men more than I do, and next time you start to criticize me as a mother, you ought to take a hard look at your contributions to Lucy's development. I mean, who the hell's she like?"

"Lucy's not like anyone I know," I said.

"Bullshit. She's your spitting image. And now she's a drunk, and I think she's queer." She burst into tears again.

"Are you suggesting I'm a lesbian?" I was beyond anger.

"Well, she got it from someone."

"I think you should go inside now."

She opened her door and looked surprised when I made no move to get out of the car. "Aren't you coming in?"

I gave her the key and the alarm code. "I'm going to the grocery store," I said.

At Ukrop's I bought gingersnaps and apples, and wandered the aisles for a while because I did not want to go home. In truth, I never enjoyed Lucy when her mother was around, and this visit certainly had started worse than usual. I understood some of what Dorothy felt, and her insults and jealousies came as no great surprise because they were not new.

It was not her behavior that had me feeling so bad but, rather, the reminder that I was alone. As I passed cookies, candies, dips, and spreadable cheeses, I wished what I had could be cured by an eating binge. Or if filling up with Scotch could have filled up the empty spaces, I might have done that. Instead, I went home with one small bag and served dinner to my pitifully small family.

Afterward, Dorothy retired to a chair before the fire. She read and sipped Rumple Minze while I got Lucy ready for bed.

"Are you hurting?" I asked.

"Not too much. But I can't stay awake. All of a sudden my eyes cross."

"Sleep is exactly what you need."

"I have these awful dreams."

"Do you want to tell me about them?"

"Someone's coming after me, chasing me, usually in a car. And I hear noises from the wreck that wake me up."

"What sort of noises?"

"Metal clanging. The air bag going off. Sirens. Sometimes it's like I'm asleep but not asleep and all these images dance behind my eyes. I see lights throbbing red on the pavement and men in yellow slickers. I thrash around and sweat."

"It's normal for you to experience posttraumatic stress, and it may go on for a while."

"Aunt Kay, am I going to be arrested?" Her frightened eyes stared out from bruises that broke my heart.

"You're going to be fine, but there's something I want to suggest that you probably won't like."

I told her about the private treatment center in Newport, Rhode Island, and she began to cry.

"Lucy, with a DUI conviction you're likely to have to do this anyway as part of your sentencing. Wouldn't it be better to decide on your own and get it over with?"

She gingerly dabbed her eyes. "I can't believe this is happening to me. Everything I've ever dreamed of is gone."

"That couldn't be further from the truth. You are alive. No one else was hurt. Your problems can be fixed, and I want to help you do that. But you need to trust me and listen."

She stared down at her hands on top of the covers, tears flowing.

"And I need for you to be honest with me, too."

She did not look at me.

"Lucy, you didn't eat at the Outback—not unless they've suddenly added spaghetti to their menu. There was spaghetti all over the inside of the car that I assume is from your carrying out leftovers. Where did you go that night?"

She looked me in the eye. "Antonio's."

"In Stafford?"

She nodded.

"Why did you lie?"

"Because I don't want to talk about it. It's nobody's business where I went."

"Who were you with?"

She shook her head. "It's not germane."

"It was Carrie Grethen, wasn't it? And some weeks ago she

had convinced you to participate in a little research project, which is why you got in so much trouble. In fact, she was stirring the liquid rubber when I came to see you at ERF."

My niece looked away.

"Why won't you tell me the truth?"

A tear slid down her cheek. To discuss Carrie with her was hopeless, and taking a deep breath, I went on, "Lucy, I think somebody tried to run you off the road."

Her eyes widened.

"I've looked at the car and where it happened, and there are many details that disturb me a great deal. Do you remember dialing Nine-one-one?"

"No. Did I?" She looked bewildered.

"Whoever used the phone last did, and I'll assume that was you. A state police investigator is tracking down the tape, and we'll see exactly when the call was made and what you said."

"My God."

"Plus, there are indications that someone may have been on your rear with lights on high. You had the night mirror flipped on and the sunscreen up. And the only reason I can imagine you might have the sunscreen up on a dark highway was that light was coming in the back windshield making it difficult to see." I paused, studying her shocked face. "You don't remember any of this?"

"No."

"Do you remember anything about a car that may have been green? Perhaps a pale green?"

"No."

"Do you know anybody who has a car that color?"

"I'll have to think."

"Does Carrie?"

She shook her head. "She has a BMW convertible. It's red."

"What about a man she works with? Has she ever mentioned someone named Jerry to you?"

"No."

"Well, a vehicle left greenish paint on a damaged area on the rear of my car and took out the taillight, too. The long and short of it is that after you left Green Top, somebody followed you and hit you from the rear.

"Then several hundred feet later you suddenly accelerated, lost control of the car, and went off the road. My conjecture is that you accelerated about the same time you dialed Nine-one-one. You were frightened, and it may be that the person who struck you was on your tail again."

Lucy pulled the covers up around her chin. She was pale. "Someone tried to kill me."

"It looks to me like someone almost did kill you, Lucy. Which is why I've asked what seem very personal questions. Someone's going to ask them. Wouldn't you rather tell me?"

"You know enough."

"Do you see a relation between what's happened to you at ERF and this?"

"Of course I do," she said with feeling. "I was set up, Aunt Kay. I never went inside the building at three A.M. I never stole any secrets!"

"We must prove that."

She stared hard at me. "I'm not sure you believe me."

I did, but I could not tell her that. I could not tell her about my meeting with Carrie. I had to muster all the discipline I could to be lawyerly with my niece right then because I knew it would be wrong to lead her.

"I can't really help if you don't talk freely to me," I said. "I'm doing my best to keep an open mind and clear head so I can do the right thing. But frankly, I don't know what to think."

"I can't believe you would . . . Well, fuck it. Think what you want." Her eyes filled with tears.

"Please don't be angry with me. This is a very serious matter we're dealing with, and how we handle it will affect the rest of your life. There are two priorities.

"The first is your safety, and after hearing what I've just told you about your accident, maybe you have a better idea why I want you in the treatment center. No one will know where you are. You will be perfectly safe. The other priority is to get you out of these snarls so your future isn't jeopardized."

"I'll never be an FBI agent. It's too late."

"Not if we clear your name at Quantico and get a judge to reduce the DUI charge."

"How?"

"You asked for a big gun. Maybe you've got one."

"Who?"

"Right now all you need to know is your chances are good if you listen to me and do what I say."

"I'll feel like I'm being sent to a detention center."

"The therapy will be good for you for a lot of reasons."

"I'd rather stay here with you. I don't want to be labeled an alcoholic the rest of my life. Besides, I don't think I am one."

"Maybe you aren't. But you need to gain some insight into why you've been abusing alcohol."

"Maybe I just like the way it feels when I'm not here. Nobody's ever wanted me here anyway. So maybe it makes sense," she said bitterly.

We talked a while longer, then I spent time on the phone with airlines, hospital personnel, and a local psychiatrist who was a good friend. Edgehill, a well-respected treatment center in Newport, could admit her as early as the next afternoon. I wanted to take her, but Dorothy would not hear of it. This was a time when a mother should be with her daughter, she said, and my presence was neither necessary nor appropriate. I was feeling very out of sorts when the phone rang at midnight.

"I hope I didn't wake you," Wesley said.

"I'm glad you called."

"You were right about the print. It's a reversal. Lucy couldn't have left it unless she made the cast herself."

"Of course she didn't make it herself. My God," I said impatiently. "I was hoping this would be over, Benton."

"Not quite yet."

"What about Gault?"

"No sign of him. And the asshole at Eye Spy denies Gault was ever there." He paused. "You're sure you saw him?"

"I would swear to it in court."

I would have recognized Temple Gault anywhere. Sometimes I saw his eyes in my sleep, saw them bright like blue glass staring through a barely opened door leading into a strange, dark room filled with a putrid smell. I would envision Helen the prison guard in her uniform and decapitated. She was propped up in the chair where Gault had left her, and I wondered about the poor farmer who had made the mistake of opening the bowling bag he had found on his land.

"I'm sorry, too," Wesley was saying. "You can't imagine how sorry I am."

Then I told him I was sending Lucy to Rhode Island. I told him everything I could think of that I had not already told him, and when it was his turn to fill me in I switched the lamp off on the table by my bed and listened to him in the dark.

"It's not going well here. As I've said, Gault's vanished again. He's screwing with our minds. We don't know what he's involved in and what he isn't. We have this case in North Carolina and now one in England, and suddenly he shows up in Springfield and appears to be involved in the espionage that's gone on at ERF."

"There's no *appears to be* about it, Benton. He's been inside the Bureau's brain. The question is, what are you going to do about it?"

"At present, ERF's changing codes, passwords, that sort of thing. We're hoping he's not been in too deep."

"Hope on."

"Kay, Black Mountain's got a search warrant for Creed Lindsey's house and truck."

"Have they found him?"

"No."

"What does Marino have to say?" I asked.

"Who the hell knows?"

"You haven't seen him?"

"Not much. I think he's spending a lot of time with Denesa Steiner."

"I thought she was out of town."

"She's back."

"How serious is this with them, Benton?"

"Pete's obsessed. I've never seen him like this. I don't believe we're going to be able to pull him out of here."

"And you?"

"I'll probably be in and out for a while, but it's hard to say." He sounded discouraged. "All I can do is give my advice, Kay. But the cops are listening to Pete, and Pete's not listening to anybody."

"What does Mrs. Steiner have to say about Lindsey?"

"She says it could have been him in her house that night. But she really didn't get much of a look."

"His speech is distinctive."

"That's been mentioned to her. She says she doesn't remember much about the intruder's voice except that he sounded white."

"He also has a strong body odor."

"We don't know if he would have that night."

"I doubt his hygiene is good on any night."

"The point is, her not being sure only makes the case against him stronger. And the cops are getting all kinds of calls about him. He was spotted here and there doing suspicious things like staring at some kid he drove past. Or a truck like his was seen near Lake Tomahawk shortly after Emily disappeared. You know what happens when people make up their minds about something."

"What have you made up your mind about?" Darkness clung to me like a soft, comforting cover, and I was aware of the timbre of the tones in the sounds he made. He had a lean, muscular voice. Like his physique, it was very subtle in its beauty and power.

"This guy, Creed, doesn't fit, and I'm still disturbed about Ferguson. By the way, we got the DNA results and the skin was hers."

"No big surprise."

"Something just doesn't feel right about Ferguson."

"Do you know anything more about him?"

"I'm running down some things."

"And Gault?"

"We still have to consider him. That he did her." He paused. "I want to see you."

My eyelids were heavy and my voice sounded dreamy to me as I lay against my pillows in the dark. "Well, I've got to go to Knoxville. That's not very far from you."

"You're seeing Katz?"

"He and and Dr. Shade are running my experiment. They should be about finished."

"The Farm is one place I have no desire to visit."

"I guess you're saying you won't meet me there."

"That's not why I won't."

"You'll go home for the weekend," I said.

"In the morning."

"Is everything all right?" It was awkward to ask about his family, and rarely did either of us mention his wife.

"Well, the kids are too old for Halloween, so at least there are no parties or costume making to worry about."

"No one's ever too old for Halloween."

"You know, trick-or-treating used to be a big production in my house. I had to drive the kids around and all that."

"You probably carried a gun and X-rayed their candy."

"You're one to talk," he said.

[illegible]

[illegible] and not once sounded directly to me [illegible]

[illegible]

17

In the early hours of Saturday morning I packed for Knoxville and helped Dorothy put together the appropriate accoutrements for someone going where Lucy was. It was not easy to make my sister understand that Lucy would need no clothing that was expensive or required dry cleaning or ironing. When I emphasized that nothing valuable should be taken, Dorothy got quite upset.

"Oh my God. It's like she's going off to a penitentiary!"

We were working in the bedroom where she was staying so we would not wake Lucy.

I tucked a folded sweatshirt into the suitcase open on the bed. "Listen, I don't even recommend taking expensive jewelry when you're staying in a fine hotel."

"I have a lot of expensive jewelry and stay in fine hotels all the time. The difference is I don't have to worry about drug addicts being down the hall."

"Dorothy, there are drug addicts everywhere. You don't have to go to Edgehill to find them."

"She's going to pitch a fit when she finds out she can't have her laptop."

"I'll explain to her that it's not allowed, and I am confident she'll understand."

"I think it's very rigid on their part."

"The point of Lucy's being there is to work on herself, not on computer programs."

I picked up Lucy's Nikes and thought of the locker room at Quantico, of her being muddy from head to toe and bleeding and burned from running the Yellow Brick Road. She had seemed so happy then, and yet she could not have been. I felt sick that I had not known of her difficulties earlier. If only I had spent more time with her, maybe none of this would have happened.

"I still think it's ridiculous. If I had to go to a place like that, they certainly couldn't stop me from doing my writing. It's my best therapy. It's just a shame Lucy doesn't have something like that because if she did I'm convinced she wouldn't have so many problems. Why didn't you pick the Betty Ford Clinic?"

"I see no reason to send Lucy to the West Coast, and it takes longer to get in."

"I suppose they would have quite a waiting list." Dorothy looked thoughtful as she folded a pair of faded jeans. "Imagine, you might end up spending a month with movie stars. Why, you might end up in love with one of them and next thing you know you're living in Malibu."

"Meeting movie stars is not what Lucy needs right now," I said irritably.

"Well, I just hope you know that she's not the only one who has to worry about how this looks."

I stopped what I was doing and stared at her. "Sometimes I'd like to slap the hell out of you."

Dorothy looked surprised and slightly frightened. I had never shown her the full range of my rage. I had never held up a mirror to her narcissistic, niggling life so she could see herself as I did. Not that she would have, and that, of course, was the problem.

"You're not the one who has a book about to come out. We're talking days, and then I'm on tour again. And what am I supposed to say when some interviewer asks about my daughter? How do you think my publisher is going to feel about this?"

I glanced around to see what else needed to go into the suitcase. "I really don't give a damn how your publisher feels about this. Frankly, Dorothy, I don't give a damn how your publisher feels about anything."

"This could actually discredit my work," she went on as if she had not heard me. "And I *will* have to tell my publicist so we can figure out the best strategy."

"You will not breathe a word about Lucy to your publicist."

"You are getting very violent, Kay."

"Maybe I am."

"I suppose that's an occupational hazard when you cut people up all the livelong day," she snapped.

Lucy would need her own soap because they wouldn't have what she liked. I went into the bathroom and got her bars of Lazlo mud soap and Chanel as Dorothy's voice followed me. I went into the bedroom where Lucy was and found her sitting up.

"I didn't know you were awake." I kissed her. "I'm heading out in a few minutes. A car will be coming a little later to get you and your mother."

"What about the stitches in my head?"

"They can come out in a few more days and someone in the infirmary will take care of it. I've already discussed these things with them. They're very aware of your situation."

"My hair hurts." She made a face as she touched the top of her head.

"You've got a little nerve damage. It will go away eventually."

I drove to the airport through another dreary rain. Leaves

covered pavement like soggy cereal, and the temperature had dropped to a raw fifty-two degrees.

I flew to Charlotte first, for it did not seem possible to go anywhere from Richmond without stopping in another city that wasn't always on the way. When I arrived in Knoxville many hours later, the weather was the same but colder, and it had gotten dark.

I got a taxi, and the driver, who was local and called himself Cowboy, told me he wrote songs and played piano when he wasn't in a cab. By the time he got me to the Hyatt, I knew he went to Chicago once a year to please his wife, and that he regularly drove ladies from Johnson City who came here to shop in the malls. I was reminded of the innocence people like me had lost, and I gave Cowboy an especially generous tip. He waited while I checked into my room, then took me to Calhoun's, which overlooked the Tennessee River and promised the best ribs in the USA.

The restaurant was extremely busy, and I had to wait at the bar. It was the University of Tennessee's homecoming weekend, I discovered, and everywhere I looked I found jackets and sweaters in flaming orange, and alumni of all ages drinking and laughing and obsessing about this afternoon's game. Their raucous instant replays rose from every corner, and if I did not focus on any one conversation, what I heard was a constant roar.

The Vols had beat the Gamecocks, and it had been a battle as serious as any fought in the history of the world. When men in UT hats on either side occasionally turned my way for agreement, I was very sincere in my nods and affirmations, for to admit in that room that I had not *been there* would surely come across as treason. I was not taken to my table until close to ten P.M., by which time my anxiety level was quite high.

I ate nothing Italian or sensible this night, for I had not eaten well in days and finally I was starving. I ordered baby back ribs, biscuits, and salad, and when the bottle of Tennessee

Sunshine Hot Pepper Sauce said "Try Me," I did. Then I tried the Jack Daniel's pie. The meal was wonderful. Throughout it I sat beneath Tiffany lamps in a quiet corner looking out at the river. It was alive with lights reflected from the bridge in varying lengths and intensities, as if the water were measuring electronic levels for music I could not hear.

I tried not to think about crime. But blaze orange burned like small fires around me, and then I would see the tape around Emily's little wrists. I saw it over her mouth. I thought of the horrible creatures housed in Attica and of Gault and people like him. By the time I asked the waiter to call for my cab, Knoxville seemed as scary as any city I had ever been in.

My unease grew only worse when I found myself waiting outside on the porch for fifteen minutes, then half an hour, waiting for Cowboy to come. But it seemed he had ridden off to other horizons, and by midnight I was stranded and alone watching waiters and cooks go home.

I went back into the restaurant one last time.

"I've been waiting for the taxi you called for more than an hour now," I said to a young man cleaning up the bar.

"It's homecoming weekend, ma'am. That's the problem."

"I understand, but I must get back to my hotel."

"Where are you staying?"

"The Hyatt."

"They have a shuttle. Want me to try it for ya?"

"Please."

The shuttle was a van, and the chatty young driver asked all about a football game I never saw as I thought how easy it would be to find yourself helped by a stranger who was a Bundy or a Gault. That was how Eddie Heath had died. His mother sent him to a nearby convenience store for a can of soup, and hours later he was naked and maimed with a bullet in his head. Tape was used in his case, too. It could have been any color because we never saw it.

Gault's weird little game had included taping Eddie's wrists after he was shot, and then removing the tape before dumping the body. We were never clear on why he had done this. Rarely were we clear on so many things that were manifestations of aberrant fantasies. Why a hangman's noose versus a simple, safer slip knot? Why a duct tape that was blaze orange? I wondered if that bright orange tape was something Gault would use, and felt it was. He certainly was flamboyant. He certainly loved bondage.

Killing Ferguson and placing Emily's skin in the freezer also sounded like him. But sexually molesting her did not, and that had continued to nag at me. Gault had killed two women and had shown no sexual interest in them. It was the boy he had stripped and bitten. It was Eddie he had impulsively snatched so he could have his perverted fun. It was another boy in England, or so it seemed now.

Back at the hotel, the bar was jammed and there were many lively people in the lobby. I heard much laughter on my floor as I quietly returned to my room, and I was contemplating turning on a movie when my pager began to vibrate on the dresser. I thought Dorothy was trying to get hold of me, or perhaps Wesley was. But the number displayed began with 704, which was the area code for western North Carolina. Marino, I thought, and I was both startled and thrilled. I sat on the bed and returned the call.

"Hello?" a woman's soft voice asked.

For a moment, I was too confused to speak.

"Hello?"

"I'm returning a page," I said. "Uh, this number was on my pager."

"Oh. Is this Dr. Scarpetta?"

"Who is this?" I demanded, but I already knew. I had heard the voice before in Judge Begley's chambers and in Denesa Steiner's house.

"This is Denesa Steiner," she said. "I apologize for calling so late. But I'm just so glad I got you."

"How did you get my pager number?" I did not have it on my business card because I would be bothered all the time. In fact, I did not let many people have it.

"I got it from Pete. From Captain Marino. I've been having just such a hard time and I told him I thought it would help if I could talk to you. I'm so sorry to bother you."

I was shocked that Marino would have done such a thing, and it was just one more example of how much he had changed. I wondered if he was with her now. I wondered what could be so important that she would page me at this hour.

"Mrs. Steiner, what can I help you with?" I asked, for I could not be ungracious to this woman who had lost so much.

"Well, I heard about your car wreck."

"Excuse me?"

"I'm just so grateful you're all right."

"I wasn't the person in the accident," I said, perplexed and unsettled. "Someone else was driving my car."

"I'm so glad. The Lord is looking after you. But I had a thought that I wanted to pass on—"

"Mrs. Steiner," I interrupted her, "how did you know about the accident?"

"There was a mention of it in the paper here and my neighbors were talking about it. People know you've been here helping Pete. You and that man from the FBI, Mr. Wesley."

"What exactly did the article say?"

Mrs. Steiner hesitated as if embarrassed. "Well, I'm afraid it indicated that you were arrested for being under the influence, and that you'd run off the road."

"This was in the Asheville paper?"

"And then it ended up in the *Black Mountain News* and someone heard it on the radio, too. But I'm just so relieved you're okay. You know, accidents are terribly traumatic, and unless you've been in one yourself, you can't imagine how it feels. I was in a very bad one when I lived in California, and I still have nightmares about it."

"I'm sorry to hear that," I told her, because I did not know what else to say. I was finding this entire conversation bizarre.

"It was at night and this man changed lanes and I guess I was in his blind spot. He hit me from behind and I lost control of the car. I ended up cutting across the other lanes and hitting another car. That person was killed instantly. A poor old woman in a Volkswagen. I've never gotten over it. Memories like that certainly can scar you."

"Yes," I said. "They can."

"And when I think about what happened to Socks. I suppose that's really why I called."

"Socks?"

"You remember. The kitten he killed."

I was silent.

"You see, he did that to me and as you know I've gotten phone calls."

"Are you still getting them, Mrs. Steiner?"

"I've gotten a few. Pete wants me to get Caller I.D."

"Maybe you should."

"What I'm trying to say is these things have been happening to me, and then to Detective Ferguson, and Socks, and then you have the accident. So I'm worried it's all connected. I've certainly been telling Pete to look over his shoulder, too, especially after he tripped yesterday. I'd just mopped the kitchen floor and his feet went right out from under him. It's like some kind of curse straight out of the Old Testament."

"Is Marino all right?"

"He's a little bruised. But it could have been bad since he usually has that big gun stuck in the back of his pants. He's such a fine man. I don't know what I'd do without him these days."

"Where is he?"

"I imagine he's asleep," she said, and I was beginning to see how skillful she was at evading questions. "I'll be glad to tell him to call you if you'll tell me where he can reach you."

"He has my pager number," I said, and I sensed in her pause that she knew I did not trust her.

"Well, that's right. Of course he does."

I did not sleep well after that conversation, and finally called Marino's pager. My phone rang minutes later and immediately stopped before I could pick it up. I dialed the front desk.

"Did you just try to put a call through for me?"

"Yes, ma'am. I guess the person hung up."

"Do you know who it was?"

"No, ma'am. I'm sorry, but I wouldn't have any idea."

"Was it a man or a woman?"

"It was a woman who asked for you."

"Thank you."

Fright jolted me wide awake as I realized what had happened. I thought of Marino asleep in her bed with the pager on a table, and the hand I saw reach for it in the dark was hers. She had read the number displayed and gone into another room to call it.

When she had discovered it was for the Hyatt in Knoxville, she asked for me to see if I were a guest. Then she hung up as the desk rang my room, because she did not want to talk to me. She simply wanted to know where I was, and now she did. Damn! Knoxville was a two-hour drive from Black Mountain. Well, she wouldn't come here, I reasoned. But I could not shake how unsettled I felt, and I was afraid to follow my thoughts into the dark places they were trying to creep.

I started making calls as soon as the sun rose. The first was to Investigator McKee with the Virginia State Police, and I could tell by his voice that I had awakened him from a deep sleep.

"It's Dr. Scarpetta. I'm sorry to call so early," I said.

"Oh. Hold on a minute." He cleared his throat. "Good morning. Listen, it's a good thing you called. I've got some information for you."

"That's wonderful," I said, enormously relieved. "I was hoping you would."

"Okay. The taillight is made out of methylacrylate like most of them are these days, but we were able to fracture-match pieces back to the single unit you removed from your Mercedes. Plus there was a logo on one of these pieces that identified it as being from a Mercedes."

"Good," I said. "That's what we suspected. What about the headlight glass?"

"It's a little trickier, but we got lucky. They analyzed the headlight glass you recovered, and based on its refraction index, density, design, logo, and so on, we know it came from an Infiniti J30. And that helped us narrow down possibilities for the origin of the paint. When we started looking at Infiniti J30s, there's a model painted a pale green called Bamboo Mist. To make a long story short, Dr. Scarpetta, you got hit by a '93 Infiniti J30 painted Bamboo Mist green."

I was shocked and confused. "My God," I muttered as chills swept up my body.

"Is that familiar?" He sounded surprised.

"This can't be right." I had blamed Carrie Grethen and had threatened her. I had been so sure.

"You know someone who has a car like that?" he asked.

"Yes."

"Who?"

"The mother of the eleven-year-old girl who was murdered in western North Carolina," I answered. "I'm involved in that case and have had several contacts with the woman."

McKee did not respond. I knew what I was saying sounded crazy.

"She also was not in Black Mountain when the accident occurred," I went on. "She supposedly had headed north to visit a sick sister."

"Her car should be damaged," he said. "And if she's the one

who did this, you can bet she's already getting it fixed. In fact, it may already be fixed."

"Even if it is, the paint left on my car could be matched back to it," I said.

"We'll hope so."

"You sound doubtful."

"If the paint job on her car is original and has never been touched up since it came off the assembly line, we could have a problem. Paint technology's changed. Most car manufacturers have gone to a clear base coat, which is a polyurethane enamel. Even though it's cheaper, it looks really rich. But it's not as many layers, and what's unique in vehicle paint identification is the layer sequence."

"So if ten thousand Bamboo Mist Infinitis came off the assembly line at the same time, we're screwed."

"Big-time screwed. A defense attorney will say you can't prove the paint came from her car, especially since the accident occurred on an interstate that's used by people from all over the country. So it won't even do any good to try to find out how many Infinitis painted that color were shipped to certain regions. And she's not from the area where the accident occurred, anyway."

"What about the Nine-one-one tape?" I asked.

"I've listened to it. The call was made at eight forty-seven P.M., and your niece said, "This is an emergency." That's as much as she got out before she was cut off by a lot of noise and static. She sounded like she was in a panic."

The story was awful, and I felt no better when I called Wesley at home and his wife answered.

"Hold on, and I'll get him to the phone." She was as friendly and gracious as she had always been.

I had weird thoughts while I waited. I wondered if they slept in separate bedrooms, or if she simply had gotten up earlier than he had and this was why she had to go someplace to tell him I was on the phone.

Of course, she might be in their bed and he was in the bathroom. My mind spun on, and I was unnerved by what I was feeling. I liked Wesley's wife, and yet I did not want her to be his wife. I did not want anyone to be his wife. When he got on the phone, I tried to talk calmly but did not succeed.

"Kay, wait a minute," he said, and he sounded as if I had awakened him, too. "Have you been up all night?"

"More or less. You've got to get back out there. We can't rely on Marino. If we even try to contact him, she'll know."

"You can't be certain it was her who called your pager."

"Who else could it have been? No one knows I'm here, and I'd just left the hotel number on Marino's pager. It was only minutes before I got called back."

"Maybe it was Marino who called."

"The clerk said it was a woman's voice."

"Dammit," Wesley said. "Today is Michele's birthday."

"I'm sorry." I was about to cry and didn't know why. "We've got to find out if Denesa Steiner's car has been damaged. Someone's got to go look. I've got to know why she was after Lucy."

"Why would she go after Lucy? How could she have known where Lucy was going to be that night and what kind of car she would be in?"

I recalled Lucy telling me that Marino had advised her on her gun purchase. It may have been that Mrs. Steiner overheard their telephone conversation, and I voiced this theory to Wesley.

"Did Lucy have a time when she was going to be there, or did she impulsively stop there on her way back from Quantico?" he asked.

"I don't know, but I'll find out." I began to shake with rage. "The bitch. Lucy could have been killed."

"Christ, *you* could have been killed."

"The goddam bitch."

"Kay, be still and listen to me." He said the words slowly

and in a way that was meant to soothe. "I will get back down to North Carolina and see what the hell's going on. We'll get to the bottom of this. I promise. But I want you to get out of that hotel as soon as you can. How long are you supposed to be in Knoxville?"

"I can leave after I meet Katz and Dr. Shade at the Farm. Katz is picking me up at eight. God, I hope it isn't still raining. I haven't even looked out the window yet."

"It's sunny here," he said as if that meant it had to be sunny in Knoxville. "If something comes up and you decide not to leave, then change hotels."

"I will."

"Then go back to Richmond."

"No," I said. "I can't do anything about this in Richmond. And Lucy's not there. At least I know she's safe. If you talk to Marino, don't tell him anything about me. Don't breathe a word about where Lucy is. Just assume he will tell Denesa Steiner. He's out of control, Benton. He's confiding in her now, I know it."

"I don't think it would be wise for you to come to North Carolina right now."

"I've got to."

"Why?"

"I've got to find Emily Steiner's old medical records. I need to go through all of them. I also want you to find out for me every place Denesa Steiner has lived. I want to know about other children or husbands and siblings. There may be other deaths. There may be other exhumations we have to do."

"What are you thinking?"

"For one thing, I'll bet you'll find there is no sick sister who lives in Maryland. Her purpose in driving north was to run my car off the road and hope Lucy died."

Wesley did not say anything. I sensed his equivocation and did not like it. I was afraid to say what was really on my mind, but I could not be silent.

"And so far there's no record of the SIDS. Her first child. Vital Records can't find anything about that in California. I don't think the child ever existed, and that fits the pattern."

"What pattern?"

"Benton," I said, "we don't know that Denesa Steiner didn't kill her own daughter."

He let out a deep breath. "You're right. We don't know that. We don't know much."

"And Mote pointed out in the consultation that Emily was sickly."

"What are you getting at?"

"Munchausen's by proxy."

"Kay, no one will want to believe that. I don't think I want to believe that."

It is an almost unbelievable syndrome in which primary care givers—usually mothers—secretly and cleverly abuse their children to get attention. They cut their flesh and break their bones, poison and smother them almost to death. Then these women rush to doctors' offices and emergency rooms and tell teary tales of how their little one got sick or hurt, and the staff feels so sorry for Mother. She gets so much attention. She becomes a master at manipulating medical professionals and her child may eventually die.

"Imagine the attention Mrs. Steiner has gotten because of her daughter's murder," I said.

"I won't argue that. But how would Munchausen's explain Ferguson's death or what you're alleging happened to Lucy?"

"Any woman who could do what was done to Emily could do anything to anyone. Besides, maybe Mrs. Steiner is running out of relatives to kill. I'll be surprised if her husband really died of a heart attack. She probably killed him in some disguised, subtle manner, too. These women are pathological liars. They are incapable of remorse."

"What you're suggesting goes beyond Munchausen's. We're talking serial killings now."

"Cases aren't always one thing, because people aren't always one thing, Benton. You know that. And women serial killers often murder husbands, relatives, significant others. Their methods are usually different from those of male serial killers. Women psychopaths don't rape and strangle people. They like poisons. They like to smother people who can't defend themselves because they're either too young or too old or incapacitated for some other reason. The fantasies are different because women are different from men."

"No one around her is going to want to believe what you're proposing," Wesley said. "It will be hell to prove, if you're right."

"Cases like this are always hell to prove."

"Are you suggesting I present this possibility to Marino?"

"I hope you won't. I certainly don't want Mrs. Steiner privy to what we're thinking. I need to ask her questions. I need her to cooperate."

"I agree," he said, and I knew it had to be very hard for him when he added, "Truth is, we really can't have Marino working this case any longer. At the very least, he's personally involved with a potential suspect. He may be sleeping with the killer."

"Just like the last investigator was," I reminded him.

He did not respond. Our shared fear for Marino's safety did not need to be said. Max Ferguson had died, and Denesa Steiner's fingerprint was on an article of clothing he was wearing at the time. It would have been so simple to lure him into unusual sex play and then kick the stool out from under him.

"I really hate for you to get more deeply into this, Kay," Wesley said.

"One of the complications of our knowing each other so well," I said. "I hate it, too. I wish you weren't, either."

"It's different. You're a woman and a doctor. If what you're thinking is right, you'll push her buttons. She's going to want to draw you into her game."

"She's already drawn me into it."

"She'll draw you in deeper."

"I hope she does." I felt the rage again.

He whispered, "I want to see you."

"You will," I said. "Soon."

18

The University of Tennessee's Decay Research Facility was simply known as The Body Farm, and had gone by that name for as long as I could remember. People like me intended no irreverence when we called it that, for no one respects the dead more than those of us who work with them and hear their silent stories. The purpose is to help the living.

That was the point when The Body Farm came into being more than twenty years before, when scientists got determined to learn more about time of death. On any given day its several wooded acres held dozens of bodies in varying stages of decomposition. Research projects had brought me here periodically over the years, and though I would never be perfect in determining time of death, I had gotten better.

The Farm was owned and run by the university's Anthropology Department, headed by Dr. Lyall Shade and oddly located in the basement of the football stadium. At 8:15, Katz and I went downstairs, passing the zooarchaeology mollusk and neotropical primates labs, and the tamarin and marmuses collection and strange projects named with roman numerals.

Many of the doors were plastered with Far Side cartoons and pithy quotations that made me smile.

We found Dr. Shade at his desk looking over fragments of charred human bone.

"Good morning," I said.

"Good morning, Kay," he said with a distracted smile.

Dr. Shade was well served by his name for more reasons than the apparent ironical one. It was true he communed with the ghosts of people past through their flesh and bones and what they revealed as they lay for months on the ground.

But he was unassuming and introverted, a very gentle spirit much older than his sixty years. His hair was short and gray, his face pleasant and preoccupied. Tall, he was hard bodied and weathered like a farmer, which was yet another irony, for Farmer Shade was one of his nicknames. His mother lived in a nursing home and made skull rings for him from fabric remnants. The ones he had sent to me looked like calico doughnuts, but they functioned very well when I was working with a skull, which is unwieldy and tends to roll no matter whose brain it once held.

"What have we got here?" I moved closer to bits of bone reminiscent of burned wood chips.

"A murdered woman. Her husband tried to burn her after he killed her, and did amazingly well. Better than any crematorium, really. But it was rather stupid. He built the fire in his own backyard."

"Yes, I would say that was rather stupid. But then so are rapists who drop their wallets as they leave the scene."

"I had a case like that once," said Katz. "Got a fingerprint from her car and was so proud until I was told the guy left his wallet in the backseat. The print wasn't needed much after that."

"How's your contraption doing?" Dr. Shade asked Katz.

"I won't get rich from it."

"He got a great latent from a pair of panties," I said.

"He was a *latent*, all right. Any man who'd dress like that." Katz smiled. He could be corny now and then.

"Your experiment's ready, and I'm eager to take a look." Shade got up from his chair.

"You haven't looked yet?" I asked.

"No, not today. We wanted you here for the final unveiling."

"Of course, you always do that," I said.

"And I always will unless you don't want to be present. Some people don't."

"I will always want to be present. And if I don't, I think I should change careers," I said.

"The weather really cooperated," Katz added.

"It was perfect." Dr. Shade was pleased to announce. "It was exactly what it must have been during the interval between when the girl vanished and her body was found. And we got lucky with the bodies because I needed two and thought that was never going to happen at the last minute. You know how it goes."

I did.

"Sometimes we get more than we can handle. Then we don't get any," Dr. Shade went on.

"The two we got are a sad story," Katz said, and we were going up the stairs now.

"They're all a sad story," I said.

"So true. So true. He had cancer and called to see if he could donate his body to science. We said yes, so he filled out the paperwork. Then he went into the woods and shot himself in the head. The next morning, his wife, who wasn't well, either, took a bottle of Nembutal."

"And they're the ones?" My heart seemed to lose its rhythm for a moment the way it often did when I heard stories like this.

"It happened right after you told me what you wanted to do," Dr. Shade said. "It was interesting timing, because I had no fresh bodies. And then the poor man calls. Well. The two of them have done some real good."

"Yes, they have." I wished I could somehow thank those poor sick people who had wanted to die because life was leaving in a way that was unbearably painful.

Outside we climbed into the big white truck with university seals and camper shell that Katz and Dr. Shade used to pick up donated or unclaimed bodies and bring them to where we were about to go. It was a clear, crisp morning, and had Calhoun's not taught me a lesson about the fierce loyalty of football fans, I would have called the sky Carolina blue.

Foothills rolled into the distant Smoky Mountains, trees around us blazed, and I thought of the shacks I had seen on that unpaved road near the Montreat gate. I thought of Deborah with her crossed eyes. I thought of Creed. At moments I could be overwhelmed by a world that was both so splendid and so horrible. Creed Lindsey would go to prison if I did not stop it from happening soon. I was afraid Marino would die, and I did not want my last vision of him to be like the one of Ferguson.

We chatted as we drove and soon passed farms for the veterinary school, and corn and wheat fields used for agricultural research. I wondered about Lucy at Edgehill and was afraid for her, too. I seemed to be afraid for anyone I loved. Yet I was so reserved, so logical. Perhaps my greatest shame was that I could not show what I should, and I worried no one would ever know how much I cared. Crows picked at the roadside, and sunlight breaking through the windshield made me blind.

"What did you think of the photographs I sent?" I asked.

"I've got them with me," said Dr. Shade. "We put a number of things under his body to see what would happen."

"Nails and an iron drain," said Katz. "A bottle cap. Coins and other metal things."

"Why metal?"

"I'm pretty sure of that."

"Did you have an opinion before your experiments?"

"Yes," said Dr. Shade. "She lay on something that began to oxidize. Her body did. After she was dead."

"Like what? What could have made that mark?"

"I really don't know. We'll know a lot more in a few minutes. But the discoloration that caused the strange mark on the little girl's buttock is from something oxidizing as she lay on top of it. That's what I think."

"I hope the press isn't here," said Katz. "I have a real hard time with that. Especially this time of year."

"Because of Halloween," I said.

"You can imagine. I've had them hung up in the razor wire before and end up in the hospital. Last time it was law school students."

We pulled into a parking lot that in warm months could be quite unpleasant for hospital employees assigned there. A tall unpainted wooden fence topped with coiled razor wire began where pavement ended, and beyond was The Farm. A trace of a foul odor seemed to darken the sun as we got out, and no matter how often I had smelled that smell, I never really got used to it. I had learned to block it without ignoring it, and I never diminished it with cigars, perfume, or Vicks. Odors were as much a part of the language of the dead as scars and tattoos were.

"How many residents today?" I asked as Dr. Shade dialed the combination of a large padlock securing the gate.

"Forty-four," he said.

"They've all been here for a while, except for yours," Katz added. "We've had the two of them exactly six days."

I followed the men inside their bizarre but necessary kingdom. The smell was not too bad because the air was refrigerator cold and most of the clients had been here long enough to have gone through their worst stages. Even so, the sights were abnormal enough that they always gave me pause. I saw a parked body sled, a gurney, and piles of red clay, and there were plastic-lined pits where bodies tethered to cinder blocks were submerged in water. Old rusting cars held foul surprises in their trunks or behind the wheel. A white Cadillac, for example, was being driven by a man's bare bones.

Of course, there were plenty of people on the ground, and they blended so well with their surroundings that I might have missed some of them were it not for a gold tooth glinting or mandibles gaping. Bones looked like sticks and stones, and words would never hurt anyone here again except for amputated limbs, whose donors, I hoped, were still among the living.

A skull grinned at me from beneath a mulberry tree, and the bullet hole between its orbits looked like a third eye. I saw a perfect case of pink teeth (probably caused by hemolysis, and still argued about at almost every forensic meeting). Walnuts were all around, but I would not have eaten one of them because death saturated the soil and body fluids streaked the hills. Death was in the water and the wind, and rose to the clouds. It rained death on the Farm, and the insects and animals were fed up with it. They did not always finish what they started, because the supply was too vast.

What Katz and Dr. Shade had done for me was to create two scenes. One was to simulate a body in a basement by monitoring the postmortem changes that take place in dark, refrigerated conditions. The other was to place a body outside in similar conditions for the same length of time.

The basement scene had been staged in the only building on the Farm, which was nothing more than a cinder-block shed. Our helper, the husband with cancer, had been placed on a cement slab inside, and a plyboard box had been built around him to protect him from predators and changes in the weather. Photographs had been taken daily, and Dr. Shade was showing them to me now. The first few days revealed virtually no change to the body. Then I began to note that the eyes and fingers were drying.

"Are you ready to do this?" Dr. Shade asked.

I returned the photographs to their envelope. "Let's take a look."

They lifted off the crate, and I squatted near the body to study it carefully. The husband was a small, thin man who had died with white stubble on his chin and a perfect Popeye tattoo of an anchor on an arm. After six days in his plyboard crypt, his eyes were sunken, his skin doughy, and there was discoloration of his left lower quadrant.

His wife, on the other hand, had not fared nearly so well, even though the weather conditions outside the hut were very similar to those inside. But it had rained once or twice, my colleagues said. At times she had been in the sun, and buzzard feathers nearby helped explain some of the damage I saw. The discoloration of her body was much more marked, the skin slipping badly and not the least bit doughy.

I silently observed her for a while in a wooded area not far from the shed, where she lay on her back, naked, on leaves from surrounding locust, hickory, and ironwood trees. She looked older than her husband and was so stooped and wizened by age that her body had reverted to a childlike androgynous state. Her nails were painted pink, and she had dentures and pierced ears.

"We've got him turned over if you want to look," Katz called out.

I went back to the shed and squatted by the husband again while Dr. Shade directed a flashlight at the marks on the back. The pattern left by an iron drain was easy to recognize, but those left by nails were straight red streaks that looked more like burns. It was the marks left by coins that fascinated us the most, especially one left by a quarter. Upon close scrutiny, I could barely make out the partial outline of an eagle left on the man's skin, and I got out Emily's photographs and made comparisons.

"What I've figured out," Dr. Shade said, "is the impurities in the metal cause the coin to oxidize unevenly while the body's on top of it. So you get blank spots, an irregular imprint, very much like a shoe print, which usually isn't complete, either, unless the weight is distributed uniformly and you're standing on a perfectly flat surface."

"Have they done image enhancement with the Steiner photographs?" Katz asked.

"The FBI labs are working on it," I said.

"Well, they can really be slow," Katz said. "They're so backed up, and it just gets worse all the time because there are so many more cases."

"And you know how it goes with budgets."

"Ours is already bare bones."

"Thomas, Thomas, that's a terrible pun."

In fact, I had personally paid for the plyboard in this experiment. I had offered to furnish an air conditioner, too, but because of the weather, that had not been needed.

"It's hard as hell to get politicians excited about what we do out here. Or about what you do, Kay."

"The problem is, the dead don't vote," I said.

"I've heard of cases where they did."

We drove back along Neyland Drive, and I followed the river with my eyes. At a bend in it I could see the top of the Farm's back fence peeking above trees, and I thought of the River Styx. I thought of crossing the water and ending up in that place as the husband and wife from our work had done. I thanked them in my mind, for the dead were silent armies I mustered to save us all.

"Too bad you couldn't have gotten here earlier," said Katz, who was always so kind.

"You missed quite a game yesterday," Dr. Shade added.

"I feel like I saw it," I said.

19

I did not follow Wesley's advice but returned to my same room at the Hyatt. I did not want to spend the rest of the day moving into someplace new when I had many calls to make and a plane to catch.

But I was very alert as I walked through the lobby and got on the elevator. I looked at every woman, and then remembered I should pay attention to men, too, for Denesa Steiner was very clever. She had spent most of her life in deceptions and incredible schemes, and I knew how intelligent evil could be.

I saw no one who caught my eye as I walked briskly to my room. But I got my revolver out of the briefcase I had checked in baggage. I had it next to me on the bed as I got on the phone. First, I called Green Top, and Jon, who answered, was very nice. He had waited on me many times, and I did not hesitate to ask pointed questions about my niece.

"I can't tell you how sorry I am," he said again. "I just couldn't believe it when I read the papers."

"She is doing well," I said. "Her guardian angel was with her that night."

"She's a special young lady. You must be proud of her."

It occurred to me that I was no longer sure, and the thought made me feel terrible. "Jon, I need to know several important details. Were you working when she came in that night and bought the Sig?"

"Sure. I'm the one who sold it to her."

"Did she get anything else?"

"An extra magazine, several boxes of hollow points. Uhhhh. I think they were Federal Hydra-Shok. Yup, pretty sure of that. Let's see. I also sold her an Uncle Mike's paddle holster, and the same ankle holster I sold to you last spring. A top-of-the-line Bianchi in leather."

"How did she pay?"

"Cash, and that surprised me a little, to be honest. Her bill was pretty high, as you might imagine."

Lucy had been good about saving money over the years, and I had given her a substantial check when she turned twenty-one. But she had charge cards, so I assumed she didn't use them because she didn't want a record of her purchase, and that didn't necessarily surprise me. She was afraid and very paranoid, as are most people who have been intensely exposed to law enforcement. For people like us, everybody is a suspect. We tend to overreact, look over our shoulders, and cover our tracks when we feel the slightest bit threatened.

"Did Lucy have an appointment with you or did she just stop in?" I asked.

"She had called first and said exactly when she would be here. In fact, she even called again to confirm."

"Did she talk to you both times?"

"No, just the first time. The second time Rick answered the phone."

"Can you tell me exactly what she said to you when she called the first time?"

"Not much. She said she'd been talking to Captain Marino,

who had recommended the Sig P230 and he had also recommended that she deal with me. As you may know, the captain and I fish together. Anyway, she asked if I would still be here around eight P.M. on Wednesday."

"Do you remember what day she called?"

"Well, it was just a day or two before she wanted to come in. I think it was the Monday before. And by the way, I asked her early on if she was twenty-one."

"Did she tell you she is my niece?"

"Yes, she did, and she sure reminded me a lot of you—even your voices sound alike. You both have sort of deep, quiet voices. But she really was very impressive on the phone. Extremely intelligent and polite. She seemed familiar with guns and clearly had done a fair amount of shooting. In fact, she told me that the captain's given her lessons."

I was relieved Lucy had identified herself as my niece. It told me she wasn't terribly concerned about my finding out she had purchased a gun. I supposed Marino eventually would have told me, too. I was sad only because she had not talked to me first.

"Jon," I went on, "you said she called a second time. Can you tell me about that? First of all, when was it?"

"That same Monday. Maybe a couple hours later."

"And she talked to Rick?"

"Very briefly. I remember I was waiting on a customer and Rick had answered the phone. He said it was Scarpetta and she couldn't remember when she told me we would meet. I said Wednesday at eight, which he relayed to her. And that was the end of it."

"Excuse me," I said. "She said *what*?"

Jon hesitated. "I'm not sure what you're asking."

"Lucy identified herself as *Scarpetta* when she called the second time?"

"That's what Rick told me. He just said it was Scarpetta on the line."

"Her last name is not Scarpetta."

"Jeez," he said after a startled pause. "You're kidding. I just assumed. Well, that's kinda weird."

I thought of Lucy paging Marino, who then returned her call, quite likely from the Steiner home. Denesa Steiner must have thought he was talking to me, and how simple it would have been for her to wait until Marino was out of the room and get directory assistance to give her the number for Green Top. Then all she had to do was call and ask the questions she did. It was an odd sense of relief mingled with fury I felt. Denesa Steiner had not attempted to kill Lucy, nor had Carrie Grethen or anyone else. The intended victim had been me.

I asked Jon one last question. "I don't want to put you on the spot, but did Lucy seem intoxicated when you waited on her?"

"If she had, I never would have sold her anything."

"What was her demeanor?"

"She was in a hurry but joking around and very nice."

If Lucy had been drinking as much as I suspected she had for months or longer, she could have had a .12 and seemed to function fine. But her judgment and reflexes would have been impaired. She would not have reacted as well to what happened on the road. I hung up and got the number for the *Asheville-Citizen Times*, and was told by the city desk that the name of the person who had written about the accident was Linda Mayfair. Fortunately, she was in, and momentarily I had her on the line.

"This is Dr. Kay Scarpetta," I said.

"Oh! Gosh, what can I do for you?" She sounded very young.

"I wanted to ask about a story you wrote. It was about an accident involving my car in Virginia. Are you aware that you were incorrect to say that I was driving and subsequently arrested for DUI?" I was very calm but firm.

"Oh, yes, ma'am. I'm really sorry, but let me tell you what

happened. Something brief about the wreck came over the wire very late the night of the accident. All it said was that the car, a Mercedes, was identified as yours and it was suspected the driver was you and alcohol was involved. I happened to be working late finishing up something else when the editor came over with the printout. He told me to run it if I could confirm that the driver was you. Well, by now we're on deadline and I didn't think there was a chance.

"Then out of the blue, a call gets rolled over to my desk. And it's this lady who says she's a friend of yours and is calling from a hospital in Virginia. She wants us to know that you were not badly injured in the accident. She thought we should know since Dr. Scarpetta—you—have colleagues still in our area working on the Steiner case. She says she doesn't want us hearing about the accident some other way and printing something that would alarm your colleagues when they pick up the paper."

"And you took the word of a stranger and ran a story like that?"

"She gave her name and number and both of them checked out. And if she wasn't someone familiar with you, how could she have known about the accident and that you have been here working on the Steiner case?"

She could have known all of that if she were Denesa Steiner and were in a phone booth in Virginia after attempting to kill me.

I asked, "How did you check her out?"

"I called the number right back and she answered, and it was a Virginia area code."

"Do you still have the number?"

"Gosh, I think so. It should be in my notepad."

"Will you look for it now?"

I heard pages flipping and a lot of shuffling around. A long minute passed, and she gave me the number.

"Thank you very much. I hope you've gotten around

to printing a retraction," I said, and I could tell she was intimidated. I felt sorry for her and did not believe she had intended harm. She was just young and inexperienced, and was certainly no match for a psychopath determined to play games with me.

"We ran a We Were Wrong the next day. I can send you a copy."

"That won't be necessary," I said as I recalled the reporters turning up at the exhumation. I knew who had tipped them off. Mrs. Steiner. She couldn't resist more attention.

The phone rang for a long time when I dialed the number the reporter had given me. Finally, it was answered by a man.

"Excuse me," I said.

"Hello?"

"Yes, I need to know where this phone is."

"Which phone. Yours or mine?" The man laughed. "'Cause if you don't know where yours is, you're in trouble."

"Yours."

"I'm at a pay phone outside a Safeway getting ready to call my wife to ask what kind of ice cream she wants. She forgot to tell me. The phone started ringing so I answered it."

"Which Safeway?" I asked. "Where?"

"On Cary Street."

"In *Richmond*?" I asked in horror.

"Yeah. Where are you?"

I thanked him and hung up and began pacing around the room. She had been to Richmond. Why? To see where I lived? Had she driven past my house?

I looked out at the bright afternoon, and the clear blue sky and vivid colors of the leaves seemed to say that nothing bad like this could happen. No dark power was at work in the world, and none of what I was finding out was real. But I always felt the same disbelief when the weather was exquisite, when snow was falling, or the city was filled with Christmas lights and music. Then morning after morning I would go into the morgue and there would be new cases. There would be people raped and shot, and killed in mindless accidents.

Before I vacated the room, I tried the FBI labs and was surprised the scientist I intended to leave a message for was in. But like so many of us who seemed to do nothing but work, weekends were for others.

"The truth is I've done all with it I can," he said of the image enhancement he had been working on for days.

"And nothing?" I asked, disappointed.

"I've filled it out a little. It's a little clearer, but I can't begin to recognize whatever it is that's there."

"How long will you be in the lab today?"

"For another hour or two."

"Where do you live?"

"Aquia Harbor."

I would not have enjoyed that commute every day, but a surprising number of Washington agents with families lived there and in Stafford and Montclair. Aquia Harbor was maybe a half hour drive from where Wesley lived.

"I hate to ask you this," I went on. "But it's extremely important that I get a printout of this enhancement as soon as I can. Is there any possibility you could drop one by Benton Wesley's house? Round trip, it would be about an hour out of your way."

He hesitated before saying, "I can do that if I leave now. I'll call him at home and get directions."

I grabbed my overnight bag. I did not return my revolver to my briefcase until I was at the Knoxville airport behind a shut door in the ladies' room. I went through the usual routine of checking that one bag and letting them know what was in it, and they marked it with the usual fluorescent orange tag, which brought to mind the duct tape again. I wondered why Denesa Steiner would have blaze orange duct tape and where she might have gotten it. I could see no reason for her to have any connection to Attica and decided as I crossed the tarmac to board the small prop plane that the penitentiary had nothing to do with this case.

I took my aisle seat and was completely caught up in my contemplations, so I did not notice the tension among the other twenty or so passengers until I was suddenly aware of police on board. One of them was saying something to a person on the ground, eyes darting furtively from face to face. Then my eyes did the same as I went into their mode. I knew the demeanor so well, and my mind went into gear as I wondered what fugitive they were looking for and what he might have done. I raced through what action I would take if he suddenly jumped out of his seat. I would trip him. I would tackle him from behind as he went past.

There were three officers panting and sweating, and one of them stopped right by me and his eyes dropped to my belt. His hand subtly dropped to his semiautomatic pistol and released the thumb snap. I did not move.

"Ma'am," he said in his most official police voice, "you're going to have to come with me."

I was shocked.

"Are those your bags under the seat?"

"Yes." Adrenaline was roaring through me. The other passengers were absolutely still.

The officer quickly stooped to pick up my purse and overnight bag, his eyes not leaving me. I got up and they led me out. All I could think was that someone had planted drugs in one of my bags. Denesa Steiner had, and I crazily looked around the tarmac and at the plate glass windows of the terminal. I looked for someone looking at me, a woman who was back in the shadows watching the latest dilemma she had caused me.

A member of the ground crew in a red jumpsuit pointed at me. "That's her!" he said excitedly. "It's on her belt!"

I suddenly knew what this was about.

"It's just a phone." I slowly raised my elbows so they could see beneath my suit jacket. Often when I wore slacks, I carried my portable phone on my belt so I didn't have to keep digging it out of my bags.

One of the officers rolled his eyes. The ground crewman looked horrified.

"Oh, no," he said. "It looked exactly like a nine-millimeter, and I've been around FBI agents before and she looks like one of them."

I just stared at him.

"Ma'am," one of the officers said, "do you have a firearm in either of these bags?"

I shook my head. "No, I do not."

"We're really sorry, but he thought you were wearing a gun on your belt, and when the pilots checked the passenger list, they didn't see anyone on it who was authorized to carry a gun on the plane."

"Did someone tell you I was wearing a gun?" I demanded of the man in the jumpsuit. "If so, who?" I glanced around some more.

"No. No one told me. I thought I saw it when you walked past," he lamely went on. "It's that black case it's in. I'm sure sorry."

"It's all right," I said, my graciousness strained. "You were just doing your job."

An officer said, "You can go back on the plane."

By the time I returned to my seat, I was trembling so violently my knees were almost knocking, and I felt eyes on me. I did not look at anyone as I tried to read the paper. The pilot was considerate enough to announce what had happened.

"She was armed with a nine-millimeter portable phone," he continued to explain the delay as everybody laughed.

This was one upset I could not blame on her, but I realized with stunning clarity that assuming she had caused it was automatic. Denesa Steiner was controlling my life. People I loved had become her pawns. She had come to dominate what I thought and did, and was always at my heels, and the revelation sickened me. It made me feel half crazy. A soft hand touched my arm and I jumped.

"We really feel bad about this," a flight attendant said quietly. She was pretty, with permed blond hair. "At least let us buy you a drink."

"No, thank you," I said.

"Would you like a snack? I'm afraid all we've got are peanuts."

I shook my head. "Don't feel bad. I would hope you would check out anything that might jeopardize the safety of your passengers." I talked on, saying exactly the right words as my mind soared in flight patterns that had nothing to do with where we were.

"It's nice of you to be such a good sport."

We landed in Asheville as the sun went down, and my briefcase quickly came off the one carousel in the small baggage department. I went back into a ladies' room and transferred my handgun to my purse, then I went out on the curb and got a cab. The driver was an old fellow in a knit cap that he had pulled below his ears. His nylon jacket was dingy and frayed around the cuffs, and his big hands looked raw on the wheel as he drove at a prudent speed and made sure I understood it was quite a distance to Black Mountain. He was worried on my behalf about the fare because it could be close to twenty dollars. I closed my eyes as they began to water, and I blamed it on the heat blasting to drive out the cold.

The roar inside the ancient red-and-white Dodge reminded me of the plane as we headed east toward a town that had been shattered without being aware of it. Its citizens could not even begin to understand what really had happened to a little girl walking home with her guitar. They could not comprehend what was happening to those of us who had been called in to help.

We were being destroyed one by one because the enemy had an uncanny ability to sense where we were weak and where we could be hurt. Marino was prisoner and weapons carrier for this woman. My niece, who was like my daughter, was head injured in a treatment center, and it was a miracle she had not died. A simple man who swept floors and sipped moonshine in the mountains was about to be lynched for a hideous crime he had not committed, and Mote would retire on disability, while Ferguson was dead.

The cause and effect of evil spread out like a tree that blocked all light inside my head. It was impossible to know where the wickedness had started and where it would end, and I was afraid to analyze too closely if one of its twisted limbs had caught me up. I did not want to think my feet might no longer be in contact with the ground.

"Ma'am, is there anything else I can do for you?" I was vaguely aware that the driver was speaking to me.

I opened my eyes. We were parked in front of the Travel-Eze, and I wondered how long we had been there.

"I hated to wake you. But it'd be a lot more comfortable to get in your bed instead of sitting out here. Maybe cheaper, too."

The same yellow-haired clerk welcomed me back as he checked me in. He asked me which side of the motel I'd like to be on. As I recalled, one side viewed the school where Emily had gone and the other offered a panorama of the interstate. It didn't matter because the mountains were all around, blazing in the day and black against the starry night sky.

"Just put me in nonsmoking, please. Is Pete Marino still here?" I asked.

"He sure is, though he don't come in much. Would you rather be next to him?"

"No, I'd rather not. He's a smoker and I'd like to be as far away from that as I can." This was not my reason, of course.

"Then I'll just put you on a different wing."

"That would be fine. And when Benton Wesley gets in, will you have him ring my room immediately?" Then I asked him to call a car rental company and have something with an air bag delivered to me early in the morning.

I went to my room and locked and chained the door and propped a chair beneath the knob. I kept my revolver on top of the toilet while I took a long, hot bath with several drops of Hermes perfuming the water. The fragrance stroked me like warm, loving hands, moving up my throat and face and lightly through my hair. For the first time in a while I felt soothed, and at intervals I ran more hot water and the perfume's sweet oily splashes swirled like clouds. I had pulled the shower curtain shut, and in this fragrant sauna I dreamed.

The times I had relived loving Benton Wesley could not be counted. I did not want to admit how often the images leaned against my thoughts until I could no longer resist giving myself up to their embrace. They were more powerful than anything I had ever known, and I had stored every detail of our first encounter here, though it had not happened exactly here. I had memorized the number of that room and would know it forever.

In truth, my lovers had been few, but they had all been formidable men who were not without sensitivity and a certain acceptance that I was a woman who was not a woman. I was the body and sensibilities of a woman with the power and drive of a man, and to take away from me was to take away from themselves. So they gave the best they had, even my ex-husband, Tony, who was the least evolved in the lot, and sexuality was a shared erotic competition. Like two creatures of equal strength who had found each other in the jungle, we tumbled and took as much as we gave.

But Benton was so different I still could not quite believe it. Our male and female pieces had interlocked in a manner unparalled and unfamiliar, for it was as if he was the other side of me. Or maybe we were the same.

I did not quite know what I had expected, and certainly I had imagined us together long before we were. He would be soft beneath his hard reserve, like a warrior sleepy and warm in a hammock tethered between mighty trees. But when we had begun to touch on the porch in the early morning, his hands had surprised me.

As his fingers undid clothing and found me, they moved as if they knew a woman's body as well as a woman did, and I felt more than his passion. I felt his empathy, as if he wanted to heal those places he had seen so hated and harmed. He seemed sorrowed by everyone who had ever raped or battered or been unkind—as if their collective sins had cost him the right to enjoy a woman's body as he was enjoying mine.

I had told him in bed that I had never known a man to truly enjoy a woman's body, that I did not like to be devoured or overpowered, which was why sex for me was rare.

"I can see why anyone would want to devour your body," he matter-of-factly had said in the dark.

"I can see why anyone would want to devour yours," I said with candor, too. "But people overpowering people is why you and I have the work we do."

"Then we won't use *devour* and *overpower* anymore. No more words like that. We'll come up with a new language."

The words of our new language came easily, and we had gotten fluent fast.

I felt much improved after my bath and rummaged through my carry-on bag for something new and different to wear. But that was an impossibility, and I put on the deep blue jacket, pants, and turtleneck sweater I had been wearing for days. The bottle of Scotch was low, and I sipped slowly as I watched the national news. Several times I thought of calling Marino's room, only to put the receiver down before I dialed. My thoughts traveled north to Newport, and I wanted to talk to Lucy. I resisted that impulse, too. If I could get through, it would not be good for her. She needed to concentrate on her treatment and not on what she had left at home. I called my mother instead.

"Dorothy's staying the night up there in the Marriott and flying back to Miami in the morning," she told me. "Katie, where are you? I've been trying you at home all day."

"I'm on the road," I said.

"Well, a lot that says. All this cloak-and-dagger stuff you do. But you would think you could tell your mother."

I could see her in my mind puffing a cigarette and holding the phone. My mother liked big earrings and bright makeup, and she did not look northern Italian like I did. She was not fair.

"Mother, how is Lucy? What has Dorothy said?"

"She says Lucy's queer, for one thing, and she blames it on you. I told her that was ridiculous. I told her just because you're never with men and probably don't like sex doesn't mean you're a homo. It's the same thing with nuns. Though I've heard the rumors—"

"Mother," I interrupted, "is Lucy okay? How was the trip to Edgehill? What was her demeanor?"

"What? She's a witness now? Her *demeanor*? The way you talk to your simple mother and don't even realize. She got drunk on the way up, if you want to know."

"I don't believe it!" I said, furious with Dorothy yet again. "I thought the point of Lucy being with her mother was so something like that wouldn't happen."

"Dorothy says that unless Lucy was drunk when they put her in detox, insurance won't pay. So Lucy drank screwdrivers on the plane the entire trip."

"I don't give a damn if insurance pays. And Dorothy isn't exactly poor."

"You know how she is about money."

"I will pay for anything Lucy needs. You know that, Mother."

"You talk as if you're Ross Perot."

"What else did Dorothy say?"

"All I know, in summary, is Lucy was in one of her moods and upset with you because you couldn't be bothered to take her to Edgehill. Especially since you picked it out and are a doctor and all."

I groaned, and it was like arguing with the wind. "Dorothy didn't want me to go."

"As usual, it's your word against hers. When are you coming home for Thanksgiving?"

Needless to say, when our conversation was ended, which simply meant I could take no more and got off the phone, my bath had been undone. I started to pour more Scotch, but stopped, because there was not enough alcohol in the world when my family made me angry. And I thought of Lucy. I put away the bottle and not many minutes later there was a knock on my door.

"It's Benton," his voice said.

We hugged for a long time, and he could feel my desperation in the way I clung to him. He led me over to the bed and sat beside me.

"Start from the beginning," he said, holding both my hands.

I did. When I was finished, his face held that impervious look I knew from work, and I was unnerved by it. I did not want that look in this room when we were alone.

"Kay, I want you to slow down. Do you realize the magnitude of our going forward with an accusation like that? We can't just close our minds off to the possibility that Denesa Steiner is innocent. *We just don't know.*

"And what happened on the plane should tell you that you're not being a hundred percent analytical. I mean, this really disturbs me. Some bozo on the ground crew's just being a hero, and you immediately think the Steiner woman's behind that, too; that she's screwing with your mind again."

"It isn't just my mind she's screwing with," I said, removing one of my hands from his. "She tried to kill me."

"Again, that's speculative."

"Not according to what I was told after making several phone calls."

"You can't prove it. I doubt you'll ever be able to prove it."

"We've got to find her car."

"Do you want to drive by her house tonight?"

"Yes. But I don't have a car yet," I said.

"I have one."

"Did you get the printout of the image enhancement?"

"It's in my briefcase. I looked at it." He got up and shrugged. "It meant nothing to me. Just a hazy blob that's been washed with a zillion shades of gray until it's now a denser, more detailed blob."

"Benton, we've got to do something."

He looked a long time at me and pressed his lips together the way he did when he was determined but skeptical. "That's why we're here, Kay. We're here to do something."

He had rented a dark red Maxima, and when we went outside, I realized that winter was not far off, especially here in the mountains. I was shivering by the time I got into the car, and I knew this was partially due to stress.

"How are your hand and leg, by the way?" I asked.

"Pretty much good as new."

"Well, that's rather miraculous, since they weren't new when you cut them."

He laughed, more out of surprise than anything else. At the moment, Wesley wasn't expecting humor.

"I've got one piece of information about the duct tape," he then said. "We've been looking into who from this area might have worked at Shuford Mills during the time the tape was manufactured."

"A very good idea," I said.

"There was a guy named Rob Kelsey who was a foreman there. He lived in the Hickory area during the time the tape was made, but he retired to Black Mountain five years ago."

"Does he live here now?"

"He is deceased, I'm afraid."

Damn, I thought. "What do you know about him?"

"White male, died at age sixty-eight of a stroke. Had a son in Black Mountain, which was why Kelsey wanted to retire here, I guess. The son's still here."

"Do you have his address?"

"I can get it." He looked over at me.

"What about the son's first name?"

"Same as his father's. Her house is right around this bend. Look how dark the lake is. It's like a tar pit."

"That's right. And you know Emily wouldn't have followed its shore at night. Creed's story verifies that."

"I'm not arguing. I wouldn't take that route."

"Benton, I don't see her car."

"She could be out."

"Marino's car is there."

"That doesn't mean they aren't out."

"It doesn't mean they are."

He said nothing.

The windows were lit up, and I felt as if she were home. I had no proof, no indication, really, but I sensed her sensing me, even if she was not conscious of it.

"What do you think they're doing in there?" I asked.

"Now, what do you think?" he said, and his meaning was clear.

"That's cheap. It's so easy to assume people are having sex."

"It's so easy to assume because it's so easy to do."

I was quite offended because I wanted Wesley to be deeper. "That surprises me, coming from you."

"It should not surprise you coming from them. That was my point."

Still, I was not sure.

"Kay, we're not talking about our relationship here," he added.

"I certainly didn't think we were."

He knew I wasn't telling the whole truth. Never had I

been so clear on why it is ill-advised for colleagues to have affairs.

"We should go back. There's nothing more we can do right now," he said.

"How will we find out about her car?"

"We will find out in the morning. But we've already found out something now. It's not there right this minute looking like it hasn't been in an accident."

The next morning was Sunday, and I woke up to bells tolling and wondered if I was hearing the small Presbyterian church where Emily was buried. I squinted at my watch and decided probably not, since it was only a few minutes past nine. I assumed their service would start at eleven, but then, I knew so little about what Presbyterians did.

Wesley was asleep on what I considered my side of the bed. That was perhaps our only incompatibility as lovers. We both were accustomed to the side of the bed farthest from the window or door an intruder was most likely to come in, as if the space of several feet of mattress would make all the difference in grabbing for your gun. His pistol was on his bedside table and my revolver was on mine. Odds were, if an intruder did come in, Wesley and I would shoot each other.

Curtains glowed like lamp shades, announcing a sunny day. I got up and ordered coffee sent to the room, then inquired about my rental car, which the clerk promised was on its way. I sat in a chair with my back to the bed so I would not be distracted by Wesley's naked shoulders and arms outside the tangled covers. I fetched the printout of the image enhancement, several coins, and a lens, and went to work. Wesley had been right when he'd said the enhancement seemed to do nothing but add more shades of gray to an indistinguishable blob. But the longer I looked at what had been left on the little girl's buttock, the more I began to see shapes.

The density of grayness was greatest in an off-center part of the incomplete circular mark. I could not say where the density would be in terms of the hours on a clock, because I did not know which way was up or down or sideways for the object that had begun to oxidize beneath her body.

The shape that interested me was reminiscent of the head of a duck or some other bird. I saw a dome, then a protrusion that looked like a thick beak or bill, yet this could not be the eagle on the back of a quarter because it was much too big. The shape I was studying filled a good fourth of the mark, and there was what appeared to be a slight dent in what would be the back of the bird's neck.

I picked up the quarter I was using and turned it over. I rotated it slowly as I stared, and suddenly the answer was there. It was so simple, so exact in its match, and I was startled and thrilled. The object that had begun to oxidize beneath Emily Steiner's dead body was indeed a quarter. But it had been face up, and the birdlike shape was the indentation of George Washington's eyes, and the bird's head and bill were our first president's proud pate and curl at the back of his powdered wig. This only worked, of course, if I turned the quarter so Washington was staring at the tabletop, his aristocratic nose pointed at my knee.

Where, I wondered, might Emily's body have been lying? I supposed any place might inadvertently have a quarter on the floor. But there had been traces of paint and pithwood, too. Where might one find pithwood and a quarter? Well, a basement, of course—a basement where something once had gone on that involved pithwood, paints, other woods like walnut and mahogany.

Perhaps the basement had been used for someone's hobby. Cleaning jewelry? No, that didn't seem to make sense. Someone who fixed watches? That didn't seem right, either. Then I thought of the clocks in Denesa Steiner's house and my pulse picked up some more. I wondered if her late husband had repaired clocks on the side. I wondered if he might have used the basement for that, and if he might have used pithwood to hold and clean small gears.

Wesley was breathing the deep, slow breaths of sleep. He brushed his cheek as if something had alighted there, then pulled the sheet up to his ears. I got out the phone book and looked for the son of the man who had worked at Shuford Mills. There were two Robert Kelseys, a junior and a Kelsey the third. I picked up the phone.

"Hello?" a woman asked.

"Is this Mrs. Kelsey?" I asked.

"Depends on whether you're looking for Myrtle or me."

"I'm looking for Rob Kelsey, Junior."

"Oh." She laughed, and I could tell she was a sweet, friendly woman. "Then you're not looking for me to begin with. But Rob's not here. He's gone on to the church. You know, some Sundays he helps with communion, so he has to head on early."

I was amazed as she divulged this information without asking who I was, and I was touched again that there were still places in the world where people were trusting.

"Which church might that be?" I asked Mrs. Kelsey.

"Third Presbyterian."

"And their service starts at eleven?"

"Just like it always has. Reverend Crow is mighty good, by the way, if you've never heard him. May I give Rob a message?"

"I'll try him later."

I thanked her for her help and hung up. When I turned around, Wesley was sitting straight up in bed staring sleepily at me. His eyes roamed around, stopping at the printout, coins, and lens on the table by my chair. He started laughing as he stretched.

"What?" I asked rather indignantly.

He just shook his head.

"It's ten-fifteen," I said. "If you're going to church with me you'd better hurry."

"Church?" He frowned.

"Yes. A place where people worship God."

"They have a Catholic church around here?"

"I have no idea."

He was very puzzled now.

"I'm going to a Presbyterian service this morning," I said. "And if you have other things to do, I might need a lift. As of an hour ago, my rental car still wasn't here."

"If I give you a lift, how will you get back here?"

"I'm not going to worry about that." In this town where people helped strangers on the phone, I suddenly felt like having few plans. I felt like seeing what might happen.

"Well, I've got my pager," Wesley said as he placed his feet on the floor and I got an extra battery from the charger plugged in near the TV.

"That's fine." I tucked my portable phone into my handbag.

20

Wesley dropped me off at the front steps of the fieldstone church a little early, but people were already arriving. I watched them get out of their cars and squint in the sun as they accounted for their children and doors thudded shut up and down the narrow street. I felt curious eyes on my back as I followed the stone walkway, veering off to the left toward the cemetery.

The morning was very cold, and though the sunlight was blinding, it felt thin, like a cool bed sheet against my skin. I pushed open the rusting wrought-iron gate that served no purpose, really, except to be respectful and ornamental. It would keep no one out and certainly there was no need to keep anybody in.

New markers of polished granite shone coldly, and very old ones tilted different ways like bloodless tongues speaking from the mouths of graves. The dead talked here, too. They spoke every time we remembered them. Frost crunched softly beneath my shoes as I walked to the corner where she was. Her grave was a raw, red clay scar from having been reopened and reclosed, and tears came to my eyes as I looked again at the monument with its sweet angel and sad epitaph.

> There is no other in the World—
> Mine was the only one.

But the line from Emily Dickinson held a different meaning for me now. I read it with a new mind and a totally different awareness of the woman who had selected it. It was the word *mine* that jumped out at me. *Mine.* Emily had had no life of her own but had been an extension of a narcissistic, demented woman with an insatiable appetite for ego gratification.

To her mother, Emily was a pawn as all of us were pawns. We were Denesa's dolls to dress and undress, hug and rip apart, and I recalled the inside of her house, its fluffs and frills and little girl designs on fabric. Denesa was a little girl craving attention who had grown up knowing how to get it. She had destroyed every life she had ever touched, and each time wept in the warm bosom of a compassionate world. Poor, poor Denesa, everyone said of this murderous maternal creature with blood on her teeth.

Ice rose in slender columns from the red clay on Emily's grave. I did not know the physics for a fact but concluded that when the moisture in the nonporous clay froze, it expanded as ice does and had nowhere to go but up. It was as if her spirit had gotten caught in the cold as it tried to rise from the ground, and she sparkled in the sun as pure crystal and water do. I realized with a wave of grief that I loved this little girl I knew only in death. She could have been Lucy, or Lucy could have been her. Both were not mothered well, and one had been sent back home, so far the other spared. I knelt and said a prayer, and with a deep breath turned back toward the church.

The organ was playing "Rock of Ages" as I walked in, because by now I was late and the congregation was singing the first hymn. I sat as inconspicuously in the back as I could but still caused glances and heads to turn. This was a church that would spot a stranger because it most likely had so few. The service moved on, and I blessed myself after prayer as a little boy in my pew stared while his sister drew on the bulletin.

Reverend Crow, with his sharp nose and black robe, looked like his name. His arms were wings as he gestured while he preached, and during more dramatic moments it almost seemed he might fly away. Stained-glass windows depicting the miracles of Jesus glowed like jewels, and fieldstone flecked with mica seemed dusted with gold.

We sang "Just As I Am" when it was time for communion, and I watched those around me to follow their lead. They did not file up to the front for the wafer and wine. Instead, ushers silently came down aisles with thimbles full of grape juice and small crusts of dry bread. I took what was passed to me, and everyone sang the doxology and benediction, and suddenly they were leaving. I took my time. I waited until the preacher was at the door alone, having greeted every parishioner; then I called him by name.

"Thank you for your meaningful sermon, Reverend Crow," I said. "I have always loved the story of the importunate neighbor."

"There is so much we can learn from it. I tell it to my children a lot." He smiled as he gripped my hand.

"It's good for all of us to hear," I agreed.

"We're so glad to have you with us today. I believe you must be the FBI doctor I've been hearing about. Saw you the other day on the news, too."

"I'm Dr. Scarpetta," I said. "And I'm wondering if you might point out Rob Kelsey? I hope he hasn't already left."

"Oh, no," the reverend said, as I had expected. "Rob helped with communion. He's probably putting things away." He looked toward the sanctuary.

"Would you mind if I tried to find him?" I asked.

"Not a bit. And by the way"—his face got sad—"we sure

do appreciate what you're trying to do around here. Not a one of us will ever be the same." He shook his head. "Her poor, poor mother. Some folks would turn on God after all she's been through. But no ma'am. Not Denesa. She's here every Sunday, one of the finest Christians I've ever known."

"She was here this morning?" I asked as a creepy feeling crawled up my spine.

"Singing in the choir like she always does."

I had not seen her. But there were at least two hundred people present and the choir had been in the balcony behind me.

Rob Kelsey, Jr., was in his fifties, a wiry man in a cheap blue pin-striped suit collecting communion glasses from holders in the pews. I introduced myself and was very worried I would alarm him, but he seemed the unflappable type. He sat next to me on a pew and thoughtfully tugged at an earlobe as I explained what I wanted.

"That's right," he said in a North Carolina drawl as thick as I'd heard yet. "Papa worked at the mill his whole entire life. They gave him a mighty nice console color TV when he retired and a solid gold pin."

"He must have been a fine foreman," I said.

"Well, he wasn't that until he got up in years. Before that he was their top box inspector and before that he was just a boxer."

"What did he do exactly? As a boxer, for example?"

"He'd see to it the rolls of tape was boxed, and then eventually he supervised everybody else doing it to make sure it was right."

"I see. Do you ever remember the mill manufacturing a duct tape that was blaze orange?"

Rob Kelsey, with his near crew cut and eyes dark brown, thought about the question. Recognition registered in the expression on his face. "Why, sure. I remember that because it was an unusual tape. Never seen it before or since. Believe it was for a prison somewhere."

"It was," I said. "But I'm wondering if a roll or two of it might have ended up local. You know, here."

"It wasn't supposed to. But these things happen because they get rejects and stuff like that. Rolls of tape that aren't just right."

I thought of the grease stains on the edges of the tape used to bind Mrs. Steiner and her daughter. Perhaps a run had gotten caught in a piece of machinery or had gotten greasy some other way.

"And generally, when you have items that don't pass inspection," I interpolated, "employees might take them or buy them for a bargain."

Kelsey didn't say anything. He looked a little perplexed.

"Mr. Kelsey, do you know of anyone your father might have given a roll of that orange tape to?" I asked.

"Only one person I know of. Jake Wheeler. Now, he passed on a while back, but before that he owned the Laundromat near Mack's Five-and-Dime. As I recollect, he also owned the drugstore on the corner."

"Why would your father give him a roll of the tape?"

"Well, Jake liked to hunt. I remember my daddy saying Jake was so afraid of getting shot out there in the woods by someone mistaking him for a turkey that no one wanted to go out with him."

I said nothing. I did not know where this was leading.

"He'd make too dadgum much noise and then wear reflector-type clothing in the blinds. He scared other hunters off all right. I don't think he ever shot a thing except squirrels."

"What does this have to do with the tape?"

"I'm pretty sure my daddy gave it to him as a joke. Maybe Jake was supposed to wrap his shotgun up in it or wear it on his clothes." Kelsey grinned, and I noticed that he was missing several teeth.

"Where did Jake live?" I asked.

"Near the Pine Lodge. Sort of halfway between downtown Black Mountain and Montreat."

"Any chance he might have passed on that roll of tape to someone else?"

Kelsey stared down at the tray of communion glasses in his hands, his brow wrinkled in thought.

"For example," I went on, "did Jake hunt with anybody else? Maybe someone else who might have had a need for the tape, since it was the blaze orange that hunters use?"

"I got no way to know if he passed it along. But I will tell you that he was close to Chuck Steiner. They went out looking for bear every season while the rest of us hoped they didn't find none. Don't know why anyone'd want a grizzle bear coming their way. And you shoot one and what're you expectin' to do with it except make it into a rug? You can't eat it 'less you're Daniel Boone and Mingo about to starve to death."

"Chuck Steiner was Denesa Steiner's husband?" I asked, and I did not let my voice show what I felt.

"He was. A mighty nice man, too. It just killed us all when he passed on. If we'd known he had such a bad heart, we would've sat on him more, made him take it easier."

"But he hunted?" I had to know.

"Oh, he sure did. I went out with him and Jake a number of times. Those two liked to go out in the woods. I always told 'em they ought to go to Aferca. That's where the big game is. You know, I personally couldn't shoot a stick bug."

"If that's the same as a praying mantis, you shouldn't shoot a stick bug. It would be bad luck."

"It's not the same thing," he said matter-of-factly. "A praying mantis is a whole 'nother insect. But I think the same way you do about that. No, ma'am, I wouldn't touch one."

"Mr. Kelsey, did you know Chuck Steiner well?"

"I knew him from huntin' and church."

"He taught school."

"He taught Bible at that private religious school. If I coulda sent my son there, I would'ave."

"What else can you tell me about him?"

"He met his wife in California when he was in the military."

"Did you ever hear him mention a baby that died? An infant girl named Mary Jo who may have been born in California?"

"Why, no." He looked surprised. "I always had the impression Emily was their only young'un. Did they lose a little baby girl, too? Oh me, oh my." His expression was pained.

"What happened after they left California?" I went on. "Do you know?"

"They came here. Chuck didn't like it out west, and he used to come here as a boy when his family vacationed. They generally stayed in a cabin on Gray Beard Mountain."

"Where is that?"

"Montreat. Same town where Billy Graham lives. Now the reverend's not here much, but I've seen his wife." He paused. "Did anybody tell you about Zelda Fitzgerald burning up in a hospital around here?"

"I know about that," I said.

"Chuck was real good about fixin' clocks. He did it for a hobby and eventually got to where he was fixin' all the clocks for the Biltmore House."

"Where did he fix them?"

"He went to the Biltmore House to fix those. But people in the area would bring theirs directly to him. He had a shop in his basement."

Mr. Kelsey would have talked all day, and I extricated myself as kindly as I could. Outside, I called Wesley's pager with my portable phone and left the police code 10-25, which simply meant "Meet me." He would know where. I was contemplating returning to the foyer to get out of the cold when I realized from the conversations of the few people still trickling out that they were members of the choir. I almost panicked. The very instant she entered my mind she was there. Denesa Steiner waited at the church door, smiling at me.

"Welcome," she said warmly with eyes as hard as copper.

"Good morning, Mrs. Steiner," I said. "Did Captain Marino come with you?"

"He's Catholic."

She had on a black wool coat that touched the top of her black T-strapped shoes, and she was pulling on black kid gloves. She wore no makeup except for a blush of color on her sensuous lips, her honey-blond hair falling in loose curls over her shoulders. I found her beauty as cold as the day, and I wondered how I ever could have felt sympathy for her or believed her pain.

"What brings you to this church?" she next asked. "There's a Catholic church in Asheville."

I wondered what else she knew about me. I wondered what Marino had told her. "I wanted to pay my respects to your daughter," I said, looking directly into her eyes.

"Well, now, isn't that sweet." Still smiling, she did not avert her gaze.

"Actually, it's good we just happened to run into each other," I said. "I need to ask you some questions. Perhaps it would be convenient if I did that now?"

"Here?"

"I would prefer your house."

"I was going to have BLTs for lunch. I just didn't feel like making a big Sunday dinner, and Pete's trying to cut back."

"I'm not interested in eating." I made very little effort to disguise my feelings. My heart was as hard as the expression on my face. She had tried to kill me. She had almost killed my niece.

"Then I guess I'll meet you there."

"I would appreciate a ride. I don't have a car."

I wanted to see her car. I had to see it.

"Mine's in the shop."

"That's unusual. It's quite new, as I recall." If my eyes had been lasers, they would have burned holes in her by now.

"I'm afraid I got a lemon and had to leave it at a dealership out of state. The thing conked out on me during a trip. I rode with a neighbor, but you're welcome to ride with us. She's waiting in her car."

I followed her down fieldstone steps and along a sidewalk to more steps. There were a few cars still parked along the street and one or two pulling away. Her neighbor was an elderly woman wearing a pink pillbox hat and a hearing aid. She was behind the wheel of an old white Buick, the heater blasting and gospel music on. Mrs. Steiner offered me the front seat and I refused. I did not want her behind my back. I wanted to see everything she did at all times, and I wished I had my .38. But it had not seemed right to take a gun to church, and it had not occurred to me that any of this would happen.

Mrs. Steiner and her neighbor chatted in the front seat and I was silent in the back. The trip lasted but a few minutes; then we were at the Steiner house, and I noted that Marino's car was in the same spot where it had been parked last night when Wesley and I had slowly driven past. I could not imagine what it would be like to see Marino. I had no idea what I would say or what his demeanor toward me would be. Mrs. Steiner opened her front door. We went in, and I noticed Marino's motel room and car keys on a Norman Rockwell plate on the foyer table.

"Where's Captain Marino?" I asked.

"Upstairs, asleep." She pulled off her gloves. "He wasn't feeling well last night. You know, there's a bug going around."

She unbuttoned her coat and lightly shook her shoulders to get out of it. She glanced away as she took it off as if she were accustomed to giving anybody interested an opportunity to look at breasts no matronly clothing could hide. The language of her body was seductive, and it was speaking for my benefit now. She was teasing me, but not for the same reasons she might tease a man. Denesa Steiner was flaunting herself. She was very competitive with women and this told me even more about what her relationship with Emily had been like.

"Maybe I should check on him," I said.

"Pete just needs to sleep. I'll take him up some hot tea and be right with you. Why don't you make yourself comfortable in the living room? Would you like coffee or tea?"

"Nothing, thank you," I said, and the silence in the house disturbed me.

As soon as I heard her go upstairs, I looked around. I went back into the foyer, slipped Marino's car keys in my pocket, and walked into the kitchen. To the left of the sink was a door leading outside. Opposite it was another one locked with a slide bolt. I slid back the bolt and turned the knob.

Cold musty air announced the basement, and I felt along the wall for a light switch. My fingers hit it and I flipped it up, flooding dark red painted wooden stairs. I went down them because I had to see what was there. Nothing was going to stop me, not even fear of her finding me. My heart was beating hard against my ribs as if it were trying to escape.

Chuck Steiner's worktable was still there, cluttered with tools and gears and an old clock face frozen in time. Pith buttons were scattered about, most of them imprinted with the greasy shapes of the delicate parts they once had cleaned and held. Some were on the concrete floor here and there, along with bits of wire, small nails and screws. Empty hulls of old grandfather clocks stood silent sentry in shadows, and I spotted ancient radios and televisions, too, along with miscellaneous furniture thick with dust.

Walls were white cinder block without windows, and arranged on an expansive pegboard were neat coils of extension cords and other cords and ropes of different materials and thicknesses. I thought of the macramé draped over furniture upstairs, of the intricate lacework of knotted cords covering armrests, chair backs, and cradling plants hanging from eye bolts in ceilings. I envisioned the noose with its hangman's knot that had been cut from Max Ferguson's neck. In retrospect, it seemed unbelievable no one had searched this basement before. Even as the police had looked for little Emily, she probably had been down here.

I pulled a string to turn on another light, but the bulb was burned out. I was still without a flashlight, and my heart was drumming so hard I almost couldn't breathe as I wandered. Near a wall stacked with firewood coated with cobwebs, I found another shut door leading outside. Near a water heater another door led to a full bathroom, and I switched on the light.

I looked around at old white porcelain spattered with paint. The toilet probably had not been flushed in years, for standing water had stained the bowl the color of rust. A brush with bristles stiff and bent like a hand was in the sink, and then I looked inside the tub. I found the quarter almost in the middle of it, with George Washington faceup, and I detected a trace of blood around the drain. I backed out as the door at the top of the stairs suddenly shut, and I heard the bolt slide. Denesa Steiner had just locked me in.

I ran in several directions, my eyes darting around as I tried to think what to do. Dashing to the door near the woodpile, I turned the lock on the knob, threw back the burglar chain, and suddenly found myself in the sunny backyard. I did not see or hear anyone, but I believed she was watching me. She had to know I would come out this way, and I realized with growing horror what was happening. She wasn't trying to trap me at all. She was locking me out of her house, making certain I couldn't come back upstairs.

I thought of Marino, and my hands were shaking so hard I almost couldn't get his keys out of my pocket as I ran around the corner to the driveway. I unlocked the passenger's door of his polished Chevrolet. The stainless steel Winchester was under the front seat where he always kept his shotgun.

The gun was as cold as ice in my hands as I ran back to the house, leaving the car door wide open. The front door was locked, as I had expected. But there were glass panes on either side of it and I tapped one with the butt of the gun. Glass shattered and lightly fell to carpet on the other side. Wrapping my scarf around my hand, I carefully reached inside and unlocked the door. Then I was running up carpeted stairs, and it was as if someone else were me or I had vacated my own mind. I was in a mode that was more machine than human. I remembered the room lit up last night and ran that way.

The door was shut, and when I opened it she was there, sitting placidly on the edge of the bed where Marino lay, a plastic trash bag over his head and taped around his neck. What happened next was simultaneous. I released the safety and racked the shotgun as she grabbed his pistol off the table and stood. Our guns raised together and I fired. The deafening blast hit her like a fierce gust of wind, and she fell back against the wall as I pumped and fired and pumped and fired again and again.

She slid down the wall, and blood streaked the girlish wallpaper. Smoke and burned powder filled the air. I ripped the bag off Marino's head. His face was blue and I felt no pulse in his carotids. I pounded his chest, blew into his mouth once, and compressed his chest four times, and he gasped. He began to breathe.

Grabbing the phone, I called 911 and screamed as if I were on a police radio during a mayday.

"Officer down! Officer down! Send an ambulance!"

"Ma'am, where are you?"

I had no idea of the address. "The Steiner house! Please hurry!" I left the phone off the hook.

I tried to sit Marino up in bed but he was too heavy.

"Come on. Come on."

I turned his face to one side and slipped my fingers under his jaw to keep it pulled forward so his airway would stay clear. I glanced around for pill bottles, for any indication of what she might have given him. Empty liquor glasses were on the table by the bed. I sniffed them and smelled bourbon, and I stared at her numbly. I saw blood and brains everywhere as I trembled like a creature in its agonal stages. I shook and twitched as if in the throes of death. She was slumped, almost sitting, with her back against the wall in a spreading puddle of blood. Her black clothes were soaked and riddled with holes, her head hanging to one side and dripping on the floor.

When sirens sounded they seemed to wail forever before I was aware of many feet hurrying upstairs, of the sounds of a stretcher banging and being unfolded, and then somehow Wesley was there. He put his arms around me and held me hard as men in jumpsuits surrounded Marino. Red and blue lights throbbed outside the window and I realized I had shot out the glass. Air blowing in was very cold. It stirred blood-spattered curtains of balloons flying free through a sky pale yellow. I looked at the ice-blue duvet and stuffed animals all around. There were rainbow decals on the mirror and a poster of Winnie the Pooh.

"It's her room," I told Wesley.

"It's all right." He stroked my hair.

"It's Emily's room," I said.

21

I left Black Mountain the next morning, which was a Monday, and Wesley wanted to go with me but I chose to go alone. I had unfinished business, and he needed to stay with Marino, who was in the hospital after having Demerol pumped out of his stomach. He would be fine, at least physically, then Wesley was bringing him to Quantico. Marino needed to be debriefed like an agent who's been under deep cover. He needed rest, security, and his friends.

On the plane I had a row to myself and made many notes. The case of Emily Steiner's murder had been cleared when I had killed her mother. I had given my statement to the police, and the case would be under investigation for a while. But I was not worried and had no reason to be. I just did not know what to feel. It bothered me some that I did not feel sorry.

I was aware only of feeling so tired that the slightest exertion was an effort. It was as if I had been transfused with lead. Even moving the pen was hard, and my mind would not work fast. At intervals I found myself staring without seeing or blinking, and I would not know how long I had been doing that or where I had gone.

My first job was to write up the case, and in part this was for the FBI investigation, and in part it was for the police investigating me. The pieces were fitting together well, but some questions would never be answered because there was no one left to tell. For example, we would never know exactly what happened the night of Emily's death. But I had developed a theory.

I believed she hurried home before her meeting ended and got into a fight with her mother. This may have happened over dinner, when I suspected Mrs. Steiner may have punished Emily by heavily salting her food. Salt ingestion is a form of child abuse that, horrifically, is not uncommon.

Emily may have been forced to drink salt water. She would have begun to vomit, which would only have served to make her mother madder. The child would have gone into hypernatremia, finally a coma, and she would have been near death or already dead when Mrs. Steiner carried her down to the basement. Such a scenario would explain Emily's seemingly contradictory physical findings. It would explain her elevated sodium and lack of vital response to her injuries.

As for why the mother chose to emulate Eddie Heath's murder, I could only imagine that a woman suffering from Munchausen's syndrome by proxy would have been intensely interested in such a notorious case. Only Denesa Steiner's reaction would not have been like someone else's. She would have imagined the attention a mother would get if she lost a child in such a ghastly fashion.

It was a fantasy that would have been exciting for her, and she might have worked it out in her head. She might have deliberately poisoned and killed her daughter that Sunday night to carry out her plan. Or she might have carried out her plan after accidentally poisoning Emily while enraged. I would never know the answer, but at this point it did not matter. This case would never see a courtroom.

In the basement, Mrs. Steiner placed her daughter's body in

the tub. I suspected it was at this point she shot her in the back of the head so blood would go down the drain. She undressed her, which would explain the coin Emily had not tithed that night because she had left her meeting before the boy she loved had taken up the collection. The quarter inadvertently slipped out of Emily's pocket when her pants were being pulled off, and her bare buttock rested on top of it for the next six days.

I imagined it was night when, almost a week later, Mrs. Steiner retrieved Emily's body, which essentially had been refrigerated all this time. She might have wrapped it in a blanket, explaining wool fibers we found. She might have placed it in plastic leaf bags. The microscopic traces of pithwood made sense, too, since Mr. Steiner had used pith buttons in the basement for years when he worked on clocks. So far, the blaze orange duct tape Mrs. Steiner had torn off in strips to tape her daughter and herself had not turned up, nor had the .22-caliber gun. I doubted they ever would. Mrs. Steiner was too smart to hold on to those items, for they were incriminating.

In retrospect, it all seemed so simple, in many ways so obvious. For example, the sequence in which the duct tape was torn off the roll was exactly right for what had happened. Of course, Mrs. Steiner would have bound her daughter first, and there would have been no need to tear off all the strips and stick them on the edge of a piece of furniture. Her mother did not need to subdue her, since Emily wasn't moving. Both of Mrs. Steiner's hands, therefore, would have been free.

But when Mrs. Steiner bound herself, that was a little trickier. She tore off all the strips at once and stuck them on her dresser. She made a token effort of taping herself, so she could get out, and she did not realize she used the strips out of sequence, not that she would have had reason to know it mattered.

In Charlotte, I changed planes for Washington, and from there I took a taxi to the Russell Building, where I had an appointment to see Senator Lord. He was on the Senate floor voting when I arrived at half past three. I waited patiently in the reception area while young women and men answered telephones nonstop, for everyone in the world wanted his help. I wondered how he lived with the burden. He walked in soon enough and smiled at me. I could tell from his eyes he knew everything that had happened.

"Kay, it's so good to see you."

I followed him through another room with more desks and people on more telephones; then we were in his private office, and he shut the door. He had many beautiful paintings by very fine artists, and it was clear he loved good books.

"The Director called me earlier today. What a nightmare. I'm not sure I know what to say," he said.

"I'm doing all right."

"Here, please." He directed me to the couch and faced me from an unimposing chair. Senator Lord rarely put his desk between himself and others. He did not need to, for as was true with every powerful person I had known, and there were but a few, his greatness made him humble and kind.

"I'm walking around in a stupor. A weird state of mind," I went on. "It's later I'll be in trouble. Posttraumatic stress and that sort of thing. Knowing about it doesn't make you immune."

"I want you to take good care of yourself. Go someplace and rest for a while."

"Senator Lord, what can we do about Lucy? I want her name cleared."

"I believe you've already managed to do that."

"Not entirely. The Bureau knows it couldn't have been Lucy's thumb scanned into the biometric lock system. But this doesn't entirely exculpate my niece. At least that's the impression I've gotten."

"Not so. Not so at all." Senator Lord recrossed his long legs and stared off. "Now, there may be a problem in terms of what circulates throughout the Bureau. The gossip, I mean. Since

Temple Gault has become part of the picture, there is much that cannot be discussed."

"So Lucy will just have to hold up under everybody's stare because she won't be permitted to divulge what happened," I said.

"That's correct."

"Then there will be those who do not trust her and will think she shouldn't be at Quantico."

"There may be those."

"That's not good enough."

He regarded me patiently. "You can't protect her forever, Kay. Let her take her licks and suffer her slights. In the long run, she will be the better for it. Just keep her legal." He smiled.

"I'm going to do my best to do that," I said. "She still has a DUI hanging over her head."

"She was the victim of a hit-and-run or even an attempted murder. I should think that might change the scenario a bit in the eyes of the judge. I also will suggest she volunteer to perform some sort of community service."

"Do you have something in mind?" I knew he did or he would not have mentioned it.

"As a matter of fact I do. I wonder if she would be willing to return to ERF? We don't know how much of CAIN Gault has tampered with. I'd like to suggest to the Director that the Bureau use Lucy to follow Gault's tracks through the system to see what can be salvaged."

"Frank, I know she would be thrilled," I said as my heart filled with gratitude.

"I can't think of anyone better qualified," he went on. "And it will give her a chance for restitution. She did not willingly do anything wrong, but she used poor judgment."

"I will tell her," I said.

From his office I went to the Willard and got a room. I was too tired to return to Richmond, and what I really wanted to do was fly to Newport. I wanted to see Lucy, even if only for an hour or two. I wanted her to know what Senator Lord had done, that her name was cleared, her future bright.

Everything was going to be just fine. I knew it. I wanted to tell her how much I loved her. I wanted to see if I could find words that for me were so hard. I tended to hold love hostage in my heart because, if expressed, I feared it might abandon me as many people in my life had. So it had been my habit to bring what I feared upon me.

In my room I called Dorothy and got no answer. Next I called my mother.

"Where are you this time?" she asked, and I could hear water running.

"I'm in Washington," I said. "Where's Dorothy?"

"It just so happens she's right here helping me with dinner. We're having lemon chicken and salad—you should see the lemon tree, Katie. And the grapefruits are huge. I'm washing the lettuce even as we speak. If you would visit your mother once in a blue moon, we could eat together. Normal meals. We could be a family."

"I would like to speak to Dorothy."

"Hold on."

The phone clunked against something, then Dorothy was on.

"What's the name of Lucy's counselor at Edgehill?" I asked right off. "I'm assuming they've assigned someone to her by now."

"Doesn't matter. Lucy's not there anymore."

"I beg your pardon?" I asked. "What did you just say?"

"She didn't like the program and told me she wanted to leave. I couldn't force her. She's a grown woman. And it's not like she was committed or something."

"What?" I was shocked. "Is she there? She returned to Miami?"

"No," said my sister, who was quite calm. "She wanted to stay in Newport for a while. She said it wasn't safe to come back to Richmond right now, or some nonsense like that. And she didn't want to come down here."

"She's in Newport alone with a goddam head injury and a problem with alcohol and you're not doing anything about it?"

"Kay, you're overreacting, as usual."

"Where is she staying?"

"I have no idea. She said she just wanted to bum around for a while."

"Dorothy!"

"Let me remind you she's my daughter, not yours."

"That will always be the biggest tragedy of her life."

"Why don't you just for once keep your fucking nose out of it!" she snapped.

"Dorothy!" I heard my mother in the background. "I don't allow the F word!"

"Let me tell you something." I spoke in the cold, measured words of homicidal rage. "If anything has happened to her, I will hold you one hundred percent accountable. You are not only a terrible mother, you are a horrible human being. I am truly sorry you are my sister."

I hung up the phone. I got out the telephone directory and began calling airlines. There was one flight to Providence that I could get on if I hurried. I ran out of the room and kept going just as fast through the Willard's elegant lobby. People stared.

The doorman got me a cab and I told the driver I would double his fare if he could get me to National *fast*. He drove like hell. I got to the terminal as my flight was being called, and when I found my seat, tears welled up in my throat and I fought them back. I drank hot tea and closed my eyes. I was unfamiliar with Newport and had no idea where to stay.

The taxi from Providence to Newport was going to take more than an hour, the driver told me, because it was snowing. Through water-streaked windows I looked out at dark faces of sheer walls of granite on roadsides. The stone was lined with drill holes and dripping with ice, and a draft creeping in from the floor was damp and miserably cold. Big flakes of snow spiraled into the windshield like fragile white bugs, and if I stared too hard at them I started to get dizzy.

"Do you have any recommendations for a hotel in Newport?" I asked the driver, who spoke in the manner peculiar to Rhode Islanders.

"The Marriott would be your best bet. It's right on the water and all the shopping and restaurants are within walking distance. There's also a Doubletree on Goat Island."

"Let's try the Marriott."

"Yes, ma'am. The Marriott it is."

"If you were a young lady looking for work in Newport, where would you go? My twenty-one-year-old niece would like to spend some time here." It seemed stupid to pose such a question to a perfect stranger. But I did not know what else to do.

"In the first place, I wouldn't pick this time of year. Newport's pretty damn dead."

"But if she did pick it this time of year. If she had time off from school, for example."

"Umm." He thought as I got caught up in the rhythm of the windshield wiper blades.

"Maybe in the restaurants?" I ventured.

"Oh, sure. Lots of young people working in the restaurants. The ones on the water. The money's pretty good because the main industry's tourists in Newport. Don't let anybody tell you it's fishing. These days, a boat with a thirty-thousand-pound hold comes back in with maybe three thousand pounds of fish. And that's on a good day."

He continued to talk as I thought about Lucy, about where she would go. I tried to get into her mind, to read it, to somehow reach her through my thoughts. I said many silent prayers and fought back tears and the most terrible of all fears. I could not deal with another tragedy. Not Lucy. That loss would be the last. It would be too much.

"How late do most of these places stay open?" I asked.

"What places?"

I realized he had been talking about butterfish, something about them being used in cat food.

"The restaurants," I said. "Would they still be open now?"

"No ma'am. Not most of 'em. It's almost one A.M. Your best bet if you want to find your niece a job is to go out in the morning. Most places open by eleven, some earlier than that if they serve breakfast."

My taxi driver, of course, was right. I could do nothing now but go to bed and try to get some sleep. The room I got at the Marriott overlooked the harbor. From my window the water was black, and the lights of men out fishing bobbed on a horizon I could not see.

I got up at seven because there was no point in lying in bed any longer. I had not slept and had been afraid to dream.

Ordering breakfast, I opened curtains and looked out at a day that was steely gray, water almost indistinguishable from sky. In the distance, geese flew in formation like fighter planes, and snow had turned to rain. Knowing not much would be open this early did not stop me from trying, and by eight I was out of the hotel with a list of popular inns, pubs, and restaurants I had gotten from the concierge.

For a while I walked the wharfs, where sailors were dressed for the weather in yellow slickers and bib pants. I stopped to talk to anyone who would listen, and my question each time was the same, just as their answers were all the same. I described my niece, and they did not know if they had seen her. There were so many young women working in places along the water.

I walked without an umbrella, the scarf around my head not keeping out the rain. I walked by sleek sailboats and yachts battened down with heavy plastic for the winter, past piles of massive anchors broken and eaten with rust. Not many people were around, but many places were open for the day, and it did not occur to me until I saw ghosts, goblins, and other spooky creatures in the shop windows of Brick Market Place that today was Halloween.

I walked for hours along the cobblestone of Thames Street, looking in the windows of shops selling everything from scrimshaw to fine art. I turned up Mary Street and passed Inntowne Inn, where the clerk had never heard my niece's name. Nor did anyone know her at Christie's, where I drank coffee before a window and looked out at Narragansett Bay. Docks were wet and dotted white with sea gulls all facing the same way, and I watched as two women walked out to look at the water. They were bundled up in hats and gloves, and something about them that made me think they were more than friends. I got upset about Lucy again and had to leave.

I ducked inside the Black Pearl at Bannister's Wharf, then Anthony's, the Brick Alley Pub, and the Inn at Castle Hill. Callahan's Cafe Zelda and a quaint place that sold strudels and cream could not help me, and I went into so many bars I lost track and wound up in some of them twice. I saw no sign of her. No one could help me. I wasn't sure anyone cared, and I walked along Bowden Wharf in despair as rain fell harder. Water swept down in sheets from a slate-gray sky, and a lady hurrying past gave me a smile.

"Honey, don't drown," she said. "Nothing's that bad."

I watched her go inside the Aquidneck Lobster Company at the end of the wharf, and I chose to follow her because she had been friendly. I watched her go into a small office behind a partition of glass so smoky and taped with invoices that I could see only dyed curls and hands moving between the slips of paper.

To get to her I passed green tanks the size of boats filled with lobsters, clams, and crabs. They reminded me of the way we stacked gurneys in the morgue. Tanks were stacked to the ceiling, and bay water pumped through overhead pipes poured into them and spilled onto the floor. The inside of the lobster house sounded like a monsoon and smelled like the sea. Men in orange bib pants and high rubber boots had faces as weathered as the docks, and they spoke in loud voices to one another.

"Excuse me," I said at the small office door, and I did not know that a fisherman was with the woman because I had not been able to see him. He had raw red hands and was sitting in a plastic chair, smoking.

"Honey, you're drenched. Come in and get warm." The lady, who was overweight and worked too hard, smiled again. "You want to buy some lobsters?" She started to get up.

"No," I quickly said. "I've lost my niece. She wandered off or we got our directions mixed up or something. I was supposed to meet her. Well, I just wonder if you might have seen her."

"What does she look like?" asked the fisherman.

I described her.

"Now, where was it you saw her last?" The woman looked confused.

I took a deep breath, and the man had me figured out. He read every word of me. I could see it in his eyes.

"She ran off. They do it sometimes, kids do," he said, taking a drag on a Marlboro. "Question is, where'd she run off from? You tell me that, and maybe I'll have a better idea about where she might be."

"She was at Edgehill," I said.

"She just got out?" The fisherman was from Rhode Island, his last syllables flattened as if he were stepping on the end of his words.

"She walked out."

"So she didn't do the program or her insurance quit. Happens a lot around here. I got buddies been in that joint and have to leave after four or five days because insurance won't pay. A lot of good it does."

"She didn't do the program," I said.

He lifted his soiled cap and smoothed back wild black hair.

"I know you must be worried sick," said the woman. "I can make you some instant coffee."

"You are very kind, but no, thank you."

"When they get out early like that, they usually start drinking and drugging again," the man went on. "I hate to tell you, but it's the way it goes. She's probably working as a waitress or bartender so she can be near what she wants. The restaurants around here pay pretty good. I'd try Christie's, the Black Pearl over there on Bannister's Wharf, Anthony's on Waites Wharf."

"I've tried all those."

"How about the White Horse? She could make good money there."

"Where's that?"

"Over there." He pointed away from the bay. "Off Marlborough Street, near the Best Western."

"Where would someone stay?" I asked. "She's not likely to want to spend a lot of money."

"Honey," said the woman, "I'll tell you what I'd try. I'd try the Seaman's Institute. It's just right over there. You had to walk right past it to get here."

The fisherman nodded as he lit another cigarette. "There you go. That'd be a good place to start. And they got waitresses, too, and girls working in the kitchen."

"What is it?" I asked.

"A place where fishermen down on their luck can stay. Sort of like a small YMCA, with rooms upstairs and a dining hall and snack bar."

"The Catholic church runs it. You might talk to Father Ogren. He's the priest there."

"Why would a twenty-one-year-old girl go there versus some of these other places you've mentioned?" I asked.

"She wouldn't," the fisherman said, "unless she don't want to drink. No drinking in that place." He shook his head. "That's exactly where you go if you leave a program early but don't want to be drinking and drugging anymore. I've known a bunch of guys to go there. I even stayed there once."

It was raining so hard when I left that water coming down bounced off pavement back up toward the loud, liquid sky. I was soaked to my knees, hungry, cold, and with no place left to go, as was true of many people who came to the Seaman's Institute.

It looked like a small brick church with a menu out front written with chalk on a chalkboard and a banner that said EVERYONE IS WELCOME. I stepped inside and saw men sitting at a counter drinking coffee while others were at tables in a plain dining room across from the front door. Eyes turned to me with mild curiosity, and the faces reflected years of cruel weather and drink. A waitress who looked no older than Lucy asked if I would like a meal.

"I'm looking for Father Ogren," I said.

"I've not seen him lately, but you can check the library or the chapel."

I climbed stairs and entered a small chapel that was empty save for saints painted in frescoes on plaster walls. It was a lovely chapel with needlepoint cushions in nautical designs and a floor of varying colors of marble inlaid with shapes of shells. I stood very still looking around at Saint Mark holding a mast while Saint Anthony of Padua blessed the creatures of the sea. Saint Andrew carried nets, and words from the Bible were painted along the top of the wall.

> For he maketh the storm to cease so that the waves thereof are still. Then are they glad because they are at rest and so he bringeth them unto their desired haven.

I dipped my hand into a large shell filled with holy water and blessed myself. Praying a while before the altar, I placed a gift in a small straw basket. I left a bill for Lucy and me and a quarter for Emily. Beyond the door I heard cheery voices and whistling of residents on the stairs. Rain on the roof sounded like drum rolls on a mattress and beyond opaque windows gulls cried.

"Good afternoon," a quiet voice behind me said.

I turned around to find Father Ogren, dressed in black.

"Good afternoon, Father," I said.

"You must have had a long walk in the rain." His eyes were kind, his face very gentle.

"I am looking for my niece, Father, and am in despair."

I did not have to talk about Lucy long. In fact, I'd scarcely described her before I could tell the priest knew who she was, and my heart seemed to open like a rose.

"God is merciful and good," he said with a smile. "He led you here as he leads others here who have been lost at sea. He led your niece here days ago. I believe she's in the library. I put her to work there cataloging books and doing other odds and ends. She's very smart and has a marvelous idea about our computerizing everything."

I found her at a refectory table in a dim room of dark paneling and shopworn books. Her back was to me as she worked out a program on paper without benefit of a computer, the way fine musicians compose their symphonies in silence. I thought she looked thinner. Father Ogren patted my arm as he left, and he quietly shut the door.

"Lucy," I said.

She turned and looked at me in astonishment.

"Aunt Kay? My God," she said in the hushed tone of libraries. "What are you doing here? How did you know?" Her cheeks were flushed, a scar on her forehead bright red.

I pulled up a chair and took one of her hands in both of mine.

"Please come home with me."

Lucy continued to stare at me as if I had been dead.

"Your name has been cleared."

"Completely?"

"Completely."

"You got me my big gun."

"I said I would."

"You're the big gun, aren't you, Aunt Kay?" she whispered, looking away.

"The Bureau has accepted that it was Carrie who did this to you," I said.

Her eyes filled with tears.

"What she did was horrible, Lucy. I know how hurt and angry you must be. But you are fine. The truth is known and ERF wants you back. We'll work on your DUI. The judge will have more sympathy since someone ran you off the road and the evidence proves that. But I still want you to get treatment."

"Can't I do it in Richmond? Can't I stay with you?"

"Of course you can."

She looked down as tears spilled over.

I did not want to hurt her further but I had to ask. "It was Carrie you were with in the picnic area the night I saw you out there. She must smoke."

"Sometimes." She wiped her eyes.

"I'm so sorry."

"You wouldn't understand it."

"Of course I understand it. You loved her."

"I still do." She began to sob. "That's what's so stupid. How could I? But I can't help it. And all along . . ." She blew her nose. "All along she was with Jerry or whoever. *Using me.*"

"She uses everyone, Lucy. It wasn't only you."

She wept as if she would the rest of her life.

"I understand how you feel," I said, pulling her close. "You can't just stop loving somebody. Lucy, it will take time."

I held her for a long while, my neck wet with her tears. I held her until the horizon was a dark blue line across the night, and in her spartan room we packed up her belongings. We walked along cobblestone and pavement deep with puddles as Halloween glowed in windows and the rain began to freeze.

FROM POTTER'S FIELD

This book is for Dr. Erika Blanton
(Scarpetta would call you friend)

And he said, What hast thou done? the voice of thy brother's blood crieth unto me from the ground.

—Genesis 4:10

'TWAS THE NIGHT BEFORE CHRISTMAS

He walked with sure steps through snow, which was deep in Central Park, and it was late now, but he was not certain how late. Toward the Ramble rocks were black beneath stars, and he could hear and see his breathing because he was not like anybody else. Temple Gault had always been magical, a god who wore a human body. He did not slip as he walked, for example, when he was quite certain others would, and he did not know fear. Beneath the bill of a baseball cap, his eyes scanned.

In the spot – and he knew precisely where it was – he squatted, moving the skirt of a long black coat out of the way. He set an old army knapsack in the snow and held his bare bloody hands in front of him, and though they were cold, they weren't impossibly cold. Gault did not like gloves unless they were made of latex, which was not warm, either. He washed his hands and face in soft new snow, then patted the used snow into a bloody snowball. This he placed next to the knapsack because he could not leave them.

He smiled his thin smile. He was a happy dog digging on the beach as he disrupted snow in the park, eradicating footprints, looking for the emergency door. Yes, it was where he thought, and he brushed aside more snow until he found the folded aluminum foil he had placed between the door and the frame. He gripped the ring that was the handle and opened the lid in the ground. Below were the dark bowels of the subway and the screaming of a train. He dropped the knapsack and snowball inside. His boots rang on a metal ladder as he went down.

1

Christmas Eve was cold and treacherous with black ice, and crime crackling on scanners. It was rare I was driven through Richmond's housing projects after dark. Usually, I drove. Usually, I was the lone pilot of the blue morgue van I took to scenes of violent and inexplicable death. But tonight I was in the passenger seat of a Crown Victoria, Christmas music drifting in and out of dispatchers and cops talking in codes.

'Sheriff Santa just took a right up there.' I pointed ahead. 'I think he's lost.'

'Yeah, well, I think he's fried,' said Captain Pete Marino, the commander of the violent precinct we were riding through. 'Next time we stop, take a look at his eyes.'

I wasn't surprised. Sheriff Lamont Brown drove a Cadillac for his personal car, wore heavy gold jewelry, and was beloved by the community for the role he was playing right now. Those of us who knew the truth did not dare say a word. After all, it is sacrilege to say that Santa doesn't exist, and in this case, Santa truly did not. Sheriff Brown snorted cocaine and probably stole half of what was donated to be delivered by him to the poor each year. He was a scumbag who recently had made certain I was summoned for jury duty because our dislike of each other was mutual.

Windshield wipers dragged across glass. Snowflakes brushed and swirled against Marino's car like dancing maidens, shy in white. They swarmed in sodium vapor lights and turned as black as the ice coating the streets. It was very cold. Most of the city was home with family, illuminated trees filling windows and fires lit. Karen Carpenter was dreaming of a white Christmas until Marino rudely changed the radio station.

'I got no respect for a woman who plays the drums.' He punched in the cigarette lighter.

'Karen Carpenter's dead,' I said, as if that granted her immunity from further slights. 'And she wasn't playing the drums just now.'

'Oh yeah.' He got out a cigarette. 'That's right. She had one of those eating problems. I forget what you call it.'

The Mormon Tabernacle Choir soared into the 'Hallelujah' chorus. I was supposed to fly to Miami in the morning to see my mother, sister and Lucy, my niece. Mother had been in the hospital for weeks. Once she had smoked as much as Marino did. I opened my window a little.

He was saying, 'Then her heart quit – in fact, that's really what got her in the end.'

'That's really what gets everybody in the end,' I said.

'Not around here. In this damn neighborhood it's lead poisoning.'

We were between two Richmond police cruisers with lights flashing red and blue in a motorcade carrying cops, reporters and television crews. At every stop, the media manifested its Christmas spirit by shoving past with notepads, microphones and cameras. Frenzied, they fought for sentimental coverage of Sheriff Santa beaming as he handed out presents and food to forgotten children of the projects and their shell-shocked mothers. Marino and I were in charge of blankets, for they had been my donation this year.

Around a corner, car doors opened along Magnolia Street in Whitcomb Court. Ahead, I caught a glimpse of blazing red as Santa passed through headlights, Richmond's chief of police and other top brass not far behind. Television cameras lit up and hovered in the air like UFOs, and flashguns flashed.

Marino complained beneath his stack of blankets, 'These things smell cheap. Where'd you get them, a pet store?'

'They're warm, washable, and won't give off toxic gases like cyanide in the event of a fire,' I said.

'Jesus. If that don't put you in a holiday mood.'

I wondered where we were as I looked out the window.

'I wouldn't use one in my doghouse,' he went on.

'You don't have a dog or a doghouse, and I didn't offer to give you one to use for anything. Why are we going into this apartment? It's not on the list.'

'That's a damn good question.'

Reporters and people from law enforcement agencies and social services were outside the front door of an apartment that looked like all the others in a complex reminiscent of cement barracks. Marino and I squeezed through as camera lights floated in the dark, headlights burned and Sheriff Santa bellowed, 'HO! HO! HO!'

We pushed our way inside as Santa sat a small black boy on his knee and gave him several wrapped toys. The boy's name, I overheard, was Trevi, and he wore a blue cap with a marijuana leaf over the bill. His eyes were huge and he looked bewildered on this man's red velvet knee near a silver tree strung with lights. The overheated small room was airless and smelled of old grease.

'Coming through, ma'am.' A television cameraman nudged me out of the way.

'You can just put it over here.'

'Who's got the rest of the toys?'

'Look, ma'am, you're going to have to step back.' The cameraman practically knocked me over. I felt my blood pressure going up.

'We need another box . . .

'No we don't. Over there.'

'. . . of food? Oh, right. Gotcha.'

'If you're with social services,' the cameraman said to me, 'then how 'bout standing over there?'

'If you had half a brain you'd know she ain't with social services.' Marino glared at him.

An old woman in a baggy dress had started crying on the couch, and a major in white shirt and brass sat beside her to offer comfort. Marino moved close to me so he could whisper.

'Her daughter was whacked last month, last name King. You remember the case?' he said in my ear.

I shook my head. I did not remember. There were so many cases.

'The drone we think whacked her is a badass drug dealer named Jones,' he continued, to prod my memory.

I shook my head again. There were so many badass drug dealers, and Jones was not an uncommon name.

The cameraman was filming and I averted my face as Sheriff Santa gave me a contemptuous, glassy stare. The cameraman bumped hard into me again.

'I wouldn't do that one more time,' I warned him in a tone that made him know I meant it.

The press had turned their attention to the grandmother because this was the story of the night. Someone had been murdered, the victim's mother was crying, and Trevi was an orphan. Sheriff Santa, out of the limelight now, set the boy down.

'Captain Marino, I'll take one of those blankets,' a social worker said.

'I don't know why we're in this crib,' he said, handing her the stack. 'I wish someone would tell me.'

'There's just one child here,' the social worker went on. 'So we don't need all of these.' She acted as if Marino hadn't followed instructions as she took one folded blanket and handed the rest back.

'There's supposed to be four kids here. I'm telling you, this crib ain't on the list,' Marino grumbled.

A reporter came up to me. 'Excuse me, Dr. Scarpetta? So what brings you out this night? You waiting for someone to die?'

He was with the city newspaper, which had never treated me kindly. I pretended not to hear him. Sheriff Santa disappeared into the kitchen, and I thought this odd since he did not live here and had not asked permission. But the grandmother on the couch was in no frame of mind to see or care where he had gone.

I knelt beside Trevi, alone on the floor, lost in the wonder of new toys. 'That's quite a fire truck you've got there,' I said.

'It lights up.' He showed me a red light on the toy truck's roof that flashed when he turned a switch.

Marino got down beside him, too. 'They give you any extra batteries for that thing?' He tried to sound gruff, but couldn't disguise the smile in his voice. 'You gotta get the size right. See this little compartment here? They go in there, okay? And you got to use size C . . .'

The first gunshot sounded like a car backfire coming from the kitchen. Marino's eyes froze as he yanked his pistol from its holster and Trevi curled up on the floor like a centipede. I folded my body over the boy, gunshots exploding in rapid succession as the magazine of a semiautomatic was emptied somewhere near the back door.

'Get *down*! GET DOWN!'

'Oh my God!'

'Oh Jesus!'

Cameras, microphones crashed and fell as people screamed and fought for the door and got flat on the floor.

'EVERYBODY GET DOWN!'

Marino headed toward the kitchen in combat stance, nine-millimeter drawn. The gunfire stopped and the room fell completely still.

I scooped up Trevi, my heart hammering. I began shaking. Grandmother remained on the couch, bent over, arms covering her head as if her plane were about to crash. I sat next to her, holding the boy close. He was rigid, his grandmother sobbing in terror.

'Oh Jesus. Please no Jesus.' She moaned and rocked.

'It's all right,' I firmly told her.

'Not no more of this! I can't stand no more of this. *Sweet Jesus!*'

I held her hand. 'It's going to be all right. Listen to me. It's quiet now. It's stopped.'

She rocked and wept, Trevi hugging her neck.

Marino reappeared in the doorway between the living room and kitchen, face tense, eyes darting. 'Doc.' He motioned to me.

I followed him out to a paltry backyard strung with sagging clotheslines, where snow swirled around a dark heap on the frosted grass. The victim was young, black and on his back, eyes barely open as they stared blindly at the milky sky. His blue down vest bore tiny rips. One bullet had entered through his right cheek, and as I compressed his chest and blew air into his mouth, blood covered my hands and instantly turned cold on my face. I could not save him. Sirens wailed and whelped in the night like a posse of wild spirits protesting another death.

I sat up, breathing hard. Marino helped me to my feet as shapes moved in the corner of my eye. I turned to see three officers leading Sheriff Santa away in handcuffs. His stocking cap had come off and I spotted it not far from me in the yard where shell casings gleamed in the beam of Marino's flashlight.

'What in God's name?' I said, shocked.

'Seems Old Saint Nick pissed off Old Saint Crack and they had a little tussle out here in the yard,' Marino said, very agitated and out of breath. 'That's why the parade got diverted to this particular crib. The only schedule it was on was the sheriff's.'

I was numb. I tasted blood and thought of AIDS.

The chief of police appeared and asked questions.

Marino began to explain. 'It appears the sheriff thought he'd deliver more than Christmas in this neighborhood.'

'Drugs?'

'We're assuming.'

'I wondered why we stopped here,' said the chief. 'This address isn't on the list.'

'Well, that's why.' Marino stared blankly at the body.

'Do we have an identity?'

'Anthony Jones of the Jones Brothers fame. Seventeen years old, been in jail more'n the Doc there's been to the opera. His older brother got whacked last year by a Tec 9. That was in Fairfield Court, on Phaup Street. And last month we think Anthony murdered Trevi's mother, but you know how it goes around here. Nobody saw nothing. We had no case. Maybe now we can clear it.'

'Trevi? You mean the little boy in there?' The chief's expression did not change.

'Yo. Anthony's probably the kid's father. Or was.'

'What about a weapon?'

'In which case?'

'In this case.'

'Smith and Wesson thirty-eight, all five rounds fired. Jones hadn't dumped his brass yet and we found a speedloader in the grass.'

'He fired five times and missed,' said the chief, resplendent in dress uniform, snow dusting the top of his cap.

'Hard to say. Sheriff Brown's got on a vest.'

'He's got on a bulletproof vest beneath his Santa suit.' The chief continued repeating the facts as if he were taking notes.

'Yo.' Marino bent close to a tilting clothesline pole, the beam of light licking over rusting metal. With a gloved thumb, he rubbed a dimple made by a bullet. 'Well, well,' he said, 'looks like we got one black and one Pole shot tonight.'

The chief was silent for a moment, then said, 'My wife is Polish, Captain.'

Marino looked baffled as I inwardly cringed. 'Your last name ain't Polish,' he said.

'She took my name and I am not Polish,' said the chief, who was black. 'I suggest you refrain from ethnic and racial jokes, Captain,' he warned, jaw muscles bunching.

The ambulance arrived. I began to shiver.

'Look, I didn't mean . . .' Marino started to say.

The chief cut him off. 'I believe you are the perfect candidate for cultural diversity class.'

'I've already been.'

'You've already been, *sir*, and you'll go again, *Captain*.'

'I've been three times. It's not necessary to send me again,' said Marino, who would rather go to the proctologist than another cultural diversity class.

Doors slammed and a metal stretcher clanked.

'Marino, there's nothing more I can do here.' I wanted to shut him up before he talked himself into deeper trouble. 'And I need to get to the office.'

'What? You're posting him tonight?' Marino looked deflated.

'I think it's a good idea in light of the circumstances,' I said seriously. 'And I'm leaving town in the morning.'

'Christmas with the family?' said Chief Tucker, who was young to be ranked so high.

'Yes.'

'That's nice,' he said without smiling. 'Come with me, Dr. Scarpetta, I'll give you a lift to the morgue.'

Marino eyed me as he lit a cigarette. 'I'll stop by as soon as I clear up here,' he said.

2

Paul Tucker had been appointed Richmond's chief of police several months ago, but we had encountered each other only briefly at a social function. Tonight was the first time we had met at a crime scene, and what I knew about him I could fit on an index card.

He had been a basketball star at the University of Maryland and a finalist for a Rhodes scholarship. He was supremely fit, exceptionally bright and a graduate of the FBI's National Academy. I thought I liked him but wasn't sure.

'Marino doesn't mean any harm,' I said as we passed through a yellow light on East Broad Street.

I could feel Tucker's dark eyes on my face and sense their curiosity. 'The world is full of people who mean no harm and cause a great deal of it.' He had a rich, deep voice that reminded me of bronze and polished wood.

'I can't argue with that, Colonel Tucker.'

'You can call me Paul.'

I did not tell him he could call me Kay, because after many years of being a woman in a world such as this, I had learned.

'It will do no good to send him to another cultural diversity class,' I went on.

'Marino needs to learn discipline and respect.' He was staring ahead again.

'He has both in his own way.'

'He needs to have both in the proper way.'

'You will not change him, Colonel,' I said. 'He's difficult, aggravating, ill-mannered, and the best homicide detective I've ever worked with.'

Tucker was silent until we got to the outer limits of the Medical College of Virginia and turned right on Fourteenth Street.

'Tell me, Dr. Scarpetta,' he said. 'Do you think your friend Marino is a good precinct commander?'

The question startled me. I had been surprised when Marino had advanced to lieutenant and was stunned when he had become a captain. He had always hated the brass, and then he had become the thing he hated, and he still hated *them* as if he were not *them*.

'I think Marino is an excellent police officer. He's unimpeachably honest and has a good heart,' I said.

'Do you intend to answer my question or not?' Tucker's tone hinted of amusement.

'He is not a politician.'

'Clearly.'

The clock tower of Main Street Station announced the time from its lofty position high above the old domed train station with its terra-cotta roof and network of railroad tracks. Behind the Consolidated Laboratory building, we parked in a slot designated *Chief Medical Examiner*, an unimpressive slip of blacktop where my car spent most of its life.

'He gives too much time to the FBI,' Tucker then said.

'He gives an invaluable service,' I said.

'Yes, yes, I know, and you do, too. But in his case, it poses a serious difficulty. He is supposed to be commanding First

Precinct, not working other cities' crimes, and I am trying to run a police department.'

'When violence occurs anywhere, it is everybody's problem,' I said. 'No matter where your precinct or department is.'

Tucker stared thoughtfully ahead at the shut steel bay door. He said, 'I sure as hell couldn't do what you do when it's this late at night and there's nobody around except the people in the refrigerator.'

'It isn't them I fear,' I matter-of-factly stated.

'Irrational as it may be, I would fear them a great deal.'

Headlights bored into dingy stucco and steel all painted the same insipid beige. A red sign on a side door announced to visitors that whatever was inside was considered a biological hazard and went on to give instruction about the handling of dead bodies.

'I've got to ask you something,' Colonel Tucker said.

The wool fabric of his uniform whispered against upholstery as he shifted positions, leaning closer to me. I smelled Hermès cologne. He was handsome, with high cheekbones and strong white teeth, his body powerful beneath his skin as if its darkness were the markings of a leopard or a tiger.

'Why do you do it?' he asked.

'Why do I do what, Colonel?'

He leaned back in the seat. 'Look,' he said as lights danced across the scanner. 'You're a lawyer. You're a doctor. You're a chief and I'm a chief. That's why I'm asking. I don't mean disrespect.'

I could tell he didn't. 'I don't know why,' I confessed.

He was silent for a moment. Then he spoke again. 'My father was a yardman and my mother cleaned houses for rich people in Baltimore.' He paused. 'When I go to Baltimore now I stay in fine hotels and eat in restaurants at the harbor. I am saluted. I am addressed "The Honorable" in some mail I get. I have a house in Windsor Farms.

'I command more than six hundred people who wear guns

in this violent town of yours. I know why I do what I do, Dr. Scarpetta. I do it because I had no power when I was a boy. I lived with people who had no power and learned that all the evil I heard preached about in church was rooted in the abuse of this one thing I did not have.'

The tempo and choreography of the snow had not changed. I watched it slowly cover the hood of his car.

'Colonel Tucker,' I said, 'it is Christmas Eve and Sheriff Santa has allegedly just shot someone to death in Whitcomb Court. The media must be going crazy. What do you advise?'

'I will be up all night at headquarters. I will make sure your building is patrolled. Would you like an escort home?'

'I would imagine that Marino will give me a ride, but certainly I will call if I think an additional escort is necessary. You should be aware that this predicament is further complicated by the fact that Brown hates me, and now I will be an expert witness in his case.'

'If only all of us could be so lucky.'

'I do not feel lucky.'

'You're right.' He sighed. 'You shouldn't feel lucky, for luck has nothing to do with it.'

'My case is here,' I said as the ambulance pulled into the lot, lights and sirens silent, for there is no need to rush when transporting the dead.

'Merry Christmas, Chief Scarpetta,' Tucker said as I got out of his car.

I entered through a side door and pressed a button on the wall. The bay door slowly screeched open, and the ambulance rumbled inside. Paramedics flung open the tailgate. They lifted the stretcher and wheeled the body up a ramp as I unlocked a door that led inside the morgue.

Fluorescent lighting, pale cinder block and floors gave the corridor an antiseptic ambience that was deceptive. Nothing was sterile in this place. By normal medical standards, nothing was even clean.

'Do you want him in the fridge?' one of the squad members said to me.

'No. You can wheel him into the X-ray room.' I unlocked more doors, the stretcher clattering after me, leaving drips of blood on tile.

'You going solo tonight?' asked a paramedic who looked Latin.

'I'm afraid so.'

I opened a plastic apron and slipped it over my head, hoping Marino would show up soon. In the locker room, I fetched a green surgical gown off a shelf. I pulled on shoe covers and two pairs of gloves.

'Can we help you get him on the table?' a paramedic asked.

'That would be terrific.'

'Hey, guys, let's get him on the table for the Doc.'

'Sure thing.'

'Shoot, this pouch is leaking, too. We gotta get some new ones.'

'Which way do you want his head to go?'

'This end for the head.'

'On his back?'

'Yes,' I said. 'Thank you.'

'Okay. One-two-three *heave.*'

We lifted Anthony Jones from the stretcher to the table, and one of the paramedics started to unzip the pouch.

'No, no, leave him in,' I said. 'I'll X-ray him through it.'

'How long will it take?'

'Not long.'

'You're going to need some help moving him again.'

'I'll take all the help I can get,' I told them.

'We can hang around a few more minutes. Were you really going to do all this alone?'

'I'm expecting someone else.'

A little later, we moved the body into the autopsy suite and

I undressed it on top of the first steel table. The paramedics left, returning the morgue to its usual sounds of water running into sinks and steel instruments clattering against steel. I attached the victim's films to light boxes where the shadows and shapes of his organs and bones brightly bared their souls to me. Bullets and their multitude of ragged pieces were lethal snowstorms in liver, lungs, heart and brain. He had an old bullet in his left buttock and a healed fracture of his right humerus. Mr. Jones, like so many of my patients, had died the way he had lived.

I was making the Y-incision when the buzzer sounded in the bay. I did not pause. The security guard would take care of whoever it was. Moments later I heard heavy footsteps in the corridor, and Marino walked in.

'I would've got here sooner but all the neighbors decided to come out and watch the fun.'

'What neighbors?' I looked quizzically at him, scalpel poised midair.

'This drone's neighbors in Whitcomb Court. We were afraid there was going to be a friggin' riot. Word went down he was shot by a cop, and then it was Santa who whacked him, and next thing there's people crawling out of cracks in the sidewalk.'

Marino, still in dress uniform, took off his coat and draped it over a chair. 'They're all gathered around with their two-liter bottles of Pepsi, smiling at the television cameras. Friggin' unbelievable.' He slid a pack of Marlboros out of his shirt pocket.

'I thought you were doing better with your smoking,' I said.

'I am. I get better at it all the time.'

'Marino, it isn't something to joke about.' I thought of my mother and her tracheotomy. Emphysema had not cured her habit until she had gone into respiratory arrest.

'Okay.' He came closer to the table. 'I'll tell you the serious truth. I've cut it down by half a pack a day, Doc.'

I cut through ribs and removed the breastplate.

'Molly won't let me smoke in her car or house.'

'Good for Molly,' I said of the woman Marino began dating at Thanksgiving. 'How are the two of you doing?'

'Real good.'

'Are you spending Christmas together?'

'Oh yeah. We'll be with her family in Urbana. They do a big turkey, the whole nine yards.' He tapped an ash to the floor and fell silent.

'This is going to take a while,' I said. 'The bullets have fragmented as you can see from his films.'

Marino glanced around at the morbid chiaroscuro displayed on light boxes around the room.

'What was he using? Hydra-Shok?' I asked.

'All the cops around here are using Hydra-Shok these days. I guess you can see why. It does the trick.'

'His kidneys have a finely granular surface. He's very young for that.'

'What does that mean?' Marino looked on curiously.

'Probably an indication of hypertension.'

He was quiet, probably wondering if his kidneys looked the same, and I suspected they did.

'It really would help if you'd scribe,' I said.

'No problem, as long as you spell everything.'

He went to a counter and picked up clipboard and pen. He pulled on gloves. I had just begun dictating weights and measurements when his pager sounded.

Detaching it from his belt, he held it up to read the display. His face darkened.

Marino went to the phone at the other end of the autopsy suite and dialed. He talked with his back to me and I caught only words now and then. They drifted through the noise at my table, and I knew whatever he was being told was bad.

When he hung up, I was removing lead fragments from the brain and scribbling notes with a pencil on an empty, bloody glove packet. I stopped what I was doing and looked at him.

'What's going on?' I said, assuming the call was related to this case, for certainly what had happened tonight was bad enough.

Marino was perspiring, his face dark red. 'Benton sent me a 911 on my pager.'

'He sent you what?' I asked.

'That's the code we agreed to use if Gault hit again.'

'Oh God,' I barely said.

'I told Benton not to bother calling you since I'm here to tell you the news in person.'

I rested my hands on the edge of the table. 'Where?' I said tensely.

'They've found a body in Central Park. Female, white, maybe in her thirties. It looks like Gault decided to celebrate Christmas in New York.'

I had feared this day. I had hoped and prayed Gault's silence might last forever, that maybe he was sick or dead in some remote village where no one knew his name.

'The Bureau's sending a chopper for us,' Marino went on. 'As soon as you finish up this case, Doc. We gotta get out of here. Goddam son of a bitch!' He started pacing furiously. 'He had to do this Christmas Eve!' He glared. 'It's deliberate. His timing's deliberate.'

'Go call Molly,' I said, trying to remain calm and work more quickly.

'And wouldn't you know I'd have this thing on.' He referred to his dress uniform.

'You have a change of clothes?'

'I'll have to stop by my house real fast. I gotta leave my gun. What are you going to do?'

'I always keep things here. While you're out, would you mind calling my sister's house in Miami? Lucy should have gotten down there yesterday. Tell her what's happened, that I'm not going to make it down, at least not right now.' I gave him the number and he left.

* * *

At almost midnight, the snow had stopped and Marino was back. Anthony Jones had been locked inside the refrigerator, his every injury, old and new, documented for my eventual day in court.

We drove to the Aero Services International terminal, where we stood behind plate glass and watched Benton Wesley descend turbulently in a Belljet Ranger. The helicopter settled neatly on a small wooden platform as a fuel truck glided out of deep shadows. Clouds slid like veils over the full face of the moon.

I watched Wesley climb out and hurry away from flying blades. I recognized anger in his bearing and impatience in his stride. He was tall and straight and carried himself with a quiet power that made people afraid.

'Refueling will take about ten minutes,' he said when he got to us. 'Is there any coffee?'

'That sounds like a good idea,' I said. 'Marino, can we bring you some?'

'Nope.'

We left him and walked to a small lounge tucked between rest rooms.

'I'm sorry about this,' Wesley said softly to me.

'We have no choice.'

'He knows that, too. The timing is no accident.' He filled two Styrofoam cups. 'This is pretty strong.'

'The stronger the better. You look worn out.'

'I always look that way.'

'Are your children home for Christmas?'

'Yes. Everyone is there – except, of course, me.' He stared off for a moment. 'His games are escalating.'

'If it's Gault again, I agree.'

'I know it's him,' he said with an iron calm that belied his rage. Wesley hated Temple Brooks Gault. Wesley was incensed and bewildered by Gault's malignant genius.

The coffee was not very hot and we drank it fast. Wesley

made no show of our familiarity with each other except with his eyes, which I had learned to read quite well. He did not depend on words, and I had become skilled at listening to his silence.

'Come on,' he said, touching my elbow, and we caught up with Marino as he was heading out the door with our bags.

Our pilot was a member of the Bureau's Hostage Rescue Team, or HRT. In a black flight suit and watchful of what went on around him, he looked at us to acknowledge he was aware we existed. But he did not wave, smile or say a word as he opened the helicopter's doors. We ducked beneath blades, and I would forever associate the noise and wind caused by them with murder. Whenever Gault struck, it seemed, the FBI arrived in a maelstrom of beating air and gleaming metal and lifted me away.

We had chased him now for several years, and a complete inventory of the damage he had caused was impossible to take. We did not know how many people he had savaged, but there were at least five, including a pregnant woman who once had worked for me and a thirteen-year-old boy named Eddie Heath. We did not know how many lives he had poisoned with his machinations, but certainly mine was one of them.

Wesley was behind me with his headset on, and my seat back was too high for me to see him when I glanced around. Interior lights were extinguished and we began to slowly lift, sailing sideways and nosing northeast. The sky was scudded with clouds, and bodies of water shone like mirrors in the winter night.

'What kind of shape's she in?' Marino's voice sounded abruptly in my headset.

Wesley answered, 'She's frozen.'

'Meaning, she could've been out for days and not started decomposing. Right, Doc?'

'If she's been outside for days,' I said, 'you would think someone would have found her before now.'

Wesley said, 'We believe she was murdered last night. She was displayed, propped against . . .'

'Yo, the squirrel likes that. That's his thing.'

'He sits them up or kills them while they're sitting,' Wesley went on. 'Every one so far.'

'Every one we know about so far,' I reminded them.

'The victims we're aware of.'

'Right. Sitting up in cars, a chair, propped against a Dumpster.'

'The kid in London.'

'Yes, he wasn't.'

'Looks like he was just dumped near railroad tracks.'

'We don't know who did that one.' Wesley seemed certain. 'I don't believe it was Gault.'

'Why do you think it's important to him that the bodies are sitting?' I asked.

'It's his way of giving us the finger,' said Marino.

'Contempt, taunting,' Wesley said. 'It's his signature. I suspect there is a deeper meaning.'

I suspected there was, too. All of Gault's victims were sitting, heads bowed, hands in their laps or limply by their sides, as if they were dolls. The one exception was a woman prison guard named Helen. Though her body, dressed in uniform, was propped up in a chair, she was missing her head.

'Certainly the positioning . . .' I started to say, and the voice-activated microphones were never quite in sync with the tempo of conversation. It was an effort to talk.

'The bastard wants to rub our noses in it.'

'I don't think that's his only . . .'

'Right now, he *wants* us to know he's in New York . . .'

'Marino, let me finish. Benton? The symbolism?'

'He could display the bodies any number of ways. But so far he's always chosen the same position. *He sits them up*. It's part of his fantasy.'

'What fantasy?'

'If I knew that, Pete, maybe this trip wouldn't be happening.'

Sometime later our pilot took the air: 'The FAA's issued a SIGMET.'

'What the hell is that?' Marino asked.

'A warning about turbulence. It's windy in New York City, twenty-five knots gusting at thirty-seven.'

'So we can't land?' Marino, who hated to fly, sounded slightly panicky.

'We're going to be low and the winds are going to be much higher.'

'What do you mean *low*? You ever seen how *high* the buildings are in New York?'

I reached back between my seat and the door and patted Marino's knee. We were forty nautical miles from Manhattan, and I could just barely make out a light winking on top of the Empire State Building. The moon was swollen, planes moving in and away from La Guardia like floating stars, and from smokestacks steam rose in huge white plumes. Through the chin bubble at my feet I watched twelve lanes of traffic on the New Jersey Turnpike, and everywhere lights sparkled like jewels, as if Fabergé had crafted the city and its bridges.

We flew behind the Statue of Liberty's back, then passed Ellis Island, where my grandparents' first introduction to America was a crowded immigration station on a frigid winter day. They had left Verona, where there had been no future for my grandfather, born the fourth son of a railroad worker.

I came from a hearty, hardworking people who emigrated from Austria and Switzerland in the early eighteen hundreds, thus explaining my blond hair and blue eyes. Despite my mother's assertion that when Napoleon I ceded Verona to Austria, our ancestors managed to keep the Italian bloodline pure, I believed otherwise. I suspected there was genetic cause for some of my more Teutonic traits.

Macy's, billboards and the golden arches of McDonald's appeared, as New York slowly became concrete and parking lots and street sides banked high with snow that looked dirty even from the air. We circled the VIP Heliport on West Thirtieth Street, lighting up and ruffling the Hudson's murky waters as a bright wind sock stood on end. We swayed into a space near a gleaming Sikorsky S-76 that made all other birds seem common.

'Watch out for the tail rotor,' our pilot said.

Inside a small building that was only vaguely warm, we were greeted by a woman in her fifties with dark hair, a wise face and tired eyes. Bundled in a thick wool coat, slacks, lace-up boots and leather gloves, she introduced herself as Commander Frances Penn of the New York Transit Police.

'Thank you so much for coming,' she said, offering her hand to each of us. 'If we're ready, I have cars waiting.'

'We're ready,' Wesley said.

She led us back out into the bitter cold, where two police cruisers waited, two officers in each, engines running and heat on high. There was an awkward moment as we held doors open and decided who would ride with whom. As so often happens, we divided by gender, and Commander Penn and I rode together. I began to ask her about jurisdiction, because in a high-profile case like this one, there would be many people who thought they should be in charge.

'The Transit Police has an interest because we believe the victim met her assailant on the subway,' explained the commander, who was one of three command chiefs in the sixth-largest police department in America. 'This would have been late yesterday afternoon.'

'How do you know this?'

'It's really rather fascinating. One of our plainclothes officers was patrolling the subway station at Eighty-first and Central Park West, and at around five-thirty in the afternoon – this was yesterday – he noticed a peculiar couple emerge from the Museum of Natural History exit that leads directly into the subway.'

We bumped over ice and potholes that shook the bones in my legs.

'The man immediately lit a cigarette while the woman held a pipe.'

'That's interesting,' I commented.

'Smoking is against the law in the subway, which is another reason the officer remembers them.'

'Were they given a summons?'

'The man was. The woman wasn't because she hadn't lit the pipe. The man showed the officer his driver's license, which we now believe was false.'

'You said the couple was strange looking,' I said. 'How so?'

'She was dressed in a man's topcoat and an Atlanta Braves baseball cap. Her head was shaved. In fact, the officer wasn't certain she was a she. At first he assumed this was a homosexual couple.'

'Describe the man she was with,' I said.

'Medium height, thin, with strange sharp features and very weird blue eyes. His hair was carrot red.'

'The first time I saw Gault his hair was platinum. When I saw him last October, it was shoe-polish black.'

'It was definitely carrot red yesterday.'

'And is probably yet another color today. He does have weird eyes. Very intense.'

'He's very clever.'

'There is no description for what he is.'

'Evil comes to mind, Dr. Scarpetta,' she said.

'Please call me Kay.'

'If you call me Frances.'

'So it appears they visited the Museum of Natural History yesterday afternoon,' I said. 'What is the exhibit?'

'Sharks.'

I looked over at her, and her face was quite serious as the young officer driving deftly handled New York traffic.

'The exhibit right now is sharks. I suppose every sort you can imagine from the beginning of time,' she said.

I was silent.

'As best we can reconstruct what happened to this woman,' Commander Penn went on, 'Gault – we may as well call him that since we believe this is who we're dealing with – took her to Central Park after leaving the subway. He led her to a section called Cherry Hill, shot her and left her nude body propped against the fountain.'

'Why would she have gone with him into Central Park after dark? Especially in this weather?'

'We think he may have enticed her into accompanying him into the Ramble.'

'Which is frequented by homosexuals.'

'Yes. It is a meeting place for them, a very overgrown, rocky area with twisting footpaths that don't seem to lead anywhere. Even NYPD's Central Park Precinct officers don't like to go in there. No matter how often you've been, you still get lost. It's high-crime. Probably twenty-five percent of all crime committed in the park occurs there. Mostly robberies.'

'Then Gault must be familiar with Central Park if he took her to the Ramble after dark.'

'He must be.'

This suggested that Gault may have been hiding out in New York for a while, and the thought frustrated me terribly. He had been virtually in our faces and we had not known.

Commander Penn said to me, 'The crime scene is being secured overnight. I assumed you would want to look before we get you safely to your hotel.'

'Absolutely,' I said. 'What about evidence?'

'We recovered a pistol shell from inside the fountain that bears a distinctive firing pin mark consistent with a Glock nine-millimeter. And we found hair.'

'Where was the hair?'

'Close to where her body was displayed, in the scrollwork of an ornate wrought iron structure inside the fountain. It may be that when he was positioning the body, a strand of his hair got caught.'

'What color?'

'Bright red.'

'Gault is too careful to leave a cartridge shell or hair,' I said.

'He wouldn't have been able to see where the shell went,' said Commander Penn. 'It was dark. The shell would have been very hot when it hit the snow. So you can see what would have happened.'

'Yes,' I said. 'I can see.'

3

Within minutes of each other, Marino, Wesley and I arrived at Cherry Hill, where lights had been set up to aid old post lamps at the periphery of a circular plaza. What once had been a carriage turnaround and watering hole for horses was now thick with snow and encircled with yellow crime scene tape.

Central to this eerie spectacle was a gilt and wrought iron ice-coated fountain that did not work any time of year, we were told. It was here a young woman's nude body had been propped. She had been mutilated, and I believed Gault's purpose this time was not to remove bite marks, but to leave his signature so we would instantly identify the artist.

As best we could tell, Gault had forced his latest victim to strip and walk barefoot to the fountain where her frozen body had been found this morning. He had shot her at close range in the right temple and excised areas of skin from her inner thighs and left shoulder. Two sets of footprints led to the fountain, and only one led away. The blood of this woman whose name we did not know brightly stained snow, and beyond the arena of her hideous death Central Park dissolved into thick, foreboding shadows.

I stood close to Wesley, our arms touching, as if we needed each other for warmth. He did not speak as he intensely studied footprints and the fountain and the distant darkness of the Ramble. I felt his shoulder lift as he took a deep breath, then settle more heavily against me.

'Jeez,' Marino muttered.

'Did you find her clothes?' I asked Commander Penn, though I knew the answer.

'Not a trace.' She was looking around. 'Her footprints are not shoeless until the edge of this plaza, right over here.' She pointed about five yards west of the fountain. 'You can clearly see where her bare footprints start. Before that she had on some sort of boot, I guess. Something with no tread and a heel, like a dingo or cowboy boot, maybe.'

'What about him?'

'We may have found his footprints as far west as the Ramble, but it's hard to say. There are so many footprints over there and a lot of churned-up snow.'

'So the two of them left the Museum of Natural History through the subway station, entered the west side of the park, possibly walked to the Ramble, then headed over here.' I tried to piece it together. 'Inside the plaza, he apparently forced her to disrobe and take off her shoes. She walked barefoot to the fountain, where he shot her in the head.'

'That's the way it appears at this time,' said a stocky NYPD detective who introduced himself as T. L. O'Donnell.

'What is the temperature?' asked Wesley. 'Or better put, what was it late last night?'

'It got down to eleven degrees last night,' said O'Donnell, who was young and angry, with thick black hair. 'The windchill was about ten below zero.'

'And she took off her clothes and shoes,' Wesley seemed to say to himself. 'That's bizarre.'

'Not if someone's got a gun stuck to your head.' O'Donnell lightly stomped his feet. His hands were burrowed deep inside the pockets of a dark blue police jacket, which was not warm enough for temperatures this low, even with body armor on.

'If you are forced to disrobe outside in this cold,' Wesley reasonably said, 'you know you are going to die.'

No one spoke.

'You wouldn't be forced to take off clothes and shoes otherwise. The very act of disrobing is to go against any survival instinct, because obviously, you could not survive naked out here long.'

Still, everyone was silent as we stared at the fountain's grisly display. It was filled with snow stained red, and I could see the indentations made by the victim's bare buttocks when her body was positioned. Her blood was as bright as when she had died because it was frozen.

Then Marino spoke. 'Why the hell didn't she run?'

Wesley abruptly moved away from me and squatted to look at what we assumed were Gault's footprints. 'That's the question of the day,' he said. 'Why didn't she?'

I got down beside him to look at the footprints, too. The tread pattern of the impression clearly left in snow was curious. Gault had been wearing some type of footwear with intricate raised diamond-shaped and wavy tread, and a manufacturer's mark in the instep, and a wreathed logo in the heel. I estimated he wore a size seven and a half or eight.

'How is this being preserved?' I asked Commander Penn.

Detective O'Donnell answered, 'We've photographed the shoe impressions, and over there' – he pointed to a cluster of police officers some distance away on the opposite side of the fountain – 'are some better ones. We're trying to make a cast.'

Casting footwear impressions in snow was rife with perils. If the liquid dental stone wasn't cool enough and the snow wasn't frozen hard enough, one ended up melting the evidence. Wesley and I got up. We walked in silence to where the detective had pointed, and as I glanced around I saw Gault's steps.

He did not care that he had left very distinctive footprints. He did not care that he had left a trail in the park that we would painstakingly follow until we reached its end. We were determined to know every place he had been, and yet it did not matter to him. He did not believe we would catch him.

The officers on the other side of the fountain were spraying two shoe impressions with Snow Print Wax, holding aerosol cans a safe distance away and at an angle so the blast of pressurized red wax would not eradicate delicate tread detail. Another officer was stirring liquid dental stone in a plastic bucket.

By the time several layers of wax had been applied to the shoe prints, the dental stone would be cool enough to pour and make casts. The conditions were actually good for what was ordinarily a risky procedure. There was neither sun nor wind, and apparently the NYPD crime scene technicians had properly stored the wax at room temperature, because it had not lost its pressure. Nozzles were not spitting or clogged as I had so often seen with attempts in the past.

'Maybe we'll be lucky this time,' I said to Wesley as Marino headed our way.

'We're going to need all the luck we can get,' he said, staring off into dark woods.

East of us was the outer limits of the thirty-seven acres known as the Ramble, the isolated area of Central Park famous for bird-watching and winding footpaths through dense, rocky terrain. Every guidebook I had ever seen warned tourists that the Ramble was not recommended for lone hikers at any season or time of day. I wondered how Gault had enticed his victim into the park. I wondered where he had met her and what it was that had set him into motion. Perhaps it was simply that she had been an opportunity and he had been in the mood.

'How does one get from the Ramble to here?' I asked anybody who would listen.

The officer stirring dental stone met my eyes. He was about Marino's age, cheeks fleshy and red from the cold.

'There's a path along the lake,' he said, breath smoking.

'What lake?'

'You can't see it real well. It's frozen and covered with snow.'

'Do you know if this path is the one they took?'

'This is a big park, ma'am. The snow's real messed up in most other places, like the Ramble, for example. Over there, nothing – not ten feet of snow – is going to keep away people after drugs or an encounter. Now here in Cherry Hill, you got another story. You got no cars allowed and for sure the horses aren't coming up here in weather like this. So we're lucky. We got a crime scene left.'

'Why are you thinking the perpetrator and the victim started in the Ramble?' asked Wesley, who was always direct and often terse when his profiler's mind was going through its convoluted subroutines and searching its scary database.

'One of the guys thinks he may have spotted her shoe prints over there,' said the officer, who liked to talk. 'Problem is, as you can see, hers aren't very distinctive.'

We looked around snow that was getting increasingly marred by law enforcement feet. The victim's footwear had no tread.

'Plus,' he went on, 'since there may be a homosexual component, we're considering the Ramble might have been a primary destination.'

'What homosexual component?' Wesley blandly asked.

'Based on earlier descriptions of both of them, they appeared to be a homosexual couple.'

'We're not talking about two men,' Wesley stated.

'At a glance, the victim did not look like a female.'

'At whose glance?'

'The Transit Police. You really need to talk to them.'

'Hey, Mossberg, you ready with the dental stone?'

'I'd do another layer.'

'We've done four. We got a really good shell, I mean, if your stuff is cool enough.'

The officer whose surname was Mossberg squatted and began to carefully pour viscous dental stone into a red wax-coated impression. The victim's footprints were near the ones we wanted to save, her foot about the same size as Gault's. I wondered if we would ever find her boots as my eyes followed the trail to an area some fifteen feet from the fountain, where impressions became those of bare feet. In fifteen steps, her bare footprints went straight to the fountain where Gault had shot her in the head.

As I looked around at shadows pushed back from the lighted plaza, as I felt the bite of intense cold, I could not understand this woman's mind-set. I could not understand her compliance last night.

'Why didn't she resist?' I said.

'Because Gault had her scared out of her mind,' said Marino, now by my side.

'Would you take off your clothes out here for any reason?' I asked him.

'I'm not her.' Anger flexed beneath his words.

'We do not know anything about her,' Wesley logically added.

'Except that she had shaved her head for some wacko reason,' Marino said.

'We don't know enough to get a handle on her behavior,' Wesley said. 'We don't even know who she is.'

'What do you think he did with her clothes?' Marino asked, looking around, hands in the pockets of a long camel's hair coat that he had begun to wear after several dates with Molly.

'Probably the same thing he did with Eddie Heath's clothes,' Wesley said, and he could no longer resist walking into the woods, just a little way.

Marino looked at me. 'We know what Gault did with Eddie Heath's clothes. It's not the same here,'

'I suppose that's the point.' I watched Wesley with a heavy heart. 'Gault does whatever he pleases.'

'Me, I personally don't think the squirrel keeps shit like that for souvenirs. He don't want a lot of crap to haul around when he's on the move.'

'Sometimes he disposes of them,' I said.

A Bic lighter sparked several times before begrudgingly offering Marino a small flame.

'She was completely under his control,' I thought aloud some more. 'He led her here and told her to undress, and she did. You can see where her shoe prints stop and her bare footprints begin. There was no struggle, no thought of running away. No resistance.'

He lit a cigarette. Wesley backed away from the woods, careful where he stepped. I felt him look at me.

'They had a relationship,' I said.

'Gault don't have relationships,' Marino said.

'He has his own type of them. Bent and warped as they may be. He had one with the warden of the penitentiary in Richmond and with Helen the guard.'

'Yeah, and he whacked both of them. He cut off Helen's head and left it in a friggin' bowling bag in a field. The farmer who found that little present still ain't right. I heard he started drinking like a fish and won't plant nothing in that field. He won't even let his cows go there.'

'I didn't say he didn't kill the people he has relationships with,' I replied. 'I just said that he has relationships.'

I stared at her footprints nearby. She had worn a size nine or ten shoe.

'I hope they're going to cast hers, too,' I said.

The officer named Mossberg was using a paint stirrer to deftly spread dental stone into every portion of the shoe print he was trying to cast. It had begun to snow again, hard small flakes that stung.

'They won't cast hers,' Marino said. 'They'll get pictures and that's it since she ain't going to be on any witness stand in this world.'

I was accustomed to witnesses who did not speak to anyone but me. 'I would like a cast of her shoe impression,' I said. 'We have to identify her. Her shoes might help.'

Marino went to Mossberg and his comrades, and they all began to talk as they periodically glanced my way. Wesley looked up at the overcast sky as snow fell harder.

'Christ,' he said. 'I hope this stops.'

Snow fell more furiously as Frances Penn drove us to the New York Athletic Club on Central Park South. There was nothing more anyone could do until the sun came up, and I feared by then Gault's homicidal trail would be covered.

Commander Penn was pensive as she drove on streets that were deserted for the city. It was almost half past two A.M. None of her officers were with us. I was in front, Marino and Wesley in the back.

'I will tell you frankly that I do not like multijurisdictional investigations,' I said to her.

'Then you have had much experience with them, Dr. Scarpetta. Anyone who has been through them doesn't like them.'

'They're a pain in the butt,' Marino offered as Wesley, typically, just listened.

'What should we expect?' I asked, and I was being as diplomatic as possible, but she knew what I wanted.

'NYPD will *officially* work this case, but it will be my officers out there digging, putting in the most hours, doing the dog work. That's always the way it is when we share a case that gets a lot of media attention.'

'My first job was with NYPD,' Marino said.

Commander Penn eyed him in the rearview mirror.

'I left this sewer because I wanted to,' he added with his usual diplomacy.

'Do you still know anybody?' she asked.

'Most of the guys I started with have probably either retired, left on disability, or else they've been promoted and are fat and chained to desks.'

I wondered if Marino considered that maybe his peers might say the latter about him.

Then Wesley spoke. 'It might not be a bad idea to see who's still around, Pete. Friends, I mean.'

'Yeah, well, don't hold your breath.'

'We don't want a problem here.'

'No way to totally avoid that,' Marino said. 'Cops are going to fight over this and be stingy with what they know. Everyone wants to be a hero.'

'We can't afford that,' Wesley went on without the slightest fluctuation of intensity or tone.

'No, we can't,' I agreed.

'Come to me whenever you wish,' Commander Penn said. 'I will do everything I can.'

'If they let you,' Marino said.

There were three commands in the Transit Police, and hers was Support and Development. She was in charge of education, training and crime analysis. The department's decentralized detectives fell under the Field Command and therefore did not answer to her.

'I am in charge of computers and, as you know, our department has one of the most sophisticated computer systems in the United States. It is because of our connection with CAIN that I was able to notify Quantico so quickly. I am involved in this investigation. Not to worry,' Commander Penn said calmly.

'Tell me more about CAIN's usefulness in this case,' Wesley spoke again.

'The minute I got details about the nature of the homicide, I thought there was something familiar. I entered what we knew on the VICAP terminal and got a hit. So I called you literally as CAIN was calling me.'

'You'd heard of Gault?' Wesley asked her.

'I can't say that I am intimately acquainted with his MO.'

'You are now,' Wesley said.

Commander Penn pulled in front of the Athletic Club and unlocked the doors.

'Yes,' she said grimly. 'I am now.'

We checked in at a deserted desk inside a lovely lobby of antiques and old wood, and Marino headed for the elevator. He did not wait for us, and I knew why. He wanted to call Molly, with whom he was still infatuated beyond good sense, and whatever Wesley and I might do was something he did not care to know about.

'I doubt the bar is open this late,' Wesley said to me as brass doors shut and Marino invisibly rose to his floor.

'I'm quite certain it isn't.'

We looked around for a moment, as if, if we stood here long enough, someone would magically appear with glasses and a bottle.

'Let's go.' He lightly touched my elbow and we headed upstairs.

On the twelfth floor, he walked me to my room and I was nervous as I tried to insert my plastic card, which at first I held upside down. Then I could not get the magnetized strip in the proper way, and the tiny light on the brass handle stayed red.

'Here,' Wesley said.

'I think I've got it.'

'Could we have a nightcap?' he asked as I opened my door and turned on a light.

'At this hour, we'd probably be better off with a sleeping pill.'

'That's sort of what a nightcap is.'

My quarters were modest but handsomely appointed, and I dropped my bag on the queen-size bed.

'Are you a member here because of your father?' I asked.

Wesley and I had never been to New York together, and it

bothered me that there was yet one more detail about him I did not know.

'He worked in New York. So yes, that's why. I used to come into the city a lot when I was growing up.'

'The minibar is under the TV,' I said.

'I need the key.'

'Of course you do.'

Amusement flickered in his eyes as he took the small steel key from my outstretched hand, his fingers touching my palm with a gentleness that reminded me of other times. Wesley had his way, and he was not like anyone else.

'Should I try to find ice?' He unscrewed the cap from a two-jigger bottle of Dewar's.

'Straight up and neat is fine.'

'You drink like a man.' He handed me my glass.

I watched him slip out of his dark wool overcoat and finely tailored jacket. His starched white shirt was wrinkled from the labors of this long day, and he removed his shoulder holster and pistol and placed them on a dresser.

'It's strange to be without a gun,' I said, for I often carried my .38 or, on more nerve-rattling occasions, the Browning High Power. But New York gun laws did not often bend for visiting police or people like me.

Wesley sat on the bed opposite the one I was on, and we sipped our drinks and looked at each other.

'We haven't been together much the last few months,' I said.

He nodded.

'I think we should try to talk about it,' I went on.

'Okay.' His gaze had not wavered from mine. 'Go ahead.'

'I see. So I have to start.'

'I could start, but you might not like what I would say.'

'I would like to hear whatever you want to say.'

He said, 'I'm thinking that it's Christmas morning and I'm inside your hotel room. Connie is home alone asleep in our bed and unhappy because I'm not there. The kids are unhappy because I'm not there.'

'I should be in Miami. My mother is very ill,' I said.

He silently stared off, and I loved the sharp angles and shadows of his face.

'Lucy is there, and as usual I'm not. Do you have any idea how many holidays with my family I've missed?'

'Yes, I have a very good idea,' he said.

'In fact, I'm not sure there has ever been a holiday when my thoughts have not been darkened by some terrible case. So it almost doesn't matter whether I am with family or alone.'

'You have to learn to turn it off, Kay.'

'I've learned that as well as it can be learned.'

'You have to leave it outside the door like stinking crime scene clothes.'

But I could not. A day never went by when a memory wasn't triggered, when an image didn't flash. I would see a face bloated by injury and death, a body in bondage. I would see suffering and annihilation in unbearable detail, for nothing was hidden from me. I knew the victims too well. I closed my eyes and saw bare footprints in snow. I saw blood the bright red of Christmas.

'Benton, I do not want to spend Christmas here,' I said with deep depression.

I felt him sit next to me. He pulled me to him and we held each other for a while. We could not be close without touching.

'We should not be doing this,' I said as we continued doing it.

'I know.'

'And it's really difficult to talk about.'

'I know.' He reached for the lamp and turned it off.

'I find that ironical,' I said. 'When you think of what we share, what we have seen. Talking should not be difficult.'

'Those darker landscapes have nothing to do with intimacy,' he said.

'They do.'

'Then why are you not intimate with Marino? Or your deputy chief, Fielding?'

'Working the same horrors does not mean the next logical step is to go to bed. But I don't think I could be intimate with someone who does not understand what it's like for me.'

'I don't know.' His hands went still.

'Do you tell Connie?' I referred to his wife, who did not know that Wesley and I had become lovers last fall.

'I don't tell her everything.'

'How much does she know?'

'She knows nothing about some things.' He paused. 'She knows very little, really, about my work. I don't want her to know.'

I did not reply.

'I don't want her to know because of what it does to us. We change color, just as when cities become sooty, moths change color.'

'I don't want to take on the dingy shade of our habitat. I refuse.'

'You can refuse all you like.'

'Do you think it's fair you hold so much back from your wife?' I said quietly, and it was very hard to think because my flesh felt hot where he traced the contours of it.

'It isn't fair for her, and it isn't fair for me.'

'But you feel you have no choice.'

'I know I don't. She understands that there are places in me beyond her reach.'

'Is that the way she wants it?'

'Yes.' I felt him reach for his Scotch. 'You ready for another round?'

'Yes,' I said.

He got up and metal snapped in the dark as he broke screw

cap seals. He poured straight Scotch into our glasses and sat back down.

'That's all there is unless you want to switch to something else,' he said.

'I don't even need this much.'

'If you're asking me to say what we've done is right, I can't,' he said. 'I won't say that.'

'I know what we've done is not right.'

I took a swallow of my drink and as I reached to set the glass on the bedside table, his hands moved. We kissed again more deeply, and he did not waste time on buttons as his hands slid under and around whatever was in their way. We were frenzied, as if our clothes were on fire and we had to get them off.

Later, curtains began to glow with morning light and we floated between passion and sleep, mouths tasting like stale whiskey. I sat up, gathering covers around me.

'Benton, it's half past six.'

Groaning, he covered his eyes with an arm as if the sun were very rude to rouse him. He lay on his back, tangled in sheets, as I took a shower and began to dress. Hot water cleared my head, and this was the first Christmas morning in years when someone other than me had been in my bed. I felt I had stolen something.

'You can't go anywhere,' Wesley said, half asleep.

I buttoned my coat. 'I have to,' I said, sadly looking down at him.

'It's Christmas.'

'They're waiting for me at the morgue.'

'I'm sorry to hear it,' he mumbled into the pillow. 'I didn't know you felt that bad.'

4

New York's Office of the Chief Medical Examiner was on First Avenue, across from the Gothic red brick hospital called Bellevue, where the city's autopsies had been performed in earlier years. Winter-brown vines and graffiti marred walls and wrought iron, and fat black bags of trash awaited pickup on top of filthy snow. Christmas music played nonstop inside the beat-up yellow cab squeaking to a halt on a street almost never this still.

'I need a receipt,' I said to my Russian driver, who had spent the last ten minutes telling me what was wrong with the world.

'How much for?'

'Eight.' I was generous. It was Christmas morning.

He nodded, scribbling, as I watched a man on the sidewalk watching me, near Bellevue's fence. Unshaven, with wild long hair, he wore a blue jean jacket lined with fleece, the cuffs of stained army pants caught in the tops of battered cowboy boots. He began playing an imaginary guitar and singing as I got out of the cab.

'Jingle bells, jingle bells, jingle all the day. OHHH what fun it is to ride to Galveston today-AAAAAYYYYY . . .'

'You have admirer,' my amused driver said as I took the receipt through an open window.

He drove off in a swirl of exhaust. There was not another person or car in sight, and the horrendous serenading got louder. Then my mentally disfranchised admirer darted after me. I was appalled when he began screaming, 'Galveston!' as if it were my name or an accusation. I fled into the chief medical examiner's lobby.

'There's someone following me,' I said to a security guard decidedly lacking in Christmas spirit as she sat at her desk.

The deranged musician pressed his face against the front door, staring in, nose flattened, cheeks blanched. He opened his mouth wide, obscenely rolling his tongue over the glass and thrusting his pelvis back and forth as if he were having sex with the building. The guard, a sturdy woman with dreadlocks, strode over to the door and banged on it with her fist.

'Benny, cut it out,' she scolded him loudly. 'You quit that right now, Benny.' She rapped harder. '*Don't you make me come out there.*'

Benny backed away from the glass. Suddenly he was Nureyev doing pirouettes across the empty street.

'I'm Dr. Kay Scarpetta,' I said to the guard. 'Dr. Horowitz is expecting me.'

'No way the chief's expecting you. It's Christmas.' She regarded me with dark eyes that had seen it all. 'Dr. Pinto's on call. Now, I can try to get hold of him, if you want.' She headed back to her station.

'I'm well aware it's Christmas' – I followed her – 'but Dr. Horowitz is supposed to meet me here.' I got out my wallet and displayed my chief medical examiner's gold shield.

She was not impressed. 'You been here before?'

'Many times.'

'Hmm. Well, I sure haven't seen the chief today. But I guess that don't mean he didn't come in through the bay and didn't tell me. Sometimes they're here half a day and

I don't know. Hmm. That's right, don't *nobody* bother to tell me.'

She reached for the phone. 'Hmm. No sir, I don't need to know.' She dialed. 'I don't need to know *nothing*, no not me. Dr. Horowitz? This is Bonita with security. I got a Dr. Scarlett.' She paused. 'I don't know.'

She looked at me. 'How you spell that?'

'S-c-a-r-p-e-t-t-a,' I patiently said.

She still didn't get it right but was close enough. 'Yes, sir, I sure will.' She hung up and announced, 'You can go on and have a seat over there.'

The waiting area was furnished and carpeted in gray, magazines arranged on black tables, a modest artificial Christmas tree in the center of the room. Inscribed on a marble wall was *Taceant Colloquia Effugiat Risus Hic Locus Est Ubi Mors Gaudet Succurrere Vitae,* which meant one would find little conversation or laughter in this place where death delighted to help the living. An Asian couple sat across from me on a couch, tightly holding hands. They did not speak or look up, Christmas for them forever wrapped in pain.

I wondered why they were here and whom they had lost, and I thought of all I knew. I wished I could somehow offer comfort, yet that gift did not seem meant for me. After all these years, the best I could say to the bereft was that death was quick and their loved one did not suffer. Most times when I offered such words, they weren't entirely true, for how does one measure the mental anguish of a woman made to strip in an isolated park on a bitterly cold night? How could any of us imagine what she felt when Gault marched her to that ice-filled fountain and cocked his gun?

Forcing her to disrobe was a reminder of the unlimited depths of his cruelty and his insatiable appetite for games. Her nudity had not been necessary. She had not needed it telegraphed to her that she was going to die alone at Christmas with no one knowing her name. Gault could have just shot her and been done with it. He could have pulled out his Glock and caught her unaware. *The bastard.*

'Mr. and Mrs. Li?' A white-haired woman appeared before the Asian couple.

'Yes.'

'I'll take you in now if you're ready.'

'Yes, yes,' said the man as his wife began to cry.

They were led in the direction of the viewing room, where the body of someone they loved would be carried up from the morgue by a special elevator. Many people could not accept death unless they saw or touched it first, and despite the many viewings I had arranged and witnessed over the years, I really could not imagine going through such a ritual. I did not think I could bear that last fleeting glance through glass. Feeling the beginning of a headache, I closed my eyes and began massaging my temples. I sat like this for a long time until I sensed a presence.

'Dr. Scarpetta?' Dr. Horowitz's secretary was standing over me, her face concerned. 'Are you all right?'

'Emily,' I said, surprised. 'Yes, I'm fine, but I certainly wasn't expecting to see you here today.' I got up.

'Would you like some Tylenol?'

'You're very kind, but I'm fine,' I said.

'I wasn't expecting to see you here today, either. But things aren't exactly normal right now. I'm surprised you managed to get in without being accosted by reporters.'

'I didn't see any reporters,' I said.

'They were everywhere last night. I assume you saw the morning *Times*?'

'I'm afraid I haven't had a chance,' I said uncomfortably. I wondered if Wesley was still in bed.

'Things are a mess,' said Emily, a young woman with long, dark hair who was always so demure and plainly dressed that she seemed to have stepped forth from another age. 'Even the mayor's called. This is not the sort of publicity the city wants or needs. I still can't believe a reporter just happened to find the body.'

I glanced sharply at her as we walked. 'A reporter?'

'Well, he's really a copy editor or some such with the *Times* – one of these nutcakes who jogs no matter the weather. So he happens to be out in the park yesterday morning and takes a turn through Cherry Hill. It was very cold and snowy and deserted. He nears the fountain and there the poor woman is. Needless to say, the description in the morning paper is very detailed and people are frightened out of their wits.'

We passed through several doorways, then she poked her head inside the chief's office to gently announce us so we would not startle him. Dr. Horowitz was getting on in years and was getting hard of hearing. His office was scented with the light perfume of many flowering plants, for he loved orchids, African violets and gardenias, and they thrived in his care.

'Good morning, Kay.' He got up from his desk. 'Did you bring someone with you?'

'Captain Marino is supposed to meet us.'

'Emily will make certain he is shown the way. Unless you'd rather wait.'

I knew Horowitz did not want to wait. There was not time. He commanded the largest medical examiner's office in the country, where eight thousand people a year – the population of a small city – were autopsied on his steel tables. A fourth of the victims were homicides, and many would never have a name. New York had such a problem with identifying their dead that the NYPD's detective division had a missing persons unit in Horowitz's building.

The chief picked up the phone and spoke to someone he did not name.

'Dr. Scarpetta's here. We're on our way down,' he said.

'I'll make sure I find Captain Marino,' Emily said. 'Seems like I know his name.'

'We've worked together for many years,' I told her. 'And he's been assisting the FBI's Investigative Support Unit at Quantico for as long as it has existed.'

'I thought it was called the Behavioral Science Unit, like in the movies.'

'The Bureau changed the name, but the purpose is the same,' I said of the small group of agents who had become famous for their psychological profiling and pursuit of violent sex offenders and killers. When I recently had become the consulting forensic pathologist for the unit, I had not believed there was much left that I had not seen. I had been wrong.

Sunlight filled windows in Horowitz's office and was caught in glass shelves of flowers and miniature trees. I knew that in the bathroom orchids grew in the steamy dark from perches around the sink and tub, and that at home he had a greenhouse. The first time I had met Horowitz he had reminded me of Lincoln. Both men had gaunt, benevolent faces shadowed by a war that was ripping society apart. They bore tragedy as if they had been chosen to, and had large, patient hands.

We went downstairs to what the N.Y. office called their mortuary, an oddly genteel appellation for a morgue set in one of the most violent cities in America. Air seeping in from the bay was very cold and smelled of stale cigarettes and death. Signs posted on aqua walls asked people not to throw bloody sheets, shrouds, loose rags or containers into Dumpsters.

Shoe covers were required, eating was prohibited and red biological hazard warnings were on many of the doors. Horowitz explained that one of his thirty deputy chiefs would be performing the autopsy on the unknown woman we believed was Gault's latest victim.

We turned into a locker room where Dr. Lewis Rader was dressed in scrubs and attaching a battery pack to his waist.

'Dr. Scarpetta,' Horowitz said, 'have you and Dr. Rader met?'

'We've known each other forever,' Rader said with a smile.

'Yes, we have,' I said warmly. 'But the last time we saw each other, I guess, was San Antonio.'

'Gee. Has it been that long?'

This had been at the American Academy of Forensic Sciences Bring Your Own Slide session, an evening once a year when people like us got together for show and tell. Rader had presented the case of a bizarre lightning death involving a young woman. Because the victim's clothing had been blown off and her head injured when she had fallen and struck concrete, she had come into the ME's office as a sexual assault. The cops were convinced until Rader showed them that the woman's belt buckle was magnetized and she had a small burn on the bottom of one foot.

I remembered after the presentation Rader had poured me a Jack Daniel's, neat and straight up in a paper cup, and we had reminisced about the old days when there were few forensic pathologists and I was the only woman. Rader was getting close to sixty and was much acclaimed by his peers. But he would not have made a good chief. He did not relish warfare with paperwork and politicians.

We looked like we were suiting up for outer space as we put on air packs, face shields and hoods. AIDS was a worry if one got a needle stick or cut while working on an infected body, but a bigger threat were infections borne on air, such as tuberculosis, hepatitis and meningitis. These days we double-gloved, breathed purified air and covered ourselves with greens and gowns that could be thrown away. Some medical examiners like Rader wore stainless steel mesh gloves reminiscent of chain mail.

I was pulling the hood over my head when O'Donnell, the detective I had met last night, walked in with Marino, who looked irritable and hungover. They put on surgical masks and gloves, no one meeting anybody's eyes or speaking. Our nameless case was in steel drawer 121, and as we filed out of the locker room, mortuary assistants hoisted the body out and set it on top of a gurney. The dead woman was nude and pitiful on her cold, steel tray.

Areas of flesh excised from her shoulder and inner thighs were ghastly patches of darkened blood. Her skin was bright pink from cold livor mortis, typical in frozen bodies or people who have died of exposure. The gunshot wound to her right temple was large caliber, and I could see at a glance the distinct muzzle mark stamped into her skin when Gault had pressed the pistol's barrel against her head and pulled the trigger.

Men in scrubs and masks rolled her into the X-ray room, where each of us was given a pair of orange-tinted plastic glasses to add to our armor. Rader set up a light energy source called a Luma-Lite, which was a simple black box with an enhanced blue fiber-optic cable. It was another set of eyes that could see what ours could not, a soft white light that turned fingerprints fluorescent and caused hairs, fibers and narcotic and semen stains to glare like fire.

'Someone hit the lights,' Rader said.

In the dark, he began going over the body with the Luma-Lite, and multiple fibers lit up like fine-gauge hot wire. With forceps, Rader collected evidence from pubic hair, feet, hands and the stubble on her scalp. Small areas of yellow got bright like the sun as he passed the light over the finger pads of her right hand.

'She's got some chemical here,' Rader said.

'Sometimes semen lights up like that.'

'I don't think that's it.'

'It could be street drugs,' I offered my opinion.

'Let's get it on a swab,' said Rader. 'Where's the hydrochloric acid?'

'Coming up.'

The evidence was recovered and Rader moved on. The small white light passed over the geography of the woman's body, into the dark recessed areas where her flesh had been removed, over the flat plain of her belly and gentle slopes of her breasts. Virtually no trace evidence clung to her wounds. This corroborated our theory that Gault had killed and maimed her where she was found, because had she been transported after the assault, debris would have adhered to drying blood. Indeed, her injuries were the cleanest areas of her body.

We worked in the dark for more than an hour, and she was revealed to me inches at a time. Her skin was fair and seemed a stranger to the sun. She was poorly muscled, thin, and five foot eight. Her left ear had been pierced three times, her right ear twice, and she wore studs and small loops, all in gold. She was dark blond with blue eyes and even features that may not have been so bland had she not shaved her head and were she not dead. Her fingernails were unpainted and chewed to the quick.

The only sign of old injuries were healed scars on her forehead and the top of her head over the left parietal bone. The scars were linear, one and a half to two inches long. The only visible gunshot residue on her hands was an ejector port mark on her right palm between her index finger and thumb, which I believed placed that hand in a defensive position when the pistol was fired. The residue most likely ruled out suicide even if all other evidence had pointed to it, which of course it did not.

'I guess we don't know which was her dominant hand.' Horowitz's voice sounded in the dark somewhere behind me.

'Her right arm is slightly more developed than her left,' I observed.

'Right-handed, then, my guess is. Her hygiene, nutrition were poor,' Horowitz said.

'Like a street person, a prostitute. That's going to be my guess,' offered O'Donnell.

'No hooker I know's gonna shave her head.' Marino's gruff voice sounded from darkness across the table.

'Depends on who she was trying to attract,' said O'Donnell. 'The plainclothes officer who spotted her in the subway thought at first she was a man.'

'This was when she was with Gault,' Marino said.

'When she was with the guy you think was Gault.'

'I don't think it,' Marino said. 'That's who she was with. I can almost smell the son of a bitch, like he leaves a bad odor everywhere he's been.'

'I think what you smell is her,' O'Donnell said.

'Move it down, right about here. Good, thanks.' Rader collected more fibers as disembodied voices continued to converse in a darkness as thick as velvet.

Finally, I confessed, 'I find this very unusual. Generally I associate so much trace with someone who has been wrapped in a dirty blanket or transported in the trunk of a car.'

'It's obvious she hasn't bathed lately, and it's winter,' Rader said as he moved the fiber-optic cable, illuminating a faint childhood scar from a smallpox inoculation. 'She may have been wearing the same clothing for days, and if she traveled on the subway or by bus, she could have collected a lot of debris.'

What this added up to was an indigent woman who had not been reported missing as far as we could tell because she had no home, no one who knew or cared she was gone. She was the tragically typical street person, we assumed, until we got her on table six in the autopsy room, where forensic dentist Dr. Graham waited to chart her teeth.

A broad-shouldered young man with an air of abstraction that I associated with medical school professors, he was an oral surgeon on Staten Island when he worked on the living. But today was his day to work on those who complained with silent tongues, which he did for a fee that probably would not cover his taxi fare and lunch. Rigor mortis was set, and like an obstinate child who hates the dentist, the dead woman would not cooperate. He finally pried her jaws open with a thin file.

'Well Merry Christmas,' he said, moving a bright light close. 'She's got a mouth full of gold.'

'Most curious,' Horowitz said, like a mathematician pondering a problem.

'These are gold foil restorations.' Graham began pointing out kidney bean-shaped gold fillings near the gum line of each front tooth. 'She has them here and here and here.' He pointed again and again. 'Six in all. This is just very rare. In fact, I've never seen it. Not in a morgue.'

'What the hell is gold foil?' Marino asked.

'It's a pain in the ass, is what it is,' said Graham. 'A very difficult, unattractive restoration.'

'I believe in the old days, they were required to pass your dental license exam,' I said.

'That's right.' Graham continued to work. 'The students hated them.'

He went on to explain that gold foil restorations required the dentist to pound gold pellets into a tooth, and the slightest bit of moisture would cause the filling to fall out. Although the restorations were very good, they were labor intensive, painful and expensive.

'And not many patients,' he added, 'want gold showing, especially on the facial surface of their front teeth.'

He continued charting various repairs, extractions, shapes and misshapes that made this woman who she was. She had a slightly open bite and a semicircular wear pattern to her front teeth possibly consistent with her biting down on a pipe, since it was reported to him that she had been seen with a pipe.

'If she was a chronic pipe smoker, wouldn't you expect her teeth to be stained from tobacco?' I said, for I saw no evidence of it.

'Possibly. But look at how eroded her tooth surfaces are – these scooped-out areas at the gum line that required the gold foil.' He showed us. 'The major damage to her teeth is consistent with obsessive overbrushing.'

'So if she brushed the hell out of her teeth ten times a day, she's not going to have tobacco stains,' Marino said.

'Brushing the hell out of her teeth doesn't fit with her poor hygiene,' I commented. 'In fact, her mouth seems inconsistent with everything else about her.'

'Can you tell when she had this work done?' Rader asked.

'Not really,' Graham said as he continued probing. 'But it is consistently good. I'd say it was probably the same dentist who did all of it, and about the only area in the country where you find gold foil restorations still being done is the West Coast.'

'I'm wondering how you can know that,' Detective O'Donnell said to him.

'You can only get these restorations done where there are dentists who still do them. I don't do them. I personally don't know anybody who does them. But there is an organization called the American Academy of Gold Foil Operators that has several hundred members – dentists who pride themselves on still doing this particular restoration. And the largest concentration of them is in Washington State.'

'Why would someone want a restoration like this?' O'Donnell then asked.

'Gold lasts a long time.' Graham glanced up at him. 'There are people who are nervous about what is put into their mouths. The chemicals in composite white fillings supposedly can cause nerve damage. They stain and wear out more quickly. Some people believe silver causes everything from cystic fibrosis to hair loss.'

Then Marino spoke. 'Yo, well, some squirrels just like the way gold looks.'

'Some do,' Graham agreed. 'She might be one of those.'

But I did not think so. This woman did not strike me as one who cared about her appearance. I suspected she had not shaved her head to make a statement or because she thought it looked trendy. As we began to explore her internally, I understood more, even as the mystery of her deepened.

She had undergone a hysterectomy that had removed her uterus vaginally and left her ovaries, and her feet were flat. She also had an old intracerebral hematoma in the frontal lobe of her brain from a coup injury that had fractured her skull beneath the scars we had found.

'She was the victim of an assault, possibly many years ago,' I said. 'And it's the sort of head injury you associate with personality change.' I thought of her wandering the world and of no one missing her. 'She probably was estranged from her family and had a seizure disorder.'

Horowitz turned to Rader. 'See if we can put a rush on tox. Let's check her for diphenylhydantoin.'

5

Little could be done the rest of the day. The city's mind was on Christmas, and laboratories and most offices were closed. Marino and I walked several blocks toward Central Park before stopping at a Greek coffee shop, where I drank coffee because I could not eat. Then we found a cab.

Wesley was not in his room. I returned to mine and for a long time stood before the window looking out at dark, tangled trees and black rocks amid snowy expanses of the park. The sky was gray and heavy. I could not see the ice-skating rink, nor the fountain where the murdered woman was found. Though I had not been on the scene when her body was, I had studied the photographs. What Gault had done was horrible, and I wondered where he was right now.

I could not count the violent deaths I had worked since my career began, yet I understood many of them better than I let on from the witness stand. It is not difficult to comprehend people being so enraged, drugged, frightened or crazy that they kill. Even psychopaths have their own twisted logic. But Temple Brooks Gault seemed beyond description or deciphering.

His first encounter with the criminal justice system had been less than five years ago when he was drinking White Russians in a bar in Abingdon, Virginia. An intoxicated truck driver, who did not like effeminate males, began to harass Gault, who had a black belt in karate. Without a word, Gault smiled his strange smile. He got up, spun around and kicked the man in the head. Half a dozen off-duty state troopers happened to be at a nearby table, which was perhaps the only reason Gault was caught and charged with manslaughter.

His career in Virginia's state penitentiary was brief and bizarre. He became the pet of a corrupt warden, who falsified Gault's identity, facilitating his escape. Gault had been out but a very short time before he happened upon a boy named Eddie Heath and killed him in much the same style he had butchered the woman in Central Park. He went on to murder my morgue supervisor, the prison warden and the prison guard named Helen. At the time, Gault was thirty-one years old.

Flakes of snow had begun to drift past my window and in the distance were caught like fog in trees. Hoofs rang against pavement as a horse-drawn carriage went by with two passengers bundled in plaid blankets. The white mare was old and not surefooted, and when she slipped the driver beat her savagely. Other horses looked on in sad relief against the weather, heads down, coats unkempt, and I felt rage rise in my throat like bile. My heart beat furiously. I suddenly swung around as someone knocked on my door.

'Who is it?' I demanded.

Wesley said, after a pause, 'Kay?'

I let him in. A baseball cap and the shoulders of his overcoat were wet from snow. He pulled off leather gloves and stuffed them in pockets, and removed his coat without taking his eyes off me.

'What is it?' he asked.

'I'll tell you exactly what it is.' My voice shook. 'Come right over here and look.' I grabbed his hand and pulled him to the window. 'Just look! Do you think those poor, pathetic horses ever get a day off? Do you think they are properly cared for? Do you think they're ever groomed or adequately shod? You know what happens when they stumble – when it's icy and they're old as hell and almost fall?'

'Kay . . .'

'*They're just beaten harder.*'

'Kay . . .'

'So why don't you do something about it?' I railed on.

'What would you like me to do?'

'Just do something. The world is full of people who don't do anything and I'm goddam tired of it.'

'Would you like me to file a complaint with the SPCA?' he asked.

'Yes, I would,' I said. 'And I will, too.'

'Would it be okay if we did that tomorrow since I don't think anything's open today?'

I continued looking out the window as the driver beat his horse again. 'That's it,' I snapped.

'Where are you going?' He followed me out of the room.

He hurried after me as I headed to the elevator. I strode across the lobby and out the hotel's front door without a coat. By now, snow was falling hard, and the icy street was smooth with it. The object of my wrath was an old man in a hat hunched over in the driver's seat. He sat up straighter when he saw this middle-aged lady coming with a tall man in her wake.

'You like nice carriage ride?' he asked in a heavy accent.

The mare strained her neck toward me and cocked her ears as if she knew what was coming. She was scarred skin and bones with overgrown hoofs, her eyes dull and rimmed in pink.

'What is your horse's name?' I inquired.

'Snow White.' He looked as miserable as his pitiful mare as he started to cite his fares.

'I'm not interested in your fares,' I said as he looked wearily down at me.

He shrugged. 'So how long you want ride?'

'I don't know,' I said curtly. 'How long do I need to ride before you start beating Snow White again? And do you beat the shit out of her more or less when it's Christmas?'

'I am good to my horse,' he said stupidly.

'You are cruel to this horse and probably to everything alive and breathing,' I said.

'I have job to do,' he said as his eyes narrowed.

'I am a doctor and I am reporting you,' I said as my voice got tighter.

'What?' he chortled. 'You horse doctor?'

I stepped closer to the driver's box until I was inches from his blanket-covered legs. 'You whip this mare one more time, and I will see it,' I said with the iron calm I reserved for people I hated. 'And this man behind me will see it. From that window right up there—' I pointed. 'And one day you will wake up and find I have bought your company and fired you.'

'You do not buy company.' He glanced up curiously at the New York Athletic Club.

'You do not understand reality,' I said.

He tucked his chin into his collar and ignored me.

I was silent as I returned to my room, and Wesley did not speak, either. I took a deep breath and my hands would not stop shaking. He went to the minibar and poured us each a whiskey, then sat me on the bed, propped several pillows behind me, and took off his coat and spread it over my legs.

He turned lights off and sat next to me. For a while he rubbed my neck while I stared out the window. The snow-sky looked gray and wet, but not dreary as when it rained. I wondered about the difference, why snow seemed soft while rain felt hard and somehow colder.

It had been bitterly cold and raining in Richmond the Christmas when police discovered Eddie Heath's frail, naked body. He was propped against a Dumpster behind an abandoned building with windows boarded up, and though he would never regain consciousness, he was not yet dead. Gault had abducted him from a convenience store where Eddie had been sent by his mother to pick up a can of soup.

I would never forget the desolation of that filthy spot where the boy had been found or Gault's gratuitous cruelty of placing near the body the small bag containing the can of soup and candy bar Eddie had purchased before his death. The details made him so real that even the Henrico County officer wept. I envisioned Eddie's wounds and remembered the warm pressure of his hand when I examined him in pediatric intensive care before he was disconnected from life support.

'Oh God,' I muttered in this dim room. 'Oh God, I'm so tired of all this.'

Wesley did not reply. He had gotten up and was standing before the window, drink in hand.

'I'm so tired of cruelty. I'm so tired of people beating horses and killing little boys and head-injured women.'

Wesley did not turn around. He said, 'It's Christmas. You should call your family.'

'You're right. That's just what I need to cheer me up.' I blew my nose and reached for the phone.

At my sister's house in Miami, no one answered. I dug an address book out of my purse and called the hospital where my mother had been for weeks. A nurse in the intensive care unit said Dorothy was with my mother and she would get her.

'Hello?'

'Merry Christmas,' I said to my only sibling.

'I guess that's an irony when you consider where I am. There's certainly nothing merry about this place, not that you would know since you aren't here.'

'I'm quite familiar with intensive care,' I said. 'Where is Lucy and how is she?'

'She's out running errands with her friend. They dropped me off and will be back in an hour or so. Then we're going to Mass. Well, I don't know if the friend will since she's not Catholic.'

'Lucy's friend has a name. Her name is Janet, and she is very nice.'

'I'm not going to get into that.'

'How is Mother?'

'The same.'

'The same as what, Dorothy,' I said, and she was beginning to get to me.

'They've had to suction her a lot today. I don't know what the problem is, but you can't imagine what it's like to watch her try to cough and not make a sound because of that awful tube in her throat. She only made it five minutes off the ventilator today.'

'Does she know what day it is?'

'Oh yes,' Dorothy said ominously. 'Oh yes indeed. I put a little tree on her table. She's been crying a lot.'

A dull ache welled in my chest.

'When are you getting here?' she went on.

'I don't know. We can't leave New York right now.'

'Does it ever strike you, Katie, that you've spent most of your life worrying about dead people?' Her voice was getting sharp. 'I think all your relationships are with dead—'

'Dorothy, you tell Mother I love her and that I called. Please tell Lucy and Janet that I'll try again later tonight or tomorrow.'

I hung up.

Wesley was still standing before the window with his back to me. He was quite familiar with my family difficulties.

'I'm sorry,' he said kindly.

'She would be like that even if I were there.'

'I know. But the point is, you should be there and I should be home.'

When he talked about home I got uncomfortable, because his home and mine were different. I thought again about this case, and when I closed my eyes I saw the woman who looked like a manikin without clothing or wig. I envisioned her awful wounds.

I said, 'Benton, who is he really killing when he kills these people?'

'Himself,' he said. 'Gault is killing himself.'

'That can't be all of it.'

'No, but it is part of it.'

'It's a sport to him,' I said.

'That, too, is true.'

'What about his family? Do we know anything more?'

'No.' He did not turn around. 'Mother and father are healthy and in Beaufort, South Carolina.'

'They moved from Albany?'

'Remember the flood.'

'Oh yes. The storm.'

'South Georgia was almost washed away. Apparently the Gaults left and are in Beaufort now. I think they're also looking for privacy.'

'I can only imagine.'

'Right. Tour buses were rolling past their house in Georgia. Reporters were knocking on their door. They will not cooperate with the authorities. As you know, I have repeatedly requested interviews and have been denied.'

'I wish we knew more about his childhood,' I said.

'He grew up on the family plantation, which was basically a big white frame house set on hundreds of acres of pecan trees. Nearby was the factory that made nut logs and other candies you see in truck stops and restaurants, mostly in the South. As for what went on inside that house while Gault lived there, we don't know.'

'And his sister?'

'Still on the West Coast somewhere, I guess. We can't find her to talk to her. She probably wouldn't anyway.'

'What is the likelihood that Gault would contact her?'

'Hard to say. But we've not learned anything that would indicate the two of them have ever been close. It doesn't appear that Gault has been close – in the normal sense – to anyone his entire life.'

'Where have you been today?' My voice was gentler and I felt more relaxed.

'I talked to several detectives and did a lot of walking.'

'Walking for exercise or work?'

'Mostly the latter, but both. By the way, Snow White is gone. The driver just left with an empty carriage. And he didn't hit her.'

I opened my eyes. 'Please tell me more about your walk.'

'I walked through the area where Gault was seen in the subway station with the victim at Central Park West and Eighty-first. Depending on the weather and what route you take, that particular subway entrance is maybe a five-, ten-minute walk from the Ramble.'

'But we don't know that they went in there.'

'We don't know a damn thing,' he said, letting out a long, weary breath. 'Certainly, we have recovered footwear impressions. But there are so many other footprints, hoof prints, dog prints and God knows what. Or at least there were.' He paused as snow streaked past the glass.

'You're thinking he's been living around there.'

'That subway station's not a transfer station. It's a destination station. People who get off there either live on the Upper West Side or are going to one of the restaurants, the museum or events in the park.'

'Which is why I don't think Gault has been living in that neighborhood,' I said. 'In a station like the one at Eighty-first or others nearby, you probably see the same people over and over again. It seems that the transit officer who gave Gault a ticket would have recognized him if Gault was local and used the subway a lot.'

'That's a good point,' Wesley said. 'It appears Gault was

familiar with the area where he chose to commit the crime. Yet there's no indication he ever spent time in that area. So how could he be familiar with it?' He turned around to face me.

The lights were off in the room, and he was in the shadows before a marbled background of gray sky and snow. Wesley looked thin, dark trousers hanging from his hips, a belt pulled to a new notch.

'You've lost weight,' I said.

'I'm flattered you would notice,' he wryly said.

'I know your body well only when you have no clothes on,' I said matter-of-factly. 'And then you are beautiful.'

'Then is the only time it matters, I guess.'

'No it isn't. How much have you lost and why?'

'I don't know how much. I never weigh myself. Sometimes I forget to eat.'

'Have you eaten today?' I asked as if I were his primary care physician.

'No.'

'Get your coat on,' I said.

We walked hand in hand along the wall of the park, and I could not recall if we had shown affection before in public. But the few people out could not see our faces clearly, not that they would have cared. For a moment my heart was light, and snow hitting snow sounded like snow hitting glass.

We walked without talking for many blocks, and I thought about my family in Miami. I probably would call them again before the end of the day, and my reward would be more complaints. They were unhappy with me because I had not done what they wanted, and whenever that was the case, I furiously wanted to quit them as if they were a bad job or a vice. In truth, I worried most about Lucy, whom I had always loved as if she were my daughter. Mother I could not please, and Dorothy I did not like.

I moved closer to Benton and took his arm. He reached over

with his other hand to take mine as I pressed my body against him. Both of us wore caps, which made it difficult to kiss. So we stopped on the sidewalk in the gathering dark, turned our caps backward like hoodlums and resolved the problem. Then we laughed at each other because of how we looked.

'Damn, I wish I had a camera.' Wesley laughed some more.

'No, you don't.'

I returned the cap to its proper position as I thought of anyone taking a picture of us together. I was reminded that we were outlaws, and the merry moment vanished. We walked on.

'Benton, this can't go on forever,' I said.

He did not speak.

I went on, 'In your real world you are a committed husband and father, and then we go out of town.'

'How do you feel about it?' he said, tension returning to his voice.

'I suppose I feel the same way most people do when they're having an affair. Guilt, shame, fear, sadness. I get headaches and you lose weight.' I paused. 'Then we get around each other.'

'What about jealousy?' he asked.

I hesitated. 'I discipline myself not to feel that.'

'You can't discipline yourself not to feel.'

'Certainly you can. We both do it all the time when we're working cases like this one.'

'Are you jealous of Connie?' he persisted as we walked.

'I have always been fond of your wife and think she is a fine person.'

'But are you jealous of her relationship with me? It would be very understandable—'

I interrupted him. 'Why must you push this, Benton?'

'Because I want us to face the facts and sort through them, somehow.'

'All right, then you tell me something,' I said. 'When I was with Mark while he was your partner and best friend, were you ever jealous?'

'Of whom?' He tried to be funny.

'Were you ever jealous of my relationship with Mark?' I said.

He did not answer right away.

'I would be lying if I didn't admit that I've always been attracted to you. Strongly attracted,' he finally said.

I thought back to times when Mark, Wesley and I had been together. I searched for the faintest hint of what he had just said. I could not remember. But when I had been with Mark, I was focused only on him.

'I have been honest,' Wesley went on. 'Let's talk about you and Connie again. I need to know.'

'Why?'

'I need to know if all of us could ever be together,' he said. 'Like the old days when you had dinner with us, when you came to visit. My wife has begun to ask why you don't do that anymore.'

'You're saying that you fear she is suspicious.' I felt paranoid.

'I'm saying that the subject has come up. She likes you. Now that you and I work together, she wonders why that means she sees less of you rather than more.'

'I can see why she might wonder,' I said.

'What are we going to do?'

I had been in Benton's home and watched him with his children and his wife. I remembered the touching, the smiles and allusions to matters beyond my ken as they briefly shared their world with friends. But in those days it was different because I had been in love with Mark, who now was dead.

I let go of Wesley's hand. Yellow cabs rushed by in sprays of snow, and lights were warm in apartment building windows. The park glowed the whiteness of ghosts beneath tall iron lamps.

'I can't do it,' I said to him.

We turned onto Central Park West.

'I'm sorry, but I just don't think I can be around you and Connie,' I added.

'I thought you said you could discipline your emotions.'

'That's easy for you to say because I don't have someone else in my life.'

'You're going to have to do it at some point. Even if we break this off, you're going to have to deal with my family. If we are to continue working together, if we are to be friends.'

'So now you're giving me ultimatums.'

'You know I'm not.'

I quickened my pace. The first time we had made love I had made my life a hundred times more complicated. Certainly, I had known better. I had seen more than one poor fool on my autopsy table who had decided to get involved with someone married. People annihilated themselves and others. They became mentally ill and got sued.

I passed Tavern on the Green. I stared up at the Dakota on my left, where John Lennon was killed on a corner years ago. The subway station was very close to Cherry Hill, and I wondered if Gault might have left the park and come here. I stood and stared. That night, December 8, I was driving home from a court case when I heard on the radio that Lennon had been shot dead by a nobody carrying a copy of *Catcher in the Rye*.

'Benton,' I said, 'Lennon used to live there.'

'Yes,' he said. 'He was killed right over there by that entrance.'

'Is there any possibility Gault cared about that?'

He paused. 'I haven't thought about it.'

'Should we think about it?'

He was silent as he looked up at the Dakota with its sandblasted brick, wrought iron and copper trim.

'We probably should think about everything,' he said.

'Gault would have been a teenager when Lennon was murdered. As I recall from Gault's apartment in Richmond, he seemed to prefer classical music and jazz. I don't remember that he had any albums by Lennon or the Beatles.'

'If he's preoccupied with Lennon,' Wesley said, 'it's not for musical reasons. Gault would be fascinated by such a sensational crime.'

We walked on. 'There just aren't enough people to ask the questions we need answered,' I said.

'We would need an entire police department. Maybe the entire FBI.'

'Can we check to see if anyone fitting his description has been seen around the Dakota?' I asked.

'Hell, he could be staying there,' Wesley said bitterly. 'So far, money hasn't seemed to be his problem.'

Around the corner of the Museum of Natural History was the snowcapped pink awning of a restaurant called Scaletta, which I was surprised to find lit up and noisy. A couple in fur coats turned in and went downstairs, and I wondered if we shouldn't do the same. I was actually getting hungry, and Wesley didn't need to lose any more weight.

'Are you up for this?' I asked him.

'Absolutely. Is Scaletta a relative of yours?' he teased.

'I think not.'

We got as far as the door, where the maître d' informed us that the restaurant was closed.

'You certainly don't look closed,' I said, suddenly exhausted and unwilling to walk any more.

'But we are, signora.' He was short, balding and wearing a tuxedo with a bright red cummerbund. 'This is a private party.'

'Who is Scaletta?' Wesley asked him.

'Why you want to know?'

'It is an interesting name, much like mine,' I said.

'And what is yours?'

'Scarpetta.'

He looked carefully at Wesley and seemed puzzled. 'Yes, of course. But he is not with you this evening?'

I stared blankly at him. 'Who is not with me?'

'Signor Scarpetta. He was invited. I'm most sorry, I did not realize you were in his party . . .'

'Invited to what?' I had no idea what he was talking about. My name was rare. I had never encountered another Scarpetta, not even in Italy.

The maître d' hesitated. 'You are not related to the Scarpetta who comes here often?'

'What Scarpetta?' I said, getting uneasy.

'A man. He has been here many times recently. A very good customer. He was invited to our Christmas party. So you are not his guests?'

'Tell me more about him,' I said.

'A young man. He spends much money.' The maître d' smiled.

I could feel Wesley's interest pique. He said, 'Can you describe him?'

'I have many people inside. We reopen tomorrow . . .'

Wesley discreetly displayed his shield. The man regarded it calmly.

'Of course.' He was polite but unafraid. 'I find you a table.'

'No, no,' Wesley said. 'You don't have to do that. But we need to ask more about this man who said his last name was Scarpetta.'

'Come in.' He motioned us. 'We talk, we may as well sit. You sit, you may as well eat. My name is Eugenio.'

He led us to a pink-covered table in a corner far removed from guests in party clothes filling most of the dining room. They were toasting, eating, talking and laughing with the gestures and cadences of Italians.

'We do not have full menu tonight,' Eugenio apologized. 'I can bring you *costoletta di vitello alla griglia* or *pollo al limone* with maybe a little *cappellini primavera* or *rigatoni con broccolo.*'

We said yes to all and added a bottle of Dolcetto D'Alba, which was a favorite of mine and difficult to find.

Eugenio went to get our wine while my mind spun slowly and sick fear pulled at my heart.

'Don't even suggest it,' I said to Wesley.

'I'm not going to suggest anything yet.'

He didn't have to. The restaurant was so close to the subway station where Gault had been seen. He would have noticed Scaletta's because of the name. It would have made him think of me, and I was someone he probably thought about a lot.

Almost instantly, Eugenio was back with our bottle. He peeled off foil and twisted in the corkscrew as he talked. 'See, 1979, very light. More like a Beaujolais.' He pulled the cork out and poured a little for me to taste.

I nodded, and he filled our glasses.

'Have a seat, Eugenio,' Wesley said. 'Have some wine. Tell us about Scarpetta.'

He shrugged. 'All I can say is he first come in here several weeks ago. I know he had not been in before. To tell the truth, he was unusual.'

'In what way?' Wesley asked.

'Unusual looking. Very bright red hair, thin, dressed unusual. You know, long black leather coat and Italian trousers with maybe T-shirt.' He looked up at the ceiling and shrugged again. 'If you can imagine wearing nice trousers and shoes like Armani and then wearing T-shirt. It was not ironed, either.'

'Was he Italian?' I asked.

'Oh no. He could fool some people, but not me.' Eugenio shook his head and poured himself a glass of wine. 'He was American. But he maybe spoke Italian because he used the Italian part of the menu. He ordered that way, you know? He would not order in English. Actually, he was very good.'

'How did he pay?' Wesley asked.

'Always charge card.'

'And the name on the charge card was Scarpetta?' I asked.

'Yes, I'm certain. No first name, just the initial *K*. He said his name was Kirk. Not exactly Italian.' He smiled and shrugged.

'He was friendly, then,' Wesley said as my mind kept slamming into this information.

'He was very friendly sometimes and not so friendly other times. He always had something to read. Newspapers.'

'He was alone?' Wesley asked.

'Always.'

'What kind of charge card?' I said.

He thought. 'American Express. A gold card, I believe.'

I looked at Wesley.

'Do you have yours with you?' he asked me.

'I would assume so.'

I got out my billfold. The card wasn't there.

'I don't understand.' I felt the blood rise to the roots of my hair.

'Where did you have it last?' Wesley asked.

'I don't know.' I was stunned. 'I don't use it much. So many places won't take it.'

We were silent. Wesley sipped his wine and looked around the room. I was frightened and bewildered. I did not understand what any of this meant. Why would Gault come here and pretend to be me? If he had my gold card, how did he get it? And even as I asked that last question, a dark suspicion stirred. Quantico.

Eugenio had gotten up to see about our food.

'Benton,' I said as my blood roared. 'I let Lucy use that card last fall.'

'When she began her internship with us?' He frowned.

'Yes. I gave it to her after she left UVA and was on her way to the Academy. I knew she'd be back and forth to visit me. She'd be flying to Miami for the holidays and so on. I gave her my American Express card to use mostly for plane and Amtrak tickets.'

'And you haven't seen it since then?' He looked dubious.

'I haven't thought about it, to tell you the truth. I generally use MasterCard or Visa, and it seems to me that the Amex card expires this February. So I must have figured Lucy could have it until then.'

'You'd better call her.'

'I will.'

'Because if she doesn't have it, Kay, then I'm going to suspect Gault stole it when the Engineering Research Facility was broken into last October.'

This was what I feared.

'What about your bills?' he asked. 'Have you noticed any strange charges over recent months?'

'No,' I said. 'I don't recall there being any charges at all during October or November.' I paused. 'Should we cancel the card or use it to track him?'

'Tracking him with it may be a problem.'

'Because of money.'

Wesley hesitated. 'I'll see what I can do.'

Eugenio returned with our pasta. He said he was trying to remember if there might be anything else.

'I think his last time here was Thursday night.' He counted his fingers. 'Four days ago. He likes the *bistecca*, the *carpaccio*. Uhhh, let me see. He got *funghi e carciofi* one time and *cappellini* plain. No sauce. Just a little butter. We invite him to the party. Every year we do this to show appreciation to friends and special customers.'

'Did he smoke?' Wesley asked.

'Yes, he did.'

'Do you remember what?'

'Yes, brown cigarettes. Nat Shermans.'

'What about drinking?'

'He like expensive Scotch and nice wine. Only he was' – he lifted his nose – 'snobbish. He think only the French make wine.' Eugenio laughed. 'So he usually got Château Carbonnieux or Château Olivier, and the vintage could be no earlier than 1989.'

'He only got white wine?' I said.

'No red, none. He would not touch red. I send him glass on the house once and he send it back.'

Eugenio and Wesley exchanged cards and other information, then our maître d' returned his attention to his party, which by now was going strong.

'Kay,' Wesley said, 'can you think of any other explanation for what we've just learned?'

'No,' I said. 'The description of the man sounds like Gault. Everything sounds like Gault. Why is he doing this to me?' My fear was turning to fury.

Wesley's gaze was steady. 'Think. Is there anything else of late that you should tell me about? Weird phone calls, weird mail, hang ups?'

'No weird phone calls or hang ups. I get some strange mail, but that's fairly routine in my business.'

'Nothing else? What about your burglar alarm? Has that gone off more than usual?'

I slowly shook my head. 'It's gone off a couple times this month, but there was no sign of anything out of order. And I really don't think Gault has been spending time in Richmond.'

'You've got to be very careful,' he said almost irritably, as if I had not been careful.

'I'm always very careful,' I said.

6

The next day, the city was at work again, and I took Marino to lunch at Tatou because I thought both of us needed an uplifting atmosphere before we went to Brooklyn Heights to meet Commander Penn.

A young man was playing the harp, and most tables were occupied by attractive, well-dressed men and women who probably knew little about life beyond the publishing houses and high-rise businesses that consumed their days.

I was struck by my sense of alienation. I felt lonely as I looked across the table at Marino's cheap tie and green corduroy jacket, at the nicotine stains on his broad furrowed nails. Although I was glad for his company, I could not share my deeper thoughts with him. He would not understand.

'Looks to me like you could use a glass of wine with lunch, Doc,' Marino said, eyeing me closely. 'Go ahead. I'm driving.'

'No, you're not. We're taking a taxi.'

'Point is, you're not driving so you may as well relax.'

'What you're really saying is that you'd like a glass of wine.'

'Don't mind if I do,' he said as the waitress appeared. 'What you got by the glass that's worth drinking?' he asked her.

She did a good job of not looking offended as she went through an impressive list that left Marino lost. I suggested he try a Beringer reserve cabernet that I knew was good, and then we ordered cups of lentil soup and spaghetti bolognese.

'This dead lady's driving me crazy,' Marino said after the waitress was gone.

I leaned closer to the table's edge and encouraged him to lower his voice.

He leaned closer, too, adding, 'There's a reason he picked her.'

'He probably picked her because she was there,' I said, pricked by anger. 'His victims are nothing to him.'

'Yeah, well, I think there's more to it than that. And I'd also like to know what brought his ass here to New York City. You think he met up with her in the museum?'

'He might have,' I said. 'Maybe we'll know more when we get there.'

'Don't it cost money to go in there?'

'If you look at the exhibits it does.'

'She may have a lot of gold in her mouth, but it don't look to me like she had much money when she died.'

'I would be surprised if she did. But she and Gault got in the museum somehow. They were seen leaving.'

'So maybe he met her earlier, took her there and paid her way.'

'I'm hoping it will be helpful when we look at what he was looking at,' I said.

'I know what the squirrel was looking at. Sharks.'

The food was wonderful, and it would have been easy to sit for hours. I was tired beyond explanation, as I sometimes got. My disposition was built upon many layers of pain and sadness that had started with my own when I was young. Then over the years, I had added. Every so often I got in moods that were dark, and I was in one now.

I paid the check because when Marino and I were together,

if I picked the restaurant, I picked up the bill. Marino really could not afford Tatou. He really could not afford New York. Looking at my MasterCard made me think of my American Express card, and my mood got worse.

To get to the shark exhibit in the Museum of Natural History, we had to pay five dollars each and go up to the third floor. Marino climbed stairs more slowly than I and tried to disguise his labored breathing.

'Damn, you would think they got an elevator in this joint,' he complained.

'They do,' I said. 'But stairs are good for you. Today this may be the only exercise we get.'

We entered the exhibit of reptiles and amphibians, passing a fourteen-foot American crocodile killed a hundred years ago in the Biscayne Bay. Marino couldn't help but linger at each display, and I got an eyeful of lizards, snakes, iguanas and Gila monsters.

'Come on,' I whispered.

'Look at the size of this thing,' Marino marveled before the twenty-three-foot reticulated python remains. 'Can you imagine stepping on that in the jungle?'

Museums always made me cold no matter how much I loved them. I blamed the phenomenon on hard marble floors and high ceilings. But I hated snakes and their pit organs. I despised spitting cobras, frilled lizards and alligators with bared teeth. A guide was giving a tour to a group of young people who were enthralled before a showcase populated with Komodo reptiles of Indonesia and leatherback sea turtles who would never traverse sand or water again.

'I beg of you, when you're at the beach and have plastic, shove it in the trash, because these fellows don't have Ph.D.'s,' the guide was saying with the passion of an evangelist. 'They think it's jellyfish . . .'

'Marino, let's move on.' I tugged his sleeve.

'You know, I haven't been to a museum since I was a kid.

Wait a minute.' He looked surprised. 'That's not true. Well, I'll be damned. Doris took me here once. I thought this joint looked familiar.'

Doris was his ex-wife.

'I'd just signed on with the NYPD and she was pregnant with Rocky. I remember looking at stuffed monkeys and gorillas and telling her it was bad luck. I told her the kid was going to end up swinging through trees and eating bananas.'

'I beg of you. Their numbers are dwindling and dwindling and dwindling!' The tour guide went on and on about the plight of sea turtles.

'So maybe that's what the hell happened to him,' Marino continued. 'It was coming in this joint.'

I had rarely heard him even allude to his only child. In fact, as well as I knew Marino, I knew nothing about his son.

'I didn't know your son's name was Rocky,' I quietly said as we started walking again.

'It's really Richard. When he was a kid we called him Ricky, which somehow turned into Rocky. Some people call him Rocco. He gets called a lot of things.'

'Do you have much contact with him?'

'There's a gift shop. Maybe I should get a shark key chain or something for Molly.'

'We can do that.'

He changed his mind. 'Maybe I'll just bring her some bagels.'

I did not want to push him about his son, but the topic was within reach, and I believed their estrangement from each other was the root of many of Marino's problems.

'Where is Rocky?' I cautiously asked.

'An armpit of a town called Darien.'

'Connecticut? And it's not an armpit of a town.'

'This Darien's in Georgia.'

'It surprises me I haven't known that before now.'

'He don't do anything you'd have any reason to know about.'

Marino bent over, his face against glass as he stared at two small nurse sharks swimming along the bottom of a tank outside the exhibit.

'They look like big catfish,' he said as the sharks stared with dead eyes, tails silently fanning water.

We wandered into the exhibit and did not have to wait in line, for few visitors were here in the middle of this workday. We drifted past Kiribati warriors in suits of woven coconut husks, and Winslow Homer's painting of the Gulf Stream. Shark images had been painted on airplanes, and it was explained that sharks can detect odors from the length of a football field and electric charges as weak as one-millionth of a volt. They have as many as fifteen rows of backup teeth, are shaped the way they are to more efficiently torpedo through water.

During a short film we were shown a great white battering a cage and lunging for a tuna on a rope. The narrator explained that sharks are legendary hunters of the deep, the perfect killing machine, the jaws of death, the master of the sea. They can smell one drop of blood in twenty-five gallons of water and feel the pressure waves of other animals passing by. They can outswim their prey, and no one is quite certain why some sharks attack humans.

'Let's get out of here,' I said to Marino as the movie ended.

I buttoned my coat and put on my gloves, imagining Gault watching monsters ripping flesh as blood spread darkly through water. I saw his cold stare and the twisted spirit behind his thin smile. In the most frightening reaches of my mind, I knew he smiled as he killed. He bared his cruelty in that strange smile I had seen on the several occasions I had been near him.

I believed he had sat in this dark theater with the woman whose name we did not know, and she unwittingly had watched her own death on screen. She had watched her own blood spilled, her own flesh sliced. Gault had given her a preview of what he had in store for her. The exhibit had been his foreplay.

We returned to the rotunda, where a barosaurus fossil was surrounded by schoolchildren. Her elongated neck bones rose to the lofty ceiling as she eternally tried to protect her baby from an attacking allosaurus. Voices carried, and the sounds of feet echoed off marble as I glanced around. People in uniforms were quiet behind their ticket counters as they guarded the entrances of exhibits from people who had not paid. I looked out glass front doors at dirty snow piled along the cold, crowded street.

'She came in here to get warm,' I said to Marino.

'What?' He was preoccupied with dinosaur bones.

'Maybe she came in here to get out of the cold,' I said. 'You can stand here all day looking at these fossils. As long as you don't go into the exhibits, it doesn't cost you anything.'

'So you're thinking this is where Gault met her for the first time?' He looked skeptical.

'I don't know if it was the first time,' I said.

Brick smokestacks were quiet, and beyond guardrails of the Queens Expressway were bleak edifices of concrete and steel.

Our taxi passed depressing apartments, and stores selling smoked and cured fish, marble and tile. Coils of razor wire topped chain-link fences, and trash was on roadsides and caught in trees as we headed into Brooklyn Heights, to the Transit Authority on Jay Street.

An officer in navy blue uniform pants and commando sweater escorted us to the second floor, where we were shown to the three-star command executive office of Frances Penn. She had been thoughtful enough to have coffee and Christmas cookies waiting for us at the small table where we were to confer about one of the most gruesome homicides in Central Park's history.

'Good afternoon,' she said, firmly shaking our hands. 'Please have a seat. And we did take the calories out of the cookies. We always do that. Captain, do you take cream and sugar?'

'Yeah.'

She smiled a little. 'I guess that means both. Dr. Scarpetta, I have a feeling you drink your coffee black.'

'I do,' I said, regarding her with growing curiosity.

'And you probably don't eat cookies.'

'I probably won't.' I removed my overcoat and took a chair.

Commander Penn was dressed in a dark blue skirt suit with pewter buttons and a high-collared white silk blouse. She needed no uniform to look imposing, yet she was neither severe nor cold. I would not have called her bearing militaristic, but dignified, and I thought I detected anxiety in her hazel eyes.

'It appears Mr. Gault may have met the victim in the museum versus the two of them having met prior to that,' she began.

'It's interesting you would say that,' I said. 'We were just at the museum.'

'According to one of the security guards, a woman fitting the victim's description was seen loitering in the rotunda area. At some point she was observed talking with a man who bought two tickets for the exhibits. In fact, they were observed by several museum employees because of their odd appearance.'

'What is your theory as to why she was inside the museum?' I asked.

'It was the impression of those who remember her that she was a homeless person. My guess is she went in to get warm.'

'Don't they run street people out?' said Marino.

'If they can.' She paused. 'Certainly if they're causing a disturbance.'

'Which she wasn't, I assume,' I said.

Commander Penn reached for her coffee. 'Apparently she was quiet and unobtrusive. She seemed to be interested in the dinosaur bones, walking round and around them.'

'Did she speak to anyone?' I asked.

'She did ask where the ladies' room was.'

'That would suggest to me she'd never been there before,' I said. 'Did she have an accent?'

'If she did, no one remembers.'

'Then it is unlikely she is foreign,' I said.

'Any description on her clothing?' Marino asked.

'A coat – maybe brown or black, short. An Atlanta Braves baseball cap, maybe navy or black. Possibly she was wearing jeans and boots. That's as much as anyone seems to remember.'

We were silent, lost in thought.

I cleared my throat. 'Then what?' I said.

'Then she was spotted talking with a man, and the description of his clothing is interesting. He's remembered as having worn a rather dramatic overcoat. It was black, cut like a long trench coat – the sort you associate with what the Gestapo wore during World War Two. Museum personnel also believe he had on boots.'

I thought of the unusual footwear impressions at the scene, and of the black leather coat mentioned by Eugenio at Scaletta.

'The two of them were spotted in several other areas of the museum, and they did go into the shark exhibit,' Commander Penn went on. 'In fact, the man bought a number of books in the gift shop.'

'You know what kind of books?' Marino asked.

'Books on sharks, including one containing graphic photographs of people who have been attacked by sharks.'

'Did he pay cash for the books?' I asked.

'I'm afraid so.'

'Then he leaves the museum and gets a summons in the subway station,' Marino said.

She nodded. 'I'm sure you're interested in the identification he produced.'

'Yo, lay it on.'

'The name on his driver's license was Frank Benelli, Italian male thirty-three years old from Verona.'

'Verona?' I asked. 'That's interesting, my ancestors are from there.'

Marino and the commander looked briefly at me.

'You saying this squirrel spoke with an Italian accent?' Marino asked.

'The officer recalled that his English was broken. He had a heavy Italian accent, and I'm assuming Gault does not?' Commander Penn said.

'Gault was born in Albany, Georgia,' I said. 'So no, he does not have an Italian accent, but that doesn't mean he didn't imitate one.'

I explained to her what Wesley and I had discovered last night at Scaletta.

'Has your niece confirmed that your charge card is stolen?' she asked.

'I have not been able to get hold of Lucy yet.'

She pinched off a small piece of a cookie and slipped it between her lips, then said, 'The officer who wrote the summons grew up in an Italian family here in New York, Dr. Scarpetta. He thought the man's accent seemed authentic. Gault must be very good.'

'I'm sure he is.'

'Did he ever take Italian in high school or college?'

'I don't know,' I said. 'But he didn't finish college.'

'Where did he go?'

'A private college in North Carolina called Davidson.'

'It's very expensive and difficult to get into,' she said.

'Yes. His family has money and Gault is extremely intelligent. From what I understand, he lasted about a year.'

'Kicked out?' I could tell she was fascinated by him.

'As I understand it.'

'Why?'

'I believe he violated the honor code.'

'I know it's hard to believe,' Marino said sarcastically.

'And then what? Another college?' Commander Penn inquired.

'I don't think so,' I said.

'Has anyone gone down to Davidson to ask about him?' She

looked skeptical, as if those who had been working this case had not done enough.

'I don't know if anyone has, but I doubt it, to be frank.'

'He's only in his early thirties. We're not talking that long ago. People there should remember him.'

Marino had begun picking apart his Styrofoam coffee cup. He looked up at the commander. 'You checked out this Benelli guy to see if he really exists?'

'We're in the process. So far we have no confirmation,' she replied. 'These things can be slow, especially this time of year.'

'The Bureau has a legal attaché at the American Embassy in Rome,' I said. 'That might expedite the matter.'

We talked a while longer, and then Commander Penn walked us to the door.

'Dr. Scarpetta,' she said, 'I wonder if I could have a quick word with you before you go.'

Marino glanced at both of us and said, as if the question had been posed to him, 'Sure. Go ahead, I'll be out here.'

Commander Penn shut her door.

'I'm wondering if we could get together later,' she said to me.

I hesitated. 'I suppose that would be possible. What did you have in mind?'

'Might you be free for dinner tonight, say around seven? I thought we could talk some more and relax.' She smiled.

I had hoped Wesley and I could have dinner together. I told her, 'That is very gracious of you. Of course I will come.'

She slipped a card from a pocket and handed it to me. 'My address,' she said. 'I'll see you then.'

Marino did not ask what Commander Penn had said to me, but it was clear he wondered and was bothered that he had been excluded from the communication.

'Everything all right?' he asked as we were shown to the elevator.

'No,' I said. 'Everything is not all right. If it were, we would not be in New York right now.'

'Hell,' he said sourly, 'I quit having holidays when I became a cop. Holidays aren't for people like us.'

'Well, they should be,' I said, waving at a cab that was already engaged.

'That's bullshit. How many times have you been called out on Christmas Eve, Christmas Day, Thanksgiving, Labor Day weekend?'

Another cab flew by.

'Holidays is when squirrels like Gault got no place to go and no one to see, so they entertain themselves the way he did the other night. And half the rest of the world gets depressed and leaves their husband, wife, blows their brains out or gets drunk and dies in a car wreck.'

'Darn,' I muttered, searching up and down the busy street. 'If you'd like to assist in this endeavor, it would be appreciated. Unless you'd like to walk across the Brooklyn Bridge.'

He stepped out into the street and waved his arms. Instantly, a cab veered toward us and halted. We got in. The driver was Iranian and Marino was not nice to him. When I returned to my room, I took a long hot bath and tried to call Lucy again. Dorothy, unfortunately, answered the phone.

'How is Mother?' I said right off.

'Lucy and I spent the morning with her at the hospital. She's very depressed and looks horrible. I think of all those years I told her not to smoke, and look at her. A machine breathes for her. She has a hole cut in her neck. And yesterday I caught Lucy smoking a cigarette in the backyard.'

'When did she start smoking?' I said, dismayed.

'I have no idea. You see her more than I do.'

'Is she there?'

'Hold on.'

The receiver bumped loudly against whatever Dorothy set it on.

'Merry Christmas, Aunt Kay,' Lucy's voice came over the line, and she did not sound merry.

'It hasn't been a very merry one for me, either,' I said. 'How was your visit with Grans?'

'She started crying and we couldn't understand what she was trying to tell us. Then Mother was in a hurry to leave because she had a tennis match.'

'Tennis?' I said. 'Since when?'

'She's on another one of her fitness kicks.'

'She says you're smoking.'

'I don't do it much.' Lucy dismissed my remark as if it were nothing.

'Lucy, we need to talk about this. You don't need another addiction.'

'I'm not going to get addicted.'

'That's what I thought when I started at your age. Quitting was the hardest thing I've ever done. It was absolute hell.'

'I know all about how hard it is to quit things. I have no intention of putting myself in a situation that I can't control.'

'Good.'

She added, 'I'm flying back to Washington tomorrow.'

'I thought you were going to stay in Miami at least a week.'

'I've got to get back to Quantico. Something's going on with CAIN. ERF paged me early this afternoon.'

The Engineering Research Facility was where the FBI worked on researching and designing highly classified technology ranging from surveillance devices to robots. It was here that Lucy had been developing the Crime Artificial Intelligence Network.

CAIN was a centralized computer system linking police departments and other investigative agencies to one massive database maintained by the FBI's Violent Criminal Apprehension Program, or VICAP. The point was to alert police that they might be dealing with a violent offender who has raped or murdered elsewhere before. Then, if requested, Wesley's unit could be called in, as we had been by New York City.

'Is there a problem?' I asked uneasily, for there had been a serious problem in the recent past.

'Not according to the audit log. There's no record of anyone being in the system who isn't supposed to be. But CAIN seems to be sending messages that he hasn't been instructed to send. Something strange has been going on for a while, but so far I've been unable to track it. It's as if he's thinking for himself.'

'I thought that was the point of artificial intelligence,' I said.

'Not quite,' said my niece, who had a genius IQ. 'These are not normal messages.'

'Can you give me an example?'

'Okay. Yesterday, the British Transport Police entered a case in their VICAP terminal. It was a rape that occurred in Central London in one of the subways. CAIN processed the information, ran details against its database and called back the terminal where the case had been entered. The investigating officer in London got the message that further information was requested on the description of the assailant. Specifically, CAIN wanted to know the color of the assailant's pubic hair and if the victim had had an orgasm.'

'You aren't serious,' I said.

'CAIN has never been programmed to ask anything remotely similar to that. Obviously, it's not part of VICAP's protocol. The officer in London was upset and reported what had happened to an assistant chief constable, who called the director at Quantico, who then called Benton Wesley.'

'Benton called you?' I asked.

'Well, he actually had someone from ERF call me. He's heading back to Quantico tomorrow, too.'

'I see.' My voice was steady and I did not show I cared that Wesley was leaving tomorrow or anytime without having told me first. 'Are we certain that the officer in London was telling the truth – that maybe he didn't make up something like this as a joke?'

'A printout was faxed, and according to ERF the message looks authentic. Only a programmer intimately familiar with CAIN could have gotten in and faked a transmission like that. And again, from what I've been told, there is no evidence in the audit log that anyone has tampered with anything.'

Lucy went on to explain again that CAIN was run on a UNIX platform with Local Area Networks connected to Greater Area Networks. She talked about gateways and ports and passwords that automatically changed every sixty days. Only the three superusers, of which she was one, could really tamper with the brains of the system. Users at remote sites, like the officer in London, could do nothing beyond entering their data on a dumb terminal or PC connected to the twenty-gigabyte server that resided at Quantico.

'CAIN is probably the most secure system I've ever heard of,' Lucy added. 'Keeping it airtight is our top priority.'

But it wasn't always airtight. Last fall ERF had been broken into, and we had reason to believe Gault was involved. I did not need to remind Lucy of this. She had been interning there at the time and now was responsible for undoing the damage.

'Look, Aunt Kay,' she said, reading my mind. 'I have turned CAIN inside out. I've been through every program and rewritten major portions of some to ensure there's no threat.'

'No threat from whom?' I asked. 'CAIN or Gault?'

'No one will get in,' she said flatly. 'No one will. No one can.'

Then I told her about my American Express card, and her silence was chilling.

'Oh no,' she said. 'It never even entered my mind.'

'You remember I gave it to you last fall when you started your internship at ERF,' I reminded her. 'I said you could use it for train and plane tickets.'

'But I never needed it because you ended up letting me use

your car. Then the wreck happened and I didn't go anywhere for a while.'

'Where did you keep the card? In your billfold?'

'No.' She confirmed my fears. 'At ERF, in my desk drawer in a letter from you. I figured that was as safe as any place.'

'And that's where it was when the break-in occurred?'

'Yes. It's gone, Aunt Kay. The more I think about it, the more I'm sure. I would have seen it since then,' she stammered. 'I would have come across it while digging in the drawer. I'll check when I get back, but I know it's not going to be there.'

'That's what I thought,' I said.

'I'm really sorry. Has someone rung up a lot of charges on it?'

'I don't think so.' I did not tell her who that someone was.

'You've canceled it by now, right?'

'It's being taken care of,' I said. 'Tell your mother I will be down to see Grans as soon as I can.'

'As soon as you can is never soon,' my niece said.

'I know. I'm a terrible daughter and a rotten aunt.'

'You're not always a rotten aunt.'

'Thank you very much,' I said.

7

Commander Frances Penn's private residence was on the west side of Manhattan where I could see the lights of New Jersey on the other side of the Hudson River. She lived fifteen floors up in a dingy building in a dirty part of the city that was instantly forgotten when she opened her white front door.

Her apartment was filled with light and art and the fragrances of fine foods. Walls were whitewashed and arranged with pen-and-ink drawings and abstracts in watercolor and pastel. A scan of books on shelves and tables told me that she loved Ayn Rand and Annie Leibovitz and read numerous biographies and histories, including Shelby Foote's magnificent volumes on that terrible, tragic war.

'Let me take your coat,' she said.

I relinquished it, gloves and a black cashmere scarf I was fond of because it had been a gift from Lucy.

'You know, I didn't think to ask if there's anything you can't eat,' she said from the hall closet near the front door. 'Can you eat shellfish? Because if you can't, I have chicken.'

'Shellfish would be wonderful,' I said.

'Good.' She showed me into the living room, which offered

a magnificent view of the George Washington Bridge spanning the river like a necklace of bright jewels caught in space. 'I understand you drink Scotch.'

'Something lighter would be better,' I said, sitting on a soft leather couch the color of honey.

'Wine?'

I said that would be fine, and she disappeared into the kitchen long enough to pour two glasses of a crisp chardonnay. Commander Penn was dressed in black jeans and a gray wool sweater with sleeves shoved up. I saw for the first time that her forearms were horribly scarred.

'From my younger, more reckless days.' She caught me looking. 'I was on the back of a motorcycle and ended up leaving quite a lot of my hide on the road.'

'Donorcycles, as we call them,' I said.

'It was my boyfriend's. I was seventeen and he was twenty.'

'What happened to him?'

'He slid into oncoming traffic and was killed,' she said with the matter-of-factness of someone who has freely talked about a loss for a long time. 'That was when I got interested in police work.' She sipped her wine. 'Don't ask me the connection because I'm not sure I know.'

'Sometimes when one is touched by tragedy he becomes its student.'

'Is that your explanation?' She watched me closely with eyes that missed little and revealed less.

'My father died when I was twelve,' I simply said.

'Where was this?'

'Miami. He owned a small grocery store, which my mother eventually ran because he was sick many years before he died.'

'If your mother ran the store, so to speak, then who ran your household while your father lingered?'

'I suppose I did.'

'I thought as much. I probably could have told you that before you said a word. And my guess is you are the oldest child, have no brothers, and have always been an overachiever who cannot accept failure.'

I listened.

'Therefore, personal relationships are your nemesis because you can't have a good one by overachieving. You can't earn a happy love affair or be promoted into a happy marriage. And if someone you care about has a problem, you think you should have prevented it and most certainly should fix it.'

'Why are you dissecting me?' I asked directly but without defensiveness. Mostly, I was fascinated.

'Your story is my story. There are many women like us. Yet we never seem to get together, have you ever noticed that?'

'I notice it all the time,' I said.

'Well' – she set down her wine – 'I really didn't invite you over to interview you. But I would be less than honest if I told you that I didn't want an opportunity for us to get better acquainted.'

'Thank you, Frances,' I said. 'I am pleased you feel that way.'

'Excuse me a minute.'

She got up and returned to the kitchen. I heard a refrigerator door shut, water run and pots and pans quietly bang. Momentarily, she was back with the bottle of chardonnay inside an ice bucket, which she set on the glass coffee table.

'The bread is in the oven, asparagus is in the steamer, and all that's left is to sauté the shrimp,' she announced, reseating herself.

'Frances,' I said, 'your police department has been on-line with CAIN for how long now?'

'Only for several months,' she replied. 'We were one of the first departments in the country to hook up with it.'

'What about NYPD?'

'They're getting around to it. The Transit Police have a

more sophisticated computer system and a great team of programmers and analysts. So we got on-line very early.'

'Thanks to you.'

She smiled.

I went on, 'I know the Richmond Police Department is on-line. So are Chicago, Dallas, Charlotte, the Virginia State Police, the British Transport Police. And quite a number of other departments both here and abroad are in the process.'

'What's on your mind?' she asked me.

'Tell me what happened when the body of the unidentified woman we believe Gault killed was found Christmas Eve. How was CAIN a factor?'

'The body was found in Central Park early in the morning, and of course I heard about it immediately. As I've already mentioned, the MO sounded familiar, so I entered details into CAIN to see what came back. This would have been by late afternoon.'

'And what came back?'

'Very quickly CAIN called our VICAP terminal with a request for more information.'

'Can you recall exactly what sort of information?'

She thought for a moment. 'Well, let's see. It was interested in the mutilation, wanting to know from which parts of the body skin had been excised and what class cutting instrument had been used. It wanted to know if there had been a sexual assault, and if so, was the penetration oral, vaginal, anal or other. Some of this we couldn't know since an autopsy had not yet been performed. However, we did manage to get other information by calling the morgue.'

'What about other questions?' I asked. 'Did CAIN ask anything that struck you as peculiar or inappropriate?'

'Not that I'm aware of.' She regarded me quizzically.

'Has CAIN ever sent any messages to the Transit Police terminal that have struck you as peculiar or confusing?'

She thought some more. 'We've entered, at the most, twenty

cases since going on-line in November. Rapes, assaults, homicides that I thought might be relevant to VICAP because the circumstances were unusual or the victims were unidentified.

'And the only messages from CAIN that I'm aware of have been routine requests for further information. There has been no sense of urgency until this Central Park case. Then CAIN sent an *Urgent mail waiting* message in flashing bold because the system had gotten a hit.'

'Should you get any messages that are out of the ordinary, Frances, please contact Benton Wesley immediately.'

'Would you mind telling me what it is you're looking for?'

'There was a breach of security at ERF in October. Someone broke in at three in the morning, and circumstances indicate Gault may have been behind it.'

'Gault?' Commander Penn was baffled. 'How could that have happened?'

'One of ERF's system analysts, as it turned out, was connected to a spy shop in northern Virginia that was frequented by Gault. We know this analyst – a woman – was involved in the break-in, and the fear is that Gault put her up to it.'

'Why?'

'What wouldn't he like better than to get inside CAIN and have at his disposal a database containing the details of the most horrendous crimes committed in the world?'

'Isn't there some way to keep him out?' she asked. 'To tighten security so there is no way he or anyone else can slip through the system?'

'We thought that had been taken care of,' I replied. 'In fact, my niece, who is their top programmer, was certain the system was secure.'

'Oh yes. I think I've heard about your niece. She's really CAIN's creator.'

'She has always been gifted with computers and would rather be around them than most people.'

'I'm not sure I blame her. What is her name?'

'Lucy.'

'And she's how old?'

'Twenty-one.'

She got up from the couch. 'Well, maybe there's just some glitch that is causing these weird messages you're speaking of. A bug. And Lucy will figure it out.'

'We can always hope.'

'Bring your wine and you can keep me company in the kitchen,' she said.

But we did not get that far before her telephone rang. Commander Penn answered it and I watched the pleasant evening drain from her face.

'Where?' she quietly said, and I knew the tone of voice quite well. I recognized the frozen stare.

I was already opening the hall closet door to fetch my coat when she said, 'I'll be right there.'

Snow had begun drifting down like ashes when we arrived at the Second Avenue subway station in the squalid section of lower Manhattan known as the Bowery.

Wind howled and blue and red lights throbbed as if the night were injured, and stairs leading into that hellhole had been cordoned off. Derelicts had been herded out, commuters had been detoured, and news vans and cars were arriving in droves because an officer with the Transit Police Homeless Unit was dead.

His name was Jimmy Davila. He was twenty-seven. He had been a cop one year.

'You better put these on.' An officer with an angry, pale face handed me a reflective vest and surgical mask and gloves.

Police were pulling flashlights and more vests out of the back of a van, and several officers with darting eyes and riot guns flashed past me down the stairs. Tension was palpable. It pulsed in the air like a dark pounding heart, and the voices of legions who had come to aid their gunned-down comrade blended with scuffing feet and the strange language radios speak. Somewhere far off a siren screamed.

Commander Penn handed me a high-powered flashlight as we were escorted down by four officers who were husky in Kevlar and coats and reflective vests. A train blew by in a stream of liquid steel, and we inched our way along a catwalk that led us into dark catacombs littered with crack vials, needles, garbage and filth. Lights licked over hobo camps set up on pallets and ledges within inches of rails, and the air was fetid with the stench of human waste.

Beneath the streets of Manhattan were forty-eight acres of tunnels where in the late eighties as many as five thousand homeless people had lived. Now the numbers were substantially smaller, but their presence was still found in filthy blankets piled with shoes, clothes and odds and ends.

Grimy stuffed animals and fuzzy fake insects had been hung like fetishes from walls. The squatters, many of whom the Homeless Unit knew by name, had vanished like shadows from their subterranean world, except for Freddie, who was roused from a drugged sleep. He sat up beneath an army blanket, looking about, dazed.

'Hey, Freddie, get up.' A flashlight shone on his face.

He raised a bandaged hand to his eyes, squinting as small suns probed the darkness of his tunnel.

'Come on, get up. What'd you do to your hand?'

'Frostbite,' he mumbled, staggering to his feet.

'You got to take care of yourself. You know you can't stay here. We got to walk you out. You want to go to a shelter?'

'No, man.'

'Freddie,' the officer went on in a loud voice, 'you know what's happened down here? You heard about Officer Davila?'

'I dunno nothing.' Freddie swayed and caught himself, squinting in the lights.

'I know you know Davila. You call him Jimbo.'

'Yeah, Jimbo. He's all right.'

'No, I'm afraid he's not all right, Freddie. He got shot down here tonight. Someone shot Jimbo and he's dead.'

Freddie's yellow eyes got wide. 'Oh no, man.' He cast about as if the killer might be looking on – as if someone might want to blame him for this.

'Freddie, you seen anybody down here tonight you didn't know? You seen anybody down here who might have done something like that?'

'No, I ain't seen nothing.' Freddie almost lost his balance and steadied himself against a concrete support. 'Not nobody or nothing, I swear.'

Another train burst out of the darkness and blew past on southbound tracks. Freddie was led away and we moved on, sidestepping rails and rodents moiling beneath trash. Thank God I had worn boots. We walked for at least ten minutes more, my face perspiring beneath my mask as I got increasingly disoriented. I could not tell if round bright lights far down the tracks were police flashlights or oncoming trains.

'Okay, we've got to step over the third rail,' Commander Penn said, and she had stayed close to me.

'How much farther?' I asked.

'Just down there, where those lights are. We're going to step over now. Do it sideways, slowly, one foot at a time, and don't touch.'

'Not unless you want the shock of your life,' an officer said.

'Yeah, six hundred volts that won't let go,' said another in the same hard tone.

We followed rails deeper into the tunnel as the ceiling got lower. Some men had to duck as we passed through an arch. On the other side, crime scene technicians were scouring the area while a medical examiner in hood and gloves examined the body. Lights had been set up, and needles, vials, and blood glistened harshly in them.

Officer Davila was on his back, his winter jacket unzipped,

revealing the stiff shape of a bulletproof vest beneath a navy blue commando sweater. He had been shot between the eyes with the .38 revolver on top of his chest.

'Is this exactly as he was found?' I asked, stepping close.

'Exactly as we found him,' said a detective with NYPD.

'His jacket was unzipped and the revolver was just like that?'

'Just like that.' The detective's face was flushed and sweating, and he would not meet my eyes.

The medical examiner looked up. I could not make out the face behind the plastic hood. 'We can't rule out suicide here,' she said.

I leaned closer and directed my light at the dead man's face. His eyes were open, head turned a little to the right. Blood pooled beneath him was bright red and getting thick. He was short, with the muscular neck and lean face of someone who was seriously fit. My light traveled to his hands, which were bare, and I squatted to take a closer look.

'I see no gunshot residue,' I said.

'You don't always,' said the medical examiner.

'The wound to his forehead is not contact and looks to me as if it's slightly angled.'

'I would expect it to be slightly angled if he shot himself,' the medical examiner replied.

'It's angled down. I wouldn't expect that,' I said. 'And how did his gun come to rest so neatly on his chest?'

'One of the street people in here might have moved it.'

I was beginning to get annoyed. 'Why?'

'Maybe someone picked it up and then had second thoughts about keeping it. So he put it where it is.'

'We really should bag his hands,' I said.

'One thing at a time.'

'He didn't wear gloves?' I squinted up in the circle of bright light. 'It's very cold down here.'

'We haven't finished going through his pockets, ma'am,' said the woman medical examiner, who was the young, rigid sort I associated with anal-retentive autopsies that took half a day.

'What is your name?' I asked her.

'I'm Dr. Jonas. And I'm going to have to ask you to back away, ma'am. We're trying to preserve a crime scene here and it's best you don't touch or disturb anything in any way.' She held up a thermometer.

'Dr. Jonas' – and it was Commander Penn who spoke – 'this is Dr. Kay Scarpetta, the chief medical examiner of Virginia and consulting forensic pathologist for the FBI. She is quite familiar with preserving crime scenes.'

Dr. Jonas looked up and I caught a glint of surprise behind her face shield. I detected embarrassment in the long moment it required her to read the chemical thermometer.

I leaned closer to the body, paying attention to the left side of his head.

'His left ear is lacerated,' I said.

'That probably happened when he fell,' said Dr. Jonas.

I scanned the surroundings. We were on a smooth concrete platform. There were no rails to strike. I shone my light over concrete supports and walls, scanning for blood on any structure that Davila might have hit.

Squatting near the body, I looked more closely at his injured ear and a reddish area below it. I began to see the class characteristics of a tread pattern that was wavy with small holes. Under his ear was the curve from the edge of a heel. I stood, sweat rolling down my face. Everyone was watching me as I stared down the dark corridor at a light getting closer.

'He was kicked in the side of the head,' I said.

'You don't know that he didn't hit his head,' Dr. Jonas said defensively.

I stared at her. 'I do know,' I asserted.

'How do we know he wasn't stomped?' an officer asked.

'His injuries are inconsistent with that,' I replied. 'People usually stomp more than once and in other areas of the body.

I would also expect there to be injury to the other side of his face, which would have been against the concrete when the stomping occurred.'

A train blew by in a rush of warm, screeching air. Lights floated in the distant dark, the figures attached to them shadows with voices that faintly carried.

'He was disabled by a kick, then shot with his own gun,' I said.

'We need to get him to the morgue,' the medical examiner said.

Commander Penn's eyes were wide, her face upset and angry.

'It's him, isn't it?' she said to me as we began to walk.

'He's kicked people before,' I said.

'But why? He has a gun, a Glock. Why didn't he use his own gun?'

'The worst thing that can happen to a cop is to be shot with his own gun,' I said.

'So Gault would have done that deliberately because of how it would make the police . . . make us feel?'

'He would have thought it was funny,' I said.

We walked back over rails and through trash alive with rats. I sensed Commander Penn was crying. Minutes passed.

She said, 'Davila was a good officer. He was so helpful, never complained, and his smile. He brightened a room.' Her voice was clenched in fury now. 'He was just a goddam kid.'

Her officers were around us but not too close, and as I looked down the tunnel and across the tracks, I thought of the subterranean acres of twists and turns of the subway system. The homeless had no flashlights, and I did not understand how they could see. We passed another squalid camp where a white man who looked vaguely familiar sat up smoking crack from a piece of car antenna as if there were no such thing as law and order in the land. When I noticed his baseball cap the meaning didn't register at first. Then I stared.

'Benny, Benny, Benny. Shame on you,' one of the officers impatiently said. 'Come on. You know you can't do this, man. How many times are we going to go through this, man?'

Benny had chased me into the medical examiner's office yesterday morning. I recognized his filthy army pants, cowboy boots and blue jean jacket.

'Then just go on and lock me up,' he said, lighting his rock again.

'Oh yeah, your ass is gonna be locked up, all right. I've had it with you.'

I quietly said to Commander Penn, 'His cap.'

It was a dark blue or black Atlanta Braves cap.

'Hold on,' she told her troops. She asked Benny, 'Where did you get your cap?'

'I don't know nothing,' he said, snatching it off a tuft of dirty gray hair. His nose looked as if something had chewed on it.

'Of course you do know,' the commander said.

He stared crazily at her.

'Benny, where did you get your cap?' she asked again.

Two officers lifted him up and cuffed him. Beneath a blanket were paperback books, magazines, butane lighters, small Ziploc bags. There were several energy bars, packages of sugarless gum, a tin whistle and a box of saxophone reeds. I looked at Commander Penn, and she met my eyes.

'Gather up everything,' she told her troops.

'You can't take my place.' Benny struggled against his captors. 'You can't take my motherfucking place.' He stomped his feet. 'You goddam son of a bitch . . .'

'You're just making this harder, Benny.' They tightened his cuffs, a cop on each arm.

'Don't touch anything without gloves,' Commander Penn ordered.

'Don't worry.'

They put Benny's worldly belongings in trash bags, which we carried out with their owner. I followed with my flashlight, the vast darkness a silent void that seemed to have eyes. Frequently, I turned back and saw nothing but a light I thought was a train, until it suddenly moved sideways. Then it became a flashlight illuminating a concrete arch Temple Gault was passing through. He was a sharp silhouette in a long dark coat, his face a white flash. I grabbed the commander's sleeve and screamed.

8

More than thirty police officers searched the Bowery and its subways throughout the overcast night. No one knew how Gault had gotten into the tunnels, unless he never left after murdering Jim Davila. We were clueless as to how he had gotten out after I spotted him, but he had.

The next morning, Wesley headed for La Guardia while Marino and I returned to the morgue. I did not encounter Dr. Jonas from the night before, nor was Dr. Horowitz in, but I was told Commander Penn was here with one of her detectives and we would find them in the X-ray room.

Marino and I slipped in with the silence of a couple arriving late for a movie, then we lost each other in the dark. I suspected he found a wall, since he had trouble with his balance in situations like this. It was easy to get almost mesmerized and begin to sway. I moved close to the steel table, where dark shapes surrounded Davila's body, a finger of light exploring his ruined head.

'I would like one of the casts for comparison,' someone was saying.

'We've got photos of the shoe prints. I've got some here.' I recognized Commander Penn's voice.

'That would be good.'

'The labs have the casts.'

'Yours?'

'No, not ours,' said Commander Penn. 'NYPD's.'

'This area of abrasion and patterned contusion right here is from the heel.' The light stopped below the left ear. 'The wavy lines are fairly clear and I see no trace embedded in the abrasion. There's also this pattern right here. I can't make it out. This contusion, uh, sort of a blotch with a little tail. I don't know what that is.'

'We can try image enhancement.'

'Right, right.'

'What about his ear itself? Any pattern?'

'It's hard to tell, but it's split versus cut. The jagged edges are nonabraded and connected by tissue bridges. And I would say based on this curved laceration right down here' – the latex-sheathed finger pointed – 'the heel smashed the ear.'

'That's why it's split.'

'A single blow delivered with great force.'

'Enough to kill him?'

'Maybe. We'll see. My guess is he's going to have fractures of the left temporal parietal skull and a big epidural hemorrhage.'

'That's what I bet.'

The gloved hands manipulated forceps and the light. A hair, black and about six inches long, clung to the bloody collar of Davila's commando sweater. The hair was collected and placed in an envelope as I worked my way through thick darkness, finding the door. Returning my tinted glasses to a cart, I slipped out. Marino was right behind me.

'If that hair's his,' he said in the corridor, 'then he's dyed it again.'

'I would expect him to have done that,' I said, envisioning the silhouette I had seen last night. Gault's face was very white but, I could not tell about his hair.

'So he's not a redhead anymore.'

'By now he may have purple hair, for all we know.'

'He keeps changing his hair like that, maybe it will fall out.'

'Not likely,' I said. 'But the hair may not be his. Dr. Jonas has dark hair about that long, and she was hovered over the body for a while last night.'

We were in gowns, gloves and masks and looked like a team of surgeons about to perform some remarkable procedure like a heart transplant. Men were carrying in a shipment of pitiful pine boxes destined for Potter's Field, and behind glass, the morning's autopsies had begun. There were only five cases so far, one of them a child who obviously had died violently. Marino averted his gaze.

'Shit,' he muttered, his face dark red. 'What a way to start your day.'

I did not respond.

'Davila'd only been married two months.'

There was nothing I could say.

'I talked to a couple guys who knew him.'

The personal effects of the crack addict named Benny had been unceremoniously heaped on table four, and I decided to move them farther away from the dead child.

'He always wanted to be a cop. I hear that all the damn time.'

The trash bags were heavy, a foul odor drifting from the top of them, where they were tied. I began carrying them over to table eight.

'You tell me why anybody wants to do this?' Marino was getting more furious as he grabbed a bag and followed me.

'We want to make a difference,' I said. 'We want to somehow make things better.'

'Right,' he said sarcastically. 'Davila sure as hell made a difference. He sure as hell made things better.'

'Don't take that away from him,' I said. 'The good he did and might have done is all he has left.'

A Stryker saw started, water drummed and X rays bared bullets and bones in this theater with its silent audience and actors that were dead. Momentarily, Commander Penn walked in, eyes exhausted above her mask. She was accompanied by a dark young man she introduced as Detective Maier. He showed us the photographs of tread patterns left in the snows of Central Park.

'They're pretty much to scale,' he explained. 'I will admit that the casts would be better if we could get them.'

But NYPD had those, and I was willing to bet that the Transit Police would never see them. Frances Penn almost did not look like the same woman I had visited last night, and I wondered why she really had invited me to her apartment. What might she have confided had we not been summoned to the Bowery?

We began untying bags and placing items on the table, except for the fetid wool blankets that had been Benny's home. These we folded and stacked on the floor. The inventory was an odd one that could be explained in only two ways. Either Benny had been living with someone who owned a pair of size seven and a half men's boots. Or he had somehow acquired the possessions of someone who owned a pair of size seven and a half men's boots. Benny's shoe size, we were told, was eleven.

'What's Benny got to say this morning?' Marino asked.

Detective Maier answered, 'He says the stuff in that pile just showed up on his blankets. He went up on the street, came back and there it was, inside the knapsack.' He pointed to a soiled green canvas knapsack that had many stories to tell.

'When was this?' I asked.

'Well now, Benny isn't real clear on that. In fact, he's not real clear on just about anything. But he thinks it was in the last few days.'

'Did he see who left the knapsack?' Marino asked.

'He says he didn't.'

I held a photograph close to the bottom of one of the boots to compare the sole, and the size and stitching were the same.

Benny had somehow acquired the belongings of the woman we believed Gault had savaged in Central Park. The four of us were silent for a while as we began going through each item we believed was hers. I felt lightheaded and weary as we began reconstructing a life from a tin whistle and rags.

'Can't we call her something?' Marino said. 'It's bugging me she's got no name.'

'What would you like to call her?' Commander Penn asked.

'Jane.'

Detective Maier glanced up at Marino. 'That's very original. What's her last name, Doe?'

'Any possibility the saxophone reeds are Benny's?' I asked.

'I don't think so,' Maier said. 'He said all this stuff was in the knapsack. And I'm not aware Benny's musically inclined.'

'He plays an invisible guitar sometimes,' I said.

'So would you if you smoked crack. And that's all he does. He begs and smokes crack.'

'He used to do something before he did that,' I said.

'He was an electrician and his wife left him.'

'That's no reason to move into a sewer,' said Marino, whose wife also had left him. 'There's gotta be something else.'

'Drugs. He ended up across the street in Bellevue. Then he'd sober up and they'd let him out. Same old thing, over and over.'

'Might there have been a saxophone that went with the reeds, and perhaps Benny hocked it?' I asked.

'I got no way to know,' Maier answered. 'Benny said this is all there was.'

I thought of the mouth of this woman we now called Jane, of the cupping of the front teeth that the forensic dentist blamed on smoking a pipe.

'If she has a long history of playing a clarinet or saxophone,' I said, 'that could explain the damage to her front teeth.'

'What about the tin whistle?' Commander Penn asked.

She bent closer to a gold metal whistle with a red mouthpiece.

The brand was Generation, it was British made and did not look new.

'If she played it a lot, then that probably just added to the damage to her front teeth,' I said. 'It's also interesting that it's an alto whistle and the reeds are for an alto sax. So she may have played an alto sax at some point in her life.'

'Maybe before her head injury,' Marino said.

'Maybe,' I said.

We continued sifting through her belongings and reading them like tea leaves. She liked sugarless gum and Sensodyne toothpaste, which made sense in light of her dental problems. She had one pair of men's black jeans, size thirty-two in the waist and thirty-four in length. They were old and rolled up at the cuffs, suggesting they were hand-me-downs or she had gotten them in a secondhand clothing store. Certainly they were much too big for the size she was when she died.

'Are we certain these don't belong to Benny?' I asked.

'He says they don't,' Maier replied. 'The stuff he says belongs to him is in that bag.' He pointed to a bulging bag on the floor.

When I slipped a gloved hand into a back pocket of the jeans, I found a red-and-white paper tag that was identical to the ones Marino and I had been given when we visited the American Museum of Natural History. It was round, the size of a silver dollar and attached to a loop of string. Printed on one side was *Contributor*, with the museum's logo on the other.

'This should be processed for prints,' I said, placing the tag in an evidence bag. 'She should have touched it. Or Gault may have touched it if he paid for admission into the exhibits.'

'Why would she save something like that?' Marino said. 'Usually you take it off your shirt button and drop it in the trash on your way out.'

'Perhaps she put it in her pocket and forgot,' Commander Penn said.

'It could be a souvenir,' suggested Maier.

'It doesn't look like she collects souvenirs,' I said. 'In fact, she seems very deliberate about what she kept and what she didn't.'

'Are you suggesting she might have kept the tag so someone would eventually find it?'

'I don't know,' I said.

Marino lit a cigarette.

'That makes me wonder if she knew Gault,' Maier said.

I replied, 'If she did, and if she knew she was in danger, then why did she go with him into the park at night?'

'See, that's what don't add up.' Marino exhaled a large cloud of smoke, his mask pulled down.

'It doesn't if she was a complete stranger to him,' I said.

'So maybe she knew him,' Maier said.

'Maybe she did,' I agreed.

I slid my hand into other pockets of the same black pants and found eighty-two cents, a saxophone reed that had been chewed and several neatly folded Kleenex tissues. An inside-out blue sweatshirt was size medium, and whatever had been written on the front of it was too faded to read.

She also had owned two pairs of gray sweatpants and three pairs of athletic socks with different-colored stripes. In a compartment of the knapsack was a framed photograph of a spotted hound sitting in the dappled shadows of trees. The dog seemed to be grinning at whoever was taking the picture while a figure in the far background looked on.

'This needs to be processed for prints,' I said. 'In fact, if you hold it obliquely you can see latents on the glass.'

'I bet that's her dog,' Maier said.

Commander Penn said, 'Can we tell what part of the world it was taken in?'

I studied the photograph more closely. 'It looks flat. It's sunny. I don't see any tropical foliage. It doesn't look like a desert.'

'In other words, it could be almost anywhere,' Marino said.

'Almost,' I said. 'I can't tell anything about the figure in the background.'

Commander Penn examined the photograph. 'A man, maybe?'

'It could be a woman,' I said.

'Yeah, I think it is,' said Maier. 'A real thin one.'

'So maybe it's Jane,' Marino said. 'She liked baseball caps, and this person has on some kind of cap.'

I looked at Commander Penn. 'I'd appreciate copies of any photographs, including this one.'

'I'll get them to you ASAP.'

We continued our excavation of this woman who seemed to be in the room with us. I felt her personality in her paltry possessions and believed she had left us clues. Apparently, she had worn men's undershirts instead of bras, and we found three pairs of ladies' panties and several bandannas.

All of her belongings were worn and dirty, but there was a suggestion of order and care in neatly mended tears, and the needles, thread and extra buttons she had kept in a plastic box. Only the black jeans and faded sweatshirt had been rudely wadded or were inside out, and we suspected this was because she had been wearing them when Gault forced her to disrobe in the dark.

By late morning, we had gone through every item with no success in getting closer to identifying the victim we had begun to call Jane. We could only assume that Gault got rid of any identification she might have carried, or else Benny had taken what little money she might have owned and disposed of what she had kept it in. I didn't understand the chronology of when Gault might have left the knapsack on Benny's blanket, if that was, in fact, what Gault had done.

'How much of this stuff are we checking for prints?' Maier said.

'In addition to the items we've already gotten,' I suggested, 'the tin whistle has a good surface for prints. You might try an alternate light source on the knapsack. Especially the inside of the flap, since it's leather.'

'The problem's still her,' Marino said. 'Nothing here's going to tell us who she is.'

'Well, I got news for you,' said Maier. 'I don't think identifying *Jane*'s gonna help us catch the guy who killed her.'

I looked at him and watched his interest in her fade. The light went out of his eyes, and I had seen this before in deaths where the victim was no one. Jane had gotten as much time as she was going to get. Ironically, she would have gotten even less had her killer not been notorious.

'Do you think Gault shot her in the park, then went from there to the tunnel where her knapsack was found?' I asked.

'He might have,' Maier said. 'All he had to do was leave Cherry Hill and catch the subway at, say, Eighty-sixth or Seventy-seventh Streets. It would take him straight to the Bowery.'

'Or he could have taken a taxi, for that matter,' Commander Penn said. 'What he couldn't have done was walk. It's quite a distance.'

'What if the knapsack was left at the scene, right out there by the fountain?' Marino then asked. 'Possible Benny might have found it?'

'Why would he be in Cherry Hill at that hour? Remember what the weather was like,' Commander Penn said.

A door opened and several attendants wheeled in a gurney carrying Davila's body.

'I don't know why,' Maier said. 'Did she have her knapsack with her at the museum?' he asked Commander Penn.

'I believe it was mentioned that she had some sort of bag slung over one shoulder.'

'That could have been the knapsack.'

'It could have.'

'Does Benny sell drugs?' I asked.

'After a while you gotta sell if you're gonna buy,' Maier said.

'There may be a connection between Davila and the murdered woman,' I said.

Commander Penn watched me with interest.

'We shouldn't discount that possibility,' I went on. 'At a glance, it seems unlikely. But Gault and Davila were both down in that tunnel at the same time. Why?'

'Luck of the draw.' Maier stared off.

Marino didn't comment. His attention had drifted to autopsy table five, where two medical examiners were photographing the slain officer from different angles. An attendant with a wet towel scrubbed blood off the face in a manner that would have been rough could Davila feel. Marino was unaware anyone was watching him, and for a moment his vulnerability showed. I saw the ravages from years of storms, and the weight pressing his shoulders.

'And Benny was in that same tunnel, too,' I said. 'He either got the knapsack from the murder scene or from someone, or it was dropped on his blankets as he claims.'

'Frankly, I don't think it just turned up on his blankets,' Maier said.

'Why?' Commander Penn asked him.

'Why would Gault want to carry it from Cherry Hill? Why not just leave it and be on his way?' he said.

'Maybe there was something in it,' I said.

'Like what?' Marino asked.

'Like anything that might identify her,' I said. 'Maybe he didn't want her identified and needed a chance to go through her effects.'

'That could be,' Commander Penn said. 'Certainly we have found nothing among her belongings that would seem to identify her.'

'But in the past Gault hasn't seemed to care whether we identified his victims,' I said. 'Why care now? Why would he care about this head-injured, homeless woman?'

Commander Penn did not seem to hear me, and no one

else answered. The medical examiners had begun undressing Davila, who did not want their help. He held his arms rigidly folded across his torso, as if blocking blows in football. The doctors were having a terrible time getting the commando sweater free of limbs and over his head when a pager went off. We involuntarily touched our waistbands, then stared toward Davila's table as the beeping continued.

'It's not mine,' one of the doctors said.

'Damn,' the other doctor said. 'It's his.'

A chill swept through me as he removed a pager from Davila's belt. Everyone was silent. We could not take our eyes off table five or Commander Penn, who walked there because this was her murdered officer and someone had just tried to call him. The doctor handed her the pager and she held it up to read the display. Her face colored. I could see her swallow.

'It's a code,' she said.

Neither she nor the doctor had thought not to touch the pager. They did not know it might matter.

'A code?' Maier looked mystified.

'A police code.' Her voice was tight with fury. 'Ten-dash-seven.'

Ten-dash-seven meant *End of tour*.

'Fuck,' Maier said.

Marino took an involuntary step, as if he were about to engage in a foot pursuit. But there was no one to chase that he could see.

'Gault,' he said, incredulous. He raised his voice. 'The son of a bitch must've got his pager number after he blew his brains all over the subway. You understand what that means?' He glared at us. 'It means he's watching us! He knows we're here doing this.'

Maier looked around.

'We don't know who sent the message,' said the doctor, who was completely disconcerted.

But I knew. I had no doubt.

'Even if Gault did it, he didn't have to see what was going on this morning to know what's going on,' Maier said. 'He would know the body was here, that we would be here.'

Gault would know that I would be here, I thought. He wouldn't have necessarily known the others would.

'He's somewhere where he just used a phone.' Marino glanced wildly around. He could not stand still.

Commander Penn ordered Maier, 'Put it on the air, an all-units broadcast. Send a teletype, too.'

Maier pulled his gloves off and angrily slammed them into a trash can as he ran from the room.

'Put the pager in an evidence bag. It needs to be processed for prints,' I said. 'I know we've touched it, but we can still try. That's why his coat was unzipped.'

'Huh?' Marino looked stunned.

'Davila's coat was unzipped and there was no reason for that.'

'Yeah, there was a reason. Gault wanted Davila's gun.'

'It wasn't necessary to unzip his coat to get his gun,' I said. 'There's a slit in the jacket's side where the holster is. I think Gault unzipped Davila's coat to find the pager. Then he got the number off it.'

The doctors had returned their efforts to the body. They pulled off boots and socks and unfastened an ankle holster holding a Walther .380 that Davila shouldn't have been carrying and had never had a chance to use. They took off his Kevlar vest, a navy police T-shirt, and a silver crucifix on a long chain. On his right shoulder was a small tattoo of a rose entwining a cross. In his wallet was a dollar.

9

I left New York that afternoon on a USAir shuttle and got into Washington National at three. Lucy could not meet me at the airport because she had not driven since her accident, and there was no appropriate reason for me to find Wesley waiting at my gate.

Outside the airport I suddenly felt sorry for myself as I struggled alone with briefcase and bag. I was tired and my clothes felt dirty. I was hopelessly overwhelmed and ashamed to admit it. I couldn't even seem to get a taxi.

Eventually, I arrived at Quantico in a dented cab painted robin's-egg blue with glass tinted purple. My window in back would not roll down, and it was impossible for my Vietnamese driver to communicate who I was to the guard at the FBI Academy entrance.

'Lady doctor,' the driver said again, and I could tell he was unnerved by the security, the tire shredders, the many antennae on tops of buildings. 'She okay.'

'No,' I said to the back of his head. 'My *name* is Kay. Kay Scarpetta.'

I tried to get out, but doors were locked, the buttons removed. The guard reached for his radio.

'Please let me out,' I said to the driver, who was staring at the nine-millimeter pistol on the guard's belt. 'I need for you to let me out.'

He turned around, frightened. 'Out here?'

'No,' I said as the guard emerged from the booth.

The driver's eyes widened.

'I mean, I do want out here, but just for a minute. So I can explain to the guard.' I pointed and spoke very slowly. 'He doesn't know who I am because I can't open the window and he can't see through the glass.'

The driver nodded some more.

'I must get out,' I said firmly and with emphasis. 'You must open the doors.'

The locks went up.

I got out and squinted in the sun. I showed my identification to the guard, who was young and militaristic.

'The glass is tinted and I couldn't see you,' he said. 'Next time just roll your window down.'

The driver had started taking my luggage out of the trunk and setting it on the road. He glanced about frantically as artillery fire cracked and gunshots popped from Marine Corps and FBI firing ranges.

'No, no, no.' I motioned him to put the luggage back in the trunk. 'Drive me there, please.' I pointed toward Jefferson, a tall tan brick building on the other side of a parking lot.

It was clear he did not want to drive me anywhere, but I got back in the car before he could get away. The trunk slammed and the guard waved us through. The air was cold, the sky bright blue.

Inside Jefferson's lobby a video display above the reception desk welcomed me to Quantico and wished me a happy and safe holiday. A young woman with freckles signed me in and gave me a magnetic card to open doors around the Academy.

'Was Santa good to you, Dr. Scarpetta?' she cheerfully asked, sorting through room keys.

'I must have been bad this year,' I said. 'I mostly got switches.'

'I can't imagine that. You're always so sweet,' she said. 'We've got you on the security floor, as usual.'

'Thank you.' I could not recall her name and had a feeling she knew it.

'How many nights will you be with us?'

'Just one.' I thought her name might be Sarah, and for some reason it seemed very important that I remember it.

She handed me two keys, one plastic, one metal.

'You're Sarah, aren't you?' I took a risk and asked.

'No, I'm Sally.' She looked hurt.

'I meant Sally,' I said, dismayed. 'Of course. I'm sorry. You always take such good care of me, and I thank you.'

She gave me an uncertain look. 'By the way. Your niece walked through maybe thirty minutes ago.'

'Which way was she headed?'

She pointed toward glass doors leading from the lobby into the heart of the building and clicked the lock free before I had a chance to insert my card. Lucy could have been en route to the PX, post office, Boardroom, ERF. She could have been heading toward her dormitory room, which was in this building but on a different wing.

I tried to imagine where my niece might be at this hour of the afternoon, but where I found her was the last place I would have looked. She was in my suite.

'Lucy!' I exclaimed when I opened the door and she was standing on the other side. 'How did you get in?'

'The same way you did,' she said none too warmly. 'I have a key.'

I carried my bags into the living room and set them down. 'Why?' I studied her face.

'My room's on this side, yours is on that.'

The security floor was for protected witnesses, spies or any other person the Department of Justice decided needed extra protection. To get into rooms, one had to pass through two sets of doors, the first requiring a code entered on a digital keypad that was reconfigured each time it was used. The second needed a magnetized card that was also often changed. I'd always suspected the telephones were monitored.

I was assigned these quarters more than a year ago because Gault was not the only worry in my life. I was baffled that Lucy had now been assigned here, too.

'I thought you were in Washington dorm,' I said.

She went into the living room and sat down. 'I was,' she said. 'And as of this afternoon, I'm here.'

I took the couch across from her. Silk flowers had been arranged, curtains drawn back from a window filled with sky. My niece wore sweatpants, running shoes, and a dark FBI sweatshirt with a hood. Her auburn hair was short, her sharp-featured face flawless except for the bright scar on her forehead. Lucy was a senior at UVA. She was beautiful and brilliant, and our relationship had always been one of extremes.

'Did they put you here because I'm here?' I was still trying to understand.

'No.'

'You didn't hug me when I came in.' It occurred to me as I got up. I kissed her cheek, and she stiffened, pulling away from my arms. 'You've been smoking.' I sat back down.

'Who told you that?'

'No one needs to tell me. I can smell it in your hair.'

'You hugged me because you wanted to see if I smell like cigarettes.'

'And you didn't hug me because you know you smell like cigarettes.'

'You're nagging me.'

'I most certainly am not,' I said.

'You are. You're worse than Grans,' she said.

'Who is in the hospital because she smoked,' I said, holding her intense green gaze.

'Since you know my secret, I may as well light up now.'

'This is a nonsmoking room. In fact, nothing is allowed in this room,' I said.

'Nothing?' She did not blink.

'Absolutely nothing.'

'You drink coffee in here. I know. I've heard you zap it in the microwave when we've been on the phone.'

'Coffee is all right.'

'You said *nothing*. To many people on this planet, coffee is a vice. I bet you drink alcohol in here, too.'

'Lucy, please don't smoke.'

She slipped a pack of Virginia Slim menthols out of a pocket. 'I'll go outside,' she said.

I opened windows so she could smoke, unable to believe she had taken up a habit I had shed much blood to quit. Lucy was athletic and superbly fit. I told her I did not understand.

'I'm flirting with it. I don't do it much.'

'Who moved you into my suite? Let's get back to that,' I asked as she puffed away.

'They moved me.'

'Who is they?'

'Apparently, the order came from the top.'

'Burgess?' I referred to the assistant director in charge of the Academy.

She nodded. 'Yes.'

'What would his purpose be?' I frowned.

She tapped an ash into her palm. 'No one's told me a reason. I can only suppose it's related to ERF, to CAIN.' She paused. 'You know, the weird messages, et cetera.'

'Lucy,' I said, 'what exactly is going on?'

'We don't know,' she spoke levelly. 'But something is.'

'Gault?'

'There's no evidence that anyone's been in the system – no one who isn't supposed to be.'

'But you believe someone has.'

She inhaled deeply, like veteran smokers do. 'CAIN is not doing what we're telling him to do. He's doing something else, getting his instruction from somewhere else.'

'There's got to be a way to track that,' I said.

Her eyes sparked. 'Believe me, I'm trying.'

'I'm not questioning your efforts or ability.'

'There's no trail,' she went on. 'If someone is in there, he's leaving no tracks. And that's not possible. You can't just go into the system and tell it to send messages or do anything else without the audit log reflecting it. And we have a printer running morning, noon and night that prints every keystroke made by anybody for any reason.'

'Why are you getting angry?' I said.

'Because I'm tired of being blamed for the problems over there. The break-in wasn't my fault. I had no idea that someone who worked right next to me . . .' She took another drag. 'Well, I only said I'd fix it because I was asked to. Because the senator asked me to. Or asked you, really . . .'

'Lucy, I'm not aware that anyone is blaming you for problems with CAIN,' I said gently.

Anger burned brighter in her eyes. 'If I'm not being blamed, I wouldn't have been assigned to a room up here. What this constitutes is house arrest.'

'Nonsense. I stay here every time I come to Quantico, and I'm certainly not under house arrest.'

'They put you here for security and privacy,' she said. 'But that's not why I'm here. I'm being blamed again. I'm being watched. I can tell it in the way certain people are treating me over there.' She nodded in the direction of ERF, which was across the street from the Academy.

'What happened today?' I asked.

She went into the kitchen, ran water over the cigarette butt and dropped it into the disposal. She sat back down and didn't say anything. I studied her and got more unsettled. I did not know why she was this angry, and whenever she acted in a way that could not be explained, I was frightened again.

Lucy's car accident could have been fatal. Her head injury could have ruined her most remarkable gift, and I was assaulted by images of hematomas and a skull fractured like a hard-boiled egg. I thought of the woman we called Jane with her shaved head and scars, and I imagined Lucy in places where no one knew her name.

'Have you been feeling all right?' I asked my niece.

She shrugged.

'What about the headaches?'

'I still get them.' Suspicion shadowed her eyes. 'Sometimes the Midrin helps. Sometimes it just makes me throw up. The only thing that really works is Fiorinal. But I don't have any of that.'

'You don't need any of that.'

'You're not the one who gets the headaches.'

'I get plenty of headaches. You don't need to be on barbiturates,' I answered. 'You're sleeping and eating all right, and getting exercise?'

'What is this, a doctor's appointment?'

'In a matter of speaking, since it just so happens I'm a doctor. Only you didn't make an appointment but I'm nice enough to see you anyway.'

A smile tugged at the corner of her mouth. 'I'm doing fine,' she said less defensively.

'Something happened today,' I said again.

'I guess you haven't talked to Commander Penn.'

'Not since this morning. I didn't know you knew her.'

'Her department's on-line with us, with CAIN. At twelve noon CAIN called the Transit Police VICAP terminal. I guess you had already left for the airport.'

I nodded, my stomach tightening as I thought of Davila's

beeper going off in the morgue. 'What was the message this time?' I asked.

'I have it if you want to see it.'

'Yes,' I said.

Lucy went into her room and returned carrying a briefcase. She unzipped it and pulled out a stack of papers, handing me one that was a printout from the VICAP terminal located in the Communications Unit, which was under Frances Penn's command. It read:

- - -MESSAGE PQ21 96701 001145 BEGINS- - -

FROM: – CAIN

TO: – ALL UNITS & COMMANDS

SUBJECT: – DEAD COPS

TO ALL COMMANDS CONCERNED:

MEMBERS WILL, FOR THE PURPOSE OF SAFETY WHEN RESPONDING TO OR BEING ON PATROL IN THE SUBWAY TUNNELS, WEAR HELMETS.

- - -MESSAGE PQ21 96701 001145 ENDS- - -

I stared at the printout for a while, unnerved and inflamed. Then I asked, 'Is there a username associated with whoever logged on to type this?'

'No.'

'And there's absolutely no way to trace this?'

'Not by conventional means.'

'What do you think?'

'I think when ERF was broken into, whoever got into CAIN planted a program.'

'Like a virus?' I asked.

'It is a virus, and it has been attached to a file that we just haven't thought of. It's allowing someone to move inside our system without leaving tracks.'

I thought of Gault backlit by his flashlight in the tunnel last night, of endless rails leading deeper into darkness and disease.

Gault moved freely through spaces most people could not see. He nimbly stepped over greasy steel, needles and the fetid nests of humans and rats. He was a virus. He had somehow gotten into our bodies and our buildings and our technology.

'CAIN is infected by a virus,' I said. 'In summary.'

'An unusual one. This isn't a virus oriented toward crashing the hard disk or trashing data. This virus isn't generic. It is specific for the Crime Artificial Intelligence Network because its purpose is to allow someone access to CAIN and the VICAP database. This virus is like a master key. It opens up every room in the house.'

'And it's attached to an existing program.'

'You might say it has a host,' she said. 'Yes. Some program routinely used. A virus can't cause its damage unless the computer goes through a routine or subroutine which causes a host program – like autoexec.bat in DOS – to be read.'

'I see. And this virus is not embedded in any files that are read when the computer is booted, for example.'

Lucy shook her head.

'How many program files are there in CAIN?'

'Oh my God,' she said. Thousands. And some of them are long enough to wrap around this building. The virus could be attached anywhere, and the situation is further complicated because I didn't do all of the programming. I'm not as familiar with files others wrote.'

Others meant Carrie Grethen, who had been Lucy's programming partner and intimate friend. Carrie had also known Gault and was responsible for the ERF break-in. Lucy would not talk about her and avoided saying her name.

'Is there any possibility this virus might be attached only to programs Carrie wrote?' I asked.

The expression did not change on Lucy's face. 'It might be attached to one of the programs I didn't write. It might also be attached to one I did. I don't know. I'm looking. It may take a long time.'

The telephone rang.

'That's probably Jan.' She got up and went into the kitchen.

I glanced at my watch. I was due down in the unit in half an hour. Lucy placed her hand over the receiver. 'Do you care if Jan drops by? We're going running.'

'I don't mind in the least,' I said.

'She wants to know if you want to run with us.'

I smiled and shook my head. I couldn't keep up with Lucy even if she smoked two packs a day, and Janet could pass for a professional athlete. The two of them gave me the vague sensation of being old and left in the wrong drawer.

'How about something to drink?' Lucy was off the phone and inside the refrigerator.

'What are you offering?' I watched her slight figure bent over, one arm holding open the door while the other slid cans around on shelves.

'Diet Pepsi, Zima, Gatorade and Perrier.'

'Zima?'

'You haven't had it?'

'I don't drink beer.'

'It's not like beer. You'll like it.'

'I didn't know they had room service here,' I said with a smile.

'I got some stuff at the PX.'

'I'll have Perrier.'

She came over with our drinks.

'Aren't there antivirus programs?' I said.

'Antivirus programs only find known viruses like Friday the Thirteenth, the Maltese Amoeba, the Stoned virus, Michelangelo. What we're dealing with inside CAIN was created specifically for CAIN. It was an inside job. There is no antivirus program unless I write one.'

'Which you can't do until you find the virus first.'

She took a big swallow of Gatorade.

'Lucy, should CAIN be shut down?'

She got up. 'Let me check on Jan. She can't get through those outer doors and I doubt we'll hear her knocking.'

I got up too and carried my bags into my bedroom with its plain decor and simple pine wardrobe. Unlike other rooms, the security suite had private baths. Through windows I had an unspoiled view of snow-patched fields unrolling into endless woods. The sun was so bright it felt like spring, and I wished there were time to bathe. I wanted to scrub New York away.

'Aunt Kay? We're out of here,' Lucy called as I brushed my teeth.

I quickly rinsed my mouth and returned to the living room. Lucy had slipped on a pair of Oakleys and was stretching by the door. Her friend had one foot propped up on a chair as she tightened a shoelace.

'Good afternoon, Dr. Scarpetta,' Janet said to me, quickly straightening up. 'I hope you don't mind my stopping by. I didn't mean to disturb you.'

Despite my efforts at putting her at ease, she always acted like a corporal startled by Patton walking in. She was a new agent, and I had first noticed her when I was a guest lecturer here last month. I remembered showing slides about violent death and crime scene preservation while she kept her eyes on me from the back of the room. In the dark I could feel her studying me from her chair, and it made me curious that during breaks she did not speak to anyone. She would disappear downstairs.

Later I learned she and Lucy were friends, and perhaps that and shyness explained Janet's demeanor toward me. Well built from hours in the gym, she had shoulder-length blond hair and blue eyes that were almost violet. If all went well, she would graduate from the Academy in less than two months.

'If you'd ever like to run with us, Dr. Scarpetta, you'd be welcome,' Janet politely repeated her invitation.

'You are very kind.' I smiled. 'And I am flattered that you would think I could.'

'Of course you could.'

'No, she couldn't.' Lucy finished her Gatorade and set the empty bottle on the counter. 'She hates running. She thinks negative thoughts the whole time she's doing it.'

I returned to the bathroom as they went out the door, and I washed my face and stared in the mirror. My blond hair seemed grayer than it had this morning and the cut had somehow gotten worse. I wore no makeup, and my face looked like it had just come out of the dryer and needed to be pressed. Lucy and Janet were unblemished, taut and bright, as if nature took joy in sculpting and polishing only the young. I brushed my teeth again and that made me think of Jane.

Benton Wesley's unit had changed names many times and was now part of HRT. But its location remained sixty feet below the Academy in a windowless area that once had been Hoover's bomb shelter. I found Wesley in his office talking on the phone. He glanced at me as he flipped through paperwork in a thick file.

Spread out in front of him were scene photographs from a recent consultation that had nothing to do with Gault. This victim was a man who had been stabbed and slashed 122 times. He had been strangled with a ligature, his body found facedown on a bed in a motel room in Florida.

'It's a signature crime. Well, the blatant overkill and the unusual configuration of the bindings,' Wesley was saying. 'Right. A loop around each wrist, handcuff style.'

I sat down. Wesley had reading glasses on and I could tell he had been running his fingers through his hair. He looked tired. My eyes rested on fine oil paintings on his walls and autographed books behind glass. He was often contacted by people writing novels and scripts, but he did not flaunt celebrity connections. I think he found them embarrassing and in poor taste. I did not believe he would talk to anyone if the decision were left completely up to him.

'Yes, it was a very bloody method of attack, to say the

least. The others were, too. We're talking about a theme of domination, a ritual driven by rage.'

I noticed he had several pale blue FBI manuals on his desk that were from ERF. One of them was an instruction manual for CAIN that Lucy had helped write, and pages were marked in numerous places with paper clips. I wondered if she had marked them or if he had, and my intuition answered the question as my chest got tight. My heart hurt the way it always did when Lucy was in trouble.

'That threatened his sense of domination.' Wesley met my eyes. 'Yes, the reaction's going to be anger. Always, with someone like this.'

His tie was black with pale gold stripes, and typically his shirt was white and starched. He wore Department of Justice cuff links, his wedding band and an understated gold watch with a black leather band that Connie had given him for their twenty-fifth wedding anniversary. He and his wife came from money, and the Wesleys lived quietly well.

He hung up the phone and took off his glasses.

'What's the problem?' I asked, and I hated the way he made my pulse pick up.

He gathered photographs and dropped them inside a manilla envelope. 'Another victim in Florida.'

'The Orlando area again?'

'Yes. I'll get you reports as soon as we get them.'

I nodded and changed the subject to Gault. 'I'm assuming you know what happened in New York,' I said.

'The pager.'

I nodded again.

'I'm afraid I know.' He winced. 'He's taunting us, showing his contempt. He's playing his games, only it's getting worse.'

'It's getting much worse. But we shouldn't focus only on him,' I said.

He listened, eyes locked on mine, hands folded on the case file of the murdered man he had just been discussing on the phone.

'It would be all too easy to become so obsessed with Gault that we don't really work the cases. For example, it is very important to identify this woman we think he murdered in Central Park.'

'I would assume everyone thinks that's important, Kay.'

'Everyone will say they think it is important,' I replied, and anger began quietly stirring. 'But in fact, the cops, the Bureau want to catch Gault, and identifying this homeless lady isn't a priority. She's just another poor, nameless person prisoners will bury in Potter's Field.'

'Obviously, she is a priority to you.'

'Absolutely.'

'Why?'

'I think she has something yet to say to us.'

'About Gault?'

'Yes.'

'On what are you basing this?'

'Instinct,' I said. 'And she's a priority because we are bound morally and professionally to do everything we can for her. She has a right to be buried with her name.'

'Of course she does. NYPD, the Transit Police, the Bureau – we all want her identified.'

But I did not believe him. 'We really don't care,' I flatly said. 'Not the cops, not the medical examiners, and not this unit. We already know who killed her, so who she is no longer matters. That's the black and white of it when you're talking about a jurisdiction as overwhelmed by violence as New York is.'

Wesley stared off, running his tapered fingers over a Mont Blanc pen. 'I'm afraid there's some truth in what you're saying.' He looked back at me. 'We don't care because we can't. It isn't because we don't want to. I want Gault caught before he kills again. That's my bottom line.'

'As it should be. And we don't know that this dead woman can't help with that. Maybe she will.'

I saw depression and felt it in the weariness of his voice.

'It would seem her only link to Gault is that they met in the museum,' he said. 'We've been through her personal effects, and nothing among them might lead us to him. So my question is, what else might you learn from her that would help us catch him?'

'I don't know,' I said. 'But when I have unidentified cases in Virginia, I don't rest until I've done all I can to solve them. This case is in New York, but I'm involved because I work with your unit and you have been invited into the investigation.'

I talked with conviction, as if the case of Jane's vicious murder were being tried in this room. 'If I am not allowed to uphold my own standards,' I went on, 'then I cannot serve as a consultant for the Bureau any longer.'

Wesley listened to all this with troubled patience. I knew he felt much of the same frustration that I did, but there was a difference. He had not grown up poor, and when we had our worst fights, I held that against him.

'If she were an important person,' I said, 'everyone would care.'

He remained silent.

'There is no justice if you're poor,' I said, 'unless the issue is forced.'

He stared at me.

'Benton, I'm forcing the issue.'

'Explain to me what you want to do,' he said.

'I want to do whatever it takes to find out who she is. I want you to support me.'

He studied me for a moment. He was analyzing. 'Why this victim?' he asked.

'I thought I'd just explained that.'

'Be careful,' he said. 'Be careful that your motivation isn't subjective.'

'What are you suggesting?'

'Lucy.'

I felt a rush of irritation.

'Lucy could have been as badly head injured as this woman was,' he said. 'Lucy's always been an orphan, of sorts, and not so long ago she was missing, wandering around in New England, and you had to go find her.'

'You're accusing me of projecting.'

'I'm not accusing you. I'm exploring the possibility with you.'

'I'm simply attempting to do my job,' I said. 'And I have no desire to be psychoanalyzed.'

'I understand.' He paused. 'Do whatever you need to do. I'll help in any way I can. And I'm sure Pete will, too.'

Then we switched to the more treacherous subject of Lucy and CAIN, and this Wesley did not want to talk about. He got up for coffee as the phone in the outer office rang, and his secretary took another message. The phone had not stopped ringing since my arrival, and I knew it was always like this. His office was like mine. The world was full of desperate people who had our numbers and no one else to call.

'Just tell me what you think she did,' I said when he got back.

He set my coffee before me. 'You're speaking like her aunt,' he said.

'No. Now I'm speaking like her mother.'

'I would rather you and I talk about this like two professionals,' he said.

'Fine. You can start by filling me in.'

'The espionage that began last October when ERF was broken into is still going on,' he said. 'Someone is inside CAIN.'

'That much I know.'

'We don't know who is doing it,' he said.

'We assume it's Gault, I suppose,' I said.

Wesley reached for his coffee. He met my eyes. 'I'm certainly no expert in computers. But there's something you need to see.'

He opened a thin file folder and withdrew a sheet of paper.

As he handed it to me I recognized it as a printout from a computer screen.

'That's a page of CAIN's audit log for the exact time that the most recent message was sent to the VICAP terminal in the Transit Police Department's Communications Unit,' he said. 'Do you notice anything unusual?'

I thought of the printout Lucy had shown me, of the evil message about 'Dead Cops.' I had to stare for a minute at the log-ins and log-outs, the IDs, dates and times before I realized the problem. I felt fear.

Lucy's user ID was not traditional in that it was not comprised of the initial of her first name and first seven letters of her surname. Instead, she called herself LUCYTALK, and according to this audit trail she had been signed on as the superuser when CAIN had sent the message to New York.

'Have you questioned her about this?' I asked Wesley.

'She's been questioned and wasn't concerned because as you can see from the printout, she's on and off the system all day long, and sometimes after hours, as well.'

'She is concerned. I don't care what she said to you, Benton. She feels she's been moved to the security floor so she can be watched.'

'She is being watched.'

'Just because she was signed on at the same time the message was sent to New York doesn't mean she sent it,' I persisted.

'I realize that. There's nothing else in the audit log to indicate she sent it. There's nothing to indicate anybody sent it, for that matter.'

'Who brought this to your attention?' I then asked, for I knew Wesley did not routinely look at audit logs.

'Burgess.'

'Then, someone from ERF brought it to his attention first.'

'Obviously.'

'There are still people over there who don't trust Lucy, because of what happened last fall.'

His gaze was steady. 'I can't do anything about that, Kay. She has to prove herself. We can't do that for her. You can't do that for her.'

'I'm not trying to do anything for her,' I said hotly. 'All I ask is fairness. Lucy is not to blame for the virus in CAIN. She did not put it there. She's trying to do something about it, and frankly, if she can't, I don't think anyone will be able to help. The entire system will be corrupted.'

He picked up his coffee but changed his mind and set it back down.

'And I don't believe she's been put on the security floor because some people think she's sabotaging CAIN. If you really thought that, you'd send her packing. The last thing you'd do is keep her here.'

'Not necessarily,' he said, but he could not fool me.

'Tell me the truth.'

He was thinking, looking for a way out.

'You assigned Lucy to the security floor, didn't you?' I went on. 'It wasn't Burgess. It wasn't because of this log-in time you just showed me. That's flimsy.'

'Not to some people it isn't,' he said. 'Someone over there raised a red flag and asked me to get rid of her. I said not now. We would watch her first.'

'Are you telling me you think Lucy *is* the virus?' I was incredulous.

'No.' He leaned forward in his chair. 'I think Gault is the virus. And I want Lucy to help us track him.'

I looked at him as if he had just pulled out a gun and shot it into the air. 'No,' I said with feeling.

'Kay, listen to me . . .'

'Absolutely not. Leave her out of this. She's not a goddam FBI agent.'

'You're overreacting . . .'

But I would not let him talk. 'She's *a college student,* for God's sake. She has no business—' My voice caught. 'I know her. She'll try to communicate with him. Don't you see?' I looked fiercely at him. 'You don't know her, Benton!'

'I think I do.'

'I won't let you use her like this.'

'Let me explain.'

'You should shut CAIN down,' I said.

'I can't do that. It might be the only trail Gault leaves.' He paused as I continued to glare at him. 'Lives are at stake. Gault hasn't finished killing.'

I blurted, 'That's exactly why I don't want Lucy even thinking about him!'

Wesley was silent. He looked toward the shut door, then back at me. 'He already knows who she is,' he said.

'He doesn't know much about her.'

'We don't know how much he knows about her. But at the very least he probably knows what she looks like.'

I could not think. 'How?'

'From when your American Express gold card was stolen,' he said. 'Hasn't Lucy told you?'

'Told me what?'

'The things she kept in her desk.' When he could see I did not know what he was talking about, he abruptly caught himself. I sensed he had brushed against details he would not tell me.

'What things?' I asked.

'Well,' he went on, 'she kept a letter in her desk at ERF – a letter from you. The one that had the credit card in it.'

'I know about that.'

'Right. Also inside this letter was a photograph of you and Lucy together in Miami. You were sitting in your mother's backyard, apparently.'

I shut my eyes for a moment and took a deep breath as he grimly went on.

'Gault also knows Lucy is your point of greatest vulnerability. I don't want him fixing on her, either. But what I'm trying to suggest to you is that he probably already has. He's broken into a world where she is god. He has taken over CAIN.'

'So that's why you moved her,' I said.

Wesley watched me as he struggled for a way to help. I saw the hell behind his cool reserve and sensed his terrible pain. He, too, had children.

'You moved her on the security floor with me,' I said. 'You're afraid Gault might come after her.'

Still he did not speak.

'I want her to return to UVA, to Charlottesville. I want her back there tomorrow,' I said with a ferocity I did not feel. What I really wanted was for Lucy not to know my world at all, and that would never be possible.

'She can't,' he simply said. 'And she can't stay with you in Richmond. To tell you the truth, she really can't stay anywhere right now but here. This is where she's safest.'

'She can't stay here the rest of her life,' I said.

'Until he's caught . . .'

'He may never be caught, Benton!'

He looked wearily at me. 'Then both of you may end up in our Protected Witness Program.'

'I will not give up my identity. My life. How is that any better than being dead?'

'It is better,' he said quietly, and I knew he was seeing bodies kicked, decapitated, and with bullet wounds.

I got up. 'What do I do about my stolen credit card?' I numbly asked.

'Cancel it,' he said. 'I was hoping we could use money from seized assets, from drug raids. But we can't.' He paused as I shook my head in disbelief. 'It's not my choice. You know the budget problems. You have them, too.'

'Lord,' I said. 'I thought you wanted to trail him.'

'Your credit card isn't likely to show us where he is, only where he's been.'

'I can't believe this.'

'Blame it on the politicians.'

'I don't want to hear about *budget problems or politicians,*' I exclaimed.

'Kay, the Bureau can barely afford ammunition for the ranges these days. And you know our staffing problems. I'm personally working a hundred and thirty-nine cases even as we speak. Last month two of my best people retired.

'Now my unit's down to nine. *Nine.* That's a total of ten of us trying to cover the entire United States plus any cases submitted from abroad. Hell, the only reason we have you is we don't pay you.'

'I don't do this for money.'

'You can cancel your Amex card,' he said wearily. 'I'd do it immediately.'

I looked a long time at him and left.

10

Lucy had finished her run and showered by the time I returned to the room. Dinner was being served in the cafeteria, but she was at ERF working.

'I'm going back to Richmond tonight,' I said to her on the phone.

'I thought you were spending the night,' she said, and I detected disappointment.

'Marino's coming to get me,' I said.

'When?'

'He's on his way. We could have dinner before I go.'

'Okay. I'd like Jan to come.'

'That's fine,' I said. 'We should include Marino, though. He's already on the road.'

Lucy was silent.

'Why don't you and I visit alone first?' I suggested.

'Over here?'

'Yes. I'm cleared as long as you let me through all those scanners, locked doors, X-ray machines and heat-seeking missiles.'

'Well, I'll have to check with the attorney general. She hates it when I call her at home.'

'I'm on my way.'

The Engineering Research Facility was three concrete-and-glass pods surrounded by trees, and one could not get into the parking lot without stopping at a guard booth that was no more than a hundred feet from the one at the Academy's entrance. ERF was the FBI's most classified division, its employees required to scan their fingerprints into biometric locks before Plexiglas doors would let them in. Lucy was waiting for me in front. It was almost eight P.M.

'Hi,' she said.

'There are at least a dozen cars in the parking lot,' I said. 'Do people usually work this late?'

'They drift in and out at all hours. Most of the time I never see them.'

We walked through a vast space of beige carpet and walls, passing shut doors leading into laboratories where scientists and engineers worked on projects they could not discuss. I had only vague notions of what went on here beyond Lucy's work with CAIN. But I knew the mission was to technically enhance whatever job a special agent might have, whether it was surveillance, or shooting or rappelling from a helicopter, or using a robot in a raid. For Gault to have gotten inside here was the equivalent of him wandering freely through NASA or a nuclear power plant. It was unthinkable.

'Benton told me about the photograph that was in your desk,' I said to Lucy as we boarded an elevator.

She keyed us up to the second floor. 'Gault already knows what you look like, if that's what you're worried about. He's seen you before – at least twice.'

'I don't like that he might now know what you look like,' I said pointedly.

'You're assuming he has the photograph.'

We entered a gray rabbit warren of cubicles with workstations and printers and stacks of paper. CAIN himself was behind glass in an air-conditioned space filled with monitors, modems and miles of cable hidden beneath a raised floor.

'I've got to check something,' she said, scanning her fingerprint to unlock CAIN's door.

I followed her into chilled air tense with the static of invisible traffic moving at incredible speeds. Modem lights blinked red and green, and an eighteen-inch video display announced CAIN in bold bright letters that looped and whorled like the fingerprint of the person who was just scanned in.

'The photograph was in the envelope with the American Express card he apparently now has,' I said. 'Logic would tell you that he may have both.'

'Someone else could have it.' She was intensely watching the modems, then glancing at the time on her screen and making notes. 'It depends on who actually went through my desk.'

We had always assumed it was Carrie alone who had broken in and taken whatever she wanted. Now I was not so sure.

'Carrie may not have been by herself,' I said.

Lucy did not reply.

'In fact, I don't believe Gault could have resisted the opportunity to come in here. I think he was with her.'

'That's awfully risky when you're wanted for murder.'

'Lucy, it's awfully risky to break into here to begin with.'

She continued making notes while CAIN's colors swirled on the screen and lights glowed on and off. CAIN was a space-age squid with tentacles connecting law enforcement entities here and abroad, his head an upright beige box with various buttons and slots. As cold air whirred, I almost wondered if he knew what we were saying.

'What else might have disappeared from your office?' I then said. 'Is there anything else missing?'

She was studying a modem's flashing light, her face perplexed. She glanced up at me. 'It's got to be coming in through one of these modems.'

'What is?' I asked, puzzled.

She sat before a keyboard, struck the space bar and the CAIN screen saver vanished. She logged on and began typing UNIX commands that made no sense to me. Next she pulled up the System Administrator Menu and got into the audit log.

'I've been coming in here routinely and checking the traffic on the modems,' she said, scanning. 'Unless this person is physically located in this building and hardwired into the system, he's got to be dialing in by modem.'

'There's no other way,' I said.

'Well' – she took a deep breath – 'theoretically you could use a receiver to pick up keyboard input via Van Eck radiation. Some Soviet agents were doing that not so long ago.'

'But that wouldn't actually get you inside the system,' I said.

'It could get you passwords and other information that might get you in if you had the dial-in number.'

'Were those changed after the break-in?'

'Of course. I changed everything I could think of, and in fact, the dial-in numbers have been changed again since. Plus we have callback modems. You call CAIN and he calls you back to make certain you're legit.' She looked discouraged and angry.

'If you attached a virus to a program,' I said, trying to help, 'wouldn't it change the size of the file? Couldn't that be a way to find out where the virus is?'

'Yes, it would change the file size,' she said. 'But the problem is that the UNIX program used to scan files for something like that is called *checksum,* and it's not cryptographically secure. I'm sure who ever did this included a balancing *checksum* to cause the bytes in the virus program to disappear.'

'So the virus is invisible.'

She nodded, distracted, and I knew she was thinking about Carrie. Then Lucy typed a *who* command to see what law enforcement agencies were logged on, if any. New York was. So were Charlotte and Richmond, and Lucy pointed out their modems to me. Lights danced across the front of them as data was transmitted over telephone lines.

'We should go eat dinner,' I said gently to my niece.

She typed more commands. 'I'm not hungry now.'

'Lucy, you can't let this take over your life.'

'You're one to talk.'

She was right.

'War has been declared,' she added. 'This is war.'

'This is not Carrie,' I said of the woman who, I suspected, had been more than Lucy's friend.

'It doesn't matter who it is.' She continued typing.

But it did. Carrie Grethen did not murder people and mutilate their bodies. Temple Gault did.

'Was anything else of yours taken during the break-in?' I tried again.

She stopped what she was doing and looked at me, her eyes glinting. 'Yes, if you must know,' she said. 'I had a big manilla envelope that I didn't want to leave in my dorm rooms at UVA or here because of roommates and other people in and out. It was personal. I thought it was safer in my desk up here.'

'What was in this envelope?'

'Letters, notes, different things. Some of them were from you, including the letter with the photograph and charge card. Most were from her.' Her face colored. 'There were a few notes from Grans.'

'Letters from Carrie?' I did not understand. 'Why would she write you? Both of you were here at Quantico and you didn't know each other before last fall.'

'We sort of did,' she said, her face turning a brighter red.

'How?' I asked, baffled.

'We met through a computer bulletin board, through Prodigy over the summer. I saved all the printouts of the notes we sent.'

'Did you deliberately try to arrange it so you could be at ERF together?' I said as my disbelief grew.

'She was already in the process of getting hired by the Bureau,' Lucy answered. 'She encouraged me to try to get an internship here.'

My silence was heavy.

'Look,' she demanded. 'How could I have known?'

'I guess you couldn't have,' I said. 'But she set you up, Lucy. She wanted you here. This was planned long before she met you through Prodigy. She probably had already met Gault in that northern Virginia spy shop, then they decided she should meet you.'

She angrily stared off.

'God,' I said with a loud sigh. 'You were lured right into it.' I stared off, almost sick. 'It's not just because of how good you are at what you do. It's also because of me.'

'Don't try to turn this into your fault. I hate it when you do that.'

'You are my niece. Gault has probably known that for a while.'

'I am also well known in the computer world.' She looked defiantly at me. 'Other people in the computer world have heard of me. Everything doesn't have to be because of you.'

'Does Benton know how you met Carrie?'

'I told him a long time ago.'

'Why didn't you tell me?'

'I didn't want to. I feel bad enough. It's personal.' She wouldn't look at me. 'It was between Mr. Wesley and me. And more to the point, I didn't do anything wrong.'

'Are you telling me that this large manilla envelope was missing after the break-in?'

'Yes.'

'Why would someone want it?'

'She would,' she said bitterly. 'It had things in it that she'd written to me.'

'Has she tried to contact you since then?'

'No,' she said as if she hated Carrie Grethen.

'Come on,' I said in the firm tone of a mother. 'Let's go find Marino.'

He was in the Boardroom, where I tried a Zima and he ordered another beer. Lucy was off to find Janet, and this gave Marino and me a few minutes to talk.

'I don't know how you stand that stuff,' he said, disdainfully eyeing my drink.

'I don't know how I'll stand it either since I've never had one before.' I took a sip. It was actually quite good, and I said so.

'Maybe you should try something before you judge it,' I added.

'I don't drink queer beer. And I don't have to try a lot of things to know they ain't for me.'

'I guess one of the major differences between us, Marino, is I am not constantly worried about whether people think I'm gay.'

'Some people think you are,' he said.

I was amused. 'Well, rest assured nobody thinks you are,' I said. 'The only thing most people assume about you is that you are a bigot.'

Marino yawned without covering his mouth. He was smoking and drinking Budweiser from the bottle. He had dark circles under his eyes, and though he had yet to divulge intimate details about his relationship with Molly, I recognized the symptoms of someone in lust. There were times when he looked as if he had been up and athletic for weeks on end.

'Are you all right?' I inquired.

He set down his bottle and looked around. The Boardroom was busy with new agents and cops drinking beer and eating popcorn while a television blared.

'I'm beat,' he said, and he seemed very distracted.

'I appreciate your coming to get me.'

'Just poke me if I start falling asleep at the wheel,' he said.

'Or you can drive. Those things you're drinking probably don't have any booze in them anyway.'

'They have enough. I won't be driving, and if you're that tired, perhaps we should stay here.'

He got up to get another beer. I followed him with my eyes. Marino was going to be difficult tonight. I could sense his storm fronts better than any meteorologist.

'We got a lab report back from New York that you might find interesting,' he said as he sat back down. 'It's got to do with Gault's hair.'

'The hair found in the fountain?' I asked with interest.

'Yeah. And I don't got the sort of scientific detail I know you want, okay? So you'll have to call up there yourself for that. But the bottom line is they found drugs in his hair. They said he had to be drinking and doing coke for this stuff to have shown up in his hair.'

'They found cocaethylene,' I said.

'I think that's the name. It was all through his hair, from the roots to the ends, meaning he's been drinking and drugging for a while.'

'Actually, we can't be certain how long he's been doing it,' I said.

'The guy I talked to said we're looking at five months of growth,' Marino said.

'Testing hair for drugs is controversial,' I explained. 'It's not certain that some positive results for cocaine in hair aren't due to external contamination. Say, smoke in crack houses that gets absorbed by the hair just like cigarette smoke does. It's not always easy to distinguish between what has been absorbed and what has been ingested.'

'You mean he could be contaminated.' Marino pondered this.

'Yes, he could be. But that doesn't mean he isn't drinking and drugging, too. In fact, he has to be. Cocaethylene is produced in the liver.'

Marino thoughtfully lit another cigarette. 'What about him dyeing his hair all the time?'

'That can affect test results, too,' I said. 'Some oxidizing agents might destroy some of the drug.'

'Oxidizing?'

'As in peroxides, for example.'

'Then it's possible some of this cocaethylene's been destroyed,' Marino reasoned. 'Meaning it's also possible his drug level was really higher than it looks.'

'It could be.'

'He has to be getting drugs somewhere.' Marino stared off.

'In New York that certainly wouldn't be hard,' I said.

'Hell, it's not hard anywhere.' The expression on his face was getting more tense.

'What are you thinking?' I asked.

'I'll tell you what I'm thinking,' he started in. 'This drug connection ain't working out so hot for Jimmy Davila.'

'Why? Do we know his toxicology results?' I asked.

'They're negative.' He paused. 'Benny's started singing. He's saying Davila dealt.'

'I should think people might consider the source on that one,' I said. 'Benny doesn't exactly strike me as a reliable narrator.'

'I agree with you,' Marino said. 'But some people are trying to paint Davila as a bad cop. There's a rumor they want to pin Jane's murder on him.'

'That's crazy,' I said, surprised. 'That makes absolutely no sense.'

'You remember the stuff on Jane's hand that glowed in the Luma-Lite?'

'Yes.'

'Cocaine,' he said.

'And her toxicology?'

'Negative. And that's weird.' Marino looked frustrated. 'But the other thing Benny's saying now is that it was Davila who gave the knapsack to him.'

'Oh come on,' I said with irritation.

'I'm just telling you.'

'It wasn't Davila's hair found in the fountain.'

'We can't prove how long that had been there. And we don't know it's Gault's,' he said.

'DNA will verify it's Gault's,' I said with conviction. 'And Davila carried a .380 and a .38. Jane was shot with a Glock.'

'Look' – Marino leaned forward, resting his arms on the table – 'I'm not here to argue with you, Doc. I'm just telling you that things aren't looking good. New York politicians want this case cleared, and a good way to do that is to pin the crime on a dead man. So what do you do? You turn Davila into a dirtbag and nobody feels sorry for him. Nobody cares.'

'And what about what happened to Davila?'

'That dumbshit medical examiner who went to the scene still thinks it's possible he committed suicide.'

I looked at Marino as if he'd lost his mind. 'He kicked himself in the head?' I said. 'Then shot himself between the eyes?'

'He was standing up when he shot himself with his own gun, and when he fell he hit concrete or something.'

'His vital reaction to his injuries shows he received the blow to his head first,' I said, getting angrier. 'And please explain how his revolver ended up so neatly on his chest.'

'It's not your case, Doc.' Marino looked me in the eye. 'That's the bottom line. You and me are both guests. We got invited.'

'Davila did not commit suicide,' I said. 'And Dr. Horowitz is not going to allow such a thing to come out of his office.'

'Maybe he won't. Maybe they'll just say that Davila was a dirtbag who got whacked by another drug dealer. Jane ends up in a pine box in Potter's Field. End of story. Central Park and the subway are safe again.'

I thought of Commander Penn and felt uneasy. I asked Marino about her.

'I don't know what she's got to do with any of this,' he said. 'I've just been talking to some of the guys. But she's jammed.

On the one hand, she wouldn't want anyone to think she had a bad cop. On the other, she don't want the public to think there's a crazed serial killer running through the subway.'

'I see,' I said as I thought of the enormous pressure she must be under, for it was her department's mandate to take the subway back from the criminals. New York City had allocated the Transit Police tens of millions of dollars to do that.

'Plus,' he added, 'it was a friggin' reporter who found Jane's body in Central Park. And this guy's relentless as a jackhammer from what I've heard. He wants to win a Nobel Prize.'

'Not likely,' I said irritably.

'You never know,' said Marino, who often made predictions about who would win a Nobel Prize. By now, according to him, I had won several.

'I wish we knew whether Gault is still in New York,' I said.

Marino drained his second beer and looked at his watch. 'Where's Lucy?' he asked.

'Looking for Janet, last I heard.'

'What's she like?'

I knew what he was wondering. 'She's a lovely young woman,' I said. 'Bright but very quiet.'

He was silent.

'Marino, they've put my niece on the security floor.'

He turned toward the counter as if he were thinking about another beer. 'Who did? Benton?'

'Yes.'

'Because of the computer mess?'

'Yes.'

'You want another Zima?'

'No, thank you. And you shouldn't have another beer, since you're driving. In fact, you're probably driving a police car and shouldn't have had the first one.'

'I've got my truck tonight.'

I was not at all happy to hear that, and he could tell.

'Look, so it don't have a damn air bag. I'm sorry, okay?

But a taxi or limo service wouldn't have had an air bag, either.'

'Marino . . .'

'I'm just going to buy you this huge air bag. And you can drag it around with you everywhere you go like your own personal hot-air balloon.'

'A file was stolen from Lucy's desk when ERF was broken into last fall,' I said.

'What sort of file?' he asked.

'A manilla envelope containing personal correspondence.' I told him about Prodigy and how Lucy and Carrie had met.

'They knew each other before Quantico?' he said.

'Yes. And I think Lucy believes it was Carrie who went into her desk drawer.'

Marino glanced around as he restlessly moved his empty beer bottle in small circles on the table.

'She seems obsessed with Carrie and can't see anything else,' I went on. 'I'm worried.'

'Where is Carrie these days?' he asked.

'I have no earthly idea,' I said.

Because it could not be proven that she had broken into ERF or had stolen Bureau property, she had been fired but not prosecuted. Carrie had never been locked up, not even for a day.

Marino thought for a moment. 'Well, that bitch isn't what Lucy should be worried about. It's him.'

'Certainly, I am more concerned about him.'

'You think he's got her envelope?'

'That's what I'm afraid of.' I felt a hand on my shoulder and turned around.

'We sitting here or moving on?' Lucy asked, and she had changed into khaki slacks and a denim shirt with the FBI logo embroidered on it. She wore hiking boots and a sturdy leather belt. All that was missing was a cap and a gun.

Marino was more interested in Janet, who could fill a polo shirt in a manner that was riveting. 'So, let's talk about what was in this envelope,' he said to me, unable to shift his eyes from Janet's chest.

'Let's don't do it here,' I said.

Marino's truck was a big blue Ford he kept much cleaner than his police car. His truck had a CB radio and a gun rack, and other than cigarette butts filling the ashtray, there was no trash to be seen. I sat in front, where air fresheners suspended from the rearview mirror gave the darkness a potent scent of pine.

'Tell me exactly what was in the envelope,' Marino said to Lucy, who was in back with her friend.

'I can't tell you *exactly*,' Lucy said, scooting forward and resting a hand on top of my seat.

Marino crept past the guard booth, then shifted gears as his truck loudly got interested in being alive.

'Think.' He raised his voice.

Janet quietly spoke to Lucy, and for a moment they conversed in murmurs. The narrow road was black, firing ranges unusually still. I had never ridden in Marino's truck, and it struck me as a bold symbol of his male pride.

Lucy started talking. 'I had some letters from Grans, Aunt Kay, and E-mail from Prodigy.'

'From Carrie, you mean,' Marino said.

She hesitated. 'Yes.'

'What else?'

'Birthday cards.'

'From who?' Marino asked.

'The same people.'

'What about your mother?'

'No.'

'What about your dad?'

'I don't have anything from him.'

'Her father died when she was very small,' I reminded Marino.

'When you wrote Lucy did you use a return address?' he asked me.

'Yes. My stationery would have that.'

'A post office box?'

'No. My personal mail is delivered to my house. Everything else goes to the office.'

'What are you trying to find out?' Lucy said with a trace of resentment.

'Okay,' Marino said as he drove through dark countryside, 'let me tell you what your thief knows so far. He knows where you go to school, where your aunt Kay lives in Richmond, where your grandmother in Florida lives. He knows what you look like and when you were born.

'Plus he knows about your friendship with Carrie because of the E-mail thing.' He glanced into the rearview mirror. 'And that's just the minimum of what this toad knows about you. I haven't read the letters and notes to see what else he's found out.'

'She knew most of all that anyway,' Lucy said angrily.

'*She?*' Marino pointedly asked.

Lucy was silent.

It was Janet who gently spoke. 'Lucy, you've got to get over it. You've got to give it up.'

'What else?' Marino asked my niece. 'Try to remember the smallest thing. What else was in the envelope?'

'A few autographs and a few old coins. Just things from when I was a kid. Things that would have no value to anyone but me. Like a shell from the beach I picked up when I was with Aunt Kay one time when I was little.'

She thought for a moment. 'My passport. And there were a few papers I did in high school.'

The pain in her voice tugged at my heart, and I wanted to hug her. But when Lucy was sad she pushed everyone away. She fought.

'Why did you keep them in the envelope?' Marino was asking.

'I had to keep them somewhere,' she snapped. 'It was my

damn stuff, okay? And if I'd left it in Miami my mother probably would have thrown it in the trash.'

'The papers you did in high school,' I said. 'What were they about, Lucy?'

The truck got quiet, filled with no voice but its own. The sound of its engine rose and fell with acceleration and the shifting of gears as Marino drove into the tiny town of Triangle. Roadside diners were lit up, and I suspected many of the cars out were driven by marines.

Lucy said, 'Well, it's sort of ironical now. One of the papers I did back then was a practical tutorial on UNIX security. My focus was basically passwords, you know, what could happen if users chose poor passwords. So I talked about the encryption subroutine in C libraries that—'

'What was the other paper about?' Marino interrupted her. 'Brain surgery?'

'How did you guess?' she said just as snootily.

'What was it on?' I asked.

'Wordsworth,' she said.

We ate at the Globe and Laurel, and as I looked around at Highland plaid, police patches and beer steins hanging over the bar, I thought of my life. Mark and I used to eat here, and then in London a bomb detonated as he walked past. Wesley and I once came here often. Then we began knowing each other too well, and we no longer went out in public much.

Everyone had French onion soup and tenderloin. Janet was typically quiet, and Marino would not stop staring at her and making provocative comments. Lucy was getting increasingly infuriated with him, and I was surprised at his behavior. He was no fool. He knew what he was doing.

'Aunt Kay,' Lucy said, 'I want to spend the weekend with you.'

'In Richmond?' I asked.

'That's where you still live, isn't it?' She did not smile.

I hesitated. 'I think you need to stay where you are right now.'

'I'm not in prison. I can do what I want.'

'Of course you're not in prison,' I said quietly. 'Let me talk to Benton, all right?'

She was silent.

'So tell me what you think of the Sig-nine,' Marino was saying to Janet's bosom.

She boldly looked him in the eye and said, 'I'd rather have a Colt Python with a six-inch barrel. Wouldn't you?'

Dinner continued to deteriorate, and the ride back to the Academy was tensely silent except for Marino's unrelenting attempts to engage Janet in a dialogue. After we let her and Lucy out of the truck, I turned to him and boiled over.

'For God's sake,' I exploded. 'What has gotten into you?'

'I don't know what you're talking about.'

'You were obnoxious. Absolutely obnoxious, and you know exactly what I'm talking about.'

He sped through the darkness along J. Edgar Hoover Road, heading toward the interstate as he fumbled for a cigarette.

'Janet will probably never want to be around you again,' I went on. 'I wouldn't blame Lucy for avoiding you, either. And that's a shame. The two of you had become friends.'

'Just because I've given her shooting lessons don't mean we're friends,' he said. 'As far as I'm concerned she's a spoiled brat just like she's always been, and a smart-ass. Not to mention, I don't like her type and I sure as hell don't understand why you let her do the things she does.'

'What *things*?' I said, getting more put out with him.

'Has she ever dated a guy?' He glanced over at me. 'I mean, even once?'

'Her private life is none of your concern,' I replied. 'It is not relevant to how you behaved this evening.'

'Bullshit. If Carrie hadn't been Lucy's girlfriend, ERF probably never would have been broken into, and we wouldn't have Gault running around inside the computer.'

'That's a ridiculous statement not based on a single fact,' I said. 'I suspect Carrie would have completed her mission whether Lucy was part of the scenario or not.'

'I tell you' – he blew smoke toward his slightly opened window – 'queers are ruining this planet.'

'God help us,' I said with disgust. 'You sound like my sister.'

'I think you need to send Lucy someplace. Get her some help.'

'Marino, you simply must stop this. Your opinions are based on ignorance. They are hateful. If my niece prefers women instead of men, please tell me why that is so threatening to you.'

'It don't threaten me in the least. It's just unnatural.' He tossed the cigarette butt out the window, a tiny missile extinguished by the night. 'But hey, it's not that I don't understand it. It's a known fact that a lot of women go for each other because it's the best they can do.'

'I see,' I said. 'A known fact.' I paused. 'So tell me, would that be the case with Lucy and Janet?'

'That's why I recommend them getting help, because there's hope. They could get guys easy. Especially Janet could with the way she's built. If I wasn't so tied up, I'd have half a mind to ask her out.'

'Marino,' I said, and he was making me tired, 'leave them alone. You're just setting yourself up to be disliked and snubbed. You're setting yourself up to look like a damn fool. The Janets of the world are not going to date you.'

'Her loss. If she had the right experience, it might straighten her out. What women do with each other's not what I consider the real thing. They have no idea what they're missing.'

The thought that Marino might consider himself an expert on what women needed in bed was so absurd that I forgot to be annoyed. I laughed.

'I feel protective of Lucy, okay?' he went on. 'I sort of feel like an uncle, and see, the problem is she's never been around men. Her dad died. You're divorced. She's got no brothers and her mother is in and out of bed with goofballs.'

'That much is true,' I said. 'I wish Lucy could have had a positive male influence.'

'I guarantee if she had she wouldn't have turned out queer.'

'That's not a kind word,' I said. 'And we really don't know why people turn out the way they do.'

'Then you tell me.' He glanced my way. 'You explain what went wrong.'

'In the first place, I'm not going to say that anything went wrong. There may be a genetic component to one's sexual orientation. Maybe there isn't. But what's important is that it doesn't matter.'

'So you don't care.'

I thought about this for a minute. 'I care because it is a harder way to live,' I said.

'And that's it?' he said skeptically. 'You mean you wouldn't rather she was with a man?'

Again, I hesitated. 'I guess at this point, I just want her with good people.'

He got quiet as he drove. Then he said, 'I'm sorry about tonight. I know I was a jerk.'

'Thank you for apologizing,' I said.

'Well, the truth is, things aren't going so good for me personally right now. Molly and me were doing fine until about a week ago when Doris called.'

I wasn't terribly surprised. Old spouses and lovers have a way of resurfacing.

'Seems she found out about Molly because Rocky said something. Now all of a sudden she wants to come home. She wants to get back with me.'

When Doris had left, Marino was devastated. But at this stage in my life I somewhat cynically believed that fractured relationships could not be set and healed like bones. He lit another cigarette as a truck bore down on our rear and swung past. A vehicle rushed up behind us, its high beams in our eyes.

'Molly wasn't happy about it,' he went on with difficulty. 'Truth is, we hadn't been getting along so hot since and it's just as well we didn't spend Christmas together. I think she's started going out on me, too. This sergeant she met. Wouldn't you know. I introduced them at the FOP one night.'

'I'm very sorry.' I looked over at his face and thought he might cry. 'Do you still love Doris?' I gently asked.

'Hell, I don't know. I don't know nothing. Women may as well be from another planet. You know? It's just like tonight. Everything I do is wrong.'

'That's not true. You and I have been friends for years. You must be doing something right.'

'You're the only woman friend I got,' he said. 'But you're more like a guy.'

'Why, thank you.'

'I can talk to you like a guy. And you know what you're doing. You didn't get where you are because you're a woman. Goddam it' – he squinted into the rearview mirror, then adjusted it to diminish the glare – 'you got where you are in spite of your being one.'

He glanced again in the mirrors. I turned around. A car was practically touching our bumper, high beams blinding. We were going seventy miles an hour.

'That's weird,' I said. 'He has plenty of room to go around us.'

Traffic on I-95 was light. There was no reason for anyone to tailgate, and I thought of the accident last fall when Lucy had flipped my Mercedes. Someone had been on her rear bumper, too. Fear ran along my nerves.

'Can you see what kind of car it is?' I asked.

'Looks like a Z. Maybe an old 280 Z, something like that.'

He reached inside his coat and slid a pistol from its holster. He placed the gun in his lap as he continued to watch the mirrors. I turned around again and saw a dark shape of a head that looked male. The driver was staring straight at us.

'All right,' Marino growled. 'This is pissing me off.' He firmly tapped the brakes.

The car shot around us with a long, angry blare of the horn. It was a Porsche and the driver was black.

I said to Marino, 'You don't still have that Confederate flag bumper sticker on your truck, do you? The one that glows when headlights hit it?'

'Yeah, I do.' He returned the gun to its holster.

'Maybe you ought to consider removing it.'

The Porsche was tiny taillights far ahead. I thought of Chief Tucker threatening to send Marino to cultural diversity class. Marino could go the rest of his life and I wasn't sure it would cure him.

'Tomorrow's Thursday,' he said. 'I've got to go to First Precinct and see if anyone remembers that I still work for the city.'

'What's happening with Sheriff Santa?'

'He's scheduled for a preliminary hearing next week.'

'He's locked up, I presume,' I said.

'Nope. Out on bond. When do you start jury duty?'

'Monday.'

'Maybe you can get cut loose.'

'I can't ask for that,' I said. 'Somebody would make a big deal of it, and even if they didn't, it would be hypocritical. I'm supposed to care about justice.'

'Do you think I should see Doris?' We were in Richmond now, the downtown skyline in view.

I looked over at his profile, his thinning hair, big ears and face, and the way his huge hands made the steering wheel disappear. He could not remember his life before his wife. Their relationship had long ago left the froth and fire of sex and moved into an orbit of safe but boring stability. I believed they had parted because they were afraid of growing old.

'I think you should see her,' I said to him.

'So I should go up to New Jersey.'

'No,' I said. 'Doris is the one who left. She should come here.'

11

Windsor Farms was dark when we turned into it from Cary Street, and Marino did not want me entering my house alone. He pulled into my brick driveway and stared ahead at the shut garage door illuminated by his headlights.

'Do you have the opener?' he asked.

'It's in my car.'

'A lot of friggin' good that does when your car's inside the garage with the door shut.'

'If you would drop me off in front as I requested I could unlock my front door,' I said.

'Nope. You're not walking down that long sidewalk anymore, Doc.' He was very authoritative, and I knew when he got this way there was no point in arguing.

I handed him my keys. 'Then you go on in through the front and open the garage door. I'll wait right here.'

He opened his door. 'I got a shotgun between the seats.'

He reached down to show me a black Benelli twelve-gauge with an eight-round magazine extension. It occurred to me that Benelli, a manufacturer of fine Italian shotguns, was also the name on Gault's false driver's license.

'The safety's right there.' Marino showed me. 'All you do is push it in, pump it and fire.'

'Is there a riot about to happen that I've not been told about?'

He got out of the truck and locked the doors.

I cranked open the window. 'It might help if you knew my burglar alarm code,' I said.

'Already do.' He started walking across frosted grass. 'You're DOB.'

'How did you know that?' I demanded.

'You're predictable,' I heard him say before disappearing around a hedge.

Several minutes later the garage door began to lift and a light went on inside, illuminating yard and garden tools neatly arranged on walls, a bicycle I rarely rode, and my car. I could not see my new Mercedes without thinking of the one Lucy had wrecked.

My former 500E was sleek and fast with an engine partially designed by Porsche. Now I just wanted something big. I had a black S500 that probably would hold its own with a cement truck or a tractor trailer. Marino stood near my car, looking at me as if he wished I would hurry up. I honked the horn to remind him I was locked inside his truck.

'Why do people keep trying to lock me inside their vehicles?' I said as he let me out. 'A taxi this morning, now you.'

'Because it's not safe when you're loose. I want to look around your house before I leave,' he said.

'It's not necessary.'

'I'm not asking. I'm telling you I'm going to look,' he said.

'All right. Help yourself.'

He followed me inside, and I went straight to the living room and turned on the gas fire. Next I opened the front door and brought in the mail and several newspapers that one of my neighbors had forgotten to pick up. To anybody watching my gracious brick house, it would have been obvious that I was gone over Christmas.

I glanced around as I returned to the living room, looking for anything even slightly out of order. I wondered if anyone had thought about breaking in. I wondered what eyes had turned this way, what dark thoughts had enveloped this place where I lived.

My neighborhood was one of the wealthiest in Richmond, and certainly there had been problems before, mostly with gypsies who tended to walk in during the day when people were home. I was not as worried about them, for I never left doors unlocked, and the alarm was activated constantly. It was an entirely different breed of criminal I feared, and he was not as interested in what I owned as in who and what I was. I kept many guns in the house in places where I could get to them easily.

I seated myself on the couch, the shadow from flames moving on oil paintings on the walls. My furniture was contemporary European, and during the day the house was filled with light. As I sorted mail, I came across a pink envelope similar to several I had seen before. It was note size and not a good grade of paper, the stationery the sort one might buy in a drugstore. The postmark this time was Charlottesville, December 23. I slit it open with a scalpel. The note, like the others, was handwritten in black fountain ink.

Dear Dr. Scarpetta,
I hope you have a very special Christmas!
CAIN

I carefully set the letter on my coffee table.

'Marino?' I called out.

Gault had written the note before he had murdered Jane. But the mail was slow. I was just getting it now.

'Marino!' I got up.

I heard his feet moving loudly and quickly on stairs. He rushed into the living room, gun in hand.

'What?' he said, breathing hard as he looked around. 'Are you all right?'

I pointed to the note. His eyes fell to the pink envelope and matching paper.

'Who's it from?'

'Look,' I said.

He sat beside me, then got right back up. 'I'm going to set the alarm first.'

'Good idea.'

He came back and sat down again. 'Let me have a couple pens. Thanks.'

He used the pens to keep the notepaper unfolded so he could read without jeopardizing any fingerprints I hadn't already destroyed. When he was finished, he studied the handwriting and postmark on the envelope.

'Is this the first time you've gotten one of these?' he asked.

'No.'

He looked accusingly at me. 'And you didn't say nothing?'

'It's not the first note, but it's the first one signed *CAIN*,' I said.

'What have the rest of them been signed?'

'There's only been two others on this pink stationery, and they weren't signed.'

'Do you have them?'

'No. I didn't think they were important. The postmarks were Richmond, the notes kooky but not alarming. I frequently get peculiar mail.'

'Sent to your house?'

'Generally to the office. My home address isn't listed.'

'Shit, Doc!' Marino got up and started pacing. 'Didn't it disturb you when you got notes delivered to your home address when it's not listed?'

'The location of my home certainly isn't a secret. You know

how often we've asked the media not to film or photograph it, and they do it anyway.'

'Tell me what the other notes said.'

'Like this one, they were short. One asked me how I was and if I was still working too hard. It seems to me the other was more along the lines of missing me.'

'Missing you?'

I searched my memory. 'Something like, "It's been too long. We really must see each other."'

'You're certain it's the same person.' He glanced down at the pink note on the table.

'I think so. Obviously, Gault has my address, as you predicted he would.'

'He's probably been by your crib.' He stopped pacing and looked at me. 'You realize that?'

I did not answer.

'I'm telling you that Gault has seen where you live.' Marino ran his fingers through his hair. 'You understand what I'm saying?' he demanded.

'This needs to go to the lab first thing in the morning,' I said.

I thought of the first two notes. If they, too, were from Gault, he had mailed them in Richmond. He had been here.

'You can't stay here, Doc.'

'They can analyze the postage stamp. If he licked it, he left saliva on it. We can use PCR and get DNA.'

'You can't stay here,' he said again.

'Of course I can.'

'I'm telling you, you can't.'

'I have to, Marino,' I said stubbornly. 'This is where I live.'

He was shaking his head. 'No. It's out of the question. Or else I'm moving in.'

I was devoted to Marino but could not bear the thought of him in my house. I could see him wiping his feet on my oriental rugs and leaving rings on yew wood and mahogany. He would watch wrestling in front of the fire and drink Budweiser out of the can.

'I'm going to call Benton right now,' he went on. 'He's going to tell you the same thing.' He walked toward the phone.

'Marino,' I said. 'Leave Benton out of this.'

He walked over to the fire and sat on the sandstone hearth instead. He put his head in his hands, and when he looked up at me his face was exhausted. 'You know how I'll feel if something happens to you?'

'Not very good,' I said, ill at ease.

'It will kill me. It will, I swear.'

'You're getting maudlin.'

'I don't know what that word means. But I do know Gault's going to have to waste my ass first, you hear me?' He stared intensely at me.

I looked away. I felt the blood rise to my cheeks.

'You know, you can get whacked like anybody else. Like Eddie, like Susan, like Jane, like Jimmy Davila. Gault's fixed on you, goddam it. And he's probably the worst killer in this friggin' century.' He paused, watching me. '*Are you listening?*'

I lifted my eyes to his. 'Yes,' I said. 'I'm listening. I'm hearing every word.'

'You got to leave for Lucy's sake, too. She can't come see you here ever. And if something happens to you, just what do you think is going to happen to her?'

I shut my eyes. I loved my home. I had worked so hard for it. I had labored intensely and tried to be a good business-woman. What Wesley had predicted was happening. Protection was to be at the expense of who I was and all that I had.

'So I'm supposed to move somewhere and spend my savings?' I asked. 'I'm supposed to just give all of this up?' I swept my hand around the room. 'I'm supposed to give that monster that much power?'

'You can't drive your ride, either,' he went on, thinking aloud.

'You got to drive something he won't recognize. You can take my truck, if you want.'

'Hell no,' I said.

Marino looked hurt. 'It's a big thing for me to let someone use my truck. I never let anybody.'

'That's not it. I want my life. I want to feel Lucy is safe. I want to live in my house and drive my car.'

He got up and brought me his handkerchief.

'I'm not crying,' I said.

'You're about to.'

'No, I'm not.'

'You want a drink?' he asked.

'Scotch.'

'I think I'll have a little bourbon.'

'You can't. You're driving.'

'No, I'm not,' he said as he stepped behind the bar. 'I'm camping on your couch.'

Close to midnight, I carried in a pillow and blanket and helped him get settled. He could have slept in a guest room, but he wanted to be right where he was with the fire turned low.

I retreated upstairs and read until my eyes would no longer focus. I was grateful Marino was in my house. I did not know when I had ever been this frightened. So far Gault had always gotten his way. So far he had not failed in a single evil task he had set out to accomplish. If he wanted me to die, I had no confidence I could evade him. If he wanted Lucy to die, I believed that would happen, too.

It was the latter I feared most. I had seen his work. I knew what he did. I could diagram every piece of bone and ragged excision of skin. I looked at the black metal nine-millimeter pistol on the table by my bed, and I wondered what I always did. Would I reach for it in time? Would I save my life or someone else? As I surveyed my bedroom and adjoining study, I knew Marino was right. I could not stay here alone.

I drifted to sleep pondering this and had a disturbing dream.

A figure with a long dark robe and a face like a white balloon was smiling insipidly at me from an antique mirror. Every time I passed the mirror the figure in it was watching with its chilly smile. It was both dead and alive and seemed to have no gender. I suddenly woke up at one A.M. I listened for noises in the dark. I went downstairs and heard Marino snoring.

Quietly, I called his name.

The rhythm of his snoring did not alter.

'Marino?' I whispered as I drew closer.

He sat up, loudly fumbling for his gun.

'For God's sake don't shoot me.'

'Huh?' He looked around, his face pale in the low firelight. He realized where he was and put the gun back on the table. 'Don't sneak up on me like that.'

'I wasn't sneaking.'

I sat next to him on the couch. It occurred to me that I had a nightgown on and he had never seen me like this, but I did not care.

'Is something wrong?' he asked.

I laughed ruefully. 'I don't think there's much that isn't.'

His eyes began to wander, and I could feel the battle inside him. I had always known Marino had an interest in me that I could not gratify. Tonight the situation was more difficult, for I could not hide behind walls of lab coats, scrubs, business suits and titles. I was in a low-cut gown made of soft flannel the color of sand. It was after midnight and he was sleeping in my house.

'I can't sleep,' I went on.

'I was sleeping just fine.' He lay back down and put his hands behind his head, watching me.

'I start jury duty next week.'

He made no comment.

'I have several court cases coming up and an office to run. I can't just pack up and leave town.'

'Jury duty's no problem,' he said. 'We'll get you out of it.'

'I don't want to do that.'

'You're going to get struck anyway,' he said. 'No defense attorney alive is going to want you on his jury.'

I was silent.

'You may as well go on leave. The court cases can be continued. Hey, maybe head off skiing for a couple weeks. Out west someplace.'

The more he talked the more upset I got.

'You'll have to use an alias,' he went on. 'And you got to have security. You can't be off at some ski resort all by yourself.'

'Well,' I snapped, 'no one is going to assign an FBI or Secret Service agent to me, if that's what you're thinking. Rights are honored only in the breach. Most people don't get agents or cops assigned to them until they're already raped or dead.'

'You can hire someone. He can drive, too, but you shouldn't be in your own ride.'

'I am not hiring anybody and I insist on driving my own car.'

He thought for a minute, staring up at the vaulted ceiling. 'How long have you had it?'

'Not even two months.'

'You got it from McGeorge, right?' He referred to the Mercedes dealership in town.

'Yes.'

'I'll talk to them and see if they'll let you borrow something less conspicuous than that big black Nazimobile of yours.'

Furious, I got up from the couch and moved closer to the fire.

'And just what else should I give up?' I said bitterly as I stared at flames wrapping around artificial logs.

Marino did not answer.

'I won't let him turn me into Jane.' I launched into a diatribe. 'It's as if he's prepping me so he can do the same thing to me he did to her. He's trying to take away everything I have.

'Even my name. I'm supposed to have an alias. I'm supposed

to be less conspicuous. Or generic. I'm not to live anywhere or drive anything and can't tell people where to find me. Hotels, private security are very expensive.

'So, eventually, I will go through my savings. I'm the chief medical examiner of Virginia and hardly in the office anymore. The governor may fire me. Little by little I will lose all that I have and all that I've been. Because of him.'

Still, Marino did not answer, and I realized he was asleep. A tear slid down my cheek as I pulled the covers to his chin and went back upstairs.

12

I parked behind my building at a quarter after seven and for a while sat in my car, staring at cracked blacktop, dingy stucco and the sagging chain-link fence around the parking lot.

Behind me were railroad trestles and the I-95 overpass, then the outer limits of a downtown boarded up and battered by crime. There were no trees or plantings and very little grass. My appointment to this position certainly had never included a view, but right now I did not care. I missed my office and my staff, and all that I looked at was comforting.

Inside the morgue, I stopped by the office to check on the day's cases. A suicide needed to be viewed along with an eighty-year-old woman who had died at home from untreated carcinoma of the breast. An entire family had been killed yesterday afternoon when their car was struck by a train, and my heart was heavy as I read their names. Deciding to take care of the views while I waited for my assistant chiefs, I unlocked the walk-in refrigerator and doors leading into the autopsy suite.

The three tables were polished bright, the tile floor very clean. I scanned cubbyholes stacked with forms, carts neatly lined with instruments and test tubes, steel shelves arranged with camera equipment and film. In the locker room I checked linens and starchy lab coats as I put on plastic apron and gown, then went out in the hall to a cart of surgical masks, shoe covers, face shields.

Pulling on gloves, I continued my inspection as I went inside the refrigerator to retrieve the first case. Bodies were in black pouches on top of gurneys, the air properly chilled to thirty-four degrees and adequately deodorized considering we had a full house. I checked toe tags until I found the right one, and I wheeled the gurney out.

No one else would be in for another hour, and I cherished the silence. I did not even need to lock the autopsy suite doors because it was too early for the elevator across the hall to be busy with forensic scientists going upstairs. I couldn't find any paperwork on the suicide and checked the office again. The report of sudden death had been placed in the wrong box. The date scribbled on it was incorrect by two days, and much of the form had not been completed. The only other information it offered was the name of the decedent and that the body had been delivered at three o'clock this morning by Sauls Mortuary, which made no sense.

My office used three removal services for the pickup and delivery of dead bodies. These three local funeral homes were on call twenty-four hours a day, and any medical examiner case in central Virginia should be handled by one of them. I did not understand why the suicide had been delivered by a funeral home we had no contract with, and why the driver had not signed his name. I felt a rush of irritation. I had been gone but a few days and the system was falling apart. I went to the phone and called the night-time security guard, whose shift did not end for another half hour.

'This is Dr. Scarpetta,' I said when he answered.

'Yes, ma'am.'

'To whom am I speaking, please?'

'Evans.'

'Mr. Evans, an alleged suicide was delivered at three o'clock this morning.'

'Yes, ma'am. I let him in.'

'Who delivered him?'

He paused. 'Uh, I think it was Sauls.'

'We don't use Sauls.'

He got quiet.

'I think you'd better come over here,' I said to him.

He hesitated. 'To the morgue?'

'That's where I am.'

He stalled again. I could feel his strong resistance. Many people who worked in the building could not deal with the morgue. They did not want to come near it, and I had yet to employ a security guard who would so much as poke his head inside the refrigerator. Many guards and most cleaning crews did not work for me long.

While I waited for this fearless guard named Evans, I unzipped the black pouch, which looked new. The victim's head was covered by a black plastic garbage bag that had been tied around the neck with a shoelace. He was clothed in blood-soaked pajamas and wore a thick gold bracelet and Rolex watch. Peeking out of the breast pocket of his pajama top was what appeared to be a pink envelope. I took a step back, getting weak in the knees.

I ran to the doors, slammed them shut and turned dead bolt locks as I fumbled inside my pocketbook for my revolver. Lipsticks and hairbrush clattered to the floor. I thought of the locker room, of places one could hide as I dialed the telephone, my hands trembling. Depending on how warmly he was dressed, he could hide inside the refrigerator, I frantically thought as I envisioned the many gurneys and black body bags on top of them. I hurried to the great steel door and snapped the padlock on the handle while I waited for Marino to return my page.

The phone rang in five minutes just as Evans began tentatively knocking on the locked autopsy suite doors.

'Hold on,' I called out to him. 'Stay right there.' I picked up the phone.

'Yo,' Marino said over the line.

'Get here right now,' I said, fighting to hold my voice steady as I tightly gripped the gun.

'What is it?' He got alarmed.

'Hurry!' I said.

I hung up and dialed 911. Then I spoke through the door to Evans.

'The police are coming,' I said loudly.

'The police?' His voice went up.

'We've got a terrible problem in here.' My heart would not slow down. 'You go on upstairs and wait in the conference room, is that clear?'

'Yes, ma'am. I'm on my way there now.'

A Formica counter ran half the length of the wall and I climbed on top of it, positioning myself in such a way that I was sitting near the telephone and could see every door. I held the Smith & Wesson .38 and wished I had my Browning or Marino's Benelli shotgun. I watched the black pouch on the gurney as if it might move.

The telephone rang and I jumped. I grabbed the receiver.

'Morgue.' My voice trembled.

Silence.

'Hello?' I asked more strongly.

No one spoke.

I hung up and got off the counter as anger began pumping through me and quickly turned to rage. It dispelled my fear like sun burning off mist. I unlocked the double doors leading into the corridor and stepped inside the morgue office again. Above the telephone were four strips of Scotch tape and corners of torn paper left when someone had ripped the in-house telephone list off the wall. On that list was the morgue's number and my direct line upstairs.

'Dammit!' I exclaimed under my breath. 'Dammit, dammit, dammit!'

The buzzer sounded in the bay as I wondered what else had been tampered with or taken. I thought about my office upstairs as I went out and pushed a button on the wall. The great door screeched open. Marino, in uniform, stood on its other side with two patrolmen and a detective. They ran past me to the autopsy suite, holsters unsnapped. I followed them and set my revolver on the counter because I did not think I would need it now.

'What the hell's going on?' Marino asked as he looked blankly at the body in its unzipped pouch.

The other officers looked on, not seeing anything wrong. Then they looked at me and the revolver I had just set down.

'Dr. Scarpetta? What seems to be the problem?' asked the detective, whose name I did not know.

I explained about the removal service while they listened with no expression on their faces.

'And he came in with what appears to be a note in his pocket. What police investigator would allow that? What police department is working this, for that matter? There's no mention of one,' I said, next pointing out that the head was bagged with a garbage bag tied with a shoelace.

'What does the note say?' asked the detective, who wore a belted dark coat, cowboy boots, and a gold Rolex that I was certain was counterfeit.

'I haven't touched it,' I said. 'I thought it wise to wait until you got here.'

'I think we'd better look,' he said.

With gloved hands, I slid the envelope out of the pocket, touching as little of the paper as I could. I was startled to see my name and home address neatly written on the front of it in black fountain ink. The letter also was affixed with a stamp. Carrying it to the counter, I carefully slit it open with a scalpel and unfolded a single sheet of stationery that by now was chillingly familiar. The note read:

HO! HO! HO!
CAIN

'Who's CAIN?' an officer asked as I untied the shoelace and removed the trash bag from the dead man's head.

'Oh shit,' the detective said, taking a step back.

'Holy Christ,' Marino exclaimed.

Sheriff Santa had been shot between the eyes, a nine-millimeter shell stuck in his left ear. The firing pin impression was distinctly Glock. I sat down in a chair and looked around. No one seemed quite sure what to do. This had never happened before. People didn't commit homicides and then deliver their victims to the morgue.

'The night-shift security guard is upstairs,' I said, trying to catch my breath.

'He was here when this was delivered?' Marino lit a cigarette, eyes darting.

'Apparently.'

'I'm gonna go talk to him,' said Marino, who was in command, for we were in his precinct. He looked at his officers. 'You guys poke around down here and out in the bay. See what you find. Put something out over the air without tipping off the media. Gault's been here. He may still be in the area.' He glanced at his watch, then looked at me. 'What's the guy's name upstairs?'

'Evans.'

'You know him?'

'Vaguely.'

'Come on,' he said.

'Is someone going to secure this room?' I looked at the detective and two uniformed men.

'I will,' one of them said. 'But you might not want to leave your gun sitting there.'

I returned my revolver to my purse, which I carried with me. Marino stabbed the cigarette in an ash can, and we boarded the elevator across the hall. The instant the doors shut his face turned red. He lost his captain's composure.

'I'm not believing this!' He looked at me, eyes filled with fury. 'This can't happen, it just can't happen!'

Doors opened and he angrily strode down the hall on the floor where I had spent so much of my life.

'He should be in the conference room,' I said.

We passed my office and I barely glanced inside. I did not have time now to see if Gault had been in there. All he had to do was get on the elevator or climb the stairs, and he could have walked into my office. At three o'clock in the morning, who was going to check?

Inside the conference room, Evans sat stiffly in a chair about halfway between the head and foot of the table. Around the room many photographs of former chiefs gazed at me as I sat across from this security guard who had just allowed my workplace to be turned into a crime scene. Evans was an older black man who needed his job. He wore a khaki uniform with brown flaps over the pockets and carried a gun that I wondered if he knew how to use.

'Do you know what's going on?' Marino pulled out a chair and asked him.

'No, sir. I sure don't.' His eyes were scared.

'Someone made a delivery they wasn't supposed to make.' Marino got out his cigarettes again. 'It was while you was on.'

Evans frowned. He looked genuinely clueless. 'You mean a body?'

'Listen.' I stepped in. 'I know what the SOP is. We all do. You know about the suicide case. We just talked about it on the phone . . .'

Evans interrupted, 'Like I said, I let him in.'

'What time?' Marino asked.

He looked up at the ceiling. 'I guess it would've been around three in the morning. I was next door at the desk where I always sit and this hearse pulls up.'

'Pulls up where?' Marino asked.

'Behind the building.'

'If it was behind the building, how could you see it? The lobby where you sit's in front of the building,' Marino bluntly said.

'I didn't see it,' the guard went on. 'But this man walks up and I see him through the glass. I go out to ask what he wants, and he says he has a delivery.'

'What about paperwork?' I asked. 'He didn't show you anything?'

'He says the police hadn't finished their report and told him to go on. He says they'll bring it by later.'

'I see,' I said.

'He says his hearse is parked out back,' Evans continued. 'He says a wheel on his stretcher's stuck and asks if he can use one of ours.'

'Did you know him?' I asked, containing my anger.

He shook his head.

'Can you describe him?' I then asked.

Evans thought for a minute. 'To tell you the truth, I didn't look close. But it seems like he was light skinned with white hair.'

'His hair was white?'

'Yes, ma'am. I'm sure of that.'

'He was old?'

Evans frowned again. 'No, ma'am.'

'How was he dressed?'

'Seems like he had on a dark suit and tie. You know, the way most funeral home folks dress.'

'Fat, thin, tall, short?'

'Thin. Medium height.'

'Then what happened?' Marino said.

'Then I told him to pull up to the bay and I'd let him in. I cut through the building like I always do and open the bay door. He come in and there's a stretcher in the hall. So he takes it, gets the body and comes back. He signs him in and all that.' Evans's eyes drifted. 'And he put the body in the fridge and went on.' He wouldn't look at us.

I took a deep, quiet breath and Marino blew out smoke.

'Mr. Evans,' I said, 'I just want the truth.'

He glanced at me.

'You've got to tell us what happened when you let him in,' I said. 'That's all I want. Really.'

Evans looked at me and his eyes got bright. 'Dr. Scarpetta, I don't know what's happened, but I can tell it's bad. Please don't be getting mad at me. I don't like it down there at night. I'd be a liar if I said I did. I try to do a good job.'

'Just tell the truth.' I measured my words. 'That's all we want.'

'I take care of my mama.' He was about to cry. 'I'm all she's got and she's got terrible heart trouble. I been going over there every day and doing her shopping since my wife passed on. I got a daughter raising three young'uns on her own.'

'Mr. Evans, you are not going to lose your job,' I said, even though he deserved to.

He briefly met my eyes. 'Thank you, ma'am. I believe what you're saying. But it's what other people will say that worries me.'

'Mr. Evans.' I waited until he held my gaze. 'I'm the only other people you should worry about.'

He wiped away a tear. 'I'm sorry about whatever it is I done. If I caused somebody to be hurt, I don't know what I'm gonna do.'

'You didn't cause anything,' Marino said. 'That son of a bitch with white hair did.'

'Tell us about him,' I said. 'What exactly did he do when you let him in?'

'He rolled the body in like I said, and left it parked in the hall in front of the refrigerator. I had to unlock it, you know, and I said he could roll the body on in there. Which he did. Then I took him in the morgue office and showed him what he needed to fill out. I told him he needed to put in for his mileage so he could get reimbursed. But he didn't pay no attention to that.'

'Did you escort him back out?' I asked.

Evans sighed. 'No, ma'am. I'm not going to lie to you.'

'What did you do?' Marino asked.

'I left him down there filling out paperwork. I'd locked the fridge back up and wasn't worried about shutting the bay door after him. He didn't pull into the bay 'cause there's one of your vans in there.'

I thought for a minute. 'What van?' I asked.

'That blue one.'

'There's no van in the bay,' Marino said.

Evans's face went slack. 'There sure was at three this morning. I saw it sitting right in there when I held open the door so he could roll the body in.'

'Wait a minute,' I said. 'What was the man with white hair driving?'

'A hearse.'

I could tell he did not know that for a fact. 'You saw it,' I said.

He exhaled in frustration. 'No, I didn't. He said he had one, and I just assumed it was parked in the back lot near the bay door.'

'So when you pushed the button to open the bay door, you didn't actually wait and watch what drove in.'

He looked down at the tabletop.

'Was there a van parked in the bay when you originally went out to push the button on the wall? Before the body was wheeled in?' I asked.

Evans thought for a minute, the expression on his face getting more miserable. 'Damn,' he said, eyes cast down. 'I don't remember. I didn't look. I just opened the door in the hallway, hit the button on the wall and went back inside. I didn't look.' He paused. 'It may be that nothing was in there then.'

'So the bay could have been empty at that time.'

'Yes, ma'am. I guess it could have been.'

'And when you held the door open a few minutes later so the body could be rolled in, you didn't notice a van in the bay?'

'That's when I did notice it,' he said. 'I just thought it belonged to your office. It looked like one of your vans. You know, dark blue with no windows except in front.'

'Let's get back to the man rolling the body inside the refrigerator and your locking up,' Marino said. 'Then what?'

'I figured he'd leave after he finished his paperwork,' Evans said. 'I went back to the other side of the building.'

'Before he'd left the morgue.'

Evans hung his head again.

'Do you have any idea at all when he finally left?' Marino then asked.

'No, sir,' the security guard quietly said. 'I guess I can't swear he ever did.'

Everyone was silent, as if Gault might this minute walk in. Marino pushed his chair back and looked at the empty doorway.

It was Evans who next spoke. 'If that was his van, I guess he shut the bay door himself. I know it was shut at five because I walked around the building.'

'Well, it don't exactly require a rocket scientist to do that,' Marino said unkindly. 'You just drive out, go back inside and hit the damn button. Then you walk out through the side door.'

'The van certainly isn't in there now,' I said. 'Someone drove it out.'

'Are both vans outside?' Marino asked.

'They were when I got here,' I said.

Marino asked Evans, 'If you saw him in a lineup, could you pick him out?'

He looked up, terrified. 'What did he do?'

'Could you pick him out?' Marino said again.

'I think I could. Yes, sir. I sure would try.'

I got up and quickly walked down the hall. At my office I stopped in the doorway and looked around the same way I had last night when I had walked inside my house. I tried to sense the slightest shift in the environment – a rug disturbed, an object out of place, a lamp on that shouldn't be.

My desk was neatly stacked with paperwork waiting for my review, and the computer screen on the return told me I had mail waiting. The in basket was full, the out basket empty, and my microscope was shrouded in plastic because when I had last looked at slides I was about to fly to Miami for a week.

That seemed incredibly long ago, and it shocked me to think Sheriff Santa had been arrested Christmas Eve, and since then the world had changed. Gault had savaged a woman named Jane. He had murdered a young police officer. He had killed Sheriff Santa and broken into my morgue. In four days he had done all that. I moved closer to my desk, scanning, and as I got near my computer terminal I could almost smell a presence, or feel it, like an electrical field.

I did not have to touch my keyboard to know he had. I watched the mail-waiting message quietly flash green. I hit several keys to go into a menu that would show me my messages. But the menu did not come up, a screen saver did. It was a black background with CAIN in bright red letters that dripped as if they were bleeding. I walked back down the hall.

'Marino,' I said. 'Please come here.'

He left Evans and followed me to my office. I pointed to my computer. Marino stared stonily at it. There were wet rings under the arms of his white uniform shirt, and I could smell his sweat. Stiff black leather creaked when he moved. He was constantly rearranging the fully loaded belt beneath his full belly as if everything he'd amounted to in life was in his way.

'How hard would that be to do?' he asked, mopping his face with a soiled handkerchief.

'Not hard if you have a program ready to load.'

'Where the hell did he get the program?'

'That's what worries me,' I said, thinking of a question we didn't ask.

We returned to the conference room. Evans was standing, numbly looking at photographs on the wall.

'Mr. Evans,' I said. 'Did the man from the funeral home speak to you?'

He turned around, startled. 'No, ma'am. Not much.'

'Not much?' I puzzled.

'No, ma'am.'

'Then how did he convey what he wanted?'

'He said what he had to say.' He paused. 'He was a real quiet type. He spoke in a real quiet voice.' Evans was rubbing his face. 'The more I think about it, the stranger it is. He was wearing tinted glasses. And to tell you the truth' – he stopped – 'well, I had my impressions.'

'What impressions?' I asked.

Evans said, after a pause, 'I thought he might be homosexual.'

'Marino,' I said. 'Let's take a walk.'

We escorted Evans out of the building and waited until he'd rounded a corner because I did not want him to see what we did next. Both vans were parked in their usual spaces not far from my Mercedes. Without touching door or glass, I looked through the driver's window of the one nearest the bay and could plainly see the plastic on the steering column was gone, wires exposed.

'It's been hot-wired,' I said.

Marino snapped up his portable radio and held it close to his mouth.

'Unit eight hundred.'

'Eight hundred,' the dispatcher came back.

'Ten-five 711.'

The radio called the detective inside my building whose unit number was 711, and then Marino was saying, 'Ten-twenty-five me out back.'

'Ten-four.'

Marino next radioed for a tow truck. The van was to be processed for prints on the door handles. It was to be impounded and carefully processed inside and out after that. Unit 711 had yet to walk out the back door fifteen minutes later.

'He's dumb as a bag of hammers,' Marino complained, walking around the van, radio in hand. 'Lazy son of a bitch. That's why they called him *Detective 711*. Because he's so *quick*. Shit.' He glanced irritably at his watch. 'What'd he do? Get lost in the men's room?'

I waited on the tarmac, getting unbearably cold, for I had not changed out of my greens and was without a coat. I walked around the van several times, too, desperate to look in the back of it. Five more minutes passed and Marino got the dispatcher to call the other officers inside my building. Their response was immediate.

'Where's Jakes?' Marino growled at them the instant they came out the door.

'He said he was going to look around,' one of the officers replied.

'I raised him twenty damn minutes ago and told him to ten-twenty-five me out here. I thought he was with one of you.'

'No, sir. Not for the past half hour, at least.'

Marino again tried 711 on the radio and got no answer. Fear shone in his eyes.

'Maybe he's in some part of the building where he can't copy,' an officer suggested, looking up at windows. His partner had his hand near his gun and was looking around, too.

Marino radioed for backups. People had begun pulling into the parking lot and letting themselves into the building. Many of the scientists with their topcoats and briefcases were braced against the raw, cold day and paid no attention to us. After all, police cars and those who drove them were a common sight. Marino tried to raise Detective Jakes on the air. Still he did not answer.

'Where did you see him last?' Marino asked the officers.

'He got on the elevator.'

'Where?'

'On the second floor.'

Marino turned to me. 'He couldn't have gone up, could he?'

'No,' I said. 'The elevator requires a security key for any floor above two.'

'Did he go down to the morgue again?' Marino was getting increasingly agitated.

'I went down there a few minutes later and didn't see him,' an officer said.

'The crematorium,' I suggested. 'He could have gone down to that level.'

'All right. You check the morgue,' Marino said to the officers. 'And I want you staying together. The doc and I will look around the crematorium.'

Inside the bay, left of the loading dock, was an old elevator that serviced a lower level where at one time bodies donated to science were embalmed and stored and cremated after medical students were through with them. It was possible Jakes might have gone there to look. I pushed the down button. The elevator slowly rose with much clanking and complaining. I pulled a handle and shoved open heavy, paint-chipped doors. We ducked inside.

'Damn, I don't like this already,' Marino said, releasing the thumb snap on his holster as we descended.

He slipped out his pistol as the elevator bumped to a halt and doors opened onto my least favorite area of the building. I did not like this dimly lit windowless space even though I appreciated its importance. After I moved the Anatomical Division to MCV, we began using the oven to dispose of biological hazardous waste. I got out my revolver.

'Stay behind me,' Marino said, intensely looking around.

The large room was silent save for the roar of the oven behind a shut door midway along the wall. We stood silently scanning abandoned gurneys draped with empty body bags, and hollow blue drums that once contained the formalin used to fill vats in floors where bodies were stored. I saw Marino's eyes fix on tracks in the ceiling, on heavy chains and hooks that in a former time had lifted the vats' massive lids and the people stored beneath them.

He was breathing hard and sweating profusely as he moved closer to an embalming room and ducked inside. I stayed nearby as he checked abandoned offices. He looked at me and wiped his face on his sleeve.

'It must be ninety degrees,' he muttered, detaching his radio from his belt.

Startled, I stared at him.

'What?' he said.

'The oven's not supposed to be on,' I said, looking at the crematorium room's shut door.

I started walking toward it.

'There's no waste to be disposed of that I know of, and it's strictly against policy for the oven to run unattended,' I said.

Outside that door, we could hear the inferno on the other side. I placed my hand on the knob. It was very hot.

Marino stepped in front of me, turned the knob and shoved the door open with his foot. His pistol was combat ready in both hands as if the oven were a brute he might have to shoot.

'Jesus,' he said.

Flames showed in spaces around the monstrous old iron door,

and the floor was littered with bits and chunks of chalky burned bone. A gurney was parked nearby. I picked up a long iron tool with a crook at one end and hooked it through a ring on the oven door.

'Stand back,' I said.

We were hit with a blast of enormous heat, and the roar sounded like a hateful wind. Hell was through that square mouth, and the body burning on the tray inside had not been there long. The clothes had incinerated, but not the leather cowboy boots. They smoked on Detective Jakes's feet as flames licked the skin off his bones and inhaled his hair. I shoved the door shut.

I ran out and found towels in the embalming room while Marino got sick near a pile of metal drums. Wrapping my hands, I held my breath and went past the oven, throwing the switch that turned off the gas. Flames died immediately, and I ran back out of the room. I grabbed Marino's radio as he gagged.

'Mayday!' I yelled to the dispatcher. 'Mayday!'

13

I spent the rest of the morning working on two homicide cases I had not counted on while a SWAT team swarmed my building. Police were on the lookout for the hot-wired blue van. It had vanished while everyone was looking for Detective Jakes.

X rays revealed he had received a crushing blow to the chest prior to death. Ribs and sternum were fractured, his aorta torn, and a STAT carbon monoxide showed he was no longer breathing when he was set on fire.

It seemed Gault had delivered one of his karate blows, but we did not know where the assault had occurred. Nor could we come up with a reasonable scenario that might explain how one person could have lifted the body onto a gurney. Jakes weighed 185 pounds and was five foot eleven, and Temple Brooks Gault was not a big man.

'I don't see how he could do it,' Marino said.

'I don't either,' I agreed.

'Maybe he forced him at gunpoint to lie down on the gurney.'

'If he was lying down, Gault could not have kicked him like that.'

'Maybe he gave him a chop.'

'It was a very powerful blow.'

Marino paused. 'Well, it's more likely he wasn't alone.'

'I'm afraid so,' I said.

It was almost noon, and we were driving to the house of Lamont Brown, also known as Sheriff Santa, in the quiet neighborhood of Hampton Hills. It was across Cary Street from the Country Club of Virginia, which would not have wanted Mr. Brown for a member.

'I guess sheriffs get paid a whole lot more than I do,' Marino said ironically as he parked his police car.

'This is the first time you've seen his house?' I asked.

'I've been by it when I've been back here on patrol. But I've never been inside.'

Hampton Hills was a mixture of mansions and modest homes tucked in woods. Sheriff Brown's brick house was two stories with a slate roof, a garage and a swimming pool. His Cadillac and Porsche 911 were still parked in the drive, as were a number of police vehicles. I stared at the Porsche. It was dark green, old, but well maintained.

'Do you think it's possible?' I started to say to Marino.

'That's bizarre,' he said.

'Do you remember the tag?'

'No. Dammit.'

'It could have been him,' I went on as I thought about the black man tailing us last night.

'Hell, I don't know.' Marino got out of the car.

'Would he recognize your truck?'

'He sure could know about it if he wanted to.'

'If he recognized you he might have been harassing you,' I said as we followed a brick sidewalk. 'That might be all there was to it.'

'I got no idea.'

'Or it simply could have been your racist bumper sticker. A coincidence. What else do we know about him?'

'Divorced, kids grown.'

A Richmond officer neat and trim in dark blue opened the front door and we stepped into a hardwood foyer.

'Is Neils Vander here?' I asked.

'Not yet. ID's upstairs,' the officer said, referring to the police department's Identification Unit, which was responsible for collecting evidence.

'I want the alternate light source,' I explained.

'Yes, ma'am.'

Marino spoke gruffly, for he had worked homicide far too many years to be patient with other people's standards. 'We need more backups than this. When the press catches wind, all hell's gonna break loose. I want more cars out front and I want a wider perimeter secured. The tape's got to be moved back to the foot of the driveway. I don't want anybody walking or driving on the driveway. And tape's got to go around the backyard. This whole friggin' property's got to be treated like a crime scene.'

'Yes, sir, Captain.' He snapped up his radio.

The police had been working out here for hours. It had not taken them long to determine that Lamont Brown was shot in bed in the master suite upstairs. I followed Marino up a narrow staircase covered with a machine-made Chinese rug, and voices drew us down a hallway. Two detectives were inside a bedroom paneled in dark-stained knotty pine, the window treatments and bedding reminiscent of a brothel. The sheriff was fond of maroon and gold, tassels and velvet, and mirrors on the ceiling.

Marino did not voice an opinion as he looked around. His judgment of this man had been made before now. I stepped closer to the king-size bed.

'Has this been rearranged in any way?' I asked one of the detectives as Marino and I put on gloves.

'Not really. We've photographed everything and looked under the covers. But what you see is pretty much how we found it.'

'Were the doors locked when you got here?' Marino asked.

'Yeah. We had to break the glass out of the one in back.'

'So there was no sign of forced entry whatsoever.'

'Nothing. We found traces of coke downstairs on a mirror in the living room. But that could have been there for a while.'

'What else have you found?'

'A white silk handkerchief with some blood on it,' said the detective, who was dressed in tweed, and chewing gum. 'It was right there on the floor, about three feet from the bed. And looks like the shoelace used to tie the trash bag around Brown's head came from a running shoe there in the closet.' He paused. 'I heard about Jakes.'

'It's real bad.' Marino was distracted.

'He wasn't alive when . . .'

'Nope. His chest was crushed.'

The detective stopped chewing.

'Did you recover a weapon?' I asked as I scanned the bed.

'No. We're definitely not dealing with a suicide.'

'Yeah,' said the other detective. 'It'd be a little hard to commit suicide and then drive yourself to the morgue.'

The pillow was soaked with reddish-brown blood that had clotted and separated from serum at the margins. Blood dripped down the side of the mattress, but I saw none on the floor. I thought of the gunshot wound to Brown's forehead. It was a quarter of an inch with a burned, lacerated and abraded margin. I had found smoke and soot in the wound and burned and unburned powder in the underlying tissue, bone and dura. The gunshot wound was contact, and the body had no other injuries that might indicate a defensive gesture or struggle.

'I believe he was lying on his back in bed when he was shot,' I said to Marino. 'In fact, it's almost as if he were asleep.'

He came closer to the bed. 'Well, it'd be kind of hard to stick a gun between the eyes of somebody awake and not have them react.'

'There's no evidence he reacted at all. The wound is perfectly centered. The pistol was placed snugly against his skin and it doesn't seem he moved.'

'Maybe he was passed out,' Marino said.

'His blood alcohol was .16. He could have been passed out but not necessarily. We need to go over the room with the Luma-Lite to see if we find blood we might be missing,' I said.

'But it would appear he was moved from the bed directly into the body pouch.' I showed Marino the drips on the side of the mattress. 'If he had been carried very far, there would be more blood throughout the house.'

'Right.'

We walked around the bedroom, looking. Marino began opening drawers that had already been gone through. Sheriff Brown had a taste for pornography. He especially liked women in degrading situations involving bondage and violence. In a study down the hall we found two racks filled with shotguns, rifles and several assault weapons.

A cabinet underneath had been pried open, and it was difficult to determine how many handguns or boxes of ammunition were missing since we did not know what had been there originally. Remaining were nine-millimeters, ten-millimeters, and several .44 and .357 Magnums. Sheriff Brown owned a variety of holsters, extra magazines, handcuffs, and a Kevlar vest.

'He was into this big time,' Marino said. 'He's got to have had heavy connections in DC, New York, maybe Miami.'

'Maybe there were drugs in those cabinets,' I said. 'Maybe the guns weren't what Gault was after.'

'I'm thinking *they*,' Marino said as feet sounded on the stairs. 'Unless you think Gault could have handled that body pouch all by himself. What did Brown weigh?'

'Almost two hundred pounds,' I replied as Neils Vander rounded the corner, holding the Luma-Lite by its handle. An assistant followed with cameras and other equipment.

Vander wore an oversize lab coat and white cotton gloves that looked ridiculously incongruous with his wool trousers and snow boots. He had a way of looking at me as if we had never met. He was the mad scientist, as bald as a lightbulb, always in a rush and always right. I was terribly fond of him.

'Where do you want me to set up this thing?' he asked nobody in particular.

'The bedroom,' I said. 'Then the study.'

We returned to the sheriff's bedroom to watch Vander shine his magic wand around. Lights out and glasses on, and blood dully lit up, but nothing else important did until several minutes later. The Luma-Lite was set to its widest beam and looked like a flashlight shining through deep water as it worked its way around the room. A spot on a wall, high above a chest of drawers, luminesced like a small, irregular moon. Vander got close and looked.

'Someone get the lights, please,' he said.

Lights went on and we took our tinted glasses off. Vander was standing on his tiptoes, staring at a knothole.

'What the hell is it?' Marino asked.

'This is very interesting,' said Vander, who rarely got excited about anything. 'There's something on the other side.'

'The other side of what?' Marino moved next to him and stared up, frowning. 'I don't see anything.'

'Oh yes. There's something,' Vander said. 'And somebody touched this area of paneling while they had some type of residue on their hands.'

'Drugs?' I inquired.

'It certainly could be drugs.'

All of us stared at the paneling, which looked quite normal when the Luma-Lite wasn't shining on it. But when I pulled a chair closer, I could see what Vander was talking about. The tiny hole in the center of the knothole was perfectly round. It had been drilled. On the other side of the wall was the sheriff's study, and we had just searched it.

'That's weird,' Marino said as he and I went back out the bedroom door.

Vander, oblivious to adventure, resumed what he was doing while Marino and I walked inside the study and went straight to the wall where the knothole should be. It was covered by an entertainment center that we had gone through once. Marino opened the doors again and slid out the television. He pulled books off shelves overhead, not seeing anything.

'Hmmm,' he said, studying the entertainment center. 'Interesting that it's out about six inches from the wall.'

'Yes,' I said. 'Let's move it.'

We pulled it out more, and directly in line with the knothole was a tiny video camera with a wide-angle lens. It was simply situated on a shallow ledge, a cord running from it into the base of the entertainment center, where it could be activated by a remote control that looked like it belonged to the television set. By doing a little bit of experimentation, we discovered that the camera was completely invisible from Brown's bedroom, unless one put his eye right up to the knothole and the camera was on, a red light glowing.

'Maybe he was doing a few lines of coke and decided to have sex with somebody,' Marino said. 'And at some point he got up close to look through the hole to make sure the camera was going.'

'Maybe,' I said. 'How fast can we look at the tape?'

'I don't want to do it here.'

'I don't blame you. The camera's so small we couldn't see much anyway.'

'I'll take it to the Intelligence Division as soon as we finish up.'

There was little left for us to do at the scene. As he suspected, Vander found significant residues in the gun cabinet, but no blood anywhere else in the house. The neighbors on either side of Sheriff Brown's property were cloistered amid trees and had not heard or seen any activity late last night or early this morning.

'If you'll just drop me by my car,' I said as we drove away.

Marino glanced suspiciously at me. 'Where are you going?'

'Petersburg.'

'What the hell for?' he said.

'I've got to talk to a friend about boots.'

There were many trucks and much construction along a stretch of I-95 South that I always found bleak. Even the Philip Morris plant with its building-high pack of Merits was stressful, for the fragrance of fresh tobacco bothered me. I desperately missed smoking, especially when I was driving alone on a day like this. My mind streaked, eyes constantly on mirrors as I looked for a dark blue van.

The wind flailed trees and swamps, and snowflakes were flying. As I got closer to Ft. Lee I began to see barracks and warehouses where breastworks once had been built upon dead bodies during this nation's cruelest hour. That war seemed close when I thought of Virginia swamps and woods and missing dead. Not a year passed when I didn't examine old buttons and bones, and Minié balls turned into the labs. I had touched the fabrics and faces of old violence, too, and it felt different from what I put my hands on now. Evil, I believed, had mutated to a new extreme.

The US Army Quartermaster Museum was located in Ft. Lee, just past Kenner Army Hospital. I slowly drove past offices and classrooms housed in rows of white trailers, and squads of young men and women in camouflage and athletic clothes. The building I wanted was brick with a blue roof and columns and the heraldry of an eagle, crossed sword and key just left of the door. I parked and went inside, looking for John Gruber.

The museum was the attic for the Quartermaster Corps, which since the American Revolution had been the army's innkeeper. Troops were clothed, fed and sheltered by the QMC, which also had supplied Buffalo soldiers with spurs and saddles, and General Patton with bullhorns for his jeep. I was familiar with the museum because the corps was also responsible for collecting, identifying and burying the army's dead. Ft. Lee had the only Graves Registration Division in the country, and its officers rotated through my office regularly.

I walked past displays of field dress, mess kits, and a World War II trench scene with sandbags and grenades. I stopped at Civil War uniforms that I knew were real and wondered if tears in cloth were from shrapnel or age. I wondered about the men who had worn them.

'Dr. Scarpetta?'

I turned around.

'Dr. Gruber,' I said warmly. 'I was just looking for you. Tell me about the whistle.' I pointed at a showcase filled with musical instruments.

'That's a Civil War pennywhistle,' he said. 'Music was very important. They used it to tell the time of day.'

Dr. Gruber was the museum's curator, an older man with bushy gray hair and a face carved of granite. He liked baggy trousers and bow ties. He called me when an exhibit was related to war dead, and I visited him whenever unusual military objects turned up with a body. He could identify virtually any buckle, button or bayonet at a glance.

'I take it you've got something for me to look at?' he asked, nodding at my briefcase.

'The photographs I mentioned to you over the phone.'

'Let's go to the office. Unless you'd like to look around a bit.' He smiled like a bashful grandfather talking about his grandchildren. 'We have quite an exhibit on Desert Storm. And General Eisenhower's mess uniform. I don't believe that was here when you were here last.'

'Dr. Gruber, please let me do it another time.' I did not put up any pretenses. My face showed him how I felt.

He patted my shoulder and led me through a back door that took us out of the museum into a loading area where an old trailer painted army green was parked.

'Belonged to Eisenhower,' Dr. Gruber said as we walked. 'He

lived in there at times, and it wasn't too bad unless Churchill visited. Then the cigars. You can imagine.'

We crossed a narrow street, and the snow was blowing harder. My eyes began to water as I again envisioned the pennywhistle in the showcase and thought about the woman we called Jane. I wondered if Gault had ever come here. He seemed to like museums, especially those displaying artifacts of violence. We followed a sidewalk to a small beige building I had visited before. During World War II it had been a filling station for the army. Now it was the repository for the Quartermaster archives.

Dr. Gruber unlocked a door and we entered a room crowded with tables and manikins wearing uniforms from antiquity. Tables were covered with the paperwork necessary to catalog acquisitions. In back was a large storage area where the heat was turned low and aisles were lined with large metal cabinets containing clothing, parachutes, mess kits, goggles, glasses. What we were interested in was found in large wooden cabinets against a wall.

'May I see what you've got?' Dr. Gruber asked, turning on more lights. 'I apologize about the temperature, but we've got to keep it cold.'

I opened my briefcase and pulled out an envelope, from which I slid several eight-by-ten black-and-white photographs of the footprints found in Central Park. Mainly, I cared about those we believed had been left by Gault. I showed the photographs to Dr. Gruber, and he moved them closer to a light.

'I realize it's rather difficult to see since they were left in snow,' I said. 'I wish there were a little more shadow for contrast.'

'This is quite all right. I'm getting a very good idea. This is definitely military, and it's the logotype that fascinates me.'

I looked on as he pointed to a circular area on the heel that had a tail on one side.

'Plus you've got this area of raised diamonds down here and two holes, see?' He showed me. 'Those could be shoe grip holes for climbing trees.' He handed the photographs to me. 'This looks very familiar.'

He went to a cabinet and opened its double doors, revealing rows of army boots on shelves. One by one he picked up boots and turned them over to look at the soles. Then he went to the second cabinet, opened its doors and started again. Toward the back he pulled out a boot with green canvas uppers, brown leather reinforcements and two brown leather straps with buckles at the top. He turned it over.

'May I see the photographs again, please?'

I held them close to the boot. The sole was black rubber with a variety of patterns. There were nail holes, stitching, wavy tread and pebble grain. A large oval at the ball of the foot was raised diamond tread with the shoe grip holes that were so clear in the photographs. On the heel was a wreath with a ribbon that seemed to match the tail barely visible in the snow and also on the side of Davila's head where we believed Gault's heel had struck him.

'What can you tell me about this boot?' I said.

He was turning it this way and that, looking. 'It's World War Two and was tested right here at Ft. Lee. A lot of tread patterns were developed and tested here.'

'World War Two was a long time ago,' I said. 'How would someone have a boot like this now? Could someone even be wearing a boot like this now?'

'Oh sure. These things hold up forever. You might find a pair in an Army Surplus store somewhere. Or it could have been in someone's family.'

He returned the boot to its crowded locker, where I suspected it would be neglected again for a very long time. As we left the building and he locked it behind us, I stood on a sidewalk turning soft with snow. I looked up at skies solid gray and at the slow traffic on streets. People had turned their headlights on, and the day was still. I knew what kind of boots Gault had but wasn't sure it mattered.

'Can I buy you coffee, my dear?' Dr. Gruber said, slipping a little. I grabbed his arm. 'Oh my, it's going to be bad again,' he said. 'They're predicting five inches.'

'I've got to get back to the morgue,' I said, tucking his arm in mine. 'I can't thank you enough.'

He patted my hand.

'I want to describe a man to you and ask if you might have seen him here in the past.'

He listened as I described Gault and his many shades of hair. I described his sharp features and eyes as pale blue as a malamute's. I mentioned his odd attire, and that it was becoming clear he enjoyed military clothing or designs suggestive of it, such as the boots and the long black leather coat he was seen wearing in New York.

'Well, we get types like that, you know,' he said, reaching the museum's back door. 'But I'm afraid he doesn't ring a bell.'

Snow frosted the top of Eisenhower's mobile home. My hair and hands were getting wet, and my feet were cold. 'How hard would it be to run down a name for me?' I said. 'I'd like to know if a Peyton Gault was ever in the Quartermaster Corps.'

Dr. Gruber hesitated. 'I'm assuming you believe he was in the army.'

'I'm not assuming anything,' I said. 'But I suspect he's old enough to have served in World War Two. The only other thing I can tell you is at one time he lived in Albany, Georgia, on a pecan plantation.'

'Records can't be obtained unless you're a relative or have power of attorney. That would be St. Louis you'd call, and I'm sorry to say records A through J were destroyed in a fire in the early eighties.'

'Great,' I said dismally.

He hesitated again. 'We do have our own computerized list of veterans here at the museum.'

I felt a surge of hope.

'The veteran who wants to pull his record can do so for a twenty-dollar donation,' Dr. Gruber said.

'What if you want to pull the record of someone else?'

'Can't do it.'

'Dr. Gruber' – I pushed wet hair back – 'please. We're talking about a man who has viciously murdered at least nine people. He will murder many more if we don't stop him.'

He looked up at snow coming down. 'Why on earth are we having this conversation out here, my dear?' he said. 'We're both going to catch pneumonia. I assume Peyton Gault is this awful person's father.'

I kissed his cheek. 'You've got my pager number,' I said, walking off to find my car.

As I navigated through the snowstorm, the radio was nonstop about the murders at the morgue. When I reached my office I found television vans and news crews surrounding the building, and I tried to figure out what to do. I needed to go inside.

'The hell with it,' I muttered under my breath as I turned into the parking lot.

Instantly, a school of reporters darted toward me as I got out of my black Mercedes. Cameras flashed as I walked with purpose, eyes straight ahead. Microphones appeared from every angle. People yelled my name as I hurried to unlock the back door and slam it shut behind me. I was alone in the quiet, empty bay, and I realized everyone else probably had gone home for the day because of the weather.

As I suspected, the autopsy suite was locked, and when I took the elevator upstairs, the offices of my assistant chiefs were empty, and the receptionists and clerks were gone. I was completely alone on the second floor, and I started feeling frightened. When I entered my office and saw CAIN's dripping red name on my computer screen, I felt worse.

'All right,' I said to myself. 'No one is here right now. There's no reason to be afraid.'

I sat behind my desk and placed my .38 within reach.

'What happened earlier is the past,' I went on. 'You've got to get control of yourself. You're decompensating.' I took another deep breath.

I could not believe I was talking to myself. That wasn't in character, either, and I worried as I began dictating the morning's cases. The hearts, livers and lungs of the dead policemen were normal. Their arteries were normal. Their bones and brains and builds were normal.

'Within normal limits,' I said into the tape recorder. 'Within normal limits.' I said it again and again.

It was only what had been done to them that was not normal, for Gault was not normal. He had no limits.

At a quarter of five I called the American Express office and was fortunate that Brent had not left for the day.

'You should head home soon,' I said. 'Roads are getting bad.'

'I have a Range Rover.'

'People in Richmond do not know how to drive in the snow,' I said.

'Dr. Scarpetta, what can I help you with?' asked Brent, who was young and quite capable and had helped me with many problems in the past.

'I need you to monitor my American Express bill,' I said. 'Can you do that?'

He hesitated.

'I want to be notified about every charge. As it comes in, I'm saying, versus waiting until I get the statement.'

'Is there a problem?'

'Yes,' I said. 'But I can't discuss it with you. All I need from you this moment is what I just requested.'

'Hold on.'

I heard keys click.

'Okay. I've got your account number. You realize your card expires in February.'

'Hopefully, I won't need to do this by then.'

'There are very few charges since October,' he said. 'Almost none, actually.'

'I'm interested in the most recent charges.'

'There are five for the twelfth through the twenty-first. A place in New York called Scaletta. Do you want the amounts?'

'What's the average?'

'Uh, average is, let's see, I guess about eighty bucks a pop. What is that, a restaurant?'

'Keep going.'

'Most recent.' He paused. 'Most recent is Richmond.'

'When?' My pulse picked up.

'Two for Friday the twenty-second.'

That was two days before Marino and I delivered blankets to the poor and Sheriff Santa shot Anthony Jones. I was shocked to think Gault might have been in town, too.

'Please tell me about the Richmond charges,' I then said to Brent.

'Two hundred and forty-three dollars at a gallery in Shockhoe Slip.'

'A gallery?' I puzzled. 'You mean an art gallery?'

Shockhoe Slip was just around the corner from my office. I couldn't believe Gault would be so brazen as to use my credit card there. Most merchants knew who I was.

'Yes, an art gallery.' He gave me the name and address.

'Can you tell what was purchased?'

There was a pause. 'Dr. Scarpetta, are you *certain* there isn't a problem here that I can help you with?'

'You are helping me. You're helping me a great deal.'

'Let's see. No, it doesn't say what was purchased. I'm sorry.' He sounded more disappointed than I was.

'And the other charge?'

'To USAir. A plane ticket for five hundred and fourteen dollars. This was round trip from La Guardia to Richmond.'

'Do we have dates?'

'Only of the transaction. You'd have to get the actual departure and return dates from the airline. Here's the ticket number.'

I asked him to contact me immediately if further charges showed up on the bank's computer. Glancing up at the clock, I flipped through the telephone directory. When I dialed the number of the gallery, the phone rang a long time before I gave up.

Then I tried USAir and gave them the ticket number Brent had given me. Gault, using my American Express card, had flown out of La Guardia at 7:00 A.M. on Friday, December 22. He had returned on the 6:50 flight that night. I was dumbfounded. He was in Richmond an entire day. What did he do during that time besides visit an art gallery?

'I'll be damned,' I muttered as I thought about New York laws.

I wondered if Gault had come here to buy a gun, and I called the airline again.

'Excuse me,' I said, identifying myself one more time. 'Is this Rita?'

'Yes.'

'We just spoke. This is Dr. Scarpetta.'

'Yes, ma'am. What can I do for you?'

'The ticket we were just discussing. Can you tell if bags were checked?'

'Please hold on.' Keys rapidly clicked. 'Yes, ma'am. On the return flight to La Guardia one bag was checked.'

'But not on the original flight out of La Guardia.'

'No. No bags were checked on the La Guardia to Richmond leg of the trip.'

Gault had served time in a penitentiary that once was located in this city. There was no telling who he knew, but I was certain if he wanted to buy a Glock nine-millimeter pistol in Richmond, he could. Criminals in New York commonly came here for guns. Gault may have placed the Glock in the bag he checked and the next night he shot Jane.

What this suggested was premeditation, and that had never been part of the equation. All of us had supposed Jane was someone Gault chanced upon and decided to murder, much as he had his other victims.

I made myself a mug of hot tea and tried to calm down. It was only the middle of the afternoon in Seattle, and I pulled my National Academy of Medical Examiners directory off a shelf. I flipped through it and found the name and number of Seattle's chief.

'Dr. Menendez? It's Dr. Kay Scarpetta in Richmond,' I said when I got him on the phone.

'Oh,' he said, surprised. 'How are you? Merry Christmas.'

'Thank you. I'm sorry to bother you, but I need your help.'

He hesitated. 'Is everything all right? You sound very stressed.'

'I have a very difficult situation. A serial killer who is out of control.' I took a deep breath. 'One of the cases involves an unidentified young woman with a lot of gold foil restorations.'

'That's most curious,' he said thoughtfully. 'You know, there are still some dentists out here who do those.'

'That's why I'm calling. I need to talk to someone. Maybe the head of their organization.'

'Would you like me to make some calls?'

'What I'd like you to do is find out if by some small miracle their group is on a computer system. It sounds like a small and unusual society. They might be connected through E-mail or a bulletin board. Maybe something like Prodigy. Who knows? But I've got to have a way to get information to them instantly.'

'I'll put several of my staffers on it immediately,' he said. 'What's the best way for me to reach you?'

I gave him my numbers and hung up. I thought of Gault and the missing dark blue van. I wondered where he had gotten the body pouch he zipped Sheriff Brown in, and then I remembered. We always kept a new one in each van as a backup. So he had come here first and stolen the van. Then he had gone to Brown's house. I thumbed through the telephone directory again to see if the sheriff's residence was listed. It was not.

I picked up the phone and called directory assistance. I asked for Lamont Brown's number. The operator gave it to me and I dialed it to see what would happen.

'I can't get to the phone right now because I'm out delivering presents in my sleigh . . . ,' the dead sheriff's voice sounded strong and healthy from his answering machine. 'Ho! Ho! Ho! Merrrrrry Christmas!'

Unnerved, I got up to go to the ladies' room, revolver in hand. I was walking around my office armed because Gault had ruined this place where I had always felt safe. I stopped in the hall and looked up and down it. Gray floors had a buildup of wax and walls were eggshell white. I listened for any sound. He had gotten in here once. He could get in again.

Fear gripped me strongly, and when I washed my hands in the bathroom sink, they were trembling. I was perspiring and breathing hard. I walked swiftly to the other end of the corridor and looked out a window. I could see my car covered in snow, and just one van. The other van remained missing. I returned to my office and resumed dictating.

A telephone rang somewhere and I started. The creaking of my chair made me jump. When I heard the elevator across the hall open, I reached for the revolver and sat very still, watching the doorway as my heart hammered. Quick, firm footsteps sounded, getting louder as they got nearer. I raised the gun, both hands on the rubber grips.

Lucy walked in.

'Jesus,' I exclaimed, my finger on the trigger. 'Lucy, my God.'

I set the gun on my desk. 'What are you doing here? Why didn't you call first? How did you get in?'

She looked oddly at me and the .38. 'Jan drove me down, and I've got a key. You gave me a key to your building a long time ago. I did call, but you weren't here.'

'What time did you call?' I was light-headed.

'A couple hours ago. You almost shot me.'

'No.' I tried to fill my lungs with air. 'I didn't almost shoot you.'

'Your finger wasn't on the side of the trigger guard, where it was supposed to be. It was on the trigger. I'm just glad you didn't have your Browning right now. I'm just glad you didn't have anything that's single action.'

'Please stop it,' I quietly said, and my chest hurt.

'The snow's more than two inches, Aunt Kay.'

Lucy was standing by the door, as if she were unsure about something. She was typically dressed in range pants, boots and a ski jacket.

An iron hand was squeezing my heart, my breathing labored. I sat motionless, looking at my niece as my face got colder.

'Jan's in the parking lot,' she was saying.

'The press is back there.'

'I didn't notice any reporters. But anyway, we're in the pay lot across the street.'

'They've had several muggings there,' I said. 'There was a shooting, too. About four months ago.'

Lucy was watching my face. She looked at my hands as I tucked the revolver in my pocketbook.

'You've got the shakes,' she said, alarmed. 'Aunt Kay, you're white as a sheet.' She stepped closer to my desk. 'I'm getting you home.'

Pain skewered my chest, and I involuntarily pressed a hand there.

'I can't.' I could barely talk.

The pain was so sharp and I could not catch my breath.

Lucy tried to help me up, but I was too weak. My hands were going numb, fingers cramping, and I leaned forward in the chair and shut my eyes as I broke out in a profuse cold sweat. I was breathing rapid, shallow breaths.

She panicked.

I was vaguely aware of her yelling into the phone. I tried to tell her I was all right, that I needed a paper bag, but I could not talk. I knew what was happening, but I could not tell her. Then she was wiping my face with a cool, wet cloth. She was massaging my shoulders, soothing me as I blearily stared down at my hands curled in my lap like claws. I knew what was going to happen, but I was too exhausted to fight it.

'Call Dr. Zenner,' I managed to say as pain stabbed my chest again. 'Tell her to meet us there.'

'Where is there?' Terrified, Lucy dabbed my face again.

'MCV.'

'You're going to be all right,' she said.

I did not speak.

'Don't you worry.'

I could not straighten my hands, and I was so cold I was shivering.

'I love you, Aunt Kay,' Lucy cried.

14

The Medical College of Virginia had saved my niece's life last year, for no hospital in the area was more adept at guiding the badly injured through their golden hour. She had been medflighted here after flipping my car, and I was convinced the damage to her brain would have been permanent had the Trauma Unit not been so skilled. I had been in the MCV emergency room many times, but never as a patient before this night.

By nine-thirty, I was resting quietly in a small, private room on the hospital's fourth floor. Marino and Janet were outside the door, Lucy at my bedside holding my hand.

'Has anything else happened with CAIN?' I asked.

'Don't think about that right now,' she ordered. 'You need to rest and be quiet.'

'They've already given me something to be quiet. I am being quiet.'

'You're a wreck,' she said.

'I'm not a wreck.'

'You almost had a heart attack.'

'I had muscle spasms and hyperventilated,' I said. 'I know

exactly what I had. I reviewed the cardiogram. I had nothing that a paper bag over my head and a hot bath wouldn't have fixed.'

'Well, they're not going to let you out of here until they're sure you don't have any more spasms. You don't fool around with chest pain.'

'My heart is fine. They will let me out when I say so.'

'You're noncompliant.'

'Most doctors are,' I said.

Lucy stared stonily at the wall. She had not been gentle since coming into my room. I was not sure why she was angry.

'What are you thinking about?' I asked.

'They're setting up a command post,' she said. 'They were talking about it in the hall.'

'A command post?'

'At police headquarters,' she said. 'Marino's been back and forth to the pay phone, talking to Mr. Wesley.'

'Where is he?' I asked.

'Mr. Wesley or Marino?'

'Benton.'

'He's coming here.'

'He knows I'm here,' I said.

Lucy looked at me. She was no fool. 'He's on his way here,' she said as a tall woman with short gray hair and piercing eyes walked in.

'My, my, Kay,' Dr. Anna Zenner said, leaning over to hug me. 'So now I must make house calls.'

'This doesn't exactly constitute a house call,' I said. 'This is a hospital. You remember Lucy?'

'Of course.' Dr. Zenner smiled at my niece.

'I'll be outside the door,' Lucy said.

'You forget I do not come downtown unless I have to,' Dr. Zenner went on. 'Especially when it snows.'

'Thank you, Anna. I know you don't make house calls,

hospital calls or any other kinds of calls,' I said sincerely as the door shut. 'I'm so glad you're here.'

Dr. Zenner sat by my bed. I instantly felt her energy, for she dominated a room without trying. She was remarkably fit for someone in her early seventies and was one of the finest people I knew.

'What have you done to yourself?' she asked in a German accent that had not lessened much with time.

'I fear it is finally getting to me,' I said. 'These cases.'

She nodded. 'It is all I hear about. Every time I pick up a newspaper or turn on TV.'

'I almost shot Lucy tonight.' I looked into her eyes.

'Tell me how that happened?'

I told her.

'But you did not fire the gun?'

'I came close.'

'No bullets were fired?'

'No,' I said.

'Then you did not come so close.'

'That would have been the end of my life.' I shut my eyes as they welled up with tears.

'Kay, it would also have been the end of your life had someone else been coming down that hall. Someone you had reason to fear, you know what I mean? You reacted as best you could.'

I took a deep, tremulous breath.

'And the result is not so bad. Lucy is fine. I just saw her and she is healthy and beautiful.'

I wept as I hadn't in a very long time, covering my face with my hands. Dr. Zenner rubbed my back and pulled tissues from a box, but she did not try to talk me out of my depression. She quietly let me cry.

'I'm so ashamed of myself,' I finally said between sobs.

'You mustn't be ashamed,' she said. 'Sometimes you have to let it out. You don't do that enough and I know what you see.'

'My mother is very ill and I have not been down to Miami to see her. Not once.' I was incapable of being consoled. 'I am a stranger at my office. I can no longer stay in my house – or anywhere else for that matter – without security.'

'I noticed many police outside your room,' she observed.

I opened my eyes and looked at her. 'He's decompensating,' I said.

Her eyes were fastened to mine.

'And that's good. He's more daring, meaning he's taking greater risks. That's what Bundy did in the end.'

Dr. Zenner offered what she did best. She listened.

I went on, 'The more he decompensates, the greater the likelihood he'll make a mistake and we'll get him.'

'I would also assume he is at his most dangerous right now,' she said. 'He has no boundaries. He even killed Santa Claus.'

'He killed a sheriff who plays Santa once a year. And this sheriff also was heavily involved in drugs. Maybe drugs were the connection between the two of them.'

'Tell me about you.'

I looked away from her and took another deep breath. At last I was calmer. Anna was one of the few people in this world who made me feel I did not need to be in charge. She was a psychiatrist. I had known her since my move to Richmond, and she had helped me through my breakup with Mark, then through his death. She had the heart and hands of a musician.

'Like him, I am decompensating,' I confessed in frustration.

'I must know more.'

'That's why I'm here.' I looked at her. 'That's why I'm in this gown, in this bed. It's why I almost shot my niece. It's why people are outside my door worried about me. People are driving the streets and watching my house, worrying about me. Everywhere, people are worrying about me.'

'Sometimes we have to call in the troops.'

'I don't want troops,' I said impatiently. 'I want to be left alone.'

'Ha. I personally think you need an entire army. No one can fight this man alone.'

'You're a psychiatrist,' I said. 'Why don't you dissect him?'

'I don't treat character disorders,' she said. 'Of course he is sociopathic.'

She walked to the window, parted curtains and looked out. 'It is still snowing. Do you believe that? I may have to stay here with you tonight. I have had patients over the years who were almost not of this world, and I did try to disengage from them quickly.

'That's the thing with these criminals who become the subject of legend. They go to dentists, psychiatrists, hairstylists. We cannot help but encounter them just like we encounter anyone. In Germany once I treated a man for a year until I realized he had drowned three women in the bathtub.

'That was his thing. He would pour them wine and wash them. When he would get to their feet, he would suddenly grab their ankles and yank. In those big tubs, you cannot get out if someone is holding your feet up in the air.' She paused. 'I am not a forensic psychiatrist.'

'I know that.'

'I could have been,' Dr. Zenner went on. 'I considered it many times. Did you know?'

'No, I didn't.'

'So I will tell you why I avoided that specialty. I cannot spend so much time with monsters. It is bad enough for people like you who take care of their victims. But I think to sit in the same room with the Gaults of the world would poison my soul.' She paused. 'You see, I have a terrible confession to make.'

She turned around and looked at me.

'I don't give a damn why any of them do it,' she said, eyes flashing. 'I think they should all be hanged.'

'I won't disagree with you,' I said.

'But this does not mean I don't have an instinct about him. I would call it a woman's instinct, actually.'

'About Gault?'

'Yes. You have met my cat, Chester,' she said.

'Oh, yes. He is the fattest cat I have ever seen.'

She did not smile. 'He will go out and catch a mouse. And he will play with it to death. It is really quite sadistic. Then he finally kills it and what does he do? He brings it in the house. He carries it up on the bed and leaves it on my pillow. This is his present to me.'

'What are you suggesting, Anna?' I was chilled again.

'I believe this man has a weird significant relationship with you. As if you are mother, and he brings you what he kills.'

'That is unthinkable,' I said.

'It excites him to get your attention, it is my guess. He wants to impress you. When he murders someone, it is his gift to you. And he knows you will study it very carefully and try to discover his every stroke, almost like a mother looking at her little boy's drawings he brings home from school. You see, his evil work is his art.'

I thought of the charge made at the gallery in Shockhoe Slip. I wondered what art Gault had bought.

'He knows you will analyze and think of him all the time, Kay.'

'Anna, you're suggesting these deaths might be my fault.'

'Nonsense. If you start believing that then I need to start seeing you in my office. Regularly.'

'How much danger am I in?'

'I must be careful here.' She stopped to think. 'I know what others must say. That's why there are many police.'

'What do you say?'

'I personally do not feel you are in great physical danger from him. Not this minute. But I think everyone around you is. You see, he is making his reality yours.'

'Please explain.'

'He has no one. He would like for you to have no one.'

'He has no one because of what he does,' I said angrily.

'All I can say is every time he kills, he is more isolated. And these days, so are you. There is a pattern. Do you see it?'

She had moved next to me. She placed her hand on my forehead.

'I'm not sure.'

'You have no fever,' she said.

'Sheriff Brown hated me.'

'See, another present. Gault thought you would be pleased. He killed the mouse for you and dragged it into your morgue.'

The thought made me sick.

She withdrew a stethoscope from a jacket pocket and put it around her neck. Rearranging my gown, she listened to my heart and lungs, her face serious.

'Breathe deeply for me, please.' She moved the head of the stethoscope around my back. 'Again.'

She took my blood pressure and felt my neck. She was a rare, old-world physician. Anna Zenner treated the whole person, not just the mind.

'Your pressure's low,' she said.

'So what else is new.'

'What do they give you here?'

'Ativan.'

The cuff made a ripping sound as she removed it from my arm. 'Ativan is okay. It has no appreciable effect on the respiratory or cardiovascular systems. It is fine for you. I can write a prescription.'

'No,' I said.

'An antianxiety agent is a good idea just now, I think.'

'Anna,' I said. 'Drugs are not what I need just now.'

She patted my hand. 'You are not decompensating.'

She got up and put on her coat.

'Anna,' I said, 'I have a favor to ask. How is your house at Hilton Head?'

She smiled. 'It is still the best antianxiety agent I know. And I've told you so how many times?'

'Maybe this time I will listen,' I said. 'I may have to take a trip near there, and I would like to be as private as possible.'

Dr. Zenner dug keys from her pocketbook and took one off the ring. Next she dashed off something on a blank prescription and set it and the key on a table by my bed.

'No need to do anything,' she said simply. 'But I leave for you the key and instructions. Should you get the urge in the middle of the night, you don't even need to let me know.'

'That is so kind of you,' I said. 'I doubt I'll need it long.'

'But you should need it long. It is on the ocean in Palmetto Dunes, a small, modest house near the Hyatt. I will not be using it anytime soon and don't think you will be bothered there. In fact, you can just be Dr. Zenner.' She chuckled. 'No one knows me there anyway.'

'Dr. Zenner,' I mused dryly. 'So now I'm German.'

'Oh, you are always German.' She opened the door. 'I don't care what you have been told.'

She left and I sat up straighter, energetic and alert. I got out of bed and was in the closet when I heard my door open. I walked out, expecting Lucy. Instead, Paul Tucker was inside my room. I was too surprised to be embarrassed as I stood barefoot with nothing on but a gown that barely covered anything.

He averted his gaze as I returned to bed and pulled up the covers.

'I apologize. Captain Marino said it was all right to come in,' said Richmond's chief of police, who did not seem particularly sorry, no matter what he claimed.

'He should have told me first,' I stated, looking him straight in the eye.

'Well, we all know about Captain Marino's manners. Do you mind?' He nodded at the chair.

'Please. I'm clearly a captive audience.'

'You are a captive audience because I have half my police

department looking out for you right now.' His face was hard.

I watched him carefully.

'I'm very aware of what happened in your morgue this morning.' Anger glinted in his eyes. 'You are in grave danger, Dr. Scarpetta. I'm here to plead with you. I want you to take this seriously.'

'How could you possibly assume I'm not taking this seriously?' I said with indignation.

'We'll start with this. You should not have returned to your office this afternoon. Two law enforcement officers were just murdered, one of them there while you were in the building.'

'I had no choice but to return to my office, Colonel Tucker. Just who do you think did those officers' autopsies?'

He was silent. Then he asked, 'Do you think Gault has left town?'

'No.'

'Why?'

'I don't know why, but I don't think he has.'

'How are you feeling?'

I could tell he was fishing for something, but I could not imagine what.

'I'm feeling fine. In fact, as soon as you leave, I'm going to get dressed and then I'm going to leave,' I replied.

He started to speak but didn't.

I watched him for a moment. He was dressed in dark blue FBI National Academy sweats and high-top leather cross-training shoes. I wondered if he had been working out in the gym when someone had called him about me. It suddenly struck me that we were neighbors. He and his wife lived in Windsor Farms just a few blocks from me.

'Marino's told me to evacuate my house,' I said in an almost accusatory tone. 'Are you aware of that?'

'I'm aware.'

'How much of a hand have you had in his suggestion to me?'

'Why would you think I've had anything to do with what Marino suggests to you?' he asked calmly.

'You and I are neighbors. You probably drive past my house every day.'

'I don't. But I know where you live, Kay.'

'Please don't call me Kay.'

'If I were white would you let me call you Kay?' he said with ease.

'No, I would not.'

He did not seem offended. He knew I did not trust him. He knew I was slightly afraid of him and probably of most people right now. I was getting paranoid.

'Dr. Scarpetta.' He got up. 'I've had your house under surveillance for weeks.' He paused, looking down at me.

'Why?' I asked.

'Sheriff Brown.'

'What are you talking about?' My mouth was getting dry.

'He was very involved in an intricate drug network that stretches from New York to Miami. Some of your patients were involved in it. At least eight that we know of at this time.'

'Drug shootings.'

He nodded, staring toward the window. 'Brown hated you.'

'That was clear. The reason was not.'

'Let's just say that you did your job too well. Several of his comrades were locked up for a very long time because of you.' He paused. 'We had reason to fear he planned to have you taken care of.'

I stared at him, stunned. 'What? What reason?'

'Snitches.'

'More than one?'

Tucker said, 'Brown had already offered money to somebody we had to take very seriously.'

I reached for my water glass.

'This was earlier in the month. Maybe three weeks ago.' His eyes wandered around the room.

'Who did he hire?' I asked.

'Anthony Jones.' Tucker looked at me.

My astonishment grew and I was shocked by what he told me next.

'The person who was supposed to get shot Christmas Eve was not Anthony Jones but you.'

I was speechless.

'That entire scenario of going to the wrong apartment in Whitcomb Court was for the purpose of taking you out. But when the sheriff went through the kitchen and into the backyard, he and Jones got into an argument. You know what happened.'

He got up. 'Now the sheriff is dead too and, frankly, you're lucky.'

'Colonel Tucker,' I said.

He stood by my bed.

'Did you know about this before it happened?'

'Are you asking me if I'm clairvoyant?' His face was grim.

'I think you know what I'm asking.'

'We had our eye on you. But no, we did not know until after the fact that Christmas Eve was when you were supposed to be killed. Obviously, had we known, you never would have been out riding around, delivering blankets.'

He looked down at the floor, thinking, before he spoke again. 'You're sure you're ready to check out of here.'

'Yes.'

'Where do you plan to go tonight?'

'Home.'

He shook his head. 'Out of the question. Nor do I recommend a local hotel.'

'Marino has agreed to stay with me.'

'Oh, now I bet that's safe,' he said wryly as he opened the door. 'Get dressed, Dr. Scarpetta. We have a meeting to attend.'

* * *

When I emerged from my hospital room not much later, I was met by stares and few words. Lucy and Janet were with Marino, and Paul Tucker was alone, a Gortex jacket on.

'Dr. Scarpetta, you ride with me.' He nodded at Marino. 'You follow with the young ladies.'

We walked along a polished white hallway toward elevators and headed down. Uniformed officers were everywhere, and when glass doors slid open outside the emergency room, three of them appeared to escort us to our cars. Marino and the chief had parked in police slots, and when I saw Tucker's personal car, I felt another spasm in my chest. He drove a black Porsche 911. It was not new, but it was in excellent condition.

Marino saw the car, too. He remained silent as he unlocked his Crown Victoria.

'Were you on 95 South last night?' I asked Tucker as soon as we were inside his car.

He pulled his shoulder harness across his chest and started the engine. 'Why would you ask me that?' He did not sound defensive, only curious.

'I was coming home from Quantico and a car similar to this one was tailgating us.'

'Who is us?'

'I was with Marino.'

'I see.' He turned right outside the parking deck, toward headquarters. 'So you were with the Grand Dragon.'

'Then it was you,' I said as wipers pushed away snow.

Streets were slick and I felt the car slip as Tucker slowed at a traffic light.

'I did see a Confederate flag bumper sticker last night,' he said. 'And I did express my lack of appreciation for it.'

'The truck it was on is Marino's.'

'I did not care whose truck it was.'

I looked over at him.

'Serves the captain right.' He laughed.

'Do you always act so aggressively?' I asked. 'Because it's a good way to get shot.'

'One is always welcome to try.'

'I don't recommend tailgating and taunting rednecks.'

'At least you admit he is a redneck.'

'I meant the comment in general,' I said.

'You are an intelligent, refined woman, Dr. Scarpetta. I fail to understand what you see in him.'

'There is a lot to see in him if one takes the trouble to look.'

'He is racist. He is homophobic and chauvinistic. He's one of the most ignorant human beings I've ever met, and I wish he were some other person's problem.'

'He doesn't trust anything or anyone,' I said. 'He's cynical, and not without reason, I'm sure.'

Tucker was quiet.

'You don't know him,' I added.

'I don't want to know him. What I'd like is for him to disappear.'

'Please don't do anything that wrong,' I said with feeling. 'You would be making such a mistake.'

'He is a political nightmare,' the chief said. 'He should never have been placed in charge of First Precinct.'

'Then transfer him back to the detective division, to A Squad. That's really where he belongs.'

Tucker quietly drove. He did not wish to discuss Marino anymore.

'Why was I never told someone wanted to kill me?' I asked, and the words sounded weird, and I really could not accept their meaning. 'I want to know why you did not tell me I was under surveillance.'

'I did what I thought was best.'

'You should have told me.'

He looked in his rearview mirror to make sure Marino was still behind us as he drove around the back of Richmond police department headquarters.

'I believed telling you what snitches had divulged would only place you in more danger. I was afraid you might become . . .' He paused. 'Well, aggressive, anxious. I did not want your demeanor substantially changing. I did not want you going on the offense and perhaps escalating the situation.'

'I do not think you had a right to be so secretive,' I said with feeling.

'Dr. Scarpetta.' He stared straight ahead. 'I honestly did not care what you thought and still don't. I only care about saving your life.'

At the police entrance to the parking lot, two officers with pump shotguns stood guard, their uniforms black against snow. Tucker stopped and rolled his window down.

'How's it going?' he asked.

A sergeant was stern, shotgun pointing at the planets. 'It's quiet, sir.'

'Well, you guys be careful.'

'Yes, sir. We will.'

Tucker shut his window and drove on. He parked in a space to the left of double glass doors that led into the lobby and lockup of the large concrete complex he commanded. I noticed few cruisers or unmarked cars in the lot. I supposed there were accidents to be worked this slippery night, and everyone else was out looking for Gault. To law enforcement, he had earned a new rank. He was a cop killer now.

'You and Sheriff Brown have similar cars,' I said, unfastening my seat belt.

'And there the similarity ends,' Tucker said, getting out.

His office was along a dreary hallway, several doors from A Squad, where the homicide detectives lived. The chief's quarters were surprisingly simple, furniture sturdy but utilitarian. He had no nice lamps or rugs, and walls were absent the expected photographs of himself with politicians or celebrities. I saw no certificates or diplomas that might tell where he had gone to school or what commendations he had won.

Tucker looked at his watch and showed us into a small adjoining conference room. Windowless, and carpeted in deep blue, it was furnished with a round table and eight chairs, a television and a VCR.

'What about Lucy and Janet?' I asked, expecting the chief to exclude them from the discussion.

'I already know about them,' he said, getting comfortable in a swivel chair as if he were about to watch the Super Bowl. 'They're agents.'

'I'm not an agent,' Lucy respectfully corrected him.

He looked at her. 'You wrote CAIN.'

'Not entirely.'

'Well, CAIN's a factor in all this, so you may as well stay.'

'Your department's on-line.' She held his gaze. 'In fact, yours was the first to be on-line.'

We turned as the door opened and Benton Wesley walked in. He was wearing corduroys and a sweater. He had the raw look of one too exhausted to sleep.

'Benton, I trust you know everyone,' Tucker said as if he knew Wesley quite well.

'Right.' Wesley was all business as he took a chair. 'I'm late because you're doing a good job.'

Tucker seemed perplexed.

'I got stopped at two checkpoints.'

'Ah.' The chief seemed pleased. 'We have everybody out. We're lucky as hell with the weather.'

He wasn't joking.

Marino explained to Lucy and Janet, 'The snow keeps most people home. The fewer people out, the easier for us.'

'Unless Gault's not out, either,' Lucy said.

'He's got to be somewhere,' Marino said. 'The toad don't exactly have a vacation home here.'

'We don't know what he has,' Wesley said. 'He could know someone in the area.'

'Where do you predict he might have gone after leaving the morgue this morning?' Tucker asked Wesley.

'I don't think he's left the area.'

'Why?' Tucker asked.

Wesley looked at me. 'I think he wants to be where we are.'

'What about his family?' Tucker then asked.

'They are near Beaufort, South Carolina, where they recently bought a sizable pecan plantation on an island. I don't think Gault will go there.'

'I don't think we can assume anything,' Tucker said.

'He's estranged from his family.'

'Not entirely. He's getting money from somewhere.'

'Yes,' Wesley said. 'They may give him money so he will stay away. They are in a dilemma. If they don't help him, he may come home. If they help him, he stays out there killing people.'

'They sound like fine upstanding citizens,' Tucker said sardonically.

'They won't help us,' Wesley said. 'We've tried. What else are you doing here in Richmond?'

Tucker answered, 'Everything we can. This asshole's killing cops.'

'I don't think cops are his primary target,' Wesley stated matter-of-factly. 'I don't think he cares about cops.'

'Well,' Tucker said hotly, 'he fired the first shot and we'll fire the next.'

Wesley just looked at him.

'We've got two-person patrol cars,' Tucker went on. 'We've got guards in the parking lot, primarily for shift change. Every car's got a photo of Gault, and we've been handing them out to local businesses – those we can find open.'

'What about surveillance?'

'Yes. Places he might be. They're being watched.' He looked at me. 'Including your house and mine. And the medical examiner's office.' He turned back to Wesley. 'If there are other places he might be, I wish you'd tell me.'

Wesley said, 'There can't be many. He has a nasty little habit of murdering his friends.' He stared off. 'What about State Police helicopters and fixed-wing aircraft?'

'When the snow stops,' Tucker said. 'Absolutely.'

'I don't understand how he can sneak around so easily,' said Janet, who most likely would spend the rest of her working life asking questions like that. 'He doesn't look normal. Why don't people notice him?'

'He's extremely cunning,' I said to her.

Tucker turned to Marino. 'You have the tape.'

'Yes, sir, but I'm not sure . . .' He stopped.

'You're not sure of what, Captain?' Tucker lifted his chin a little.

'I'm not sure they should see it.' He looked at Janet and Lucy.

'Please proceed, Captain,' the chief said curtly.

Marino inserted the tape into the VCR and cut the lights.

'It's about half an hour long,' his voice sounded as numbers and lines went by on the television screen. 'Anybody mind if I smoke?'

'I definitely mind,' Tucker said. 'Apparently, this was what we found in the video camera inside Sheriff Brown's house. I have not seen it yet.'

The tape started.

'Okay, what we got here is Lamont Brown's upstairs bedroom,' Marino began to narrate.

The bed I had looked at earlier today was neatly made, and in the background we could hear the sound of someone moving.

'I think this was when he was making sure his camera was working,' Marino said. 'Maybe it's when the white residue got on the wall. See. Now it's jumping ahead.'

He hit the pause button and we stared at a blurred image of the empty bedroom.

'Do we know if Brown was positive for cocaine?' the chief asked in the dark.

'It's too early to know if he had cocaine or it's metabolite, benzoyleconine, on board,' I said. 'All we have right now is his alcohol level.'

Marino resumed, 'It's like he turned the camera on and then off and then back on. You can tell because the time's different. First it was ten-oh-six last night. Now it's suddenly ten-twenty.'

'Clearly, he was expecting somebody,' Tucker spoke.

'Or else they was already there. Maybe doing a few lines of coke downstairs. Here we go.' Marino hit the play button. 'This is where the good stuff starts.'

The darkness in Tucker's conference room was absolutely silent save for the creaking of a bed and groaning that sounded more like pain than passion. Sheriff Brown was nude and on his back. From the rear we watched Temple Gault, wearing surgical gloves and nothing else. Dark clothes were laid out on the bed nearby. Marino got quiet. I could see the profiles of Lucy and Janet. Their faces were without expression, and Tucker seemed very calm. Wesley was beside me, coolly analyzing.

Gault was unhealthily pale, every vertebra and rib clearly defined. Apparently, he had lost a lot of weight and muscle tone, and I thought about the cocaine in his hair, which now was white, and as he shifted his position I saw his full breasts.

My eyes shot across the table as Lucy stiffened.

I felt Marino look at me as Carrie Grethen worked to give her client ecstasy. It seemed drugs had interfered, and no matter what she did, Sheriff Brown could not rise to receive what would prove to be the most he ever paid for pleasure. Lucy bravely kept her eyes on the television screen. She stared, shocked, as her former lover performed one lewd act after another on this big-bellied, intoxicated man.

The ending seemed predictable. Carrie would produce a gun and blow him away. But not so. Eighteen minutes into the video, footsteps sounded in Brown's bedroom, and her accomplice walked in. Temple Gault was dressed in a black suit and also wearing gloves. He seemed to have no clue that his every blink and sniffle were on camera. He stopped at the foot of the bed and watched. Brown had his eyes shut. I wasn't sure if he was conscious.

'Time's up,' Gault said impatiently.

His intense blue eyes seemed to penetrate the screen. They looked right into our conference room. He had not dyed his hair. It was still carrot red, long and slicked back from his forehead and behind his ears. He unbuttoned his jacket and withdrew a Glock nine-millimeter pistol. Nonchalantly, he walked toward the head of the bed.

Carrie looked on as Gault placed the barrel of the pistol between the sheriff's eyes. She placed her hands over her ears. My stomach tightened and I clenched my fists as Gault depressed the trigger, and the gun recoiled as if horrified by what it had just done. We sat in shock as the sheriff's agonal jerks and twitches stopped. Carrie dismounted.

'Oh damn,' Gault said, looking down at his chest. 'I got splashed.'

She snatched the handkerchief out of the breast pocket of his suit jacket and dabbed his neck and lapels.

'It won't show. It's a good thing you wore black.'

'Go put something on,' he said as if her nudity disgusted him. His voice was adolescent and uneven, and he was not loud.

He went to the foot of the bed and picked up the dark clothing.

'What about his watch?' She looked down at the bed. 'It's a Rolex. It's real, baby, and it's gold. The bracelet's real, too.'

Gault snapped, 'Get dressed now.'

'I don't want to get dirty,' she said.

She dropped the bloody handkerchief on the floor where the police would later find it.

'Then bring the bags in,' he ordered.

He seemed to be fooling with the clothing as he placed it on the dresser, but the angle of the camera made it impossible for us to see him well. She came back with the bags.

Together they disposed of Brown's body in a way that seemed careful and well planned. First, they dressed him in pajamas, for reasons we did not understand. Blood spilled on the pajama top as Gault pulled the garbage bag over the sheriff's head and tied it with a shoelace that came from a running shoe in the closet.

They lowered the body from the bed into the black pouch on the floor, Gault holding Brown under the arms while Carrie got his ankles. They tucked him in and zipped it up. We saw them carry Lamont Brown out and heard them on the stairs. Minutes later, Carrie ducked back in, got the clothing and left. Then the bedroom was empty.

Tucker tensely said, 'Certainly we can't ask for better evidence. Did the gloves come from the morgue?'

'Most likely from the van they stole,' I answered. 'We keep a box of gloves in each van.'

'It's not quite over,' Marino said.

He began advancing the film, speeding past scene after scene of the empty bedroom, until suddenly a figure was there. Marino rewound and the figure quickly walked backward out of the room.

Marino said, 'Look what happens exactly an hour and eleven minutes later.' He hit the play button again.

Carrie Grethen walked into the bedroom, dressed like Gault. Were it not for her white hair, I might have thought she was him.

'What? She's got on his suit?' Tucker asked, amazed.

'Not his suit,' I said. 'She's got on one like it, but it's not the suit Gault was wearing.'

'How can you tell?' Tucker said.

'There's a handkerchief in the pocket. She took Gault's handkerchief to wipe blood off him. And if you go back you'll see his jacket had no flaps on the pockets, but hers does.'

'Yeah,' Marino said. 'That's right.'

Carrie looked around the room, on the floor, on the bed, as if she had lost something. She was agitated and angry, and I was certain she was on the wrong side of a cocaine high. She looked around a minute longer, then left.

'I wonder what that was about,' Tucker said.

'Hold on,' Marino told us.

He advanced the film and Carrie was back. She searched some more, scowling, pulling covers back from the bed and looking under the bloody pillow. She got down on the floor and looked under the bed. She spewed a stream of profanities, eyes casting about.

'Hurry up,' Gault's impatient voice sounded from somewhere beyond the room.

She looked in the dresser mirror and smoothed her hair. For an instant, she was staring straight into the camera at close range, and I was startled by her deterioration. I once had thought her beautiful, with her clean complexion, perfect features and long brown hair. The creature standing before us now was gaunt and glassy eyed, with harsh white hair. She buttoned the suit jacket and walked off.

'What do you make of that?' Tucker asked Marino.

'I don't know. I've looked at it a dozen times and can't figure it out.'

'She's misplaced something,' Wesley said. 'That seems obvious.'

'Maybe it was just a last check,' Marino said. 'To make certain nothing was overlooked.'

'Like a video camera,' Tucker wryly said.

'She didn't care if something was overlooked,' Wesley said. 'She left Gault's bloody handkerchief on the floor.'

'But both of them was wearing gloves,' Marino said. 'I'd say they were pretty careful.'

'Was any money stolen from the house?' Wesley asked.

Marino said, 'We don't know how much. But Brown's wallet was cleaned out. He was probably missing guns, drugs, cash.'

'Wait a minute,' I said. 'The envelope.'

'What envelope?' Tucker asked.

'They didn't put it in his pocket. We watched them dress him and zip him up inside the pouch, but no envelope. Rewind it,' I said. 'Go back to that part to make certain I'm right.'

Marino rewound the tape and replayed the footage of Carrie and Gault moving the body out of the room. Brown was definitely zipped inside the pouch without the pink note that I had found in the breast pocket of his pajamas. I thought of other notes I had gotten and of all the problems Lucy was having with CAIN. The envelope had been addressed to me and fixed with a stamp as if the author's intention were to mail it.

'That may be what Carrie couldn't find,' I said. 'Maybe she's been the one sending me the letters. She intended to mail this most recent one, too, explaining why it was addressed and stamped. Then, unbeknownst to her, Gault put it in Brown's pajama pocket.'

Wesley asked, 'Why would Gault do that?'

'Perhaps because he knew the effect it would have,' I replied. 'I would see it in the morgue and instantly know that Brown was murdered and Gault was involved.'

'But what you're saying is that Gault isn't CAIN. You're saying that Carrie Grethen is,' Marino said.

It was Lucy who spoke. 'Neither of them is CAIN. They are spies.'

We were silent for a moment.

'Obviously,' I said, 'Carrie has continued helping Gault with the FBI computer. They are a team. But I think he took the note she wrote to me and did not tell her. I think that's what she was looking for.'

'Why would she look for it in Brown's bedroom?' Tucker wondered. 'Is there a reason she might have had it in there?'

'Certainly,' I said. 'She took her clothes off in there. Perhaps it was in a pocket. Play that part, Marino. When Gault is moving the dark clothing off the bed.'

He went back to that segment, and though we could not specifically see Gault remove the letter from a pocket, he did tamper with Carrie's clothing. He certainly could have gotten her letter at that time. He could have placed it in Brown's pocket later, in the back of the van or perhaps in the morgue.

'So you're really thinking she's the one who's been sending the notes to you?' Marino asked skeptically.

'I think it's probable.'

'But why?' Tucker was confounded. 'Why would *she* do this to you, Dr. Scarpetta? Do you know her?'

'I do not,' I said. 'I've only met her, but our last encounter was quite confrontational. And the notes don't seem like something Gault would do. They never have.'

'She would like to destroy you,' Wesley calmly said. 'She would like to destroy both Lucy and you.'

'Why?' Janet asked.

'Because Carrie Grethen is a psychopath,' Wesley said. 'She and Gault are twins. It's interesting that they are now dressing alike. They look alike.'

'I don't understand what he did with the letter,' Tucker said. 'Why not just ask Carrie for it instead of taking it without telling her?'

'You're asking me to tell you how Gault's mind works,' Wesley said.

'Indeed I am.'

'I don't know why.'

'But it must mean something.'

'It does,' Wesley said.

'What?' Tucker asked.

'It means she thinks she has a relationship with him. She thinks she can trust him, and she's wrong. It means he will eventually kill her, if he can,' Wesley said as Marino turned on lights.

Everybody squinted. I looked at Lucy, who had nothing to say, and sensed her anguish in one small way. She had put her glasses on when she did not need them to see unless she was sitting at a computer.

'Obviously, they're working tag team,' Marino said.

Janet spoke again. 'Who's in charge?'

'Gault is,' Marino said. 'That's why he's the one with the gun and she's the one giving the blow job.'

Tucker pushed back his chair. 'They somehow met Brown. They didn't just show up at his house.'

'Would he have recognized Gault?' Lucy asked.

'Maybe not,' Wesley said.

'I'm thinking they got in touch with him – or she did, anyway – to get drugs.'

'His phone number is unpublished but not unlisted,' I said.

'There weren't any significant messages on his answering machine,' Marino added.

'Well, I want to know the link,' Tucker said. 'How did these two know him?'

'Drugs would be my guess,' Wesley said. 'It may also be that Gault got interested in the sheriff because of Dr. Scarpetta. Brown shot someone Christmas Eve, and the media covered it ad infinitum. It was no secret that Dr. Scarpetta was there and would end up testifying. In fact, she might have ended up in the jury pool since, ironically, Brown summoned her for jury duty.'

I thought of what Anna Zenner said about Gault bringing gifts to me.

'And Gault would have been aware of all this,' Tucker said.

Wesley said, 'Possibly. If we ever find where he lives, we may discover that he gets the Richmond newspaper by mail.'

Tucker thought for a while and looked at me. 'Then who

killed the officer in New York? Was it this woman with white hair?'

'No,' I said. 'She could not have kicked him like that. Unless she is a black belt in karate.'

'And were they working together that night in the tunnel?' Tucker asked.

'I don't know that she was there,' I said.

'Well, you were there.'

'I was,' I said. 'I saw one person.'

'A person with white hair or red hair?'

I thought of the figure illuminated in the arch. I remembered the long dark coat and pale face. I had not been able to see the hair.

'I suspect it was Gault down there that night,' I said. 'I can't prove it. But there is nothing to suggest that he had an accomplice when Jane was killed.'

'Jane?' Tucker asked.

Marino said, 'That's what we call the lady he killed in Central Park.'

'Then the implication is he did not form a violent partnership with this Carrie Grethen until he returned to Virginia, after New York.' Tucker continued trying to fit the pieces together.

'We really don't know,' Wesley said. 'It's never going to be an exact science, Paul. Especially when we're dealing with violent offenders rotting their brains with drugs. The more they decompensate, the more bizarre the behavior.'

The chief of police leaned forward, looking hard at him. 'Please tell me what the hell you make of all this.'

'They were connected before. I suspect they met through a spy shop in northern Virginia,' Wesley said. 'That is how CAIN was compromised – is compromised. Now it appears the connection has moved to a different level.'

'Yeah,' Marino said. 'Bonnie's found Clyde.'

15

We drove to my home on streets barely touched by traffic. The late night was perfectly still, snow covering the earth like cotton and absorbing sound. Bare trees were black against white, the moon an indistinct face behind fog. I wanted to go for a walk, but Wesley would not let me.

'It's late and you've had a traumatic day,' he said as we sat in his BMW, which was parked behind Marino's car in front of my house. 'You don't need to be walking around out here.'

'You could walk with me.' I felt vulnerable and very tired, and did not want him to leave.

'Neither of us needs to be walking around out here,' he said as Marino, Janet and Lucy disappeared inside my house. 'You need to go inside and get some sleep.'

'What will you do?'

'I have a room.'

'Where?' I asked as if I had a right to know.

'Linden Row. Downtown. Go to bed, Kay. Please.' He paused, staring out the windshield. 'I wish I could do more, but I can't.'

'I know you can't and I'm not asking you to. Of course,

you can't any more than I could if you needed comfort. If you needed someone. That's when I hate loving you. I hate it so much. I hate it so much when I need you. Like now.' I struggled. 'Oh damn.'

He put his arms around me and dried my tears. He touched my hair and held my hand as if he loved it with all his heart. 'I could take you downtown with me tonight if that's what you really want.'

He knew I did not want that because it was impossible. 'No,' I said with a deep breath. 'No, Benton.'

I got out of his car and scooped up a handful of snow. I scrubbed my face with it as I walked around to the front door. I did not want anyone to know I had been crying in the dark with Benton Wesley.

He did not drive off until I had barricaded myself inside my house with Marino, Janet and Lucy. Tucker had ordered an around-the-clock surveillance, and Marino was in charge. He would not entrust our safety to uniformed men parked somewhere in a cruiser or van. He rallied us like Green Berets or guerrillas.

'All right,' he said as we walked into my kitchen. 'I know Lucy can shoot. Janet, you sure as hell better be able to if you're ever gonna graduate from the Academy.'

'I could shoot before the Academy,' she said in her quiet, unflappable way.

'Doc?'

I was looking inside the refrigerator.

'I can make pasta with a little olive oil, Parmesan and onion. I've got cheese if anybody wants sandwiches. Or if you give me a chance to thaw it, I've got *le piccagge col pesto di ricotta* or *tortellini verdi*. I think there's enough for four if I warm up both.'

Nobody cared.

I wanted so much to do something normal.

'I'm sorry,' I said in despair. 'I haven't been to the store lately.'

'I need to get into your safe, Doc,' Marino said.

'I've got bagels.'

'Hey. Anybody hungry?' Marino asked.

No one was. I closed the freezer. The gun safe was in the garage.

'Come on,' I told him.

He followed me out and I opened it for him.

'Do you mind telling me what you're doing?' I asked.

'I'm arming us,' he said as he picked up one handgun after another and looked at my stash of ammunition. 'Damn, you must own stock in Green Top.'

Green Top was an area gun shop that catered not to felons, but to normal citizens who enjoyed sports and home security. I reminded Marino of this, although I could not deny that by normal standards I owned too many guns and too much ammunition.

'I didn't know you had all this,' Marino went on, half inside my large, heavy safe. 'When the hell did you get all this? I wasn't with you.'

'I do shop alone now and then,' I said sharply. 'Believe it or not, I am perfectly capable of buying groceries, clothing and guns all by myself. And I'm very tired, Marino. Let's wind this up.'

'Where are your shotguns?'

'What do you want?'

'What do you have?'

'Remingtons. A Marine Magnum. An 870 Express Security.'

'That'll do.'

'Would you like me to see if I can round up some plastic explosives?' I said. 'Maybe I can put my hands on a grenade launcher.'

He pulled out a Glock nine-millimeter. 'So you're into combat Tupperware, too.'

'I've used it in the indoor range for test fires,' I said. 'That's what I've used most of these guns for. I've got several papers to present at various meetings. This is making me crazy. Are you going into my dresser drawers next?'

Marino tucked the Glock in the back of his pants. 'Let's see. And I'm gonna swipe your stainless steel Smith and Wesson nine-mil and your Colt. Janet likes Colts.'

I closed the safe and angrily spun the dial. Marino and I returned to the house and I went upstairs because I did not want to see him pass out ammunition and guns. I could not cope with the thought of Lucy downstairs with a pump shotgun, and I wondered if anything would faze or frighten Gault. I was to the point of thinking he was the living dead and no weapon known to us could stop him.

In my bedroom I turned out lights and stood before the window. My breath condensed on glass as I stared at a night lit up by snow. I remembered occasions when I had not been in Richmond long and woke up to a world quiet and white like this. Several times, the city was paralyzed and I could not go to work. I remembered walking my neighborhood, kicking snow up in the air and throwing snowballs at trees. I remembered watching children pull sleds along streets.

I wiped fog off the glass and was too sad to tell anyone my feelings. Across the street, holiday candles glowed in every window of every house but mine. The street was bright but empty. Not a single car went by. I knew Marino would stay up half the night with his female SWAT team. They would be disappointed. Gault would not come here. I was beginning to have an instinct about him. What Anna had said about him was probably right.

In bed I read until I fell to sleep, and I woke up at five. Quietly, I went downstairs, thinking it would be my luck to die from a shotgun blast inside my own home. But the door to one guest bedroom was shut, and Marino was snoring on the couch. I sneaked into the garage and backed my Mercedes out. It did wonderfully on the soft, dry snow. I felt like a bird and I flew.

I drove fast on Cary Street and thought it was fun when I fishtailed. No one else was out. I shifted the car into low gear and plowed through drifts in International Safeway's parking lot. The grocery store was always open, and I went in for fresh orange juice, cream cheese, bacon and eggs. I was wearing a hat and no one paid me any mind.

By the time I returned to my car, I was the happiest I had been in weeks. I sang with the radio all the way home and skidded when I safely could. I drove into the garage, and Marino was there with his flat black Benelli shotgun.

'What the hell do you think you're doing!' he exclaimed as I shut the garage door.

'I'm getting groceries.' My euphoria fled.

'Je-sus Christ. I can't believe you just did that,' he yelled at me.

'What do you think this is?' I lost my temper. 'Patty Hearst? Am I kidnapped now? Should we just lock me inside a closet?'

'Get in the house.' Marino was very upset.

I stared coldly at him. 'This is my house. Not your house. Not Tucker's house. Not Benton's house. This, goddam it, is my house. And I will get in it when I please.'

'Good. And you can die in it just like you can die anywhere else.'

I followed him into the kitchen. I yanked items out of the grocery bag and slammed them on the counter. I cracked eggs into a bowl and shoved shells down the disposal. I snapped on the gas burner and beat the hell out of omelets with onions and fontina cheese. I made coffee and swore because I had forgotten low-fat Cremora. I tore off squares of paper towel because I had no napkins, either.

'You can set the table in the living room and start the fire,' I said, grinding fresh pepper into frothy eggs.

'The fire's been started since last night.'

'Are Lucy and Janet awake?' I was beginning to feel better.

'I got no idea.'

I rubbed olive oil into a frying pan. 'Then go knock on their door.'

'They're in the same bedroom,' he said.

'Oh for God's sake, Marino.' I turned around and looked at him in exasperation.

We ate breakfast at seven-thirty and read the newspaper, which was wet.

'What are you going to do today?' Lucy asked me as if we were on vacation, perhaps at some lovely resort in the Alps.

She was dressed in her same fatigues, sitting on an ottoman before the fire. The nickel-plated Remington was nearby on the floor. It was loaded with seven rounds.

'I have errands to run and phone calls to make,' I said.

Marino had put on blue jeans and a sweatshirt. He watched me suspiciously as he slurped coffee.

I met his eyes. 'I'm going downtown.'

He did not respond. 'Benton's already headed out.'

I felt my cheeks get hot.

'I already tried to call him and he already checked out of the hotel.' Marino glanced at his watch. 'That would have been about two hours ago, around six.'

'When I mentioned downtown,' I said evenly, 'I was referring to my office.'

'What you need to do, Doc, is drive north to Quantico and check into their security floor for a while. Seriously. At least for the weekend.'

'I agree,' I said. 'But not until I've taken care of a few matters here.'

'Then take Lucy and Janet with you.'

Lucy was looking out the sliding glass doors now, and Janet was still reading the paper.

'No,' I said. 'They can stay here until we head out to Quantico.'

'It's not a good idea.'

'Marino, unless I've been arrested for something I know nothing about, I'm leaving here in less than thirty minutes and going to my office. And I'm going there *alone*.'

Janet lowered the paper and said to Marino, 'There comes a point when you've got to go on with your life.'

'This is a security matter,' Marino dismissed her.

Janet's expression did not change. 'No, it isn't. This is a matter of your acting like a man.'

Marino looked puzzled.

'You're being overly protective,' she added reasonably. 'And you want to be in charge and control everything.'

Marino did not seem angry because she was soft-spoken. 'You got a better idea?' he asked.

'Dr. Scarpetta can take care of herself,' Janet said. 'But she shouldn't be alone in this house at night.'

'He won't come here,' I said.

Janet got up and stretched. 'He probably won't,' she said. 'But Carrie would.'

Lucy turned away from the glass doors. Outside, the morning was blinding, and water dripped from eaves.

'Why can't I go into the office with you?' my niece wanted to know.

'There's nothing for you to do,' I said. 'You'd be bored.'

'I can work on the computer.'

Later, I drove Lucy and Janet to work with me and left them at the office with Fielding, my deputy chief. At eleven A.M., roads were slushy in the Slip, and businesses were opening late. Dressed in waterproof boots and a long jacket, I waited on a sidewalk to cross Franklin Street. Road crews were spreading salt, and traffic was sporadic this Friday before New Year's Eve.

James Galleries occupied the upper floor in a former tobacco warehouse near Laura Ashley and a record store. I entered a side door, followed a dim hallway and got on an elevator too small to carry more than three people my size. I pushed the button for the third floor, and soon the elevator opened onto another dimly lit hallway, at the end of which were glass doors with the name of the gallery painted on them in black calligraphy.

James had opened his gallery after moving to Richmond from New York. I had purchased a monoprint and a carved bird from him once, and the art glass in my dining room had come from him as well. Then I quit shopping here about a year ago after a local artist came up with inappropriate silk-screened lab coats in honor of me. They included blood and bones, cartoons and crime scenes, and when I asked James not to carry them, he increased his order.

I could see him behind a showcase, rearranging a tray of what looked like bracelets. He looked up when I rang the bell. He shook his head and mouthed that he was not open. I removed hat and sunglasses and knocked on the glass. He stared blankly until I pulled out my credentials and showed him my shield.

He was startled, then confused when he realized it was me. James, who insisted the world call him James because his first name was Elmer, came to the door. He took another look at my face and bells rattled against glass as he turned a key.

'What in the world?' he said, letting me in.

'You and I must talk,' I said, unzipping my coat.

'I'm all out of lab coats.'

'I'm delighted to hear it.'

'Me too,' he said in his petty way. 'Sold every one of them for Christmas. I sell more of those silly lab coats than anything in the gallery. We're thinking of silk-screened scrubs next, the same style you folks wear when you're doing autopsies.'

'You're not disrespectful of me,' I said. 'You're disrespectful of the dead. You will never be me, but you will someday be dead. Maybe you should think about that.'

'The problem with you is you don't have a sense of humor.'

'I'm not here to talk about what you perceive the problem with me is,' I calmly said.

A tall, fussy man with short gray hair and a mustache, he specialized in minimalist paintings, bronzes and furniture, and unusual jewelry and kaleidoscopes. Of course, he had a penchant for the irreverent and bizarre, and nothing was a bargain. He treated customers as if they were lucky to be spending money in his gallery. I wasn't sure James treated anyone well.

'What are you doing here?' he asked me. 'I know what happened around the corner, at your office.'

'I'm sure you do,' I said. 'I can't imagine how anybody could not know.'

'Is it true that one of the cops was put in . . .'

I gave him a stony stare.

He returned behind the counter, where I could now see he had been tying tiny price tags on gold and silver bracelets fashioned to look like serpents, soda can flip tops, braided hair, even handcuffs.

'Special, aren't they?' He smiled.

'They are different.'

'This is my favorite.' He held up one. It was a chain wrought of rose-gold hands.

'Several days ago someone came into your gallery and used my charge card,' I said.

'Yes. Your son.' He returned the bracelet to the tray.

'My *what*?' I said.

He looked up at me. 'Your son. Let's see. I believe his name is Kirk.'

'I do not have a son,' I told him. 'I have no children. And my American Express gold card was stolen several months ago.'

James chided me, 'Well, for crummy sake, why haven't you canceled it?'

'I didn't realize it was stolen until very recently. And I'm not here to talk to you about that,' I said. 'I need you to tell me exactly what happened.'

James pulled out a stool and sat down. He did not offer me

a chair. 'He came in the Friday before Christmas,' he said. 'I guess about four o'clock in the afternoon.'

'This was a man?'

James gave me a disgusted look. 'I *do* know the difference. Yes. He was a man.'

'Please describe him.'

'Five-ten, thin, sharp features. His cheeks were a little sunken. But I actually found him rather striking.'

'What about his hair?'

'He was wearing a baseball cap, so I didn't see much of it. But I got the impression it was a really terrible red. A Raggedy Andy red. I can't imagine who got hold of him, but he ought to sue for malpractice.'

'And his eyes?'

He was wearing dark-tinted glasses. Sort of Armani-ish.' He got amused. 'I was so surprised you had a son like that. I would have figured your boy wore khakis, skinny ties and went to MIT . . .'

'James, there is nothing lighthearted about this conversation,' I abruptly said.

His face lit up and his eyes got wide as the meaning became clear. 'Oh my God. The man I've been reading about? That's who . . . My God. *He* was in my gallery?'

I made no comment.

James was ecstatic. 'Do you realize what this will do?' he said. 'When people find out he shopped here?'

I said nothing.

'It will be fabulous for my business. People from all over will come here. My gallery will be on the tour routes.'

'That's right. Be certain to advertise something like that,' I said. 'And character disorders from everywhere will stand in line. They'll touch your expensive paintings, bronzes, tapestries, and ask you endless questions. And they won't buy a thing.'

He got quiet.

'When he came in,' I said, 'what did he do?'

'He looked around. He said he was looking for a last-minute gift.'

'What was his voice like?'

'Quiet. Kind of high-pitched. I asked who the present was for, and he said his mother. He said she was a doctor. That's when I showed him the pin he ended up buying. It's a caduceus. Two white gold serpents twined around a yellow gold winged staff. The serpents have ruby eyes. It's handmade and absolutely spectacular.'

'That's what he bought for two hundred and fifty dollars?' I asked.

'Yes.' He was appraising me, crooked finger under his chin. 'Actually, it's you. The pin is really you. Would you like for me to have the artist make another one?'

'What happened after he bought the pin?'

'I asked if he wanted it gift wrapped, and he didn't. He pulled out the charge card. And I said, "Well, small, small world. Your mother works right around the corner." He didn't say anything. So I asked if he was home for the holidays, and he smiled.'

'He didn't talk,' I said.

'Not at all. It was like pulling hens' teeth. I wouldn't call him friendly. But he was polite.'

'Do you remember how he was dressed?'

'A long black leather coat. It was belted, so I don't know what he had on under it. But I thought he looked sharp.'

'Shoes?'

'It seems he had on boots.'

'Did you notice anything else about him?'

He thought for a while, looking past me at the door. He said, 'Now that you mention it, he had what looked like burns on his fingers. I thought that was a little scary.'

'What about his hygiene?' I then asked, for the more addicted a crack user got, the less he cared about clothing or cleanliness.

'He seemed clean to me. But I really didn't get close to him.'

'And he bought nothing else while he was here?'

'Unfortunately not.'

Elmer James propped an elbow on the showcase and rested his cheek on his fist. He sighed. 'I wonder how he found me.'

I walked back, avoiding slushy puddles on streets and the cars that drove through them heedlessly. I got splashed once. I returned to my office, where Janet was in the library watching a teaching videotape of an autopsy while Lucy worked in the computer room. I left them alone and went down to the morgue to check on my staff.

Fielding was at the first table, working on a young woman found dead in the snow below her bedroom window. I noted the pinkness of the body and could smell alcohol in the blood. On her right arm was a cast scribbled with messages and autographs.

'How are we doing?' I asked.

'She's got a STAT alcohol of .23,' he replied, examining a section of aorta. 'So that didn't get her. I think she's going to be an exposure death.'

'What are the circumstances?' I could not help but think of Jane.

'Apparently, she was out drinking with friends and by the time they took her home around eleven P.M. it was snowing pretty hard. They let her out and didn't wait to see her in. The police think her keys fell in the snow and she was too drunk to find them.'

He dropped the section of aorta into a jar of formalin. 'So she tried to get in a window by breaking it with her cast.'

He lifted the brain out of the scale. 'But that didn't work. The window was too high up, and with one arm she couldn't have climbed in it anyway. Eventually she passed out.'

'Nice friends,' I said, walking off.

Dr. Anderson, who was new, was photographing a ninety-one-year-old woman with a hip fracture. I collected paperwork from a nearby desk and quickly reviewed the case.

'Is this an autopsy?' I asked.

'Yes,' Dr. Anderson said.

'Why?'

She stopped what she was doing and looked at me through her face shield. I could see intimidation in her eyes. 'The fracture was two weeks ago. The medical examiner in Albemarle was concerned her death could be due to complications of that accident.'

'What are the circumstances of her death?'

'She presented with pleural effusion and shortness of breath.'

'I don't see any direct relationship between that and a hip fracture,' I said.

Dr. Anderson rested her gloved hands on the edge of the steel table.

'An act of God can take you at any time,' I said. 'You can release her. She's not a medical examiner's case.'

'Dr. Scarpetta,' Fielding spoke above the whining of the Stryker saw. 'Did you know that the Transplant Council meeting is Thursday?'

'I've got jury duty.' I turned to Dr. Anderson. 'Do you have court on Thursday?'

'Well, it's been continued. They keep sending me subpoenas even though they've stipulated my testimony.'

'Ask Rose to take care of it. If you're free and we don't have a full house on Thursday, you can go with Fielding to the council meeting.'

I checked carts and cupboards, wondering if any other boxes of gloves were gone. But it seemed Gault had taken only those that were in the van. I wondered what else he might find in my office, and my thoughts darkened.

I went directly to my office without speaking to anyone I passed and opened a cabinet door beneath my microscope. In back I had tucked a very fine set of dissecting knives Lucy had given to me for Christmas. German made, they were stainless steel with smooth light handles. They were expensive and incredibly sharp. I moved aside cardboard files of slides, journals, microscope lightbulbs and batteries and reams of printer paper. The knives were gone.

Rose was on the phone in her office adjoining mine, and I walked in and stood by her desk.

'But you've already stipulated her testimony,' she was saying. 'If you've stipulated her testimony, then you obviously don't need to subpoena her to appear so she can give you her testimony . . .'

She looked at me and rolled her eyes. Rose was getting on in years, but she was ever vigilant and forceful. Snow or shine she was always here, the headmistress of *Les Misérables*.

'Yes, yes. Now we're getting somewhere.' She scribbled something on a message pad. 'I can promise you Dr. Anderson will be very grateful. Of course. Good day.'

My secretary hung up and looked at me. 'You're gone entirely too much.'

'Tell me about it,' I said.

'You'd better watch out. One of these days you may find me with someone else.'

I was too worn out to joke. 'I wouldn't blame you,' I said.

She regarded me like a shrewd mother who knew I had been drinking or making out or sneaking cigarettes. 'What is it, Dr. Scarpetta?' she said.

'Have you seen my dissecting knives?'

She did not know what I was talking about.

'The ones Lucy gave me. A set of three in a hard plastic box. Three different sizes.'

Recognition registered on her face. 'Oh yes. I remember now. I thought you kept them in your cabinet.'

'They're not there.'

'Shoot. Not the cleaning crew, I hope. When was the last time you saw them?'

'Probably right after Lucy gave them to me, which was actually before Christmas because she didn't want to take them down to Miami. I showed the set to you, remember? And then I put them in my cabinet because I didn't want to keep them downstairs.'

Rose was grim. 'I know what you must be thinking. Uh.' She shivered. 'What a gruesome thought.'

I pulled up a chair and sat. 'The thought of him doing something like that with my—'

'You can't think about it,' she interrupted me. 'You have no control over what he does.'

I stared off.

'I'm worried about Jennifer,' my secretary then said.

Jennifer was one of the clerks in the front office. Her major responsibility was sorting photographs, answering the phones, and entering cases into our database.

'She's traumatized.'

'By what's just happened,' I assumed.

Rose nodded. 'She's been in the bathroom crying quite a lot today. Needless to say, what happened is awful and there are many tales circulating. But she's so much more upset than anyone else. I've tried to talk to her. I'm afraid she's going to quit.' She pointed the mouse at the WordPerfect icon and clicked a button. 'I'll print out the autopsy protocols for your review.'

'You've already typed both of them?'

'I came in early this morning. I've got four-wheel drive.'

'I'll talk to Jennifer,' I said.

I walked down the corridor and glanced into the computer room. Lucy was mesmerized by the monitor, and I did not bother her. Up front, Tamara was answering one line while two others rang and someone else was unhappily flashing on hold. Cleta made photocopies while Jo entered death certificates at a workstation.

I walked back down the hall and pushed open the door to the ladies' room. Jennifer was at one of the sinks, splashing cold water on her face.

'Oh!' she exclaimed when she saw me in the mirror. 'Hello, Dr. Scarpetta,' she said, unnerved and embarrassed.

She was a homely young woman who would forever struggle with calories and the clothes that might hide them. Her eyes were puffy and she had protruding teeth and flyaway hair. She wore too much makeup even at times like this when her appearance should not matter.

'Please sit down,' I said kindly, motioning to a red plastic chair near lockers.

'I'm sorry,' she said. 'I know I've not done right today.'

I pulled up another chair and sat so I would not tower over her.

'You're upset,' I said.

She bit her bottom lip to stop it from quivering as her eyes filled with tears.

'What can I do to help you?' I asked.

She shook her head and began to sob.

'I can't stop,' she said. 'I can't stop crying. And if someone even scrapes their chair across the floor I jump.' She wiped tears with a paper towel, hands shaking. 'I feel like I'm going crazy.'

'When did this all start?'

She blew her nose. 'Yesterday. After the sheriff and the policeman were found. I heard about the one downstairs. They said even his boots was on fire.'

'Jennifer, do you remember the pamphlets I passed out about Post Traumatic Stress Syndrome?'

'Yes, ma'am.'

'It's something everybody's got to worry about in a place like this. Every single one of us. I have to worry about it, too.'

'You do?' Her mouth fell open.

'Certainly. I have to worry about it more than anyone.'

'I just thought you was used to it.'

'God forbid that any of us should get used to it.'

'I mean' – she lowered her voice as if we were talking about sex – 'do you get like I am right now?' She quickly added, 'I mean, I'm sure you don't.'

'I'm sure I do,' I said. 'I get very upset sometimes.'

Her eyes brimmed with tears again and she took a deep breath. 'That makes me feel a whole lot better. You know, when I was little my daddy always was telling me how stupid and fat I was. I didn't figure someone like you would ever feel like I do.'

'No one should have ever said such a thing to you,' I replied with feeling. 'You are a lovely person, Jennifer, and we are very fortunate to have you here.'

'Thank you,' she said quietly, eyes cast down.

I got up. 'I think you should go home for the rest of the day and have a nice long weekend. How about it?'

She continued looking down at the floor. 'I think I saw him,' she said, biting her bottom lip.

'Who did you see?'

'I saw that man.' She glanced at my eyes. 'When I saw the pictures on TV, I couldn't believe it. I keep thinking if only I had told somebody.'

'Where is it you think you saw him?'

'Rumors.'

'The bar?' I asked.

She nodded.

'When was this?'

'Tuesday.'

I looked closely at her. 'This past Tuesday? The day after Christmas?'

That night Gault had been in New York. I had seen him in the subway tunnel, or at least I thought I had.

'Yes, ma'am,' Jennifer said. 'I guess it was about ten. I was dancing with Tommy.'

I did not know who Tommy was.

'I seen him hanging back from everyone. I couldn't help but notice because of his white hair. I'm not used to seeing anybody his age with hair that white. He was in a real cool black suit with a black T-shirt under it. I remember that. I figured he was from out of town. Maybe from a big place like Los Angeles or something.'

'Did he dance with anyone?'

'Yes, ma'am, he danced with a girl or two. You know, he'd buy them a drink. Then next thing I know he was gone.'

'Did he leave alone?'

'It looked to me like one girl went with him.'

'Do you know who?' I asked with dread. I hoped the woman, whoever she was, had lived.

'It wasn't anybody I knew,' Jennifer said. 'I just remember he was dancing with this one girl. He must've danced with her three times and then they walked off the floor together, holding hands.'

'Describe her,' I said.

'She was black. She was real pretty in this little red dress. It was low cut and kind of short. I remember she had bright red lipstick and all these little braids with little lights winking in them.' She paused.

'And you're certain they left the club together?' I asked.

'As far as I could tell. I never saw either one of them again that night, and me and Tommy stayed till two.'

I said to her, 'I want you to call Captain Marino and tell him what you just told me.'

Jennifer got out of the chair and felt important. 'I'll get started right this minute.'

I returned to my office as Rose was walking through the door.

'You need to call Dr. Gruber,' she said.

I dialed the number for the Quartermaster Museum, and he had stepped out. He called me back two hours later.

'Is the snow bad in Petersburg?' I asked him.

'Oh, it's just wet and messy.'

'How are things?'

'I've got something for you,' Dr. Gruber said. 'I feel real bad about it.'

I waited. When he offered nothing more, I said, 'What do you feel bad about, exactly?'

'I went into the computer and ran the name you wanted. I shouldn't have.' He got quiet again.

'Dr. Gruber, I'm dealing with a serial killer.'

'He was never in the army.'

'You mean his father wasn't,' I said, disappointed.

'Neither of them was,' Dr. Gruber said. 'Not Temple or Peyton Gault.'

'Oh,' I said. 'So the boots probably came from a surplus store.'

'Might have, but he may have an uncle.'

'Who has an uncle?'

'Temple Gault. That's what I'm wondering. There's a Gault in the computer, only his name is Luther. Luther Gault. He served in the Quartermaster Corps during World War Two.' He paused. 'In fact, he was right here at Ft. Lee a lot of the time.'

I had never heard of Luther Gault.

'Is he still alive?' I asked.

'He died in Seattle about five years ago.'

'What makes you suspicious this man might be Temple Gault's uncle?' I asked. 'Seattle's on the other side of the country from Georgia, which is where the Gaults are from.'

'The only real connection I can make is the last name and Ft. Lee.'

I then asked, 'Do you think it's possible the jungle boots once belonged to him?'

'Well, they're World War Two, and were tested here at Ft. Lee, which is where Luther Gault was stationed for most of his career. What would typically happen is soldiers, even some officers, would be asked to try out boots and other gear before any of it was sent to the boys in the trenches.'

'What did Luther Gault do after the army?'

'I don't have any information on him after the army except that he died at the age of seventy-eight.' He paused. 'But it might interest you to know he was a career man. He retired with the rank of major general.'

'And you had never heard of him before this?'

'I didn't say I've never heard of him.' He paused. 'I'm sure the army has quite a file on him if you could get your hands on it.'

'Would it be possible for me to get a photograph?'

'I have one on the computer – just your run-of-the-mill file photo.'

'Can you fax it?'

He hesitated again. 'Sure.'

I hung up as Rose walked in with yesterday's autopsy protocols. I reviewed them and made corrections while I waited for the fax machine to ring. Momentarily, it did, and the black-and-white image of Luther Gault materialized in my office. He stood proudly in dark mess jacket and pants with gold piping and buttons, and satin lapels. The resemblance was there. Temple Gault had his eyes.

I called Wesley.

'Temple Gault may have had an uncle in Seattle,' I said. 'He was a major general in the army.'

'How did you find that out?' he asked.

I did not like his coolness. 'It doesn't matter. What does is that I think we need to find out all we can about it.'

Wesley maintained his reserve. 'How is it germane?'

I lost my temper. 'How is anything germane when you're trying to stop somebody like this? When you've got nothing, you look at everything.'

'Sure, sure,' he said. 'It's no problem, but we can't schedule it just now. You too.' He hung up.

I sat there stunned, my heart gripped by pain. Someone must have been in his office. Wesley had never hung up on me before. My paranoia got more inflamed as I went to find Lucy.

'Hi,' she said before I spoke from the doorway.

She could see my reflection in the monitor.

'We've got to go,' I said.

'Why? Is it snowing again?'

'No. The sun's out.'

'I'm almost finished here,' she said, typing as she talked.

'I need to get you and Janet back to Quantico.'

'You need to call Grans,' she said. 'She's feeling neglected.'

'She is neglected and I feel guilty,' I said.

Lucy turned around and looked at me as my pager went off.

'Where is Janet?' I asked.

'I think she went downstairs.'

I pressed the display button and recognized Marino's home number. 'Well, you round her up and I'll meet you downstairs in a minute.'

I returned to my office and this time shut the doors. When I called Marino, he sounded as if he were on amphetamines.

'They're gone,' he said.

'Who is?'

'We found out where they was staying. The Hacienda Motel on US 1, that roach trap not too far from where you buy all your guns and ammo. That's where that bitch took her girlfriend.'

'What girlfriend?' I still did not know what he was talking about. Then I remembered Jennifer. 'Oh. The woman Carrie picked up at Rumors.'

'Yo.' He was so excited he sounded as if he had been on a Mayday. 'Her name's Apollonia and—'

'She's alive?' I interrupted.

'Oh yeah. Carrie took her back to the motel and they partied.'

'Who drove?'

'Apollonia did.'

'Did you find my van in the motel parking lot?'

'Not when we hit the joint a little while ago. And the rooms were cleared out. It's like they was never there.'

'Then Carrie wasn't in New York this past Tuesday,' I said.

'Nope. She was here partying while Gault was up there whacking Jimmy Davila. Then I'm thinking she got a place ready for him and probably helped intercept him wherever he was.'

'I doubt he flew from New York to Richmond,' I said. 'That would have been too risky.'

'I personally think he flew to DC on Wednesday . . .'

'Marino,' I said. 'I flew to DC on Wednesday.'

'I know you did. Maybe you and him was on the same plane.'

'I didn't see him.'

'You don't know that you didn't. But the point is, if you were on the same plane, you can bet he saw you.'

I remembered leaving the terminal and getting into that old, beat-up taxi with the windows and locks that didn't work. I wondered if Gault had been watching.

'Does Carrie have a car?' I asked.

'She's got a Saab convertible registered to her. But she sure as hell isn't driving it these days.'

'I'm not certain why she picked up this Apollonia woman,' I said. 'And how did you find her?'

'Easy. She works at Rumors. I'm not sure what all she sells, but it isn't just cigarettes.'

'Damn,' I muttered.

'I'm assuming the connection is coke,' Marino said. 'And it might interest you to know that Apollonia was acquainted with Sheriff Brown. In fact, they dated, you might say.'

'Do you think she could have had anything to do with his murder?' I asked.

'Yeah, I do. She probably helped lead Gault and Carrie to

him. I'm beginning to think the sheriff was pretty much a last-minute thing. I think Carrie asked Apollonia where she could score some coke, and Brown's name came up. Then Carrie tells Gault and he orchestrates another one of his impetuous nightmares.'

'That could very well be,' I said. 'Did Apollonia know Carrie was a woman?'

'Yeah. It didn't matter.'

'Damn,' I said again. 'We were so close.'

'I know. I just can't believe they slipped through the net like that. We got everything but the National Guard looking for them. We got choppers out, the whole nine yards. But in my gut I feel they've left the area.'

'I just called Benton and he hung up on me,' I said.

'What? You guys have a fight?'

'Marino, something is very wrong. I had a sense that someone was in his office and he didn't want this person to know he was talking to me.'

'Maybe it was his wife.'

'I'm heading up there now with Lucy and Janet.'

'You staying the night?'

'That all depends.'

'Well, I wish you wouldn't be driving around. And if anybody tries to pull you over for any reason, don't you stop. Not for lights or sirens or nothing. Don't stop for anything but a marked patrol car.' He gave me one of his lectures. 'And keep your Remington between the front seats.'

'Gault's not going to stop killing,' I said.

Marino got quiet on the line.

'When he was in my office he stole my set of dissecting knives.'

'You sure someone from the cleaning crew didn't do it? Those knives would be good for fileting fish.'

'I know Gault did it,' I said.

16

We returned to Quantico shortly after three, and when I tried to reach Wesley, he was not in. I left a message for him to find me at ERF, where I planned to spend the next few hours with my niece.

No engineers or scientists were on her floor because it was a holiday weekend, and we were able to work alone and in quiet.

'I could definitely get global mail out,' Lucy said, sitting at her desk. She glanced at her watch. 'Look, why not just throw something out there and see who bites?'

'Let me try the chief from Seattle again.'

I had his number on a slip of paper and called it. I was told he had left for the day.

'It's very important that I reach him,' I explained to the answering service. 'Perhaps he can be reached at home?'

'I'm not at liberty to give that out. But if you'll give me your phone number, when he calls in for his messages . . .'

'I can't do that,' I said as my frustration grew. 'I'm not at a number he can call.' I told her who I was, adding, 'What I'm going to do is give you my pager number. Please have him call me and then I'll call him.'

That didn't work. An hour later my pager remained silent.

'She probably didn't get it straight about putting pound signs after everything,' Lucy said as she cruised around inside CAIN.

'Any strange messages anywhere?' I asked.

'No. It's a Friday afternoon and a lot of people are on holiday. I think we should send something out over Prodigy and see what comes back.'

I sat next to her.

'What's the name of the group?'

'American Academy of Gold Foil Operators.'

'And their highest concentration is Washington State?'

'Yes. But it can't hurt to include the entire West Coast.'

'Well, this will include the entire United States,' Lucy said as she typed *Prodigy* and entered her service ID and password. 'I think the best way to do this is through the mail.' She pulled up a Jump Window. 'What do you want me to say?' She looked over at me.

'How about this? *To all American Academy of Gold Foil Operators. Forensic pathologist desperately needs your help ASAP*. And then give them the information to contact us.'

'All right. I'll give them a mailbox here and carbon copy it to your mailbox in Richmond.' She resumed typing. 'The replies may come in for a while. You may find you get a lot of dentists for pen pals.'

She tapped a key as if it were a coda and pushed back her chair. 'There. It's gone,' she said. 'Even as we speak, every Prodigy subscriber should have a *New Mail* message. Let's just hope someone out there is playing with their computer and can help.'

Even as she spoke, her screen suddenly went black, and bright green letters started flowing across it. A printer turned on.

'That was quick,' I started to stay.

But Lucy was out of her chair. She ran to the room where CAIN lived and scanned her fingerprint to get in. Glass doors unlocked with a firm click and I followed her inside. The same writing was flowing across the system monitor, and Lucy snatched a small beige remote control off the desk and pressed a button. She glanced at her Breitling and activated the stopwatch.

'Come on, come on, come on!' she said.

She sat before CAIN, staring into the screen as the message flowed. It was one brief paragraph repeated numerous times. It said:

- - -MESSAGE PQ43 76301 001732 BEGINS- - -
TO: – All COPS
FROM: – CAIN
IF CAIN KILLED HIS BROTHER, WHAT DO YOU THINK HE'D DO TO YOU?
IF YOUR PAGER GOES OFF IN THE MORGUE, IT'S JESUS CALLING.
- - -MESSAGE PQ43 76301 001732 ENDS- - -

I looked at the shelves of modems filling one wall, at lights flashing. Though I was not a computer expert, I saw no correlation between their activity and what was occurring on screen. I looked around some more and noticed a telephone jack below the desk. A cord that was plugged into it disappeared beneath the raised floor, and I found that odd.

Why would a device plugged into a telephone jack be stored beneath a floor? Telephones were on tables and desks. Modems were on shelves. I got down and lifted a panel that covered a third of the floor inside CAIN's room.

'What are you doing?' Lucy exclaimed, unable to take her eyes off the screen.

The modem beneath the floor looked like a small cube puzzle with rapid flashing lights.

'Shit!' Lucy said.

I looked up. She stared at her watch and wrote something

down. The activity on the screen had stopped. The lights on the modem quit flashing.

'Did I do something?' I asked in dismay.

'You bastard!' She pounded her fist on the desk, and the keyboard jumped. 'I almost had you. One more time and I would have had your ass!'

I got up. 'I didn't disconnect anything, I hope?' I said.

'No. Dammit! He logged off. I had him,' she said, still staring at her monitor as if the green words might begin to flow again.

'Gault?'

'CAIN's imposter.' She blew out a big breath of air and looked down at the naked guts of the creation she had named after the world's first murderer. 'You found it,' she blandly said. 'That's pretty good.'

'That's how he's been getting in,' I said.

'Yes. It's so obvious no one noticed.'

'You noticed.'

'Not at first.'

'Carrie put it there before she left last fall,' I said.

Lucy nodded. 'Like everybody else, I was looking for something more technologically recondite. But it was brilliant in its simplicity. She hid her own private modem and the dial-in is the number of a diagnostics line almost never used.'

'How long have you known?'

'As soon as the weird messages started, I knew.'

'So you just had to play the game with him,' I said, upset. 'Do you realize how dangerous this game is?' I asked.

She began typing. 'He tried it four times. God, we were close.'

'For a while you thought Carrie was doing this,' I said.

'She set it up, but I don't think she's the one getting in.'

'Why not?'

'Because I've been following this intruder day and night. This is someone unskilled.' For the first time in months, she spoke her former friend's name. 'I know how Carrie's mind works. And Gault's too narcissistic to let anyone be CAIN except him.'

'I got a note, possibly from Carrie, that was signed CAIN,' I said.

'And I'll bet Gault didn't know she mailed it. And I'll also bet that if he found out, he took that little pleasure away from her.'

I thought of the pink note we suspected Gault had spirited away from Carrie at Sheriff Brown's house. When Gault placed it in the pocket of the bloody pajama top, the act certainly served to reassert his dominance. Gault would use Carrie. In a sense, she always waited in the car except when he needed her help to move a body or perform a degrading act.

'What just happened here?' I said.

Lucy did not look at me when she answered, 'I found the virus and have planted my own. Every time he tries to send a message to any terminal connected to CAIN, I have the message replicate itself on his screen – like it's bouncing back in his face instead of going out anywhere. And he gets a prompt that says *Please Try Again*. So he tries again. The first time this happened to him, the system icon gave him a thumbs-up after two tries, so he thought the message was sent.

'But when he tried the next time, the same thing happened, but I made him try one additional time. The point is to keep him on the line long enough for us to trace the call.'

'Us?'

Lucy picked up the small beige remote control I had seen her grab earlier. 'My panic button,' she said. 'It goes via radio signal straight to HRT.'

'I assume Wesley has known about this hidden modem since you discovered it.'

'Right.'

'Explain something to me,' I said.

'Sure.' She gave me her eyes.

'Even if Gault or Carrie had this secret modem and its secret number, what about your password? How could either of them log on as a superuser? And aren't there UNIX commands you could type that would tell you if another user or device was logged on?'

'Carrie programmed the virus to capture my username and password whenever I changed them. The encrypted forms were reversed and sent to Gault via E-mail. Then he could log on as me, and the virus wouldn't let him log on unless I was logged on, too.'

'So he hides behind you.'

'Like a shadow. He's used my device name. My same username and password. I figured out what was going on when I did a WHO command one day and my username was there twice.'

'If CAIN calls users back to verify their legitimacy, why hasn't Gault's telephone number shown up on ERF's monthly bill?'

'That's part of the virus. It instructs the system on callbacks to bill the call to an AT&T credit card. So the calls never showed up on the Bureau's bills. They show up on the bills of Gault's father.'

'Amazing,' I said.

'Apparently, Gault has his father's phone card number and PIN.'

'Does he know his son has been using it?'

A telephone rang. She picked it up.

'Yes, sir,' she said. 'I know. We were close. Certainly, I will bring you the printouts immediately.' She hung up.

'I don't think anyone's told him,' Lucy said.

'No one here has told Peyton Gault.'

'Right. That was Mr. Wesley.'

'I must talk to him,' I said. 'Do you trust me to take him the printouts?'

Lucy was staring at the monitor again. The screen saver

had come back on, and brilliant triangles were slowly slipping through and around each other like geometry making love.

'You can take it to him,' she said, and she typed *Prodigy*. 'Before you go . . . Wow, you've got new mail waiting.'

'How much?' I moved closer to her.

'Oops. Just one so far.' She opened it.

It read: *What is gold foil?*

Lucy said, 'We're probably going to get a lot of that.'

Sally was working the front desk again when I walked into the Academy lobby, and she let me through without the bother of registration and a visitors' pass. I walked with purpose down the long tan corridor, around the post office and through the gun cleaning room. I will always love the smell of Hoppes Number 9.

A lone man in fatigues was blasting compressed air into the barrel of a rifle. Rows of long black countertops were bare and perfectly clean, and I thought of years of classes, of the men and women I had seen, and of the times I had stood at a counter cleaning my own handgun. I had watched new agents come and go. I had watched them run, fight, shoot and sweat. I had taught them and cared.

I pressed the elevator button, boarded and went down to the lower level. Several profilers were in their offices, and they nodded at me as I walked by. Wesley's secretary was on vacation, and I passed her desk and knocked on the shut door. I heard Wesley's voice. A chair moved and he walked to the door and pulled it open.

'Hello,' he said, surprised.

'These are the printouts you wanted from Lucy.' I handed them over.

'Thank you. Please come in.' He slipped on reading glasses, reviewing the message Gault had sent.

His jacket was off, a white shirt wrinkled around woven

leather suspenders. Wesley had been perspiring and he needed to shave.

'Have you lost more weight?' I asked.

'I never weigh myself.' He glanced at me over the top of his glasses as he seated himself behind his desk.

'You don't look healthy.'

'He's decompensating more,' he said. 'You can see that from this message. He's getting more reckless, more brazen. I would predict that by the end of the weekend, we will nail his location.'

'Then what?' I was not convinced.

'We deploy HRT.'

'I see,' I said dryly. 'They will rappel from helicopters and blow up the building.'

Wesley glanced at me again. He placed the paperwork on the desk. 'You're angry,' he said.

'No, Benton. I'm angry with you, versus being angry in general.'

'Why?'

'I asked you not to involve Lucy.'

'We have no choice,' he said.

'There are always choices. I don't care what anybody says.'

'In terms of locating Gault, she's really our only hope right now.' He paused, looking directly at me. 'She has a mind of her own.'

'Yes, she does. That's my point. Lucy doesn't have an off button. She doesn't always understand limits.'

'We won't let her do anything that might place her at risk,' he said.

'She's already been placed at risk.'

'You've got to let her grow up, Kay.'

I stared at him.

'She's going to graduate from the university this spring. She's a grown woman.'

'I don't want her coming back here,' I said.

He smiled a little, but his eyes were exhausted and sad. 'I hope she'll be back here. We need agents like her and Janet. We need all we can get.'

'She keeps many secrets from me. It seems the two of you conspire against me and I'm left in the dark. It's bad enough that . . .' I caught myself.

Wesley looked into my eyes. 'Kay, this has nothing to do with my relationship with you.'

'I would certainly hope not.'

'You want to know everything Lucy is doing,' he said.

'Of course.'

'Do you tell her everything you're doing when you're working a case?'

'Absolutely not.'

'I see.'

'Why did you hang up on me?'

'You got me at a bad time,' he answered.

'You've never hung up on me before, no matter how bad the time.'

He took his glasses off and carefully folded them. He reached for his coffee mug, looked inside and saw it was empty. He held it in both hands.

'I had someone in my office, and I didn't want this individual to know you were on the line,' he said.

'Who was it?' I said.

'Someone from the Pentagon. I won't tell you his name.'

'The Pentagon?' I said, mystified.

He was quiet.

'Why would you be concerned that someone from the Pentagon might know I was calling you?' I then asked.

'It seems you've created a problem,' Wesley simply said, setting the coffee mug down. 'I wish you hadn't started poking around Ft. Lee.'

I was astonished.

'Your friend Dr. Gruber may be fired. I would advise you

to refrain from contacting him further.'

'This is about Luther Gault?' I asked.

'Yes, General Gault.'

'They can't do anything to Dr. Gruber,' I protested.

'I'm afraid they can,' Wesley said. 'Dr. Gruber conducted an unauthorized search in a military database. He got you classified information.'

'Classified?' I said. 'That's absurd. It's one page of routine information that you can pay twenty dollars to see while you're visiting the Quartermaster Museum. It's not like I asked for a damn Pentagon file.'

'You can't pay the twenty dollars unless you are the individual or have power of attorney to access that individual's file.'

'Benton, we're talking about a serial killer. Has everybody lost their minds? Who the hell cares about a generic computer file?'

'The army does.'

'Are we dealing with national security?'

Wesley did not answer me.

When he offered nothing more, I said, 'Fine. You guys can have your little secret. I'm sick and tired of your little secrets. My only agenda is to prevent more deaths. I'm no longer certain what your agenda is.' My stare was unforgiving and hurt.

'Please,' Wesley snapped. 'You know, some days I wish I smoked like Marino does.' He blew out in exasperation. 'General Gault is not important in this investigation. He does not need to be dragged into it.'

'I think anything we know about Temple Gault's family could be important. And I can't believe you don't feel that way. Background information is vital to profiling and predicting behavior.'

'I'm telling you, General Gault is off limits.'

'Why?'

'Respect.'

'My God, Benton.' I leaned forward in my chair. 'Gault may

have killed two people with a pair of his uncle's damn jungle boots. And just how is the army going to like it when that hits *Time* magazine and *Newsweek*?'

'Don't threaten.'

'I most certainly will. I will do more than threaten if people don't do the right thing. Tell me about the general. I already know his nephew inherited his eyes. And the general was a bit of a peacock, since it seems he preferred being photographed in a splendid mess uniform like Eisenhower would have worn.'

'He may have had an ego but was a magnificent man, by all accounts,' Wesley said.

'Was he Gault's uncle, then? Are you admitting it?'

Wesley hesitated. 'Luther Gault is Temple Gault's uncle.'

'Tell me more.'

'He was born in Albany and graduated from the Citadel in 1942. Two years later, when he was a captain, his division moved to France, where he became a hero in the Battle of the Bulge. He won the Medal of Honor and was promoted again. After the war, he was sent to Ft. Lee as officer in charge of the uniform research division of the Quartermaster Corps.'

'Then the boots were his,' I said.

'They certainly could have been.'

'Was he a big man?'

'I am told that he and his nephew would have been the same size when General Gault was younger.'

I thought of the photograph of the general in the dress mess jacket. He was slender and not particularly tall. His face was strong, eyes unwavering, but he did not look unkind.

'Luther Gault also served in Korea,' Wesley went on. 'For a while he was assigned to the Pentagon as the assistant chief of staff, then it was back to Ft. Lee as the deputy commander. He finished his career in MAC-V.'

'I don't know what that is,' I said.

'Military Assistance Command – Vietnam.'

'After which he retired to Seattle?' I said.

'He and his wife moved there.'

'Children?'

'Two boys.'

'What about the general's interaction with his brother?'

'I don't know. The general is deceased and his brother will not talk to us.'

'So we don't know how Gault might have wound up with his uncle's boots.'

'Kay, there is a code with Medal of Honor winners. They are in their own class. The army gives them a special status and they are stringently protected.'

'That's what all this secrecy is about?' I said.

'The army isn't keen on having the world know that their Medal of Honor-winning two-star general is the uncle of one of the most notorious psychopaths our country has seen. The Pentagon is not exactly keen on having it known that this killer – as you have already pointed out – may have kicked several people to death with General Gault's boots.'

I got up from my chair. 'I'm tired of boys and their codes of honor. I'm tired of male bonding and secrecy. We are not kids playing cowboys and Indians. We're not neighborhood children playing *war*.' I was drained. 'I thought you were more highly evolved than that.'

He stood up, too, as my pager went off. 'You're taking this the wrong way,' he said.

I looked at the display. The area code was Seattle, and without asking Wesley's permission I used his phone.

'Hello,' said a voice I did not know.

'This number just paged me.' I was confused.

'I didn't page anybody. Where are you calling from?'

'Virginia.' I was about to hang up.

'I just called Virginia. Wait a minute. Are you calling about Prodigy?'

'Oh. Perhaps you talked to Lucy?'

'LUCYTALK?'

'Yes.'

'We just this minute sent mail to each other. I'm responding to the gold foil query. I'm a dentist in Seattle and a member of the Academy of Gold Foil Operators. Are you the forensic pathologist?'

'Yes,' I said. 'Thank you so much for responding. I'm trying to identify a dead young woman with extensive gold foil restorations.'

'Please describe them.'

I told him about Jane's dental work and the damage to her teeth. 'It's possible she was a musician,' I added. 'She may have played the saxophone.'

'There was a lady from out here who sounds a lot like that.'

'She was in Seattle?'

'Right. Everyone in our academy knew about her because she had such an incredible mouth. Her gold foil restorations and dental anomalies were used in slide presentations at a number of our meetings.'

'Do you recall her name?'

'Sorry. She wasn't my patient. But it seems I remember hearing she was a professional musician until she was in some terrible accident. That was when her dental problems began.'

'The lady I'm talking about has a lot of enamel loss,' I said. 'Probably from overbrushing.'

'Oh absolutely. The lady out here did, too.'

'It doesn't sound to me as if the lady out there was a street person,' I said.

'Couldn't be. Someone paid for that mouth.'

'My lady was a street person when she died in New York,' I said.

'Geez, that makes me sad. I guess whoever she was, she really couldn't care for herself.'

'What is your name?' I asked.

'I'm Jay Bennett.'

'Dr. Bennett? Do you remember anything else that might have been said during one of these slide presentations?'

A long silence followed. 'Okay, yes. This is very vague.' He hesitated again. 'Oh, I know,' he said. 'The lady out here was related to someone important. In fact, that might be who she lived with out here before she disappeared.'

I gave him further information so he could call me again. I hung up the phone and met Wesley's stare.

'I think Jane is Gault's sister,' I said.

'What?' He was genuinely shocked.

'I think Temple Gault murdered his sister,' I repeated. 'Please tell me you didn't already know that.'

He got upset.

'I've got to verify her identity,' I said, and I had no emotion left in me right now.

'Won't her dental records do that?'

'If we find them. If she still has X rays left. If the army stays out of my way.'

'The army doesn't know about her.' He paused, and for an instant his eyes were bright with tears. He looked away from me. 'He just told us what he did when he sent the message from CAIN today.'

'Yes,' I said. 'He said CAIN killed his brother. The description of Gault with her in New York sounded more like two men than a woman and a man.' I paused. 'Are there other siblings?'

'Just a sister. We've known she lived on the West Coast but have never been able to locate her because apparently she doesn't drive. DMV has no record of a valid license. Truth is, we've never been certain she is alive.'

I said to him, 'She's not.'

He flinched and looked away.

'She hadn't lived anywhere – at least not in recent years,' I said, thinking of her pitiful belongings and malnourished body.

'She'd been on the street for a while. In fact, I'd say she survived out there all right until her brother came to town.'

His voice caught and he looked wrecked as he said, 'How could anyone do something like that?'

I put my arms around him. I did not care who walked in. I hugged him as a friend.

'Benton,' I said. 'Go home.'

17

I spent the weekend and the New Year at Quantico, and though there was considerable mail on Prodigy, verifying Jane's identity was not promising.

Her dentist had retired last year and her Panorex X-rays had been reclaimed for silver. The missing films, of course, were the biggest disappointment, for they might have shown old fractures, sinus configurations, bony anomalies, that could have effected a positive identification. As for her charts, when I touched upon that subject, her dentist, who was retired and now living in Los Angeles, got evasive.

'You do have them, don't you?' I asked him point-blank on Tuesday afternoon.

'I've got a million boxes in my garage.'

'I doubt you have a million.'

'I have a lot.'

'Please. We're talking about a woman we're unable to identify. All human beings have a right to be buried with their name.'

'I'm going to look, okay?'

Minutes later, I said to Marino on the phone, 'We're going to have to try for DNA or a visual ID.'

'Yo,' he said drolly. 'And just what are you going to do? Show Gault a photograph and ask if the woman he did this to looks like his sister?'

'I think her dentist took advantage of her. I've seen it before.'

'What are you talking about?'

'Occasionally, someone takes advantage. They chart work they didn't do so they can collect from Medicare or the insurance company.'

'But she had a hell of a lot of work done.'

'He could have charted a hell of a lot more. Trust me. Twice as many gold foil restorations, for example. That would have meant thousands of dollars. He says he did them when he didn't. She's mentally impaired, living with an elderly uncle. What do they know?'

'I hate assholes.'

'If I could get hold of his charts, I would report him. But he's not going to give them up. In fact, they probably no longer exist.'

'You got jury duty at eight in the morning,' Marino said. 'Rose called to let me know.'

'I guess that means I leave here very early tomorrow.'

'Go straight to your house and I'll pick you up.'

'I'll just go straight to the courthouse.'

'No you won't. You ain't driving downtown by yourself right now.'

'We know Gault's not in Richmond,' I said. 'He's back wherever he usually hides out, an apartment or room where he has a computer.'

'Chief Tucker hasn't rescinded his order for security for you.'

'He can't order anything for me. Not even lunch.'

'Oh yeah he can. All he does is assign certain cops to you. You either accept the situation or try to outrun them. If he wants to order your damn lunch, you'll get that, too.'

The next morning, I called the New York Medical Examiner's

Office and left a message for Dr. Horowitz that suggested he begin DNA analysis on Jane's blood. Then Marino picked me up at my house while neighbors looked out windows and opened handsome front doors to collect their newspapers. Three cruisers were parked in front, Marino's unmarked Ford in the brick drive. Windsor Farms woke up, went to work and watched me squired away by cops. Perfect lawns were white with frost and the sky was almost blue.

When I arrived at the John Marshall Courthouse, it was as I had done so many times in the past. But the deputy at the scanner did not understand why I was here.

'Good morning, Dr. Scarpetta,' he said with a broad smile. 'How about that snow? Don't it just make you feel like you're living in the middle of a Hallmark card? And Captain, a nice day to you, sir,' he said to Marino.

I set off the X-ray machine. A female deputy appeared to search me while the deputy who enjoyed snow went through my bag. Marino and I walked downstairs to an orange-carpeted room filled with rows of sparsely populated orange chairs. We sat in the back, where we listened to people dozing, crackling paper, coughing and blowing their noses. A man in a leather jacket with shirt-tail hanging out prowled for magazines while a man in cashmere read a novel. Next door a vacuum cleaner roared. It butted into the orange room's door and quit.

Including Marino, I had three uniformed officers around me in this deadly dull room. Then at eight-fifty A.M. the jury officer walked in late and went to a podium to orient us.

'I have two changes,' she said, looking directly at me. 'The sheriff on the videotape you're about to see is no longer the sheriff.'

Marino whispered in my ear, 'That's because he's no longer alive.'

'And,' the jury officer went on, 'the tape will tell you the fee for jury duty is thirty dollars, but it's still twenty dollars.'

'Nuts.' Marino was in my ear again. 'Do you need a loan?'

We watched the video and I learned much about my important civic duty and its privileges. I watched Sheriff Brown on tape as he thanked me again for performing this important service. He told me I had been called up to decide the fate of another person and then showed the computer he had used to select me.

'Names called are then drawn from a jury ballot box,' he recited with a smile. 'Our system of justice depends on our careful consideration of the evidence. Our system depends on us.'

He gave a phone number I could call and reminded all of us that coffee was twenty-five cents a cup and no change was available.

After the video, the jury officer, a handsome black woman, came over to me.

'Are you police?' she whispered.

'No,' I said, explaining who I was as she looked at Marino and the other two officers.

'We need to excuse you now,' she whispered. 'You shouldn't be here. You should have called and told us. I don't know why you're here at all.'

The other draftees were staring. They had been staring since we walked in, and the reason crystallized. They were ignorant of the judicial system, and I was surrounded by police. Now the jury officer was over here, too. I was the defendant. They probably did not know that defendants don't read magazines in the same room with the jury pool.

By lunchtime I was gone and wondering if I would ever be allowed to serve on a jury even once in my life. Marino let me out at the front door of my building and I went into my office. I called New York again and Dr. Horowitz got on the phone.

'She was buried yesterday,' he said of Jane.

I felt a great sadness. 'I thought you usually wait a little longer than that,' I said.

'Ten days. It's been about that, Kay. You know the problem we have with storage space.'

'We can identify her with DNA,' I said.

'Why not dental records?'

I explained the problem.

'That's a real shame.' Dr. Horowitz paused and was reluctant when he spoke next. 'I'm very sorry to tell you that we've had a terrible snafu here.' He paused again. 'Frankly, I wish we hadn't buried her. But we have.'

'What happened?'

'No one seems to know. We saved a blood sample on filter paper for DNA purposes, just like we typically do. And of course we kept a stock jar with sections of all major organs, et cetera. The blood sample seems to have been misplaced, and it appears the stock jar was accidentally thrown out.'

'That can't have happened,' I said.

Dr. Horowitz was quiet.

'What about tissue in paraffin blocks for histology?' I then asked, for fixed tissue could also be tested for DNA, if all else failed.

'We don't take tissue for micros when the cause of death is clear,' he said.

I did not know what to say. Either Dr. Horowitz ran a frighteningly inept office, or these mistakes were not mistakes. I had always believed the chief was an impeccably scrupulous man. Maybe I had been wrong. I knew how it was in New York City. The politicians could not stay out of the morgue.

'She needs to be brought back up,' I said to him. 'I see no other way. Was she embalmed?'

'We rarely embalm bodies destined for Hart Island,' he said of the island in the East River where Potter's Field was located. 'Her identification number needs to be located and then she'll be dug up and brought back by ferry. We can do that. That's all we can do, really. It might take a few days.'

'Dr. Horowitz?' I carefully said. 'What is going on here?'

His voice was steady but disappointed when he answered, 'I have no earthly idea.'

I sat at my desk for a while, trying to figure out what to do. The more I thought, the less sense anything made. Why would the army care if Jane was identified? If she was General Gault's niece and the army knew she was dead, one would think they would want her identified and buried in a proper grave.

'Dr. Scarpetta.' Rose was in the doorway adjoining her office to mine. 'It's Brent from the Amex.'

She transferred the call.

'I've got another charge,' Brent said.

'Okay.' I tensed.

'Yesterday. A place called Fino in New York. I checked it out. It's on East Thirty-sixth Street. The amount is $104.13.'

Fino had wonderful northern Italian food. My ancestors were from northern Italy, and Gault had posed as a northern Italian named Benelli. I tried Wesley, but he was not in. Then I tried Lucy, and she was not at ERF, nor was she in her room. Marino was the only person I could tell that Gault was in New York again.

'He's just playing more games,' Marino said in disgust. 'He knows you're monitoring his charges, Doc. He's not doing anything he doesn't want you to know about.'

'I realize that.'

'We're not going to catch him through American Express. You ought to just cancel your card.'

But I couldn't. My card was like the modem Lucy knew was under the floor. Both were tenuous lines leading to Gault. He was playing games, but one day he might overstep himself. He might get too reckless and high on cocaine and make a mistake.

'Doc,' Marino went on, 'you're getting too wound up with this. You need to chill out.'

Gault might want me to find him, I thought. Every time he used my card he was sending a message to me. He was telling me more about himself. I knew what he liked to eat and that he did not drink red wine. I knew about the cigarettes he smoked, the clothes he wore, and I thought of his boots.

'Are you listening to me?' Marino was asking.

We had always assumed that the jungle boots were Gault's.

'The boots belonged to his sister,' I thought out loud.

'What are you talking about?' Marino said impatiently.

'She must have gotten them from her uncle years ago, and then Gault took them from her.'

'When? He didn't do it at Cherry Hill in the snow.'

'I don't know when. It may have been shortly before she died. It could have been inside the Museum of Natural History. They basically wore the same shoe size. They could have traded boots. It could be anything. But I doubt she gave them up willingly. For one thing, the jungle boots would be very good in snow. She would have been better off with them than the ones we found in Benny's hobo camp.'

Marino was silent a moment longer. Then he said, 'Why would he take her boots?'

'That's easy,' I said. 'Because he wanted them.'

That afternoon, I drove to the Richmond airport with a briefcase packed full and an overnight bag. I had not called my travel agent because I did not want anyone to know where I was going. At the USAir desk, I purchased a ticket to Hilton Head, South Carolina.

'I hear it's nice down there,' said the gregarious attendant. 'A lot of people play golf and tennis down there.' She checked my one small bag.

'You need to tag it.' I lowered my voice. 'It has a firearm in it.'

She nodded and handed me a blaze orange tag that proclaimed I was carrying an unloaded firearm.

'I'll let you put it inside,' the woman said to me. 'Does your bag lock?'

I locked the zipper and watched her set the bag on the conveyor belt. She handed me my ticket and I headed upstairs to the gate, which was very crowded with people who did not look happy to be going home or back to work after the holidays.

The flight to Charlotte seemed longer than an hour because I could not use my cellular phone and my pager went off twice. I went through the *Wall Street Journal* and the *Washington Post* while my thoughts slalomed through a treacherous course. I contemplated what I would say to the parents of Temple Gault and the slain woman we called Jane.

I could not even be sure the Gaults would see me because I had not called. Their number and address were unlisted. But I believed it could not be so hard to find the place they had bought near Beaufort. Live Oaks Plantation was one of the oldest in South Carolina, and the local people would know about this couple whose homestead in Albany had recently washed away in a flood.

There was enough time in the Charlotte airport for me to return my calls. Both were from Rose, who wanted me to verify void dates because several subpoenas had just come in.

'And Lucy tried to get you,' she said.

'She has my pager number,' I puzzled.

'I asked her if she had that,' my secretary said. 'She said she'd try you another time.'

'Did she say where she was calling from?'

'No. I assume she was calling from Quantico.'

I had no time to question further because Terminal D was a long walk, and the plane to Hilton Head left in fifteen minutes. I ran the entire way and had time for a soft pretzel without salt. I grabbed several packages of mustard and carried on board the only meal I'd had this day. The businessman I sat beside stared at my snack as if it told him I were a rude housewife who knew nothing about traveling on planes.

When we were in the air, I got into the mustard and ordered Scotch on the rocks.

'Would you by chance have change for a twenty?' I asked the man next to me, because I had overheard the flight attendant complaining about not having adequate change.

He got his wallet out as I opened the *New York Times*. He gave me a ten and two fives, so I paid for his drink. 'Quid pro quo,' I said.

'That's mighty nice,' he said in a syrupy southern accent. 'I guess you must be from New York.'

'Yes,' I lied.

'You by chance going to Hilton Head for the Carolina Convenience Store convention? It's at the Hyatt.'

'No. The funeral home convention,' I lied again. 'It's at the Holiday Inn.'

'Oh.' He shut up.

The Hilton Head airport was parked with private planes and Learjets belonging to the very wealthy who had homes on the island. The terminal was not much more than a hut, and baggage was stacked outside on a wooden deck. The weather was cool with volatile dark skies, and as passengers hurried to awaiting cars and shuttles, I overheard their complaints.

'Oh shit,' exclaimed the man who had been seated beside me. He was hauling golf clubs when thunder crashed and lightning lit up parts of the sky as if a war had begun.

I rented a silver Lincoln and spent some time ensconced inside it at the airport parking lot. Rain drummed the roof, and I could not see out the windshield as I studied the map Hertz had given to me. Anna Zenner's house was in Palmetto Dunes, not far from the Hyatt, where the man on the plane was headed. I looked in vain to see if his car might still be in the parking lot, but as far as I could tell, he and his golf clubs were gone.

The rain eased and I followed the airport exits to the William Hilton Parkway, which took me to Queens Folly Road. I just wandered for a while after that until I found the house. I had expected something smaller. Anna's hideaway was not a bungalow. It was a splendid rustic manor of weathered wood and glass. The yard in back where I parked was dense with tall palmettos and water oaks draped in Spanish moss. A squirrel ran down a tree as I climbed steps leading to the porch. He came close and stood on his hind legs, cheeks going fast as if he had a lot to say to me.

'I bet she feeds you, doesn't she?' I said to him as I got out the key.

He stood with his front paws up, as if protesting something.

'Well, I don't have a thing except memories of a pretzel,' I said. 'I'm really very sorry.' I paused as he hopped a little closer. 'And if you're rabid I'll have to shoot you.'

I went inside, disappointed there was no burglar alarm.

'Too bad,' I said, but I wasn't going to move.

I locked the door and turned the dead bolt. No one knew I was here. I should be fine. Anna had been coming to Hilton Head for years and saw no need for a security system. Gault was in New York and I did not see how he could have followed me. I walked into the living room, with its rustic wood and windows from floor to sky. Hardwood was covered in a bright Indian rug, and furniture was bleached mahogany upholstered in practical fabrics in lovely bright shades.

I wandered from room to room, getting hungrier as the ocean turned to molten lead and a determined army of dark clouds marched in from the north. A long boardwalk led from the house, over dunes, and I carried coffee to its end. I watched people walking and riding bicycles, and an occasional jogger. Sand was hard and gray, and squadrons of brown pelicans flew in formation as if mounting an air attack on a country of unfriendly fish or perhaps the weather.

A porpoise surfaced as men drove golf balls into the sea, and then a small boy's Styrofoam surfboard blew out of his hands. It cartwheeled across the beach while he madly ran. I watched the chase for a quarter of a mile, until his prize tumbled through sea oats up my dune and leapt over my fence. I ran down steps and grabbed it before the wind could abduct it again, and the boy's gait faltered as he watched me watching him.

He could not have been older than eight or nine, dressed in jeans and sweatshirt. Down the beach his mother was trying to catch up with him.

'May I have my surfboard, please?' he said, staring at the sand.

'Would you like me to help you get it back to your mother?' I asked kindly. 'In this wind it will be hard for one person to carry.'

'No, thank you,' he shyly mumbled with outstretched hands.

I felt rejected as I stood on Anna's boardwalk, watching him fight the wind. He finally flattened the surfboard against himself like an ironing board and trudged across damp sand. I watched him with his mother until they were scratches on a horizon I eventually could not see. I tried to imagine where they went. Was it a hotel or a house? Where did little boys and mothers stay on stormy nights out here?

I had not taken one vacation when I was growing up because we had no money, and now I had no children. I thought of Wesley and wanted to call him as I listened to the loud wash of surf rushing to shore. Stars showed through cloudy veils and voices carried on the wind and I could not decipher a word. I may as well have been hearing frogs scream or birds crying. I carried my empty coffee cup inside and did not feel afraid for once.

It occurred to me that there was probably nothing to eat in this house and all I'd had today was that pretzel.

'Thank you, Anna,' I said when I found a stack of Lean Cuisines.

I heated turkey and mixed vegetables, turned on the gas fire and fell asleep on a white couch, my Browning not too far away. I was too tired to dream. The sun and I rose together, and the reality of my mission did not seem real until I spied my briefcase and thought about what was in it. It was too early to leave, and I put on sweater and jeans and went out for a walk.

The sand was firm and flat toward Sea Pines, the sun white gold on water. Birds embroidered the noisy surf with their songs. Willets wandered for mole crabs and worms, gulls glided on the wind, and crows loitered like black-hooded highwaymen.

Older people were out now while the sun was weak, and as I walked I concentrated on the sea air blowing through me. I felt I could breathe. I warmed to the smiles of strangers strolling past, hand in hand, and I waved if they did. Lovers had arms around each other, and solitary people drank coffee on boardwalks and looked out at the water.

Back in Anna's house, I toasted a bagel I found in the freezer and took a long shower. Then I put on my same black blazer and slacks. I packed and closed up the house as if I would not be back. I had no sense of being watched until the squirrel reappeared.

'Oh no,' I said, unlocking the car door. 'Not you again.'

He stood on his hind legs, giving me a lecture.

'Listen, Anna said I could stay here. I am her very good friend.'

His whiskers twitched as he showed me his small white belly.

'If you're telling me your problems, don't bother.' I threw my bag in the backseat. 'Anna's the psychiatrist. Not me.'

I opened the driver's door. He hopped a few steps closer. I couldn't stand it any longer and dug inside my briefcase, where I found a pack of peanuts from the plane. The squirrel was on his hind legs chewing furiously as I backed out of the drive beneath the shade of trees. He watched me leave.

I took 278 West and drove through a landscape lush with cattails, marsh lace, spartina grass and rushes. Ponds were tiled in lotus and lily pads, and at almost every turn, hawks hovered. Away from the islands it seemed most people were poor except in land. Narrow roads offered tiny white painted churches and mobile homes still strung with Christmas lights. Closer to Beaufort, I found auto repairs, small motels on barren plots, and a barbershop flying a Confederate flag. Twice I stopped to read my map.

On St. Helena Island I crept around a tractor on the roadside stirring up dust and began looking for a place to stop for directions. I found abandoned cinder block buildings that once had been stores. There were tomato packers, farmhouses and funeral homes along streets lined with dense live oaks and gardens guarded by scarecrows. I did not stop until I was on Tripp Island and found a place where I could have lunch.

The restaurant was the Gullah House, the woman who seated me big and dark black. She was brilliant in a flowing dress of tropical colors, and when she spoke over a counter to a waiter their language was musical and filled with strange words. The Gullah dialect is supposed to be a blend of West Indian and Elizabethan English. It was the spoken language of slaves.

I waited at my wooden table for iced tea and worried that no one who worked here could communicate to me where the Gaults lived.

'What else I get for you, honey?' My waitress returned with a glass jar of tea full of ice and lemons.

I pointed to *Biddy een de Fiel* because I could not say it. The translation promised a grilled chicken breast on Romaine lettuce.

'You want sweet-potato chips or maybe some crab frittas to start?' Her eyes roamed around the restaurant as she talked.

'No, thank you.'

Determined her customer would have more than a diet lunch, she showed me fried low-country shrimp on the back of the menu. 'We also got fresh fried shrimp today. It so good it'll make you tongue slap you brains out.'

I looked at her. 'Well, then I guess I'd better try a small side dish.'

'So you want all two of 'em.'

'Please.'

The service maintained its languid pace, and it was almost one o'clock when I paid my bill. The lady in the bright dress, who I decided was the manager, was outside in the parking lot talking to another dark woman who drove a van. The side of it read *Gullah Tours*.

'Excuse me,' I said to the manager.

Her eyes were like volcanic glass, suspicious but not unfriendly. 'You want a tour of the island?' she asked.

'Actually, I need directions,' I said. 'Are you familiar with Live Oaks Plantation?'

'It's not on no tour. Not no more.'

'So I can't get there?' I asked.

The manager turned her face and looked askance at me. 'Some new folks is moved there. They don't take kindly to tours, you hear my meaning?'

'I hear you,' I said. 'But I need to get there. I don't want a tour. I just want directions.'

It occurred to me that the dialect I was speaking wasn't the one the manager – who no doubt owned Gullah Tours – wanted to hear.

'How about if I pay for a tour,' I said, 'and you get your van driver to lead me to Live Oaks?'

That seemed a good plan. I handed over twenty dollars and was on my way. The distance was not far, and soon the van slowed and an arm in a wildly colorful sleeve pointed out the window at acres of pecan trees behind a neat white fence. The gate was open at the end of a long, unpaved drive, and about half a mile back I caught a glimpse of white wood and an old copper roof. There was no sign to indicate the owner's name and not a clue that this was Live Oaks Plantation.

I turned left into the drive and scanned spaces between old pecan trees that had already been harvested. I passed a pond covered with duckweed where a blue heron walked at the water's edge. I did not see anyone, but when I got close to what was a magnificent antebellum house, I found a car and a pickup truck. An old barn with a tin roof was in back next to a silo built of tabby. The day had gotten dark and my jacket felt too thin as I climbed steep porch steps and rang the bell.

I could tell instantly by the expression on the man's face that the gate at the end of the driveway was not supposed to have been left open.

'This is private property,' he flatly stated.

If Temple Gault was his son, I saw no resemblance. This man was wiry with graying hair, and his face was long and weathered. He wore Top-Siders, khaki slacks and a plain gray sweatshirt with a hood.

'I'm looking for Peyton Gault,' I said, meeting his gaze as I gripped my briefcase.

'The gate's suppose to be shut. Didn't you see the *No Trespassing* signs? I've only got them nailed up every other fence post. What do you want Peyton Gault for?'

'I can only tell Peyton Gault what I want him for,' I said.

He studied me carefully, indecision in his eyes. 'You aren't some kind of reporter, are you?'

'No, sir, I most certainly am not. I'm the chief medical examiner of Virginia.' I handed him my card.

He leaned against the door frame as if he felt sick. 'Good God have mercy,' he muttered. 'Why can't you people leave us be?'

I could not imagine his private punishment for what he had created, for somewhere in his father's heart he still loved his son.

'Mr. Gault,' I said. 'Please let me talk to you.'

He dug his thumb and index fingers into the corners of his eyes to stop from crying. Wrinkles deepened in his tan brow, and a sudden blaze of sunlight through clouds turned stubble to sand.

'I'm not here out of curiosity,' I said. 'I'm not here doing research. Please.'

'He's never been right from the day he was born,' Peyton Gault said, wiping his eyes.

'I know this is awful for you. It is an unapproachable horror. But I understand.'

'No one can understand,' he said.

'Please let me try.'

'There's no good to come of it.'

'There is only good to come of it,' I said. 'I am here to do the right thing.'

He looked at me with uncertainty. 'Who sent you?'

'Nobody. I came on my own.'

'Then how'd you find us?'

'I asked directions,' I said, and I told him where.

'You don't look too warm in that jacket.'

'I'm warm enough.'

'All right,' he said. 'We'll go out on the pier.'

His dock cut through marshlands that spread as far as I could see, the Barrier Islands an infrequent water tower on the horizon. We leaned against rails, watching fiddler crabs rustle across dark mud. Now and then an oyster spat.

'During Civil War times there were as many as two hundred and fifty slaves here,' he was saying as if we were here to have a friendly chat. 'Before you leave you should stop by the Chapel of Ease. It's just a tabby shell now, with rusting wrought iron around a tiny graveyard.'

I let him talk.

'Of course, the graves have been robbed for as long as anyone remembers. I guess the chapel was built around 1740.'

I was silent.

He sighed, looking out toward the ocean.

'I have photographs I want to show you,' I quietly said.

'You know' – his voice got emotional again – 'it's almost like that flood was punishment for something I did. I was born on that plantation in Albany.' He looked over at me. 'It withstood almost two centuries of war and bad weather.

Then that storm hit and the Flint River rose more than twenty feet.

'We had state police, military police barricading everything. The water reached the damn ceiling of what had been my family home, and forget the trees. Not that we've ever depended on pecans to keep food on the table. But for a while my wife and I were living like the homeless in a center with about three hundred other people.'

'Your son did not cause that flood,' I gently said. 'Even he can't bring about a natural disaster.'

'Well, it's probably just as well we moved. People were coming around all the time trying to see where he grew up. It's had a bad effect on Rachael's nerves.'

'Rachael is your wife?'

He nodded.

'What about your daughter?'

'That's another sorry story. We had to send Jayne west when she was eleven.'

'That's her name?' I said, astonished.

'Actually, it's Rachael. But her middle name's Jayne with a *y*. I don't know if you knew this, but Temple and Jayne are twins.'

'I had no idea,' I said.

'And he was always jealous of her. It was a terrible sight to behold, because she was just crazy about him. They were the cutest little blond things you'd ever want to see, and it's like from day one Temple wanted to squash her like a bug. He was cruel.' He paused.

A herring gull flew by, screaming, and troops of fiddler crabs charged a clump of cattails.

Peyton Gault smoothed back his hair and propped one foot on a lower rail. He said, 'I guess I knew the worst when he was five and Jayne had a puppy. Just the nicest little dog, a mutt.' He paused again. 'Well' – his voice caught – 'the puppy disappeared and that night Jayne woke up to find it dead in her bed. Temple probably strangled it.'

'You said Jayne eventually lived on the West Coast?' I asked.

'Rachael and I didn't know what else to do. We knew it was a matter of time before he killed her – which he almost succeeded in doing later on, it's my belief. You see, I had a brother in Seattle. Luther.'

'The general,' I said.

He continued staring straight ahead. 'I guess you folks do know a lot about us. Temple's made damn sure of that. And next thing I'll be reading about it in books and seeing it on movies.' He pounded his fist softly on the rail.

'Jayne moved in with your brother and his wife?'

'And we kept Temple in Albany. Believe me, if I could have sent him off and held on to her, that's what I would have done. She was a sweet, sensitive child. Real dreamy and kind.' Tears rolled down his cheeks. 'She could play the piano and the saxophone, and Luther loved her like one of his. He had sons.

'All went as well as could be expected, in light of the trouble we had on our hands. Rachael and I went out to Seattle several times a year. I'm telling you, it was hard on me, but it nearly broke her heart. Then we made a big mistake.'

He paused until he could talk again, clearing his throat several times. 'Jayne insisted she wanted to come home one summer. And I guess this was when she was about to turn twenty-five, and she wanted to spend her birthday with everyone. So she, Luther and his wife, Sara, flew to Albany from Seattle. Temple acted like he wasn't fazed a bit, and I remember . . .'

He cleared his throat. 'I remember so clearly thinking that maybe everything would be okay. Maybe he'd finally outgrown whatever it was that possessed him. Jayne had a grand time at her party, and she decided to take our old hound dog, Snaggletooth, out for a walk. She wanted her picture taken, and we did that. Among the pecan trees. Then we all went back into the house except her and Temple.

'He came in around suppertime and I said to him, "Where's your sister?"

'He replied, "She said she was going horseback riding."

'Well, we waited and we waited, and she didn't come back. So Luther and I went out to hunt for her. We found her horse still saddled up and wandering about the stable, and she was there on the ground with all this blood everywhere.'

He wiped his face with his hands, and I could not describe the pity I felt for this man or for his daughter, Jayne. I dreaded telling him his story had an ending.

'The doctor,' he struggled on, 'figured she just got kicked by the horse, but I was suspicious. I thought Luther would kill the boy. You know, he didn't win a Medal of Honor for handing out mess kits. So after Jayne recovered enough to leave the hospital, Luther took her back home. But she was never right.'

'Mr. Gault,' I said. 'Do you have any idea where your daughter is now?'

'Well, she eventually went out on her own four or five years ago when Luther passed on. We usually hear from her at birthdays, Christmas, whenever the mood strikes.'

'Did you hear from her this Christmas?' I asked.

'Not directly on Christmas Day, but a week or two before.' He thought hard, an odd expression on his face.

'Where was she?'

'She called from New York City.'

'Do you know what she was doing there, Mr. Gault?'

'I never know what she's doing. I think she just wanders around and calls when she needs money, to tell you the truth.' He stared out at a snowy egret standing on a stump.

'When she called from New York,' I persisted, 'did she ask for money?'

'Do you mind if I smoke?'

'Of course not.'

He fished a pack of Merits from his breast pocket and fought to light one in the wind. He turned this way and that, and finally I cupped a hand on top of his and held the match. He was shaking.

'It's very important you tell me about the money,' I said. 'How much and how did she get it?'

He paused. 'You see, Rachael does all that.'

'Did your wife wire the money? Did she send a check?'

'I guess you don't know my daughter. No way anybody is going to cash a check for her. Rachael wires money to her on a regular basis. You see, Jayne has to be on medicine to prevent seizures. Because of what happened to her head.'

'Where is the money wired?' I asked.

'A Western Union office. Rachael could tell you which one.'

'What about your son? Do you communicate with him?'

His face got hard. 'Not a bit.'

'He's never tried to come home?'

'Nope.'

'What about here? Does he know you're here?'

'About the only communicating I intend to do with Temple is with a double-barrel shotgun.' His jaw muscles bunched. 'I don't give a damn if he is my son.'

'Are you aware that he is using your AT&T charge card?'

Mr. Gault stood up straight and tapped an ash that scattered in the wind. 'That can't be.'

'Your wife pays the bills?'

'Well, those kind she does.'

'I see,' I said.

He flicked the cigarette into the mud and a crab went after it.

He said, 'Jayne's dead, isn't she? You're a coroner and that's why you're here.'

'Yes, Mr. Gault. I'm so sorry.'

'I had a feeling when you told me who you are. My little girl's that lady they think Temple murdered in Central Park.'

'That's why I'm here,' I said. 'But I need your help if I'm going to prove she is your daughter.'

He looked me in the eye, and I sensed bone-weary relief. He drew himself up and I felt his pride. 'Ma'am, I don't want her in some godforsaken pauper's grave. I want her here with Rachael and me. For once she can live with us because it's too late for him to hurt her.'

We walked along the pier.

'I can make certain that happens,' I said as wind flattened the grass and tore through our hair. 'All I need is your blood.'

18

Before we went inside his house, Mr. Gault warned me that his wife did not have good coping skills. He explained as delicately as he could that Rachael Gault had never faced the reality of her offsprings' blighted destinies.

'It's not that she's going to pitch a fit,' he explained in a soft voice as we climbed the porch steps. 'She just won't accept it, if you know what I mean.'

'You may want to look at the pictures out here,' I said.

'Of Jayne.' He got very tired again.

'Of her and of footprints.'

'Footprints?' He ran callused fingers through his hair.

'Do you remember her owning a pair of army jungle boots?' I then asked.

'No.' He slowly shook his head. 'But Luther had all kinds of things like that.'

'Do you know what size shoe he wore?'

'His foot was smaller than mine. I guess he wore a seven and a half or an eight.'

'Did he ever give a pair of his boots to Temple?'

'Huh,' he said shortly. 'The only way Luther would have

given that boy boots would be if Luther still had 'em on and was kicking Temple's butt.'

'The boots could have belonged to Jayne.'

'Oh sure. She and Luther probably wore close to the same size. She was a big girl. In fact, she was about the size of Temple. And I always suspected that was part of his problem.'

Mr. Gault would have stood out in prevailing winds and talked all day. He did not want me opening my briefcase because he knew what was inside.

'We don't have to do this. You don't have to look at anything,' I said. 'We can use DNA.'

'If it's all the same to you,' he said, eyes bright as he reached for the door. 'I guess I'd better tell Rachael.'

The entrance of the Gault house was whitewashed and bordered in a pale shade of gray. An old brass chandelier hung from the high ceiling, and a graceful spiral stairway led to the second floor. In the living room were English antiques, oriental rugs and formidable oil portraits of people from lives past. Rachael Gault sat on a prim sofa, needlepoint in her lap. I could see through a spacious archway that needlepoint covered the dining room chairs.

'Rachael?' Mr. Gault stood before her like a bashful bachelor with hat in hand. 'We have company.'

She dipped her needle in and out. 'Oh, how nice.' She smiled and put down her work.

Rachael Gault once had been a fair beauty with light skin, eyes and hair. I was fascinated that Temple and Jayne had gotten their looks from their mother and their uncle, and I chose not to speculate but to attribute this to Mendel's law of dominance or his statistics of genetic chance.

Mr. Gault sat on the sofa and offered me the high-back chair.

'What's the weather doing out there?' Mrs. Gault asked with her son's thin smile and the hypnotic cadences of a Deep South drawl. 'I wonder if there are any shrimp left.' She looked directly at me. 'You know, I don't know your name. Now, Peyton, let's not be rude. Introduce me to this new friend you've made.'

'Rachael,' Mr. Gault tried again. Hands on his knees, he hung his head. 'She's a doctor from Virginia.'

'Oh?' Her delicate hands plucked at the canvas in her lap.

'I guess you'd call her a coroner.' He looked over at his wife. 'Honey, Jayne's dead.'

Mrs. Gault resumed her needlework with nimble fingers. 'You know, we had a magnolia out there that lasted nearly a hundred years before lightning struck it in the spring. Can you imagine?' She sewed on. 'We do get storms here. What's it like where you're from?'

'I live in Richmond,' I replied.

'Oh yes,' she said, the needle dipping faster. 'Now see, we were lucky we didn't get all burned up in the war. I bet you had a great-granddaddy who fought in it?'

'I'm Italian,' I said. 'I'm from Miami, originally.'

'Well, it certainly gets hot down there.'

Mr. Gault sat helpless on the couch. He gave up looking at anyone.

'Mrs. Gault,' I said, 'I saw Jayne in New York.'

'You did?' She seemed genuinely pleased. 'Why, tell me all about it.' Her hands were like hummingbirds.

'When I saw her she was awfully thin and she'd cut her hair.'

'She never is satisfied with her hair. When she wore it short she looked like Temple. They're twins and people used to confuse them and think she was a boy. So she's always worn it long, which is why I'm surprised you would say she's cut it short.'

'Do you talk to your son?' I asked.

'He doesn't call as often as he should, that bad boy. But he knows he can.'

'Jayne called here a couple weeks before Christmas,' I said.

She said nothing as she sewed.

'Did she say anything to you about seeing her brother?'

She was silent.

'I'm wondering because he was in New York, too.'

'Certainly, I told him he ought to look up his sister and wish her a Merry Christmas,' Mrs. Gault said as her husband winced.

'You sent her money?' I went on.

She looked up at me. 'Now I believe you're getting a bit personal.'

'Yes, ma'am. I'm afraid I have to get personal.'

She threaded a needle with bright blue yarn.

'Doctors get personal.' I tried a different tack. 'That's part of our job.'

She laughed a little. 'Well now, they do. I suppose that's why I hate going to them. They think they can cure everything with milk of magnesia. It's like drinking white paint. Peyton? Would you mind getting me a glass of water with a little ice? And see what our guest would like.'

'Nothing,' I told him quietly as he reluctantly got up and left the room.

'That was very thoughtful of you to send your daughter money,' I said. 'Please tell me how you did it in a city as big and busy as New York.'

'I had Western Union wire it, same as I always do.'

'Where exactly did you wire it?'

'New York, where Jayne is.'

'Where in New York, Mrs. Gault? And have you done this more than once?'

'A drugstore up there. Because she has to get her medicine.'

'For her seizures. Her diphenylhydantoin.'

'Jayne said it wasn't a very good part of town.' She sewed some more. 'It was called Houston. Only it's not pronounced like the city in Texas.'

'Houston and what?' I asked.

'Why, I don't know what you mean.' She was getting agitated.

'A cross street. I need an address.'

'Why in the world?'

'Because that may be where your daughter went right before she died.'

She sewed faster, her lips a thin line.

'Please help me, Mrs. Gault.'

'She rides the bus a lot. She says she can see America flow by like a movie when she's on the bus.'

'I know you don't want anyone else to die.'

She squeezed her eyes shut.

'Please.'

'Now I lay me.'

'What?' I said.

'Rachael.' Mr. Gault returned to the room. 'There isn't any ice. I don't know what happened.'

'Down to sleep,' she said.

Dumbfounded, I looked at her husband.

'Now I lay me down to sleep, I pray the Lord my soul to keep,' he said, looking at her. 'We prayed that with the kids every night when they were small. Is that what you're thinking of, honey?'

'Test question for Western Union,' she said.

'Because Jayne had no identification,' I said. 'Of course. So they made her answer a test question to pick up the money and her prescription.'

'Oh yes. It was what we always used. For years now.'

'And what about Temple?'

'For him, too.'

Mr. Gault rubbed his face. 'Rachael, you haven't been giving him money, too. Please don't tell me . . .'

'It's my money. I have my own from my family just like you do.' She resumed sewing, turning the canvas this way and that.

'Mrs. Gault,' I said, 'did Temple know Jayne was due money from you at Western Union?'

'Of course he knew. He is her brother. He said he'd pick it up for her because she hasn't been well. When that horse threw her off. She's never been as clearheaded as Temple is. And I was sending him a little, too.'

'How often have you been sending money?' I asked again.

She tied a knot and cast about as if she had lost something.

'Mrs. Gault, I will not leave your house until you answer my question or throw me out.'

'After Luther died there wasn't anyone to care about Jayne, and she didn't want to come here,' she said. 'Jayne didn't want to be in one of those homes. So wherever she went she let me know, and I helped when I could.'

'You never told me.' Her husband was crushed.

'How long had she been in New York?' I asked.

'Since the first of December. I've been sending money regularly, just a little at a time. Fifty dollars here, a hundred dollars there. I wired some last Saturday, as usual. That's why I know she's fine. She passed the test. So she was standing right there in line.'

I wondered how long Gault had been intercepting his poor sister's money. I despised him with a zeal that was scary.

'She didn't like Philadelphia,' Mrs. Gault went on, talking faster. 'That's where she was before New York. Some city of brotherly love that is. Someone stole her flute there. Stole it right out of her hand.'

'Her tin whistle?' I asked.

'Her saxophone. You know, my father played the violin.'

Mr. Gault and I stared at her.

'Maybe it was her saxophone that got taken. Lawww, I don't know where all she's been. Honey? Remember when she came here for her birthday and went out in the pecan trees with the dog?' Her hands went still.

'That was Albany. That's not where we are now.'

She shut her eyes. 'Why, she was twenty-five and had never been kissed.' She laughed. 'I remember her at the piano playing up a storm, singing "Happy Birthday" to beat the band. Then Temple took her to the barn. She'd go anywhere with him. I never understood why. But Temple can be charming.'

A tear slipped between her lashes.

'She went out to ride that darn horse Priss and never came back.' More tears spilled. 'Oh Peyton, I never saw my little girl again.'

He said in a voice that shook, 'Temple killed her, Rachael. This can't go on.'

I drove back to Hilton Head and got an early evening flight to Charlotte. From there I flew to Richmond and retrieved my car. I did not go home. I felt a sense of urgency that set me on fire. I could not reach Wesley at Quantico, and Lucy had returned none of my calls.

It was almost nine o'clock when I drove past pitch-black artillery ranges and barracks, trees hulking shadows on either side of the narrow road. I was rattled and exhausted as I watched for signs and deer crossing, then blue lights flashed in my rearview mirror. I tried to see what was behind me. I could not tell, but I knew it was not a patrol car because those had light bars in addition to lights in the grille.

I drove on. I thought of cases I had worked in which a woman alone stopped for what she thought was a cop. Many times over the years I had warned Lucy never to stop for an unmarked car, not for any reason, especially not at night. The car was dogged, but I did not pull over until I reached the Academy guard booth.

The unmarked car halted at my rear, and instantly an MP in uniform was at my driver's door with pistol drawn. My heart seemed to stop.

'Get out and put your hands up in the air!' he ordered.

I sat perfectly still.

He stepped back and I realized the guard was saying something to him. Then the guard emerged from his booth and the MP tapped on my glass. I rolled down my window while the MP lowered his gun, his eyes not leaving me. He did not look a day over nineteen.

'You're going to have to get out, ma'am.' The MP was hateful because he was embarrassed.

'I will if you'll holster your weapon and move out of my way,' I said as the Academy guard stepped back. 'And I have a pistol on the console between the front seats. I'm just telling you so you aren't startled.'

'Are you DEA?' he demanded as he surveyed my Mercedes.

He had what looked like gray adhesive residue for a mustache. My blood was roaring. I knew he was going to put on a manly show because the Academy guard was watching.

I was out of my car now, blue lights throbbing on our faces.

'Am I DEA?' I glared at him.

'Yes.'

'No.'

'Are you FBI?'

'No.'

He was getting more disconcerted. 'Then what are you, ma'am?'

'I am a forensic pathologist,' I said.

'Who is your supervisor?'

'I don't have a supervisor.'

'Ma'am, you have to have a supervisor.'

'The governor of Virginia is my supervisor.'

'I'll have to see your driver's license,' he said.

'Not until you tell me what I am being charged with.'

'You were going forty-five in a thirty-five-mile-an-hour zone. And you attempted to elude.'

'Do all people who attempt to elude military police drive straight to a guard booth?'

'I must have your driver's license.'

'And let me ask you, Private,' I said, 'just why do you imagine I didn't pull over on this godforsaken road after dark?'

'I really don't know, ma'am.'

'Unmarked cars rarely make traffic stops, but psychopaths often do.'

Bright blue pulsed on his pathetically young face. He probably did not know what a psychopath was.

'I will never stop for your unmarked Chevrolet if you and I repeat this misadventure for the rest of our lives. Do you understand?' I said.

A car sped from the direction of the Academy and halted on the other side of the guard booth.

'You drew down on me,' I said, outraged, as a car door shut. 'You pulled a goddam nine-millimeter pistol and pointed it at me. Has no one in the Marine Corps taught you the meaning of *unnecessary force*?'

'Kay?' Benton Wesley appeared in the pulsing dark.

I realized the guard must have called him, but I did not understand why Wesley would be here at this hour. He could not have come from home. He lived almost in Fredericksburg.

'Good evening,' he sternly said to the MP.

They stepped aside and I could not hear what they said. But the MP walked back to his small, bland car. Blue lights quit and he drove away.

'Thanks,' Wesley said to the guard. 'Come on,' he said to me. 'Follow me.'

He did not drive into the parking lot I usually used but to reserved spaces behind Jefferson. There was no other car in the lot but a big pickup truck I recognized as Marino's. I got out.

'What is going on?' I asked, my breath smoky in the cold.

'Marino's down in the unit.' Wesley was dressed in a dark sweater and dark slacks, and I sensed something had happened.

'Where's Lucy?' I quickly said.

He did not answer as he inserted his security card into a slot, opening a back door.

'You and I need to talk,' he said.

'No.' I knew what he meant. 'I am too worried.'

'Kay, I am not your enemy.'

'You have seemed like it at times.'

We walked quickly and did not bother with the elevator.

'I'm sorry,' he said. 'I love you and don't know what to do.'

'I know.' I was shaken. 'I don't know what to do, either. I keep wanting someone to tell me. But I don't want this, Benton. I want what we've had and I don't want it ever.'

For a while he did not speak.

'Lucy got a hit on CAIN,' he eventually said. 'We've deployed HRT.'

'Then she's here,' I said, relieved.

'She's in New York. We're on our way there.' He looked at his watch.

'I don't understand,' I said as our feet sounded on stairs.

We moved swiftly down a long corridor where hostage negotiators spent their days when they weren't abroad talking terrorists out of buildings and hijackers out of planes.

'I don't understand why she's in New York,' I said, unnerved. 'Why does she need to be there?'

We walked into his office, where Marino was squatting by a tote bag. It was unzipped, and next to it on the carpet were a shaving kit and three loaded magazines for his Sig Sauer. He was looking for something else and glanced up at me.

He said to Wesley, 'Can you believe it? I forgot my razor.'

'They have them in New York,' Wesley said, his mouth grim.

'I've been in South Carolina,' I said. 'I talked to the Gaults.'

Marino stopped digging and stared up at me. Wesley sat behind his desk.

'I hope they don't know where their son is staying,' he said oddly.

'I have no indication that they do.' I looked curiously at him.

'Well, maybe it doesn't matter.' He rubbed his eyes. 'I just don't want anyone tipping him off.'

'Lucy kept him on CAIN long enough for the call to be traced,' I assumed.

Marino got up and sat in a chair. He said, 'The squirrel's got a crib right on Central Park.'

'Where?' I asked.

'The Dakota.'

I thought of Christmas Eve when we were at the fountain in Cherry Hill. Gault could have been watching. He could have seen our lights from his room.

'He can't afford the Dakota,' I said.

'You remember his fake ID?' Marino asked. 'The Italian guy named Benelli?'

'It's his apartment?'

'Yes,' Wesley answered. 'Mr. Benelli apparently is a flamboyant heir to a considerable family fortune. Management has assumed the current occupant – Gault – is an Italian relative. At any rate, they don't ask many questions there, and he's been speaking with an accent. It also is very convenient because Mr. Benelli does not pay his rent. His father in Verona does.'

'Why can't you go into the Dakota and get Gault?' I asked. 'Why can't HRT do that?'

'We could, but I'd rather not. It's too risky,' Wesley said. 'This isn't war, Kay. We don't want any casualties, and we are bound by law. There are people inside the Dakota who could get hurt. We don't know where Benelli is. He could be in the room.'

'Yeah, in a plastic bag in a steamer trunk,' Marino said.

'We know where Gault is and we have the building under surveillance. But Manhattan is not where I would have chosen to catch this guy. It's too damn crowded. You get in an exchange of firepower – I don't care how good you are – and someone's going to get hit. Someone else is going to die. A woman, a man, a child who just happens to walk out at the wrong time.'

'I understand,' I said. 'I'm not disagreeing with you. Is Gault in the apartment now? And what about Carrie?'

Wesley said, 'Neither has been sighted, and we have no reason to suspect Carrie travels with him.'

'He hasn't used my charge card to buy her plane tickets,' I considered. 'That much I can tell.'

'We do know Gault was in the apartment as recently as eight o'clock this evening,' Wesley said. 'That's when he got on the line and Lucy trapped him.'

'She trapped him?' I looked at both men. 'She trapped him from here and now she's gone? Did she get deployed with HRT?'

I had a bizarre image of Lucy in black boots and fatigues being loaded on a plane at Andrews Air Force Base. I imagined her with a group of supremely fit helicopter pilots, snipers and experts in explosives, and my incredulity grew.

Wesley met my eyes. 'She's been in New York for the past couple of days. She's working on the Transit Police computer. She got the hit in New York.'

'Why not work here where CAIN is located?' I wanted to know, because I did not want Lucy in New York. I did not want her in the same state where Temple Gault was.

'Transit's got an extremely sophisticated system,' he said.

Marino spoke. 'It's got things we don't have, Doc.'

'Like what?'

'Like a computerized map of the entire subway system.' Marino leaned closer to me, forearms resting on his knees. He understood what I was feeling. I could see it in his eyes. 'We think that's how Gault's been getting around.'

Wesley explained, 'We think Carrie Grethen somehow got Gault into the Transit Police computer, through CAIN. He was able to map out for himself a way to move around the city through the tunnels, so he could get his drugs and commit his crimes. He has had access to detailed diagrams that include stations, catwalks, tunnels and escape hatches.'

'What escape hatches?' I asked.

'The subway system has emergency exits that lead out of the tunnels, in the event a train should have to stop for some reason down there. Passengers can be routed through an emergency exit that will bring them back above ground. Central Park has a number of them.'

Wesley got up and went to his suitcase. He opened it and pulled out a thick roll of white paper. Removing the rubber band, he spread open very long drawings of New York's subway system that included all tracks and structures, every manhole, trash can, car marker, platform edge. The diagrams covered most of his office floor, some more than six feet long. I studied them, fascinated.

'This is from Commander Penn,' I said.

'Right,' Wesley replied. 'And what's on her computer is even more detailed. For example' – he squatted, pointing and moving his tie out of the way – 'in March of 1979, turnstiles at CB number 300 were removed. That's right here.' He showed me on a drawing of the 110th Street station at Lenox Avenue and 112th Street.

'And a change like that now,' he went on, 'goes directly into the Transit Police computer system.'

'Meaning that any changes are instantly reflected on the computerized maps,' I said.

'Right.' He pulled another drawing closer, this one of the Eighty-first Street Museum of Natural History station. 'Now the reason we think Gault is using these maps is right here.' He tapped an area on the field survey that indicated an emergency exit very near Cherry Hill.

'If Gault was looking at this drawing,' Wesley went on, 'he most likely would choose this emergency exit as the one to come in and out of when he committed the murder in Central Park. That way he and his victim could travel unseen through the tunnels after leaving the museum, and when they surfaced in the park they would be very close to the fountain where he planned to display the body.

'But what you don't know from looking at this three-month-old printout is the day before the murder, the Maintenance of Way Department bolted that escape door shut for repairs. We think that might be why Gault and his victim started out closer to the Ramble,' he said. 'Some footwear impressions recovered in that area, as it turns out, are consistent with theirs. And the tracks were found near an emergency exit.'

'So you have to ask how he knew that exit in Cherry Hill was bolted shut,' Marino said.

'I suppose he could have checked it first,' I said.

'You can't do that above ground because the doors don't open except from inside the tunnels,' Marino said.

'Maybe he was down in the tunnel and saw from the inside that the door was bolted,' I argued, because I sensed where this was leading and did not like it.

'Of course that's possible,' Wesley reasonably said. 'But Transit cops go down into the tunnels a lot. They're all over the platforms and the stations, and none of them remembers seeing Gault. I believe he travels down there by computer until it suits his purposes to make an appearance.'

'What is Lucy's role?' I asked.

'To manipulate,' Marino said.

'I'm not a computer person,' Wesley added. 'But as best I can understand, she has worked it so when he logs on to this computerized map, he's really seeing one she is altering.'

'Altering for what purpose?'

'We're hoping to come up with a way of trapping him like a rat in a maze.'

'I thought HRT had been deployed.'

'We are going to try whatever it takes.'

'Well then, let me suggest you consider one other plan,' I said. 'Gault goes to Houston Professional Pharmacy when he wants money.'

They looked at me as if I were crazy.

'That's where his mother has been wiring money to Temple's sister, Jayne—'

'Wait a minute,' Marino interrupted

But I went on, 'I tried to call earlier to tell you. I know that Temple has been intercepting the money because Mrs. Gault wired money after Jayne was already dead. And someone signed for it. This person knew the test question.'

'Hold on,' Marino said. 'Hold on one damn minute. Are you telling me that son of a bitch murdered his own sister?'

'Yes,' I answered. 'She was his twin.'

'Jesus. No one told me.' He looked accusingly at Wesley.

'You just got here two minutes before Kay got arrested,' Wesley said to him.

'I didn't get arrested,' I said. 'Her middle name actually is Jayne, with a *y*,' I added, and then I filled them in.

'This changes everything,' Wesley said, and he called New York.

It was almost eleven when he got off the phone. He stood and picked up his briefcase and his bag and a portable radio that was on his desk. Marino rose from his chair, too.

'Unit three to unit seventeen,' Wesley spoke into the radio.

'Seventeen.'

'We're heading your way.'

'Yes, sir.'

'I'm coming with you,' I said to Wesley.

He looked at me. I was not on the original passenger list.

'All right,' he said. 'Let's go.'

19

We discussed the plan in the air as our pilot flew toward Manhattan. The Bureau's New York field office would assign an undercover agent to the pharmacy at Houston and Second Avenue, while a pair of agents from Atlanta would be dispatched to Live Oaks Plantation. This was happening even as we talked into our voice-activated microphones.

If Mrs. Gault maintained the usual schedule, money was due to be wired again tomorrow. Since Gault had no way of knowing his parents had been told their daughter was dead, he would assume the money would arrive as usual.

'What he's not going to do is just take a taxi to the pharmacy.' Wesley's voice filled my headset as I looked out at plains of darkness.

'Naw,' Marino said. 'I doubt it. He knows everybody but the queen of England is out looking for him.'

'We want him to go underground.'

'It seems riskier down there,' I said, thinking of Davila. 'No lights. And the third rails and the trains.'

'I know,' said Wesley. 'But he has the mentality of a terrorist. He doesn't care who he kills. We can't have a shoot-out in

Manhattan in the middle of the day.'

I understood his point.

'So how do you make certain he travels through the tunnels to get to the pharmacy?' I asked.

'We turn up the heat without scaring him off.'

'How?'

'Apparently, there's a March Against Crime parade tomorrow.'

'That's appropriate,' I said ironically. 'It's through the Bowery?'

'Yes. The route can easily be changed to go along Houston and Second Avenue.'

Marino cut in. 'All you do is move traffic cones.'

'Transit PD can send out a computerized communication notifying police in the Bowery that there is a parade at such and such a time. Gault will see on the computer that the parade is supposed to go through the area at the exact time he is supposed to pick up the money. He'll see that the subway station at Second Avenue has been temporarily closed.'

A nuclear power plant in Delaware glowed like a heating element on high, and cold air seeped in.

I said, 'So he'll know it's not a good time to be traveling above ground.'

'Exactly. When there's a parade, there are cops.'

'I worry about him deciding not to go for the money,' Marino said.

'He'll go for it,' Wesley said as if he knew.

'Yes,' I said. 'He's addicted to crack. That is a more powerful motivator than any fear he might have.'

'Do you think he killed his sister for money?' Marino asked.

'No,' Wesley said. 'But the small sums her mother sent her were just one more thing he appropriated. In the end, he took everything his sister ever had.'

'No, he didn't,' I said. 'She was never evil like him. That's the best thing she had, and Gault couldn't take it.'

'We're arriving in the Big Apple with guns,' Marino's voice blurted over the air.

'My bag,' I said. 'I forgot.'

'I'll talk to the commissioner first thing in the morning.'

'It is first thing in the morning,' Marino said.

We landed at the helipad on the Hudson near the *Intrepid* aircraft carrier, which was strung with Christmas lights. A Transit Police cruiser was waiting, and I remembered arriving here not that long ago and meeting Commander Penn for the first time. I remembered seeing Jayne's blood in the snow when I did not know the unbearable truth about her.

We arrived at the New York Athletic Club again.

'Which room is Lucy in?' I asked Wesley as we checked in with an old man who looked as if he had always worked unearthly hours.

'She isn't.' He handed out keys.

We walked away from the desk.

'Okay,' I said. 'Now tell me.'

Marino yawned. 'We sold her to a small factory in the Garment District.'

'She's in protective custody, sort of.' Wesley smiled a little as brass elevator doors opened. 'She's staying with Commander Penn.'

In my room I took my suit off and hung it in the shower. I steamed it as I had the last two nights and considered throwing it out should I ever get a chance to change my clothes again. I slept under several blankets and with windows open wide. At six I got up before the alarm. I showered and ordered a bagel and coffee.

At seven, Wesley called and then he and Marino were at my door. We went down to the lobby and on to an awaiting police car. My Browning was in my briefcase, and I hoped Wesley got special permits and did it fast, because I did not wish to be in violation of New York gun laws. I thought of Bernhard Goetz.

'Here's what we're going to do,' Wesley said as we drove toward lower Manhattan. 'I'm going to spend the morning on the phone. Marino, I want you out on the street with Transit cops. Make damn sure those traffic cones are exactly where they ought to be.'

'Got it.'

'Kay, I want you with Commander Penn and Lucy. They'll be in direct contact with the agents in South Carolina and the one at the pharmacy.' Wesley looked at his watch. 'The agents in South Carolina, as a matter of fact, should be reaching the plantation within the hour.'

'Let's just hope the Gaults don't screw this up,' said Marino, who was riding shotgun.

Wesley looked over at me.

'When I left the Gaults they seemed willing to help,' I said. 'But can't we just wire the money in her name and keep her out of it?'

Wesley said, 'We could. But the less attention we draw to what we're doing, the better. Mrs. Gault lives in a small town. If agents go in and wire the money, someone might talk.'

'And what someone might say might get back to Gault?' I asked skeptically.

'If the Western Union agent in Beaufort somehow tips his hand to the one here in New York, you just never know what might happen to scare off Gault. We don't want to take the chance, and the fewer people we involve, the better.'

'I understand,' I said.

'That's another reason I want you with the commander,' Wesley went on. 'Should Mrs. Gault decide to interfere in any way, I'm going to need you to talk to her and get her back in the right frame of mind.'

'Gault just might show up at the pharmacy anyway,' Marino said. 'He might not know until he gets to the counter that the money's not coming, if that's what happens because his old lady wimps out on us.'

'We don't know what he'll do,' Wesley said. 'But I would suspect he'd call first.'

'She's got to wire the money,' I agreed. 'She absolutely must go through with it. And that's hard.'

'Right, it's her son,' Wesley said.

'Then what happens?' I asked.

'We've arranged it so the parade starts at two, which is about the time the money has been wired in the past. We'll have HRT out – some of them will actually be in the parade. And there will be other agents as well. Plus plainclothes police. These will be mostly positioned in the subway and in areas where there are emergency exits.'

'What about in the pharmacy?' I asked.

Wesley paused. 'Of course, we'll have a couple agents in there. But we don't want to grab Gault in the store or near it. He might start spraying bullets. If there are to be any casualties, it will be just one.'

'All I ask is let me be the lucky guy who does him,' Marino said. 'After that I could retire.'

'We absolutely must get him underground.' Wesley was emphatic. 'We don't know what weapons he has at present. We don't know how many people he could take out with karate. There's so much we don't know. But I believe he's fired up on coke and rapidly decompensating. And he's not afraid. That's why he's so dangerous.'

'Where are we going?' I asked, watching dreary buildings flow by as a light rain fell. It was not a good day for a parade.

'Penn's set up a command post at Bleecker Street, which is close to Houston Pharmacy but a safe distance, too,' Wesley said. 'Her team's been at it all night, bringing in computer equipment and so on. Lucy's with them.'

'This is inside the actual subway station?'

The officer driving answered, 'Yes, ma'am. It's a local stop that operates only during the week. Trains don't stop here on the weekends, so it should be quiet. Transit PD's got a miniprecinct here that covers the Bowery.'

He was parking in front of the stairs going down into a station.

Sidewalks and streets were busy with people carrying umbrellas and holding newspapers over their heads.

'You just go down and you'll see the wooden door to the left of the turnstiles. It's next to the information window,' the officer said.

He unhooked his mike. 'Unit one-eleven.'

'Unit one-eleven,' the dispatcher came back.

'Ten-five unit three.'

The dispatcher contacted unit three and I recognized Commander Penn's voice. She knew we had arrived. Wesley, Marino and I carefully descended slick steps as rain fell harder. The tile floor inside was wet and dirty, but no one was around. I was getting increasingly anxious.

We passed the information window, and Wesley knocked on a wooden door. It opened and Detective Maier, whom I had first met at the morgue after Davila's death, let us into a space that had been turned, essentially, into a control room. Closed-circuit television monitors were on a long table, and my niece sat at a console equipped with telephones, radio equipment and computers.

Frances Penn, wearing the dark commando sweater and pants of the troops she commanded, came straight to me and warmly grasped my hand.

'Kay, I'm so happy you're here,' she said, and she was full of nervous energy.

Lucy was absorbed in a row of four monitors. Each showed a blueprint of a different section of the subway system.

Wesley said to Commander Penn, 'I've got to go on to the field office. Marino will be out with your guys, as we discussed.'

She nodded.

'So I'll leave Dr. Scarpetta here.'

'Very good.'

'Where is this going down, exactly?' I inquired.

'Well, we're closing Second Avenue station, which is right there at the pharmacy,' Commander Penn answered me. 'We'll block the entrance with traffic cones and sawhorses. We can't risk a confrontation when civilians are in the area. We expect him to come up through the tunnel along the northbound track or leave that way, and he's more likely to be enticed by Second Avenue if it's not open.' She paused, looking over at Lucy. 'It will make more sense when your niece shows you on the screen.'

'Then you hope to grab him somewhere inside that station,' I said.

'That's what we hope,' Wesley said. 'We'll have guys out there in the dark. HRT will be out there and all around. The bottom line is we want to grab him away from people.'

'Of course,' I said.

Maier was watching us closely. 'How did you figure out the lady from the park was his sister?' he asked, looking straight at me.

I gave him a quick summary, adding, 'We'll use DNA to verify it.'

'Not from what I heard,' he said. 'I heard they lost her blood and shit at the morgue.'

'Where did you hear that?' I asked.

'I know a bunch of guys who work over there. You know, detectives in the Missing Persons Division for NYPD.'

'We will get her identified,' I said, watching him closely.

'Well, you ask me, it's a shame if they figure it out.'

Commander Penn was listening carefully. I sensed she and I were arriving at the same conclusion.

'Why would you say that?' she asked him.

Maier was getting angry. 'Because the way the stinking system works in this stinking city is we nab the asshole here, right? So he gets charged with killing that lady because there isn't enough evidence to convict him of killing Jimmy Davila. And we don't have capital punishment in New York. And the case just gets weaker if the lady's got no name – if no one knows who she is.'

'It sounds as if you're saying you want the case to be weak,' Wesley said.

'Yeah. It sounds that way because I do.'

Marino was staring at him with no expression. He said, 'The toad whacked Davila with his own service revolver. The way it ought to work is Gault ought to fry.'

'You're damn right he should.' Maier's jaw muscles clenched. 'He wasted a cop. A goddam good cop who's getting accused of a bunch of bullshit because that's what happens when you get killed in the line of duty. People, politicians, internal affairs – they speculate. Everybody's got an agenda. The whole world does. We'd all be better off if Gault gets tried in Virginia, not here.'

He looked at me again. I knew what had happened to Jayne's biological samples. Detective Maier had gotten his friends at the morgue to do him a favor in honor of their slain comrade. Though what they had done was terribly wrong, I almost could not blame them.

'You got the electric chair in Virginia, where Gault's also committed murders,' he said. 'And word has it that the Doc here breaks the record for getting these animals convicted of capital murder. Only if the bastard gets tried in New York, you probably won't be testifying, right?'

'I don't know,' I said.

'See. She don't know. That means forget it.' He looked around at everyone as if he'd argued his case and there could be no rebuttal. 'The asshole needs to go to Virginia and get cooked, if he don't get nailed here first by one of us.'

'Detective Maier,' Commander Penn quietly said, 'I need to see you in private. Let's go back to my office.'

They left and went through a door in back. She would pull him from the assignment because he could not be controlled. She would give him a Complaint and he would probably be suspended.

'We're out of here,' Wesley said.

'Yeah,' Marino said. 'Next time you see us it will be on TV.' He referred to the monitors around the control room.

I was taking off my coat and gloves and about to talk to Lucy when the door in back opened and Maier emerged. He walked with quick, angry strides until he got to me.

'Do it for Jimbo,' he said with emotion. 'Don't let that asshole get away with it.'

The veins were standing out in his neck and he looked up at the ceiling. 'I'm sorry.' He blinked back tears and almost could not talk as he flung open the door and left.

'Lucy?' I said, and we were alone.

She was typing and concentrating intensely. 'Hi,' she said.

I went to her and kissed the top of her head.

'Have a seat,' she said without looking away from what she was doing.

I scanned monitors. There were arrows for Manhattan-bound, Brooklyn-, Bronx- and Queens-bound trains and an intricate grid showing streets, schools and medical centers. All were numbered. I sat beside her and got my glasses out of my briefcase as Commander Penn reappeared, her face stressed.

'That was no fun to do,' she said, standing behind us, the pistol on her belt almost touching my ear.

'What are these flashing symbols that look like twisted ladders?' I asked, pointing out several on the screen.

'They're the emergency exits,' Commander Penn said.

'Can you explain what you're doing here?' I asked.

'Lucy, I'll let you do that,' the commander said.

'It's really pretty simple,' Lucy said, and I never believed her when she said that. 'I'm supposing that Gault is looking at these maps, too. So I'm letting him see what I want him to see.'

She hit several keys and another part of the subway was there before me, with its symbols and long linear depictions of tracks. She typed and a hatchwork appeared in red.

'This is the route we believe he'll take,' she said. 'Logic would tell you that he'll penetrate the subway here.'

Lucy pointed to the monitor left of the one directly in front of her. 'This is for the Museum of Natural History station. And as you can see there are three emergency exits right here near Hayden Planetarium and one up by Beresford Apartments. He also could go southbound closer to Kenilworth Apartments and get into the tunnels that way and then pick any platform he wants when it's time to get on a train.

'I haven't altered anything on these field surveys,' Lucy went on. 'It's more important to confuse him at the other end, when he gets to the Bowery.'

She rapidly typed and one after another images appeared on each monitor. She was able to tilt, move and manipulate them as if they were models she was turning in her hands. On the center screen in front of her the symbol for an emergency exit was lit up and a square had been drawn around it.

'We think this is his snake hole,' Lucy resumed. 'It is an emergency exit where Fourth and Third merge into the Bowery.' She pointed. 'Here behind this big brownstone. The Cooper Union Foundation Building.'

Commander Penn spoke. 'The reason we think he has been using this exit is we've discovered it has been tampered with. A folded strip of aluminum foil has been wedged between the door and its frame so someone could access the exit from above ground.

'It's also the closest exit to the pharmacy,' Commander Penn continued. 'It's remote, back here behind this building, basically in an alleyway between Dumpsters. Gault could go in and out whenever he pleased, and it's unlikely anyone would see him, even in broad daylight.'

'And there's another thing,' Lucy said. 'At Cooper Square there's a famous music store. The Carl Fischer Music Store.'

'Right,' Commander Penn said. 'Someone who works there recalls Jayne. Now and then she wandered in and browsed. This would have been during December.'

'Did anyone talk to her?' I asked, and the image made me sad.

'All they recalled was that she was interested in jazz sheet music. My point is, we don't know what Gault's connections to this area are. But they could be more involved than we think.'

'What we've done,' Lucy said, 'is take away this emergency exit. The police have bolted it shut, and boom.'

She hit more keys. The symbol was no longer lit up and a message next to it said *Disabled.*

'It seems that might be a good location to catch him,' I said. 'Why don't we want him there behind the Cooper Union Building?'

'Again,' the commander said, 'it's too close to a crowded area, and should Gault duck back into the tunnel, he would be very deep inside it. Literally, in the bowels of the Bowery. A pursuit would be terribly dangerous and we might not catch him. My guess is he knows his way around down there even better than we do.'

'All right,' I said. 'Then what happens?'

'What happens is, since he can't use his favorite emergency exit, he has two choices. He can pick another exit that's farther north along the tracks. Or he can continue walking through the tunnels and surface at the Second Avenue platform.'

'We don't think he'll pick another emergency exit,' Commander Penn said. 'It would place him above ground too long. And with a parade in progress, he's going to know there will be a lot of cops out. So our theory is he will stay in the tunnels for as long as he can.'

'Right,' Lucy said. 'It's perfect. He knows the station has been temporarily closed. No one's going to see him when he comes up from the tracks. And then he's right there at the pharmacy – practically next door to it. He gets his money and goes back the same way he came.'

'Maybe he will,' I said. 'And maybe he won't.'

'He knows about the parade,' Lucy said adamantly. 'He knows the Second Avenue station is closed. He knows the emergency exit he's tampered with has been disabled. He knows everything we want him to know.'

I looked skeptically at her. 'Please tell me how you can be so sure.'

'I've worked it so I get a message the minute those files are accessed. I know all of them were and I know when.' Anger flashed in her eyes.

'Someone else couldn't have?'

'Not the way I rigged it.'

'Kay,' Commander Penn said. 'There's another big part of all this. Look over here.' She directed my attention to the closed-circuit TV monitors set up on a long, high table. 'Lucy, show her.'

Lucy typed, and the televisions came on, each showing a different subway station. I could see people walking past. Umbrellas were closed and tucked under arms, and I recognized shopping bags from Bloomingdale's, Dean & DeLuca food market and the Second Avenue Deli.

'It's stopped raining,' I said.

'Now watch this,' Lucy said.

She typed more commands, synchronizing closed-circuit TV with the computerized diagrams. When one was on-screen, so was the other.

'What I can do,' she explained, 'is act as an air traffic controller, in a sense. If Gault does something unexpected, I will be in constant contact with the cops, the feds, via radio.'

'For example, if, God forbid, he should break free and head deep into the system, along these tracks here' – Commander Penn pointed to a map on screen – 'then Lucy can apprise police by radio that there is a wooden barricade coming up on the right. Or a platform edge, express train tracks, an emergency exit, a passageway, a signal tower.'

'This is if he escapes and we must chase him through the hell where he killed Davila,' I said. 'This is if the worst happens.'

Frances Penn looked at me. 'What is the worst when you're dealing with him?'

'I pray we have already seen it,' I said.

'You know that Transit's got a touch screen telephone system.' Lucy showed me. 'If the numbers are in the computer, you can dial anywhere in the world. And what's really cool is 911. If it's dialed above ground, the call goes to NYPD. If it's dialed in the subway, it comes to Transit Police.'

'When do you close Second Avenue station?' I got up and said to Commander Penn.

She looked at her watch. 'In a little less than an hour.'

'Will the trains run?'

'Of course,' she said, 'but they won't stop there.'

20

The March Against Crime began on time with fifteen church groups and a miscellaneous contingent of men, women and children who wanted to take their neighborhoods back. The weather had worsened and snow blew on frigid winds that drove more people into taxis and the subways because it was too cold to walk.

At two-fifteen, Lucy, Commander Penn and I were in the control room, every monitor, television and radio turned on. Wesley was in one of several Bureau cars that ERF had painted to look like yellow cabs and equipped with radios, scanners, and other surveillance devices. Marino was on the street with Transit cops and plainclothes FBI. HRT was divided among the Dakota, the drugstore and Bleecker Street. We were unclear on the precise location of anyone because no one on the outside was standing still, and we were in here, not moving.

'Why hasn't anyone called?' Lucy complained.

'He hasn't been sighted,' said Commander Penn, and she was steady but uptight.

'I assume the parade has started,' I said.

Commander Penn said, 'It's on Lafayette, headed this way.'

She and Lucy were wearing headphones that plugged into the base station on the console. They were on different channels.

'All right, all right,' Commander Penn said, sitting up straighter. 'We've spotted him. The number seven platform,' she exclaimed to Lucy, whose fingers flew. 'He's just come in from a catwalk. He's entered the system from a tunnel that runs under the park.'

Then the number seven platform was on black-and-white TV. We watched a figure in a long dark coat. He wore boots, a hat and dark glasses, and stood back from other passengers at the platform's edge. Lucy brought up another subway survey on the screen as Commander Penn stayed on the radio. I watched passengers walking, sitting, reading maps and standing. A train screamed by and got slower as it stopped. Doors opened and he got on.

'Which way is he bound?' I asked.

'South. He's coming this way,' Commander Penn said, excited.

'He's on the A line,' Lucy said, studying her monitors.

'Right.' Commander Penn got on the air. 'He can only go as far as Washington Square,' she told someone. 'Then he can transfer and take the F line straight to Second Avenue.'

Lucy said, 'We'll check one station after another. We don't know where he might get off. But he's got to get off somewhere so he can go back into the tunnels.'

'He has to do that if he comes in the Second Avenue way,' Commander Penn relayed to the radio. 'He can't take the train in there because it's not stopping there.'

Lucy manipulated the closed-circuit television monitors. At rapid intervals they showed a different station as a train we could not see headed toward us.

'He's not at Forty-second,' she said. 'We don't see him at Penn Station or Twenty-third.'

Monitors blinked on and off, showing platforms and people who did not know they were being watched.

'If he stayed on that train he should be at Fourteenth Street,' Commander Penn said.

But if he was, he did not disembark, or at least we did not see him. Then our luck suddenly changed in an unexpected way.

'My God,' Lucy said. 'He's at Grand Central Station. How the hell did he get there?'

'He must have turned east before we thought he would and cut through Times Square,' Commander Penn said.

'But why?' Lucy said. 'That doesn't make sense.'

Commander Penn radioed unit two, which was Benton Wesley. She asked him if Gault had called the pharmacy yet. She took her headphones off and set the microphone so we could hear what was said.

'No, there's been no call,' came Wesley's reply.

'Our monitors have just picked him up at Grand Central,' she explained.

'What?'

'I don't know why he's gone that way. But there are so many alternative routes he could take. He could get off anywhere for any reason.'

'I'm afraid so,' Wesley said.

'What about in South Carolina?' Commander Penn then asked.

'Everything's ten-four. The bird has flown and landed,' Wesley said.

Mrs. Gault had wired the money, or the Bureau had. We watched while her only son casually rode with other people who did not know he was a monster.

'Wait a minute,' Commander Penn continued to broadcast information. 'He's at Fourteenth Street and Union Square, going south right at you.'

It drove me crazy that we could not stop him. We could see him and yet it did no good.

'It sounds like he's changing trains a lot,' Wesley said.

Commander Penn said, 'He's gone again. The train's left.

We've got Astor Place on-screen. That's the last stop unless he goes past us and gets out at the Bowery.'

'The train's stopping,' Lucy announced.

We watched people in the monitors and did not see Gault.

'All right, he must be staying on,' Commander Penn said into the microphone.

'We've lost him,' Lucy said.

She changed pictures like a frustrated person flipping television channels. We did not see him.

'Shit,' she muttered.

'Where could he be?' The commander was baffled. 'He's got to get out somewhere. If he's going into the pharmacy, he can't use the exit at Cooper Union.' She looked at Lucy. 'That's it. Maybe he's going to try. But he won't get out. It's bolted. But he might not know.'

She said. 'He's got to know. He read the electronic messages we sent.'

She scanned some more. Still, we did not see him and the radio remained tensely silent.

'Damn,' Lucy said. 'He should be on the number six line. Let's look at Astor Place and Lafayette again.'

It did no good.

We sat without talking for a while, looking at the shut wooden door that led into our empty station. Above us, hundreds of people were walking sodden streets to demonstrate they were fed up with crime. I began looking at a subway map.

Commander Penn said, 'He should be at Second Avenue now. He should have gotten off at an earlier or later stop and walked the rest of the way through the tunnel.'

A terrible thought occurred to me. 'He could do the same thing here. We're not as close to the pharmacy, but we're on the number six line too.'

'Yeah,' Lucy said, turning around to look at me. 'The walk from here to Houston is nothing.'

'But we're closed,' I said.

Lucy was typing again.

I got up out of my chair and looked at Commander Penn. 'We're here alone. It's just the three of us. The trains don't stop here on the weekends. There is no one. Everyone is at Second Avenue and the pharmacy.'

'Base station to unit two,' Lucy was saying into the radio.

'Unit two,' Wesley said.

'Everything ten-four? Because we've lost him.'

'Stand by.'

I opened my briefcase and got out my gun. I cocked it and pushed on the safety.

'What's your ten-twenty?' Commander Penn got on the air to ask for their location.

'Holding steady at the pharmacy.'

Screens were flashing by crazily as Lucy tried to locate Gault.

'Hold on. Hold on,' Wesley's voice came over the air.

Then we heard Marino. 'It looks like we've got him.'

'You've got him?' Commander Penn, incredulous, asked the radio. 'What is the location?'

'He's walking into the pharmacy.' Wesley was back. 'Wait a minute. Wait a minute.'

There was silence. Then Wesley said, 'He's at the counter getting the money. Stand by.'

We waited in frantic silence.

Three minutes passed. Wesley was back on the air. 'He's leaving. We're going to close in once he gets inside the terminal. Stand by.'

'What's he wearing?' I asked. 'Are we sure it's the person who got on at the museum?'

Nobody paid me any mind.

'Oh Christ,' Lucy suddenly exclaimed, and we looked at the monitors.

We could see the platforms of Second Avenue station, and HRT exploding out of the darkness of the tracks. Dressed in black fatigues and combat boots, they ran across the platform and up steps leading to the street.

'Something's gone wrong,' Commander Penn said. 'They're grabbing him above ground!'

Voices ricocheted on the radio.

'We've got him.'

'He's trying to run.'

'Okay, okay, we've got his gun. He's down.'

'Have you got him cuffed?'

A siren went off inside the control room. Lights along the ceiling began flashing blood red, and a red code 429 began flashing on a computer screen.

'Mayday!' Commander Penn exclaimed. 'An officer is down! He's hit the emergency button on his radio!' She stared at the computer screen in stunned disbelief.

'What's happening?' Lucy demanded into the radio.

'I don't know,' Wesley's voice crackled. 'Something's wrong. Stand by.'

'That's not where it is. The Mayday isn't at Second Avenue station,' Commander Penn said, awed. 'This code on the screen is Davila's.'

'Davila?' I said numbly. 'Jimmy Davila?'

'He was unit four twenty-nine. That's his code. It hasn't been reassigned. It's right here.'

We stared at the screen. The flashing red code was changing locations along a computerized grid. I was shocked no one had thought of it before.

'Was Davila's radio with him when his body was found?' I asked.

Commander Penn didn't react.

'Gault's got it,' I said. 'He's got Davila's radio.'

Wesley's voice came back, and he could not know of our difficulty. He could not know about the Mayday.

'We're not sure we have him,' Wesley said. 'We're not sure who we have.'

Lucy intensely looked over at me. 'Carrie,' she said. 'They're not sure if they have her or Gault. She and Gault are probably dressed alike again.'

Inside our small control room with no windows and no people nearby, we watched the flashing red Mayday code move along the computer screen, getting closer to where we sat.

'It's in the southbound tunnel heading straight at us,' Commander Penn said with growing urgency.

'She didn't get the messages we sent.' Lucy had it figured out.

'She?' Commander Penn asked, looking oddly at her.

'She doesn't know about the parade or that Second Avenue is closed,' Lucy went on. 'She may have tried the emergency exit in the alleyway and couldn't get out because it's been bolted. So she just stayed under and has been moving around since we sighted her at Grand Central Station.'

'We didn't see Gault or Carrie on the platforms of the stations closer to us,' I said. 'And you don't know it's her.'

'There are so many stations,' Commander Penn said. 'Someone could have gotten out and we just didn't see them.'

'Gault sent her to the pharmacy for him,' I said, more unnerved by the minute. 'He somehow knows every goddam thing we're doing.'

'CAIN,' Lucy muttered.

'Yes. That and he's probably been watching.'

Lucy had our location, the Bleecker Street local stop, on closed-circuit TV. Three of the monitors showed the platform and turnstiles from different angles, but one monitor was dark.

'Something's blocking one of the cameras,' she said.

'Was it blocked earlier?' I asked.

'Not when we first got here,' she said. 'But we haven't been monitoring this station where we are. There didn't seem to be a reason to check here.'

We watched the red code slowly move across the grid.

'We've got to stay off the air,' I told Commander Penn. 'He has a radio,' I added, because I knew Gault was the red code on our screen. I had no doubt. 'You know it's on and he's hearing every word we say.'

'Why's the Mayday light still on?' Lucy asked. 'Does she want us to know where she is?'

I stared at her. It was as if Lucy were in a trance.

'The button may have been hit inadvertently,' Commander Penn said. 'If you don't know about the button, you wouldn't realize it's for Maydays. And since it's a silent alarm, you could have it on and not know it.'

But I did not believe anything happening was inadvertent. Gault was coming to us because this was where he wanted to be. He was a shark swimming through the blackness of the tunnel, and I thought of what Anna had said about his hideous gifts to me.

'It's almost at the signal tower.' Lucy was pointing at the screen. 'Goddam that's close.'

We did not know what to do. If we radioed Wesley, Gault would overhear and disappear back through the tunnels. If we did not make contact, the troops would not know what was happening here. Lucy was at the door, and she opened it a little.

'What are you doing?' I almost screamed at her.

She quickly shut the door. 'It's the ladies' room. I guess a janitor propped open the door while cleaning and left it that way. The door's blocking the camera.'

'Did you see anybody out there?' I asked.

'No,' she said, hatred in her eyes. 'They think they have her. How do they know it's not Gault? It may be her who's got Davila's radio. I know her. She probably knows I'm in here.'

Commander Penn was tense when she said to me, 'There's some gear in the office.'

'Yes,' I said.

We hurried back to a cramped space with a beat-up wooden

desk and chair. She opened a cabinet and we grabbed shotguns, boxes of shells, and Kevlar vests. We were gone minutes, and when we returned to the control room Lucy was not there.

I looked at the closed-circuit TV monitors and saw a picture blink onto the fourth screen as someone shut the ladies' room door. The flashing red code on the survey grid was deeper inside the station now. It was on a catwalk. At any second it would be on the platform. I looked for my Browning pistol, but it was not on the console where I had left it.

'She took my gun,' I said in amazement. 'She's gone out there. She's gone after Carrie!'

We loaded shotguns as fast as we could but did not take the time for vests. My hands were clumsy and cold.

'You've got to radio Wesley,' I said, frantic. 'You've got to do something to get them here.'

'You can't go out there alone,' Commander Penn said.

'I can't leave Lucy out there alone.'

'We'll both go. Here. Take a flashlight.'

'No. You get help. Get someone here.'

I ran out not knowing what I would find. But the station was deserted. I stood perfectly still with the shotgun ready. I noticed the fixed camera bracketed to the green tile wall near the restrooms. The platform was empty, and I heard a train in the distance. It rushed by without pause because it did not have to stop at this station on Saturdays. Through windows I saw commuters sleeping, reading. Few seemed to notice the woman with a shotgun or even think it odd.

I wondered if Lucy could be in the bathroom, but that didn't make sense. There was a toilet just off the control room, inside our shelter where we had been all day. I walked closer to the platform as my heart pounded. The temperature was biting and I did not have my coat. My fingers were getting stiff around the stock of the gun.

It occurred to me with some relief that Lucy might have gone for help. Perhaps she shut the bathroom door and ran toward

Second Avenue. But what if she hadn't? I stared at that shut door and did not want to go through it.

I walked closer, one slow step at a time, and wished I had a pistol. A shotgun was awkward in confined spaces and around corners. When I reached the door my heart was pounding in my throat. I grabbed the handle, yanked hard and thrust myself inside with the shotgun aimed. The area around the sink was blank. I did not hear a sound. I looked under the stalls and stopped breathing when I saw blue trousers and a pair of brown leather work boots that were too big to be a woman's. Metal clanked.

I racked the shotgun, shaking as I demanded, 'Come out with your hands in the air!'

A big wrench clanged to the tile floor. The maintenance man in his coveralls and coat looked as if he might have a heart attack when he emerged from the stall. His eyes bulged from his head as he stared at me and the shotgun.

'I'm just fixing the toilet in here. I don't have any money,' he said in terror, hands straight up as if someone had just scored a touchdown.

'You're in the middle of a police operation,' I exclaimed, pointing the shotgun at the ceiling and pushing the safety on. 'You must get out of here now!'

He did not need the suggestion twice. He did not collect his tools or put the padlock back on the bathroom door. He fled up steps to the street as I began walking around the platform again. I located each of the cameras, wondering if Commander Penn saw me on the monitors. I was about to return to the control room when I looked down dark tracks and thought I heard voices. Suddenly there was scuffling and what sounded like a grunt. Lucy began to scream.

'No! No! Don't!'

A loud pop sounded like an explosion inside a metal drum. Sparks showered the darkness where the sound came from as the lights inside Bleecker Street station flickered.

* * *

Along the tracks there was no light, and I could not see because I did not dare turn on the one in my hand. I felt my way to a metal catwalk and carefully descended narrow stairs that led into the tunnel.

As I inched my way along, breathing rapid, shallow breaths, my eyes began to adjust. I could barely see the shapes of arches, rails and concrete places where the homeless made their beds. My feet hit trash and were loud when they knocked objects made of metal or glass.

I held the shotgun out in front to shield my head from any projection I might not see. I smelled filth and human waste, and flesh burning. The farther I walked, the more intense the stench, and then a strong light rose loudly like a moon as a train appeared on northbound tracks. Temple Gault was no more than fifteen feet ahead of me.

He held Lucy in a choke hold, a knife at her throat. Not far from them Detective Maier was welded to the third rail of southbound tracks, hands and teeth clenched as electricity flowed through his dead body. The train screamed past, returning the darkness.

'Let her go,' my voice quavered as I turned on the flashlight.

Squinting, Gault shielded his face from the light. He was so pale he looked like an albino, and I could see small muscles and tendons in his bare hands as he held the steel dissecting knife he had stolen from me. In one quick motion he could cut Lucy's throat to her spine. She stared at me in frozen terror.

'It's not her you want.' I stepped closer.

'Don't shine that light in my face,' he said. 'Set it down.'

I did not turn the flashlight off but slowly set it on a concrete ledge, where it cast an irregular light and shone directly on Detective Maier's burned, bloody head. I wondered why Gault did not tell me to put the shotgun down. Maybe he couldn't see it. I held it pointed up. I was no more than six feet from them now.

Gault's lips were chapped and he sniffed loudly. He was emaciated and disheveled, and I wondered if he were high on crack or on his way down. He wore jeans and jungle boots and a black leather jacket that was scraped and ripped. In a lapel was the caduceus pin I imagined he had bought in Richmond several days before Christmas.

'She's no fun.' I could not stop my voice from trembling.

His terrible eyes seemed to focus as a thread of blood ran down Lucy's neck. I tightened my grip on the gun.

'Let her go. Then it's just you and me. I'm who you want.'

Light sparked in his eyes, and I could almost see their weird blue color in the incomplete dark. His hands suddenly moved, violently shoving Lucy toward the third rail, and I lunged for her. I grabbed her sweater, yanking her on top of me, and together we fell to the ground and the shotgun clattered. Fire popped and sparks flew as the greedy rail grabbed it.

Gault smiled, my Browning in hand as he tossed the knife out of his way for now. He snapped the slide back, gripping the pistol with both hands, pointing the barrel at Lucy's head. He was used to his Glock and did not seem to know that my Browning had a safety. He squeezed the trigger and nothing happened. He did not understand.

'Run!' I yelled to Lucy, pushing her. 'RUN!'

Gault cocked the gun, but it was already cocked, and no cartridge ejected, so now he had a double-feed. Enraged, he squeezed the trigger, but the pistol was jammed.

'RUN!' I screamed.

I was on the ground and did not try to get away because I did not believe he would go after Lucy if I stayed here. He was forcing the slide open, shaking the gun as Lucy began to cry, stumbling through the dark. The knife was close to the third rail, and I groped for it as a rat ran over my legs and I cut myself on broken glass. My head was dangerously close to Gault's boots.

He could not seem to fix the gun and then I saw him tense as he looked at me. I could feel his thought as I tightened my grip on the cold steel handle. I knew what he could do with his feet, and I could not reach his chest or a major vessel in his neck because there was not time. I was on my knees. I raised the knife as he got in position to kick and plunged the surgical blade into his upper thigh. With both hands I cut as much as I could as he shrieked.

Arterial blood squirted across my face as I pulled the knife out and his transected femoral artery hemorrhaged to the rhythm of his horrible heart. I ducked out of the way because I knew HRT would have him in their sights and were waiting.

'You stabbed me,' Gault said with childlike disbelief. Hunched over, he stared with shocked fascination at blood spurting between his fingers clutching his leg. 'It won't stop. You're a doctor. Make it stop.'

I looked at him. His head was shaved beneath his cap. I thought of his dead twin, of Lucy's neck. A sniper rifle cracked twice from inside the tunnel in the direction of the station, bullets pinged, and Gault fell close to the rail he had almost thrown Lucy on. A train was coming and I did not move him free of the tracks. I walked away and did not look back.

Lucy, Wesley and I left New York on Monday, and first the helicopter flew due east. We passed over cliffs and the mansions of Westchester, finally reaching that ragged, wretched island not found on any tourist map. A crumbling smokestack rose from the ruins of an old brick penitentiary. We circled Potter's Field while prisoners and their guards gazed up into an overcast morning.

The BellJet Ranger went as low as it could go, and I hoped nothing would force us to land. I did not want to be near the men from Rikers Island. Grave markers looked like white teeth protruding from patchy grass, and someone had fashioned a cross from rocks. A flatbed truck was parked near the open grave, and men were lifting out the new pine box.

They stopped to look up as we churned air with more force than the harsh winds they knew. Lucy and I were in the helicopter's backseat, holding hands. Prisoners, bundled for winter, did not wave. A rusting ferry swayed on the water, waiting to take the coffin into Manhattan for one last test. Gault's twin sister would cross the river today. Jayne, at last, would go home.